# There is no Time Limit

# There is no Time Limit

J. Michael O'Connor

ISBN-13: 9781533578990
ISBN-10: 1533578990

This book is dedicated to:
My beloved son, Sean Patrick O'Connor
12.20.1976-10.02.2007
My adoring soul mate, Christine Jane O'Connor
03.22.1951-11.25.2014

Achknowledgements:

**EDITOR:** Sally Shupe
**COVER ART:** Create Space Staff
**Thanks to Craig and Myra for their assistance.**

**A special thank you to Mrs. Sharon Clevenger; in your celestial domain; for inspiring and encouraging me to write this entire story.**

# Contents

# Narrator

HIS DESTINY LIED WITH HIS students. He had no intentions of becoming a high school teacher, nor had his plans included moving to the Appalachian mountains of Southwestern Virginia.

James Patrick O'Francis gift was his ability to communicate with teen agers. He seemed to understand them more than most. He never breached their trust nor did he ever betray their deepest secrets. He listened, counseled and advised. He even helped directly when requested. His teaching ability was not just the knowledge of the subject, it was his delivery. He made the subject easy for his students to understand the material. He required effort from each of them, and a lot of it. It was said, by many, "he was hard." I have learned from my own sources, "hard," no; demanding; yes. To reach the zenith of an individual's ability to obtain knowledge. In addition he made learning fun, he had fun in his classes, he enjoyed teaching, passing knowledge on to the students that graced his "think tank."

He believed he was directed to where he was for a reason. He questioned why many times, but the answer always came back, "The Students."

It took years for J.P. to put the small insignificant pieces of the large puzzle of his life in a small rural mountain community together. He had been for years unable to see the big picture because he was so deep in the forest that he actually could not see the trees. His loyalty and devotion to a small high school program had blinded him.

But in his defense, perception and deceit was everything. It ruled anything that had a political connection to it. Large, medium and very small. The scale of politics was irrelevant, it was the same game.

Egos of men in power and with power drive them to befriend and betray and cloak themselves in dishonor. Men who are dissembled are weak in character. Their mendacity was endless and they were experts at the art of preforming these qualities.

However to tell J.P's. story of his revenge for the character assassination in which he had to suffer through, I will have to fill in a few gaps in his daily routine as a simple teacher as he was slowly putting the little pieces of the puzzle of his life in a small insignificant mountain town together. But when it was completed and he stepped back to view the picture, his anger was overwhelming.

I think at this point in his story, I should add that people should always know who they are character assassinating. Because if the assassinator does not know with whom they are dealing with and who they have connections to, one may find in the end that it was not worth the small reward they had received for the price in which they would ultimately have to pay.

There is no promise for tomorrow to anyone. In the real world, people are tortured, and people actually die. In the isolated world of education, most people live in a pretend world. Although in this modern day and time, there has been changes in the world of the educator, not for all, but for some that have had to experience the real world of terror. But for those who have not had to endure the real world, that pretend world in which they lived in and felt they would always be safe and secure, was about to enter into the world of harsh reality. An exclusive group of self-deemed important people who thought they were untouchable and could control everything in "their world" had hurt the wrong person.

Death, it is not such a bad thing. It is inevitable. It is the living that have to suffer. So, what is a good death? The answer should be any death that rids the world/society, community, town, city or humanity of some form of human social disease. That should be defined as a good death. A good death is awarded to some evil someone who in the course of their existence causes pain, suffering, misery, personal humiliation, character assassination and heartache for some other human being.

However, most of society makes excuses for these types of people, most but not quite all, of society reverts to the "Book" and all of its so-called good words to "live" by. The fractured fairy tale "Book" that is in circulation around the world leading the mindless sheep with excuses for all evil beings. The "Book" that has left out, changed or altered as much as is actually printed in the modern day and time, of which of course, is a complete oxymoron.

So right about now, you are asking yourself, should I continue to read on? What is this story about? What is a bad death?

A bad death is one that takes away the innocent, the young, the youth, the fun loving, happy honest law abiding individual who goes about their daily lives trying to make a good living for themselves and their families.

❧ ❧ ❧ ❧

I am John Frederick O'Donovan, a freelance writer and have over many years traveled the world writing down the stories about people whose paths I have crossed. I have seen and written about the suffering of humans and their deaths caused by not just nature in its cruelest form, but by the evilness that exists on this earth.

I am six feet tall and weigh one hundred and eighty pounds. My once strawberry blond hair is now a gray white. I am clean shaven, and my physique remains trim. I have been very successful financially and now I am semi-retired and have been for several years. I settled in the Appalachian mountains of Eastern Tennessee in 1980, to write about the people of the area as well as the people who settled in the areas of the Appalachian mountains of Southwestern Virginia, Southeastern Kentucky and Western North Carolina. I wanted to write about the hard working class of people who arrived in these areas, and who began carving out a meager living within the vast labyrinth of mountainous terrain, and turned the area into a patch-work of productive thriving small towns and communities.

This area had been part of a Native American hunting ground for seven or so tribes surrounding the forests and woodlands that had a radius of a hundred or so miles. The Germans, Scotch and Irish drove the Native Americans west, carving up the land into farms, vast areas of land that would become adjoining states. With the European invaders carving, cutting, and digging out a living over the past two hundred years, the forests had been raped, the land surface had been scarred, and the mountains had been gutted, leaving its underbelly hollow. This caused the surface of the mountainous land in many places to collapse, literally destroying the underground water system, leaving hundreds of people high and dry.

I had no idea that I would run across an Irishman that really had no con-nections to the earlier settlers of the area and that I would become obsessed with his saga. We met at a social gathering and after a brief conversation with J.P. O'Francis, my journalistic instincts took over and I was drawn to this person and the not so simple life he led. I decided to write about one man's fight against the injustices in a rural school system, and the politically corrupt county in which he resided. His enduring effort to keep his surname intact and untarnished was a fight that he would ultimate lose and his name and his char-acter would become tarnished by the callous, malicious self-serving, self-righteous, and disassembling politically connected people of the county in which he lived and worked, ultimately driving him out of the mountains he so loved.

After several years of following O'Francis throughout his semi-normal life of being a simple high school teacher and learning of his past as well as his personal philosophies, he walked out of my life on a cool August night, fog encircling the mountain midway and down to the valley floor like a Saturn ring. The night sky was filled with the celestial twinkling of millions of tiny lights as we stood looking out over a white cloud ringing my mountain sanctuary. He had but a few simple words, *"there is no time limit,"* then he turned and walked away, got in his jeep and drove off, disappearing down into the mist of a white cloud of fog.

How would I describe J.P.? I grew to know him after several years of research and conversation. He was a strong man, but was often more playful than serious. He had a pure spirit and enjoyed music. J.P. was very artistic and craved adventure. He strived to be a good-natured person. He liked to put others before himself. He loved nature and to be outside most of the time. He had a fierce side to him as well, but only to the people that deserved it. He had trust issues, because he had been betrayed and hurt so many times. He was not a religious man, yet he believed in the spirit world. He had a great sense of humor. He could be extremely tender when he wanted to. The last I saw of him he was a broken man. The once bright light that had pierced his darkened world and had made it bright, had suddenly and unexpectedly gone out. His beloved Dawn was all that kept him balanced. His loss turned him bitter toward life itself. Darkness once again overshadowed his world.

As I now sit on my upper deck looking out over the hardwood laden mountain in reflection, his voice echoing the words that come back to me loud and clear, I see him walking off into the darkness of the night. Several years have now passed and I once again find myself drawn like a moth to a bright light to investigate the connections, if any, between the events that have occurred over the past few years and the man I knew as J.P. O'Francis. He was a man of his word. I know that. He was a man with honor, a man out of his time. He was a man who wanted to be left alone to live the life of a simple teacher, build a home for his adoring wife and raise his beloved sons in a safe, clean environment. The people who had forced the changes in his life had no idea what Pandora's box held in it.

He would often state that he did not like reporters and especially media reporters, as he felt they had no honor, were rude, interruptive, and they were not without malice in any story in which they were reporting. He would often tell me after some event was reported on television, that the reporter of whatever story he or she was referring to, was done without any care about whom the story was being told. All they cared about was the ratings they would get. Ratings equated money, and that was what it was all about and nothing else. They couldn't care less about the people or person the story was being reported about, whether it was accurate or not was not the case, just get the ratings up. If it turned out that it was not accurate, maybe one would see or hear a minor blip about the correction and they would move on to some other so-called truth that had to be reported, "because it was the right of the people to know. "Yeah, right." He would always say. "Right of the people my ass. It is all about money or whom you can character assassinate and destroy their lives."

However, J.P. did give journalists and the general media a sizeable edge over politicians. Over the years of talking with him, I found he came to loathe most all politicians. The oddity of that was he loved to study the working of politics and was quite the expert on our political system. However, he would often remind me that he did not like reporters. Then he would get a big smile on his face.

Looking back on my relationship with J.P., and me being a journalist, I do not know why he ever agreed to talk to me. Nevertheless, he slowly and cautiously kept meeting with me and answering my many questions. I did my best to be honest with him and he tested me on many occasions. Maybe he kept meeting with me because of the location of my home, the remote isolation and the purity of the land surrounding it. He told me on many occasions that he always wanted to live on top of a mountain with no neighbors. Isolated and yet close enough to civilization that he and Dawn could enjoy the modern day social conveniences, and then escape back to his mountain top sanctuary.

Maybe he kept returning because of the fate topic in which we often discussed. He always reminded me, "You know John, nothing happens out of just coincidence."

I do not know. However, what I do know is the cost to J.P. would be more than he could take, and in the end, his dark side took over. His Irish characteristics of seeking revenge on those who harmed his family would rule and guide his fate.

What I have learned is that the events that led to his departing his beloved Appalachian Mountains he so enjoyed and the events that occurred sometime after he left the area is so unbelievable that I have decided to continue with the saga of James Patrick O'Francis.

# Justice Awakens

I HAD NOT SEEN J.P. in many years, as I sat on my back upper deck, my feet laid out on the wicker ottoman reading the Sunday morning paper, not really absorbing anything I was reading. I turned one page after another skimming one article after another sipping my coffee and enjoying the warm eight o'clock sun rays. The spring birds were singing and Boaz, my very large cat, front paws turned inward, was purring contently on my lap. An article on the front page re-flashed through my mind. I quickly turned back to the front page and scanned through several stories and there in the right-hand column midway down the page with a medium headliner was a short article that had subconsciously caught my attention. TEACHER FOUND DEAD IN CAR.

The article did not give a lot of details concerning the death but the name stood out in my memory, Richard Finkel. I decided that day to do some investigating as I had learned a lot about that particular person as well as a number of other people that had been a large part of a conspiracy to destroy the character and career of J. Patrick O'Francis. I remembered O'Francis' last few years and what drove him to leave the Southwestern Virginia Appalachian Mountains. I needed my file on J.P. I lifted Boaz off my lap placing him on the decking, much to his dislike, and he so informed me, as he let me know with a disapproving meow. I got up to get a refill of morning coffee and returned to my favorite chair and spot on my back upper deck to review the O'Francis file from that August night when he walked out of my life, backward, covering his last fifteen years. A lot had happened to him in his last fifteen years, almost as much as in his first twenty years. I had learned a lot about this simple teacher that turned out to be not so simple. I mentally reminded myself, as I began reviewing, that I really did not have his full and complete story. A lot of pieces were missing.

Two young boys were playing "Indiana Jones, the great explorer," in a large section of forest not far from their homes located in the eastern mountains of Tennessee. As they came down onto an old logging road they saw a yellow compact two-door Volkswagen Golf parked within a half mile of the end of the very rough logging road. Approaching the car in a cautious manner, they crouched down and snuck up on the car from the back instantly shifting their imagination to the spy world of James Bond...

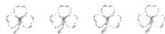

Friday after school was the last time anyone saw Mr. Richard Finkel as he did his usual come-ons and fraternization with the young seventeen and eighteen year old girls in the back parking lot. The eighteen-year-old he was seducing and the two seventeen-year-old girls were on his schedule to be violated and placed on his trophy wall.

The girls walked off toward their cars and Richard smiled and informed them he would see them later. He got into his car and started it when a black four door Chrysler 300 pulled crossways behind Finkel's car preventing him from backing up. The two men in the back of the Chrysler got out and casually walked to the driver's door of Richard's car. He looked up at the two well-dressed men in navy blue pin striped suits, white shirts, and expensive silk ties.

"Mr. Richard Finkel?" one of the men asked.

"Yeah, what can I do for you?" Finkel responded in his usual cocky ill-mannered tone.

"Would you please step out of the car, there is someone who would like to talk to you."

Finkel had become instantly irritated, however for whatever reason, a little quiver in his inner self occurred, brought on by the deep non-feeling business tone of the voice coming from the man facing him.

Richard asked, "Who is it?"

The two very large men just asked him to please step out of the car as one reached down and opened the driver's door for Finkel.

Richard unbuckled his seat belt and swung his legs around placing his feet on the ground.

He looked up at the men who had positioned themselves on either side of him. As he stood, his mid-section began to tremble again, as both expressionless men towered some five inches over him and out-weighed him by twenty-five pounds of solid well-developed physiques.

The man on his right laid out his hand toward the black Chrysler with the right back door opened, indicating for him to get into the car. Richard hesitated momentarily and then made the mistake of looking into the man's eyes at his left. He saw cold, dark, hard, steel grey eyes and a cold serge traveled up Richard 's back, leaving a wide trail of bumps. He simply nodded his head and did as the two men asked.

Finkel's involvement in illegal gambling, as well as his drug contacts and being the drop off for drug dealers, as well as his distribution to lower-rung dealers as an intermediary, the go-between at a public school, had never stopped since his departure from Honsburg High School many years earlier. His position as Athletic Director at the school he worked in after his requested resignation at Honsburg, again allowed him the freedom of communicating, as well as coming in contact with a large range of diverse and somewhat unscrupulous people, a better location than the rural school in Honsburg. The city school allowed for easier as well as more discreet contacts for his illegal product delivery, as well as a good place for somebody to come by and pick up the products. Finkel was well paid for his little service by a much larger organization. However, his usual tough persona, and arrogant image in and around the Vermillion High School, had suddenly wilted in the presence of the men he now faced. As Richard got into the back seat of the Chrysler, the man standing at Richard's little yellow Golf pulled a pair of rubber gloves out of his suit pocket and placed them on his hands. He then wiped the door handle with a clean white cloth, where he had placed his hand to open it. He then got into Richard's automobile. The man who escorted Richard to the Chrysler closed the door after Finkel had gotten into the Chrysler, and then he walked around to the back driver's side of the car and got in. There were two men in the front seat. The driver pulled slightly forward, the man on the passenger's side looked toward Richard 's car, nodded, and then they pulled out with Finkel's car following.

"Excuse me. But why is that man driving my car?"

No one spoke. And again Finkel spoke. "I asked you a question. Could someone tell me what is going on?"

The man to his left spoke, his voice had a deep, rough tone to it. "Just sit where you are and shut your mouth."

The drive took them 45 minutes, leaving the city and traveling into the countryside on a narrow very isolated road where the black Chrysler 300 pulled in behind a dark gray Jeep Grand Cherokee, which was parked on a wide spot along the isolated rural country road. Finkel had asked several times who they were and what they wanted and got no response from any of the three men. The three men in the Chrysler were listening to a selection of the best of the Eagles for the entire trip.

The man in the back with Richard got out and walked to Richard's door, opened the door and asked him to get out. Finkel had turned as pale as any Caucasian could have possible turned and sweat was running down his face, as fear permeated his eyes. He was escorted to the Jeep and placed on the left side of the back seat. The other man on the front passenger's side of the Chrysler got out and got behind the wheel of the Jeep. Finkel then panicked and attempted to get out of the back of the Jeep. The steal grey-eyed man was at the rear door of the jeep where he met Finkel with a fist to his mouth sending him stumbling backward into the Jeep. He shoved his legs into the Jeep and then closed the door, walked around to the passenger's door, and got into the front seat. He pulled out a pistol with a silencer attached to the end of the barrel, turned slightly to his left, pointed the pistol at him, and stated, "Now you sit there like a good little boy."

The Jeep pulled out with Finkel's yellow Golf following and the Chrysler turned and went in the opposite direction. The Jeep went deeper into the mountains, driving from one paved road to a graveled road to a dirt road to an old unused logging road, where the Jeep pulled over just enough for the Golf to get by and then proceeded to the near end of the road. It had been a rather steep grade and the Golf had a difficult time making it, bottoming out several times, and spinning the tires to get up the rough rutted out grade.

They came to a stop on a level area of about hundred foot squared on the logging road and proceeded to pull Richard Finkel out of the back of the Jeep, his mouth still bleeding as one of the men walked him to the left of the jeep and instructed him to remove all his clothes. He refused, and attempted to break "bad", a fist to the side of his jaw put him on the ground semi-conscience, where two of the three men removed all his clothes and placed them in a plastic bag leaving him bare naked from head to toe. The steel grey eyed man removed his suit coat and rolled his shirtsleeves up to his elbows.

"Mr. Finkel," he stated, "you no doubt question why you find yourself in such an awkward position."

Richard began crying as he rolled over and came to his knees, bending at his waist, looking up at all three men now surrounding him.

"No, no, I don't, I, I, I don't even know you guys. I have done nothing to you. What is this all about? I don't understand. You must have the wrong person."

"Now, Richard, you know!"

"No, no, no, I really don't." He sobbed some more.

"Let me refresh your memory just a little," the well-groomed, steel grey-eyed man spoke in his deep voice. "Do you remember what you and others like you have done to a very close friend of ours? Now, I know you have damaged a lot of people with your mouth. Now, this one particular person, you took part in destroying his career and tainting his character!"

Richard Finkel paused momentarily as in deep thought. He had over the years been a part of the destruction of at least four teachers' careers, not excluding the many cases of sexual violations of teenage girls in three different schools. He began making statements that he was never in charge, that he just did what he was told, that he meant no harm. He had no clue which one of the teachers the men were talking about.

"Let me help you a little Mr. Finkel. Did you ever work at a high school called Honsburg?"

"Yes." Came a meek reply. Then came the naming of people, "spilling his guts" freely, claiming he was only following their instructions.

At that, one of the men grabbed him by the hair and pulled him back hard onto the ground forcing his hands onto the ground above his head, placing his knees on the open palms of each hand. The other man grabbed his feet and spread-eagled him on the ground. As the steel grey eyed man put his rubber gloves on, he spoke.

"Mr. Finkel, how many little girls have you raped?"

"What? None I swear. None really." His voice was trembling with each word.

"Now Mr. Finkel, you mean to lie here in the state you are in and confess to us you have never seduced any teenagers?"

Richard was quick with a response, thinking with that statement, they had the wrong man. "No, no, no I have never raped any teens." Finkel was looking up at the man with the rubber gloves on.

"You lie there naked and tell me you have never had sex with any teenager in any high school you have ever worked at?"

"Ahhh, well, I..."

The man standing above him cut him off. "Now don't lie to me!" His voice was hard and stern.

"I mean I have had a few, but now they were not raped."

From a black leather case, the man removed a scalpel with a number 12 blade curved precisely for the job to be performed, and then he proceeded to castrate Richard Finkel. Richard opened his mouth to scream and just as he did a clean white cloth was placed into his mouth, muffling the sounds.

The man with the scalpel then cut his penis off, holding them in his left hand showing them to Finkel. Richard's eyes were as wide as a human's could have been, showing all white, still groaning from the sudden shock to his body. The man then leaned down close to Richard's face and in a low deep voice said, "Don't guess you will be fucking any more teens!"

Then he placed his bloody "manhood" on his bare chest. Then he reached down and quickly removed the cloth from his mouth as Finkel began to scream, and with the skill of a surgeon, he grabbed Finkel's tongue with a pair of ten-inch stainless steel curved hemostats and with the scalpel cut Finkel's tongue out placing it on Finkel's chest.

Before Richard went into an unconscious state, once again the man spoke in a deep unfeeling voice, "You will never again speak evil of our friends' good name!" Finkel began choking on his own blood as it drained down his throat, the steel grey-eyed man then pulled off his gloves and placed them into the plastic bag with the rest of Richard's clothes. He cleaned the scalpel and hemostat off with a clean white alcohol-soaked cloth and placed each back into the leather case. He walked to the hood of the Jeep where he had laid his coat. He placed the case in the inside pocket of his suit coat. He then placed the bloody cloth he had cleaned the scalpel with into the bag with the rest of Finkel's attire. The two other men were getting Finkel to his feet, the extracted parts of his body dropping to the ground. Dragging Finkel to his car, blood dripping from his mouth and groaning, they placed him in the driver's seat. The seat had been moved back as far as it would go and the back of the seat had been tilted halfway back to allow for ease of placing Finkel's now very limp body into the driver's seat. Two of the men went back to the Jeep and got into the front seat and started the engine.

The man with the cold steel grey-eyes then pulled out a pistol with a silencer on it, calmly walked to the driver's door of the yellow Golf, pointed it toward Finkel's left temple and popped the cap, splattering Richard's right skull, blood, and brains all over the passenger's side of the interior of his car. The man calmly walked back to the driver's door of the jeep pausing momentarily to replace a clean pair of rubber gloves on his hands and the man behind the wheel of the jeep handed him a dark purple lily wrapped in green wrapping paper. He went to where his "manly" parts had fallen to the ground, picked them up, returned to Finkel's car and placed the lily, less the paper, on Richard's bloody nicked lap. Then tossing his penis, testicular, and tongue on the floorboard at Finkel's feet, he then closed the door. He walked back to jeep, pulled his rubber gloves off, placed them in the plastic bag, picked his suit coat off the hood, put it on, placed the bag in the back cargo compartment of the Jeep, and got into the back seat behind the driver. They left.

As the two boys eased up to the right side of the car and looked in from the back right rear window, which was splattered with blood, they saw the nude body slumped over toward the right side of the car. "Holy shit! Let's get out of here!" The ten year old proclaimed to his nine year old adventurous playmate. Quickly they ran to the nearest house, some two miles away. The old man that lived there had no phone, but did have an old 1955 red Chevy pick-up truck. The boys told the seventy plus year old man what they had seen, and asked him to take them down the mountain to a country store where they could call for help. He did and the boys' parents as was well as the County and State Police arrived in a short time. Full rigor had set in as it had been two full days since Richard Finkel's sudden demise.

I had a few friends in the newspaper business, so I placed a call to one of them.

"Bastally Daily Chronicle may I help you?"

"Good morning. May I speak to Ted West or Anthony Krause please?"

"One moment please." Several seconds went by as my call transferred.

"Ted West here, may I help you?"

"Ted, this is John O'Donovan."

"Hey, what's up this bright sunny morning? Got a good story for me, you old retired dog."

"Well, not really. I do not think. I need some information from you first. What do you know about the Finkel story?"

Ted paused as if he was trying to remember what they had gathered on the Finkel story. Then he proceeded to tell me the bits and pieces of a story he had gathered letting me in on as many details as they had, as he did owe me several favors. He informed me that he had gotten what he could from several teachers at the school where Finkel worked.

"Several students gave me a little information, but not really much. But of course they were rather shaken up. But I guess that is understandable."

"Ted, how old were the students you talked to?"

There was a pause for several seconds. "I really don't know."

"Well give me your best guess. And were they male or female?"

"Well, both."

"So how old, would you say?"

"Welllll, I would have to say...welll, given their build, ohhh, seventeen or eighteen, maybe a few sixteen year olds. Why do you ask?"

"Oh, something I heard."

"What? Something I can use?" Ted quickly responded.

"Well, maybe, later. I want to check some of my facts out first."

As Ted and John continued their short conversation, Ted remembered the name of James Patrick O'Francis and a civil trial that had taken place several years earlier. Of course, the question any good newspaper reporter would ask, he asked, "John, do you think that O'Francis had anything to do with the torture and murder?"

I proceeded to inform Ted that I really did not think so. I told him that O'Francis had moved from the area some years ago and to my knowledge no one had heard or seen him since.

Of course, Ted wanted to know where he was, and I informed him that I did not have a clue. The truth of the matter was, I really did not know for sure. Of course, I was lying about the fact that I didn't have a clue, as I had given my word, and I knew from the long talks, that meant a great deal to

J.P., and the fact that we had a Brotherhood code I had to live by. I had to wonder as my mind flashed back to the last few conversations I had with him. Had he and his Master come to terms as to what justice was, or was this just a case of a corrupt bookie, drug dealing, statutory rapist, rotten teacher, getting his just dues by any number of people connected to the illegal businesses or enraged fathers?

The investigation revealed that there were traces of cocaine in the trunk of Finkel's car. The police concluded that he had been involved in drugs and had double-crossed someone and paid the price. The school's administrative personnel of course pretended that they had no clues as to his corrupt character or that he had been involved in any wrongdoing. Of course, they also did not know of anything in his past that would have suggested that he was involved in anything illegal. Finkel had been smooth and they may have been semi-innocent, but not completely. Money can and did buy off a lot of people, and have them look the other way. "I have no knowledge" comments became a popular saying among many school administrators throughout the entire area. It was also a known fact that most, not all, but most administrators from any of the surrounding school systems were like most politicians, liars and cheats, not to discount, corrupt.

The phone tree had started throughout Reynolds County. Damon Bales who now lived in the Abetton area called Irvin Brewer first, who also had moved to the lake area not far from Abetton. He then called LaMar Marshy who had moved on to a county in the middle of the state, doing what he did best. The phone rang at Judge Danial Edwin residence and to the eight others that were the principal conspirators in the destruction of J.P. O'Francis' career. Bales made an effort to connect with the county sheriff's department. However a new sheriff was now in charge of the county, one with honor and integrity,

Sidney Delta. He had cleaned up all but a few of the corrupt deputies within the department, and was working on cleaning out the few remaining suspected corrupt members of his department. Damon's' panic resulted in a call to their connection in the state police, who was now retired. Panic had overtaken Damon, as he was the most paranoid of all the people connected to O'Francis' past. He quickly found that nothing could be done about what he perceived to be taking place. Damon and Brewer had tried to get the county commonwealth attorney, (also new to the county and one with a degree of honor,) as well as the sheriff's department to issue a warrant for J.P. as that was whom they had automatically targeted as doing the "number" on Richard. That failed, as there was nothing of substance to their erroneous allegations. They could not get any help from the State Police level because they had nothing connecting the person being accused. They could not get any help issuing a warrant for J.P. from the adjoining counties' legal and law enforcement agencies (where the crime took place) as no one knew who or where J.P. was, and no one had any proof he was involved, which really created more panic for the guilty minded jackals from and remaining in Reynolds County that knew they had been part of the destruction of O'Francis' career, as well as what was done to his youngest son, which led J.P. to leave the area. All anyone in the law enforcement agencies had was some individual finger pointing by this small group, and their power structure, which did not extend far outside their domain. Most of the people doing the finger pointing were well known for their tainted characters as well as their methods of operation, and little credence was given to their accusations outside Reynolds County.

Sheriff Delta and several of his deputies, who had been students of O'Francis, talked among themselves, smiling at the possibility of O'Francis being the judge, jury, and executioner. Although they all were honorable police officers, one officer stated in the closed-door gathering, "Does my heart good to just think that J.P. pulled this off. Even though I really do not think he is anywhere around this area to administer the due justice."

I decided to contact a few of my reliable sources. In doing so, I learned of the finger pointing and the phone calls. I had to have a little laugh as to the reaction to Finkel's demise and the self-deemed importance of the group that had caused J.P. so much hardship for so many years. He himself was dealing with PTSD and all the mental duress that goes with it. I actually had no doubt that he himself could have performed such an act. However, I had gotten the impression from several of our talks, that he may have had sources in places with a great deal of power and many tentacles that reached far and wide. Something else I learned about the people who had cut his career short with their iniquities, they did not have a clue as to whom they were really dealing with.

# Demotion

IT WAS TO BE ANOTHER year of heartache for J.P., as he started his year of teaching. He had been demoted to the lowest grade level Marshy and Damon could place him, the middle school. His stress level was once again reaching the high-level mark with the thoughts of having to work for some-one who years earlier did everything he could to destroy his career. His emotions were like a charted heartbeat, he was joyfully happy and at peace teaching the children that graced his "Think Tank" and when some admin-istrator brought forth yet another erroneous allegation, and launched some in-depth central office investigation, it was pumping at a 150 beats per min-ute. Now, once again, he faced working for his old nemesis Bobby Simms, the man who claimed he had done nothing to supplant J.P. in the com-munity, county, or school system. Like the small town politician that he was, the words he uttered where no different from someone on the national stage, meaningless and often damaging to one's character with no absence of malice.

His very first day started out with a faculty meeting where he knew no one, as Simms introduced J.P. to the teachers. J. Patrick O'Francis' name was well known, with the "have you heard, and "did you know," gossip and whispers among the facility members at Honsburg Elementary and Middle School. However, none knew the man. A standard meeting, many papers handed out telling you everything from when to go and not go, the times of duties and dates. As J.P. surveyed the room of mostly female teachers, he began feeling apprehensive as though an enemy he could not kill surrounded him.

Then at the end of the 45-minute meeting, a woman of many years in teaching stood and stated, "I would just like to tell everyone here, that I personally am very glad that Mr. O'Francis is here at our school. I feel that he will make a much-needed addition to the faculty. I have heard that he is an excellent teacher. I think it is about high time we get quality teachers here at this school."

O'Francis did not have a clue as to who the woman was and gave little value to her words, although the words were very much appreciated. He had become 100% distrustful of all people, more especially anyone within the Reynolds School System.

As the meeting adjourned, Simms asked J.P. to come to his office, *such a formulary sound*, he thought. He had come to hate the words.

The same setting just a different school. Simms sat behind his desk, J.P. in one of two chairs in the room with the door closed. The only real exception was that Decal was not attached to Simms' hip.

"Mr. O'Francis, I really feel that we need to talk. I hope that you and I can put all the past behind us and start over on a clean slate."

J.P. sat taking notes on his legal pad. He had forgotten his tape recorder, as he had not expected to be in the principal's office so soon. His bad, he thought. I w*ill not make that mistake again.*

Simms paused momentarily and then continued, "I truly am glad you are here at this school. I am aware that you are a very good teacher. You know I have always said that. I feel we can have a very good and productive year."

He went through all the rules and policies he had and then asked if J.P. had any questions or he needed anything.

J.P. was very polite and very professional. "No sir, I do not think so at this time. I will adhere to all policies, rules, and regulations here at this school. I do want to be left alone to just teach the children. I do not think that is too much to ask."

Simms stood, as did J.P. He walked around the desk and extended his hand out to him, a moment of hesitation, and then with great reluctance, he shook Simms' hand.

"Now Mr. O'Francis, you know that you and I have a common foe, don't you?" Their hands parted, as J.P. did not respond.

"You know." Simms continued. Jim's eyes were locked on Simms.

His mind raced at lightning flash speed, his insides were tense, his anxiety level had risen, his arms and hands felt warm. *I know too much on too many people. I do not trust you and no one else within the system in which I have to work. Damn, I just need to start fresh, even if I have been demoted. I am a teacher, a real teacher. I love teaching, I love spreading knowledge that I hope will grow exponentially in all my students. Damn, I need for you and the rest of the Jackals of the possessed demoniacs of chthonic to leave me the fuck alone.*

Bobby tried once again to get J.P. to state a name. At that moment he did not know who their common foe could be, several names instantly flashed through his mind: *Marshy, Bales, Finkel, Jones, Decal, Harper, good God, I did not think we had any common foe...who was he referring to?* Jim was not really trying to come up with a name. He only wanted to get out of the office of the enemy he was now in the presence of, and could not do a damn thing to him.

"Sure you do," Simms stated as O'Francis stood in silence looking directly into his eyes. "The man over in the central office."

J.P. did not comment. "Marshy. You know what he has done to you, and you know he and I do not join at the hip."

He thought, as he stood looking directly at Bobby Simms, still not speaking, *"No. But I damn sure know that you and Decal sure the hell done a number on me over the years in this glorious County as well as outside the County! He sure was joined at the hip with you."* J.P. broke eye contact and looked at his watch on his left wrist.

"I've really got to go Mr. Simms, if there is nothing else Sir."

"No, no I don't think so." Simms broke a big warm smile. "Now Mr. O'Francis, if you need anything, you just come see me."

J. Patrick made a sharp pivoting right and walked out of the office without anything else being said. As J.P. walked the very long hallway toward his new classroom, which was the last classroom at the far end of the hall of the Junior High section of the building, a song began to play in his mind. *"Smiling faces, smiling faces, tell lies, and I got the proof...the evil that lurks within...the truth is in the eyes, 'cause the eyes don't lie..." Damn, the Temptations sure the fuck had that song right...*

# River Fishing

It had been a rather stressful day and J.P. needed somewhere to go to think, somewhere alone, somewhere no humans would be. He did not feel like journeying to the mountains, his other retreat over the years, weather permitting, he would go to the river.

J.P. changed into his tan wading shorts, his green and gold pull over tee shirt with a football and golden helmet on the front with the words in the background, Notre Dame, in large letters. Across the middle of the back of his tee shirt was the words WE ARE ND in large letters. It was not as if anyone who ever knew him did not already know where his feelings lie. His loyalty never wavered, in the good years or lean years. He was ND through and through. Putting his pocketknife in his left hip pocket, he went to his hat tree and picked his boonie hat off the rack, placed it on his head, his favorite for fishing as well as his mountain retreats. Then he picked out a pair of white ankle high socks out of his dresser drawer as he went out of the bedroom and down the hallway. He slipped on his flip-flops as he went through the utility room and went to his shed, "The Barn" as he called it, because it was shaped like a barn. He picked up his white low cut tennis shoes, which he wore each time he went fishing, took his fishing jacket off the hook he always hung it up on, reached up and retrieved his spinning reel and rod off its hanger he had made for the eight rods and reels, three of which were his youngest sons'. He put all his fishing items in the truck bed, went back in his house, picked up a bottle of water, gave Dawn a kiss, told her that he loved her and went out the front door. Dawn told J.P. to be careful, and J.P. replied as he always did.

"If I die, make damn sure the damn insurance company does not screw you out of your money, and they will if they can. Hell you know that they are nothing but legalized racketeers supported by the damn corrupt politicians anyway."

J.P. started his truck and drove out of the driveway. Ten minutes later he arrived at the river where he wanted to fish for the next three hours. He parked his truck some twenty yards down from the little church that set several hundred feet above the river as it turned down the high cliffs that extended south above the little white church. J.P. sat on the tailgate putting on his socks and tennis shoes. Then he reached into the right upper pocket, one of his many pockets on his fishing jacket, and took out a pack of sugar free chewing gum. He took out two sticks, removed the wrappers, put the wrappers in a plastic trash bag he kept in the cab of his truck, placed the gum in his mouth and chewed them for a few minutes as he put his rod together and put one of his Rebel crawfish on the end of his yellow line. J.P. then took out a pock of beechnut chewing tobacco and put a handful into his left jaw, mixing it with the gum he had gotten juicy.

Turning toward the river, he began his walk down the riverbank. Walking through the waist high grasses and what he referred to as 'hog weeds" for about one hundred yards, he came upon a red iron six foot long, four foot high farming gate. He opened it and passed to the other side, closing and latching the gate as he found it. The area he crossed over into was a pasture area along the river with a tractor road that lead along the river bank. J.P. continued to walk for half a mile down the river. He stopped and looked out at the shoals.

"Good spot to start," he stated aloud as if he was talking to someone present. J.P. spit his mouthful of amber to his right, and then stepped into the cool waters of the Clinch.

The water was only a little above his ankles, with a rocky bottom of small rocks, the kind that are easy to walk on. He took several steps toward the middle of the river as the water's depth became deeper, up to the top of his knees. He stopped and cast his line toward the middle of the swift moving water.

J.P. traversed the small and large rocks of the Clinch, occasionally losing his balance and ended up sitting down in the river with the waters swirling around his upper body and over his shoulders. Regaining his balance in the swift-flowing water, he stood in thigh high water, laughing at himself. Then he spit the tobacco juice into the water. He cast his line to the right side of the rocky shoals into a pool of bubbling oxygen-filled water at the far end, over the rocks that were protruding above the water in hopes of catching the big bass of the day. Several casts into the same general spot and he finally got a hit on the crawfish. His rod bent drastically toward the water below him as his line stretched tight and he strained at the fish on the end of it.

Slowly he reeled the bass toward him. As the fish came over the rocky shoals, it broke the surface of the water in an effort of freeing himself. The bass fought hard and J.P. gradually reeled him toward him. Now only ten yards away, the rod trembled as the large bass fought even harder. J.P. reeled the big bass slowly to within two feet of himself and lifted the two-pound bass out of the water. He put his left thumb into the bottom of the bass's mouth curving his index finger around his lower mouth. Placing his reel between his upper thighs, he reached into his left upper pocket, released the surgical hemostat, and removed the hooks from the bass's mouth. Holding the two-pound bass up looking at it for a moment, J.P. smiled, bent over and released the fish back into the river to be caught yet another day stating to the bass as if he could hear him, "Until next time big boy."

J.P. walked over a mile down the middle of the river, fishing to one side or the other of the river, falling only once, with a couple of slips but regaining his balance. He had caught ten fish of various sizes, all bass. The beauty of the sun setting to his west and the glimmer of the reflection of the sun off the bubbling waters that flowed over and gushed between the rocks and boulders caused J.P. to pause and lose himself in its beauty and sound. The temperature was still in the low eighties at six o'clock in the evening. All he could hear was the roar of the rushing water and the sound of a crow off toward the farmland that joined the river at its banks. Twenty yards to his right front stood a four and a half foot tall Blue Crane at the edge of the water. Then out of the sky from behind J.P. and thirty feet over his head, four wild ducks passed over him landing a good fifty yards down the river in front of him in the smoother deeper waters, all with the grace of a Navy 'Tom-Cat' on the deck of a carrier.

To his left the topography of the land rose quickly and was covered with the hard woods of the southwestern part of the state. To his right cattle grazed in the open fields that ran to the river's edge. He stood motionless with his reel and rod in his hand poised to cast his line just across the top of the outcropping of rocks protruding above the water, where he thought would be a good place for yet another large bass. He stood motionless at the edge of yet another rocky shoal looking down the river, the sun warm on his face, his clothes from his belt line up had dried to a very light dampness. His world moved in slow motion as he just stood in the middle of the river gazing down toward the ducks, hearing nothing as his mind slipped into a far off land in a far off time.

# The Creek

It was Rusty, Bill, Jim and three "yards" loading onto the chopper at 0500 hours for a trip into the forbidden jungle as Jim so often referred to it. Once again, the patrol was to infiltrate the domain of "Charlie", gather information on his activities, and then report their findings to Captain Thompson, who in turn would pass it along to the SOG officer who in turn would do whatever with it. Most likely Jim figured after all the "brains" mulled over the "Intel" they would be tapped for a major ambush patrol.

The "taxi" pilots were always in a joking mood, of which Jim liked and yet he did not like it as he was never in the mood for "wise cracks" and jokes when flown out on a mission, yet "Rusty" was always telling him to lighten up, that everything was going to be okay. Sometimes Jim thought his closest friend was hiding his fears behind his ever-optimistic approach to missions like the one they were embarking upon. Jim was in no mood, especially that early in the morning for chopper pilot wisecracks. Down deep, he knew that they only did it to take the tension off the mission. Jim knew the pilots knew the dangers, not only to the patrol, but also to themselves. They were as good at their job as Jim and the members of the patrols were at their jobs. They too were also a part of a very elite group of men who were placed in harm's way on a near daily basis. Their performance under fire could not be matched, and the lives they saved in the heat of a firefight were beyond heroic. As far as Jim was concerned when he had been pulled out of a compromised mission, on more than one occasion, the pilots should have been given the Congressional Medal of Honor.

However, as I have learned over the many conversations with him, he himself did not believe in medals and being glorified or put on some front-page story about anything he did while simply doing his job, just like thousands of other combat soldiers have done.

But be that as it may, the pilots were at their best. Jim did not laugh, Bill and Rusty of course did, and the "yards" did not get the humor to start with, so they were as poker faced as Jim. Jim got to know the pilots well, and they him. He was not always as hard faced toward their humor, just on certain missions, that led to locations he was not at all happy about going into.

It was not that any of the places were good places to go, but there were some that were far worse than others. Jim hated the location where they were going. Nothing ever seemed to work out correctly when they were in that particular part of the jungle, AO (Area of Operation). Moreover, this area of the jungle was an area they had never 'reconned' and they knew nothing about it other than what the maps showed them.

The flight did not last all that long, thirty minutes, but one can cover a lot of terrain in a chopper within a thirty minute span. The geographic location put the green "taxi" down on a small hill with a clearing just large enough for one "Huey" to hover six feet or so off the ground. The patrol was out and clear within seconds and the ever-dependable UH-1 Iroquois was lifting above the trees and slanting off to the east by the time the patrol set up under the thick canopy.

As Jim laid motionless listening to the sounds of the surrounding jungle and its ever-present noises as the birds and other assorted species returned to their morning wake-up calls from being disturbed by the deep popping sound of the Huey's large blades cutting through the early morning air, O'Francis looked about him, and not being able to see anything at any distance which was totally impossible, it made him feel very uneasy about this particular patrol. His thoughts were on the name of the patrol, *"Cripple Creek." Jesus Christ, why in the hell did the old man let Billy call it Cripple Creek. Shit, only a boy from North Carolina with the nickname of Hawk would do that. And, Bill thought it was funny. Oh, just like the song he said. Fuck a bunch of songs: Bad name for a patrol like this one in this area. All because on the topo map it showed that we had to descend into and travel down a fucking creek.* Then the frigging song started going over and over in his mind.

*"Going down Cripple Creek, going on the run, going down Cripple Creek, going to have me some fun... ghee's, bluegrass, damn I hate bluegrass. What was it "Hawk" said...oh yeah, Bill Monroe is the greatest."*

Ten minutes passed and the "Cripple Creek Patrol" gathered and began their descent toward the creek. It was approximately one klick (0.62 miles) straight down the mountain, or so the map showed. Going straight was out of the question.

After meandering for two hours at a snail's pace through thick jungle foliage, making little or no noise to reach the upper head waters of the creek, "Hawk" held up his left arm, his fist clinched high in the air to the man behind him. The man behind him repeated the same sign and the man behind him, until all had frozen in place. They had reached the creek, a steep 90-degree bank at least seven feet high lay before them as one by one they dropped into the calf high water. It appeared, according to the map, that they had connected to the creek about a third of the way from where it allegedly started. How far up the mountain it started, Jim was not sure, but by its size at that point, it must have been several klicks.

Jim was the fourth member back and when it was his time to drop into the water, he thought, *damn good thing we were not running, hell coming on this out of nowhere, the fall would have killed us.* As he dropped into the water the rocks being slippery he lost his balance and landed on his butt causing a splash and more noise than he would like. No one said a word, just looked to see if he was okay. He held his left hand up with his thumb in the air, regained his footing, and then moved forward allowing the man behind him to drop into the creek.

Moments later a very eerie group of men dressed in green with "war paint" covering their faces, necks, and hands with boonie hats draped on their heads, stretched out some five to seven meters apart, very slowly making their way down the creek.

The water's depth ran from calf high to waist high, and the width of the water itself was about three to five feet wide with the creek bed running from a few feet wide to touching the steep banks itself. The water flowed over a rocky creek bottom which made it most difficult to walk in, then it would just drop into a pool of water which reached to one's waist. Jim kept wondering when "Hawk" was going to go through one of the pools and just drop over his head. But they were in the upper parts of the creek, so that would most likely not happen until they got to the lower end of the creek, if they got that far, which he was hoping they would not have to travel that far down toward the valley floor.

The foliage would change from a complete overhead canopy, where even with the sun at high noon made it rather dark, even to the point that the sunlight did not penetrate through the heavy overhead canopy that would have normally created streams of light rays filtering through the trees, making it look as if some heavenly host was ready to appear in all its celestial glory before the group of men in single file wading down some blessed mountain waters. The trees that were positioned on the top edges of the creek banks had a multitude of large and medium side roots that extended openly through the sides of the steep creek banks and extended down into the creek bed.

Then as if one were coming out of a cave, there would be an opening in the canopy and the sky would be clear and the hot sunlight would pour down onto the small patrol. The foliage on the sides of the creek bank would turn to the long thick green grasses that seemed to have a razor edge to them. Rusty would tell us "it is as bad as the cord grass in Texas, cut you to shreds." These grasses were over six feet tall and so thick that one could not penetrate it without great difficultly. The grasses' long blades would drape over the sides of the top of the creek bank nearly reaching the creek bed itself, hanging loosely and moving with the slightest of breezes like long tentacles appearing to be reaching out with their rough sandpaper surface attempting to gulp you into its hundreds of waving blades. The larger broad leaf plants were often mixed in with the grasses as well as in and around the trees under the canopy.

One and a half hours of very slowly wading the creek the patrol took a break as they once again entered into another darkened overhead of canopy forest. The under-foliage in the dark shaded areas was completely different from that of the open areas. Larger and broader plants covered the ground area. Each man alternated to each side of the creek placed themselves against the banks of the creek, blending into the roots of the trees that reached down into the edge of the water like giant legs that were attached to some towering giant forest creature that guarded the secret waters flowing by its feet.

Jim welcomed the cool damp ground of the creek bank on the backs of his legs and buttocks. The creek bed area was only three feet from the water's edge. He leaned back against the side of the creek bank, which was only about six feet in height. He removed his boonie hat, then leaned forward and scooped up a hat full of water, poured it over his head letting the cool water soak his upper body, then sat back into the roots, laying his head back between them. His shaved "war painted" head and face made it almost impossible to be seen as he closed his eyes and listened for anything that was not normal to the forest in which they were descending deeper and deeper down into.

In the distance, he could hear the sharp cry of a monkey and the odd sound of some bird unknown to him. The sound of the rippling, briskly clean clear water over the rocks as it flowed to the valley far below was soothing to his mind. But mostly he heard silence, a welcomed sound to his ears. As he sat, savoring the moments of silence, his thoughts went to the creek that descended into the river that ran by the home he grew up in and the two mountains that towered high above the river across from where he was raised. He thought of how, long before the Long Hunters penetrated into the virgin forests of Southwestern Virginia, and over time how the white man had polluted the steams, as well as the creek that cascaded over a one hundred foot high falls before it emptied into the river a quarter of a mile away. The creek had over the eons cut its path between the two mountains to empty into the river directly across from his home place. A creek he had explored from its mouth to its source a three-mile journey back up into the open area of a valley between yet more mountains to the south. He thought that at one time, long ago, that it too must have been just as clean and clear. A time when the Native Americans were roaming the area and to his knowledge, it was at one time a pristine hunting ground for several tribes that filtered into the area to do their hunting.

Every inch of his clothes was wet with sweat or creek water. He was tired even before he had left for the mission. He wished he could relieve himself of the weight of personal supplies he was carrying, relaxing where he sat and sleep for just a few hours, secure in the fact that he knew his concealment was secure from anyone who might happen by. He did not feel hungry, although it had been several hours since he had eaten and whatever food for energy he had consumed for breakfast had already been burned. There had been very little conversation between any of the patrol members as they sat and ate their breakfast. No one wanted to talk about the mission and where they were heading.

He knew that a power nap was not possible and that he would be up and moving again in a matter of minutes. The food would come late in the day. Real sleep would not come at all. He opened his canteen and took a small drink of water, replaced it on his side, closed his eyes and just listened.

Another hour of walking the creek, trying not to fall on the slippery rocks and traversing between the large boulders where the creek gushed between them, since they had started their decent in the pristine water, then suddenly a fist went up from the point man. Jim went down on his right knee into the water and pivoted slightly to his left, his AR-15 at the ready quickly scanning the area in front of him. "Hawk" slowly worked his way back to the first "Yard" and informed him by whispering in his ear that he had spotted a major trail leading down into the creek on both sides of the bank. The word was passed back in the same manner.

As the patrol very alertly and slowly advanced to inspect the trail, they saw that it was well worn, and was about four feet wide, very large for a trail through the jungle. Which meant that it was a major "road-way" for the VC to haul their supplies. The bank on each side of the creek had been carved out allowing easy access down into the creek. The patrol gathered and plotted the trail on their maps at the creek crossing, then cautiously proceeded up the left side of the trail. It ran in between two ridges that ran all the way to the creek from the top of the mountain. For Jim, a hollow was all it was. Jim found himself more alert, his heart began to pump faster, not because of the incline but because it was a trail that was worn smooth which meant that many people traveled it and these people were not going to welcome the patrol with open arms if they met anywhere along the path.

The hollow twisted and turned gently upward for about a mile (two klicks) with only two branches that Jim could tell. Neither branch had any paths that intersected into the main hollow. As the patrol approached the top of the ridge, the trail led off to the west and along the ridgeline. The patrol traveled along the ridge for about 3.22 kilometers (2 miles) and stopped. After a hand only discussion, they back tracked back to the creek and followed the trail up the other side of the mountain. The same topography was on the northwest side of the creek as was on the southeast side. The trail to the southeast side of the ridge meandered along the side of the mountain instead of up any hollow and it took the patrol longer to reach the top of the ridge on the southeast side. Once at the top of the ridgeline the trail followed along the ridge and according to their maps, the ridge descended all the way to the valley like tributaries to a river. This meant that the traffic in the valley, which was already known, was coming from the area in which the "Cripple Creek Patrol" was now on. This was what they were looking for, which for Jim meant that they were in great danger. He as well as the others realized that the odds were great that they would not get out of this mission without being compromised. Now what worried him as they sat at the top of the ridge and planned where they would be for the night was if he, as well as the rest, would get out at all.

His mind wandered briefly as the rest of the patrol talked in whispers and hand signals. He looked around and realized that the entire forest was a rather enchanting and mysterious place to be. It was so peaceful and filled with great beauty and yet amidst all the beauty he saw, he felt the darkness and horror of war and death, causing him to shake as his body suddenly felt chilled and he was quickly brought back into the reality of where he was. "Hawk" asked him where he thought they should set up for the night in hopes that they would observe the traffic that they felt traveled the mountain path on a nightly basis, carrying the supplies of war.

Jim looked at Bill and then at Rusty, the long distance look in his eyes must have told them everything as his mind was yet streaking back to reality.

"You alright Jim?" Rusty whispered.

"Yes." Jim whispered and unfolded his laminated covered topographic map out on the ground looking at it for a few seconds and pointed his finger to a line he had drawn with his grease pencil, denoting the trail leading up the hollow and out of the top of the ridge on the northwest side of the creek. He quickly drew a black line on the topographic map denoting the southeast side of the trail and extended it all the way down to where the ridge ended in the valley.

"Here. I think we should recon this area here and set up for the night."

"Why there?" 'Hawk' whispered.

"Because here," still pointing and tapping the map, "we can observe them coming down the hollow. We will be on the upper side of them looking down into the hollow, and still see somewhat, enough to get an idea of how many and how often and still be safe."

"Damn that is awful thick shit over there," Rusty started in a whisper.

"Yeah, well, better not to be seen my flat landed Texas friend. Besides on this side of the creek it is too steep and too thick for us to get a good location to observe our little friends."

"We can recon the area during the day and observe during the night. That way if we have to come back we will have it plotted out for an ambush," Bill whispered as if he was excited about the entire mission.

"'Hawk,' let us not forget, this is their yard we are playing in and they may very well travel during the day. Hell, they feel safe this deep in the jungle. They figure this trail will not be found. I mean think about it, what are the odds that anyone would find this. Damn slim if you ask me. So, yeah, we can do some reconning, but we had better be damn careful. I mean there ain't but six of us and you know fuck'en well that there are going to be one hell-of a lot more of them. The PZ is damn sure to far away to be running for, and getting anyone in here, for a pick-up is out of the question."

"Yeah, yeah, I got it. But if we were not good at what we do, we would not have found this trail to start with."

Jim just looked at Bill without saying a word. Rusty never said anything, as he knew that Jim went with his intuition, that little voice he always talked about, and most of the time he was right. Two of the three "Yards" were off a few meters, one toward the valley side of the trail, the other the creek side. Y Jhon was kneeling on his left knee beside Rusty, he looked at O'Francis for a long moment, his dark eyes reading Jim's face as if he too felt the fear that was being revealed across his grease painted face.

Off they went back down the mountain, back across the creek and half way up the mountain where they reconned for the best sight to set up to observe for the next couple of days.

After finding the best place to see the trail, at a safe distance to not be seen, they settled in, spreading out along the side of the hill some 6 meters apart.

After removing his 90 pounds of gear and eating, Jim got comfortable intertwining himself into the foliage, becoming invisible. The mountain air was cool and he put on his field jacket. He closed his eyes and rested, his hearing increasing tenfold, for any sound that was not natural to the jungle. Darkness came rather quickly or so it seemed. He looked at his illuminating watch, it was 2100 hours and wondered if the traffic would come. He did not have to wait all that long. By 2230 hours he could hear the Viet Cong and most likely North Vietnamese Regular Army intermixed with the VC coming from on top of the ridge. Jim thought, *they sure the hell are not at all quiet, but, why should they be. They felt safe in their mountain sanctuary.* The length of soldiers and supply carriers stretched from the creek to somewhere on top of the ridge and then there was a lull of about an hour or so and another group traveled down the hollow.

Even though Jim could not be seen, his heart pounded so heavily he could hear it in his ears as they went by. They waited and only two columns passed the first night. He could only estimate as to how many there had been, but the number was great and he knew that it would take a major operation to pull off an ambush, if at all. As he lay and analyzed the possibilities, he concluded that there would be too many for any size of an ambush patrol from Dak Pek to put together and take on such a large force. In addition, they would be too deep into the jungle, and the terrain was too rugged for any large operation, in Jim's mind. One good thing about working with this group of soldiers, they would listen and take advice from the people who had done the reconnaissance of the area.

The next day they reconned the entire area, plotting every "inch" of the hollow from the creek to the top of the ridge. This took all day, as they had to work at a snail's pace and as quiet as a slithering snake.

The next night, the same took place, almost at the same time. Jim logged the time in his head as he was sure that Bill and Rusty had done the same. At 0600 hours, as the dawn was just breaking, giving them just enough light to move safely, they backtracked their way back up the creek and to the PZ the sound of people was heard at the top of the ridge. At once, they were down again in silent watching mode. This time they could see more clearly between all the foliage. It took 45 minutes from the first person Jim saw to the last person that passed in front of him. It appeared they were carrying everything from food supplies to weapons, including several large mortars and several were pulling two wheeled carts with supplies.

*Christ, this is not good. They are preparing a major attack on someone. This will take every "Yard" we have to ambush a patrol this size. This is not good. Hell, I hate even telling SOG that we even found this fuck'en place.* Jim's little voice kept talking to him as he lay and waited for over an hour after the VC patrol had passed.

Each one of the "Cripple Creek Patrol" slowly moved through the thick undergrowth along the side of the hillside over the top of the fingered ridge that formed the hollow, which led to the creek, down the back sloping of the ridge angling back toward the creek. They reached the creek within an hour of their descent. Jim estimated that they were a good half mile up from were the main trail crossed the creek. He felt very uneasy as they made their way back up the creek. He wished they could have moved faster but knew they could not. He felt like a turtle trying to trek up the creek, as his heart pounded with anxiety. He tried to calm himself telling himself that they would not run into any rogue patrols this far from the trail. They had seen no signs of any trails leading down from either side of the mountain as they had come down the creek. He recognized where they entered the creek as they pushed onward up the creek looking for a good place to exit the area and make their way through the jungle and to the rendezvous about 4 kilometers (2.5 miles) from where they had been let out three days earlier. The ever-dependable "Green Taxi" would be at the coordinates on time he had no doubts. The question was, could they?

Another two miles up the creek, the bank on the west side feathered out enough for the "Cripple Creek Patrol" to exit the creek area with ease and began their ever snail pace through the jungle, picking their way as quietly as possible. By the time they reached the top of the ridge, Jim was soaking wet, his legs ached, his back ached, he had a headache that was pounding like kettledrums, and he was not in a good mood. The humidity was so high that it was hard to breath. There was no breeze and the temperature had to be in the upper 90's, Jim told himself. As they rested and plotted where they were from the maps, clouds began to move over the mountain, and in a matter of minutes it was raining so hard that if one could have seen 20 yards in any direction, you couldn't. The rain felt good, it was a cool rain, and Jim welcomed it. He knew that just as soon as it was over, and it would stop just as quick as it had begun, the humidity would be just as bad if not worse, if that could have been possible.

They made their way along the ridgeline up and down the rises in the topography, then without any notice, they came upon a trail. Smaller in width, maybe two meters (two feet) wide, but well used, they all stopped and located where they were on the maps, again plotting the trail. The patrol pulled back several yards off the trail. The trail appeared to lead in the same direction in which they had to travel. One of the "Yards" headed in the opposite direction in which the patrol was traveling to see if he could determine where it may be going or coming from. He returned in ten minutes with a report that it dropped off the backside of the main ridge a short ways out the top of the ridge, maybe one kilometer at best (about a half mile).

"So what do you think?" 'Hawk' whispered.

"I say we take the fucking trail," Rusty stated. "I am fucking tired of trying to get through that shit and not make any fucking noise."

"Hawk" looked at Jim. O'Francis pulled his hat off, looked at the map, looked back at Rusty and then at Bill, then a Y Jhon. "Shit, I don't know. Sure would make it easier on us to get where we need to be."

Rusty whispered, "So how do you feel? I mean you know?"

Bill was talking to Y Jhon and the other two "Yards" and looking at the map. Jim had not responded for several seconds.

"Well?" Rusty asked again.

Jim looked at Rusty for several more seconds.

"Damn Rus, I just don't like this fucking area. I don't know. I have had a bad feeling from the time I learned we had to recon this damn place."

"Ahh, hell O'Francis, God damn-it, one place is just as bad as another. It's all fucked up. You know that, shit man. Let's take the damn trail and just get the fuck out of here. Come-on what do you say?"

"Okay, hell you are probably right, one place is just as bad as another. No telling what or when you are going to run upon a patrol, shit, we can handle it. Right?" He and Rusty looked at each other.

"Right by god! Fuck-it! We are Rangers, we can handle it!"

Bill made his way back over to Jim and Rus, "So, what do you want to do?"

"Take the trail," Rusty stated. Jim just nodded yes.

"Okay." 'Hawk' took the point once again and they were off.

They had traveled an hour and were making good time. The patrol would be at the PZ a good half day at their current pace before they were to be extracted. The trail kept to the top of the ridges most of the time, dropping off to one side or the other for several meters from time to time. They were back on top of the ridgeline for several hundred yards and then they began descending slowly straight down as the path, following the topography of the ridge into a gap between the ridgeline, crossing over several large outcroppings and then another stretch of relatively smooth trail were the jungle foliage touched them on both side as they walked along.

All Jim heard was the sound of an AR-15 and then the deep reply of the AK-47's. He saw Rusty dive to his right and Jim went to his left into the thick foliage of the jungle. He heard "Hawk" yell that they were directly to his front. Jim and the "Yard" behind him moved quickly along the side of the path toward Bill, a matter of a few meters. Rusty and Y Jhon moved through the undergrowth on the opposite side. Seeing where the enemy was, was difficult, the sounds were not. O'Francis and the "Yard" engaged about the same time Rusty and Y Jhon did. The advantage went to the "Cripple Creek Patrol" as they were on the upper side and the movement of the Viet Cong allowed them a target to shoot at.

Jim yelled at Rusty that he and Y Bang were moving up to "Hawk's" position on the down slope side. As they did, he could see the line of fire and the movement of the VC trying to circle around on Bill and Y Jhon's position. They opened fire instantly and saw a body fall. As they continued to lay down fire he could hear Rusty engaging and within a matter of minutes there was once again silence. No sounds from the forest, no sounds of rain falling, nothing. Several minutes passed before O'Francis yelled for Rusty. He got a return "Okay." Then he heard Rusty moving and in seconds, he called out to Jim as quietly as possible that 'Hawk" had been hit, Y Jhon was okay. Several more minutes passed before Y Bang and Jim moved toward Bill's position. They had not heard any movement coming from the ten to thirteen meters directly in front of them for several minutes after the firefight had stopped.

As Jim and Y Bang arrived at Bill's position, they found Rusty caring for a left shoulder wound. Y Jhon was positioned just to his front on alert, Y Bang turned and moved a few meters to their rear and took up a position. They quickly patched the "Hawk-man" up and he was on his knees sitting back on his calves, his boonie hat draped on the back of his neck supported by its string. He looked up at Rusty and then Jim.

"Damn, how close can that get? Shit. Hell, I barely saw them. Son-of-a-bitch! What the hell!"

Jim smiled for the first time in three days. "Well, I am sure glad you saw them first Mr. "Hawk," a nickname Jim had given to Bill because of his nose, and not his very good eyesight, as his nose had a beak look to it from being broken several times. Of course, it was easy as his last name was Hawkins. However, Jim always liked giving people he liked nicknames.

"Hey, we are not far from the PZ, should be there in a few hours. I'll take the point, you drop back in front of Y Bang," Jim stated.

Y Jhon worked his way down to the VC patrol and checked the dead. As he returned, Bill was just getting to his feet.

"There were six, all dead."

"We need to get them off the trail a few meters before we go," Rusty stated.

After getting "Mr. Charles" and his "Commie" buddies off to both sides of the trail several meters the "Cripple Creek Patrol" proceeded down the trail through the swag on the ridge and up the other side. As Jim crested the top of the ridge, he could hear voices and movement coming up the trail. He figured the sound of the firefight would bring any other patrols to their location and in a hurry. Quickly his arm went up, he turned and pointed to his ears and then pointed down toward where they were headed. Waving left then right the CCP quickly disappeared into the jungle on either side of the little trail. As he lay camouflaged into the jungle floor, he could hear the patrol quickly passing, almost in a run. He waited for several minutes giving them plenty of time to reach the swag in the ridgeline, which was about three hundred meters or so away. Then as if they all had some type of sixth sense they moved in unison back onto the trail and proceeded to their PZ. They settled in and waited on their ride.

A clearing on top of one of the ridges was all they needed and off in the distance the deep throb of the "Green Taxi" could be heard. Moments later it was hovering on the small opening in the jungle at the top of the mountain ridge and as the last man of the "Cripple Creek Patrol" was on board, the green UH-1 Huey lifted just above the surrounding tree line and slanted eastward gaining altitude with each passing second.

The ducks brought J.P. back to the world he now lived in. They had for whatever reason lifted off the water and turned and flew back over J.P's head in a flutter of wings and quacking. J.P. looked at his watch. It was 1930 hours by his time and he did not feel like fishing anymore, so he waded to the pasture side of the river and began his walk back to his truck.

# Middle School Adventure Begins

As Bobby Simms had stated, "If you need anything..." J.P. went to him on the last working day of the teachers' work days before the students arrived, and questioned Mr. Simms as to his qualifications to teach a sixth grade class as his certification was for secondary (9-12) and junior high (7-8). However, Simms got around that by telling him that he was qualified because they were departmentalized, and that he was certified in the subject matter. J.P. did not debate the matter, as he knew that Reynolds County bent all the rules to fit whatever they needed. He always did his best to remember the Mark Twain quote. He was well aware that no one in the upper ranks of the department of education in Richmond did any checking on such small insignificant matters as teacher qualifications in any field. J.P. had seen too many "teachers" teaching in areas they were not even close to being qualified or certified in, in the many years of working for the Reynolds County School System. That was why he had the attitude about the education in Virginia, it was "whom" you knew or "blew" or did sexual favors for that mattered, not the education of the youths.

Of course, he also knew that was one of the major reasons that Reynolds County School System was twenty-five years behind the rest of the nation in education and that they would never catch up, not with the current superintendent and his puppet School Board. They were not qualified for the lofty positions they held. It was based solely on whoever was politically connected and would move their mouths when the strings were pulled, and most of the time the combined intelligence of the entire School Board would not equal an IQ of 80, which reflected their actions and their method of thought toward education as a whole. Over the many years, School Boards would change, but the lies, corruption, and stupidity were always the same.

The months of August, September and October went about as J.P. expected them to go, semi-smooth, with his new colleagues being distant, having little communications with him as if he had some type of plague. He was the last to be informed of anything going on as to meetings or places he was to be or for his classes to be. The students kept him informed as to any changes in any schedules. J.P. of course arrived on more than one occasion a few minutes late to assemblies or programs that were suddenly changed, which made him look like he was being uncooperative, causing some of the women teachers who outnumbered the men by 20 to 1, to gossip about him and his alleged reputation of being insubordinate to the administration. J.P. was adjusting or trying to, as he had never taught a junior high class before and the age and mental capabilities were way below what he was accustomed.

It was not easy for him to get to the level of sixth and seventh graders. He found that they were ill prepared for a junior high school class setting. Of course the freshmen students he had taught for a number of years, were ill prepared for high school, which made a bold statement about the quality of middle school teaching. The student had been pampered and spoon-fed on a level below the grade they were in. The grading system was the same as at the high school, antiquated. Giving the students high-level grades was not out of the norm in order to make the teacher look good in the eyes of the administration, and to make parents happy. J.P. just did not do that. He taught a level higher than what they were, in order to bring them up, not down. He believed in making them think. They were not too young to have to think either about questions presented to them verbally in the course of his lectures or on a test. J.P. did not waver in his teaching and testing style.

He continued to lecture, slowing down until the students got used to taking notes. He would teach them how to take notes in each individual's own type of shorthand. No true and false tests, no fill in the blanks and no multiply choice, only short answer questions, which had to be in complete sentences. After a short while, he would work in at least two short essay questions. This required thinking. He carried his classroom title of O'Francis' Think Tank to the Middle School.

A few mild protests from a few parents about note taking at that level and the type of tests that were being given was passed along through the administration to J.P. He listened professionally and responded intellectually giving sound reasons for his methods of teaching as well as testing. One of the major problems, as J.P. saw it, was that most parents in the area considered the six and seventh grades to be elementary. They had not grasped the concept of a middle school, of which the school system itself had not grasped either, as the eighth grade was located at the high school. This gave the impression that "they" were in high school. In the minds of the students and parents of Reynolds County, you had two levels, elementary school and high school.

He had always tried to prepare his students for the next highest level of education. Now his work really was cut out for him. He faced more of the same gossipy criticism from any number of his new colleagues in a building that housed kindergarten through the seventh grades. The students advancing from their elementary environment into a middle school environment were ill prepared, especially when they entered J.P. O'Francis' "Think Tank."

J. Patrick was in hopes that the seven teachers located in the middle school section of the school were different from the ones he had been dealing with for the past 15 years at the high school level. He was in hopes that they were there to be real teachers, not just to collect another paycheck, padding their family yearly income with what their husbands or mates made. He was really in hopes that at 3:30 it did not look like rats scurrying to flee a burning building, that the few he would be working with was the type that put forth the effort to work at being a good educator, which in itself took many long hours outside their regular classroom on a daily basis. He was in hopes that what he had "heard" over the years was not correct, games and playtime, with little real instruction taking place.

Over time, he would learn who the real educators were and who was there for the paycheck. It always showed in the students that entered his "Think Tank," which reflected a very poor product for the next level of education. This made J.P. realize why he had gotten so many students as freshmen and sophomores that were not prepared. There were of course exceptions with his young students. Several students were standouts for their age of 12 to 13 years. Several would excel in O'Francis' "Think Tank," and go on to excel in high school as well as in college. One in particular he told me about was Josh Pickens, who would obtain a Roads Scholar and a PhD. from the University of Virginia.

O'Francis reminded me of a conversation he had when he first arrived in Honsburg. The insulting conversation with one of his fellow colleagues concerning the level of learning skills the students had in the Appalachian Mountains. He told me he hated it then, and he hated it during our conversation. J.P. had a simple philosophy, a person that carried the title of "Teacher" had an enormous responsible. Opening up the minds of the youths and inciting knowledge. It did not matter if it was in the inner-city or in the Appalachian Mountains. The student would learn if the "Teacher" would make it presentable in a manner that made them thirsty for more knowledge and not bore them to the point that they shut down the learning center, the brain.

Shortly after his first year at the Middle School level, he discovered that one of his students did not fit the age group. Young was a major understatement, when O'Francis found out that Noble Bryan was only ten years old. J.P. had a difficult time understanding how a ten year old was in his sixth grade World Geography class. However, he would soon learn that he was a child prodigy, a very quiet, excellent student. J.P. would have the young Noble for two straight years, and enjoyed his learning skills. His sponge-like brain absorbed every ounce of knowledge that J.P. put out. J.P. could not see the future, but in time, he would run across the man named Nobel, who became a computer genius, and worked for none other than the unappreciative Reynolds County School System. The typical Reynolds County School Board was ignorant about the technological world that was growing exponentially right in front of them. The School Board members had no interest in learning about such a world because of their own lack of education, and yet they sat at the head of a school system, putting on the façade of being important. J.P. once stated in one of our more intense discussions concerning the intellectual level of the elected School Board members, "Twain said it best; never argue with a stupid person. They will drag you down to their level and then beat you with experience." That was why J.P. did not attend many School Board meetings. He could not stand to be in the presence of so many stupid people playing demi-gods. Of course, as O'Francis often would state, in our lengthy conversations about the school system, "you just cannot fix stupid!"

Another one of J.P.'s students appeared on the scene on a warm August morning. Bruce Vidal. However, I am getting way ahead of my story, the tech department staff, and their relationship with J. Patrick O'Francis. This part of his story I will pick up later on in the ever-challenging world of J.P. O'Francis.

# Happy Anniversity

In late September, J. Patrick went squirrel hunting, something he had not done in many years. He enjoyed that type of hunting, no real danger in some overzealous hunter shooting him. He had been asked to go deer hunting on several occasions by a number of people, but he could not bring himself to gamble on that kind of hunting. He told me a story about an acquaintance of his, a Vietnam veteran who went deer hunting and was killed. He was covered in bright orange from head to toe. Shooting a deer for J.P. was not the problem. He liked venison, he enjoyed it very much, point of fact was, it was his favorite meat, as long as someone else did the killing and just brought it to him to clean and cut up.

Shooting a rodent was a world of difference for J.P. and besides he really did not like rodents of any kind. For him, he got great pleasure in hunting them down and killing them. He did enjoy eating the squirrels, but the game he played in hunting them was the most fun. It was the challenge of moving ever so slowly through the forest with only the sounds of nature surrounding him. Hiding and sneaking up on them and then getting them in his sights with his shotgun. He always used his old single shot he had gotten when he was thirteen years old. He earned the money for his first gun by being a caddy at the local golf course, and his grandfather helped him buy it. It had been his choice of the type and gage of gun, which was a 12 gage, model 37 Winchester. He had several shotguns now, more modern, more shots, but it was the challenge again, one shot, one "squack" that he enjoyed.

Fall was in full color the last week in October and the anniversary of J.P. and Dawn O'Francis. Their day had been carefully planned and mapped out as they stopped by the corner gas station to fill their car up with fuel. It was a little after nine in the morning and the October mountain air was crisp, as J.P. stood at the gas pump. He wore a lightweight tan jacket, jeans and a pair of soft sole high top hiking shoes. Dawn sat behind the wheel of the car, windows up and the heater on light warm to offset the chill. He did not take note of who was in the car that had pulled in beside the pumps at the island to the far side of the service station lot. He finished filling his car and placed the nozzle back into the pump holder, opened the door and told Dawn how much the cost was. She wrote out a check, which in a small town one could do, if one was known to have good credit. He picked up some two-day-old newspapers and an empty paper coffee cup to be placed in the trash can to the rear of the island. Taking the check, closing the door he turned and walked toward the closed double glass doors of the cash and carry store.

"I didn't know they let ass holes like you out this early in the morning!"

J.P. stopped and turned quickly as he recognized the voice of Richard Finkel. He thought, *"Ahhh, hell, he is not worth ruining my day, fuck him!"*

Turning away, he went in to pay for his gas. Mary Jo Bankos was the cashier that morning. She was talking to Gerry Bare who was getting a cup of coffee at the far end of the counter.

"Good morning coach, how are you today?" Mary stated with a warm tone and a smile on her face.

"Morning Mary," Then he looked toward Gerry.

"Top 'o the morning to you Gerry."

"Morning J.P. Good to see you again."

"You too Gerry, but I believe I would find a better person to ride with than the piece of shit you are riding with today!"

Gerry had a little laugh, and still smiling, said, "Well, gotta get a ride with whomever, no choice in the matter today."

J.P. turned and walked toward the double glass doors, waving back over his shoulder. "See ya Mary Jo, see ya Gerry." Then he exited the store. Finkel was walking toward the store doors as J.P. walked toward his car.

"Got rid of your ass didn't I!" Richard stated as he pointed his finger at J.P., walking in his usual cocky-strutting manner.

Enough was enough. J.P. turned from the direction of his car and walked toward Finkel.

"You have shot off the mouth for the last time." J.P.'s tone was cold and hard.

They had walked to within three feet of each other. J.P. pulled off his narrow style sunglasses and dropped them on the concrete to his left.

"Now Finkel, we are not on your protected school grounds and you have stated to several people in this community how you were going to kick my ass if you ever caught me out in public. So here I am! You want a piece of me? Then lets you and I do a little dancing!"

Finkel froze, his eyes widened, his hands began to tremble, and he lowered his head looking at the concrete at his feet.

"No." He stated in a much lower voice. His total demeanor changed from only moments earlier. He had not figured in the fact that J.P. would ever confront him with witnesses only a matter of fifty feet away inside the store. He had also figured on Gerry coming to his aid if J.P. started anything. He had miscalculated on all counts.

"What? I do not think I heard you Finkel! Now is the time to back up that big mouth of yours. I mean you made the statements to several people, so let's dance. You get to take that big shot you been bragging about!"

Inside the store, Mary and Gerry looked out the door at the two men and looked at each other. Neither spoke. Gerry simply shrugged his shoulders, smiled and took a drink of coffee.

J.P. took a step toward him bringing him to within an extended arm's length of Richard Finkel. "No." He replied again in a meek tone, not the arrogant cocky tone and posture he normally displayed. J.P. was calm, his feet slightly apart, with his right foot just to the rear of his left, his body turned ever-so slightly to his right, his arms to his side, his thumbs tightly wrapped over his fingers, forming a fist and pointing downward. There was no doubt he meant business and was baiting Finkel to find enough "man" in him to strike him. J.P. locked his vacuous eyes on Richard's downward look, a slight breeze began to blow the cool 35-degree air around the corner of the building.

"Well, Mr. BAD-ASS, here I am. I am waiting for my ASS-KICKING! What do you say? Do we get it on here so you can tell all your ass hole political buddies how you kicked old J.P.'s ass all over the street or not!" Richard had not looked up from the concrete and once again stated "No."

"Well, since we ain't going to dance, then I am telling you here and now MR., you keep your mouth shut about how you are going to kick MY ASS, and as for you "GETTING ME", you and your other pieces of shit have made a very bad mistake! You people have fucked with the wrong self-made son of a bitch this time! My time WILL come! You can BET on that one, 'Mr. Bookie.' Put a lot of money on it, because it will take place! My time, my place!"

J.P. stepped back one long step, squatted down never taking his eyes off Richard, picked his sunglasses up, placed them to his eyes, pivoted sharply, and calmly walked to the car. Dawn had no knowledge of what had taken place, as she had been grooving to the "oldies" on the radio. J.P. and Dawn drove off to spend a very happy and loving day together at the "Grand Canyon of the South." The two ended their day that evening with a bottle of fine wine and very well prepared food at an old renovated dairy barn turned into a very nice steak house restaurant called Cuzes.

Damon, Finkel, Duncan and Marshy gathered in Marshy's office for the plan to put O'Francis out of the teaching business for good. Damon would write a letter to Marshy claiming that O'Francis confronted Finkel while on assignment for the school, threatening his life as well as Finkel's. He would include in this letter that J.P. had in the past threatened Damon's life with terrorist acts as well as several other teachers in the school. He would claim that he had conducted terrorist acts toward several other members in the community and that they had personally requested that he do something about O'Francis. He would include in the letter that he as well as Finkel feared for their life and their property. He would request that the School Board remove him from the school system as a teacher. He would state in his letter to the School Board that type of person should not be allowed around children. He as well as many parents considered him unstable and unfit to teach. He would include in the letter that at the very present he feared for the safety of several of his teachers as well as several parents and their children because of personal threats made by O'Francis to parents and children.

It was conceived that day that Damon would send a copy of this letter to their good political friend Judge Edwin, all the local law enforcement departments throughout the area, as well as the State Police. A copy was to be sent especially to their ally, trooper Penrod.

"I think we should also send a copy to the FBI." Damon spoke with an evil glee in his voice. There was nothing being said among the men in LaMar's office.

LaMar was the first to respond to Damon's suggestion.

"I don't know about that. I mean…well, we are okay within our own area. Hell, we all know that. But shit, the FBI, hell I don't think we should go there."

Damon insisted. "Why not, I mean it really would be the doom for the son of a bitch!"

"Yeah, well Damon, it damn well could be the doom for all of us when you get the FBI involved in this. Hell, do you have anybody in the FBI that can pull any weight for us?" This was the first time Duncan had spoken in the meeting.

Finkel was in strong support of his principal. "I think we should. I think it is a safe bet."

More silence as Marshy was up pacing across his large office. He would look over at Duncan to try to get a political read from the leading Board of Supervisors. A very slight movement of the head, indicating a no, and Marshy spoke.

"Look, let's not bring in the Federal people. We have no control over them at all. We do not want to get in over our heads here. I mean we can handle this little matter in our own back yard. Hell, he is just a fuck'en teacher, a small pimple on our ass. Shit Damon, some time you get to god damn carried away."

Damon Bales exploded using several colorful metaphors and concluded with, "I want him gone!"

"Look Damon, lower your voice," LaMar came back in a harsh tone. "You have forgotten just who is in charge here. By-god I make the final decision here, so just calm down." LaMar walked to his desk, sat down and looked at all three men present in the office.

"Okay we send the letter to all area law enforcement people. Except the FBI! Now Damon, make it happen."

He rose and the meeting was over. Damon would do it his way. He was obsessed with the total destruction of J.P. O'Francis.

It was early December and time for O'Francis to renew his Special Police license, as William Peng had advised him after the Democratic Party had elected a new sheriff, one that they could control. J.P. had done so, and had kept them up to date for the past six years, helping with some of the honorable police officers in the area who had been loyal democrats and had been given a job as county deputies. Some were his former students.

He arrived at the courthouse at 1000 hours to meet with Judge Edwin. J.P. informed the secretary that he had an appointment with the judge, and in a moment the "good" judge came out of his office.

"Come in Mr. O'Francis." J.P. walked into his office.

"What can I do for you today?"

"Your Honor, I am here to get my Special Police license renewed for the 29th district."

He paused, and then went to the far corner of his office were several file cabinets were, opening the second drawer down from the top of one of the cabinets. He pulled out a file folder and withdrew a sheet of paper, turned and walked to the corner of a large wooden, glossy topped rectanglar table and placed a letter in front of J.P. "Have you seen this?"

J.P. looked down at the paper and asked if he may look, and the judge acknowledged for him to do so. Taking a minute or so to read the letter, he looked up at the judge, stating in total surprise, "This is a joke, correct?"

"I don't think so, or I don't take it as a joke."

"Well, your Honor, this is just an out and out lie! I mean, you don't really believe all this, do you?"

Judge Edwin picked up the letter and looked at it. "Well, Mr. O'Francis, I cannot see me having someone like you working for my court!"

J.P. protested quickly. "Your Honor, these statements are false! Lies! This is out and out slander! I have had an impeccable record working for the police department. I have assisted in many cases and never, not once ever been reprimanded. I have adhered to the law, by the book."

"I am refusing to give you a Special Police license," he said as he held the letter toward O'Francis.

"I see...well...then I would like a copy of this letter Sir." He paused for just a moment, and then walked to his door, which was never closed.

"Ann, would you make a copy of this for me?" He stood at the door while his secretary made a copy of the letter, and then walked to where J.P. was still standing, and gave him the copy. "Have a good day Mr. O'Francis."

J.P. turned and did not respond, walked out of his office and went straight to Dan's office. This would mean that he could not work private security at nights and weekends, which he was doing to offset the loss of income that had been incurred on him by the loss of his coaching duties.

Dan directed J.P. to the office of Fitzroy, Philps and Starnoc. All three attorneys read the letter and made several comments concerning the author of the letter and his connection to the superintendent, of which none were good.

One of the attorneys, Channy "Bob" Philps, came over to J.P. who was sitting in a chair at the corner of an office desk, and began touching his shoulder. J.P. looked at him as to say, *"What the hell are you doing?"* and Channy simply stated, "I just wanted to touch a terrorist, never have been this close to one. One thing that bothers me, you are a little light skinned to be what is stereo-typed as a typical terrorist."

At that, laughter erupted, but not to have Channy have all the fun of what J.P. considered to be a very serious matter, Kelly Fitzroy quickly stated, "He is Irish, part of the IRA, that type of terrorist."

Then more laughter from all three attorneys, only a slight smiled crossed J.P's face, and with coldness in his voice that stopped the laughing as if someone had turned off a radio and only the sounds of silence could be heard, he said, "I think these people have underestimated me. I know they do not know me. I want to do this by the legal system if at all possible. I have no intentions of losing one way or the other. Kelly, if I were you I would not make too lightly of ole J.P.'s connections. You just may not be too far off! But you can be assured that the statements in this letter are bogus!"

As he held the letter up, with that statement it was recommended by the associations' lawyers that J.P. file a lawsuit against Bales and Finkel for slander and defamation of character. It was dark by the time he left the attorneys' office and he walked to his car. A little voice began talking to him.

"Why did not one of the three men in the room offer to take the case? Was it because they would have to file it in Reynolds County, or were there other reasons he was not yet aware? Most likely the reasons would be political. It did not matter, he would play this game out to the end and if he could not be vindicated of the wrong that had been splattered on him like mud and dirty water from a passing car on a country road on a rainy day, then he would in due time get his justice.

Dan went to work on finding a lawyer to take the case, which turned out not to be so easy. It was after all Reynolds County, and it did have a very venal reputation. J.P. had tried diligently to get an attorney to take his case of slander and defamation in 1988, and he had gone all over southwestern Virginia. Each attorney would state that what had been done and was being done was wrong, both morally and most definitely ethnically wrong. However, all seemed to think that there was just not enough to win a lawsuit or as J.P. began to think after the tenth trip to an attorney's office, that the entire area was a den of snakes all slithering and sliding over and around each other. Of course, the teachers' association would not come to the aid of one of their own, because his job was not being threatened, according to their standards and policies and even with his current slandering letter, they still would not come to his aid.

J.P. always felt that the policy was another political escape goat for the policy makers in Richmond, which reminded him of the Vietnam policy the Washington "ass-holes" had, *"you only shoot when you are shot at!"* Now if just so happen you get hit while waiting, and if it was the shot that you did not hear, sending you home in a draped star spangled banner black rectangle box, "OH, we are very sorry about your son, and all the other meaningless rehearsed bull-shit words they verbalized for the grieving parents and wives. *Brilliant minds running this country and state*, he thought.

It was Christmas 1989, and J.P. was not at all happy. His son Michael was in his first semester of college, and Patrick was in the seventh grade, and in J.P.'s History class. The vile and despicable powers within the school system had cost J.P. and his wife ten thousand dollars in yearly income in one malicious stroke of the pen. J.P. had no money to give to his son for expenses and had taken away anything extra for Christmas. It was all they could do to keep the bills paid and their credit good, which left zero money to spend on anything of leisure. The Christmas gifts were put on credit, food was put on credit, thanks to a very kind and giving grocery store owner, by the name of David Horner, in whom J.P. and Dawn would ever be indebted and would never forget. There were months that they would even have to borrow money for the gas to be put in his car just to get to work. All was in the hopes they could find a way to juggle the only pay they had coming into the house.

Dawn had been unable to get another job in the community, not that there had not been several jobs that had come open in places like the local bank, which they did business with, but she was never given the chance. No family ties or political connections, or the most important, favors done for certain people. She could not go out of town to get a job; they had one car, now being used to take J.P. back and forth to his work place. All that had happened to the O'Francis family was not done by accident, nor did just a few individual people do it. It had been very well planned and coordinated by a long list of people with many in the wings helping to make even the little things go the way they wanted and why, and all because he would not come in line. He would not give up his principles that he lived by. More important to his adversaries, he always seemed to know too much.

His career was on its last link. J.P. had sent out several applications to several surrounding counties. He was patient, he had learned that attribute while on many recon missions where he would have to "lay-dog" for days at a time waiting for the quarry. He knew sometimes it took a while to get any type of response from schools systems. He felt that he would get some word from one of the counties about an upcoming job on the high school level and even a coaching opportunity along with the teaching. He was always a positive thinker and believed in himself and what he could contribute to the wellbeing of the youths he was privileged to have in his classroom.

Many weeks passed and then months. His little voice told him to make some phone calls to some of the old friends that dated back to his childhood, who were now in administrative positions within several of the schools' systems. He felt they would tell him straight up and that was all he ever asked of anyone. What he learned sent J.P. deeper into his dark world and awakened the side of himself that he himself feared. He once really liked that side of himself, the cold, callus, insensitive person that kept him alive in a life and death game. But now a beautiful wife and two sons in which he adored above everything placed enormous stress on his mental status.

Three of the four old time acquaintances informed J.P. of the recommendations coming out of Reynolds County, from the central office to principals and athletic directors. His career had be torpedoed. He now was black balled, according to the information he received. No one wanted to touch him, he was a bad apple and was on his last leg. He was trapped inside a system that smelled of a vile stench that would have gagged a fresh maggot. The powers in control were intent on seeing him fired as a teacher. They had destroyed him as a coach, now all they needed was enough evidence to fire him as a teacher. His enemies felt as if they had his gonads in a vice, they needed the right combination of parents and principal to end it all.

He could not escape anywhere, not even to another state. The Central Office controlled what was sent to wherever. J.P.'s sources got him details of what was in his files. After reading them, he would not have hired himself, based on what he read.

"My god, where are they getting this shit? Hell they have taken insignificant events and skewed them to the point of incomprehensible. Damn, these statements are just lies!" He went from verbally talking to himself to thinking.

# The Unknown Connection

THE PHONE RANG ONCE, TWICE and in the middle of the third ring it was answered. "Hello...

"Good morning Maria."

"Morning daddy."

"Has Joseph left yet?"

"No, would you like to talk to him?"

"Yes, please. You have a good day my dear."

"Thanks daddy, I will and you too. I love you, here's Joseph."

"Yes Sir." Joseph said.

"Joseph, Michael will be by to pick you up at eight."

"Yes Sir." The phone clicked silent. Joseph informed his wife Maria, he would not be using his car, that her dad had sent Michael to get him. It was unusual for the Don to send someone to get Joseph, he usually requested for him to come by his office.

Michael pulled in the arched driveway in the black four-door BMW on time and by 8:05 they were on the way to Don Vincent Spadolini's home. He came from a rural Sicilian, rather large farming family, to the United States to have a better life in 1960. He worked very hard, attended DePaul University, obtained a degree in Accounting and Business, and became a successful multi-millionaire in the shipping and restaurant business. His connection with the Syndicate came through his business, and his uncle, who had passed away in 1983 at 85, some fifteen years earlier. The Spadolini Family was very powerful and had connections worldwide.

Joseph had married Don Spadolini's only daughter and had entered the Family on the ground floor, required to earn his way up the ranking order of the chain of command that existed within the Family. It was Don Spadolini's way, you must work for what you get, no free rides, no give-mes because of who you are or who you "marry" or who you know. Don Spadolini was a very stern man, all business, and very candid. He required a lot from his people, but he was more than fair with them, both monetarily and in benefits. He most definitely was a man of his word and anyone who knew of him or even remotely connected to him, knew it.

Joseph gently knocked on the dark double oak, den doors. "Come in Joseph." He opened the door into a large 30 by 30 foot room filled with books on shelves on two walls from the floor to the twelve foot ceiling. There were several paintings by Remington of the old west on the walls, a twenty-foot section of glass on the far wall as you entered the den. In the middle of the glass wall was one glass door leading onto a large wooden cedar deck and beyond the deck a very large, very private yard. Don Spadolini's office desk was centered in the middle of the room, with a phone and several folders on it in a very neat order off to his left. He had a cup of coffee in front of him and a large ashtray for his cigars. As Joseph entered he was lighting his first morning cigar, a Montecristo, seven inches long and what is known in the cigar world as a 50 ring. His phone rang as Joseph closed the door behind him. He took a seat in the dark brown, deeply padded leather-back, soft pillow-top arms and T-cushion chair, the only other chair in the room directly to the front of the desk. Vincent took several more puffs of his cigar and answered the phone, the conversation was short and direct, and then he simply placed the phone on its cradle.

"Joseph, I have several items I want some answers to." He reached to his left and placed one of the folders in front of him opening it.

"I have been informed you have been busy with some out of state activity. I was not made aware of any job arranged out of state. Now do you want to let me in on what is going on?"

Just as Joseph started to speak, a peck came on the door, and it opened. The maid stepped in.

"Don Spadolini would you like for me to bring the coffee tray in?"

"Yes, please, and bring some Danish also Teresa."

Teresa Piero had been working for the Spadolini family for the past twenty years. Sophia, the wife of Vincent, had hired her. Sophia had known her family in the old country, and had been requested to help her out, by bringing her to the United States and giving her a job. Sophia had made sure she had gotten an education while she worked for the family. Teresa turned and closed the door.

"Now Joseph, what is going on, and why did I not know about this?"

Joseph had been in the Spadolini family for twenty-five years, and was very close to his father-in-law, but he also knew that his father-in-law was the head of a much larger Family, and that to do any type of business in the "Family," you went through the Don first. Joseph had worked his way up the ladder and had been given a large part of the business to run with the oversight of his father-in-law. He began telling Don Spadolini what he had ordered and why, which took a good hour to explain it all and who was involved, and how Joseph had gotten involved. He informed Vincent of his ordeal with O'Francis and how they had become acquainted. The conversation was interrupted only briefly when Teresa brought in the coffee tray and the Danish rolls. Vincent rarely got angry and listened intently to Joseph. He had a lot of questions concerning the people as well as the whole picture. Each action could lead back to the "Family," and that was taken very seriously, each action had to be calculated down to the very micro-degree.

"Where is this friend of yours now?" Vincent asked.

Joseph paused. "I really am not sure. He left the area he was living some years ago without leaving word with anyone."

Another pause as Don Spadolini looked across at Joseph. "Okay...make some inquiries, and find him."

Joseph reassured his father-in-law that James Patrick was okay, and that he was totally unaware of his actions.

Don Spadolini re-lit his cigar. "I must go to the downtown office this afternoon. I want something by Friday."

Another pause as he rose from his chair and walked to the full glass windows and looked out over the back part of his estate. Without turning around, he asked, "Do you think this...O'Francis, is that correct?"

"Yes sir, that is correct."

"Do you think he would have approved of your action?"

"Well..." as Joseph rose and walked to the window to stand by Don Spadolini. "I am not really for sure. I know his Irish background and I know how he feels, and I know he knows what the cost is and as he would phrase it, "the game" is played."

"Game, what do you mean, game?"

"For J.P. and his military background, the action that is required and has taken place, is considered a "game.""

"What was he in the military?"

"He was a Ranger / Special Forces that served two tours in Vietnam."

"Hmmmm, I see." A few moments of silence as the two stood looking out the window. "What was he specialized in?"

"I don't know. He won't talk about it. I don't believe he would even talk to his wife. I am not sure about that, but I would bet he has never talked to anyone outside his home about it. I have been informed that he did not trust many people, if any."

"How far can he be trusted?"

"Well, sir, from past experience, and from our source in that part of the country, he is a man of his word. If he tells you something he will hold to it no matter what the cost."

"Are you sure?"

"Yes sir, one hundred per cent sure."

"Then let's find out where he is and then I will talk to you about the other matters, later. Do nothing without my approval Joseph. Do not act on your own again on such a matter. I know you meant well, and I understand you owe him a few favors. But do not act on your own again when it involves this Family, *capace?*" Then he turned and looked his son-in-law in the eyes.

"*Capace,* Don Spadolini."

Vincent Spadolini smiled, and placed his hands on Joseph's shoulders. "You have done very well and I know I do not tell you that enough. Now, I have work to do and so do you."

They turned and walked to the den doors, with Don Spadolini's left arm across the back of Joseph's shoulders.

"How old is this O'Francis?"

"Ahhh, I am not for sure, a few years older than I am. Maybe about 60, but not sure. I do not think he is older than that. Let me think, I was 20 when he and I got acquainted, and he had already been in and out of the service so, I am thinking maybe he was 25 at the time, so, that would make him, ahhh yep, about 60, Vincent."

# Deer Hunting

THE FATHER OF ONE OF O'Francis' students called and asked if he would like to have some deer meat, but that he would have to do the cleaning and the cutting. He and his sons killed more than they could use and had thought of him. Given the fact that it was his favorite kind of meat he accepted, and felt that Mr. Earl Milstone knew that he was having some financial problems and could use the meat. There were a few good people in and around the little town that sat at the foot of the mountain, that were just good honest hard working people. They did not control the political machine, nor did the political machine give a damn about them, except at election time. Then and only then did they even address any of the "little" people, the working class people's concerns or problems.

It was "game" time once again and Rusty and J.P. got to work together, along with four "Yards" on this mission. The briefing was held in the pre-dawn hour, which was standard, and the SOG personnel had provided the area map, which was provided by the CIA, which was provided by the Air Force with their aerial reconnaissance. According to some of the more flamboyant pilots, "the big eye in the sky" can snap a picture of two red ants fucking on a green leaf floating down the Dak Poko River. So the "recon" team should never question their work of art.

The team loaded onto their green limousine, "the one with the lovely interior" and "the bar in the back seat," and they were off by 0500 hours. In a very short time crossing a very long and high mountain range. According to the "Huey boys" of the escort service it was over 5300 feet in altitude, they did not do high or low, it was altitude. Then suddenly they just dropped to the foothills and the valleys below, sending all of J.P.'s inner-most organs up into his throat. He just knew they did it on purpose and without any warning. Knowing they enjoyed what they were doing and laughing to themselves at the very moment. J.P. and the Huey pilots got along very well, he enjoyed their humor, sometimes, but they seemed to make him laugh just when he needed it. They were as good at their job as he was his, which for O'Francis meant they were the best, and that their "Game" was just as dangerous as his, if not more so, as they were exposed to incoming rounds often and it was for damn sure they put themselves in "Harms" way when they extracted a "recon" team out of a hot PZ in the middle of some jungle laden valley.

They then zigged and zagged east and then west through the foothills and lower valleys of the mountain ridge they had just crossed. This went on for a good five minutes or so, and then they put the brakes on as they announced that once again they had arrived at their pre-determined coordinates on time and in one piece, and that they hoped that J.P. and company had enjoyed their trip. They would return in four days to pick them up. They hoped they had a nice relaxing time watching the area animal life. More humor J.P. thought as the "Chopper" came to a semi-air stop some six feet off the ground, and in no more than a beat of one of it blades they were out and the green "lemo" was out of sight. The team was once again alone with the silence of the forest.

The temperature was in the mid-nineties by the time they started toward their observation point. The ridge ran in a multitude of double hump-back camel contours and according to their map they needed to follow the ridge that now faced them, and travel some five kilometers [8 miles] to a point where "according" to intelligence reports "heavy" traffic was taking place. Now they just had to verify all this before the super fly-boys dropped a "shit" load of 500 and 1000-pound "fire crackers" on the area. *Like they really give a big "rat's ass",* J.P. thought. He may look like a fool with his "baby-ass" face and shaved head, *but if the "big eye in the sky" could do all they said it could, then why in the hell did they need him and his team to verify a damn thing?*

It was mid-morning before they arrived at their prescribed coordinates, which was a pinnacle of a ridge that extended down sharply to the east. The ridge itself had been formed into a jagged knife-edge of outcroppings. Now it was up to Sergeant O'Francis to find an area where they could observe the hollow below. He "reconned" the entire area as quickly as he could, down to within fifty or so meters [55 yards] of the main trail as well as a kilometer and a half [1.5 miles] toward the valley but found that "Mother Nature" had provided an area some 30 meters [35 yards] long about 25 meters [28 yards] down from the end point of the ridge as the best location for their observation. From that point they could see with their binoculars through a few openings in the forest to the valley some one hundred and fifty meters [175 yards] away.

It appeared that from what they could tell that there were two major trails entering the narrow valley and then leading toward the river. Close enough he would tell himself, O'Francis and Rusty knew that the traffic would most likely be heavy, however giving the SOG officer his due, he had described it damn close in the briefing. But O'Francis knew that he did not know the difference between a hollow, or holler as it would be pronounced in the mountains of Southwestern Virginia, and a valley. For that matter the difference between a hill and a mountain which was damn sure different, *but hell,* O'Francis thought, *he probably came from the flat lands of the United States where a rolling hill was a mountain, then went to West Point, so what the hell could he expect.*

There was very little time for the four-man team to get themselves set-up for their waiting game. O'Francis thought it must be like deer hunting for the people in his mountain region back home, where men and boys position themselves to wait for the deer to come by on the trail they normally used on a daily basis. Only on this hunt, they were to bag no game, just watch and record, and afterwards slip silently back to the pre-determined PZ. But as one would expect very rarely did any mission ever go as planned, and this one would turn out to be no different. For two and a half days, they "laid dog" and observed enough traffic that one would think that these people were just going and coming to work on a daily basis like one would see on any New York Street. It was totally amazing the amount of equipment that was physically carried through the hollow and across the ridge to the next hollow and down to the tributary that led to a larger river valley.

Obtaining all the information they were asked to obtain, the team began working back through the double hump-backs to be extracted. At the same time a nonchalant V.C. patrol was working its way in the direction O'Francis' team had come two days earlier. Both patrols were working their way up the same "hump" and met at its top. The results were as expected, O'Francis' team got the edge as the V.C. patrol had no clue that anyone other than themselves were in the area and were talking among themselves casually. All ten Victor Charlies paid the ultimate price for being in the wrong place at the wrong time. Sergeant O'Francis' team suffered no loses or wounded. They laid the soldiers out alongside the trail side by side in an orderly manner. One, so they could be found, leaving a message as to who had been in "Their" back yard. He took his one trophy he was sure of, yet another message, and was very much aware they knew that the same person had been in another part of their "back yard."

Two, J.P. knew they would be missed and their comrades would come looking for them. He knew they too had families, and they too needed to know what had happened to them, or so he felt. Some of the "Yards" did not understand why O'Francis would do what he did. Rusty did, and knew the "Yards" did not know that he had a great deal of respect for their skill and their tenacity for "The Game" they played. Too often the special OP'S teams had to try and locate a downed pilot, some with success and some they came up empty, which left the question, were they MIA or were they KIA? Often the families would never know, and would in the depths of their subconscious wonder whatever happened to their loved ones, never really closing the book on the events that would change their lives forever. He had learned that their ideologies were different, however. They were human, and he felt he was doing right by them. A caring spot in his normal hard-shelled exterior persona.

I had asked J.P. once after he told me of his ordeal and after a period of time had passed. I went back to the events, "why did you lay them out like that?" His answer was slow in coming, and he told me that he would like to think that people all over the world do have the same personal feeling about their loved ones. I mean, really, it is a game. I know it is a very deadly game, but we, the elite soldiers, had to play it and have played it from, ever how long back in time. At the time, on that day, it just felt just. I laid that away in the recesses of my mind for future thought and maybe conversation with him as I still had a lot of questions about his war experiences. I also knew that getting him to talk about Vietnam was very rare and I needed to tread lightly on the matter. I did not ask, but suspected that he did not talk to just anyone about his Vietnam experiences. Now one would have to ask, why me? I do not know.

# The Legal Process

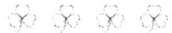

DAN INFORMED J.P. THAT HE had made arrangements for him to meet with an attorney in nearby Abetton, and he was to be there at 1600 hours on Tuesday. As he made the 45 minute trip his mind became more and more stressed. How often had he presented his case to attorneys and how often had they sat and just insulted him by pretending to be listening? One even nodded off to sleep as J.P. looked up and stopped in the middle of a sentence. The attorney never even noticed, J.P. simply stood and was walking out of the office before he snapped awake.

This was the first female attorney he had met over the years, and her office was in the upper part of the law office building, which had been at one time a very large antebellum home. It looked as if it would date back to the late 1800's or very early 1900's. It was a large room 30 feet by 40 feet with two windows in it, one to the back of her desk which was some ten feet away, and the other window six feet to the left of one of two chairs located in front of her desk. The walls were the old style wood paneling, medium brown. The floor was wood with a rug that covered the middle sections where the two chairs and the desk set on. To the back of the room was a long table with a lot of files on it. Some boxes were on the floor in front of the table with files in them. A computer was at the left of her desk against the wall.

She rose from her desk as the secretary announced, "Ms. Donatello, this is Mr. O'Francis."

She walked toward J.P. with her right arm extended out open handed. "Come in Mr. O'Francis."

Her handshake was firm for the size of body she had. A very petite woman, a warm smile and a very attractive face, short dark brown hair, with a well-proportioned body.

"Have a seat," she said, as she pointed to the two chairs facing her desk. "Okay, now, I understand you have a problem with a letter that your boss sent out to a variety of people?"

"Yes, that is correct, but ex-boss."

"Do you have the letter with you?"

"Yes I do." J.P. reached into his brief case and withdrew a folder that contained several pieces of paper. "Here is what I would consider a very damaging letter. I have been advised that it is very slanderous."

"Who did you show this letter to for you to come to this conclusion?"

"I showed it to three attorneys, Mr. Philps, Mr. Starnoc and Mr. Fitzroy."

She took a few minutes to read over the letter, and then laid the letter in front of her on the desk. "Mr. O'Francis, they were correct, it is a very damaging letter. Now what do you want to do about it?"

J.P. took a few seconds to collect his thoughts. "Well, Ms. Donatello, I want to know what I can do, legally that is, about this. And madam, I would like to say that this is only the tip of the iceberg. I mean, well...it is a very long story, and..."

" No, no, Mr. O'Francis, I would like to hear about some of your problems, that way I can get a feel of why such a letter was written in the first place."

He pulled out his yellow legal pad where he had bulleted an extensive outline of events in chronological order by date and year. For the next hour and a half, J.P. gave her a very brief synopsis about some of his problems as well as the incident at the corner gas station, and then went back to his last year at the high school working under the twisted mind of an evil dictator. He included what he had done to Dawn, and his son Michael.

"Okay, J.P., may I call you J.P.?"

"Sure."

"You may call me Holly. Now, I will take your case. I will need 2,000.00 dollars up front as a retainer fee."

"Okay," he replied.

"Now, wait one minute, just what figure were you thinking about when we file the suit."

"Figure?" J.P. asked.

"Yes, how much were you thinking about suing for, and J.P., I will receive thirty-three and a third of whatever we get from the case if we win."

"Well, I do not really know," he stated.

"Well, you must have had some figure in mind, didn't you?"

"Yes I did, but..."

"But, what?" Holly quickly responded, with an all business tone in her voice.

"Well, I would like to file a suit for one million dollars!"

A moment of silence as Holly sat back in her chair, her arms on the arms of her chair, never taking her eyes off J.P., something J.P. had taken note of and liked right away about her. The fact that she was not afraid to make eye contact and hold it, rare for women, he thought. Of course he was not exposed to Holly's caliber of women, he had been surrounded by women teachers for the past fifteen years.

"J.P., I really do not think we can get that around here. Now, if you were out east or up north in a more metropolitan area, then you can tap in the million-dollar area, but... it is just not realistic for this part of the country. I was thinking... let me... how about half a million for the two of them?"

This caught J.P. a bit off guard. "What do you mean the two of them?"

"I believe that we will name both Bales and Finkel in the suit, as they both have conspired to create this letter." J.P. looked puzzled at her use of the word, conspired.

"J.P. keep in mind, that from what you have told me, and I can at this point only assume that you are telling the truth, Richard Finkel had to take the information from the gas station to Damon Bales, and that means that they had to conspire to write the letter."

"Correct! And Ms. Donatello, I am not in any way, form, or fashion lying! You can be assured that if I tell you something it is a fact! If you ask me something, I will, and have always stated it just like it is! My word reflects me. I am a man of my word! That is why I have had so much trouble in the school system that I work in, but you would not know anything about that." J.P.'s voice had become slightly defensive.

"I believe you, and I have it from a good source that you are a man of your word." She stood, stuck her hand out to J.P. across the desk. "J.P., you would probably be very surprised at what I know about your school system. I know Dan Jakes very well. I will let my secretary draw up the proper papers. Now let us set a date for the next appointment. Let's say next Tuesday. What is a good time for you?"

"I do not get out of school until 1530, I mean..."

"Oh that is find, I understand military time. I served several years in the Army as an attorney, so you are on good ground with me with that. Okay, let's say 1630 hours."

"Fine, I will be here with a check for two thousand, correct?"

"Correct. And J.P., I also will need all your files, written documentations, and taped conversations, and a list of people you think I will need to talk to."

On the way home J.P. was not real happy with the half million figure, but he was not a lawyer so he would assume she knew what she was talking about. Still a million, he felt would have buckled their knees. *Moreover, she was a JAG officer. Wow, now I really want to see them handle her,* J.P. thought and then a smile came across his face.

# Connections

HE HAD BEEN A VETERAN of the Vietnam War, attached to a SOG unit, "Spooks" as they were called. The CIA had their hooks in him and he had spent several years doing the covert, not so legal work for our government, the kind of work (the spy game) that "THEY" do not do.

His own government had betrayed him or one should say by one of the government's elected political figures and a news reporter that thought she had a great story that would win her some great prize in journalism, which blew his cover, which almost cost him his life. Actually, technically he was dead. His CIA identity was dead. Only three people knew he had survived the "hit" on him. As far as the CIA knew, officially he was dead. His body had never been completely recovered. All that remained was a pile of ashes that had been scattered about as if "someone" had been searching for something and the remains of human bones with a hole in the left side of only a part of the skull of the victim of a blown up, burned out car and body. After repeated efforts by the forensic team, and with all the modern day and high tech methods the government had of identifying the human remains they had gathered, they had tried to match some fragment of the bones to the agent and his car. For positive identification, the best anyone in the agency could come up with was that all evidence pointed to the American agent was dead, according to the official report presented by the CIA. They had lost a good agent all because of one of the many governments' corrupt Senators. And this one was indebted to a snooping reporter who had discovered his connection to several very large corporations with ties to Wall Street as well as organized crime, as it was called, and "under the table" payroll he was receiving. The affair he had been having for the past five years that his wife and family nor anyone else of importance knew about was a side issue. It was always just another "junket" he had to take for two or three days. Of course, what the idiot Senator did not know was the woman was working for the syndicate and had with great ease dug her nails in so deep he would never get off the "hook", unless he died. But the money and the secret life, the excitement, the thrill of it all kept him going. His payback was to vote the correct way and to get votes when needed on whatever bill was to help or hurt, depending on what "His" boss needed done. The name of the game was money and a lot of it, which was of course typical of Washington politicians.

A dead agent needs a new identity, a new location, a new job, a job that related to his expertise of investigation, gathering information, spying, ease dropping, photographing and if necessary, assassinating whom he chose.

A few law firms in the local area would hire him to do what he had done in the spy world he had lived in for many years, gathering information on someone. Or as it was referred to, assets. But now he would be able to do it at his pleasure, not for his government. He really did not need a job for money. He would never have to worry about money for the remainder of his life. That had been taken care of long before his "sudden departure from this earth." He had taken precautions, and made sure that his future was well financed with Swiss as well as Cayman bank accounts and several accounts in the United States under several names. He planned carefully. His given Italian name would have to go in the vault, no more Mario Sagaria Rosso. He would need a new identity; he would take his middle name, which translated into Paul. He had a Vietnam friend by the name O'Neill, it sounded good. His olive tone skin and dark hair would be from his mother's side of the family, if an explanation was ever needed. It was called a "backstop. " To make sure an agent's cover is not blown. Of course the "cover within a cover" (in case the backstop did not work) was always ready. He needed an obscure place, a mountain city, small in size, yet large enough not to stand out.

His new life style would be for enjoyment. After a few years of buying some land on top of a mountain, building a road, designing and building a house he had always wanted, learning the lay of the nearby city and the types of people as well as businesses in the area, he came to realize that he had chosen well. A lot of Irish-Italian rooted families lived throughout the entire area. However after all the work was done and all the asset gathering, he had become bored, so he quietly started his own PI business. Most of his work was minor jobs, not very exciting, but he had in his life about all the excitement he needed between his Vietnam experiences and his post war "I Spy" experience, that was enough to last a lifetime.

Twenty years after his "death" the dull life of a small city PI checking on who was cheating on whom, or a little work for some local attorney on some civil cases here and there or even a homicide once in a while, to aid the local police department was just right for him.

He had kept right much to himself, not getting personally close to people and the ones with whom he picked to converse with outside of business he was very careful, not letting people in general know anything about his past, which was none of anyone's business anyway. But small towns and small city people were gossipy and nosey, not really that much different than "Big Brother." He literally hated reporters, they always claimed absent of malice, but that also was part of the "big lie!"

His connection to Joseph came about by accident and a case he had been working on for several months and through some very covert checking he was able to get all the information he needed on him. The local prosecuting attorney had sought his small business out for some much needed assistance in solving a homicide case that had involved a local wealthy pillar of the Community. He had figured some small outside private firm could get enough leads that he could crack the case and get some big headlines, with a possible future political advancement attached to his good work. However he had picked the wrong firm, and the information Paul had discovered was worth more to him than to the prosecuting attorney. So he sorrowfully reported that all leads had dead-ended, leaving the police and the prosecuting attorney's office with a cold case.

After more intelligence gathering on Joseph and who he was and who he worked for, Paul made a trip to Chicago. After making a professional contact with Joseph and a rather lengthy luncheon meeting with Joseph, giving him the inside information concerning the cold case assassination, along with more information about Joseph than he wanted anyone to know, as well as Paul seemed to have more information of his boss than was comfortable, this led to a meeting with Vincent Spadolini, the head of the family. The first meeting lasted several hours and then extended over several days of meetings. Vincent learned that Paul was Sagaria, and that O'Neill was Rosso. Mario (Paul) provided Vincent with information that he thought no one knew about. Sharing privileged asset validation with one another bonded an alliance and a business partnership. After several years had passed, Paul was hired to do some work for the "Family Spadolini," and the bond and trust between them grew tighter. For the most part Spadolini and his businesses were legal, for the most part. But that could also apply to the government, for the most part. In many cases, Vincent's businesses were even "cleaner" than the organization Paul had previously worked for, his dear "Uncle."

"Uncle Sam" was by no means legal in its day-to-day operations and all its agencies and splinter agencies that no one knew about. Therefore, Paul was not so quick to judge Joseph Caprotti and his connection to Vincent and the Spadolini family as to any of their business operations or their methods of dealing with business problems. He had seen, done and was very well aware of much worse by the very company, the United States Government, was "sworn" to uphold the accepted social norms, mores and laws of the Nation.

The phone rang three times before the answering machine picked-up. "Blue Ridge Investigation, leave your name and number and I will get back with you."

"This is Joseph, call me."

He had done a few small jobs for Joseph, nothing really big, information gathering on a few people, a few pictures, some daily schedules. It did not matter, he would not get directly involved, just do the job he was hired for and let it go. No one knew who he was, and he was not getting on the front page of any newspaper, no pictures of him, and no comments from him. He kept an extremely low profile and he would keep it that way, just a small city PI.

His personal residence was a remote, very nice mountain cabin with all the luxuries one could ask for along with a lot of electronic equipment and security. He kept a small apartment in the small city as a cover and would often stay there. He bought an entire building, reinvaded it to his liking, and rented the lower half out to an antique dealer. His office was on the second floor overlooking the corner of Main and Commonwealth, in the middle of downtown, in a not so fancy but classic building that had been constructed in the early 1920's.

He sat in his worn, high-backed wooden office chair, his feet resting on the low part of a very wide windowsill, typical of the era, a foot or so off the floor. Looking out one of the two windows, one on each side of the corner of his office, he rocked back and forth, thinking, holding his coffee cup with both hands to his lips, occasionally taking a sip. The windows were tall and wide with original glass panes still in them, another telltale sign of a less complex era.

The 20's, Jazz, the "Blues" good time for most people, an era of good feeling, even with all the self-righteous religious groups still lobbying the politicians, marching in protest against the flow of "booze," of dancing, of the music, the legions of Chicago, New York, and Detroit. "Boot-legers," and of course, the "Fed's." *I think I would have liked to have lived during that era,* he thought as he took another sip of hot coffee. He really liked the old art deco style office building and the old office style. He had the entire building professionally cleaned and repairs done where needed. He had a company come in and clean every inch of the interior of the building before he or anyone else moved in. He kept the old dark hardwood floors, worn with use over the many years, the old windows and windowsills worn with the dark brown color showing the wear of a time when there was no air conditioners, the doors in the office, solid oak, dark brown almost black in color. He kept the original solid brass doorknobs and long key plates. He refused to remove the old windows and had contracted custom fitted storm windows to go over the original ones making his office as well as the rest of the building's windows energy efficient. There was something about it that made him feel comfortable. He had the ceiling painted white, which did brighten up the room. The walls were plaster covered and by all accounts were original, so he had repairs done to them where needed and they were yellow stained, so he had them professionally cleaned, leaving them a cream color, with a rather rough texture.

He would take a sip of coffee and look down on the early morning busy street below as he listened to the message on the answering machine. It was 9:40 A.M., Mary J. (Fitzpatrick) Pendergrass, his secretary, was arriving. Judith was a five foot three inch one hundred and forty five pound fifty-five year old divorced mother of two grown children. Her arrival as the firm's only secretary came a month after Paul had opened his office doors. Judy was looking for work and had stopped in at the corner antique story inquiring as to any type of employment. Jonathan and Lisa Williams, a couple in their sixties, had been operating the store for four months and was having good success, primarily due to the good location. As they needed no assistance they directed Judy to the upstairs business and their landlord as they thought Paul was looking for a secretary. Her daily schedule was to stop by the post office to pick up the mail, as he had no mail delivered to his office. His office had two rooms, a large outer office and his rather large office. The rest of the entire up-stairs was just empty space and closed off. The door was slightly open. He could hear her getting a cup of coffee, as he had already made it, which meant he had arrived early. Judy started to go through the mail. He turned and reached for the phone and then opened a blue address book turning to the letter C, and then dialing Joseph Caprotti's number. On the third ring Joseph picked up.

"Hello."

"Joseph, returning your call."

"Good morning, how are things in the South?"

"They are fine, weather is nice. What can I do for you?"

"I could us some information on a friend." A pause of silence on the line. He had never asked for information on "a friend", a particular person, yes, but Joseph had never used the word "friend" seeking any type of work that was needed.

"By chance do you know where J.P. is located?" Another long pause of silence.

"Haaaa, no. He moved some time ago with no forwarding address."

"I really need to get in touch with him. No trouble, just need to talk to him. I will hire you to locate him. I will pay you our arranged fee for your time and expense."

"What is so important in locating him?"

"I owe him a few favors and I would like to talk to him concerning some details about what I owe him."

"Don't know if he wants to be found."

"I think he would want to hear what I have to tell him. Business, you understand?"

"Yes...I understand. Joseph...you know how I feel about him. He has gone through enough, don't want him to suffer any more!"

"I know...nor do I. He won't, I give you my word."

"I'll hold you to that!"

"I know you will. Again...I assure you no malice here. No grief will come to him or the remainder of his family."

"Vincent."

"He approved."

"I'll see what I can do. I'll get back with you."

# Big Sky Country

MONTANA HAD ALWAYS APPEALED TO J.P., not so for Dawn. But J.P. wanted open areas, very few people, and there he could find what he was looking for. The weather on the other hand was not to his liking, especially the winters. That was the part that Dawn would have really not liked. She hated cold weather, and Montana winters were no fun, but to choose between the heartbreaking events in his life, coupled with the local corrupt political machines, with their self-righteous norms, and the peoples associated with them, he would choose Mother Nature's harsh winters.

The remoteness of the North Western mountain state, its rugged topography, ensured that the area was one of the last areas settled by the Europeans, one of the last areas anyone would look for him.

Fort Missoula, Montana a good size town just east of the Bitterroot Mountain, sat where the Clark, Bitterroot and Blackfoot rivers joined. It was Flathead "Indian" country, to the north of Fort Missoula, a large lake named after the Native America tribe, Flathead Lake. He moved just to the west of Fort Missoula about five miles off O'Brien road, a good Irish name, so he knew it had to be a good place. He bought a ranch with a little over two thousand acres of land, small in comparison to some of the area ranches, but on the average for the state.

The place had a nice modern one story log house with lots of windows, big rooms. Four bedrooms, more than he really needed, but he would always have a room for his oldest and only living son and grandson, from his youngest son Patrick, when they came to visit and at least one guest room.

He liked lots of room, he even had a room that was just big enough for his own private Do-Jo, as his karate was part of his everyday life and would remain so as long as he could stretch daily, and do a few kata's. J.P. hated to be cramped into a small place, the living room or great room as it was referred to by the modern day designers of homes was very big and open with a large front window that allowed for a picturesque view. A very large rock fireplace that he used every chance he got, and of course during the late fall and winter and early spring that was almost daily.

He loved the smell of the wood and the flickering of the fire in the darkness of his great room late at night as he rocked in his chair. The entire house was wood flooring except for the three bathrooms, which had ceramic tile flooring. The kitchen, with its white marble floors, was as modern as any in the country, with lots of space to move about and lots of cabinets. It had an island in the middle, something Dawn would have wanted. A few of the items O'Francis replaced and upgraded were the stove and refrigerator. He got a commercial gas stove, and a double door refrigerator as well as a double door commercial freezer all in stainless steel. Dawn always wanted that for her dream kitchen, as that was her domain. Over the many years they had been together she was always cooking up something different, and using J.P. as her guinea pig. She was a very good cook, and could have hosted her own cooking show (something she enjoyed watching on TV) if she had wanted. They installed a large heat pump that kept the house temperature at a constant, year round.

J.P. added a large deck to the back of the house. He loved decks, and enjoyed spending time on them, looking off in the distance at the mountain range in the evening as the sun would set. He knew that the real estate agent never did understand why he insisted that the house he would buy had to face the east and the back to the west. But it did not matter if he understood or not, it was a Masonic thing and most people would never understand anyway. All the houses he had owned were that way and "Pop" Kuntz's house had been that way. Dawn knew and never once interfered.

It had a nice big three-car garage and a paved drive for a quarter of a mile to the main county road that led directly into town. The yard was about the right size, 100x200 feet in the front and 100 x 100 feet in the back, with about 50 feet on each side of the house. It had a natural wood fence around the entire house separating it from the farmland.

The barn was just what the doctor had ordered, about fifty yards from the house. The roof was shaped like a bent horse shoe with 45 degree angles extending from the top, and the top had a strip running the entire length of the barn about two feet wide made of thick Plexiglas letting lots of light in. The barn had an open area extending through the middle from one end to the other with eight stalls in it, four on each side. On the left side it also had a stall for storage such as grain, (sweet feed, corn...) for the horses. An open area in the loft running the length of the barn on both sides was used for storing hay. It had a large stall for saddles and all the tack equipment used for horse riding. J.P. added two features to the barn as soon as he got settled in and reorganized. Electricity was added allowing lots of lights and lots of outlets. He added water facilities to the barn also, a faucet at each end of the barn and a water hose connected to each one that would extend the length of the barn if needed.

He redid the floors of the horse stalls, by having them concreted with drains put in each, extending the drains out to one large septic tank, which was totally separate from the house septic tank. This allowed him to keep his barn clean, and he felt like his four horses liked it also. Whether they did or not or for that matter if they cared less, he felt they did and that was the way he was. At each end of the barn was a sliding door to close off the winter cold and to allow the horses to enter the barn from the field side and not have to come out to the house side. J.P. added a wooden gate to the front side to allow air flow through the barn in good weather. The horses got used to coming in and going to their stalls. Often they would just stand in the open area of the middle of the barn, or look out over the gate at the front of the barn. J.P. kept water in four of the stalls at all times for the four horses he owned.

His favorite horse was a buckskin breed with perfect black markings. He communicated well with his animals and they seemed to understand. From the front edge of the barn was a natural wood treated fence that extended some fifty yards out in both directions and then back toward an open field for about two-hundred yards square with a gate in the middle area. His entire land boundary was fenced with four runs of barbed wire. It had been subdivided into 200 acres for grazing, a hundred for spring grass and a hundred for fall grass. A hundred was fenced off for growing hay for his livestock, and about sixty for corn. The rest of the grazing land had a medium size creek running through the northwestern part of it giving his stock access to all the water they would need. A four-wheeler path had been made around the entire fenced boundary, as the repair of fencing by horseback had been outdated by time and machines. His stock was not of the cattle variety as the rest of the local ranchers had, but of the magnificent American Bison. They really did not need any real care in any season. Unlike the cow, the bison could graze on the land year round. In the harshest of winters J.P. made sure they had hay to eat, but basically left them to graze off the land, which allowed them to remain independent as well as dependent on the land as they have done for a thousand years. He had long loved the greatness of the bison, and all that it stood for. It was something he had always wanted to own, and started out with a herd of fifty with the intentions of selling off about ten to twenty as the herd grew, for profit and meat in his freezer. He had two bulls, and in the spring, April or May, the newborn calves were born. One per female, on a rare occasion you might have a set of twins born. With the help of two locals he had hired, J.P. had no problem keeping his herd up. He actually did not need the money any more, and often gave meat away to the needy and to organizations that helped the needs of the less fortunate.

It had not been his teaching profession's retirement that had left him financially secure, which he had automatically deposited in a bank in a small town in northern Georgia. It was his foresight in some investments that had paid off beyond his wildest imagination, leaving him set for life. He had used his new found wealth wisely, and had reinvested in areas that would bring in a steady income, plus his ranch, which he estimated would only net him around thirty thousand a year. Not a lot to compare with the surrounding ranchers, but he really did not need his land to survive economically, he needed it to survive mentally. None of his Montana ranch came from any teaching retirement money, which was a joke. He had invested very wisely with his "pot of gold" and had turned a mere few hundred thousand into 10 million, all to the thanks of an extremely booming economy through the late nineties and into the turn of the century. He had pulled all his money out of the high-risk investments and had it secured in a safe but less profit making account before the market took its dive. None of what he now enjoyed could have ever been possible if it were not for a little Irish "luck" and smart investments. No one outside his family knew of his "wind fall" and he would keep it that way. The illegal stash he had so carefully buried, just before his final move, he had recovered and had discretely placed in three separate bank safety deposit boxes in a small town in northern Georgia, for his future security, if ever needed.

He had his phone unlisted and unpublished with a list of everyone that had his number. His mail was delivered to a P.O. Box, with only his initial J. and last name.

J.P. had stayed up late looking up at the stars in hopes of seeing something other than a meteorite, but as usual nothing unusual crossed his line of sight so he went to bed around 0100 hours. He was asleep in a matter of minutes, what seemed to be a long time, but was in fact only a short 45 minutes. He awoke suddenly to a voice. He looked carefully around the bedroom with his eyes, not moving his head or his body. Slowly he reached across his body to his nightstand to his left, (he always slept on the left side of the bed) and grasped his .357 firmly in his right hand. His two friends, he always would say, Mr. Smith and Mr. Wesson, were always close by his side. He saw nothing, he heard nothing. It was not another Nam dream, they had not come calling in a long time and even then, they were rare. He accepted his part in history and had learned to live with it. He contributed the fact that he did not have the thrill of reliving the war over and over night after night to the fact of not being under stress and the constant battle he had for years having to fight for his name.

But the voice was so clear, so plain. It was not Dawn, it was not Patrick. He knew their voices, he always knew when they came to visit, which left him feeling warm and happy. He got up and went to his favorite rocking chair to think, to try and recall what he had heard or dreamed and why. It had been "The Man." Why? He had not thought of him in several years. How did he know he needed to contact him, and why? J.P. knew that he did not know where he was. He also knew that he knew that he had not told him the truth about where he was going. But it was something he had to do, and he knew that he, of all people, would have understood. He had told only two men where he was going, and of course did not go where he had stated he would.

Therefore, outside of his son and his wife Michaela, and his daughter-in-law Leigh O'Francis, who never remarried after the loss of Patrick, no one knew where he really was. As far as he knew both the men thought he had indeed relocated in the mountains of Northern Georgia at the foothills of the Great Appalachian Mountain chain along the North Carolina border in a little town called Mountain City. He hated lying to them but the little voice inside of him advised him to do so, and he always listened to his internal voice. He would have to give a good deal of thought to this subconscious voice. So he put it aside and went back to bed. He was awake just as the morning dawn was breaking. He heard the same voice and the same message. He rose, got dressed and by 0700 hours, he informed the spirit of Dawn that he was going for a ride and would be back in a couple of hours. The early morning ride was not something out of the ordinary. He needed the fresh air of the early morning, the sound of Mother Nature, the smell of his horse. *"Yes"* he thought, *"This would help clear my thoughts up."* The early North Western Montana air had a little chill to it, so he wore his favorite coat, cowhide, lined in sheep wool that extended out over the sleeves and collar. He wore a pair of tan goatskin gloves, Lee jeans, blue long sleeve shirt and brown western boots, and a brown leather flat brimmed "cowboy" hat. He would ride out to talk to his American icons. The Native Americans seemed to get along very well for centuries with the idea of communicating with nature and the bison before the "good Christian religions" and their holy than thou carriers of the "good word" declared that they were wrong, and "They" had the inside track to communicating with God, not the "Great Spirit".

Being the good agent Paul was, he knew that J.P. was not where he said he would be, or for that matter, in the same area. Something he would have done in his case. He ran every check he knew and that covered about every possibility as to locating J.P. in the area and the state. He was not in the Volunteer state, nor was he in the Tar Heel State. He knew he would have never re-located in the Commonwealth State of Virginia. West Virginia did not suit him, never did like it, a Civil War thing. Kentucky was too flat from the middle and west, and the eastern part was too close to Virginia. South Carolina was too flat, and he had searched all of northern Georgia, knowing he would never go to the middle or southern part. Now the question was where did he go?

Did he leave any clues in any of the conversations he had with him over the years he had communicated with him? Would he go to the northeast? Maybe? The mountains of Vermont, maybe New Hampshire, but no further north, he really do not think. It made him proud of J.P. *"Hell"*, he thought, *"He most likely would have made a very good agent, he sure had all the qualifications for it. Glad he didn't let the government get their hooks into him, he would have been fucked just like I was!"* The bitterness surfaced in him for the first time in many years, his contempt for the people running the nation, and their pompous self-righteous attitude as well as their attitude toward the agency. *God,* he thought, *fucking politicians can fuck up a one-car funeral!*

He would need a little help in finding J.P. and he was not really sure he wanted to, as he labored over the fact of why he was getting paid to do so. He did need to locate him for several reasons, of course Joseph's request, of which he felt he knew why. He had spent three weeks looking for J.P., and decided to go to his mountain home. It was time for some rest and to get a little help from some old friends. He had not contacted the only two people that knew he was in existence for at least two years. The United States was a big place and one could disappear in it and never be found, unless one had the right connections and then, over time, about anyone could be found, unless you were dead, and even then, it was conceivably possible your grave could be located and you were found.

It was late or early depending on one's point of view of night, 0200 hours. He went to his basement with its wall to wall shelves of hundreds of old and new hardbound books, antique bottles, jars, wooden carvings and a few bronze busts and statues in between the many books. The walled shelves were one of three, all looking the same. He walked to the thermostat next to the glass doors leading outside. He moved the bottom lever on the thermostat to the off position and then moved the top lever to 45 degrees. On the opposite side of the room, an entire section of the bookshelves made a click and a slight movement inward. He walked across the room to where a very slight opening had appeared in a section of the wall of the bookshelves. One could see a hairline of light along the wall. He lightly pushed the bookshelf and stepped into a very well lighted room. He pushed the door wall until it clicked closed. The thermostat levers returned to the original position.

An utterly soundproof room, measuring 30x30 foot with no windows, was located under the two-car garage. The concrete walls and ceiling measured four inches thick. An antique desk sat somewhere close to the middle of the room. A phone and one note pad was all that was on the desk. One would have thought they had entered a war room in the pentagon. To the back of the desk against the wall were two long wooden antique tables with two computers and two reel-to-reel tape players, two printers, a fax machine, a typewriter, and a shredder on a separate antique table to the right side of the desk. Against the wall were eight surveillance monitors, a set of key boards to their controls and a small antique desk with two other phones with a square black box with a place for the phone receiver to fit into them. He went to one of the phones at the small desk and took it off the hook and placed it on the black box and then dialed a number.

After three rings a sleepy voice on the other end of the line answered, "Hello."

"JFK."

A pause... then came a response, "Jacqueline Bouvier"

"Camelot"

"It never rains until after sun down"

"Ahh, do you know what time it is?"

"Of course I do, it is time that we talk. Are we secure?"

"Yes...let me double check, hold on..." a pause..."Secure," came the response on the other end of the line. "What have you been up to? I have not heard from you in over two years."

"Ah...a little work here and there, nothing earth shaking. Keeping busy, how is everything in the castle?"

"The same old same old...have you talked to *King Arthur*?"

"No, but would you have him call me on 3 if you talk to him today? I will be here all day. I need a little help from both of you on a very covert matter."

"What are you in to?"

"No, no, nothing major, just a little assistance in locating a friend, and could use some high tech sources."

"Okay, what say we call this afternoon around 1600, ahh, great number." Then he laughed.

"Yes, it is. I will talk to you then and fill you and *Arthur* in on what I need."

"Good deal. Later." As the phone clicked on the other end of the line, he sat and listened for thirty seconds before he disconnected his phone, and looked over to the reel to reel to see if it was still recording.

# The Legal System

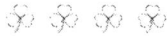

AFTER SEVERAL MEETINGS WITH HOLLY, she had formulated a plan of action. It was March and J.P. was feeling like he was going to get some form of legal justice. Friday, Holly went to the Reynolds County courthouse and filed a half million-dollar lawsuit against Damon Bales and Richard Finkel. She had timed filing the proper papers so it would be closing time, and had made all the arrangements for a U.S. Marshal to serve the papers on Monday to Bales and Finkel at Honsburg High. It would give J.P. a great deal of pleasure knowing the shock of being sued and the embarrassment from all the "Gang of Jackals" that hung around the office.

But once again J.P. would not get that small bit of joy. Saturday morning Jarvis Griffith the clerk of the county and a personal friend and political comrade of Damon's, phoned him and summoned him to his office.

"There is something you need to see." The two men walked to the courthouse doors and Griffith unlocked and opened the door with his key.

"What is it?"

"Wait, I will show you, I want to let you see, don't want to tell you." Jarvis locked the doors behind him, and went to his office, pulled out the paperwork on the suit and handed it to Damon. He looked over the front page and was halfway down the page before speaking.

"That sonavbitch! Goddamanit, I hate that bastard! Damn...I wish we would have gone along with the plan to eliminate the sonavabitch! Now what the hell am I to do?"

"I have someone who will take care of the problem. First thing to do is do nothing until they serve the papers on you. Then we can put things to work. Shit Damon, not to worry, we will take care of you. Hell, everyone knows he is a piece of shit, and has caused nothing but trouble for us for years. This is nothing to worry yourself about, it will be handled."

"What about Finkel ?"

"Well...that is another matter. Depends on how things unfold, let's wait and see. I'll let Duncan, Marshy and Daniel know what is going on. You call Bobby, then let Richard know. He worries me a little, but at any rate, we'll talk later."

Monday came and the Marshal arrived and requested to see Bales and Finkel. Damon was of course expecting him and had a bit of a "shit-eating" grin on his face, as the Marshal handed him the papers, informing him he had been duly served. He then asked to see Richard Finkel. He was informed that he was not at work. Indeed he was not, in fact he missed the next two days, and was covered by Damon and Marshy, and was not charged for missing work, but the Marshal found his home, waited for him to arrive and served him with the papers Wednesday night.

It was Saturday and the "Gang" met at Marshy's home as it was out of the way and no one could see the cars from the main road. They had a nice dinner of steak and all the trimmings of a big meal, as they sat and discussed O'Francis' move, "High level" as O'Francis would have referred to it. A judge, a clerk of the court, a superintendent of schools, a principal of a high school, a supervisor of the county and a leading political figure with a lot of powerful political connections. The major power players were in place to determine the fate of one lowly simple teacher and ex-coach. A small thorn that they were about to pull out and dispose of, Damon in the course of a lengthy meeting, stated in his mass of ignorance.

"I think we should have gone through with my suggestion a long time ago, eliminate him. Hell it would have cost us a lot less than it is going to now." A silence came over the group, and then Daniel spoke.

"But it is less dangerous getting him in this manner. We have more control of events this way, less worry," Marshy chimed in.

"Look, don't worry about the money Damon, it will be handled. This won't cost you a dime. Hell, he is the one that will pay out of his pocket. I can assure you of that!" Irvin stood, stretched, and walked to the window.

"You know we have done about everything to the bastard and still can't drive him out. He knows too much, he is dangerous. Most people would have given it up and left the area. It bothers me a little as to why he does not come open with what he knows. I know he is aware of some of our activities, and I am a little more than concerned about what I don't know what he knows. I just don't understand why he has not tried to, shall I say, blackmail us with what he has?" Damon responded quickly.

"That is fine, he had another son in junior high, one way or the other gentlemen, one way or the other...it will be done!" Irvin then turned to face his comrades.

"LaMar, how in the hell does he find out all the little things he does, or seems to be always dropping words here and there in the conversations with certain people in the community, that he knows that will tell us what he has stated or questioned? I don't know how many people have come to me and asked me questions about any one of us and items concerning the school system and conversations we have had in private. I am getting fed-up with explaining these damn questions away to these dumb asses. It is becoming more frequent. It is always Coach O'Francis said, or told me...Fuck him! I want to know how he knows what in the hell is going on inside the system! Our business! I want to find the leak! And I want the leak fired!"

"Calm down Irvin, shit, it will be handled."

"Well, LaMar, when? I mean you have been handling O'Francis now for four goddamn years! He is still here and is still challenging the policies as well as the administrators, and again, still sending messages."

"Hey, look, we have hurt him a lot, he is down, and I know it. He'll never coach again anywhere, I am damn sure that he will never teach again outside this county, he is financially hurting, I know that. These things take time, you have said that yourself."

"Yeah, but most people..."

"He's not most people."

"Ahh, no shit!"

Damon spoke, "Well, you all don't have to work with him on a daily basis."

LaMar laughed loudly and then stated, "And nor do you anymore. Bobby will have to deal with him again. Now boys, everyone knows I don't have anything for Bobby, and I know several of you all like him, and that is fine. Let's all pull together here. There is more at stake here than O'Francis, and we all know what I mean. He is but a small problem. Let's not let this thing get out in the open. We do not want any state and damn sure do not want any federal investigation into alleged illegal activity within our system and community. We need to keep this thing within our own boundaries so we can control whatever may occur."

"Another thing, before we move on to more important items. Has anyone questioned why he has not gone to the Feds? I mean, look, he has dropped enough hints to us that he knows, and you wonder why I have become extremely concerned. Damon just may have the right solution."

Silence permeated the room, as each one began looking at each other.

# Talking to J.P.

I FOLLOWED O'FRANCIS AND HIS saga as I have done now for many years, and he continues to surprise me. I asked him in the spring of 1990, "Why don't you just move? On the other hand, go public with the information you have on the political powers in the county, as well as all their connections." He thought for maybe thirty seconds.

"Because I have a younger son to get through this piece of shit of a public school system first, and it is not right for me to move because I am having problems with the political power players in the county. As to the going public, I will not place my family in harm's way. I know how the game is played, and I know who the real players are, and I know that even though "they" think "they" are big fish, in a big ocean, they are just big fish in a very little pond."

With that statement, I looked directly at J.P. with a very puzzled look on my face. I thought I knew what he was talking about, yet he had never revealed anything to me about any connections he might have with any type of organization or anyone who might even be remotely connected to any organization, or powerful wealthy people. He continued.

"Patrick did not ask to come into this world and it is up to me to give him every opportunity to make it. And moving from here to start in another place is not good, it would not be fair to him, since he is already established. It is very hard for a teen to relocate and make new friends and to be accepted. Hell, I still have not been accepted in Honsburg! But, what these people do not know is that my grandfather, great grandfather and great, great grandfather is from this town. Actually even before it was legally incorporated. No, I will put up with the petty bullshit, and fight these bastards with every breath I have until my sons have completed their education, as piss poor as the system is!

As to the second question, because I cannot see the legal system doing anything about what information I have. Even though it is highly illegal, what they are doing and have done, there is just too many holes in the cheese for me to go public. And if going public you mean the media, well I trust them just about as much as I do the political and legal system. For them, the media, there is no absence of malice. Not enough protection for me or my family." Then he paused and walked across the room. "I am not at all real sure that the legal system is legal. I know you figure that I have more information than I am telling you and you are very much correct on your thoughts. Correct?"

I did not respond right away, and there was a very long period of silence. "Yes you are correct J.P. However, I also figured that if you wanted me to know you would have told me."

J.P. turned to face me across the room. He just smiled. "You are a reporter..."

I quickly stated, "Retired."

He slowly answered, "However, still a reporter. Maybe not a media type, but still journalists are just as uncaring as the media. Just as hungry for a story, looking for that journalistic award that sets them apart from all others, putting them at the top of the pill, that coveted award that somebody gives to whomever, for the best story of the year."

"I have given you my word as to what I will get printed as well as when you tell me it is okay to do so, and not a letter until. I value my words just as much as you do. We do have something in common."

J.P. stood in silence looking at me. I did not continue with what I mistakenly let slip. He never asked. He just stood there looking directly at me, his mental wheels spinning as to what we had in common.

# Umpiring

J.P. CONTACTED THE COMMISSIONER OF baseball in February of '90 to take his test and re-certify himself to umpire high school games, and to let him know that he would be available to call that year. It was Edward Lowe who had just two years earlier talked to O'Francis about umpiring. In at least three conversations while Lowe was umpiring, who preferred to do the bases which gave him an opportunity to talk to Coach O'Francis at first base, he encouraged him to get certified as an umpire, even though he was coaching at the time. Then he would say:

"When you get out of this business you will have been on record as an umpire." He told J.P. that he would have to have at least three years on record as a certified umpire to call post-season games. So O'Francis did indeed take the test and certify himself as an official baseball umpire in the spring of 1988. In addition he had provided the commissioner and the umpiring association with his records of umpiring high school baseball while living "up north." Which included post season games and his ratings.

"Damon and company may stop you from coaching someday, but they will not be successful in keeping you out of baseball." J.P. remembered the statement and wondered if Edward had some type of foresight into his life.

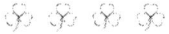

Kevin Barnard and Arthur MacFraley entered their senior year of baseball without Coach O'Francis. He had been their strength; he had made believers out of them. When he was present, the "battery" of Barnard and MacFraley could not be beat, or so they felt. He would call every pitch for them, leaving the pitching and catching jobs free from worry as to if they had called the correct pitch for the batter they were working. They knew that their coach would take the heat for a pitch that was wrong, and some batter took it out of the park. O'Francis would tell them constantly:

"Do not worry about a hit or a home run, you just concentrate on your job. I will take care of the rest." They did and they were good, they felt good, they believed in themselves.

Not only did O'Francis know the game, he knew what made players like Barnard and MacFraley tick. He was able to communicate with them on life's real problems. He was able to reach them with their own "big" problems as teens, and put it in a manner they could understand. They would come to him with what they considered problems, and to them they were problems such as teachers, grades, girlfriends, and parents, even the head coach. When they left, O'Francis made it all fit into place in the scheme of life's day in and day out education. Things just did not seem so bad after a long talk with Coach O'Francis.

Barnard had a bad year altogether, as there was no one to control his temper and there was no one to understand his emotions. No one could calm him down, and he lost his edge. He could not concentrate when he was on the mound. Arthur had lost his sharpness as a catcher, he was not as confident in his throws to second. He had passed balls that a season earlier he would have never had. No real teaching. No time was taken to stop everything and instruct. No encouraging word of "wisdom" expressed when needed to either of them. Teddy Hauler did not give them what they needed in terms of confidence. He talked a lot but nothing coming out that made a difference. It was not that Ted did not try, he did. It was just not the same. Tim Harper knew the game, but did not know the players. He could not communicate with them on the level that they had been accustomed too. He was never the communicator. He had never been the coach that could make believers out of the players. They missed the ever-present voice in their ear that made them better than most players they faced.

Coach O'Francis' presence as a baseball coach was missed greater than most people ever realized. Harper seemed to be at a loss. His "right arm" and his "eyes and ears" were gone. He had in his unwise and jealous move to regain "total control" of "his" ball club, killed the one thing that had made his command whole. But he would never tell a soul. He would play it out as if the administration was totally at fault and hope that no one would figure out how he was able to shift all the power back to himself. What he did not realize was that James Patrick O'Francis had no desire to take command of the baseball team. He was not power hungry, nor was his ego so out of control that he was undercutting the head coach. He was very happy doing what he did and the position in which he held.

# Getting Personal

WE WERE ON THE UPPER deck and had been talking about some of his more pleasant umpiring experiences, which to me was rather humorous. It had been several years since J.P. had been associated with baseball at Honsburg High School. I reluctantly brought the question to bear that had been on my list of questions to ask at the proper time.

"J.P., I had heard once that not even Harper could control you. Would you tell me about what he or they meant by control?"

J.P. took a very long time to address the question, and for a moment I thought I had crossed the line in asking such a poignant question.

"Control…now am I to assume that you mean that I was out of control? On the other hand, that they, whoever they may be, could not control me at all? Then there is the meaning of control in itself. Now John, let me think, to have power over, to have direct influence over, and to rule over."

"Well, J.P., either or both I guess?"

"Then let us talk first about my so called being out of control. First let me state I am an emotional coach. So in a lot of people's eyes I am out of control. Now that is fine if "they" (as he motions with his fingers, out into the open spaces) see one of their favorite coaches in whatever sport on TV appear to be out of control or as it is often referred to, lose it. Now "they" can do that, and that is good for the team, fires them up, it gets the team more motivated. Now that is accepted and "they" love the coach even more than "they" did before. Yes, there are times in my basketball coaching years,

I wish I would have had some foresight and not have been so emotional. However, the players also see and feel that emotion, and for the most part the players react in a positive manner to the "out of control" coach. I was never negative in my so-called out of control mode.

In addition, John, just for your record, I never got a technical foul. The so-called calm and cool coach does not always get the same reaction from his players. Point of fact is, it is just the opposite. Now John, when it came to baseball that is a different type of game. Some coaches do get emotional, however, I can only remember one time in which I did not control my emotions and that was after the game had ended. I regretted my actions the instant I reacted to the loss. Which was my fault we lost the game to one of our, my, bitter rivals. There were times in which I took certain games too personal. I got too involved in the game and forgot that I was not a player. I was a coach, so as for Coach O'Francis being out of control, in all the years of coaching baseball, I only lost my self-control once. Does that give you the answer to part one of your question John?"

"Yes I do believe I get the idea."

"Now, part two to your question. As for the controlling me over all, and having the top control over your team as well as all aspects of the team which includes all the staff. Well it is all in the perception of the person that holds the top title. I think it depends on how big his and I am sure, her, ego is. If some member of the staff is getting too much attention, well, someone has to go, and if that someone is an assistant, oh well…and the assistant does not have to be a person that is looking to take over…remember I used the term perception, look, the alpha wolf rules. And I am sure you are aware of how that works. It does not make a damn how badly the perceived challenging wolf is damaged, you get rid of him and move on, still the alpha wolf. Ego can be one's Achilles Heel in coaching."

I have often wondered in my talks to the players and a few members of the community, if Harper was not more in tune with the administration and the so called "control issue" than the vast majority would ever realize. I have learned and pieced together one dominating fact. He was quiet, inward, and cunning.

O'Francis had a mystique about him, and all that knew him felt it when they were in his presence. When he walked onto the field for practice, the players felt it. Their whole attitude would change. There was something about Coach O'Francis that swept across the park when he entered the confines of a baseball field. Players felt a level of confidence when he was around them. They listened to every word he would say, every gesture, they believed in him. He took them to a higher level and they had no clue as to why. I have interviewed several players and they would describe for me how they felt about O'Francis.

*"He just had a walk about him."*

*"The way he stood or looked, there was something that was surrounding him."*

*"It was what he would say or how he would say it or something. I really don't know, just what it was, but I felt it."*

*"He just seemed to bring out the very best in me."*

*"I wanted to do a better job for him. It was as if, ahhhhhh, it was as if I owed him something. I just seemed to welll... I just seemed to excel, it was as if things, I mean the game seemed to, well... I mean I just played better."*

*"He seemed to understand us."*

*"He could talk to us on our level, and still I respected him as a coach. Well, now looking back on it now, I just respected him as a man."*

*"I liked the stories that he told us about his days as a player, some really great stories."*

*"I don't think that I really realized the meaning of some of the things he told me, until I graduated and had to work for a living, what he was saying. It just hit me one day, and I have used his words to get me through some really hard times."*

*"He would take the time to teach us, no matter how long it took. He would be there until we got it."*

*"He would put down his bat and come running out to my position and show me exactly what he was talking about. Then he would run back to home plate and hit me the ball and if I did not get exactly what it was he wanted me to do, or the way he felt that it should be done, he would hit me another. He was hard on us, and there were times when I would cuss him under my breath, but now I realize that he really was teaching us more than just the game of baseball. Hell, I could tell you several stories about jobs that I have had over the years that Coach's words seemed to come to mind, and things seemed to work out for me."*

*"I learned more from him about the game of baseball than anyone. And hell, that is not to include what he taught me in the classroom."*

As I went to each one of these men I would ask: "What about the head coach, Tim Harper, how did he fit into all of this?"

*"Coach Harper. Well..., he was the head coach, I mean officially, I guess. But O'Francis, well, he was too or that is how I looked at it."*

*"Coach Harper, well, he was...he just was different. Don't get me wrong, he was a good baseball coach. But he, welll...he just didn't have whatever it was that Coach O'Francis had. Something, I really don't know what it was that was different, but it was something. I really can't put it into words."*

*"Coach Harper, well, he was different. He just could not communicate with us like Coach O'Francis could. He was a really good coach, I mean he really knew the game of baseball, but there was something really special about O'Francis."*

*"Harper...he really never did show any type of feelings...you never really knew if he really cared one way or the other if you lost or won...O'Francis, well he was very emotional...I, well we, all knew where he was coming from. I might add here, I do not know a player that I played with that did not like the way he coached. Oh, and before you ask, yes that includes his emotion."*

"I asked the three in which I was talking to at the time, if he yelled and screamed, when they referred to his emotions."

*"No, all three responded in unison. That is not what I, we meant. He wore his feelings on his sleeve so to speak. We could tell in his body language, his tone of voice, how he felt. He did not do all that stupid yelling we have seen from other coaches."*

"So, together as coaches, how were they?"

*"When you put all three of them together, hellll-oooo, man,..I mean, if the umpires had been fair, shit, man. They could have won at least three state championships. Shit. There is no doubt! Hell, you ask anyone who played for them back in those days. They will tell you the same thing."*

*"Okay, what about Teddy Hurler or "Humper" as you have referred to him?"*

All of the former players in which I talked to praised him with overwhelming accolades, stating that he was as good of a baseball coach as either one of the "official" high school coaches. They told me that if he had been given a chance to go to college he would have been a force in baseball to contend with. He was baseball smart, he knew the game inside and out, he was quick thinking, and he was a good teacher. I did note that in any of the discussions about Honsburg baseball, Hurler was always included. It was very apparent that the former players had a great deal of respect for Teddy Hurler.

Several proceeded to tell me about several championship games in vivid detail about how umpires had no honor, no honesty, and had taken the game away from Harper, O'Francis and Hurler. The ex-players, now men, whom I talked to, expressed how much it hurt their coaches. They could read Coach O'Francis' face, we could not really tell about Harper, but I am sure he was hurting also. *"Teddy, well even though he tried to hide it, we could tell. But he was a class person so he, like the rest of us, took the losses fair or unfair, and went on without a public word."* It was stated by several, that O'Francis showed it more than anyone of the three. They described the three as men of honor that played the game with honor, and that if they had been given a fair "shot" they would have won games that had been taken away from them. These players told me that they had played well enough to win, but that one or even two umpires could and did turn the game so that the other team would win. They informed me on more than one occasion that they had been prepared and that they would have won, but...

103

I have watched the man that replaced O'Francis, Andy Ziegler. By all accounts that I have been able to observe and receive feedback from players and parents, Ziegler actually knew the game as well as anyone, but he just did not have that something that Coach O'Francis had. By all accounts, he was a very nice man, very intelligent, an extremely hard worker, very baseball savvy, but he just did not have that mystique. He did not have that special touch with the players. In addition, he did not challenge the political power structure, nor did he challenge the egotistical power controlling head coach.

I have done a great deal of investigating into how and why O'Francis was removed and Ziegler was installed. It seems that the idea came from Tim Harper himself. He alleged that he needed Andy to take over his junior varsity program, which had been lacking in leadership and teaching of the basic skills in order for the players to be prepared for the next level of play, the varsity. Harper claimed he had gotten no help from the administration in the matter of getting a good quality junior varsity coach for several years. J.P. as well as Harper had both agreed that *"THEIR"* plan was to destroy the varsity program by inserting a lesser qualified person at a lower level, and that would ensure that the players they received would be of a lesser quality, and that they would have a losing season, or seasons. If that occurred, (which did not happen) then the administration would have cause for dismissal. They could claim that they were getting pressure from the community for a coaching staff that would produce winning teams. The three coaches overcame the shortfalls and produced one winning team after another, in spite of the efforts of the Damon's, Decal's, and Finkel's and their district School Board representative, Barnard Theodoric, of course all with the approval of the 'Fuhrer.'

I learned that it was Harper who suggested he and O'Francis pay a visit to Andy at the middle school where he was assigned to teach. They had not seen him in some several years, and only then on the opposite side of the field as he had at one time been the head baseball coach at Library High. They presented the idea to him. He was very hesitant, and had indicated that he would never coach on a varsity level again. He had been the head coach for Liberty High for ten years, but he had crossed the powers of the political machine by not playing whom *"They"* wanted him to play. He lost, they had fired him and had done so in an embarrassing manner, humiliating him in the paper, the one and only paper the county had, which was located in Liberty and was solely devoted to emphasizing the Liberty sports programs. Politics always seemed to play a hand in the teachers' and coaches' lives in Reynolds County. Control.

Both Harper and O'Francis knew that Ziegler had the qualities of a very good coach, and he had the basic philosophy they had. They knew that he had been shafted and felt that he would work with them to build a strong junior varsity program. Intellectually, he had it above most of all other coaches in the area. He knew the game well enough to have given Tim and J.P. a run for their money on several occasions. He had come up on the short end of the stick having to play against both of their wits. The one thing that O'Francis noted about him when they had faced his teams was that he had not prepared them for special game situations. Of course Andy did not have any help in preparing his teams either, something J.P. was a devoted advocate about. He created game simulations, repeating them daily in practice to where they were second nature to his players. Over the years of research, I have found that had been the secret to the Harper and O'Francis success. And even though Hurler was not on the bill, he was an intricate part of the game plan.

They had a great deal of respect for Andy and his efforts, and they knew he had been done a great wrong.

J.P. did not see it coming. He was sold on Harper's idea, so in his good-hearted effort and being totally loyal to his head coach, offered Andy a chance to get back into baseball, something J.P. knew that he truly loved. J.P. could tell in the course of the conversation that the political powers had all but destroyed Andy's will to ever coach again. Something the superintendent and school system of Reynolds County seemed to marvel in doing. Unless you were part of the "dance team." He had been out of the coaching circle for five years, and expressed a concern that he may not have it in him to do the job, but O'Francis in his ever-Irish philosophical manner, managed to get him to consider the offer. Harper as usual did little talking to promote his ideal, but J.P. was used to that, and took the lead. But that was only part of the Harper plan. To use one of Jim's baseball terms, he just did not know the type of pitch Harper was throwing, and J.P. was just not ready for it.

Deep inside the internal workings of Ziegler's baseball soul there had remained a single ember with a slight glow to it and when the two, now famous baseball coaching duo and especially the inspirational words of O'Francis had left, it seemed to glow a little brighter. Little did O'Francis know what he had helped set into motion would seal his fate as a high school baseball coach.

The next concern for the two coaches, would "They" allow Ziegler to coach again? That part of the plan was not clear and Tim Harper decided that he would have to present the idea to the administration and push it to get Andy into place. Tim, on more than one occasion in the course of the O'Francis, Harper era fell far short on the push part. It had been the unrelenting efforts of J.P. that had gotten what the baseball team had, not only in material, but more especially the facilities, which was still not completed. I have learned from several of my sources in and around the area of Honsburg, that O'Francis' enthusiasm to obtain the best baseball field in the area, and his candid outspoken character, cost him dearly.

Tim presented his plan to Mr. Damon Bales alone. Jim thought it odd that he would so, as he had never presented any innovative proposal to the administration without O'Francis present, backing him. But it really did not matter to J.P. as he did like going into Bales office for any reason.

Bale informed Harper that he would consider the matter. Tim thanked him for his time, and departed his office. Tim knew what he would do, and he knew that he had planted a good seed and that it would grow and bloom. It just would take a little time. Bales waited for several minutes, got up, walked out into the lobby of the office, and made sure that Tim was gone, and went to the phone.

"Reynolds County School Board, may I help you?"

"This is Mr. Bales. I need to speak to Mr. Marshy." A moment passed and LaMar answered the phone in a big happy go ha, ha, jovial, "How are you doing Damon?"

"LaMar, I have a new plan. I have a way of getting rid of O'Francis."

"You were supposed to get enough on him to fire him two years ago. But, so what is the plan?"

"Harper wants Andy Ziegler to coach his junior varsity."

"Why in the hell would you want him added to your staff? Shit Damon, we got rid of him, and we are close to getting rid of O'Francis. Damn-it, don't add to the fuck'en problem!"

"Would you go for firing O'Francis from coaching, and transferring him to the middle school? Moving Ziegler to the high school and putting him in O'Francis' position? Now LaMar, I think he can be controlled. I do not think he has forgotten what happened to him at Liberty. He will be much easier to deal with than O'Francis, you know that."

There was a silence on the line, and Damon continued, "I really think this will work. I will need your help on this."

LaMar cleared his throat. "Let me call you back." Then he hung up.

Damon paged Finkel to his office, and in a few minutes Richard arrived in Bales' office. Damon was smiling with an evilness that would have made his dark master very proud. This new plan that had been dumped into his lap, as he thought, by accident, would work. He felt it in his sinister bones.

"Yes sir, you wanted to see me?"

"I have a plan! I will request that O'Francis be transferred to the middle school and Andy Ziegler be transferred to the high school. Now here is what I want from you. I want you to tell Andy that he will be replacing O'Francis as the baseball assistant to Tim Harper."

"What if he refuses?"

"He won't, he will have no choice! Now once that is done, I want you to tell him he will have the head-coaching job within a year, maybe two at the most."

"How are you going to get rid of Harper?"

Bales waved his hand forward. "Ah, to hell with Harper. Tell Andy that he has indicated that he is ready to retire and that O'Francis has quit and does not want the head job. Work him and reel him in. Hell you never know Harper may fuck-up on something and we may be able to get rid of him. Andy just needs to let us know if he does."

"Do you really think he will do that?"

"Ohhh, yes, he will. He will have no choice! Mr. Marshy and I will make sure of that. You leave that to us. You just get close to him, and use him." He leaned back in his chair and smiled once again.

The phone rang as Richard was leaving. Bales reached to his left and picked up the phone.

"Mr. Bales," the secretary stated. "Mr. Marshy is on line one."

His voice was one of a happy person. He felt so good he could have jumped up and clicked his heels together. "Damon, LaMar here. Come over to my office just as soon as you can get here. I think I have a plan."

That statement made him smile even bigger, and his blood even rushed through his veins at a speed that he had not felt in years. To Damon this was better than sex. His evilness reeked throughout his entire body and his steps had a quick and bouncy gate to them as he went from the school to his car. No matter how one cut it, Tim Harper had given Damon Bales the key to destroy J.P.'s coaching career, as well as the embarrassment of being demoted to a lower level of education and out of Honsburg High School.

Andy Ziegler did not have a clue as to how evil Damon and Marshy really were. He was placed in a position that he was led to believe that he had no choice but to accept the teaching transfer as well as the coaching position. They made sure that he had not contacted Tim Harper before they made their move. As far as Andy knew at the time he was in the presence of Bales, Finkel and Marshy, O'Francis had resigned of his own accord, and had requested that he be transferred. Bales laid the story out so smoothly that most anyone would have believed him.

"Now we are placed in a really bad position here Andy. We really need your help."

LaMar never went to any meeting anywhere that he did not have to make some major statement. He never allowed anyone to out "shine" him, as he chimed in on the conversation.

"Now Andy, I know you have had a few little indifferences with the school system in the past. But really, all that is in the past. Now Andy, I know that most of that was brought on by a few radicals around Liberty. Hell, you know how things can get. Most of us really liked you and like how you ran the baseball program. You know how politics is. But you can really help us here. Get yourself back in the baseball groove. You never know, you may want to be a head coach somewhere again someday. You're a damn good coach Andy! If I were a principal at a high school, I would want you on my coaching staff."

It did not take Andy over two days before he called Harper on the phone and informed him of what had taken place. Harper listened quietly as Andy told him how his position had come to be. Then he asked Harper why J.P. had resigned as he had not indicated that he was ready to give up baseball earlier when they had met at the middle school.

Tim for the first time in what had been a one-way conversation spoke. "He didn't!" Then there was a long silence on the phone.

Andy cleared his throat. "Tim, I was told that..."

Harper interrupted him. "I have no doubts that is not what they told you. But I am telling you that Damon, Finkel and LaMar did in J.P.! He had no intentions of quitting baseball! Nor did he want to be transferred!"

"Listen, I am really sorry. I didn't know. I mean, what should I do?"

"Hell Andy, there ain't a damn thing you can do!"

Tim arrived at the O'Francis home in what appeared to be an ill mood, which was normal for him as he always seemed to portray the negative. After some bitching about the current events, which was normal for Tim as they sat at the kitchen table, usually eating supper with them. He asked if J.P. had called Dan Jakes. J.P. assured him that he had and that there was nothing that could be done. They had the power to transfer a teacher anytime and anywhere they so desired. As to the coaching job, neither the county nor the state considered coaching a job, so getting fired was not a matter for legal concern by the association.

"So what good is the damn association if they can't help you?" Tim spouted in anger.

There was a moment of pause before he replied as O'Francis sat and looked at Tim Harper. "I really do not know. It seems to me that you have to lose everything for them to come to your legal aid. Hell, then there is no guarantee that they will win. Well, here in this place at any rate. I damn sure do not have to tell you about that. Christ, they have every judge and political power person in their pocket. Good God almighty, what a place! I have never seen any place like it!"

J.P. told me in a later conversation, which included that particular day, that just for a few moments he felt something cold cross through the room. And that when he and Dawn talked after Harper left, she had expressed the same feelings. The two as I have learned were more than close as husband and wife, there was a spiritual bone between them. He told me that he did not know at the moment what it could be, but in retrospect, we both knew. Then he stated, "Hind sight is Fuck'en great is it not?"

I had to agree.

# AN Ally

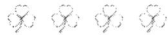

DURING O'FRANCIS' FIRST SEMESTER AT his new location of Honsburg Junior High, Bobby Simms assigned J.P. a room directly across from a good home-grown Honsburg teacher, Mrs. Bernadette Mazo who taught Science and English. She stood 5'3", short brown hair, and weighed around 115 lbs. Bernadette introduced herself to J.P. toward the end of the first six weeks of the school year and offered to help him in any way she could. She had a warm smile and a pleasant face. J.P. thanked her and assured her he would call on her if he needed anything, as he knew nothing about the way things worked at the middle school and that he had never taught students on the junior high level.

It was not long that she did help him, and appeared, at any rate, to try and keep him informed on events and procedures that he was not aware of or accustomed to. Now for J.P. the question was why she would help him. He was very aware of the Simms-Bales connection and had it figured that this being their "MO," that she would report anything O'Francis might say that they could use to get rid of him.

After several weeks had passed and several school events had taken place, Bernadette had reminded J.P., keeping him informed, always in a very polite manner, of which he had been very appreciative, but remained very skeptical.

Two months passed, and in a rare conversation one afternoon after school hours, meeting Mrs. Mazo in her room as requested, a discussion arose between the two concerning Bobby Simms. Bernadette asked J.P. if he had heard anything about Bobby and Ginger having an affair while he was at the High School.

J.P. hedged in his answer, but with care, responded, "I can tell you what I saw and what other teachers said. However, keep in mind, what was said by others does not mean that it is true. In addition, Bernadette, what I saw could have been misconstrued, and you can be assured that I did not take what was perceived by me personally to anyone else in that school. Therefore, I tell you this with great caution to not judge the information as facts. I have learned that not all is what it appears. In addition, I have a great deal of respect for Ginger. She is a very good teacher and actually does care for the students, okay?" He then related the information to her.

After doing so, Bernadette asked, "What do you think?"

"First, I think this conversation is beginning to sound like an inquest. Now, as to what I personally think of what the gossip grapevine has and still is spreading, I think that if one looks at the possibility of a very attractive woman with a great deal of intelligence, and a not so attractive man with absolutely no scruples, and if one looks at the type of female she is, and the type of male he is, and if one throws in the reputation of both, no, I do not think she would lower herself to such a level. As I stated in the beginning of this conversation, perception is everything. It does not make it a fact! In addition Bernadette, gossip is not facts. This school and this town is full of just that. No offense to your town. I like the town and most of the people in and around it. Despite what the GGV is pandering.

The following day as J.P. was preparing to leave his classroom to go home, in walked Bobby Simms. He closed the door hard and walked briskly to the front of J.P's desk, which struck O'Francis as being somewhat odd, as Simms was usually the one behind the big desk. Only J.P.'s was not quite as plush. Bobby pulled up a student's desk to the very edge of J.P.'s desk, and sat down in it, red faced and with anger in his body language.

"Mr. O'Francis, I would just like to ask you, did you see me and Ginger engaged in any sexual activity?"

J.P. remained very calm, as he had been at that point many times before, except he was not being accused by Decal of doing or saying something that did not fit his norm.

"No Sir, I did not, nor have I ever said that you did. So why are you asking me this?"

Bobby Simms continued, "Then in order to prove anything, you have to see someone first! Am I right?" He slapped his open right hand down on the top of the students desk.

"I think, Mr. Simms, I have over the many years dealing with you, in which I have had conversations concerning "hearsay," I have always stated that to see, or to be present during the course of any type of conversation, or for that matter, activities, is the most important fact in any accusation."

"Good then, that will be all of that!"

"All of what sir?"

"You know what I mean."

"Well actually, no I do not." O'Francis' voice became more firm.

"I mean any conversations to any other teacher in this school about me or anyone else."

J.P. broke a slight smile. "Well sir, just let me say this. I do not control what others may or may not say. As for myself, I am not for sure as to where you might have gotten the idea that I was engaged in any type of conversation concerning you and or Ginger. I think you and I have been in this position many times in our storied past, except, I was the one on the receiving end of the accusations and gossip. The have you heard, did you know and so on. In addition Mr. Simms," as J.P.'s voice became slightly more elevated, his facial expression became hard, "I recall quite clearly, you seemed to always agree with the people bringing you the accusations which directly concerned me!"

Simms sat for a moment looking at J.P., then got up, placed the desk back where he had gotten it and began to walk toward the door.

O'Francis waited until he just about reached the door. "Mr. Simms." J.P. said. "As for being accused of an event or events that may or may not have occurred in your past, I will tell you this. I personally do not care one way or the other. I do not, nor have I in the past made any false accusations about you or anyone else in this community. If I tell someone of some event or occurrence that reflects someone personally, it is checked out beforehand and is factual. Mr. Simms," J.P's voice became pronounced. "I have neither in the past nor at present accepted hearsay from others as fact! Now as we stand here facing each other once again with accusations of some alleged infidelities or type of out of the professed Honsburg community's norms, with a bit of a different twist to it all, you can be assured of one thing. I have and had the upmost respect for Ginger." Then after a slight pause, "I will not speak to anyone in the confines of this educational institution about any past-alleged occurrences that may have involved you personally. You have my word. That, I think you know is all you will need. Now, Mr. Simms, how about you giving me the same courtesy for once?"

Simms stood across the room looking at J.P. saying nothing.

"Sir, which is more than I can say, has taken place in my life while living in your community, according to sources that would include you, sir. You now have my word. Do I have yours?"

He stood across the room with a stark expression on his face. Before he could turn J.P. shot one more volley across his bow, with an even more deadly tone in his voice. "I do not deal in character assassination." Simms turned boldly, took two steps to the door, opened it harshly, exiting the room, leaving the door open.

J.P. scooted his chair back a bit, slowly sat down, and placed his feet up on the edge of his shabby looking desk. His hands cupped together, his two index fingers gently bouncing back and forth off his lips, as he sat pondering. *Seems that my conversation with Bernadette may have struck a nerve. The facts in the matter are that I did not state that any of it was true. I thought I had made myself clear. Oh well, it is what it is. He also did not give me his word of honor that he would not repeat gossip that was related to him concerning me, so much for honor*

*on his part. So what is new in my world. Now the question begs to be asked, where did he get his information?*

J.P. spoke aloud softly to no one there. "Mr. Martin was directly across the hall, and Bernadette's classroom door was open when we were talking. He could have easily heard the conversation as our voices would carry in an empty classroom. Or Bobby could have listened in over the intercom. He could have seen me go into Bernadette's room, that was a possibility. The only other person to come in the room or in the area was Annie Alderman, who had stopped by momentarily, then left. She could have heard them talking. Na, she did not fit the typical gossip lounge teacher. I just do not know. Oh well...sure cannot expect anything better! Just have to deal with it! My mistake! I have to get a job somewhere else! This place will kill me if I do not! What a hellhole. There is not another human being on earth that would believe all this shit!"

# Patrick's Day Off

J.P. WENT ABOUT HIS JOB as if nothing ever happened adapting to his new world of teaching pre-high school students. Bobby became friendlier and more pleasant with him as the year progressed. Bernadette would become close friends and a proven ally to O'Francis when it appeared that the "cards" were stacked against him in the years to come, leaving J.P. to believe that it was not Bernadette that had informed Bobby of their conversation.

Patrick was having problems with his Science teacher Fred Martin. J.P. tried to be professional, as he had to work with Fred. He would hear the women teachers that worked in his section of the building talk about Fred in a manner that would have chilled hell with their words. Now J.P. did not know the man and could have cared less about how the women felt as long as he treated his son fairly.

As he arrived home Dawn had a troubled looked on her face. "Bobby Simms called today."

"What did he want?"

"Patrick got in trouble in Mr. Martin's class."

"For what?"

"Well according to Patrick, Mr. Martin yelled at him for answering a question incorrectly. And it was not the first time he had done so."

"Okay."

"Well, Patrick called him a damn "fagit." And Mr. Martin sent him to the office."

"He did not say anything to me on the way home."

"Well, at any rate, Bobby told me that he was suspending him for one day."

J.P. called Patrick into the kitchen and had him to explain what happened to him in his science class.

The O'Francis family accepted the punishment and tried to get along, encouraging Patrick to work hard with his studies, that it would work out in the long haul, that he would face many types of obstacles throughout his life and that he would have to learn to deal with each of them, learning from the one before. But for their 13 year old son, it was very difficult to understand why a teacher was being unfair to him and treating him harshly class, embarrassing him in front of his classmates.

Fred copped a very bad attitude toward Patrick and his grades dropped from "B's" to "D's" to "F's", which concerned Dawn and J.P. as Martin's science class began to affect his other classes and even his father's history class. Patrick was getting to the point that he hated school, as it had become an everyday event between Fred Martin and Patrick O'Francis. Patrick had History after his Science class and would come into his father's class stressed out and upset. It would take him half the period before he would settle down to the point that he could gain any knowledge about history. This J.P. had noticed in several other students as well, and had from time to time reported his concerns to Mr. Simms, that there appeared be a problem in Fred Martin's class with certain students.

On Patrick's day off, he rode an 18 ton tri-axle rock truck with Peter Henry Stacy who went back to truck driving after he had lost his job as a police officer because of the political machine. New Sheriff, different political party, new deputies, and if you were not one of the "good ole boys" you look for a new job. It did not make a royal rats ass how much experience you had, or how good of a law enforcement person you were, you're out, cold, cut and dried!

Of course, the new "law in the county" was not qualified, nor would they have the leadership of a William Peng. The ethics and honor would also go with Peng. But William had never walked to the beat of the political powers, he walked to the beat of his own drum, and that was of course why he did not last more than one term in office as the Reynolds County Sheriff.

Patrick's day with Peter was extremely enjoyable, as Peter picked him up at 5:00 A.M. had worked until 5:00 P.M. For a 13 year old that was a full day. Peter was one of a very few people in the area that had not jumped on the band wagon of accusing J.P. of any wrong doing and had not believed all the gossip that had floated through the vast network of sewer lines in the community and the county. Peter remained a true friend to the O'Francis family, and would drop in from time to time for a brief visit and a cup of coffee.

The following six weeks J.P. made arrangements with Bobby Simms to meet with Fred Martin after his regular contract working hours. He informed Simms that he would be a parent, not a fellow colleague. He also requested that Mr. Simms be present for the parent teacher conference. J.P. was not a very happy camper, as he took it personal when some adult attacked his sons. The meeting was set for 3:45 p.m. Bobby had informed Mr. Martin that J.P. would be meeting him as a parent, and when Simms confirmed the meeting with J.P. he indicated that Fred did not have any problem with the meeting.

At 3:45 J.P. entered into Fred Martin's room. "Afternoon Mr. Martin."

"Afternoon." Martin replied.

Bobby Simms was not present and J.P. waited for five minutes before he began to address Fred Martin about his son. J.P. did not know why Simms was late. His thoughts were that he was setting him up for something he could fire him for. Bobby knew how he felt about his sons and knew that he would not let anything happen to them. Jim figured he would lose it and take Fred out, leaving him no choice but to recommend him being dismissed. That, Jim did not intend on happening. He had been through too much to lose control. He would handle the matter in a controlled manner. If Fred would not cooperate, he would walk away.

"Fred, what seems to be the problem between my son and you?" J.P. asked as he sat in one of the front row students desks. Fred on the other hand, chose to stand at the taller black topped science table located directly in the front of the room, which was basically Mr. Martin's desk.

"I didn't know that we had a problem."

"Oh, I see. Well, okay, good. Then could you tell me why his grades have dropped from "B's" to "F's"?"

"He's not doing the work."

"Well Fred, what about this past six weeks? I mean, look...he did a project, and what was his grade on that? It was a rather large project, and he spent a lot of time on it. Also, what of the test grades he received these six weeks. What were they? I have asked him to bring home each test paper so that we could go back over the ones he may have missed, but he tells me that you have not given any of his test papers back. May I see them or the grades that he received for them?" By that point in the conversation, Fred had taken a seat a few feet from J.P.

"I really don't know what I have done with his test papers."

"Well, fine. Let's look at his grades in your grade book."

"Why?"

"I beg your pardon?"

"I said why?"

"Well, Fred it is customary to show a parent their child's grades and what tests they have taken and what they made on each of the tests. Do you not do that with other parents? He was not absent a single day, so he had to have taken all the tests you had scheduled for the six weeks."

J.P. took out his pen, went to his briefcase, and got out a note pad.

"What do you think you are doing?"

"I am going to copy each test, date, and grade down, that is what I am doing Fred." J.P. looked up at Fred as he suddenly jumped up out of the student's desk.

"I don't have to put up with this!" He had out of no apparent provocation gotten angry.

"Look Fred." J.P. rose to face him. "I am here as a parent with concerns for my son. I expect you to cooperate with me. I am not here to attack you in any way. Hell man, I have been through this, what seems would be a hundred times. I am not your enemy. All I want is to get a grip on my son's progress and try to find out what is going on. Come on, how about a little cooperation here, okay?"

"I ain't saying nothing else!"

"So you are refusing to work with me on this? Is that what you are telling me Fred?"

He turned and angrily left the room, leaving J.P. standing next to the students' desk. J.P. sat back down and waited. Five minutes passed and Bobby Simms came in.

"Where is Mr. Martin?"

"Well, Mr. Simms, he has left the room. I would have presumed that you would have seen him in the hall or that he went to your office."

"Have you all started yet?"

"Yes sir, that we have." Bobby Simms looked puzzled, and pulled up a desk just to J.P.'s right. "Well, is he coming back or is the meeting over? I mean, did you two get everything worked out okay?"

"Well, not really, Mr. Simms. I would have really appreciated it if you had been here when we started. I do believe you would have found it to be very interesting."

"What does that mean?"

"Well, as a parent, and looking at it from a teacher's point of view, I have never treated any parent in the manner in which I have just been treated. And if I had, you and any number of my previous bosses would have most likely had legitimate grounds to take me in front of the school superintendent as well as the School Board. I am talking about legitimate grounds, not the ones that have been used in the past. Now as a parent, I am filing with you right now," he said as he pointed his right index finger toward the desk top, "an official complaint against Mr. Fred Martin. I would also like for you to find out why Mr. Martin is harassing my son. I expect it to stop!" At that moment Fred Martin walked back into the room, and instantly went off like a roman candle. He froze three feet into the room.

"By-god, I ain't meeting with him in here!" He pointed his figure toward Bobby Simms.

"Fred," J.P. spoke in a concerning manner, "lets." He interrupted J.P. "I told you I ain't saying nothing in front of him! Why is he in here anyway?"

"Fred, calm down. He is the principal, or have you forgotten? I asked him to stop by, it is customary, or it was when I had to meet with a parent when there was a problem with a student. I mean, what is the problem?"

"No, no, no, he goes or I go!"

"No, now Fred, look… let's iron this out today, let's you and me…"

"Hell no, not as long as HE is in here!" He turned and walked out again leaving J.P. and Simms looking at each other.

In a calm voice J.P. spoke, "Well Mr. Simms, I would call that a gross case of insubordination. If I had done just that, no let me rephrase that, anywhere near that to you…oh well, I did not, would never, and have never treated a parent anywhere near the way I have just been treated." Mr. Simms sat saying nothing.

"So Mr. Simms I guess that means we will meet in your office, in an official capacity, with my wife present. I would like to meet Friday at 0900 hr., 9:00 A.M. to you Sir. I will be taking the day off, as I will be here as a parent. Sir, I will put in for a personal leave day."

J.P. got up first leaving Simms sitting in the student's desk, walked out of the room, went home to Dawn and Patrick, and informed her of what had taken place.

Friday arrived and the O'Francis parents were at the school at 8:55 A.M., and were escorted into Mr. Simms office. A very short time later Mr. Simms entered with Mr. Martin. For J.P. it was an odd feeling being on the flip side of the pancake. He was hoping that he would not have to say anything and Dawn would do all the talking. But Fred being Fred, and having an attitude toward them and their son, it did not work out like J.P. hoped for. As much as he hated to, he finally stepped into the conversation when Fred continued to verbally attack Dawn and Patrick referring, to his son as "someone" he would expect to find on the street corner in leathers and chains and dealing in drugs. Mr. Simms seemed to have no control over Mr. Martin, and when Fred refused for the fourth time to answer Dawn's questions about her son's grades, J.P. spoke.

"Mr. Martin, you are making more out of this than needs to be. We want to clear this matter up here in Mr. Simms office and with just a little cooperation we can." Fred Martin laughed at both of them.

"Look Mr. Martin, now if you do not want to clear this up here we can take it to the superintendent. It is up to you."

"You can take it to whoever you want! I don't have to clear up anything!" He got up, opened the door and walked out.

"Mr. Simms, Fred has given us no choice but to go to the superintendent. Now I have followed all the guidelines, and chain of command."

"Well, Mr. and Mrs. O'Francis, I guess you will just have to do what you think is best."

Then Dawn spoke as J.P. rose from his chair. "We are doing what is best for our son. I want him out of his classroom today."

"Now Mrs. O'Francis, you know I can't do that."

"Excuse me! You did not seem to have a problem doing it with students in my husband's classes over the years! You and every other damn principal he has had to work for! Yes you can! And I do not want Patrick to spend another day in MR. MARTIN's room!"

"Mr. O'Francis."

"No, Mr. Simms, this time Mr. Martins is wrong, and he has not been treating Patrick fairly. It is affecting his grades overall and we cannot allow that to happen. I do not want my son to have to go to that class another day." The two left Simms' office and went straight to the superintendent's office.

After a thirty-minute conversation with the superintendent where Dawn finally became emotional, J.P. could see that LaMar was enjoying every minute of it. J.P. watched LaMar as Dawn explained the problem to him. His thoughts flashed like a lightning bolt, *he could care less. He has the political mannerisms down to a fine art. He should have been a professional politician, show that mother that real concern, make that little caring comment.*

"Now Mrs. O'Francis, I really care about the welfare of all the students in our system, and if there is something wrong, I will look into it and correct any wrong. I like old Sean, bet he is a lot like his dad."

Then a big laugh rolled out of his over boisterous mouth. *Make her think something will be done to justify the wrong being done. And I caught that demeaning comment of he is just like his dad...Of course if it was anyone else, and it was O'Francis on the hot seat, he would do something! How easy would it be for me to just eliminate him right here, God, if I only could and walk away?* LaMar interrupted J.P.'s thoughts.

"Mr. O'Francis, so you have tried to come to, let's say, terms with Mr. Martin?"

J.P. smiled. "That is correct." A momentary pause as LaMar expected J.P. to elaborate on the matter.

"Ahhh, is there anything else you want to say."

"No sir." He knew there would be no investigation into the matter and that not a thing would be done to help them or their son. The O'Francis family could expect no satisfaction from the Reynolds County School System.

Patrick did have to attend Mr. Martin's class, but he would not have to do any work for the remainder of the year. He would receive a "D" for each of the remaining six weeks left and a grade of "D" for the year. J.P. and Dawn were angry, as they knew that he would not get any preparation for his High School Science classes which would make it harder for him in the upper grades. But it would give the people who were connected to the overall conspiracy an opportunity to strike once again at J.P. through his son by giving him a bad grade in his course load and claiming that he just could not do the work. J.P. would once again come to realize that he had all the cards stack against him, which made him that much more bitter, and the hatred grew stronger and stronger. The stress mounted on him as he visualized the assassination of all that was involved. He fought to control his inner-most desires to relieve the painful hate he was going through. Once again he was brought to the forefront of reality that he was not part of the political machine and the game he was playing in.

# The Players

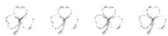

It was spring and baseball was in the air. J.P. was hurting as he was not on the field teaching the sport he so dearly loved. He had been scheduled his first umpiring game of the year and had been given the plate to call. All the years of coaching, he now found himself wearing the "blue shirt". It had been a lot of years since he had called an official game and he was a bit tight, as he knew how important each pitch was to the young men on the mound.

He had invested in a top quality set of equipment: two pairs of charcoal slacks and two blue shirts; one pair of plate shoes and a pair of base shoes; two caps, one to be used for the bases and one with the shorter bill for the plate, allowing for his mask to fit over it.

His shoes had a high gloss shine to them. His "gig line" was straight. He placed a chew of beechnut in his right cheek. Then he stepped to the plate, turned his back to the pitcher, took his plate broom out of his right pouch, bent over, and cleaned the home plate off. He straightened up, looked at the catcher, who was standing in his catchers box behind the plate, and asked, "Are you ready to play ball?"

The catcher, a junior in high school, was holding his mask in his right hand, smiled and replied "Yes sir."

J.P. smiled. "Then let's get this game going. It sure doesn't work without us."

He then turned back to the pitcher and in a loud voice stated, "Play ball!" He pulled his tan leathered padded mask over his face and stepped behind the catcher as the first batter positioned himself in the batter's box.

He was very comfortable behind home plate, as he had been a catcher himself, and enjoyed the role of chief umpire. Over the next six years he would be known among coaches as being a very fair and impartial umpire. Some of them he had faced as a coach, although the coaches often would not agree with his calls, be it as a base "ump" or a plate umpire. He was good at his job, and there was never a game that he did not do his best to improve over the last game he called. He knew the game and knew the rules, and did his best to read the rulebook as well as the casebook as many times as he could. He knew that he would never reach 100 % perfection, but intended to try. It bothered him when he missed a call. He would replay it over and over in his mind so as not to make the same mistake again. The one quality he had over many umpires he had known as a coach and as a colleague, whether he liked the coach or not, was that he never made a call in malice to get back at or even with any coach. He knew that the players were the ones playing the game not the coaches, and he would call them as he saw them. He would be requested to call many games and a lot of "big" games. Games that would determine the outcome of a conference championship, and would be selected to call many post-season games.

Once again the Damon - Finkel factor attempted to discredit O'Francis, by calling the commissioner of baseball after receiving a list of umpires that would be used for the season. Richard requested that O'Francis not be used for any of the Honsburg games, at home or away. Now what Finkel did not know most of the coaches and 90 % of all the umpires in the "umpiring" association were very much aware of the way J.P. had been treated over the years. But when Richard asked Ed Lowe if he knew anything about O'Francis, and had gotten a no for a reply, he proceeded to assassinate him verbally. Ed scheduled a game the second week of the season to work with J.P. and to evaluate him personally. He knew his quality as a coach, over many years of seeing him operate. Ed calculated that if he was anywhere as close to umpiring as he was a coach, he was going to be one of the best the association had.

It was at the pre-game outside of the confines of the playing field that he told him of the conversation with his nemesis.

"So what are you going to do Ed?" J.P. asked.

"I am going to schedule you like I do any other umpire. Now do you want to call any of the Honsburg games? I mean it is no real problem for me. Neither Richard Finkel nor Damon Bales controls this organization, nor will they ever as long as I am commissioner."

"Well, Ed, I do not think that the other coaches would appreciate me calling Honsburg's games when they had to face me and Tim last year as coaches. Now do not read me wrong, I still would call them like I see them. Point of fact is, Tim would most likely give me a harder time than any of the other coaches ever would. He really never did like my low strike zone when I would call during our practices. But I personally would not feel comfortable calling a Honsburg game. I am too close to the players. So for all of Richard's efforts to discredit me, it really went for nil. Let it go. Let him and the rest of the ass-holes… no let me correct myself, an ass-hole does have a purpose in life, these people have no purpose, they really should be exterminated. These people are a disease in our society and should be gotten rid of. Sorry Ed, it is just that I have a lot of anger in me."

"Hell, you don't have to explain a damn thing to me. Shit, I am surprised that you haven't put one of the bastards in the hospital or in the grave already with as much as you have gone through. J.P., word gets around. Every one of us knows what has gone on, you owe me no apology what so ever. And I think you will find that most, if not all the other umpires, feel the same way. I have never heard one that did not like to come to yours and Tim's place to call a game. I don't think, I am not real sure about this, but I don't think any of us has ever had a confrontation with either one of you for…how many years?"

"Tim and I were together for ten years. And you are very most correct. We have never had a problem with any umpire. Now that does not mean we liked the calls all the time, and I know you are very much aware of some of the games we have been fucked on! That most likely cost us at least one State title, and I am not so sure that we could have not have won at least two more. And I mean that, I really do believe that!"

"Oh, yes, I am very much aware of the games that you have been screwed on! But there is one thing that can never be taken away from you two. You were a class act no matter what the outcome was. And that goes for your players as well. There are not a lot of teams that I can say that about."

"All a player is, that is, with his actions on and around the game, reflects the coaches, and I thank you for the kind words." J.P. stated as they walked onto the field to start the game.

Michael was in his second semester of college as was his close friend Stacy Cross. Both had struggled as freshmen because of the lack of their high school preparation. But that did not surprise J.P. as he had said many times that for the most part the teachers at the school were a joke. There were a few exceptions, maybe five or six, but no more. He was proud to be one of the ones that did prepare the students. The courses these few taught their students that did go off to a higher education, did very well, and often times came back to thank J.P. as well as a few of the real teachers that had prepared them for college.

Dawn had been unable to get a job in the area and the money to run their household was once again depleted at the end of each month. If he could make a thousand dollars umpiring it would keep them out of the red. He stayed depressed most of the time because he was unable to give Michael any spending money. He told Dawn that he would be going to Detroit to get a summer job and stay with Dennis and Theresa.

It was Holly who suggested that J.P. see a psychoanalyst to help him with his stress, and after some thought he decided to do so. What Holly did not know, and couldn't have cared less, was that the money was not there for any doctor, mental or physical. He borrowed the money off his mother-in-law to pay for Holly's services. Of course, it was not the first time J.P. sought psychotherapy and most likely would not be the last. However, over the years he had not found any relief from any one of them. So, Dawn and J.P. sat down and did their calculations as to how to stretch the dollar just a little more, for at least a brief period. He started his mental therapy in March of that year and had to go once a week. He often times felt that he was wasting his time and valued money, but did what had been advised, as he felt that maybe it would this time help keep him balanced enough that he would not do something stupid.

It was the last six weeks of school and even though the umpiring job had turned out to be a success, and the extra money had exceeded expectations, the coffer had little left at the end of each month.

The year had gone without any major allegations of O'Francis wrong doings, and J.P. had been thankful for it. However during the last few weeks of the school year, he had been having a difficult time out of one of his seventh graders. Kent Wilfred had interrupted his lectures on more than one occasion and it seemed that no matter what he did, he could not reach the boy. The administration did not want to deal with him because of his mother, whose "bubble" did not come close to being between the lines. So they just threw him back at J.P. He noticed that if one of the female teachers sent Kent to the office they handled the matter and often sent him home for several days on more than one occasion.

It was not a particularly bad day for J.P., but Kent's outburst of "He-Haw, jack-ass" style of laughter during a lecture on Vietnam did not set well with O'Francis.

He stopped in the middle of his lecture and stated, "Kent, if you continue to act and sound like a Jack-Ass in my class, I will remove you for the remainder of the year! DO YOU UNDERSTAND ME?" His voice had become very direct, harsh and deep.

The following day as J.P. entered his room, running three minutes late, as he had gone to the restroom to empty a bladder that had been full of coffee, and walked to his podium.

"Okay...let me see... fourth period...okay, where were we? Someone give me a brief breakdown of yesterday's lecture."

Usually several students tried to talk at once, and he had to remind them that only one was to speak at a time, trying to teach them the manners of not talking over one another. Something J.P. hated and noticed that people in general did and more women than men, with the exception of media reporters and commentators, and then gender did not matter. They all were rude. However, that day no one spoke and there was total silence in the room. He looked up and scanned the room as it hit him that something was not just right in his now famous "Think Tank" as it had been called for many years on the high school level and now on the junior high level. It had not registered with him that no one had been talking as he entered the room. That was not normal, except when there was a guest in the room, and the rule was that if there was a guest, or a fellow colleague, or principal that no one spoke out of order, which he admired his students for adhering to the rule.

As he scanned the room, there in the back of the room was a woman whom he did not recognize. He had not scheduled any parent conferences, which would have been during his morning break and none had asked to sit in on his class that day, which on occasions a parent did and J.P. allowed it.

He stated that he was a professional and that he intended to be treated as such. Simms had mildly objected at the time of the conversation, whether he had been playing the "devil's advocate" or not, J.P. was not sure, but had responded.

"Do you just walk into a doctor's office and demand to see your physician? No, I do not think so. Do you walk into your lawyer's office and demand to see your attorney? No, again I do not think so. Try walking into your congressmen's office and demanding to see him. I am a professional and I will be treated like one. If someone would like to see me, they can make an appointment, and I will be more than glad to see them if I do not have something of importance scheduled at the time."

Simms had agreed that anyone just stopping by to see him for whatever reason, they would first have to contact him and would get his approval before allowing them to come to J.P.'s room.

J.P. walked to within a few feet of the woman. "Madam may I help you?"

"May I help you madam," came the sneering comeback. "Just who the fuck do you think you are?"

J.P. cut her off quickly. "Look... I do not know who you are, but you will have to leave my room. I have a class to conduct!"

"Shit! I ain't going anywhere, Mr. O'FRANCIS!" She stated in a hard drawn out manner.

J.P. turned to one of the female students sitting close to the door. "Barbara, would you please go to the office and ask Mr. Simms to come to my room? I have a problem."

She was up and gone in a flash as all saw that it was a very dangerous situation.

"You have a god damn problem alright. You're going to think problem when I get done with you!"

"Who are you?" J.P. inquired.

"I am Kent Wilfred's mother and I..."

Once again J.P. cut her off. "Will please step outside of my room Mr. Wilfred?" As he indicated with his left arm and hand to the direction of the door.

Mrs. Wilfred got up out of the student desk and in a violent manner shoved it to her right, colliding with the student to her right. "You're a piece of shit!" As she glared at O'Francis, she passed him and walked to the door in a manner that would indicate a woman was very upset. Kent was sitting in his assigned seat at the other side of the room smiling as J.P. followed Mrs. Wilfred out the door closing it behind him. His major concern was to get her away from the students, as he had been told that she was not at all stable, and he did understand that part. He was well aware that an unstable person without self-discipline was a threat to all in their presence. Several students looked back at Kent when the door closed.

"Hey, don't look at me like that," Kent stated. "Shit he brought it on and my mother will kick his ass!" Several boys laughed, lightly.

"Sure Kent, I can just see that!"

"Yeah, well, my dad will bury his ass! He ain't all that bad! Hell, my dad will blow his ass away!"

Patrick finally turned in his seat and from across the room boldly defended his father. "You know Kent, you and your whole damn family are nothing but trash!"

"Look you little fat piece of shit, I'll come up there and beat your ass!" Since the size difference was well in the favor of Kent, who was, for a 14 year old, six foot, two hundred plus pounds, and Patrick, who at thirteen, five foot five and one hundred and fifty pounds, it would have been Patrick's doom's day. However, being the O'Francis he was, and even though fearing the overbearing giant sitting in the back of the room, whom all the junior high students were afraid of, Patrick called his bluff, knowing he would get his face smashed in. However, his friend Curt, who was about the same size as well, and had a passive demeanor, to a point, and who would forever remain his friend, had Patrick's back, and it would have most likely taken both of them to have handled Kent.

Patrick challenged the brute. "Well, I don't see anyone stopping you. Of course Mommy is just outside the door, maybe you can call on her!"

The boys in the room were exited. A fight was about to take place, and for all boys in junior high school, a fight was something to behold. Now Curt was not much on the physical aspect of resolving a dispute. He was more the intellectual type and diplomacy was the better part of valor.

However, being a country boy, and having to choose between trying to talk to an idiot, and coming to the aid of his friend, Curt would opt for the physical part of resolving the matter. J.P. could hear voices raised in the room, reopened the door, and looked throughout the room. He did not have to speak, silence swept over the room like a Black Death cloud.

Mr. Simms and Mr. Cosworth, his assistant, were coming down the hallway in a manner that indicated an emergency. Barbara was only thirty feet in front of them, approaching the door to the classroom and J.P. let her in, and then closed the door.

J.P. politely and calmly stated, "Mr. Simms, I would like for you to escort Mrs. Wilfred away from my room, please."

"I have told you, you sonavabitch, that I ain't going nowhere!"

She placed her hand on the doorknob, shifted her hips to her right. "You think you are some kind of real tough guy! I have heard all about you, and I ain't afraid of you! My husband was in the Army too! He WILL put YOU in the hospital, here or downtown!"

Mr. Simms interrupted her, "Mrs. Wilfred, please come with me to the office and let's see if we can clear up whatever it is that is bothering you."

"This...THIS," as she looked at J.P., "Is what is bothering me! He'll not talk to my boy like he did and get away with it!"

"Mrs. Wilfred, I don't know what you are talking about, but..."

"OH, I AM sure you don't! I KNOW HOW YOU ALL STICK TOGETHER UP HERE! You all pick on Kent all the time and I am damn fed up with it and I intend to do something about it here and now!"

J.P. reached for the doorknob with his right hand.

"OH NO YOU DON'T! DON'T YOU...YOU EVEN THINK ABOUT IT MISTER! I'LL SLAP THE HELL OUT YOU, YOU SONAVABITCH!"

O'Francis took a deep breath, and in the most polite voice and tone he could, stated, "Please Mrs. Wilfred. I really do not think you want any problems here today. Now if you would please just go with Mr. Simms and Mr. Cosworth, I am sure they will hear your complaint and we will resolve the matter." O'Francis looked at his administrators. "Sirs, I am asking you to allow me to return to my class. Enough is enough and I am losing patience real fast."

Neither man would step closer than six feet, the same position they had come to when arriving at O'Francis' room.

"Mrs. Wilfred if you would just come with me please." Mr. Simms spoke as calmly as he could. J.P. knew that both of the administrators had more than one encounter with her, none being very pleasant.

"I will allow you to tell me all about whatever it is that is bothering you. I promise you we will take care of the matter."

O'Francis reached for the door and she slapped his hand away, glaring at him. "YEAH, SURE! I'M NOT THROUGH WITH YOU!" Her face drawn and with anger, pointing her finger at J.P., she turned toward Bobby and Darrel and walked down the hallway. Getting some thirty feet away, she turned just as J.P. was opening the door, pointing her finger at him.

"You're dead! You're dead you sonofabitch!"

After J.P.'s sixth period class had ended, Mr. Cosworth came to his room five minutes into the last class of the day and informed him that Mr. Simms wanted him in the office and that he would stay with his class. J.P. looked at Darrel with concern on his face.

"I take it that things did not go well?"

"Ahhhh, no. Not at all! But that is normal for her!"

O'Francis pecked on the door. "Come in," Mr. Simms stated, his voice indicating that he was nervous. J.P. entered. Two chairs were against the wall to the left of the door as he entered, facing Simms desk, one chair was to the right of the door against the wall to the left of Simms desk. He saw Mrs. Wilfred sitting in the far chair, facing Simms desk. He closed the door and took a seat in the one on Simms' left against the wall.

"Mr. O'Francis, Mrs. Wilfred stated that you called her son a jack-ass in front of the entire class. Is that true?"

"Yes sir."

Mrs. Wilfred jumped on that instantly. "My son doesn't use that kind of language, nor do we around him! Now, I want something done about him now!"

Mr. Simms looked at J.P. "Ahhh, Mr. O'Francis, do you have anything you would like to say?"

"Yes sir, I do." He proceeded to explain why he chose to use the terms he did, which brought on a ten minute verbalizing assault, charging J.P. with cussing her little boy. J.P. was well aware of Kent's after school curriculum, lying out on the street corner at all hours of the night with drug hustlers. J.P. uncrossed his left leg.

"Sir, may I be excused? I really do not think we are going to resolve anything here and now."

"You're right. You will apologize to my little boy and to me!" An instant response from Mrs. Wilfred as J.P. stood. He did not wait for Simms to excuse him. He turned and walked out of the office.

Within a week of Mrs. Wilfred's display of ignorance, Mr. Marshy sent his leading SS people to Honsburg Middle to conduct an investigation of the events and of J.P. Again Dan was called to come to the assistance of James Patrick O'Francis, which irritated LaMar to the point of violent vernacular verbalization of him. Once in a display of his true self, after losing to Dan in another one of his attacks on O'Francis, he stated that he would like to kill Dan Jakes. But like O'Francis, Dan had faced real death many times, and unlike Marshy who had dodged the draft during the Vietnam Conflict, and being a basic coward, he was no real match for either Dan or J.P. on or off the "playing field".

He could do his behind the scenes acts of sabotage and character assassination, keeping the pressure on in hopes that J.P. would break, using the ignorance of some of J.P.'s colleagues and his principals who were controlled by the money that Marshy made sure they received in salaries and other perks, especially his very close office staff. In the end J.P. would have to face the reality of the power of his conspirators. He would be presented a statement by Simms that informed him that any future complaints concerning the same type of issues, would result in serious disciplinary action taken against him. Bobby Simms requested that he sign the document, but O'Francis refused to sign it, informing him that he was not guilty of cussing anyone and had never in his career directly cursed a student. Simms told him that a copy would be placed in his file.

"Well, Mr. Simms, that being the case I will have Mr. Jakes respond to your document with a letter denouncing any wrong doing that I am charged with."

Pausing momentarily before walking out of the office, "Mr. Simms... if I had been one of the "boys" or a "split-tail" we would not be having this conversation!" He turned and exited the office.

It was June and J.P. was trying to repair his water heater, as they had no extra money to get a much-needed new one. Dawn walked into the laundry room.

"I am going to call Dennis after I finish here and leave for Detroit Saturday."

She just stood looking at her beloved soulmate for a good five minutes.

"I saw a help wanted sign in the Video store downtown. I think I will apply for the job. What do you think?"

"Well, if you can get the job, it would save me from leaving you all alone for the summer. How much does it pay?"

"Well I'm not sure. I need to call."

"You got the number?" J.P. asked.

"Yes, their main office is in Harriette."

As he struggled with his repairs, he stated, "Damn I hate this damn thing! Fuck, nothing works anymore!"

As he sat back on the concrete floor, he pushed himself against the wall, relit his cigar, which he had chewed half away. He looked up at his wife who was still standing in the doorway, with a look that said I wish I could make it all better.

"Look, we have to do something. Call them now, see if they will give you an interview." Dawn went to the phone and made the call, and to both of their surprises they asked if she could come for an interview the next day.

They arrived in Harriette ten minutes before her interview. Both had discussed the matter of her getting a job and what it would mean during the forty-five minute trip it took to get to Harriette, and both kept a positive approach to the job possibility.

*"Always think positive J.P. would say. If you think positive most of the time it will happen, not always, but most of the time. Got to go with the percentage."*

Thinking positive was something he was having a hard time doing as of late, but he would always tell everyone else to do it.

Dawn was in the interview for thirty minutes. The entire time J.P.'s thoughts went from extreme anger for choosing the profession he was in, to assassination, to asking his Master and Spirit Guide for help in getting Dawn a job. She came out with a smile on her face.

"So how did it go?"

"Really, really good. I believe I have a chance of getting it."

They were both excited, as Dawn went over the entire interview with J.P. on their return trip home, expressing excitement in everything, telling J.P. she seemed very happy about the whole idea.

The next day she got the call that informed her that she had gotten the job and that she would have to come to the Harriett store to be trained for the first week, before she could work in the Honsburg store. For the both of them the trip and the gas it would take for a week was well worth the time and money. So they went to their coin jar and counted out all the change they had and went to the bank and cashed it in for bills. With careful calculation they figured the miles and the amount of gas they would need. Dawn would work out very well for the owner of the video store, and would in time become very good friends with Allen Wesley. The one thing that allowed her to get the job was her good looks, her bubbling personality, and her ability to communicate well with the general public. Her knowledge of bookkeeping and management was a strong factor and for J.P. the fact that the owner was not from Honsburg or Reynolds County was a major factor. No one had their hands around his throat, or crushing his balls telling him to do what THEY wanted him to do. He was a man of his own mind and couldn't give a damn less about the powers in the town or for that matter the county. Politics to Allen was a bad disease, and he made every effort not to catch it. He owed no one anything and was intent on keeping it that way.

The job would keep J.P. home for the summer and allow him to work around his house on his usual summer projects of repairing this or that, or building this or that in which Dawn seemed to always have a new idea for the improvement of the house whether it be inside or outside.

Their summer went by quickly. Michael was home and had been working for Kleeco Construction Company building bridges, learning how to tie steel, and using a jackhammer, throughout his summer. J.P. had always been extremely proud of Michael, as he had always been a hard worker, striving to be the best at whatever he did. When August came and the football players reported back for training Michael did not go. He had decided that he would not play football his second year of college. Instead he wanted to play baseball in the fall and spring. He was more suited for the game of baseball, and enjoyed it more. His roommate and friend Stacy opted for the more physical game of football. He was the most unlikely one to play football even as a defensive back. His speed and height made up for his lack in bulk and weight, as he only weighed 170 pounds, and had reached his finial height of six feet one. His tall lanky frame, extremely good hands, and ability to read QB's, made him a very good DB for a small private college.

Patrick would be entering his last year of Junior High, and was not overly excited about going back to school. J.P. and Dawn were very worried about him and his attitude toward education. They feared that his nightmare (to him at his age, a nightmare) experience would set him behind and that he would not rebound from it, to get back on course.

J.P. had been in contact with Dan off and on throughout the summer and he had encouraged him to get more involved in the teacher association business, political as it was. J.P. loved the study of politics, and loved to teach it, but did not know if he was ready to get directly involved in the grand scheme of things as he felt he had enough enemies as it was. To get directly involved in the political game, you made enemies quick. Of course on the other hand, you could make some good allies, if of course you were able to serve the needs of the politician and come in line like everyone else. In other words, he would often use the dirtiness and corruptness of the political game.

According to Holly his case was moving along as expected, and she would give him an update from time to time by letter, or a rare phone call. He rarely had to go to her office, and when he did it was for a meaningful purpose. She was very direct and to the point every time J.P. met with her, something he liked. He felt good about Holly, and felt that she could handle Damon very well, and got the impression that she did know how to play hardball with the best, and probably better than most.

At one point in a meeting concerning her plan of operation, she asked, "J.P., are you aware of who you are suing?"

"Yes, I am."

"I really don't think you are." He looked at her with puzzlement.

"You are not just talking about two low-lives that have made your life miserable for the past...ever how many years now. No, you are about to take on the entire Democratic party of Reynolds County. Now don't sit there and look at me like that. You know who runs the county, and you know that these very same people are connected to all the other power players in the county. So... you are smart enough to know that they are going to come to the aid of one of their "good ole boys". Now make no mistake about it, they will do whatever it takes to defend Damon. Richard, welllll, he is along for the ride. Hell, if they could sacrifice him without any damage to their political comrade Damon, they would in a heartbeat. However...he could prove to jeopardize this case, too many connecting links, so they will carry him. They know that he would roll over on all of them in this case, trust me on this one. I know you are not the trusting type, but I have done my homework and I know, believe me!"

J.P. started to speak, but she interrupted him.

"Hold your question. Are you aware that the Reynolds County School Board has agreed to pay for their attorney and all legal expenses?"

"No." His thoughts raced. "Now wait one minute here Holly. I mean, I...I mean... does that mean we can file a suit against the School Board?"

"No."

"Why?"

"Because they did not write the letter."

"But,"

"No but to it. They can foot his bill all they want. That does not mean they are directly involved. I just got through telling you what you are about to face. Now do you want to carry this thing out to the end, knowing what you do at this point?"

J.P. did not waver for a moment. "Yes!"

Holly continued. "You know there is no guarantees as things stand now."

"Yes I am aware of that. But I have no choice. I have to try. I have been damaged. My name has been tarnished. I am a fighter. I do not know what the word quit means. You cannot find it in my vocabulary. Now do you think I have been damaged?"

"Yes I do, and probably more than you even realize. Now, a winning attitude is good... but bear in mind, things could and most likely will get rough before all is said and done. I want you to be aware of that right up front. There could be a lot of fallout from this, okay?"

"Okay."

"Do you have any questions?"

"Yes. I was about to ask if the School Board's insurance is going to cover them?"

"No, and I will give you two reasons. One, I think they know that he... screwed up with his letter campaign against you. And this last one went over the line. Two, I think the major power brokers in the network over there asked them not to cover him. Now before you ask, I will tell you. Because that would mean a larger sum of money and, most likely a jury would be more apt to award you a larger sum if you should win the case. And juries are more apt to find in favor of you if the insurance is picking up the tab. And believe you me, they do not want you to win this case. The money is secondary. They are less likely to award you a large sum if it is just the two that the money is coming from."

J.P. went into a total mood change almost at once.

"J.P. before you get too far down, and I can see it coming, your face gave you away. We can win this case. It is a good case, and you could get a good chunk of money out of this, but we have to face reality, like it or not, okay?"

He sat looking at his attorney. She had a very pretty face, and she was smiling. Her smile was warm, and directed a degree of confidence from it. It was not a fake smile that he got from his fellow colleagues all the time, nor from some low life politician seeking his support during an election year and would not give him the time of day in between. He got no bad vibes from her, nothing telling him to be aware, no warning signals. She did not have to say another word, he saw and felt.

On the way home that day he thought about what Holly had said about the Democratic Party. He had for the most part leaned toward the Democratic Party although he was basically an independent voter. Holly belonged to the Republican Party. J.P. did not reveal his political preference to her, but he also knew he did not have any real connections to the Party.

He was just a single vote when they needed it. In addition, J.P. as well as Dawn really did not like everything either party stood for, so they really based whomever they chose to support on the person, not on the party line.

J.P. once told me while we were engaged in a discussion on politics that to follow along with any party line was sacrificing the ability to think for yourself.

# Langley Connection

It had been a week since "The Man" had made the call to the "castle." It was 10:00 p.m. Friday night when the call came through on one of the three phone lines. Only two people had the number to his line that rang in his security office. When this phone rang a reel-to-reel tape would automatically click on in his security room. His den, which was located in his basement, had a large glass door wall leading outside to a large patio. The "man" spent a lot of his time in his den where he often would read or watch television or sit just outside in his lounge chair enjoying the late afternoon and evening. His den had a large dark maple desk located toward the middle of the room and on it was a phone, a lap top, a pencil holder, a legal tablet, a square walnut box the size of a cigar box with a small rectangular red light at the end of the box. The light would flash when he received a call, allowing him to know that the castle connection had been activated. He then would enter into his security room and call the number.

It was Sunday when he arrived back to his mountain retreat. As he made his way down to his den, he could see that the light was on. He went to his high tech "war room" and placed a call. It was 6:30 P.M. The phone rang twice and then connected.

"Hello."

"Age cannot whither her, nor custom stale." A short pause of silence was on the line.

"Her infinite variety."

"Anthony and Cleopatra."

"Act II. Sc.2."

"How you doing?"

"Good, just playing the game..." Then both laughed together.

"Ohhhh,...yeahhhh...how well I know."

"What do you have for me?"

"47 degrees latitude...114 degrees longitude...do you need a number?"

"Negative on that, we just don't operate like that."

"Understood, it just disappeared."

"I thought you would."

"You know, this guy has got one hell of a service record."

"I know."

"Seems to be a little bit of a mystery surrounding it, my kind of man."

"Mine too, and you don't know the half.... really our kind of person... need I remind you, paper trails do not always tell the real story..."

"Yes I know, do I ever know...ah, it is all what one wants to believe."

"You are very much correct on that one."

"Say I have some vacation time coming, and I was..."

"Say no more, the fishing is really good here. When can I expect you?"

"Let's say, ahhhhh, ohhhh, in 45 from lets seeeeee...ahh, hell today."

"Sounds real good. It has been at least two years since I have seen you. Oh, is the Pope traveling with you?"

"I suspect he will, might as well count on it. Stock up on the beer."

"That is a done deal."

"Oh, how long will you be on this "recon" mission?"

"Shall we say 7?"

"Seven sounds really great to me."

"Got a few new gadgets for you. I think you will really like them and they are really good for listening to..."

"Anything new for "commo?""

"Ohhh, yes. I would never leave you out on it. Haven't I always taken care of you?" Then more laughter.

"Affirmative on that."

"Look, as always…"

"Yes, I will, and you also." Then click, as he hung the phone up.

He exited the security room and entered the den and dialed a number.

A voice answered on the other end of the line, "Hello."

"Andy, meet me in the office around 09:00 hundred hours tomorrow."

"Okay, will be there."

By 1200 noon Monday Andrew was on his way to Montana. He touched down in Helena by late afternoon, picked up his rent-a-car, and was in Missoula by 2100 hours, which was some one hundred miles or so away. He checked into the pre registered Hampton Inn Hotel on North Reserve St. in the northern most part of Missoula.

The following morning Andy located the post office, and by 0900 hours Tuesday he was inquiring as to where he could locate J. Patrick O'Francis.

J.P. was off helping and getting more education on running a ranch. A local rancher had befriended him and J.P. was getting another lesson on ranching in Montana. His neighbor introduced himself because of the Masonic symbol on the back of J.P.'s truck window. J.P. went over to his very large ranch that bordered his but was four times the size of what J.P. had. He would often go by and work all day, learning an occupation that he knew very little about from his oldest son Bob Lewis III who was in his late twenties. J.P. learned that Bob Lewis II served in Vietnam and had a nice scar just below his left lower ribs made by a round from an AK-47. The Masons and Nam would bond the two and made communications between them easy. Bob raised cattle, and a lot of them. J.P. had no problem being the student, and learned quickly.

Just after 1800 hours, J.P. returned home and had not much more than stepped from his truck when Andrew arrived. O'Francis did not have a clue as he saw the car approaching his home. He re-opened the truck door and reached for his .357, which was in a holster on his seat and awaited on the approaching car to come to a stop. He laid it at the edge of the seat and stood with his back against the open door as he watched the car come to a stop about twenty yards away. Andy had only delivered "mail" to J.P. twice and that had been several years back when J.P. was a teacher. J.P. on the other hand did not recognize the man casually getting out of his car. J.P. noticed right away he had a large brown envelope in his right hand. Seeing that, he knew "The Man" had tracked him down. J.P. smiled. He thought, as Andy walked toward him, *it had to be extremely important or he would not be getting "mail".*

"Mr. O'Francis?"

"Yes, that would be me."

"Sir, I have a delivery for you. Sir, I have been instructed to tell you, and I quote, "This did not take place. You are safe.""

"Okay, I can live with that." Andy handed him the envelope, turned and began walking toward his car. J.P. stood watching what he figured to be an earlier to middle thirty-year-old man and just when he reached the car door which he had left open, O'Francis spoke.

"Say there... would you answer me a question?"

Andrew paused with his right hand on top of the edge of the driver's door. "Sure, if I can."

J.P. shoved the gun back in its holster, attached to his left hip, closed his truck door and walked toward him with the envelope in his left hand. "In all the years and of all the times someone has delivered one of these," and he held it up as if showing Andy, and continued to advance forward, "I have never asked anyone their name. Would you tell me your name?"

"Sure, Mr. O'Francis, my name is Andrew Jefferson Stone."

J.P. smiled as he reached the car. "Andy, have you had supper yet?"

"Well, no, matter of fact I have not. I just figured I would find a place in town to eat."

"If you have no objections, or I guess I should say if you can, would you like to join me for dinner?"

"I would like that, thank you."

"Good, let's go get a drink and I will tell my cook to put another plate on the table."

"Do you think it will be okay with her?"

"Well, the her is a him. And no he will not mind."

James Patrick just had to giggle. "No, nothing new in my life to have extra mouths at the dinner table. Do you drink? When Dawn was alive, she would fix dinner for any number of students on any given day. They never came to our home at feeding time and was not given a plate." J.P. giggled again, and with a warm smile, stopped, and turned to face Andy. "You know I think they always showed up at dinner just because Dawn was such a damn good cook."

"Does anyone call you A.J?"

"A few people, not many."

As they entered the house J.P. introduced Broderick Carlson to his guest, and informed him that he would be staying for dinner. The two men went to the great room.

B.C. as J.P. referred to him as, was an inspiring chief who worked at the Montana Club, breakfast through lunch, and on occasions prepared dinner. J.P. hired him to cook dinner for him five days a week, and was flexible with B.C's schedule. The extra job added to his income, of which the twenty-six year old needed. He was not the Iron chief yet, but he was good.

"Drink anything special A.J?"

"I usually like scotch, but..."

"No buts, you are in good company, unless you want a beer?"

"No-no, if you have scotch..."

"Oh, now that I do have, got some good Irish whiskey if you like?"

Later, after another fine meal prepared by Broderick, they spent a short time in some small talk, never once bringing up any business.

J.P. had retired to his great room shortly after Andy left. He sat in his rocking chair looking out the front window, as he opened the envelope. He removed the contents and began reading.

"*J.P.,*

*My apologies for intruding into your life, but I think you need to be enlightened as to some events that could affect you.*

*I do want you to know, I do respect your semi-isolation, and your new life, but if I felt that this was not of the greatest of importance I would have never located you. And by the way you did well.*

*Joseph has contacted me, and he has asked me to locate you. He stated that it was imperative that he talked to you. As of this letter I have not notified him that I have located you. I am sending you a copy of a newspaper clipping concerning someone in your past life.*

*This will be your call. I will do what you wish. My courier will be staying at the Hampton Inn, in Missoula. He will await your answer.*"

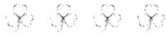

The phone rang in his living room.

"Hello."

"Sir, this is Andy."

"Did you have a good trip?"

"Sure did and no hitches."

"Did you locate him?"

"Yes sir. Sir, he asked me to stay for supper, hope you didn't mind. I spent about three hours with him." There was a short pause of silence.

"No problem, there, well, his hospitality does not surprise me."

"Really nice person. We had a very enjoyable evening. Sir, no business was discussed."

"That too does not surprise me Andy."

"Politics, weather, and farming, or I guess ranching out here."

"Okay, you did well. He will contact you, await his call and you will be bringing an envelope back with you. And Andrew, you go to his place, do not let him come to you, and he will insist, but tell him that you have your instructions, okay?"

"Yes sir, no problem here."

"I'll see you in a couple of days." Then he hung the phone up.

Andrew got up early and had breakfast and several cups of coffee awaiting his phone call.

Andy's phone rang at 10:00 A.M.

"A.J. Stone?"

"Yes, this is he."

"This is J.P. O'Francis. I have an envelope for you to take back with you. I will be at your room in about thirty minutes."

"Mr. O'Francis, Sir...I have been instructed to pick the envelope up from you at your place, Sir." A pause.

"Okay, if that is the way he wants to do it."

"Yes sir, it is. I can be there within the hour."

"Sure thing. I will have a cup of coffee for you. Oh, say have you had breakfast?"

"Yes sir, early."

"Well, you can have a good cup of coffee before you go. See you shortly."

Andrew delivered the envelope back to Paul's office by mid-day Friday. He sat with his feet propped up on the windowsill, leaning back in his chair looking out the window to the street below, something he liked to do, watching people, and his office was a very good place to do just that. He opened the envelope and pulled out the letter.

*"I am aware that you could find me with all your connections. I have no problem with you knowing my location, as I know I still remain lost (or I surely hope I am.) Thank you for the news clipping, very interesting and there was no remorse here! I did*

*not ask for the job to be done. As to Joseph...I would like for you to inform him that I wish to remain "lost". I really do not think he will have a problem with that. I will go as far as meeting him in Chicago if he needs to talk to me that bad. But I do not want anyone to know where I am! I will communicate through you and you only! No other way!*

*Thank you for keeping my privacy, private. I am enclosing my number. It of course is unlisted and unpublished, and you have just made my very short list. J.P."*

Janice Jones and her husband retired from teaching with a very good retirement as the last three years of one's working career is the basis for what you will get monthly on your retirement check. The school system had taken very good care of Janice, for she had been part of the "good ole boys" network. She had performed her duties well over the years, and she had been rewarded for her work. Her monthly pay check was standard for the years in the profession, but it was the extras that pushed her pay up from the top pay in the county from $40,000.00 per year, no matter how many years one taught, to a nice sum of $90,000.00 per year. Lots of people were aware of her "extra" pay for her "work" but none would do anything about it. She had damaged many, many students over her longevity in Reynolds County, but the job she had done on O'Francis was the one she was most proud of. A real masterpiece, one for the performing arts, an Oscar winner for sure. But her deeds and her performance would ultimately be put to the test and she would have to ask herself *was it worth the cost?*

# Jordan Black

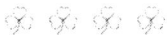

JORDAN BLACK OPENED HER EYES and blinked several times to get them focused as she viewed the mural ceiling. A collage of Native American scenes covered the entire ceiling over her queen size hand carved bed. The four large bed posts were of Native American busts with the foot and headboards displaying carvings of Native American warriors on horseback, a spectacular piece of art work.

She flipped the sheet and light blanket to her right and rolled herself to the left and onto the hardwood floor. It was 5:30 in the morning and the sun was just peeking its orange sphere up out of the gulf waters. Quintana Beach, just east of Freeport Texas, was where she made her home. A two-story house designed to her specifications. It was located at the end of Quintana drive, far enough away from the other residents to allow her a great deal of privacy. A two-car garage and a large storage area took up the first level of her home.

There was no front entrance to Jordan's house. A set of stairs from inside the garage allowed entrance into a small foyer off her kitchen. The only other doorway was to the back deck, which ran the full length of the upper level with one set of semi-circle stairs at one end leading to a small back yard. Several hundred yards of sand dunes, wild grasses, weeds, dotted with small bushes, led to the beach. She had purchased several acres surrounding her home, preventing anyone building close to her. The beach stretched several hundred feet to the blue waters of the Gulf of Mexico. The house set up high off the ground with reinforced concrete stilts for support to prevent flooding during the hurricane season, or tropical storms which did not happen often, but when it did her living quarters remained dry. The three bedroom expensively furnished home had never been lost to the ravages of Mother Nature.

She opened the heavy double glass doors and walked out onto her deck. Placing her hands on the railing and leaning her golden brown fully naked body forward tilting her head back concaving her back, she felt the disks pop down her back, stretching the caves of her legs as she closed her eyes and sucked in the fresh morning air.

Jordan was a single 40-year-old that looked like she was maybe 35, a very attractive Creek. She stood five feet five inches tall and weighed one hundred and twenty-five pounds with an hourglass figure with near perfect measurements, a firm body from the top of her head to the tip of her toes.

She was well educated, her bachelor's from the University of Texas in Sociology, her Master's from University of Michigan in Military History, and her Ph. D. from Georgetown in International Terrorism.

*"Today is a good day to go fishing,"* she told herself. Returning to her bedroom, she made the bed, slipped on a pair of tattered legged cut off blue jeans, picked out a large tee shirt, gathered it up at the bottom and tied a knot in it on her right side. She went down to the garage, slipped on her sand shoes, picked up her fishing gear, went to the storage area, got some fresh bait out of the refrigerator, opened the electric garage door, and walked her usual pathway to the beach.

While fishing, catching several and tossing them back, Jordan went through every detail in her mind of her last contract. Satisfying herself that she had made no mistakes completely assured her that there had been no errors, and after three hours of fishing she returned home. It was mid-morning and she was hungry. She got on her 21-speed bicycle, peddled out of her garage, turning and clicking the electronic door, closing it, which automatically set the alarm system. She traveled the two miles to the small gulf town of Quintana. At 830 Lamar Street she stopped at the Sand Bar and Grill. There she ordered her a BLT special and socialized with the regulars.

No one really knew a great deal about the attractive and sensuous female that regularly visited the Sand Bar. They knew she kept to herself, drove a silver BMW, rode her bike, fished off the beach as well as the pier, and made trips out of town for various periods of time. Jordan preferred it that way. From time to time she would stop by the Sand Bar and Grill at night for a few beers and a dance with a few locals with whom she was acquainted. Sometimes a male who was not acquainted with her would hit on her with flashes of a one-night stand cluttering his mind, and would inevitably ask some feckless questions about what she did for a living. Jordan's usual response was that she was retired. Of course the young stud with his testosterone in overload would press her for what she did before her retirement, hoping for a conversation that might lead to a bed. She would simply reply with a smile.

"I was in the exterminating business."

Jordan never made those mistakes. No one came by her house and she never dated nor had any one-night stands with anyone from the area. A few drinks at the bar, a dance, and that would be it. Her personal life was hers. Her professional life was another matter altogether.

Jordan Black was born into a Creek family in Broken Arrow Oklahoma, a proud Native American family dating back to Menewa or as he was known to the "Indian" world, Hothlepoya, *(Crazy War Hunter)* of the Lower Creek Nation.

Joseph and Martha Black had one daughter, *White Star.* But in the "white man's" world they had been forced for generations to live with "white man's" names. To Jordan's Native American friends and close acquaintances she was known as *White Star.*

Jordan's mother and father died in an automobile accident when she was twelve years old, caused by three drunken overly prejudiced "whites" in a pick-up truck.

It had been a pleasant Saturday night as Joseph and Martha traveled back from their friend's house. Jordan had been staying with her girlfriend that was having a slumber party.

Hanging their heads out the window yelling and driving wildly, the three drunken men played "chicken" with approaching vehicles, then swerved out of the way at the last possible moment, or caused the approaching vehicles to veer off the road to avoid a head on collision. The three men then would laugh and turn up another beer. The two-lane road gently rose and dipped through the rural Oklahoma countryside like the tide of the open ocean. The moon was full, and the night sky was clear. The driver reached to his left and turned off the lights. As he did so he drifted into the left lane. Approaching just to the opposite side of the rise in the road was Joseph and Martha Black. As their 1970 V.W. reached the top of the rise it was met by a 1980 Chevrolet pick-up. There had not been time for breaks to be applied, nor to swerve out of the way. The oncoming sixty mile per hour modified truck with its oversize tires and lift kit sheared the top of the small car off, killing the two passengers instantly.

Having no brothers or sisters Jordan had been raised by friends of the Black family. She was extremely intelligent and excelled in school. Her favorite sport was shooting, and riding horses. The school had a rifle team and Jordan was their best shot among both males and females. She continued her love of the sport in college and won many first place awards with the rifle as well as the pistol.

She bid her good nights to her acquaintances at the local pub where she had eaten dinner and had a few beers. It was ten o'clock when she mounted her bike and started her two and one half mile trek to her apartment. Jordan was in her last semester of completing her Master's, and by June she would be off to Georgetown. It was a typical April night in Ann Arbor, cool, but Jordan liked it and liked riding her bike where ever and whenever she could. As she approached North University Avenue and Observatory Street she slowed and observed no approaching vehicles. Making a left on Observation she made her way to Washington Heights and turned right. Her mind drifted to her planned studies at Georgetown University and her Ph.D. As she turned left onto North Hospital Drive she did not see the dark blue 1993 Jaguar turning onto the same street until the last moment. Jordan swerved her bike to the left but it was too late. She ricocheted off the left front fender, losing her balance. She tumbled to the pavement. Anthony stopped his car, jumped out and came to the aid of Jordan. She was sitting up as he approached her.

"Are you alright?"

She paused and looked up at the very handsome six foot one, black haired, brown skinned man.

"Yes, I think so." As he reached his right hand out toward her, she reached up and took it and he helped her to her feet.

"I am so sorry. I didn't see you. Did I damage your car?"

Anthony had not looked. It really did not matter to him, as it was a piece of metal with four wheels. Expensive yes, but money for Scarola was not a problem. Anthony looked at her bike, and saw its front wheel was warped.

"Looks as if your bike is damaged," he stated and Jordan looked over at it laying a few feet from her.

"Shit! Oh, sorry. I did not,"

Anthony cut her off. "No problem, I've used much worse. Look, ahhhh, may I take you somewhere?" Anthony asked.

Jordan paused before answering. "Ahhh,"

Scarola could see the concerned look on her face. It was late and she had no clue as to who he was. "Look Miss." He paused.

"Jordan," she responded.

"Jordan, I can put your bicycle in the trunk, and I will be more then glad to drop you where ever."

"Well, okay. It really isn't far, just to North Nichols."

Anthony picked up the bike, popped open the trunk, maneuvered the back wheel into the trunk, leaving the better part of the bike sticking out. Jordan was waiting by the passenger's door. Anthony walked to the door, opened it, and gestured with his left hand to get in. In a matter of minutes they arrived at her apartment. Anthony removed the bike from the trunk.

"Do you need any help?" he inquired.

"No thanks, I can get it. Look, Mr., ahhhh." Then she paused for a moment. "I don't know your name."

"Anthony Ryan Scarola. No Mr." Jordan stuck her hand out and Anthony shook it.

"Anthony if you would give me your address I will pay for the damage to your fender."

Scarola smiled, reached into his inside jacket pocket, pulled out a pocket planner, opened it, took a business card out, and handed it to Jordan. "Call me when you get a chance. And Jordan, don't worry about the fender." He turned, walked by the trunk and closed it, got in the "Jag" and drove off.

Two days later a 21-speed bicycle, a much more expensive one than Jordan had, along with a basket of flowers, was delivered to her apartment with a note.

*"Hope this will do. Sorry for the inconvenience. Give me a call."* It was signed Anthony Ryan Scarola.

Anthony Ryan Scarola was born in New York in 1958. He graduated from NYU, in business, attended Boston University for his master's as a financial analysis. His success was measured in his own wealth, not that of his family's.

Joseph Antonio Scarola, Anthony's father, was born in New York in 1933. He had been very successful in his business of distributing liquor to stores and hotels. Joseph Antonio was the son of Joseph Michael Scarola, who was born in Italy, and had immigrated to the United States in 1927, where he went to work on the docks as a dockworker. He would become a boss and a major player in running one of New York's largest docks.

Anthony Ryan Scarola's mother, Mary Catherine Ryan, was the daughter of Logan Kendrick Ryan. His Irish family had arrived in Boston in 1930. Mary Catherine's father went into the bar owing business and over many years became one of the largest bar owners in the Boston area. Mary Catherine became a nurse and left Boston for New York, where she met Joseph Antonio Scarola when he was brought into the hospital for treatment after an accident occurred on the dock where he was working.

# Paul O'Neill

PAUL PICKED THE PHONE UP and dialed a number. The phone rang three times before the pickup.

"Caprotti residence."

"Joseph, Paul here."

"Good morning Paul." After some pleasantries the conversation got to business.

"Good news I hope?"

"Well Joseph, yes and no." A pause occurred in their conversation.

"Okay, give me the good news."

"I did locate J.P."

"Okay, and….."

"And…, well Joseph…he wants to remain, let's say, lost." There was another long pause in the conversation.

"Did you talk to him?"

"Yes in a way. Yes."

"What exactly does that mean?"

"It means I have contacted him."

"Are you going to tell me where he is?"

"No, I can't do that."

"Look…" Joseph started to insist.

"No, Joseph. Listen to me. He will come to Chicago if you want him to. But…he does not want to be found. Now Joseph, I can understand that and so can you."

"Okay, okay, so you can contact him?"

"Yes, I can contact him."

"So...Okay...how about this. Let him know I really need for him to come to Chicago. You have my address. Let's say...." Joseph opened a daily planner. "Ahhhhh, let's see...how about next month, ahhhh, let's say Friday the 22nd."

"Okay, I can tell him that. If he so agrees and makes the trip, how about you meet him at the airport?" Paul asked.

"That will work. Tell him to plan on spending a couple of days or so with me. Tell him that Michael and I will be at the airport to pick him up."

"He will stay at your place?" Paul inquired, for information.

"Ahhhh, yeah, he can stay here. Do you think he will need any money for the flight?" Joseph asked.

"Do not know that. I can handle the cost for him."

"Okay, tell you what, I will reimburse you for any and all costs. Fair enough?"

"Fair enough. I'll get back to you to confirm the yay or nay and the flight number and time of arrival." Paul replied. Then the line clicked and a dial tone came on as Paul kept the phone to his ear for several more seconds, and then hung his phone up.

It was 2100 hours when J.P.'s phone rang. He let it ring and after the fourth ring the default answering voice informed the caller to leave a number and a short message and that a returned call would come as soon as possible. J.P. was sitting in his rocking chair to the left of a nice fire in his large rock fireplace, reading a book and enjoying a dram of Irish Whiskey.

He put the book on the floor, got up and went to the kitchen, and looked at the phone number. He did not recognize it, so he went to his "office" and clicked the answering machine. It was a very short message. "*Sit-Rap.*" J.P. knew the code, he needed to talk to him.

He pulled out an obscure list of numbers, ran his finger down the page, and found the number in which he had been instructed to call. Dialing the number, after the third ring came the words, "*OSS.*"

He responded with, "*Wild Bill.*"

Then came the response, "*General William J. Donovan.*"

"Hey, how are you doing? It's been a long time."

"Guess you received my," then J.P. stopped himself as he realized it was a rhetorical question, because "The Man" would not have called him if he had not received his letter. On the other end of the line J.P. heard a laugh.

"Yes, yes, it is good to hear your voice. I assume you are well, and enjoying your new life."

"As well as can be for me. I can assume you are calling concerning our mutual friend?"

"Yes, he wants you to come to Chicago on the 22nd of next month if at all possible." A pause for several seconds and Paul waited in silence.

"Well, I think I can make arrangements."

"Will you need help financially?" Another pause for several more seconds. Then Paul spoke, "Not to trouble yourself. It will be covered."

"By whom?" J.P. asked.

"By Joseph."

"How long of a stay?" J.P. inquired.

"I do not know. I would expect for two maybe three days. Listen, when you make the flight, do not make it direct."

Another pause occurred while J.P. thought. "Of course, I understand, do you have any suggestions?" Another pause in the conversation for a good ten seconds.

"Let me set it up for you, if you do not mind, that is?"

"No, no I do not mind at all."

"I will handle the finance of the entire flight. It will be settled up at a later date."

"Welllll, ahhhhh,"

"Look, don't worry. Our friend will reimburse me for all costs. Don't say a word. He can handle it with pocket change, and you know it! Forget pride on this one! Let me change the subject. I would like to come visit for a day or two if you do not mind? We need to do some talking face to face, okay?"

"Yes, I understand. On the visit by you, no problem, would love to see you. Yes... I think that is a grand idea. Glad I thought of it." J.P. stated. Then he laughed real big. Both began to laugh, one that reached down deep into both men, a rare moment of hearty laughter.

"Our friend told me you would be staying at his place, no hotel."

"Why?"

"Why what J.P.?"

"Why his home?"

"Can't answer that for sure, just have to speculate."

"Okay, let's hear it." Then a very quick, "No, no, no!" Came the quick response by J.P. "Let's not. This is a phone. Let it go, I can figure. Hell, I am not totally stupid. Hell, I have been there and done that."

"I know you have J.P. I do not think there is a problem, let's say, higher up?"

"Okay. I was wondering just that. Have you met him?"

"Yes, many years ago. He is a very nice man, but all business. Make no mistake about that. Very up front, pulls no punches. You should have no problems in that area. Just be you and you two should hit it off very well. You don't have to be on guard, tell it like it is, and trust me on this. He would prefer it that way, and does business that way. J.P., if you are not completely at ease with the offer, I will tell him you need to think about it and we can talk when I come out. Keep in mind, this is my area of expertise, and I can be of service to you if you want. Think of it as baseball, no clock, just innings. No time limit."

"I thank you, and I may very well do just that. I do respect your skills, and will ask for advice on the matter if that is what this is all about."

"I don't think the events that have taken place are the subject. It is the future events that are the subject. I think it is your call that will be the subject."

"Okay."

"I'll have your flight plans to you in a few days."

"Good deal, thanks."

"No problem, thank you." And then they hung up.

# Teacher's Association

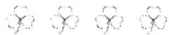

BOBBY SIMMS CAME TO J.P.'S room and asked to talk to him for a few minutes. J.P. stepped out in the hall, and in a short conversation, he learned that he was in need of his help for the next year's curriculum as he had learned that they were going to change what was to be taught on the sixth and seventh grade levels. That afternoon after school, he met Bobby in his office to discuss the matter. Simms informed him that they wanted to replace World Geography with World History in the sixth grade. J.P. objected to the idea, as he explained that the course was too deep for that age group, that they would not understand and that it could not be "watered" down enough for them to get it. He asked Bobby why the change, but he could not give him an answer.

"Well Mr. O'Francis what would you suggest?"

"Well sir, I really think that sixth graders should have the sequel to the U.S. History that they are having in the fifth grade and then give them World Geography in the seventh."

"Why World Geography, instead of World History?"

"Because Mr. Simms, World G. can be brought down to the seventh grade level, and it can be made more interesting to the student. They can use it in high school in several course areas."

"For instance?" Bobby inquired.

"Okay. It can be used in U.S. History, as the United States was involved in events in history throughout the world. They would be able to identify where these places are, Mr. Simms, as I have stated before, and, as you are aware of my statements, you cannot teach history without geography. They will of course be able to use it in World History or World Geography as it is their option to take as a freshman or sophomore."

"I like it, good sound reasons. I will do what I can to get this done. I will most likely need you to sit on a committee for adopting a textbook."

"Yes sir, I have done that and will do it again if you ask me to do so."

"Thank you Mr. O'Francis and I will let you know."

For J.P. he was having a difficult time figuring the kindness. Many years earlier, his suggestions were considered a joke and were laughed at. *Something was not fitting correctly, now what was it?* he thought, as he went on his way home for the day. *Could it be that he has seen the light? Is it because he is not influenced by Decal? Was it Decal all along? Was Bobby Simms controlled that much by Decal? Did Simms realize that he was wrong about me and now wanted to make amends? I cannot be fooled again by an act of good faith. He basically is a good natured person. I would like to trust him at this point of my career, but so much damage has been done. What about his connection to Damon? I know he and Marshy hate each other and I cannot blame Simms for his dislike of Marshy. That is a plus. However, is Simms beginning to think on his own and not listening to the ones that wish to destroy me and my career even further? I will not be fooled again. I will have to play this game out to the end, make no mistakes, and hope for the best.*

Damon arrived at Marshy's office at four o'clock. Already present were Duncan Brewer, and Barnard Theodoric, the School Board member from the Honsburg area whose usual occupation was that of a local drug pusher (pharmacist.) All three were anti-O'Francis people but they were big church going Christians. LaMar was a deacon in his church and Barnard was a "Sunday school teacher."

After a two hour session it was agreed by all that Damon Bales would retire at the end of the year. Leaving the system was payment for all the legal fees that would incur in the future. Bales had been adamant about O'Francis being fired from his teaching job, and the three "big political dogs" assured him that they were working on it and that he would be gotten rid of.

After Damon left, the three men continued their conversation concerning Damon and O'Francis. Barnard asked LaMar if in fact he could get O'Francis fired from his teaching position. LaMar assured him that it could be done. At that point he informed the other two that he was informed that Bobby Simms was going to take the early retirement plan offered, and his replacement was to be Scott Wolffe.

Duncan spoke at that point. "I can assure you Barnard, that he can get the job done. He has already been briefed on the matter and he is the man for the job. He won't take any of O'Francis' bull shit. He worked for us before and will set his goddamn ass up right! He will not leave any loose ends for him to squirm out on!"

Theodoric shook his head back and forth. "I don't know, do not forget about Jakes."

Marshy was quick in his response. "FUCK JAKES! THAT SONAVABITCH! By-god, Scott has been told, and he had damn sure better do his job. He says he had people who will help him. I'm getting damn tired of O'Francis. He's been a damn pain in the ass for too damn long! If Bales had not gotten so damn personally involved and let O'Francis get to him he could have!"

Duncan interjected, "With our help."

"Yeah, we damn sure would have had to help him, but shit, he and Richard blew it!"

Theodoric asked, "Did you ever find out how he was getting his info? I mean, it appears to me that he seems to know what we are going to do before we do it."

LaMar angrily got up from his chair. "Shit! I don't know. I have checked and rechecked, and it ain't any of our people, and I know that for a fact! Hell I even had professional people come in here and check for "bugs!" I had the phone lines checked just to make sure." LaMar's voice rose with the thought of O'Francis still in the system.

Theodoric rose and stretched. "LaMar, just what did he do to you..."

LaMar cut his question off. "By-god the sonavabitch supported that dump ass ole man, Henry Marwin for one thing! And for another he caused me a lot of problems over that damn baseball field up at Honsburg. Hell, I know he was the one who got the damn newspaper involved, by-god I have my sources. He seems to know just a little too damn much about the flow of money and some of the connections we have. And another thing, I never did like the bastard way back when I had a brief baseball season with him."

Barnard had a puzzled look on his face. "What do you mean by playing baseball with him?"

"Oh, hell I don't remember...ahhh back in...maybe the summer of '68 we played on a baseball summer team together. First time I met him. Then he left the area, wish the sonavabitch had stayed gone. I guess if it had not been for dumb ass, Don Morgan, hell, he would have...but at any rate, I just didn't like his cocky nature. Hell, I guess he was in some special type of army unit or some shit, or that is what I was told at one time. It didn't make a damn to me what he was in, he...well I just didn't like him! Asked to damn many questions, won't go along with the game plan, he won't come in line like everyone else. It appears that there is no one who can bring him in line! Is that enough reason for you?"

"Well, I remember him in high school." Theodoric began. "And I had to play basketball against him, and I damn sure didn't like him! Bubble gum blowing show off bastard. Shit, I don't know anyone who really liked him on our team. Matter of fact we talked about putting him out of the game if we ever got the chance."

"Well did you?" LaMar asked with a slight grin on his face.

"Ah, hell no, we would knee him, run him into the wall, and he still kept going!"

Duncan interrupted. "Look, all that shit is in the past, now is now, and we have a chance to get him out of the system. He creates too much trouble, not just with the students but also with parents, and with our operation. Which really is the most important item we should be concerned with. School shit can be handled. I still worry about why he has not gone public or even tried to blackmail us. I am telling you he knows about all of it. That should worry both of you. The fact he can get information about what we do and how it is done is an even greater concern for me. Another thing, now boys I am telling you, if he gets involved in that goddamn association shit, he will be a real pain in the ass. Up until now, it is my understanding, he has been out of all the internal workings and the political part of it.

I am telling you! If he gets intertwined into the political aspect of the political system outside of this county, we can't handle it. We can handle our own people, but beyond that, well…we have enough problems now with a few of the damn radical teachers spread throughout the county. It appears that none, as far as I can tell, knows a damn thing about our operation. Hell, they ain't but about a half dozen and we damn sure don't need O'Francis getting involved, especially if O'Francis starts talking about matters outside the teaching profession. Most of these people can be handled. They are scared to death any way. If he can't be brought in line, we will get rid of him, and that is the bottom line. Once that is done he will just leave, which is what we want. LaMar you will give him a good recommendation, to where ever, but away from around here! Here, LaMar, means far away. Not just a county or two over. That will be it. We can get on with business without any worries." A short pause, no one was talking.

"Shit LaMar," Duncan continued. "You know very well how to get it done, and you have people that will work with you. Decal made sure that he established his "rep", all we have to do is stir it a little and the rest will take care of itself. At least someone did get something on him that we could make damn sure will continue to cause him problems. He has no chance of getting a job anywhere close. You will have the board behind you and you know it. Bring him up on some type of bullshit charge and they will take care of the rest. All this talk about killing him is bullshit. Damn-it, you know damn good and well that will bring too much heat, especially on our friend on the court, not to mention our prosecuting attorney connection. I mean…damn boys, if it wasn't for good old Douglas…well of course I don't want to forget Trooper Penrod, but… shit… if Douglas had not been the Commonwealth, if he had not been where he was or if it had been some of our not so good friends, we would have been fucked!

Let's not forget what doing him in like that would do to them, too much heat, too much heat, just not good, just too goddamn many things that can go wrong with that type of action. Besides, watching him go down this way is much more enjoyable. Hell-far...there are enough parents out there that don't like him, use them! Shit, I know a few that will do me a few favors. Just let me know, I'll make sure they say the right things! There are too many other things at stake here. I mean we have some people depending on us to make money for them. Now I do not have to tell you these people are not the ones to be messed with. We have all enjoyed the...shall I say, the fruits of our little tree. I personally am one who is not going to kill the fruit tree. If and I mean if, things get too far out of hand with O'Francis, we can always let these people know and they will handle the matter."

The entire room was deathly silent. Duncan took a drink of coffee.

"That is if they have to get involved. We will not have anything to do with it. There will be no connection to the school system or any of its personnel what so ever. They can do these things better than we can."

Dan called and asked J.P. to meet him at St. Pete for a pre-caucus meeting for the upcoming VEA convention just to see how things worked and to start to get a feel of what the association was about. He would introduce him to some of the officers and some of the more active people in other counties that were to be present, including the people from Richmond.

J.P. arrived at 1745 hours [5:45 p.m.] and talked to several teachers he knew including a person he had not seen since his childhood. Emmanuel Reuben had been a boy who hung around with the "big boys" during his youth, a mosquito that buzzed around the older teens, very likeable, but for an older teen a mosquito. The first thing J.P. recalled when he recognized Emmanuel was one of their sandlot football games. J.P. was the quarterback and Emmanuel would attach himself to J.P. like a leech to his leg or back and hang on for dear life while J.P. scrambled to get his pass off. Each time a play ended, he would tell one of his teammates, "Keep that little shit off me!" However, to no avail, the "little shit" seemed to manage to get by the "big boys" and attach himself to J.P. in one form or another.

When J.P. and Emmanuel relived the good days of childhood innocence, they laughed a good healthy warm loving laugh, which led to another story. *"Oh yeah, do you remember..."* and then another story. After the meeting concluded, they stood outside as Reuben had a cigarette. Another funny story emerged as they had worked their way to the parking lot. It had been a very good re-union, something J.P. had not expected. As Emmanuel stood by J.P.'s car in the semi darkness of the lower parking lot smoking a cigarette, a car passed them leaving the parking lot.

Emmanuel pointed to the car. "Do you know that person?"

J.P. quickly looked at the car and did not recognize the auto now pulling out onto the street. He had a very clear view of the car as the streetlights gave off enough light, but he did not recall the car or who may have been driving it. "I do not believe I know the person, or I should say I do not recognize the car. Why?"

"Well...I really hate to spoil a good evening, but I feel you should know something."

J.P.'s smile left his face, as his defensive system went up like a flashing mediator piercing the night sky. His face turned stern and emotionless, as he looked at the onetime childhood acquaintance.

Emmanuel's older brother Lance was J.P.'s. age, maybe a couple of years older. J.P. could relate to growing up with older boys as he had experienced the same thing and was sure that his onetime "playmates", who were all older than he, felt at times that he too was a pain in the ass, tagging along, aggravating them, emulating everything they would do and say. Emmanuel was well aware that J.P. had grown up with his brother, and he felt that he was a friend to J.P. even though there was a six-year difference between them. Emmanuel looked at J.P. in the pale light of the parking lot and could tell that he no longer had his "happy face" on.

"Look, I guess there is only one way to say this, and that is to just tell it like it is." J.P. still had not responded. "Ahhhh, that person approached me while you and Dan were talking and told me that I would be wise not to have anything to do with you. That if I got involved with you in any manner that you would cause me a lot of problems, that you were nothing but trouble, and had been since you returned to Reynolds County. That you have big problems with all administrators that you worked for and that your reputation was very bad and that being associated with you would give me a bad name. Now, do you know Sabrina Wagner?"

J.P. turned his head quickly toward the road, as if to see the car that had been gone for several minutes and then turned back to look at Manuel. "Is that who that was?"

Emmanuel dropped his cigarette and crushed it out with his right foot. "Yes, that is who was in that car."

J.P. reached into his inside sports jacket and pulled out a cigar, slowly licked the cigar from one end to the other, then took out a cigar cutter, and clipped off the tip of it. Manuel stood and watched, saying nothing. J.P. lit his lighter holding it to the end of the cigar for a few seconds and then put it into his mouth. Drawing heavily on it until the end of the cigar glowed with fire and large puffs of smoke exhaled from his mouth, he continued to look at Emmanuel, saying not a word.

"Well...Emmanuel, I guess it will be your call on this one. I can say nothing as to what you should or should not do."

Manuel reached into his shirt pocket and pulled out a pack of cigarettes, took one out and lit it. As he replaced the pack in his pocket, he spoke in a stern voice. "I will pick and choose who I associate with and I will not choose my friends based on what someone else says about them." They stood looking at one another. "I mean what I say J.P."

"Okay, I have no problems with what you are saying. I do want to tell you that if Wagner has anything to do with this association as I can assume at this point she does, then..." he stopped.

"I will leave it at that Manuel. I appreciate you telling me, it was honorable of you. Thank you. I think we should call it a night."

He turned and walked to his car. Manuel got in his car and they departed.

J.P.'s thoughts were on many events that had occurred over the years and could not understand why people of Serbian's nature were allowed to disrupt the lives of other people who had really done nothing to them. He had not been around her in many years and had not known of her activities, but at that moment, figured that she had not been still. Her connections were, he figured, with the same circle that preyed on the weak and manipulated people into believing everything that they said as "gospel". Oh how the disciples of evil worked the "good book" and cloaked themselves in piety. J.P. had not known, up until that point, that she was working with the people that were out to do him in.

He knew that the little boy Emmanuel, that had been just as he had been in his days, a little boy, had become a man, and it would be up to him as to what he believed or did not believe. Time would tell, as he would get involved in the political scheme of things in the teaching profession. He would not throw caution to the wind because of a childhood acquaintance. He really did not know Emmanuel. He did not know what he had experienced along life's many roads that one had to travel. On the other hand, his feelings were to give this young man a chance. His inner alarms had not gone off, he heard no voices warning him of any danger. He would move with prudence with Manuel and let time and events take its course. He would judge him on his actions, not his words, then and only then could he place a value on his words.

# Open Wheeled Race Cars

It was May and J.P.'s attention turned from umpiring baseball to auto racing. He had been in love with the "Indy" car and the Grand Prix cars from the time he first heard their high pitched sound on the radio, thanks to his mother who listened to the Indy race every year that he could remember.

Before he met Dawn he went to a professional race driving school to earn the right to drive the open wheeled racecars. He knew from the very beginning that the odds of becoming a professional were even greater than that of a baseball player. But J.P. had a skill that allowed him to at least be tested. He had demonstrated that with great success. Then he met Dawn and it had changed his course of life forever. His passion for the open wheeled car and the beautiful sound of the high pitched whine they produced stirred his blood each and every year. His Sundays were devoted to watching any Grand Prix race he could find that ESPN or any other channel that might show the open wheeled racecars and especially the famous Indianapolis 500. He never missed watching a race in its entirety as he often wondered as he sat and watched a race, be it "Indy" or a GP race, what would have happened if he had not met Dawn? Would he have made it as a racecar driver? Could he have met the enormous challenge it took to be such a superb athlete? It took skill to drive a racecar at 200 plus miles an hour around a track, not bumping and touching your opponent, as did the famous Southern auto sport of NASCAR.

Most people could not imagine in their wildest dreams what it was like, J.P. had. In one brief moment in his life, he had experienced the thrill of driving a road course. Shifting gears at the flick of one's wrist, working one's feet from clutch to accelerator a multitude of times in a distance of a three-mile course, where the turning of the steering wheel could be measured in centimeters. The drivers would place their hands on the steering wheel at the "ten o'clock and the two o'clock" positions. They would be sitting in an open wheeled car inches from the ground, practically laying down, obtaining speeds that could not be explained in words. In many ways he was very envious of the drivers he would sit and watch as they skillfully drove the road courses of the world. The skill it took to make 500 miles on the most famous racetrack in the world at speeds that could not be felt by the millions that watched on television and the hundreds of thousands that descended on Indianapolis each year. The sheer terror that engulfed his entire body when one of the cars lost control quicker than the blinking of one's eye hitting a wall or guard rail or getting entangled with one another. In the world of the Grand Prix racers, there was no room for error. Only someone who had at least been in one and had experienced losing one, could ever understand. J.P. had been there and done that.

He would never forget the Sunday that it had rained all morning and the student drivers had been in a classroom listening to a lecture by one of the professional driving instructors. He was young, daring, and full of life. He had made it home from a war, and wanted more from whatever it was "out there". He wanted to experience it all, whatever fate had lain out in his path, and he wanted to reach out and grab hold of it and embrace it.

"Sir", he raised his hand. "What do Grand Prix drivers do when it rains? Do they do like the "Indy" racers, or do they just deal with it?" The instructor asked him his name and he proudly stated it to him.

"They drive in it, no matter what. The race goes on."

J.P. waited for a few minutes and then raised his hand again. "Sir, are we going to drive today, as it is raining?"

The instructor smiled. "Yes, we are and in about ten minutes we will see what kind of drivers you think you are." He stepped to another instructor and asked him to get J.P's file. In a few minutes he returned with it. As he opened it he addressed J.P. "I see here you have done very well to this point. I see that there is only one other person ahead of you in the class standings. I also see that you are second place because you were caught speed shifting as you came out of the last set of "S's" onto the back straight-away." He looked up at O'Francis.

He sat in his seat saying nothing for a few moments. "Yes sir, that is correct."

"You over-revved your engine in doing so. The red tachometer needle locked on how far your engine revved too. If that had been one of the hundred thousand dollar machines that you are in hopes of driving one day, you could have lost an engine, cost the owner a lot of money, and taken you out of a race worth lots of money and points toward a world title."

J.P. thought before he answered. "Yes, but sir, I am in hopes that by the time I am driving a car for someone that comes with that kind of price tag, that I will have gained enough experience that kind of mistake will not occur."

The instructor just smiled and finishing his lesson released the students to go to the track. The day did not go well for J.P., as they did begin their training in a drizzling rain. He was on his last lap of a timed ten lap series, pushing his car to what he thought was its limits when he came out of a double set of "S" turns onto a slopped back straight away of the MIS oval. Shifting to fifth gear, pressing his accelerator down hard, the back of his car gave to his left. He quickly flinched his steering wheel to his left, as he was instructed to do, and the rear would fishtail a little and straighten up on a dry road, but not on a wet one. It sent him spinning in circles at over one hundred miles an hour through the hay bales into the steel guardrail at the top of the oval backstretch.

The fiberglass surrounding the metal tube frame went into a thousand pieces, rupturing the water line running along the left side of the inside of the framing going from the small radiator to the engine, covering J.P. in hot water. Other than being embarrassed and a little red from the water, he was unhurt. A review of what he had done wrong and a good ass chewing from several instructors, he learned a lesson that he would long remember. He did not end up at the top of the class, but did maintain his second place position as he did have the skills it took to outdrive all the other drivers in his class, even the number one driver in the class as was proven in a head-to-head race between the top five drivers in class.

However, J.P.'s Master had other plans for him. His fate laid in another direction, and he had little to say about it. Nevertheless, his passion for the Grand Prix racecar remained strong as his blood and adrenaline raised each and every time he sat and watched the cars work their way through the turns and straightaways of the many worldwide courses, totally absorbed in each and every turn and pass of one of the beautiful whining machines.

His summer was devoted to working around his home, seeing his psychoanalyst on a weekly basis, and being called to Holly's office several times for the purpose of reviewing material for the court case. The one thing he really liked about her was the fact that she was all business. She never contacted him to come to her office for meaningless conversations. He would spend no less than an hour and usually longer on the average each and every time they met.

He would spend his spare time researching how the law worked in a civil suit. He wanted to understand how it all worked. He did not intend to make any mistakes. He viewed the case as a military war game. His life was at the very essence of this new battle, and he did not intend to lose. He took long walks in the hills surrounding his home, to be close to nature, to keep himself mentally fit. He kept his physical body fit by his daily workouts in the martial arts, honing his skills against his imaginary opponents and his enemies in reality.

David "Country" Higgenbottom, would call from time to time reviewing the charges of his military career seeking advice as to his next move,
whether it was good or not. His calls always seemed to lift J.P.'s spirits for
a short period of time, someone who had come into his life as a youth, and
had been a constant presence for many years. J.P. had become extremely
close to Dave, the street boy that Simms had kicked out of school, the
English teacher that had fucked over him as a senior because he was not
one of the higher social economic students. His social background had
been a weight around his neck, but J.P. had installed in him a will and a
desire that he could achieve anything in life no matter what the odds were.
He received his high school equivalence degree, and picked up his college courses whenever he could, at whatever military base he was at. He
received his military police degree, was named regimental soldier of the
month twice, had been awarded every peacetime ribbon that could have
been given to him. He became a model soldier for the United States Army.
But this call was a little different; he had to decide if he should re-enlist for
another four years.

If he did, the Army was sending him to Korea for 18 months. He had
served eight at the present and he was due another promotion, another
stripe, three up and two down. He had all the time in grade he needed and
the points that were required in the now modern day Army, a new type
of evaluation that measured soldiers in order for them to get promoted.
But "They" were holding his promotion over David's head to get him to
re-up. David told them that if they gave him his "rocker" he would enlist for
another four. But the Army recruiting officer wanted him to enlist and go
to Korea before they would give him his E-7 rank. "Country" had told the
recruiting officer that he knew he had the promotion coming, and that if
they were not going to give it to him he was out. He told the recruiting officer that if it came down to the last week before he was due to process out,
not to come to him and offer him his "rocker." That if they could not honor
it at that point in time then not to insult him his last five days of service to
his Nation for the past eight years.

Dave wanted to know if he was doing the right thing. J.P. advised him to follow his inner-most feelings, that if he stated he was going to do something, not to back off from it.

"Remember. Think before you speak."

Dave had grown into a man of honor, and believed that the words that he spoke meant something.

# Obsessed with Power

EMMANUEL HAD BEEN IN THE Reynolds County School System for fifteen years. He had little if any trouble with any principal or superintendent, and had worked for the same principal for the past twelve years. He had been a promoter of education on the upper elementary level as well as the middle school level by starting the first science fair in the county. He was a mover and a shaker in the science field. He had been a member of the teachers' association from day one. After a short time in the teacher profession, he was elected faculty representative for his school. He remained active within the association but not the fore-runner. He strongly supported the leaders of the teachers' association, without any criticizing for their methods of approach to the power brokers of the system in the futile effort to obtain a better salary and benefit agreement with the School Board. He always had the support of his principal, and had been a major supporter of his principal. If Emmanuel had been in a good school system, he would have been considered a brilliant science and math teacher. A good school system would have counted themselves fortunate to have such a teacher for their children.

Emmanuel had been appointed by the state board of education to sit on a committee for the development of a technological program, and was a major player in the development of the technological curriculum for the county. He did whatever it took to help the county to progress into the future in the field of education. He was well recognized for his efforts and his hard work. The teachers of his school as well as others that knew him placed his name in the running for the national teacher of the year award.

Emmanuel was not in the circle of social elite, the power brokers of the county. He was just a teacher, no money, no political power.

Emmanuel Lucius Reuben had not always been a teacher. He spent his earlier years in the Air Force as a medic. He volunteered for Vietnam service but had been turned down because of a blood problem. When he was a teen he had contracted hepatitis and no matter how many times he requested to be sent to Vietnam, his request was turned down.

His post military years were spent underground, the type of underground that produced black gold. Coal. Fate may have been good to Reuben, as he was laid off from the mines for a short period of time, and in that time he felt the need in going back to school. He liked science and math and felt like he would like to teach it.

His first job in the teaching field was at a juvenile prison. The years spent teaching young boys who had opted to live on the wrong side of the legal system was one that opened his eyes to how bad the nation's public schools really were. "Somebody", a "teacher", a "counselor" or the administration had failed many young men. Horror stories abounded from the young juveniles about their education from elementary through their high school or until they dropped out. If only half were true it was too many and they had been done a terrible injustice.

Reuben tried to reach as many as he could and did his best to make-up for the "somebodys" that did not do their job. However, Reuben's teaching path lay elsewhere and after several years of teaching failed juveniles, he entered Reynolds County School system.

It was another fall and school had not been in session for a long period. Signs of trouble loomed on the horizon for several of Emmanuel's students. One of his larger seventh grade students had been for several weeks bullying other students in the restroom and hallways.

His overt "hard core" attitude surfaced in Emmanuel Reuben's science class on more than one occasion. Rick Hays seemed to be the leader of the pack along with his two loyal buddies, David Kirk and Peter Edgar. Emmanuel was halfway through his science class and had explained and lectured on Acid Rain. Now it was time for some class participation.

"Now class, do we have any acid rain in these mountains? If we do, where does it come from and what does it do to our environment?"

Susan Brock quickly raised her hand, as Emmanuel walked to the corner of his desk and sat on it. "Yes Susan?"

"I think we do have acid rain in our area and I believe that the power plant causes it, and it is killing our trees."

"Correct."

The power plant Susan referred to was a large double stacked electric plant located on the Clinch River some twenty miles from where Elk Horn Middle school was located.

"But Susan, the plant is over twenty miles from here. How can it cause any damage to our environment that far away?"

Reuben rose from the desk and walked to the chalkboard to put a few more notes up.

Rick Hays spoke. "Susie you think you're so damn smart. Why don't you just keep your mouth shut and we would not have to take all these damn stupid notes!"

Even though his back was to his class as he wrote on the board, he heard the tongue-lashing Rick had given to Susan. He finished putting up his notes, put the chalk in the tray, turned and walked to the middle of the room, facing his twenty-one students.

"Okay, now let's see. Someone else answers the next question. How about you Rick. Give me some examples of what acid rain will do to the trees or anything else you may think of."

Rick laughed. His tone of voice was sarcastic. "I don't know, ask miss know it all! She wants to answer all the questions!"

"Rick, if I wanted Susan to answer I would have asked her. Now I am asking you."

Rick smiled and looked over to his two "hard core" buddies for support. "Welll, Mr. Reuben, I think that acid rain can be used to get high on!" Then the laughter from Peter and David. Rick leaned across the aisle to Peter and gave him a high five.

"Yeah, Mr. Reuben, you can bottle it and sell it on the street and make a lot of money." More laughter from the three "tough guys" in Reuben's class. No one else in the room was laughing.

Emmanuel watched as the three bullies of Elk Horn Middle made fools of themselves. Then the idea hit. *I know just what will save these three and maybe some others I don't know about*, he thought. The class bell rang and he excused them and the three left the room laughing and giggling. Reuben knew he had to do something as the three would only get worse and create problems not only in his class with the more academic enthusiastic students trying to get educated, but in the hallways, causing unneeded stress for them.

Emmanuel pecked on Harold Hobbit's office door. "Come in Manuel" he responded with a warm smile and happiness in his voice. Of course that was the way Hobbit was with all his teachers. However, he especially liked Emmanuel as they both liked pranks and jokes and got along extremely well.

"Harold I would like to take my seventh graders on a field trip."

Harold leaned back in his old worn chair, locking his hands behind his head. "Okay, where?"

"I want to take my science class to the Black Hawk juvenile facility."

Harold smiled. "Sure you would."

"No, I am serious. I really do. I believe it just may help a few of my "hard-core" boys. Well, they think they are hardcore. I would like for them to find out what hard core teens really are and what hard core attitudes will get them."

"Damn, you are serious, aren't you?"

"Yes."

Hobbit had not moved from his position the entire time Reuben was talking. He rocked backward and forward in his chair thinking, not saying anything, just looking at one of his favorite innovative teachers. Then he came forward in his chair and in one motion stood. He was somewhat taller than Emmanuel. He walked around his desk. Manuel still stood with his hands on the back of the two office chairs in the small overly crowed office.

"Okay, I'll handle our superintendent. You make all the arrangements at Black Hawk. You do know the superintendent at Black Hawk, don't you?"

"Yes, I know him very well. I do not think there will be any problem."

The outcome for the Emmanuel Lucius Reuben's futuristic idea worked and for the following four years, each fall a group of seventh graders made the trip, coming back with a totally different attitude.

His classes were filled with fun and good times while all the time learning science. Emmanuel, from the first day he had entered the public school system, had been a real teacher. He was not going to be one of the people that society called "teachers" that littered the public school systems throughout the nation, producing nothing but dry sponges without any desire for expanding their knowledge. He had seen too many byproducts of the state of Virginia's public school systems "teachers".

Lucius Reuben was a happy teacher and he enjoyed his success with his students over the years. Several returned after graduation to thank him for preparing them so well in the field of science. One of his more truly gifted science students Kelly Bantam went on to become part of the NASA team and from time to time dropped his Junior High teacher a note thanking him for guiding him into the field of science. Emmanuel used little of the Reynolds County's regular textbooks, as it was standard for most teachers to do so. Instead, he brought in his own material and only used the school text as secondary material, as it had very limited information that would inspire as well as challenge his students. He researched and kept up to date with the ever-changing world of science and taught his students beyond the standard text.

The inter-com came on in Emmanuel's room interrupting his class. "Mr. Reuben."

"Yes Sir."

"After your class is over could you come by my office, please?"

"Yes sir, Mr. Hobbit." Twenty minutes later, he was knocking on his principal's door. "Yes Sir.

You wanted to see me?"

"Yes Manuel. Come in and close the door." This was rare and Harold did not have his usual smile on his face, more of concern, of which Emmanuel detected instantly. He knew something was wrong. His mind raced to find in it something he had done wrong that would warrant a serious trip to his boss's office. However, he could not find anything in the seconds he had before he took a seat as Harold indicated with his open hand and spoke.

"Have a seat."

He took a deep breath, got up from his chair, walked to the corner of his desk, looked at his friend and employee, walked back to his chair, and sat down hard. "Look...I have just had a conversation with the superintendent. It seems that you have had a complaint filed against you by the principal at Liberty High."

"What? I..."

Hobbit held his hand up, stopping Reuben from talking. "It seems that a teacher, a science teacher, has filed the complaint with the principal. In turn he filed it with the superintendent, and shit rolls downhill, and here we are."

"I don't understand." He sat looking at his principal with a puzzled look on his face. "I have absolutely nothing to do with Liberty's science classes! I mean, come on Mr. Hobbit, and as for the science teachers, I know very few teachers out there anyway. Who filed the complaint?"

"A Mrs. Anne Albert."

"Yes I know her, and her husband. What did I.... no, no. Let me rephrase that. What was I supposed to have done?"

"Well it appears that you have been teaching too much science."

That statement sent a message to Emmanuel's brain that did not compute. It came close to causing a short circuit.

"What?"

"Yes my good friend, you heard me correctly. You have been doing your job too damn well. Your students are so well prepared, that according to Mrs. Albert she just does not have anything left to teach them. You are teaching them beyond what you should, and she is very upset. According to Mrs. Albert, this has been going on for several years and she wants to put a stop to it."

"You are joking me, right?"

"No. Really, I have been on the phone with Mr. Marshy concerning this. I mean this is a real complaint. No prank, no joke this time."

Emmanuel sat looking at Harold Hobbit, and semi-anger came over him after he realized that this was not a Hobbit joke on him. He recalled the years spent trying to teach the juveniles what was not taught by some so called teacher!

"Look, Mr. Hobbit. Maybe Mrs. Albert needs to update her science class, and teach beyond the junior high level. She needs to take them to the next level if they are already at the freshman level!"

Harold finally broke a smile. "Look Manuel. Now don't go and get your ass all bent out of shape."

"Well, I mean this is just plain stupid!" Manual stated in disgust.

"Yes I agree. However, I have a job to do and I have done my job. I have brought it to your attention. I have discussed it with you."

"Okay, so now what do I do?" Reuben asked.

"You will go back to the classroom and you will continue to teach in the same manner in which you have been for the past...past, ever how many years it has been."

"So what about the complaint and what about Mrs. Albert?"

"Don't worry about Mrs. Albert. She will just have to become a real teacher. As to the complaint, I have handled it."

"I am very sorry Mr. Hobbit, that my students have made her look, I suppose stupid, or that they know more... no I won't go there, but at any rate I am sorry this has happened."

"Hell-O Manuel you owe neither me nor anyone else any apology for doing your job." Then he laughed. "Jesus man, this is a first for me. I mean I have had some real complaints on teachers, but this one."

He shook his head back and forth, and then stood. "You are a damn good teacher, don't you forget it! You are doing a great job and don't ever stop! Hell Manuel, take this complaint as a compliment. It probably won't ever happen again. Let the Science teachers at Liberty get their shit together and start doing some real teaching!"

Harold Hobbit had been the principal at the Elk Horn elementary school for fourteen years. He was the type of principal that everyone would like to have. He did not draw lines in the sand between the teacher and the administration, or the teachers' association. His line of communication between his teachers and himself was always open and often sought and took suggestions from his staff. It had been a marriage made in heaven, but all that was about to come to an abrupt end.

Hobbit was one of the very few principals, if there was another that was not intimidated by Marshy, who would not be controlled like a marionette. He was a fun loving type of person with a great sense of humor. He knew how a school should be run, getting the max out of his teachers and yet making them feel like they were important, which to him they were. He had a real grip on what education was all about, how to reach the students, how to treat and communicate with his teachers as well as his support staff.

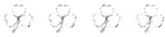

After three years under the Fuhrer he read the graffiti on the wall. Hobbit saw through Marshy and wanted no part of his evilness and would not submit to his demands for the destruction of "certain" teachers "HE" felt needed to be brought in line. Hobbit escaped the onslaught of Marshy's dictatorial reign of, "It was his way or the highway" philosophy that he would tell his administrators. Hobbit took the better road and took a job in Tennessee. He would not do the Fuhrer's evil work for him and had enough intelligence about him to see what was coming. The school system in Tennessee had gained a superb principal. Reynolds County school system had lost a man of honor. However, honor and integrity was not what Marshy was looking for and he found his replacement in a very short time. This move was a major blow to all the teachers who had been under Hobbit's immediate supervision.

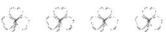

Norberta Millicent heard of the possible opening and applied for the job. She was a tall, blue eyed, very short haired blond, cold blooded, ruthless, a made to order Marshy recruit with a German ethnic background. She had been working as a title one teacher in an adjoining county when she heard about the opening. Marshy had personally asked her to come to his office for an interview. It did not take long for him to see that she was what he was looking for.

In the course of an hour of an official interview, he suggested that because it was late in the afternoon that they continue over a more pleasant environment. He asked her if she would like to join him for dinner. This was a test for Norberta. She passed the test as she accepted with glee and the two were off to one of the more elegant restaurants in Jamison City, far from the "Seeing Eyes" of the local people. A pre-dinner drink, a very nice dinner, a few after dinner drinks all on the Reynolds County tab.

Norberta was Marshy's type to the tee: immoral, corrupt, with a callously cold killer instinct, that would do for him without question. The conversation turned from school business to one of a more exotic nature, as the night took on a special glow for the two with the conversation heating, leading more and more to the sultry permissive tone. Their night out for business took a three-hour delay as they entered into a local Holiday Inn, for a round of sex, which was another way of Marshy testing the new recruit. She passed with an "A". Something he expected from the females he had working for him. Most seemed to forgo any and all of their moral beliefs whenever he requested their services. A type of power he seemed to have over the females he chose to "bed".

Norberta had no problem with the events of the evening and all its immoralities as she herself had no morals to speak of to start with. This made for a very good relationship between the two. As LaMar would tell

<br/>

her, "You are just what the doctor ordered." She would for the next couple of years pay her "dues" with joy, looking forward to a call to join him, on a sporadic basis, to keep any "off the wall" talk taking place, whenever his sexual hormones got active for "His" long legged blond, who was not all that bad looking. All for the lucrative principal's job, she obtained. She would become very good at what she did, both in the school system as well as her extracurricular activities. In turn, she was paid well for her work, along with the fringe benefits for years to come.

It was the start of the 1989 school year and Emmanuel had a new boss. In the very first faculty meeting, he knew in the back of his mind that the dark treacherous storm clouds were moving toward the mountains and fast.

Emmanuel had not been prepared for the blitz that was about to be launched on him by Millicent. She had been given her orders by her Fuhrer.

*"Emmanuel either comes in line or he goes. I do not care what you have to do to get him. If he does not come in line, just get the job done. I will take care of any repercussions that may occur. You just make sure you nail his ass!"* Marshy did not like anyone getting all the limelight, any glory for anything. It was he and he alone. He was the man in the picture, the headlines, the spotlight. It was his name, his picture that was to be first in everything. The people would come in line with what he, and he alone, wanted or else.

Emmanuel had been led to believe that LaMar really liked him. It was true; he could make people believe he really liked them. He was good at what he did, cunning, slick, mendacious, a politician. However, pure evil was good at controlling the weak minded, corruptible masses. That is what powerful evil people did. Very few ever saw him for what he really was. If a person did, they were destroyed, making it look as if it was the "victim" themselves and not that of Marshy's dictatorial rule that brought any hardship onto them. Leaving the sightless masses believing every syllable uttered from his bale mouth. Marshy hated strong willed people, especially if they had morals and had any type of honor about them. They became a threat to him and he had to work at bringing them down or controlling them. His loyal legions would, for the most part, take care of all the small details, and for doing so he would take care of them financially.

Emmanuel's paperwork for the National Teacher of the Year nomination had by the second grading period of Norberta's reign, reached Marshy's desk.

"You have got to be joking! There is no god damn way I will approve that bastard for any National nomination." He picked up the phone and called Norberta. "Did you get any paperwork on Emmanuel Reuben for teacher of the year nomination?"

"Yes sir, I did."

"Throw the shit in the trash! That just ain't going to happen! Do I make myself clear?"

"Yes sir, anything else?"

"Not over the phone. Meet me here in the office at 4:30 today." He hung the phone up.

It was late on a Friday afternoon before the students were scheduled to leave when Emmanuel was called to Norberta's office.

"Mr. Reuben you have been using the phone entirely too much for your personal calls."

"Excuse me a moment Ms.," But he did not get a chance to finish.

"You sit there and keep your mouth shut until I am finished! Then, if I want to hear what you have to say, you can speak."

Emmanuel was in a bit of a shock at the tone in which he was being addressed. His temper took over in a few moments, but even with his blood pressure rising quickly to its max, he sat in the office chair and took

Norberta's verbal lashing. Of course, he knew he had not abused nor violated any of the policies that the new principal was charging him with.

When Norberta Millicent finished, she excused Emmanuel with an abrupt, "You can go now!"

"Ms. Millicent if I may."

He was quickly cut off. "NO! You may not! What you can do is leave as I have instructed you to do!"

He stood momentarily looking at his boss in anger and shock. Slowly he turned and walked out of the office, went home for the weekend as a stressed out not so happy camper, and not fully knowing or for that matter understanding what was taking place at the school he had worked in harmony for so many years. The beginning move in the all-important human chess game played in the Reynolds School System by the Nights, Rooks, Bishops, Queens, and the all-powerful King, but not the pawns. They were to be the sacrificial humans to the powerful demi-gods of the mighty political machine.

# John F. O'Donovan

JOHN FREDERICK O'DONOVAN HAD BEEN following James Patrick O'Francis and his saga for several years, and had done extensive research into any and all of his stories and events and had found him to be of the utmost integrity. He had over the years, asked O'Francis to come to his place on many occasions for information concerning one event or another that had occurred in the county. He left an "open door" policy for him to drop in whenever he felt the need to get away from the rest of the "world."

He lived in a semi-remote area some distance from Reynolds County where he bought up all the land surrounding him in order to keep most of the people of the world away. For many years, John was a freelance writer, and traveled a good part of the world in covering many different stories. He had been very successful and semi-retired to the mountains of the extreme easternmost part of Tennessee on the western border of North Carolina. He really had not intended to do any major writing and was enjoying his time away from the triumphs and tragedies of people and their daily lives. For whatever reason he was attracted to O'Francis and his life. He began writing again but this time not just the short stories for a major magazine or newspaper. He decided to write a book. A book on a world that he had little knowledge about, and felt that the majority of the people in the United States knew little about.

He was researching and learning about the real world of education, locked behind the brick walls of the many thousands of schools throughout the nation, concentrating especially on the ones in Reynolds County. What he found was not what he had expected, nor was it what most people of most cities, towns, and communities would have expected. He had noticed that the most real information one may get about the public educational system was an occasional headline story on one of the national news networks, covering some tragedy or some teacher who had carried their affair with a student to a level of nation attention.

John became burnt out with the traveling, asking questions, seeing the horror and depression of a multitude of different races, ethnic groups, genders of people. However, for whatever reason, O'Francis' life was different. He was inspired by the life O'Francis led, and once again he began to write with great enthusiasm.

J.P. arrived at my home at 10:00 A.M., in his language 1000 hours. He just needed a place to get away for a while. We had a few cups of coffee and some small talk and then he went into one of his silent modes for a good thirty minutes as he looked out from the back deck into the woods that surrounded my home.

"You know John what I was just thinking about, for whatever reason?"

I got up from my chair, walked to his side, and leaned over on the rail with him. "No, what?"

He had a little giggle, then he rose up, stretched his back and upper shoulders, took a drink of his coffee, and asked for a refill. He returned and continued his story.

"Do you remember me telling you about the incident with Damon Bales and Richard Finkel over the son of bitch thing?"

"Yes I do."

"Well, I had something like that happen to me a long time ago. Would you like to hear about it? It has been on my mind and I wanted to tell you. Oh, guess you had better get your recorder."

So I went in the house and retrieved it from my desk, checked the batteries, removed the tape where I had taped him several months earlier, and replaced it with a blank one and quickly returned.

"Okay, I am ready."

J.P. giggled again, and with a big smile on his face began. "The Bales ordeal reminds me of an incident that occurred when I was getting ready to ship out for Nam. We, as in the troops, were working on a dock loading and moving shit, something to keep us busy. That was the Army's way you know. We were in San Francisco, and I was acting stupid, as were others. Garb-assing around. Shit, just having fun, like young boys will. I should say, young men, you know, just really killing time. Shit, I was only twenty years old. It was the first time I had not been in some type of training since I had been in the service. Hell I knew where we were going, did not know what the hell was facing me, but at any rate, we were fucking around, and this hard-ass sergeant, who had joined us at port was in charge of the "laborers". Did not know him, had not seen him before, but he was placed in charge of us.

"Well, he started barking orders at us being all serious. Several of us, as well as myself, took him and his orders lightly, and started laughing. We got the giggles, and it did not make any difference what one of us did or said, or for that matter what he said, we laughed. Wellll, he got pissed and decided to exercise his authority, and broke bad. Hell, we really were not laughing at him. Really, we were laughing at ourselves, and the entire situation. Well at any rate, he picked on good ole me out of the six or eight that were having some fun, and got in my face like we were in boot camp and we were a new group of raw recruits, like most DI's do. Something I noticed about people in uniforms was, one, if they have wings, two, if they have a Ranger tab, of which he had none. Welllll, in his zealous effort to show his authority with his E-6 rank, he called me a son of a bitch. Now at that time, being very young and being on the somewhat arrogant side with a Ranger tab on my shoulder and a set of silver wings on my chest got straight real quick. So, I was nose to nose with him and said. Now let me just interject here for a moment. My mother was more than just close. She raised me alone for the most part. She was my rock, my ear for listening, my advisor. She had a very difficult life, and worked very hard and many hours as a nurse. And she was really a good nurse. Over the years after returning to this part of the world, I have had a multitude of people tell me what a good nurse she was. We struggled financially, and she worked two jobs. Hospital and private nursing just to make ends meet. I mean I can go on and on about the heroics of my mother. The point here is, she was not a bitch. And being young, I took the comment very personal. So as I was telling you...

"'Look "Sarg", you can yell at me. You can get in my face. I can deal with that. But, DO NOT call my mother a bitch! You got that!' Now there ain't nobody laughing at that time. Point of fact is, one of the "laughing boys" stated, 'oh shit, it is on now...' Now the middle-aged gung-ho sergeant took offense to my tone of voice, given the fact that I was only a corporal and stepped close enough to be literately nose-to-nose.

"'Look you so called bad ass youngster,' looking at my left shoulder. 'Those tabs don't mean shit to me! Hell, anybody can get one of them...you sons a bitches ain't half what you are made out to be! I'll clean this fuck'en dock with all of you!' Soooo, my reaction was quick and swift, no thought was put into what I did, and I took him out with one punch, left fist under the middle of his right jaw. He hit the dock, his eyes rolled back till the whites were showing and I walked off and went up on the deck of the ship. Now keep in mind I knew after I had calmed down, which was in a matter of minutes, that I had fuckkkkk-up.

"Well, what I did not know was that another sergeant, one Gregory African, a Caucasian by the way, odd name I know, but never the less, he was an E-5 and had been close enough to see and hear the entire event. Oh yeah, by the way, he did have a set of wings on his chest. Later we became close, but that too is another story. Anyway, I had to report to the First Sergeant, and let me tell you, you really did not want to have to go to him in trouble. Hell I did not want to go to him when I was not in trouble. God, he scared the hell out of me. Shit, he was about six-six, and weighed ahhh, shit, I guess two forty or better, solid as a brick wall.

"A voice that sounded like Gods or what one would perceive as being God's voice. You know, deep, powerful, commanding, the kind that you damn sure listened to when he spoke. The kind that when you were being "dressed down" you had goose bumps all over your body and the temperature would be in the nineties. The hair on the back of your neck stood up like a dog's when he was about to meet a foe. Now, I did not know that Sergeant African had already given him a full report of the incident. Sergeant Powell, the man I decked, of course had filed charges against me. Now the First Sergeant chewed my ass out so bad that I had none when I left the office he had brought me into. Hell I do not know if it was one of the Navy personnel's offices, do not know what they call their offices, do not know anything about Navy language. But, he had to do something with me. I mean a corporal just could not deck an E-6 and get away with it. So, he assigned me to pull KP for the entire trip, which was thirty days by the way on the open sea.

"Just before we arrived in country, point of fact is it was the day before, First Sergeant called me back into the office, probably the Captain of the ship's office, hell I don't know. But he told me why he had to do what he did. Then he smiled and told me that he would have done the same thing. That he was not pressing charges against me, an article 15, which would have cost me time and grade and most likely some jail time in Nam. Damn, just think, go to Vietnam and go to jail, God what a thought. He did commend me for the job I had done on KP, which I did do a good job, hell I just had fun at doing what I had to do. I mean John, where was I going? I was out at sea, and it was really lots of fun seeing everyone get sick, puking in their food, and of course everywhere else too. Shit, we went through some damn big ass storm, the ship's front, ahhh, what the hell they call it, I do not know, anyway, it would go up, I mean, like forty-five degrees up, and then, smack. It would hit the water like it had just bottomed out, jarred the hell out you. Then just as soon as it hit, up again. Lord what a ride, and puking troops all over the ship. Now before you ask, no I did not get sick, not once, not even during the wild ride through the storm. I have no idea why, I just told myself that I was not going to get sick and I did not.

"However, for whatever reason that has been on my mind and just wanted to tell you that little story. Guess that is why I made right much of a joke out of the SOB thing with Bales. I mean we are not young now and we have over the years, done and said the same thing, to all kinds of people, in jest and being serious."

"Well J.P., do you regret telling Finkel that Damon was a son of a bitch?"

"No, not really. I mean I would like to think that his mother was not responsible for the way he turned out, but I guess it was just a means of insulting him. Which I truly intended to do, and he deserved it. So no, I do not regret one little bit of what took place in the sequence of events back then! However..." He stopped talking then walked a few steps toward the far end of the deck and then back. "I think in hind sight and all that I have uncovered, I do regret trying to get that damn trophy, which did lead to the confrontation with Finkel, which led to Bales."

We talked about several other teachers in the system and how Marshy was treating them and J.P. enlightened me on some of the facts that I did not have. Then he just up and left leaving me with a pile of unanswered questions, which was not all that unusual for J.P. He figured that I was the journalist, that it was my story, and that I was the one to find the truth, if that was what I was seeking.

# Another Principal

J.P. MADE TRIP AFTER TRIP to his psychotherapies for over a year but was not really doing any better. His court case was going slow. It seemed that Holly was having a difficult time getting material back from Damon's attorney in the allotted time. He seemed to be able to get an extension on some of the most trivial matters, which to J.P. was legal bill shit, as J.P. was beginning to really learn about the legal profession first hand. This made his mental condition worse as he was beginning to get a bad feeling about doing things by legal means. So another doctor was called in, a psychologist by the name of Celia Flora to help J.P. with his stress.

A new principal had arrived at Honsburg Middle and was making inquiries concerning O'Francis. Mr. Scott Jackson Wolffe. O'Francis did have some information concerning him, but felt that he needed to know more. He made his call and requested more info on S. J. Wolffe. "The Man" did inform O'Francis about Wolffe, things J.P. was not aware of and would have had no way or means of knowing.

Mrs. Mazo was in her room working with her science class when Scott Wolffe called her out into the hallway to talk to her.

"Bernadette you and I have been friends since high school and I would like for you to give me some information on Mr. O'Francis."

Bernadette had a cold chill run over her body at his request. She liked J.P. and they had been working together very well. They had shared ideas that both had incorporated into their own classroom. O'Francis and Mazo expounded on several topics that most people avoided. Religion and science, politics and the school system. The community and the self-righteous attitude that many people held, the manner in which the so-called social elite looked upon certain people in and around the community. They found a common bond and adjusted to each other, agreeing on some matters and disagreeing on others and remained good acquaintances and professional colleagues.

J.P. found that she was a very open-minded person and listened to his point of view on various matters they seemed to find themselves conversing about. She was very intelligent and not easily fooled by other people and did not take what she heard as fact. J.P. turned to her often for advice on how to teach on the middle school level, and took her suggestions as they seemed to work. He had never been trained to teach on the level he had been demoted to and often found himself struggling to reach the ten through thirteen-year-old students.

The earlier beginnings of doubt about her had faded to the foggy pits of his memory and he chose to leave them there. His earlier suspicions that she had gone to Simms about their conversation, proved unjust. All indications had pointed elsewhere. His little voice told him she was an ally and not an enemy or "spy" for the bastardized administrators that seemed to come and go like some revolving door operation. The how as to how Simms found out about their conversation was a file left open. However, one thing he became convinced of was that Bernadette was not the one who took the conversation to Simms. He found that she had a great deal of integrity, a lot of spirit and grit, something J.P. had grown to admire in her.

The two had reached the point of real personal Q and A's.

O'Francis was working overtime so to speak. It was 1600 hours and he was grading papers and getting some maps reorganized and in the order in which he wanted his students to work on. He was standing at the back of the room when Bernadette Mazo walked into the room. Learning from word of mouth and from her personal experience early in their professional relationship that you did not walk up behind him and announce yourself, and you never touched him from behind, she spoke softly as she stood just inside the door. "J.P., do you have a few minutes?"

As he turned he answered, "Sure, what can I do for you?"

"J.P., I would like to ask you something and I do not want you to get mad at me."

"Well, I do not know quite how to answer that, but as far as asking me a question, which by your opining is a rather, shall I say, a heavy question."

"Well it is and I really want to go to the person in which the rumor mill is still turning its wheels about. I feel as if you and I have reached a professional relationship in which we can talk about personal topics without offending one another."

At that point in the conversation, J.P. did not respond, as he felt that there was really some question or questions on her mind that was really bothering her and she needed to get a direct answer from him.

"Okay, with all this?" Bernadette continued, looking J.P. directly in his eyes.

J.P. answered with a puzzled look on his face, "Sure, why not. I mean, look, if there is something on your mind, hell Bernadette, just ask. If I think it is too personal I will tell you, and if it is something in which I can answer, I will. However, there is one thing you can be damn sure of. You will get a straight answer. In addition, Bernadette, you just may not like what you hear. Now, is that fair enough for you?"

"Fair enough. Okay, did you ever have any relationships with any of your girl basketball players?"

J.P. really was not expecting that question, and it took him aback a moment. "Well, well, that is a bit of a surprise. Wow, rumor mill, the same old shit is still gushing through the sewer line of the hall ways of the school system. Okay, let's clear a few things up first. You used the word relationship. Let me clarify that first. The answer to that is yes. But, purely fatherly, as an advisor, a counselor, and a coach. There was never, and I repeat, with an infected resounding no passionate lover type relationship ever between any of "my girls." Now, Bernadette that is a fact, and what others in this lovely community and school system would like to think, well I cannot control that. The girls are now of the age that any one of them will tell you to your face if asked, the truth. I dare say none will deviate from what I have attested to. I had and have the utmost respect for all of them. My god, they were teenagers for christ sake!"

There was a bit of sternness as well as resentfulness in J.P.'s voice, which created a bit of uneasiness in the room at the moment. Silence filled the classroom, and Bernadette just looked at J.P.

"You know Bernadette, what this good loving caring Christian community does not understand is that I have some ethics. Unlike others in which I have had to work with and around, you see these people who continue to spread the filth about me, are the very ones that have no ethics what so ever. It is called character assassination, Bernadette. There is not one damn thing a person can do about it. If you try to publicly defend yourself, you simply make matters worse. People are either going to believe what they are told via many sources, meaning from one person to another to another and so on, adding to whatever they may have heard or thought they have heard, and the slander continues to grow like a cancer until it kills the character of the person it was intended to kill." They stood facing one another, not a word was spoken for a good two minutes.

Bernadette then broke a slight smile on her face. "I did not think so. Thank you J.P." She turned and bounced her petite body out of the room.

I found that when J.P. talked to me concerning his daily teaching of the students and his problems of reaching the students at the age he was now forced to teach, he enlightened me to the fact that all "teachers" cannot just walk into a class and teach a subject. Nor can they teach any age group because they have the title of a "teacher." Nor for that matter, a degree in whatever field they choose to enter the teacher profession. A master's or even beyond does not make you a good teacher. After such a long time talking to J.P., I reflected back on my college days and remembered that all professors were not all that good of a teacher. A PhD did not make you a good teacher and now I realized that it did not make good high school teachers or any other level of educator. I, like most of the mass public really do not understand the innermost workings of any school system and that degrees in education do tend to intimidate or impress most all people on the street. At any rate, let me continue with my story...

Wolffe asked, "Do you find him hard to get along with?"

"No Scott, I don't. Why. Who said he was?"

"Well Bernadette, I was told he gave Simms a hard time. That none of you got along with him. That he had an attitude toward you."

"Well I don't know who you have been talking to. All that you have said is not true."

Scott made the mistake of asking Bernadette, "Are you sure?"

At that she became irritated with Wolffe's insinuation. "Look Mr. Wolffe. I don't know what you want me to say, but I am not going to tell you what you want to hear. You asked me and I told you. Now if you want to get someone else to tell you what you would like to hear, then I would really suggest that you go get your information from someone else." She then turned and went back to her class.

That same day, Scott Wolffe met J.P. O'Francis coming down the stairs headed toward his classroom. "Hello Mr. O'Francis. How are things going so far this year?"

J.P. continued to walk down the stairs to the first landing then paused. He could detect a devious tone in his voice. The two men stood at the top of the last flight of stairs leading to the first floor hallway and to J.P.'s classroom, which was directly across from the stairs.

"Mr. Wolffe, I have never worked for you and I think you and I should get off on the right foot. So let me say, you just come clean with me, and I will answer any questions you might have. It most likely will save you a lot of work trying to get the information from other people who really do not know me at all."

J.P.'s candidness caught Wolffe off guard, and he exposed himself for a brief moment with a quick curt response, "Well, I know you don't like administrators, but,.." and before he could finish J.P. interrupted.

"You know! How do you know that? I have never worked for you. So why would you group all administrators into one category? Unless all of **YOU**, are the same. Now, Mr. Wolffe if that is the case, then you are very correct. I do not like any administrator, starting with your Fuhrer!" At that Scott Wolffe looked at J.P. with a puzzled face, and O'Francis knew in an instant he had tripped him with the word Fuhrer.

"Mr. Wolffe, I am referring to the superintendent, your leader. The man you follow so loyally, pledging allegiance to!"

"Now what a minute. I am not like all the rest of these principals in the county. I do not agree with every little thing that Mr. Marshy does."

J.P. was quick with a response. "And I do not place ALL administrators in the same group! Point of fact is Mr. Wolffe, I have worked for a couple of very good, honest and honorable principals since I have been working for Reynolds County." Then there was a short pause in their conversation.

"And, Mr. Wolffe, let me add, I have worked for some of the most evil, malicious, mendacious and corrupt principals in this or any other county in the state of Virginia!"

Wolffe stood looking at J.P. for just a moment, and then lost eye contact and began looking from the floor to the walls or down the stairs, but not at O'Francis.

"But I will bet my "pissy" ass little pay check against yours that you will do exactly what your Fuhrer tells you to do. And I will bet without questioning him!"

"Do what?" Scott stated.

"I am referring to your statement about not agreeing with your Fuhrer."

"I think you are wrong in feeling that way Mr. O'Francis. I am here to help you in any way I can. I just want you to know that. I mean I am not like

Damon Bales. Matter of fact I don't even like him, and I think you have been done a terrible wrong."

"Well, I thank you for your deep concern Mr. Wolffe. I have one question for you. Just where did you get the idea that I hated all administrators?" J.P. emphasized all administrators in a tone that left no doubt of what he meant. "I mean you cannot personally attest to that, as you and I have never worked with each other. And just in case you may have missed that, I really want to repeat myself so that you fully understand me, worked together. Not me just working for you in this school. So, Sir, just why would you make such a sweeping generalized statement to me like that?"

At the end of J.P.'s stunning statement, Scott Wolffe began a nervous shifting of the feet and hands, and began walking down the stairs without responding to O'Francis' question. O'Francis walked a step behind his new principal. They reached the first floor hallway and walked the short fifteen feet to his classroom door.

"Well Mr. O'Francis, I hope you and I can work together this year and if there is anything you might need just come and ask and if I can help you on it, I will."

He then turned and headed off down the hall at a quick pace. J.P. stood and watched him and smiled to himself. The bell rang and the students filled the hallway. Wolffe became engulfed in the masses of students as they went to and fro to their next class. As his last student entered his famous "Think Tank" he spoke softly to himself, "shittttttttt!"

The new special education teacher was a rather young 35 year old from the far end of the county. Pat Cuffel was not very attractive, but did have a well-shaped body. Wolffe zeroed in on her from day one. By the middle of the year of his and her first year at Honsburg Middle, the two were an ongoing thing. Her marriage to a state highway department supervisor was no concern for her lust for sex with her immediate boss. His lust was for anything that would spread, lay, bend, or any other configurationally position one could imagine in one's sexually active mind. He had no real feelings for any female other than the fact that they could satisfy his unquenchable desire for sex. Pat was giving him all he wanted anywhere and anytime, on and off school grounds.

The local political machine had appointed Robert Studer to the School Board for support of LaMar, and LaMar in turn made Robert's brother John the new principal of Liberty High and had John's wife Joyce assigned to Elk Horn Middle School where Emmanuel worked.

Before Hobbit left to a more honorable working environment, he had placed Emmanuel on a steering committee as the chairperson for the school's self-study, and taking his assignment seriously, he had been doing a very good job. But LaMar felt that he had too much power and instructed Norberta to remove him as the chairperson. Emmanuel had been appointed to the technological committee and had been working with the people in Richmond to establish a future for tech labs in the schools in Reynolds County, which had been coming along very well. He had also been appointed part of a visiting team for school renewal in another county. All that came to an abrupt stop the very first week that Norberta Millicent arrived as the principal of Elk Horn School.

Emmanuel was called to her office, and upon arriving he had no idea what was about to take place, and was totally defenseless. "Come in Mr. Reuben", she said as she got up and closed the door. Motioning with her right hand for him to have a seat, she walked back behind her desk. Emmanuel still had no idea that his world as an energetic, conscientious hard working teacher was about to collapse.

"Mr. Reuben you will no longer be the reading teacher. I am assigning a new teacher to that position." He had been teaching reading for twelve years, and without a moment of hesitation, she continued, "Mr. Reuben I am also removing you as the chairman of the self-study committee."

"Ahh, Mrs. Millicent."

She did not give him a chance to speak, "Now you understand this, you will do as I tell you! I make the rules here now. I'm not Hobbit, and you are not running things here! I am! You are also off the visiting committee for the self-study of Glenn Williams Middle School!"

Reuben was in total shock at that point, and his mind was trying to recover from the illogical verbal attack on him. He normally was an easygoing person and did not get angered easily, however he was becoming very agitated at this new principal's attitude toward him, and once again started to address her in a more stern voice.

"Mrs. Millicent, I would like to." She once again cut him off.

"I told you to sit there and listen. I do the talking here, and you do the listening! You seem to have a problem understanding that MR. REUBEN! I thought I made myself very clear! Now you can go back to your classroom. I am finished for now!"

Emmanuel left the office reeling from the attack on him, and asking himself what had happened. The same week there was a scheduled reading workshop for all middle school teachers, but Emmanuel did not attend.

The day following the workshop he once again was called to her office, but this time Emmanuel was not so relaxed and his guard was up, as his past week had been uneasy and stressful. Norberta wasted no time. Emmanuel had no more than sat in the chair.

"Mr. Reuben you just don't get it do you! You did not attend the scheduled work shop you were supposed to be at yesterday!"

Emmanuel spoke with a more commanding voice his third time around with Norberta Millicent. "YOU told me that I was no longer teaching reading! YOU told me that you were assigning a new teacher to that position!"

She quickly and angrily recanted. "I did not!"

"Yes ma'am you most unequivocally did!"

"Mr. Reuben do you have anything in writing? Did I send you a memo so stating?"

"No ma'am that you did not. But it does not have to be in writing, and I was doing what you stated in our first meeting, doing as I was told!"

At that she stood with her hands on her desk, slightly bending over and toward Emmanuel. "Don't you get smart with me MR. REUBEN! You have no idea who the hell you are dealing with here! YOU are completely out of touch with this community! You need to improve your professionalism with visiting parents! You need to get your act together, or else!"

"Yes ma'am." At that, Norberta became very angry.

"Don't you patronize me with your yes ma'am bull shit! You just do as I tell you!"

"Yes ma'am! Will there be anything else Ms. Millicent?" Emmanuel stated with a curt angry tone in his voice.

With a wave of the hand, Norberta stated with a commanding voice. "No, you may leave!"

"Oh thank you."

"What?"

"You heard me!" He opened the door and let it slam hard against the wall.

# The Path Forks

J.P. O'Francis arrived at Chicago's O'Hara from a flight coming out of Atlanta. He had been provided with four different identifications to travel from Montana to Atlanta.

His trip would begin in Helena, Montana as Timothy S. Daly. That would take him to Phoenix, Arizona. There he would be William Matt Molly as he traveled to Houston, Texas. In Houston, he would present his ticket at the counter as John W. Kilpatrick, and travel to Atlanta, Georgia. None of the flights were connecting. It would appear that all originated from one origin. It took a full day and several hours for J.P. to make his trip, but he did not object and fully understood what Paul had done and as he arrived in Chicago, he felt very secure.

Joseph checked the flight from Atlanta to determine if it was on time. A mere fifteen minutes late, not bad, so he headed off to O'Brien's Restaurant and Bar, where J.P. had been instructed that he would meet Joseph and Michael, which was close to Terminal 3 where he was to arrive.

Thirty-five minutes later, J.P. entered into O'Brien's. He scanned the room. He saw Joseph and Michael sitting at a table toward the back of the room. Michael spotted J.P. first and could see him directing Joseph's attention toward him. As the two men rose, Joseph tossed twenty dollars on the table and walked toward O'Francis, greeting J.P. with a big smile on his face.

"Afternoon J.P."

"Afternoon Joseph, Michael." Michael then reached for J.P.'s garment bag.

"May I take that?"

"Sure. Thanks Michael." They then walked to the parking lot and headed for the North side of Chicago.

Arriving at the Caprotti home, J.P. was shown to a guest room, which was more like someone's master bedroom. Afterwards, Maria gave him the grand tour while Joseph was on the phone with his father-in-law.

Nina Maria was the proud daughter of a powerful executive who also happened to be the head of a "Family". Her five foot two inch small framed body was shaped like an hour glass, with a firm 36 inch breast line, a 24 inch waist and a mere one hundred and ten pounds, short dark brown hair with a naturally dark complexion. She had no children and looked ten years younger than her forty-nine years. She had been educated in a private school, and received her higher education from her father's alumni, De Paul. She majored in international business and worked for her father. She had become known in the business circles as a cold, hard driving corporate executive. Her father was extremely proud of her.

Joseph found them in the back of the house as they were touring the pool, pool house, sauna and Jacuzzi.

"So, J.P. what do you think?" he asked as he joined them entering the pool house, which had its own wet bar, small bedroom 10x12, small apartment size kitchen, and one bath.

"Well, Joseph my man, I think you have done very well for yourself, very well indeed."

"J.P., we are joining Maria's father for dinner. Do you need to shower?"

"Yes, I would like to. Is this a formal gathering?"

"No,no,no, this is a jeans gathering." As both Maria and Joseph laughed, knowing that J.P. was not quite at ease, and did not know what to expect from Vincent Spadolini. It was up to them to make him feel at ease at the Caprotti house as well as the Spadolini home.

As they approached the double iron gates, Joseph pushed the button on the box attached to the post ten feet or so from the gates. From the box a voice asked, "May I help you?"

"Tony, its Joseph." The gates opened and they proceeded. A camera began tracking them into the estate and the gates closed behind them. Another three hundred yards of concrete driveway to a thirty yard squared open area in front of the main house. Maria went in first.

"Momma, Dad we're here," she called out entering the large foyer. In Don Spadolini's homeland, it would have been called a villa. The odor of an Italian dinner permeated the lower level of the Spadolini mansion. Maria knew just where she would find her mother. She went straight to the kitchen. There was no real need for Sophia Nina Spadolini to be in the kitchen, but her love for cooking was a hobby and she would have to be considered an expert at it, as their personal chef would often tell her.

As J.P. would learn about her hobby, his thoughts were that Dawn and Sophia would have gotten along very well. However, the passing of Dawn still left a deep void in J.P.'s soul even after many years of her death.

Maria was a clone of her mother, just that Sophia was older with black hair with no graying even at the age of 67 and looked as if she had never had a child.

The house, if that is what one could call it, was immaculate and was kept that way with a full staff of maids and grounds keepers. On a normal day a cooking staff fixed all the meals unless Sophia wanted to have a hand in cooking, which was often, despite her social prominence and the gala events she attended with Vincent, pressing flesh with local and national political figures, and corporate tycoons. However, this dinner was not to be normal, and Sophia helped and directed in fixing the dinner for a special guest, a trusted friend of Joseph's, someone who had been in the right place at the right time to ensure that he lived a longer life and wed to the daughter of a Don. To Vincent and Sophia that made O'Francis special.

J.P. did not feel special. Point of fact was he felt a bit out of place. He was in the presence of a very powerful figure, an extremely wealthy man that controlled a large corporation with ties in powerful places. Not just in the Illinois government, but in the Nation's Capital. J.P. was not easily intimidated by anyone, but in this case, he felt very intimidated by Don Vincent Spadolini, even though he did not blatantly come across that way. In fact, he was very cordial. It was the fact that O'Francis was very aware of his position and his power.

A very good-looking man, six foot two, well-trimmed, one hundred and ninety pounds, salt and pepper short well-groomed hair and clean shaving. His voice was not very deep, medium with just a slight accent. He did not look as if he was 68 years old. Senators, congresspersons, attorneys, judges never got him uptight, even though they too had power in many places, and they liked to wield that power and make people feel intimidated by their position, power and stature. Those types of people did not bother O'Francis. He more or less brushed them off, like lint on his suit coat. However, this man, Vincent Spadolini was different. He had an air about him, his posture, and his walk commanded great respect without words or boastfulness of titles or positions. When he spoke, it reminded J.P. of the E. F. Hutton commercial, everyone listened. He appeared, to J.P. at any rate, to be very low keyed, not one to get overly excited, very analytical, and rarely raised his voice.

The dining area was quite large, a 30x40 foot room with a large dining table in the middle. It looked as if it had been handmade, and upon inquiring as J.P. admired the room and made a few honest but polite comments concerning the decor, found that the table was handmade and shipped in from Sicily, a family heirloom, dating back to Vincent's great grandfather. J.P. could see the pride on Sophie's face as he commented on her dining room as well as the pride in the table as Vincent went into detail about the history of a magnificent piece of woodwork.

The family gathered around the table and J.P. was given a place directly across from Don Spadolini. *Odd,* his thoughts flashed through his mind, *the Don sitting in the middle with his wife to his left.* To J.P.'s right was Maria and to his left Joseph. J.P. had not expected that type of dining arrangement. To add to the unexpected seating arrangements, Sophia instructed everyone that grace was to be said, and all bowed their heads. "Bless us O' Lord...." the well-known and traditional Catholic dinner prayer, of which

J.P. recited along with the rest of the Spadolini family, "through Christ our Lord..." and a slight pause and Vincent ended with the Amen. Something J.P. could tell was done each time they were together.

Sophia looked across at J.P. "You are Catholic I take it?" A slight smile was on her face.

"Yes. In a way. Recovering." He continued. "Being Irish, with my ancestral heritage from the County Tipperary, and being the third generation of my family here in the United States." No one commented on his statement, "in a way. Recovering."

At that point, the maid brought in the dinner and began placing the food on the table. Vincent opened a bottle of wine, and offered his guest the first glass. There was lots of wine at the meal and several bottles were consumed before the meal was over.

After J.P. took a long drink of wine, Don Spadolini asked, "So what do you think of the wine?"

"Well, I am not a wine connoisseur, but I like it. Of course I am Irish, and you know what they say about us Irish and alcohol."

All had a good laugh. As the meal proceeded, the conversation was light with a joke thrown in occasionally with lots of laughter. As all were about to finish their meal, the conversation turned a little more serious as Don Spadolini asked, "J.P. do you know a Brian Keefe O'Francis?"

J.P. thought for a few seconds. "No sir, I do not think so." There was yet another short pause in conversation.

"Do you have a brother?" J.P. looked at Vincent Spadolini.

"No sir, I am the only son from my father's loins." Then with a bit of a laugh he added, "I might add, to my knowledge and that too is somewhat of a long story, my father that is. Why do you ask?"

There was a rather long pause in the conversation from Vincent as he took the last bit of his veal and then a sip of wine to finish his meal. For the second time during the course of the meal there was silence as J.P. finished his wine, and Sophia asked if he would like more and O'Francis extended his glass across the table for her to fill his glass. Then Vincent reached his glass to his wife for her to fill his.

"Because I do some business with Mr. O'Francis and he could be your brother, looks that is. Where did you say you were from?"

"Well, I was born in Oklahoma. But I was raised in the southern part of Virginia with my grandparents and mother." A long pause occurred again in the conversation and with some degree of hesitation J.P. continued, "My mother and father separated when I was very young. I never got to know my father. I was only three when they separated."

In her Italian accent, Sophia spoke, "Ooooh, that is not good, family is very important. A son needs his father when he is growing up. Did you not go look for him?"

As J.P. started to answer, Don Spadolini spoke, "Enough of that. How about some desert?"

"Sure I think I can handle a little."

For desert they had spumoni ice cream. As the maid was bringing the desert out, Sophia asked J.P. if he had ever had spumoni ice cream.

"Yes, Mrs. Spadolini I have and quite often. My mother-in-law, Gloria Marie Rabaiotti was Italian, and I am very acquainted with spumoni ice cream."

J.P. and Sophie began a much lighter conversation between them.

"Where was she from?" J.P. was in the process of taking a small bite, and took a moment to answer.

"Her roots are in Parma, Italy." A big smile came across her face. "My grandparents are from Palermo, Sicily."

Sophia and J.P. continued a conversation about her family, and no one else did any talking during the next ten-minute. Then Maria joined in on the conversation.

"Where do you live now J.P.?" A moment passed, Joseph turned and looked at Maria as if to say do not ask that question. Joseph then looked at his father-in-law, all in a matter of a two seconds. Coffee had been served with the spumoni ice cream, and J.P. started to drink from his cup and he slowly finished before he answered Maria's question.

He then placed the cup gently down onto the soccer, and without any wavering, answered, "I live north of Atlanta Georgia. I have a home in the very southern tip of the Appalachian Mountains."

"I always thought that Georgia was flat?" Maria stated.

J.P. smiled as the moment of tension with Joseph seemed to pass with each answer J.P. would give to Maria. "Well, Maria, most of the state is. However, in the northern most part of the state, the long two thousand mile Appalachian mountain ranges come to an end. I found a place in the area between Atlanta and Chattanooga Tennessee along the North Carolina border that suited me and I retired there. The winters are not bad and yet you have your four seasons. Summers can get a little hot, but I am not far from the Great Smoky Mountains and the air in the mountains is oftentimes ten degrees cooler than it is in the flat areas or in the cities surrounding the area."

"I hear that the Smokies are real nice."

J.P. smiled. "Yes they are and it is a real nice place to visit. I think you would really enjoy the area." He looked over at Joseph. "I think Joseph should take you there for a week's vacation, and get some real good clean southern mountain air in your lungs." Joseph just smiled, and took a drink of his coffee.

After dinner Vincent took J.P. on a tour of his estate, describing the house in great detail, ending up in the back yard, where a bottle of Glenfiddish Scotch, two glasses, a bucket of ice and a box of Montecristo, 50 ring, six inches long cigars had been placed on the table in the gazebo.

"I understand that you like scotch or Irish whiskey."

"Yes sir I do, both." He proceeded to open the bottle and fill both glasses.

"With two cubes of ice, correct?"

J.P. just smiled and replied softly, "Yes."

"I am told you like a good cigar with your after dinner drink."

J.P. smiled. "Yes I do."

Vincent reached over and opened the humidor. "Get yourself one."

He pointed to the lighter and the cutter, then he clipped the end off and lit his cigar. Vencent Spadolini did the same, and with the glass of scotch in his hand, turned and faced O'Francis.

"I salute you." His statement took J.P. back, and Vincent read it.

"You ask yourself why should I salute you?" J.P. could not speak. He just nodded his head, yes.

"I will tell you. Would you like to walk while we talk, or would you rather sit?"

"Walk." O'Francis replied.

"Good, I also like to walk while I talk." With his glass of scotch in his right hand he indicated for J.P. and he to walk the very large back yard, an area of at least three acres of extremely well cared for lawn, shrubs, trees, and flowers.

"Why do I salute you, you ask? Because all these years, you have never, not once, asked anything in return for what you did for Joseph. I would not have Joseph, whom I consider a son. My daughter was deeply in love with him, and as you know, married him. She would not be happily married now if it were not for you."

J.P. said nothing, just walked alongside the "Don."

"I know that you knew that you could have asked for anything you wanted. I know this. Most people would have asked for something. I would have given it to them. But yet, you went on with your own life, leaving the area without a word, no requests, no favors, nothing. You are a man with honor. I like men with honor. I know you can be trusted. I know you are a man of your word. I know these things. It is my business to know people. Especially people I want to get to know. Joseph has enlightened me as to some of your hardships, and yet even with his offer to help you, you ask for nothing. Why? He owes you his very life, now why I ask you?"

It was time for a re-fill as they had taken a short walk and approached the gazebo. J.P. was still somewhat nervous inside, even with the wine he had consumed throughout the hour or so dinner, and a double shot of scotch. His outward appearance showed a calm, ice-cold approach to a man in a position of power he really could not relate. Yet here he was talking to J.P. as if he was of equal statue, talking carefree, as if he had known him for a long time. J.P. did not understand, and was not yet at ease with the Don of the Spadolini Family.

"Don Spadolini." Vincent Spadolini interrupted J.P.. "It is just Vincent, J.P., okay?"

"Yes sir." J.P. replied with respect to a gentleman a mere few years his senior. Then he continued. "I do not know how to answer your question. I just did not feel that Joseph owed me anything. When I did learn of his connections to you, welllll, I still did not feel you nor Joseph owed me anything. I did what I had to do at the time and that was it. He and I became very well acquainted, as you know, and I really liked Joseph. But I..." Then a long pause, a drink, a few puffs. His insides quivered ever so slightly.

"I... I... do not like getting real close to people. Friends that is. I..." Another pause, they walked, Vincent said nothing.

"I lost two very close friends a long time ago... I have never gotten over it. I did not want to get that close to another person. The word friend is used so loosely. I have tried to become friends with a few others in my life only to be betrayed. A mistake on my part. Joseph...well... Joseph was quite young and just got himself into a bad situation that night, and I just happened to be at the right place at the right time. I just did what I had to do. That is it. I did not then, I do not now, expect any reciprocity. Ahh."

Vincent interrupted. "An act of heroism." J.P. took a couple of puffs on his cigar and then took another sip.

"Well, I really do not think...I would call,"

Again Vincent interrupted. "Saving his life, from some, some... low life piece of bar...trash. A low life, that was drunk, pissed off because Joseph took a few hundred dollars of his money at the pool table! And he ambushed him in the parking lot with a gun! And would have shot and killed him if it were not for you. Yes, J.P., I would call it heroism. You put your life on the line for Joseph. He has never forgotten it. I have never forgotten it. Maria, well...she knows that something happened and that if you had not been in the right place at the right time and was willing to take action, she would have never married the man she was so much in love with and may very well not be at her side as her husband now. All she knows is that Joseph considers you his friend, and for her that is all that matters.

Do not get me wrong, she is sharp, or she would not have the position in my company as she does and she knows that it was not just a little incident. I do not give anything to anyone. They earn it, and the hard way. That's right, even my daughter! She most likely knows that there is more to the story, but she has never asked, nor will she ask. That is the way things are here. That would be up to Joseph to tell her if he ever does."

For the next three hours they talked, consumed the scotch, and smoked a couple of cigars apiece. J.P. answered all the Don's questions, expounding on several, giving the Don an idea of what his life as a teacher with no political connections, in a very corrupt county in the south, had been like for many years. The type of people he had been dealing with, J.P. did not hide anything nor did he lie about anything. He told him of the loss of his daughter, his youngest son, and the devastating loss of his beloved soul mate. Vincent listened and watched J.P. as he related his life in brief.

Vincent introduced the subject of J.P.'s connection with the law enforcement and found that J.P. had developed a bitter taste toward them. He had to explain why as Vincent listened intently.

"I really had no real problem with the policemen on patrol for the most part, but…I mean…for an example Don Spadolini, the two people I always worked with, cut people breaks, hell most cops do that, I think. The thing that really bothers me about the law is the corrupt judges, attorneys, and politicians. Drugs, illegal gun trafficking, porn, murder, and they are arrogant about it as they have no worries, as they know they have the system under control and they all have each other by the balls. Oh, I know what an attorney would say and have told me personally… "it is better than anywhere else in the world…yeah, well I think I can debate that."

Their conversation went to insignificant topics for several minutes and then it went back to a more serious subject, the United States Government. J.P. spoke on his personal feeling toward the government without hesitation. Vincent learned quickly how O'Francis felt about his country and he learned that it brought out a deep seeded emotion in J.P. They talked about the social hypocrisy as well as the religious hypocrisy in the country. Vince learned that J.P. had a major problem with the religious hypocrisy but did not have any problem with the working women of the street.

Vincent asked J.P. a simple question as he was getting to know O'Francis.

"How do you feel about the politics in Washington?"

That set off a rather lengthy oratory and then a long period of silence as they had walked the grounds again and was back at the gazebo for a refill.

"Please continue," Vincent said as he poured both a refill of scotch.

J.P. turned to the military and the political games the politicians played with them expressing a great deal of dislike toward the elected idiots that controlled the nation. The elected politicians' have no honor. They are corrupt, bough off, they are shameless, mendacious, murders. Let me clarify that last comment. They work behind the curtains, back stage, they do not have the stones to actually do the dirty work. They just make sure that the people who are connected to the people who do the real work of eliminating others do not have any legal problems. I actually loathe politicians'. I know you have to be connected to them in a multitude of ways, however, you, I think, want to see what I am made of. I am what you see.

Vince turned to the educational aspect, and found J.P. to be very candid and very bitter.

"The teaching profession, the big fish in the little pond theory, and the demigod's theory, are right in there with all the bigger fish in the bigger pond."

J.P. was on a roll, and had felt at ease and figured that if he really wanted to know about him he was going to get his personal feelings thrown into the mix. Vincent Spadolini listened and on occasion would break a slight smile.

Then after several minutes of venting J.P. paused and looked directly at Vincent, took a deep breath, reached for his scotch glass, took a sip, then placed it gently down.

"Sorry, Vincent, just a few touchy subjects and most likely too much alcohol, which appears to be loosening up my tongue a bit, which I normally do not do. Which to me personally is not a good thing, would you agree?"

"I would. But it is okay. You are in good company, and you are safe here. I can appreciate your candidness."

The two men talked about the hit on Finkel, and how J.P. felt about it.

"I have reached the point, when it comes to these people, my feelings are the same as they were when I served in Vietnam. I feel nothing, it is just business. A job you are assigned to do, and you do it with pride and with the greatest expertise one can."

They spoke at length about the relationship between him and Joseph and where he expected to go from the point they were at, and at what cost. Vincent Spadolini seemed pleased at J.P.'s responses to his questions.

They spoke on his retirement, his family what was left of it, and his feeling toward family, his son Michael and his grandson Patrick, and his total devotion to them. Their conversation turned to his Irish background and the close relationship the Irish and the Italian culture had. They had briefly touched on Religion, God, and Catholicism. Vincent learned quickly that J.P. had no religion, and loathed all religions. He learned that he was deeply spiritual, and was told face to face that he would not go into any details about his spiritual life.

"Of course the world at present is in a state of war because of religion... but I will not pursue that subject." J.P. stated.

"Okay, it is a rather complex subject at that and would take a rather long time to discuss and that is not what we are here for on this night J.P." Then another few moments of silence as the night creatures took over the conversation.

Vincent could tell that J.P. was still bothered by the bad memoirs of long ago. He could tell in the tone of his voice that he held a bitterness for the loss of his family members. He knew that in the game of politics, the power brokers could make or break people. He also knew that lying and "under-handed" tactics were only part of their weaponry. He also knew that in most cases, most people in a public position, if they were not part of some political party with connections, they were as good as dead, a living death, which was worse than death itself if you placed any value on your family name.

Vincent took over the conversation and turned the conversation to the banking business, the shipping business, and the hotel business as J.P. absorbed every word Vincent Spadolini spoke. He would from time to time, with hesitation, ask a question concerning the businesses they were talking about, and would get a short lesson pertaining to his question. Vincent told him that he had a great deal of respect for good educators, that there were not enough of them. He discussed the educational system in the Chicago area, and was both very critical as well as complimentary in some cases.

"Vincent Spadolini. I was a damn good teacher at one time. The powers to be destroyed my career! They tarnished my name, unjustly, hurt my family financially. Now that may be no big deal to many people. We made it and moved on. However, for me, no, it was a big deal and for that matter, it still is. Moreover, the old worn out line of just get over it, welllll...no, I was done an injustice in more than one way and I do not just get over it. I took it personal. When this person takes something personal, there is no time limit as to when I will seek revenge."

The two took a seat in the gazebo. The walking covered the entire area, all the gardens with extended explanations. It was time to sit. J.P. took a long drink, reached for the ice, dropping three cubs in his glass, and pouring himself a single shot, took a little sip. Vincent watched him and then slowly spoke.

"I know you did! I also know you were done a terrible wrong. I also know they tried to assassinate you and your wife and I know why. I also know what happened to your youngest son. I also want to tell you how sorry I am for the loss of your wife as well as your son and daughter. You have had a lot of heartache in your life."

That got J.P.'s attention quick, even though his mind was not working at full capacity. With both hands loosely wrapped around his glass as it set on the table, turning it in the same spot slowly, looking down into the fresh glass of scotch, his head tilted, turning it slightly to his left looking at Don Vincent Spadolini out of his left eye. Even in the very dim light provided by the elaborate lighting system, set on a medium setting for illumination, which could be adjusted to whatever level one wanted, he could see in the man's eyes there was no bullshit about him.

"J.P., I know a lot about you, and that is why you are here. Joseph and I have had several talks concerning you. Joseph has requested that I meet you personally. I know how you feel about your name. I too, have very strong feels about a family name! I think..." He finished his drink, refilled his glass with two ice cubes and poured himself a double scotch.

"I think that there is no limit a man should have in defending his family honor, his name. I have noticed over the years, that less and less people have any pride in their family name. It, for the most part, is just a name. People just do not give a damn about how it reflects on them, their ancestry. None of the old philosophies exist in these new generations. I think you will find I do understand how you feel about your name. There has been over the years a saying, What's in a Name, well, there is a lot in a name."

In all that was discussed he never once questioned J.P. as to where he lived or where his son was. Vincent knew that he would not so freely and openly reveal his current residence, but he respected his privacy, and J.P. never revealed his current residence to Vincent Spadolini. In a part of the conversation, Vincent brought up Brian O'Francis, and J.P. learned that they were in the shipping and hotel business together. He did not elaborate on the details of how they met and the extent of their business. He did learn that Brian and J.P. were born in the same part of the country and that their father had the same name. Vincent asked J.P. if he had any objections to meeting Brian. With a slight bit of hesitation, he replied that he had none. He asked J.P. if he would object to returning back to Chicago in a month or so as he had a business appointment with Brian, and that he would be in the area during that period of time. J.P. thought for a few moments as they finished off their scotch.

"I will take care of your expenses, don't worry about that, I just have a feeling about the two of you. I cannot get over the similarities. I think you will be very surprised. Bear in mind, there may be nothing to it. However, I still would like you to meet Brian. That is if you have no objections."

"No sir, I do not. But I really do not think," then he stopped himself. J.P. had reservations about the whole conversation, but went with his little voice in his head, which was much clearer than his own mind at that point and agreed to return to meet Brian O'Francis.

As they parted for the night and a gracious thanks to Sophia, as well as their staff, J.P. was still in shock about meeting Vincent Spadolini. He just could not get over why he was given such special treatment. He was worldly enough to know that not just every "swinging Dick" dined with the head of a "Family," nor had a candid lengthy conversation with him. To top the entire evening off, to be asked to return, just to meet someone who just happened to have the same last name, that Vincent Spadolini felt looked like J.P. just was not natural, not for the world Vincent operated in.

*Is it a brother?*

🍀 🍀 🍀 🍀

J.P. spent the next day with Joseph taking a guided tour of the city and the headquarters of Vincent. Michael and Joseph took J.P. to the airport the third morning of his trip. J.P. had gotten little sleep that night, reviewing all that had been talked about, what he had said, and what Vincent had said. The three said their farewells. *Til next time*, as Joseph put it. J.P. O'Francis' flight took off on time. Destination: Atlanta, Georgia.

He pondered on the short flight.

*Why me? Why would a man like that take the time out of his life for someone like me? What am I not seeing? Who is this Brian O'Francis? Shit...brother...I just do not think so. For us to have the same father? Someone I never met! The odds of some such event happening in my life, well, hell, just ain't no way!*

The airline host interrupted his thoughts. J.P. took an orange juice and thanked her, then proceeded to look out the window and the passing clouds below him, returning to his thoughts.

*This man, hell Joseph for that matter, well, even Maria, all are way out of my league. I have nothing to offer, not that much money, really do not give a damn about the evil bastards that destroyed my career as a teacher and a coach, tarnished my family name throughout the entire area, just not that important in the real world for all this. What's in a name any more, shit, no one really cares! As to what I think, wellll,..Hell I damn sure ain't the one to vindicate the wrong that has been done. I just do not understand. Is this my Master's plan? Naaaa...I do not think...well, now...why all the right connections now? Are these the right connections? Is this a test? I never really do know. Will I ever? I do not think...I will understand my own philosophy of, of, not religion, of, whatever I have. However, nothing happens out of coincidence. Got to be a reason?*

J.P. had developed a headache from all the drinking and the lack of sleep as well as all his thinking.

He became mentally stressed with his own thoughts, and forced his thoughts onto his beloved Dawn and drifted off to sleep for a short nap.

Upon arriving in Atlanta, he made his way to the Cheers restaurant, where he found "The Man" waiting for him. It was 9:15 A.M.

"So how was your trip?" Paul asked.

"Very interesting. Very interesting to say the very least."

"How is Vincent Spadolini?"

"Fine, I guess? I really do not know how to answer that. I mean...I cannot get over me even being there."

"Well, J.P. let me tell you something." He took a sip of coffee. At that moment the waitress arrived and asked if he would like more coffee and asked J.P. if he would like something to drink as well as a menu. He ordered coffee and she handed him a menu.

"I'll return in a few minutes."

"Let me tell you about Vincenzo Spadolini. First off, he knows a lot about you. Second, he liked what he has learned about you. He can't quite figure you J.P."

"Figure me? Why? I am nothing. An ex-school teacher, one that was run out of the profession at that! And by the way, how well do you know him?"

"First, I know him very well. The how, welll, is…"

J.P. interrupted. "That is fine, I do not want to know the how, it is not important."

"Now"... the server arrived, and J.P. ordered breakfast. Three eggs, four pieces of bacon, two slices of toast and two pancakes.

As soon as the server walked away, Paul smiled. "Hungry are you?"

J.P. smiled and had a little chuckle in his voice. J.P. spoke in his best Irish accent. "Well, point of fact is, I am. Hell, with all that has happened to me in the last 48 hours, I am stressed, and when I get that way I eat. T'is all the alcohol I consumed for the pass two nights. It makes an Irishman hungry." Then he laughed.

"J.P., what puzzled Vincent Spadolini you never ask for anything."

"Sooooo."

"Well, that is not normal, especially if someone has a lot of money. And shall I say, in the position he is in."

"Well, we touched on that matter. I still at this point, do not see the point in wanting to meet me, and why all the interest in me? I mean, shit Paul...come on man, I am out of everyone's picture, doing basically nothing in a place where no one knows me or anything about me, and I like it like that."

The server brought his food, and refilled both coffee cups. J.P. thanked her and she was off.

"I think I can give you some answers, don't know if I can answer all the questions. However, Joseph took it upon himself to take care of some business without Vincenzo's okay. Now that, one does not do! I don't give a fuck if you are his number one "son." Son-in-law and well entrenched into the hotel business end of the Spadolini business dealings and I might add does his job extremely well as does his wife. However, Joseph just wanted to do something for you. I'll not get into why he wanted to, you know that."

"Yes, yes, I...well I wish he would have picked Bales...but, at any rate..."

"Well, he knows that was just the tip of the "ice-berg." That the main players in your past problems, over so many years, were untouched and he has been briefed on all of them. I am sure he spoke to you as to their future?"

"Yes, but not all the details, just a few comments. There is more to a job than just a few words, or wants."

Paul quickly responded. "I know. That is why he wanted to talk to you first hand. He was assured that you could be trusted and that your word was bond. I told you he liked what he had learned about you. The man is sharp. Do not let his age fool you and it has a lot of people. Not that his age is old, I mean you and I, oh well, you know what I mean. He did not become what he is by making mistakes. Did you like him?" Paul concluded.

"Yes I did. He and Sophia were extremely gracious, no facade'. That I also question. I am nothing to these people."

"J.P.," Paul stated, "these people as you refer to them, are like everybody. Yes, they are very rich. Yes they are in big business, big politics, high in the social order of things. However, they can be and are "down to earth", if you get my drift? In addition, their daughter, well, looks, yes. Class, yes. Rich, yes. Very intelligent, yes, and she has it all. No, most are not like her either. Joseph, well, you know him."

"Well, I do and I do not. I knew him when." J.P. stated.

"He is the same Joseph, just the rough edges of the stone have been removed, and he is more honed in the manner that Vincent Spadolini wants, to fit the builders, so to speak. He still knows where he was raised and he knows very well why he has what he does. Maria loves him deeply, even with all she has going for her and at her age. Shit, she knows that she could have had any one she had wanted and even to this day she can have anyone she wants. She knew that way back when. Nevertheless, she had her sights set on Joseph and by-god she got him. He has come a long way in the business." Paul paused and thought.

"J.P., look. The Family, well it ain't like everything you see on T.V., and all these anti-mob, Justice Files, bull shit! Good-god almighty, I could tell you some stories about our own government that would make the "mob" look like a Boy Scout troop! You damn sure do not see any programs or documents about our own governments and all of its operations. Illegal at that may I state! Vincenzo's business is...wellll...for the most part is on the up and up. Moreover, the business of taking care of business so to speak, well, that too has changed. Now I damn sure ain't going to sit here and blow smoke up your ass. Yes they do "take care of business" but so does our own government, despite all the news media propaganda! It is just different than it was, ohh, thirty, or even twenty years ago."

J.P. finished his meal, accepted another cup of coffee, and requested his bill.

"Fine, I think. I am not sure, but I think I get the idea." J.P. responded to end the conversation.

Paul asked if he had all his tickets in order for his return flight to his now, semi-private world.

"Hey, don't worry; you'll be safe where you are. I know these things, you're safe!"

"One more thing, before we go, did Vincent speak of Brian?"

J.P.'s eyes quickly locked on Paul's eyes, and the look on his face told everything. "Yes!"

They rose and walked out into the open area of the airport. It was somewhat of a walk to the boarding area. Some small talk took place, as J.P. commented on the rather large mobile hanging from the top of the building, and again the assurance of his safety and privacy.

"J.P.", Paul stated, "Vincent Spadolini is very big on a man's word, and a code of honor, another point he liked about you." They shook hands and as they did Paul's thumb slipped to a spot on J.P.'s right hand. Paul smiled, J.P. did not. He just looked at Paul. He could not speak.

"Yes J.P. I am." J.P. still did not speak. They broke their hands, and Paul spoke as he placed his hand on J.P.'s left shoulder.

"I'll be in touch, enjoy your trip home. I will explain in full in due time. Just wait, a time of patience, and all will be revealed. Okay?"

O'Francis had a slight smile on his face. He did not speak, he turned and walked away.

# Privacy

EMMANUEL REUBEN CLOSED HIS BRIEFCASE, but did not lock it, turned and walked out of his classroom to make his way to the smoking area. He had fifteen minutes to go to the restroom and get in a few puffs of a cigarette before his students returned from their music class. As he descended the stairs at the west end of the building, Norberta Millicent arrived on the top floor from the east end of the building. She walked directly to Reuben's classroom knowing that he was out of the room, as it was the only morning break he had and knowing he usually went to the restroom and then to an area outside of the cafeteria to have a smoke. She boldly walked into his room and opened Reuben's briefcase. Casually and without worry, she began going through the material in various folders.

Reuben came out of the boys' restroom on the main floor of the school, snapped his right finger, saying to himself, *"damn, I have got to make a copy of the letter to Dan."* So he headed back up the stairs in a hurry in hopes he would be able to make a copy of his letter, and still get in a few puffs, which he needed as his stress level had been running high with the principal's constant attacks. As he walked through the door, he came to an abrupt halt.

"What do you think you are doing?" His voice filled with instant anger.

Norberta just casually looked over at Reuben and in a very calm voice said, "I am looking through your briefcase!"

"WHAT!" He walked quickly to his desk and with his left hand slammed the top of the case closed.

"That is my private briefcase, and what is in it is private, you have..."

She cut him off sharply. "I have the right to look at anything I want to in this school! Do you understand that! If you bring anything in this school and I so choose I will look at it, in it, through it, now is that clear!"

"Lady, you are nuts! You do not have the right to look IN, THROUGH, OR AT, anything that I consider as MY private material! DO YOU understand THAT!"

Norberta placed her hand once again on the lid of Reuben's briefcase.

Emmanuel's anger peaked. As calmly as he could, with his pulse in overdrive as he spoke very slowly trying to maintain control of his emotions, "IF I were you, I would remove your hand from that lid!"

Norberta smiled and turned and strutted out of the classroom, her head arched upward as if to parade and flaunt her authority.

The traveling music teacher sent word that she could not be at Reuben's school on their normal Monday, and that music classes would be canceled. The professional person she was, she notified Norberta Millicent a full week in advance so that rescheduling could be properly done. When it came time for Reuben's class to go to music he had them rise and in an orderly manner quietly walk to the music room. He waited for five minutes and no teacher. As he stepped out in the hallway to look to see if she was coming and may have been late for whatever reason, which really did not bother Manuel, he saw Norberta walking toward him in a manner that denoted that she was not coming to give him a kiss.

In her boldness and dictatorial manner she approached Manuel. "You just refused to follow my instructions, don't you, MR. REUBEN!" Manuel was in total darkness as to what she was talking about, as he had been the only teacher not to receive a memo from Norberta informing them the music teacher would not be at his school on her scheduled day. Not another teacher in the school had notified Manual of the absence of the music teacher. The memo had stated that they would go to the library for additional reading.

"Ms. Millicent." Once again, in her rudeness and unprofessional manner, she cut him off. *"NOW YOU, TAKE YOUR STUDENTS TO THE LIBRARY LIKE I INSTRUCTED YOU TO DO A WEEK AGO! I DON'T GIVE A DAMN ABOUT YOUR LAME-BRAINED EXCUSES! NOW MOVE!"*

Reuben did not stand and argue with her, as the scene was already way out of line for a group of sixth graders to have to witness. He gritted his teeth and took his class to the library. He went to all the teachers that had music scheduled for that Monday and asked if they had received a memo informing them of the schedule change. All had received a memo, and all told Reuben that they did not say anything because they just assumed that he received one also.

Manuel had Dan Jakes write a stern letter to Norberta outlining several unprovoked attacks on Manuel as well as her unprofessional demeanor toward him.

Norberta arrived in LaMar's office just as scheduled, 5:00 P.M... All administrative staff had left for the day, as it was a Friday and most had families and ball games to go to. Just a custodian was in the building doing her cleaning. Norberta closed the door as she entered LaMar's office. She reached into her briefcase and presented LaMar with the letter she had received from Dan.

He read it rather rapidly, and then smiled and looked up. "You want to keep this?"

"Not really. Not unless you want me to."

He wadded the letter up in his right hand and tossed it in the trash, with the comment, "Don't worry about the small things. The letter ain't shit! It's meaningless! So how is Mr. Reuben this week?"

Then he laughed, as did Norberta, and at the same time she tried to tell LaMar what she had been doing to "make his day" as difficult as she could.

"LaMar it's working. I can see it in his face. I really feel I will break him by the end of the year. I told you I could get the job done."

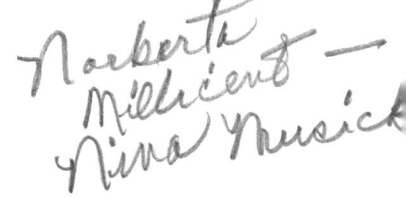

Norberta had a long blue ankle length dress on that had buttons all the way up the front.

She had unbuttoned her dress up two buttons above her knees before entering the office, and as she sat talking to LaMar she had casually slipped a few more buttons out exposing her mid-thigh as she crossed her leg. She knew it would not take but a very little enticement for him to react to her come-on. She had been amorous all day with the thought of meeting with LaMar privately in his office. She had a difficult time focusing on anything throughout the day other than her plan to seduce LaMar in his office. A place they had not yet engaged in the lustful act of intercourse. For Norberta this would be a notch in her gun, HIS office.

Indeed, his eyes did fall onto her smooth thighs, and he reacted just as she would have hoped he would. He got up and locked his door, put some music on to drown the animalistic noises they both made. Walked over to her, got down on his right knee and with his right hand unbuttoned her dress to the top, folding over the dress across her shoulders. This allowed her to pull her arms through the sleeves exposing her bra, and her bare groin area, as she had gone to the restroom before going to LaMar's office and removed her panties, placing them in her purse. The lustful act of oral sex as well as sexual intercourse was on.

The last summer Damon Bales was at Honsburg High, before his retirement, Patrick O'Francis was entering his first year of high school. He had not had a very good eighth grade year and his self-esteem was at rock bottom. His grades had slipped, his desire for education was in the darkest hole one could imagine. For many students, it only takes one or two teachers to derail them and send them spiraling down the dark tunnel of ignorance, and for Patrick this had happened, once in elementary school with a "dead-wood" worthless person that the system called a "teacher," that was so bad, that it made dead-wood seem like it was strong and vibrant. Then it occurred once again in his junior high year with a teacher that did more damage to students than they ever did any good.

Dawn and J.P. as concerned parents tried to get their son removed from the science class he was being infected with defeatism. J.P. was well aware that a student could be moved from one class to another for it had been done to several of his students over the years. Sometimes teachers and students just do not hit it off, and of course some parents are over protective and because of the work some teachers require, mommies little darlings did not get their usual "A", and they are removed to an easier teacher. The whining of overwork was not the case for the O'Francis', it was the quality of instruction that bothered Patrick's parents. None of the administrators would aid the O'Francis parents. Patrick would just have to work a little harder in getting along with his science teacher was the recommendation of the principal at the time.

Damon made a point of looking up the records of J.P. and Dawn's son Patrick. He removed his file, took it to the guidance department, and ordered them to place him in the School Drop Out and At Risk Program.

The guidance counselor called the O'Francis home.

"Coach, this is Howard, how you doing?"

Now knowing that Howard did not call him to wish him a good day or to see if his health was good, he knew something was wrong the second Howard started talking. He informed J.P. that he or Dawn needed to come to the school and meet with the SDARP director, and was informed as to why. Dawn's hours of work were from 11:00 A.M. to 11:00 P.M., so J.P. had to tell her at work what he had learned. After a few phone calls, and some legal checking, they learned that before a child could be placed in such a program the parents had to give consent, in writing. They learned that reasons for placing a student in such a program had to be documented by several teachers. J.P. did a quick and very intense investigation into the program itself, and learned that the students that were placed in such a program were from broken homes, alcohol/drug abusive parents, students with a history of violence in the home, students with parents that sexually abused them, and students with a history of violence in the classroom.

Dawn walked into Howard's office. "Good morning Howard," she stated with a big smile on her face. "I understand Patrick is being placed in a special class." Her voice was warm and friendly.

"Mrs. O'Francis, now this was not my idea. I want you to know that."

"Well, you are the guidance counselor, and it is my understanding that this new program for students that are at risk must go through you. So, if you had nothing to do with Patrick getting put into such a program, then who placed him there?"

Howard became nervous and started stuttering, never giving her an answer but directed Dawn to the head of the program for her scheduled appointment. As she entered the room with Howard leading the way, a large smile came across her face. Sitting behind the desk was Leigh Peng, the daughter of "Shihan" William Peng. After Howard introduced Dawn, Leigh was playing the role and going along with the scene without been prompted. Howard escaped as quickly as if he was a gust of wind that had just blown through the open window.

Before Dawn sat down Leigh asked, "I have to ask Dawn," holding the file of Patrick O'Francis up in the air. "What in the hell is this?"

"Leigh, I don't have a clue."

"Well, I knew it had to be some dumb-ass that placed Patrick's name on the list. I mean, of all people, with a father like he's got. Hell Dawn that is an insult to my father! Of course, these people don't know I know you and J.P. Moreover, they most likely do not know who my father is. Nor that J.P. is and has been one of his students. Christ! What a joke!" Then she began to laugh, as did Dawn.

"So, Leigh who did put him on the list?"

"Well, the only people that saw this list are the counselor, principal, and secretary. Sooo, you can figure. Not too hard, huh?"

"No not at all." Dawn replied, smiling.

"Why? I mean I know, well everyone knows how he feels about J.P., well unless you are dead from the neck up. However, to attack your son, I mean that is mean! And Dawn that is just what this is, an attack on your son!"

"Well, Leigh that is what this school is dealing with and has been for the past six years! And yes, he is mean! He is evil mean!" Dawn's tone of voice had changed to a more serious one.

"Wellll, I think I have found that this student is not the kind we are looking for. So he does not qualify for this program." Then she laughed again. Dawn momentarily placed her right hand palm outward over her forehead and in a sad voice.

"Oooooh, Leigh, I am so broke-up over this. I really…" and could not go any further as she began to laugh.

The phone rang and Patrick answered. Most children beat their parents to the phone, basically because they make little effort to challenge for the privilege to be the ones to say hello or some off the wall line like, "your quarter," used to be a dime, "you called, you talk". Or some of the older, "moldy" sayings like, "morgue, you stab'em, we slab'em", "Jake's pool hall, eight ball speaking", "hello, grape-vine, what's the juice." On the other end was Dawn's sister, Theresa, and then you would hear, "Mom, it's Theresa," and for the next hour and often as long as two hours, depended on how much "catching-up" the two had to do, Dawn was on the phone. On this day the call was one of a more serious nature and would require a great deal of talk between J.P. and Dawn. Theresa and Dennis were having a great deal of trouble out their youngest son Nicodemus who was the same age as Patrick, soon to be fourteen, and needed help. The city life was taking its toll on Nicodemus. Poor grades in school, problems related to teachers and other students, resulting in suspensions, gang related connections on the street had driven both parents to make a major request to J.P. and Dawn. Would they take him in and get him through school? They felt that the change in environment would change his life style and attitude. They already knew before asking that Nico and J.P. would cross sabers because of the strict rules already in place in his home. They knew that was asking a great deal of Dawn and J.P. but they were at the end of their rope.

They were in hopes that they could save their son from the violence and crime that seemed to be attracting him like a moth to a flame, surely to be burned and his life destroyed. It would not be an easy task, as Dawn's mother had moved into the house with them only two years earlier, and that in itself was taking a toll on J.P. as well as Dawn, even though it was her mother. "Maw-maw", as J.P. referred to her, was not the easiest person in the world to live with. Gloria was set in her ways, very reluctant to change or adapt, reared in an Old Italian family, made for some difficult times in the O'Francis home.

J.P. loved his mother-in-law, make no mistake about that, but... as he would often talk to me about her, I could hear the tone of discontent and I could understand given his mother-in-law's background, and J.P.'s Irish background, how things could reach the boiling point. As he related the story to me, and how Nico made it into his home, I asked him why he would take on such an enormous task, being under the pressure and stress he was already under. His response did not surprise me, given the fact that I had learned a great deal about the man by that point. As he would so often do, he took a deep breath, and leaned over on the top rail of the deck, looked out over the short field leading into the forest, usually taking a puff or two off his cigar.

"Well, I did give it a lot of thought, and Dawn and I really hashed it over before I gave my okay. But it had to be under my terms, and I had helped so many teens that were not even related to me, adopted, or married into family, I guess is a better way of putting it. So, I decided that I could save one more teen heading for a jail cell or death, whichever came first."

The two families met in Dayton, Ohio at their cousin's home, Dennis and Theresa at Bernadette's house and J.P. and Dawn at Jean's house. After a long evening talk and drinks and food, and still mixed into the seriousness of the matter a lot of fun and laughter, jokes and the Kuntz craziness, of which J.P had habituated himself to over the years. The final test would come the next day with a meeting with the young "stud" and the uncle teacher.

J.P. and Nico went for a long walk along the banks of the Miami River. He laid out the rules to the young street-smart boy, or he thought he was the tough street hood. J.P. did not mix any words, he addressed him on an equal basis, and Nico found that the old, in his mind, man had some of the "street" in him. He was very surprised to learn that J.P. was not so "dumb" about "what is happening" as he had once thought. He agreed that he would abide by the rules of the O'Francis house, and that any deviation would result in some degree of punishment.

   While J.P. was off on his walk and talk to Nico, Dawn told her sister, even though they were extremely close, it would all be up to how Nico responded to their talk. The greatest fear that Theresa had was that they would return from their walk and J.P. would simply say, "no". He would have if he had not felt that he could save the boy, and she and Dennis both knew him well enough that he could and would say "no" if he did not feel that there was at least a chance for Nico. The city boy was headed for the country. The Stepenian family was very grateful.

❀ ❀ ❀ ❀

J.P. had given a great deal of thought to the new principal, Henry Stafford. He had at one time gotten along very well with him, but things seemed to have changed. Henry was not as stupid as people thought he was. He had, after going through a number of women in the school system, zeroed in on Rose Bassel, a P.E. teacher, with the personality of a sour dishrag. Her social upbringing in one of the three wealthiest families in Honsburg gave her an attitude of superiority over the rest of the people in the community as well as the school. She rarely spoke to J.P. the entire time he had been at the high school. Her years at the elementary school had not been pleasant for her colleagues, and they were happy to see her transferred to the high school.

Henry started his move on her in J.P.'s last two years of coaching. It took him all of about a snap of a finger to figure his move out. Political connections, money, equal power. He told Tim that he had no doubts that his move would pay in big dividends in the future. Little did J.P. know that the future would come so quickly. Henry had started to "turn" to the LaMar Marshy side of the game shortly after his marriage to Rose. J.P. did not trust him, but knew that he had to play the little game to a point, if he ever wanted to get back on the high school level of teaching and his coaching job back.

Therefore, off he went to pay an unannounced visit to Henry to discuss the new arrival into the O'Francis home, giving Henry a brief on Nicodemus, and requesting that he help in any professional way that he could. Letting him know if there were any problems, even the smallest of ones together they might head off some major disaster. Henry seemed to be very receptive to J.P. and assured him that he would help in any way.

As J.P. was ending the conversation, he congratulated him on his promotion and asked him if he could help him, and would he have any problems if J.P. put in a request to return to the high school level to teach. He also asked him if he had any problems with him putting in a request to return to the coaching ranks. Henry assured him that he had no problems with either request, and would accept him if the request was approved. He went one step further than J.P. had expected.

Just as O'Francis was at the door, Henry stated, "J.P. one more thing. I want you to know that I personally think you were a damn good teacher and a damn good coach. I have seen you at both positions first hand and I would attest to the fact. The problems that existed with you and Damon do not in any way reflect how I feel. I just want you to know that."

J.P. smiled, nodded his head up and down, and left.

It was the following week that J.P. learned that Henry had fired Richard Finkel from all his coaching positions and his A.D. position, notifying him that he needed to start looking for another teaching position, that he did not want him at his school at the beginning of the next school year.

# Ostracize

EMMANUEL ENTERED THE LIBRARY AND went to a table toward the back of the room. Several teachers were sitting at tables toward the front, with no one sitting at the two tables at the very back. As the rest of the faculty came into the room, they looked about the room and sat with each other as a group toward the front. Mrs. Beth Elkhart came in and walked back to where Emmanuel was seated.

"May I sit with you Manuel?" she asked.

"I don't mind at all, it doesn't look like anyone else wants to. Beth, I don't know if it would be a good ideal for you to sit with me."

Beth laughed. "I will sit where I choose Emmanuel. I know very well what is going on around here, and I want no part of it. It is very unprofessional, not to mention just plan rude!"

Beth had no more ended her statement to Emmanuel when Norberta walked back to their table. "Mrs. Elkhart I want you to sit up at that table there," pointing to the other teachers sitting at the front table.

"Mrs. Millicent I think I will sit here. It's a little crowded at that table and I do believe I can hear you quite well right where I am at."

"Mrs. Elkhart, I am not asking you to move, I am telling you!"

"Well, Mrs. Millicent, I am telling you that I am very comfortable right where I am. I am not a student at this school. I am a professional staff member with many more years of experience than you have. I expect to be treated as a veteran teacher as well as a professional teacher, not as a student."

Norberta wheeled and walked to the front of the room in a hostile manner. At that point Maggie Logger walked in and looking around the room, went to the table where Beth and Emmanuel were seated. Norberta glared at her but did not challenge her as she was the wife of the director of instruction for the county. She could tell that something was wrong when she sat down and looked at her two colleagues.

Emmanuel spoke. "Maggie, I don't know if is wise for you to sit with me. Beth has just received a verbal reprimand for being at this table."

Maggie looked toward the front of the room at the principal. "Say what?" she replied in astonishment.

"Well I am just telling you what has taken place."

"I mean I... why can't I or you sit where you want? The very idea is childish, my Lord! What is wrong with Norberta?"

"She does not want anyone to sit or associate with me. Now I am sure you are aware of that."

"Ohhh, Emmanuel." Beth was moving her head up and down, as Maggie looked at her. "Welll that is just total ludicrous. Emmanuel is a staff member just like all of us. I'll not be any part of anything like that."

Norberta Millicent put out to several people that Emmanuel's job was in jeopardy. She made sure that a call had been placed to his wife Nina Jeanette, who was the director of finance at one of the more prestigious private schools in the area. Jeanette of course became worried, and discussed it with Emmanuel over supper, of which he knew nothing about what she was talking about.

He had barely arrived at his school the next day when he was called to the office of Ms. Millicent, who wasted no time in attacking him with misuse of the phone again, of which he was not aware he had, other than a few calls he had made to his representative. She then accused him of allowing ex-students to visit him without her permission, which brought a quick and angry response.

"Look Ms. Millicent! I don't call these people and tell them to come by to see me, and I am very sorry you are so upset or maybe its jealousy, I really don't know. However, they are, have been and will always be welcome in my room! One other thing, why should it matter to you if I have ex-students come back to tell me of their success, or how they are doing in high school? I mean..."

"Look, I run this school, not you! YOU just don't seem to understand that, DO YOU MR. Reubin!"

"OH, yes ma'am, I really do understand you are in charge here. I have no problem being able to see right thought that. Madam, you have made it very clear to me as well as others that YOU ARE in full control of this school."

"And by-god, YOU, and a few others, had damn well better do exactly as I tell you! You WILL NOT use any phones at this school without my personal consent, do you understand that? Do you know MR. Reubin that your job is in jeopardy, do you know that?"

"No ma'am, I was not aware that I had done anything that would put my job in jeopardy."

He never mentioned that he was aware that "someone" had been calling his wife and telling her the same story.

It was after lunch that Emmanuel saw the DARE police officer coming up the hall.

"Hell-o, Manuel, what's with your principal?"

"I don't know, why?"

"Well hell, I just stopped by to be friendly and to let her know that I was in the building like I have been doing for...well, forever how long and she goes off on me. I mean Emmanuel. I may be in big trouble with the sheriff. SHIT, now you people may have to put up with that kind of un-professionalism, but by-god I don't and I damn sure told her so! Do you want me to do the DARE program as we have planned or not?"

Emmanuel stood at his door thinking. "Well, yes I guess? I mean we have been doing it for years now, why not?"

"I thought that, excuse me for putting it to you this way, that bitch, downstairs was not happy that I was here, and told me that she knew nothing about it, so I thought I had better check with you."

"You're right about the bitch part, and she was made well aware of the fact that you would be here on this date, two weeks ago, so that is a bunch of bull!"

That afternoon before Emmanuel left for the day, Norberta called him to her office.

"Mr. Reuben, I want to know who gave you the right to have the DARE police officer here today."

"You did."

"No, I DID NOT!"

"Yes ma'am, I informed you two weeks ago that he would be here to do his program for the fourth and fifth grades."

She rose quickly from her chair, her voice harsh in her attack on Reuben.

"I told you not to do anything without my personal approval, and you did not follow my orders! A letter will be placed in your file for insubordination!"

"Well, Ms. Millicent, you do what you think you have to. I am again telling you, you did tell me to go ahead and schedule the DARE program for this week."

"Do you have that in writing?" Emmanuel knew he had made the same mistake twice, as he did not have a letter from her so stating, a mistake he would not make again. He knew that he had been set up, but he was learning quickly, and he knew he would have to contact Dan and file a letter to counter the one she would put in his file.

# Hour Glass

THE PHONE RANG..."HELLO."

"Bruce, Brian here."

"Haaaaa... how'ya been lately."

"Bruce, I need a job done. Do you have some time?"

"Yes."

Bruce ran all security for all of Brian's hotels throughout the county, as well as several other large firms and businesses.

"My jet will be there, ahhh, let's say...tomorrow at 1500 hundred, can you make that?" There was a short pause. "Yes, no problem. What's the equipment?"

"Camera, all other information will be handed to you when you get there."

Bruce knew that all accommodations, a file and transportation along with a driver would be handled. This was not anything new for him, he worked side jobs for Brian many times over the many years he had known him and was at his disposal at a moment's notice. He also knew that a lot of "recon" work would go into any mission he had. He expected no mistakes, and over the years, Bruce had made none, and all missions had been a success. Bruce also knew his people would be called on later to finish the job. Rarely did he do any heavy work anymore. He had four professionals, who were masters at their jobs to do the physical labor. His job was to gather all information, plan the operation, and make the assignments.

The private jet taxied to a stop outside a hanger. A few minutes later, the door opened and emerging was a well-dressed gentleman in beige dress slacks, black turtleneck, a brown tweed jacket, tan and brown Italian made loafers. The six foot two, two hundred-thirty pound man stood at the bottom of the steps. His gray-white hair with some black still intertwined and receding hairlines on both sides that he now brushed straight back touched the top of his jacket on his neck. He had dark eyebrows and a full dark mustache tapering down each side of his lips with a tent of gray at the ends. He stood very erect and his dark skin seemed to display his entire head. His face was hard and expressionless as he watched the approaching car. It came to a stop three feet from him, the passenger window came down, "Welcome to the mountains." He learned down slightly, and peered into the car, and then a slight smile broke across his face. The trunk popped open and he put his two pieces of luggage in it and closed the lid. Within minutes they were on the interstate headed north.

Arrangements were made for him to stay at the Courtyard Marriott Suites. Paul took him to his room and then they walked fifty yards to O'Charley's restaurant for supper. After a few hours of bar time and several drinks, the schedule was set.

It was 0600 hours when they left the hotel. Their first stop on the tour was the area of Carl Decal's house. With a Cannon camera, and an assortment of lens, including a 500 mm lens he could take as many pictures covertly as he needed of the area roads, intersections, and businesses as well as individuals. He took several of the Decal house on all sides as well as the surrounding terrain as well as the street entering the rather lavish subdivision. At 0800 hours, Carl came out his front door and walked to get his paper, all the time the camera was clicking off pictures.

At 1000 hours, the garage door opened and Carl backed his silver BMW out of his garage and drove off. Giving some space between them, he clicked off several shots of his license plate, and in ten minutes, they arrived at Lowe's. As Carl walked toward the entrance, Bruce took several more pictures.

The following day, it was mid-afternoon before Carl and his wife emerged from their seven hundred thousand dollar home. They headed north in their tan four door Mercedes-Benz, traveled for a good hour and a half deep into the lush green mountains of the southern Appalachian Mountain Range.

Bruce spoke of the beauty of the mountains and asked about the strips of land carved out of the tops of the mountains. Even though Bruce knew what strip mining was he had never been in an area where it had actually taken place. Paul explained that it was known as strip mining and then elaborated on how and why it had at one time been a major source of money and had made a lot of people very rich in the 1970's through the 1980's.

Bruce opened a file. "I read this report on Mr. Decal last night. Now," He turned several pages and then ran his finger down the page, "Here, it says here he got out of education, ahhhh, in 1987, correct?"

As Paul drove, he paused in thought. "I believe that is correct."

"Well, now just why did this man continue to involve himself with O'Francis, and his efforts to better himself? I see nothing on O'Francis giving him cause...or is there something I should know?"

"No. O'Francis is clear on that part."

"Well Paul, it really did not make a damn to me. I don't know any of these people. I'm here to assess, and make sure the job will be done correctly. Don't give a damn who did what to whom! Not my call, you know that."

"Well Bruce I know, and as to the why on Decal, I really don't know. J.P. was never a threat to him and his little power structure. He just wanted to be part of J.P.'s fall and disgrace his name I guess. I do know that he did not like him."

"Why?"

"Basically because he could not control J.P. and J.P. would not kiss his ass, and place him on some high god-like pedestal like everyone else did. Some kind of ego trip he was on. He was one of those people who worked in the backdrop, using others, the weak and stupid, to do his dirty work for him."

"I can see by this report that it cost O'Francis a rather high price, not in dollars per-say, by our standards. And by the way, are these figures correct?"

"Now which figures are you talking about?"

"The ones on this man's salary?"

"You mean J.P.'s salary?"

"Yes, here on page ten of your report, you stated what he made and lost as a family."

"Yes, the figures are on the mark." A rather long pause in their conversation, as Bruce looked out the window, and then back at the figures on the pages in front of him and then back out the window. Paul drove the mountain road, then looked over at him.

"Something bothering you Bruce?"

He slowly closed the file. "Well yes, matter of fact it is." A thirty-second pause. "I had forgotten what it was like not to have money. This guy, O'Francis I mean, shit...this man don't or didn't have a pot to piss in! He is a teacher? I mean I thought,"

Paul interrupted, "You thought that teachers made more money than that, correct?"

"Correct."

"You have been out of touch with the lower middle income people of the world Bruce. Look, I really did not know either. I was working a case and, well, came in contact with J.P. by pure accident, literally! Our world, and his...Christ, man...well they are a planet apart, believe me. You just are not used to the common people and nor was I. We have been involved in the upper political and business world of high finance, and it really is an eye opener to step down to this world." Then there was another short pause as Bruce looked out at the mountain scenery.

"As to what he has lost, well...yes, in some people's eyes, it may not mean much, but to J.P. it meant a lot. See...well, you must understand something here...J.P. lived by a code, that really just doesn't fit in this day and time. Hell, for that matter it did not fit in the 70's, 80's or the 90's. J.P.

is a rare breed of a man and that is why, as trivial as it may seem, that is why you are here. He is not, nor has he ever been, an important person, politically or business wise. But, for some reason," then he paused in thought, as Bruce Beck had changed lenses and snapped some more pictures, this time of some of the landscape. "He touches people and has affected their lives in the simplest ways. Never asked for anything in return, other than, just let him alone to do his job. J.P.'s problem was he was too honest and too damn candid. He just could not play the political game in Reynolds County, which there is some very bad people there that hurt innocent people. He and his family being one."

"Okay, how is it that one teacher make so little and you have this Decal person living in a half million dollar plus home in a multi-million dollar sub-division?"

"Don't get the two confused. Decal got his money from his wife. Her father left it to her. Her father was in the mining business and made a lot of money. Carl Decal really did not have to teach. He could have lived off his wife's money."

"Then why did he choose to give O'Francis a hard time?"

"Well, the best I can figure he just did not like him, as I have stated. He felt he was a threat to his over inflated ego. Basically Decal is a real ass-hole! I have followed his work and his efforts to character assassinate O'Francis for several years. He did a real job on him."

"And people believed this Decal?" Bruce asked with a surprised sound to his voice.

"He is smooth. He is about as spineless as they come. His mouth is more dangerous than a cocked pistol."

Bruce had laid the file down on the seat between them.

"Not that it matters, but is O'Francis some type of little college book worm?"

Paul laughed. "No. No, by no means! I realize you're just here to do a job and you are just curious, but he is nothing like that."

Paul then briefed him on a few points of J.P. and his military background, his obsession with the martial arts, and his love for teaching and helping teens, his effort to change his life, and put his past behind him. He included a few items of his coaching as part of his teaching.

Bruce listened intently and when Paul finished he just grunted and said, "Hmmmmm, I see. Sounds like a man who could have been one of us? Any connection to Brian?"

He changed lenses again and bringing his camera up to his eye and focusing in on the home the Decal's had arrived at, snapped off several pictures of Carl and his wife getting out of the car and the house as well as the surrounding area.

"Very interesting, this J.P. is. Very interesting."

They then drove back to the city and continued to talk about some of the people on the list, and how many times he would have to return to the area before all the pieces were in place. They arrived back at the hotel, and as Bruce was getting out of the car, bending down at the waist with his right hand on the top of the opened door and looking back into the car, he asked, "I'll see you for dinner, correct?"

"Yes, let's make it around eight. I have some work I need to do."

"Okay, ahhh, Paul... is J.P. and Brian related?"

Paul paused as he looked out the front window and then back at Bruce. "I really don't know." Bruce never moved, as there was a ten-second pause in their conversation. "Bruce that is something I really think you and Brian should talk about. I mean it is not my place to discuss that."

Bruce nodded his head in an affirmative manner, closed the door, and walked to the entrance of the hotel.

# Tottering Rock

J.P. ARRIVED AT HIS THERAPIST'S office at precisely 1400 hours, something the therapist noted. He was never late, nor had he ever missed an appointment. He adhered to a strict schedule in his life, and appeared, to operate in an extremely orderly manner. The receptionist buzzed his doctor, and she walked out of her office and greeted him in a warm and friendly manner. Being the alert person she was she could tell that on this day he was not in the best "frame of mind." She had put J.P. on Xanax for the past four months, and he had been more relaxed, but was still having more sleepless nights than she liked. His mood had improved greatly from the first time she had seen him, he did at least appear to be more stable. The last thread of his sanity was at least not stretched to its max, and being tattered to the point of breaking. But Dr. Celia Flora wanted him on solid ground, as she knew it would take very little for him to break. J.P. did have one good thing going in his favor, he would follow her instructions to the letter, and that was a major point in saving him.

His sessions would never go in any one direction, she found him to be a very complex man, with lots of anger and hate bottled up in him, and it had been slow getting it out. He oftentimes would look at her with mistrust, and question her reason for posing any one question. Celia Flora found that J.P. had little if any trust for the female gender. She discovered that he felt that they were the most dangerous animal on earth even more than that of the male gender, which he did not trust any more, but feared the female more than the male. His paranoia made it harder for her to extract the source of the pain that existed in his mind, some of which had been lying dormant for many years, and had been activated by the evilness that he now had to face, and he had but one way, in his mind, how to fight it and that was not an acceptable norm.

She found him very intriguing and a challenging patient. He would never start a conversation with her, everything she got came from a question, which would lead him into talking and even often times, not always but often, answered with a question. Then he would just stop, as if some computer chip keyed a program that stopped him from continuing along the path he had been traveling. She would then have to pose another question and often a series of questions to get his "computer" clicking again and then he would talk some more. Often times his emotions were over powering, and he would cover a wide array of subjects, some very "deep" philosophically. She began to understand after a lengthy period of time why her patient did not fit the norms of the area.

As he entered her office there were two large generously padded cushiony medium blue chairs with an ottoman in front of one, a sofa with an overstuffed back and heavily padded arms, which made it look more like one's living room. Her desk was a rather large one made of light oak. The chair she sat in was a high backed style made of light tan leather. The room was done in warm colors of light blue and cream, with pictures of the Aztec Indians, depicting happy family life pictures. Celia Flora was not Native American, but of the Philippine ancestral heritage, but she liked the history of the Aztec people.

J.P. took a seat, on the far right hand part of the sofa. He never sat in the same piece of furniture repeatedly. Celia Flora once asked him if he would like to sit in her chair, and he accepted, which did not surprise her.

"J.P., how has your week been?"

"Ahhh, about the same."

"Have you been sleeping well?"

"No, not really."

"Are you taking your medicine nightly?" J.P. did not respond, instead looked at her as if to say, "That is a stupid question, of course I have!"

"Before we get started I want you to try some natural medicines I have mixed for you myself. Here is a pamphlet telling you what is in it and where it comes from as well as what it will do for you."

As she handed it to him she continued, "Now, if you run out, I want you to come by here and let one of the girls working out front know, and they will refill it for you."

J.P. was looking at the little three inch, tall, dark brown glass bottle, about the circumference of a dime, then at the paper she had given him, along with an eye dropper.

"Now I want you to take five drops of this and place it under your tongue twice a day, when you first get up and thirty minutes before you go to bed, okay, J.P.?"

He looked up. "Okay." Then he paused before continuing. "Do you still want me to take the pills?"

"Yes. How is your supply?"

"I have half a bottle still yet."

"Now tell me why you think you are not sleeping well. You should be by this point be getting a full night's sleep."

"Well, I am not." Then off the wall he stated, "Why do you not have any pictures of any Aztec warriors on your walls? You know that they were mighty warriors?"

"Yes J.P. I do know that. As to why I don't have any of the warriors on the walls is because I want a pleasant and happy environment in my office."

Celia Flora continued her line of questions. "Are you having nightmares or can you just not sleep?"

He did not answer for a good minute, and she sat and waited. She knew that it was a test for her, as most people cannot sit in a room in silence, especially if they have been in a conversation with another person. She found J.P. to be good at not talking when others thought he should or would. His face broke with a slight smile.

"A little of both, sometimes the dream weaver is good to me...".

"The what?"

"The dream weaver, sometimes he takes away the pain, sometimes he does not. The dream weaver, do you not know who the dream weaver is?"

Dr. Flora just sat and looked at J.P. saying nothing, not sure exactly what he was talking about. J.P. let it go and did not carry the conversation any further, too much explaining for him to do, especially on this particular day.

In the four months she had been seeing him she had never asked him to go into the details of his military combat experience. The eight months prior to Dr. Celia Flora, he had been seeing a counselor who was in business with her. He had reached an impasse with J.P. and felt that it was time for her to go deep with him. His report was based on his problems with the people with whom he had to deal with in his teaching profession. Robert Caan had written in his file,

*James Patrick O'Francis is a very strong willed person, with deep seeded problems; he suffers from depression and has distrust for all human kind. He is extremely devoted to a spiritual being, of which is not remotely connected to any set religion. He has never revealed a name to such a Being. He seems to be having enormous difficulties with the dishonor and mendacity of the people he must work with and for. He has, up to this point, talked very little about his military experience, but I feel that he is suffering from Post Dramatic Stress Disorder. He is devoted to his two sons and it appears that he adores his wife. Has a very stable marriage. Other than a few normal marriage problems, his is a lasting marriage that is strong enough to overcome any problems that may arise between the two. I find that if he is committed to something, or has made promises, he will go to any lengths to either keep or complete whatever it is. I find that he is extremely candid, and at this point very honest in his responses. I feel that this could be part of his problem, in relation to his job. It has been very difficult to get him to open up and he has to be prodded in order to get him to talk.*

"J.P. tell me about your dreams."

" Ah yes, the dream weaver, have you ever heard the song, The Dream Weaver?"

"No J.P. I do not believe I have."

"Well it fits me to a tee; you should listen to it."

"Tell me about the latest one that woke you."

He avoided the question and asked a question, "Doctor, have you ever had an out of body experience?"

"No I have not."

"Okay, do you believe that such an event can happen?"

"Yes I do."

"Have you ever had anyone come to you with such an occurrence?'

"No I haven't."

"Wellll...you have now."

Then he paused again, for a long thirty- second count. Changed the subject matter and left his doctor hanging. He proceeded to tell an event that had occurred at his home concerning three members of a local church out recruiting. After finishing his story, O'Francis got up and walked to the other side of the room, pivoted sharply, then said, "Now keep in mind Doc,"

Then his voice turned to a bitter discussion, with hand jesters that would indicate a degree of agitation. "These are the intelligent ones. Of course they quickly denied believing in incest, concerning the "Adam and Eve" fracture fairy tale. WHYYYYY, that is against Goddddd, law!" His voice rose. He paced back and forth across the room, using his hands as if he were directing some great symphony, his voice lecturing as if he were in an advanced college class on Philosophy and Religion.

He stopped at the far end of the room and looked at Celia Flora. "Now you are really going to love this. As sincere as they could be they responded. I asked them, in response to all the questions in which they could not answer, what would happen to anyone who did not believe in their religion. And they stated, they will go to hell. At that I asked them to leave in a rather abrupt and rude manner."

"J.P., tell me about your out of body experience." As Celia Flora tried to get back on track with her client.

"No."

"Are you happy now?"

"NO!"

"Why?"

"Because!" She waited. She did not repeat the word "Because" and add why as most people would do when someone states because, and J.P. waited for her to ask.

When he saw she was not going to do the norm, he continued, "Because I am feeling hate at the moment and I will tell you what I think you want me to say. I want to strike out at the people who have been attacking my family and me! Point of fact is I would get GREAT satisfaction out of putting them through what the Viet Cong would do to some of their own people, just to extract information from them. Ohhhhh, man, could I ever get off on doing that!"

She could see and feel the anger in him. It had permeated the room when he spoke. He then got up and started pacing once again. J.P. moved with power, his back straight, and his head up always looking directly at his doctor. His voice had a powerful tone to it. He would have been intimidating in his movements and tone of voice to most people. Commanding, forceful, each of his words striking fear in whomever he might be talking to. Doctor Celia Flora watched him intently as he went through his venting.

"You have no idea what I can do to these bastards! These people are the very essence of evil! I really mean that! I can see it in them and I can feel it in their presence when I have to be around them. They do not like me because I... know what they are! Ooh, yes, I know!" At that point J.P. paused, giving her a chance to speak.

"J.P. I want you to try to think of happy things in your life when you get these feelings, or you have a bad dream. We have not talked about your dreams, but we can do that at another time." He stood at the far end of the room, very erect and silently looking at Doctor Celia Flora.

"Okay, I will try. But I will leave today by telling you that I really enjoy thinking about what I can do to these, these, ass-holes!" Then his voice softened. "For lack of another word at the present."

"I know, but try anyway, for me. Now J.P., I will be honest with you. We have a long way to go, and you will have to help me help you. You will have to try the things I have asked of you if you are to get back on stable ground. I will not bull-shit you, I will be up front and straight with you."

O'Francis just looked at her, with a question all over his face, doubt reeking from every part of him. She knew that she would have to prove herself to him, if she was going to help him.

"Take your medicine, and I will see you in two weeks." He looked at her as if something was wrong, as each week he had been seeing someone concerning his mental condition.

"Yes two weeks. I have my reasons."

J.P. did not verbally question her reasons.

# New Role in Life

J.P. HAD BEEN ASKED TO serve on the teaching association's salary committee. Emmanuel was appointed the chair of the committee. He had amassed a large folder of paperwork with lots of numbers and lots of figures. The two poured over the numbers trying to make some logical sense out of what lay in front of them. After several pots of coffee and fourteen hours of work they found they could not account for some three hundred thousand dollars. Not being certified CPAs they were very much aware that they could have easily misinterpreted some of the numbered accounts and the entire cross references they had. Since there was no real line item, they had no way of knowing what went where.

The following day was a Monday and the two requested more information from the "Fuhrer's" headquarters concerning some of the accounts and the monies that accompanied the accounts, as several had the same numbers but with different amounts. They were stonewalled, and were denied the requested information. Now for J.P., not being a math person per-say, but being very logical, and knowing what he did know about LaMar Marshy, it threw up a red flag. The superintendent was always reporting that they just did not have the money for this or for that, especially when it came to the lowly teachers' salary, and even lower on the "pecking" order was the support staff, of which the school system could not operate without but in all reality did not care one way or the other about.

J.P. was just getting his "feet" wet when it came to the business of the teachers' association and its battle with the school system, so he said very little but listened and learned, as he was a very fast learner. He had a gift of remembering details, what people would say, or do, or where they were and what they wore, who they were with, times events took place. Uncle Sam had trained him well, and over the years he was very grateful. He was at least able to use some of his training in civilian life. If his lower education had taught him as well as his military, he would have been better balanced, but as it was he was weak in his English grammar and spelling, and only slightly above average in his higher mathematical ability. A handycap he was very self-conscience of, but he was slowly finding that Emmanuel was accepting him for what he was, his candidness, his integrity, as well as his shortcomings.

On the other side of the pancake, as J.P. would so often say, Emmanuel was extremely good at Math and English and the two appeared to have made a connection and was quickly becoming closer the more they worked together. But he had made up his mind he was not going to make the same mistake he had made while teaching on a high school level and aliening himself so closely to any one individual that he did not see what was coming. He was not going to be used like he had been in the past.

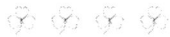

It was a Saturday and J.P. was working on repairing his privacy fence that was separating the road from the back part of his home. Patrick and Nico were helping, although as teenagers they really did not want to do the manual labor it took to re-dig the three post holes and replace them with new pressure treated posts and replace the two sections of fencing that needed to be replaced. They were putting forth what would be considered their best effort.

There had been a call for the County Sheriff to send a deputy to a neighbor's house as some lady had been creating what was considered a disturbance. Of course the neighbor who called, the Jamisons, Rob and Kitty, themselves did not have their pancake cooked in the middle, especially Kitty. J.P. did not get along with them at all, as Kitty had a mouth that would not stop, and as he described it by using the Stone's lyrics, "start me up…" and spread more rumors and did more gossiping than a tabloid newspaper. She had gone through the sub-division and the little town, especially her church group, telling what a poor teacher J.P. was and how he was not fit to teach the children, making statements that the reason so many students came to his house was that he was dealing in drugs, and would allow them to get drunk at his home. Being in a small town, it did not take long for the grapevine of slander to reach the ears of the O'Francis house.

With the reputation of being a leach on society, by drawing a paycheck from the federal government, Rob claiming some back problem, but was able to bow hunt in the fall of the year when deer season came around, did not sit well with J.P. as he hated people who was able to work and yet robbed Social Security of the money he as well as the other working class people were pouring into the system which he most likely, when it came time for him and Dawn to apply for, would not be there. He also had an opinion of the legislative branch of our government, which was that the legislators were totally oblivious to what was occurring in the world of the commoners. He became used to the gossip and mendacity that the people of Honsburg habitually practiced but never accepted it and it "rubbed" him wrong and usually made for a few days of being in an ill mood, as he knew there was nothing he could do about it.

The deputy that arrived on the scene was Ross Tipton, who knew J.P. as a coach and knew that he had worked for the Sheriff's department at one time, walked across the street to where he was working and inquired as to what seemed to be the problem. J.P. informed Ross what he had observed as well as heard. Ross left and in a short time after taking care of business he returned to where O'Francis was working to have a non-business conversation with him. As they spoke of the school problems and the coaching problems the Honsburg High School was having, J.P. noticed a Masonic ring on his finger.

"Ross, I was not aware that you were a Mason. My father-in-law was a Mason. Well for that matter all his brothers were, and I think, ahhh, now let me think for a minute. I believe that several of Dawn's cousins are." He then reached down with his hand to the ring Ross wore and requested to take a closer look at it.

"Nice, how does one become a Mason?" Before Ross could answer, J.P. continued.

"You know I have always wanted to belong to the Masons, just never seemed to find the time with coaching and teaching. But now that I am out of coaching and it appears for good, but that is another story."

Ross interjected. "I hope not, I want you back in baseball, we really need you. Hell J.P. it just ain't the same since you left. The team has lost something. Tim just doesn't seem to have that "something" that you seem to have that the players related too. And the teams are missing something, really can't put my finger on it, but the boys are not quite the same anymore. Don't get me wrong here. I think Tim is a good coach. But since you have been removed from his staff, the teams are not as sharp as they were. They seem to be lacking something."

"Welllll, Ross, I really do not know what will become of all this. I know that I have done no wrong. I just did not play my fiddle the way "they" wanted me to, if you get my drift?"

"They, who are they?"

"Hmmm, well, Ross, I really do believe that you would be extremely surprised at who belongs to the "They" club."

At that the dispatchers called for him on his radio, and he had to leave. J.P. finished his fence then finished the remaining daylight hours alone with his usual over exhausting workout in his karate.

It was nine o'clock that evening and a knock came from his front door. It was Ross and a gentleman named Vernon Story.

"Hi Coach, may we come in?" J.P. opened the door and welcomed the two men into his home. Coach you asked me this afternoon how one becomes a Mason. Well you asked the right question. Here are a couple of forms for you to fill out. Just follow the instructions and answer all the questions, attach the proper fee to the papers, and give it back to me or Vernon."

"And that is it?" J.P asked.

"Well, no, not exactly, there will be an investigation of you, and a report submitted to the other Masons, and a vote taken. Then if you are approved, then we will start your road to becoming a Mason."

"Okay, sounds fair enough to me. I have always heard that a Mason's word is as good as it can get. So I will fill these out and have them back to you in a few days." The two men bid J.P. and Dawn a good evening and left.

# The Legal Game

HOLLY SET UP THE TIME for the deposition for both Damon Bales and Richard Finkel, and J.P. arrived at the attorney's office thirty minutes before the time of the deposition. Holly pulled him aside.

"Now J.P., I want you to sit and say nothing. You can't. If you want me to ask something, write it down and pass it to me. Look, they will say things that will get you upset. Do not show your emotions. Let me deal with them. We will review all they say later, okay?"

J.P. had never been in a deposition, and he was not really ready for what he would hear, but he would do what Holly requested. He instantaneously put his mind on a major self-control mode, preparing himself for the worst, and it came.

In the course of the next four hours he would hear more lies and more denials than he had ever heard in any one period of time, all under oath. The one thing that struck him about the court system was the fact that the words, swear to God, probably not to the same god that J.P. talked to and believed in, but they swore to whatever god they paid homage to, that the truth would be told. So much for the legal system and the swear thing. O'Francis felt it was the height of hypocrisy.

J.P. laughed to himself on several occasions when Holly redirected questions she had asked earlier in the deposition, and got different answers. He found it to be very odd that Richard stated he was not afraid, nor was he intimidated by the conversation he had with J.P. on the morning in question. J.P. thought to himself as Holly went on, *"Well, dumb-ass, if that is the case then why did you take the story to Bales?"*

Holly did come back to the fact that it had not bothered Richard Finkel and did ask, "Mr. Finkel if this confrontation with Mr. O'Francis did not intimidate you as you have so stated, and you were not in fear of your health or your life, then why did you take the event that took place on the date in question to Mr. Bales?"

Richard twisted and turned in his seat, not like before when he had puffed up his chest like a big toad and played the macho man for Holly.

"I really don't know. I guess, well I thought he should know."

"Well, Mr. Finkel if it was that important why did you wait five days before you brought this to the attention of Mr. Bales?"

"Well, I really did not have time."

"According to your statement to Mr. Bales you feared for your well-being. And you are telling me that you did not have time."

"Well Mr. Bales was not at school on the days I was there. Or I was absent when he was there."

"I see. Well tell me Mr. Finkel, do you have a phone?"

"Well yes I do."

"Okay, does Mr. Bales have a phone?"

"I suppose he does."

"You suppose he does."

"Well, yes I mean I have never been in his house."

"Have you ever had an occasion to call Mr. Bales at his home after school hours?"

There was along paused before Richard answered.

"Mr. Finkel, you might want to think about how you are going to answer that question very carefully."

"Well, yes I have called him at home."

"If the events at the service station were so life threatening to you, and you and Mr. Bales could not see each other at school, then why didn't you pick up the phone and call him?"

"Ahhh, I don't know. Don't guess I thought of it."

When it came to Damon, J.P. found it odd that if J.P. was considered such a terrorist and that the two felt that their lives were in jeopardy, why did it take Richard a week to get around to telling Damon about the incident? Damon of course had a loss of memory on many questions but now when it came to his typing the letter, he could remember that and even went so far as to tell Holly how many words a minute he could type and how many he could type when he was in high school, as if he was bragging about his ability. All that did not impress Holly. Damon admitted sending the letter to the School Board, Superintendent, and all the various law enforcement agencies in the area.

When asked why he sent the letters, he responded, "Ms. Donatello," always drawing out the Ms. Part, "Terrorist acts have been conducted against me. He has threatened Mr. Finkel. We feared for our lives and that of other teachers in the school. They feared for their lives."

"Mr. Bales, could you please name some of the other teachers that have come to you concerning any of these alleged terrorist acts?"

"Welllll, Msss. Donatello, at the moment I really can't recall."

"You can't recall that a teacher in your school came to you and reported that an act of terrorism had taken place?"

"That is correct."

"Did you not write it down?"

"I really don't recall that."

"Do you know for a fact that any or all of these so called terrorist acts involved Mr. O'Francis?"

"Wellll, nowww, I really feeel that they do."

"But Mr. Bales, I asked you if you had any facts to back up your statement that terrorist acts allegedly committed against you and as you say others, including Mr. Finkel, were committed by Mr. O'Francis."

"Mssss. Donatello, I believe they could have very easily been!"

"Then if you were in such fear for your lives, why did you and Mr. Finkel wait so long to create this letter, now in front of you, and send it out to the various organizations in which you have done?"

Another dance around the mulberry tree, never giving a complete and straight answer to her question. He could not remember certain events or conversations he was involved in or what he did a matter of a few months or a short few years earlier concerning J. Patrick O'Francis. Holly hammered them hard and found lots of flaws in their answers but when it came to naming all the parents that had filed complaints against J.P. he could not recall any names.

J.P. felt his attack on his coaching was a major mistake.

"Mr. Bales, I really would like for you to at least give me just one name of a parent or even an umpiring official that has filed any complaint against my client. That you say have been filed."

"Ms. Donatello I have had many calls from parents and from umpires filing complaints against Mr. O'Francis."

"Give me an example of some of these complaints."

"His conduct on the field."

"Would you be more specific?"

"I don't really recall what they told me at this time but they called and complained how he conducted himself on the field."

"What were the names of the umpires that called and filed these alleged complaints?"

"Ahhhh, I really do not recall their names at this time."

"Will you recall their name later?"

"I may."

"Well, Mr. Bales, when you recall, I want a copy of all complaints as well as the names of the people filing the complaints."

She looked toward his attorney. He nodded in compliance.

J.P. knew that if any complaints had been filed against him, they would have to go through the commissioner and that there would be a record of the complaint in detail. He also knew that he would have been called into the office of the commissioner if any had been filed. So another lie, only this time the Reynolds County political machine did not control the commissioner. He could not be bought off, and would if called, tell the truth.

A slight pause in Holly's questions as she looked through a few notes she had made. As she leafed through notes, silence permeated the room.

Then out of his mendacious mouth, "Ms. Donatello, I have had so many parents come to me on NUMEROUS occasions and request that Mr. O'Francis be removed as a coach that it is really difficult for me to recall them all. Why, several asked if I could have him removed from the school as a teacher."

Holly asked, "What reasons would they give?"

Damon took in a deep breath and let it out as if he was tired of all the questions. "They claimed that he was rude to them, he was unfair to their sons, that he used bad language all the time. That he did not believe in God. His teaching methods were not suited for this area."

J.P. had to sit and take the verbal assault, his abdomen muscles were as tight as the top of a drum, the temples of his head throbbed in pain, his jaws hurt from the pressure of gritting his teeth. Damon repeated himself several times trying to drive home how many parents complained.

"Just how many complaints were there?" Holly asked.

"There were lots"

"Well how many is a lot Mr. Bales?"

"Well as I have stated there were so many that I can't recall."

"With that many you surely wrote them down?"

"Well, some. I think."

"You think. Mr. Bales? You are an experienced principal and you are sitting there telling me that you think you may have written some of these complaints down from ever how many of these phantom parents and umpiring officials?"

"Wellll, Ms. Donatello, I think there were at least one hundred."

"One hundred. Is that correct? Is that what you are stating for the record?"

"Yes, at least. There could have been more. There were so many I just can't recall."

Holly's voice became very hard, and rose slightly. "You mean to sit there and tell me that there were one hundred people who complained to you about Mr. O'FRANCIS and you can't remember ONE name! YOU can't name ONE person!"

"Ahhhhh, Welllll...maybe one."

"Well Mr. Bales?"

"Ahhh, well there was Mr. and Mrs. McNelson. Yes, now there is one." As he arrogantly addressed J.P.'s attorney.

"Does their son play for Mr. O'FRANCIS?"

He put a smirk grin on his face. "Well, they play for Mr. Harper. Mr. O'FRANCIS is not the coach."

"Are you telling me that Mr. O'Francis does not coach?"

"No-no, he just helps Mr. Harper. He had no authority when it comes to coaching."

Holly quickly snapped back before he could think, "Did Mr. Harper ever come to you and file any complains or suggest that Mr. O'Francis be removed from his coaching position?"

"Wellllll, noowwww, Mssssss. Donatello, Mr. Harper and Mr. O'Francis are good friends."

"I did not ask you if they were good friends. I asked you if Mr. Harper had ever, at any time, come to you and ask to have Mr. O'Francis removed as his assistant, for whatever reason?"

"I really don't recall."

"You don't recall. You are the principal of the school and you have a head coach running a baseball program and you are telling me that you have all these parents coming to you and not to the head coach, complaining about Mr. O'Francis and you don't recall Mr. O'Francis' immediate supervisor in the sport in which he is assisting, bringing even one of these numerous complaints to your attention?"

"Yes, that is what I am saying, I don't recall. He may have, I just don't recall exactly when and what the complaint was."

"So, now you think that Mr. Harper, the head of the baseball program, did file at least one complaint against Mr. O'Francis? Is that your statement Mr. Bales?"

"Yes. Maybe more than one. But I can't recall just how many."

"What was the complaint Mr. Bales?"

"Msss. Donatello, I really don't recall what it was about."

"Did Mr. Harper ever come to you and ask to have Mr. O'Francis removed as his assistant?" Damon paused a long time before answering. "Well," as he drew out the word, "He may have once."

"He may have?"

"Yes."

"When?"

"Ahhh, I really don't recall at the moment."

"Mr. Bales, did any other coaches, who Mr. O'Francis worked with, ever file a complaint with you concerning anything Mr. O'Francis may or may not have done?"

"Welll, yes."

"Who and what was the complaint?"

"Ahhh, I think the head football coach requested that he be removed as his assistant."

"You think?"

"Yes."

"Are you sure?"

"Yes, I believe I am."

"What was the reason he gave?" Holly paused, looked back in her notes, and then continued,

"Who is the head football coach?"

"That would be Coach Hobart."

"His first name please, for the record."

"Oh, ahhh, Dave."

"Thank you. Now, what was his reason for requesting that Coach O'Francis be removed from his staff?"

"The same as Mr. Harper's."

"Which was."

"I think I have stated that."

"No Mr. Bales you have not. Now what was the reason given by Mr. Hobart and Mr. Harper for removing Coach O'Francis from their staff?" Another long pause, too long for Holly. "Mr. Bales, your answer?"

"Oh yes. Ahhh, I think it was because he could not be controlled. He used misappropriate language."

"Explain what you mean by Mr. O'Francis could not be controlled."

"I have no idea."

"Mr. Bales, you have two head coaches telling you that one of their assistances cannot be controlled and you never asked as to what they meant? What specifically they were referring to when they came to you about his allegedly being out of control?

"I don't recall."

"Mr. Bales, did you make any notes concerning these meetings you had with the two coaches in which Mr. O'Francis worked under?"

"Wellll, yes."

"Do you have these documentations with you at the time?"

"No I do not."

She looked at his attorney and requested a copy of all the notes on the meeting Bales had allegedly had concerning O'Francis and his conduct.

"Mr. Bales, anything else that you might recall concerning the conduct of Mr. O'Francis as to why he was requested to be removed by his two superiors?"

"I am sure that there was Ms. Donatello. But at the moment I just don't recall."

"How many games has Mr. O'Francis won?"

"Mssss. Donatello, I don't know. To my knowledge he hasn't won any! He is not the head coach! He is given NO credit for any wins!"

"Okay, Mr. Bales. How many has he helped Mr. Harper win?"

"I have no idea."

"Well, have they had a winning season since you have been the principal at Honsburg high school?"

"I really don't recollect."

"So Mr. Bales, for the record you are stating that Mr. O'Francis has not assisted in whatever wins or loses that Mr. Harper may have?"

"That is correct."

"So then he really is not assisting Mr. Harper in coaching?"

"Welll, he may be kind-of helping him a little, but as for Mr. Harpers record, I really do not think that Mr. O'Francis had much to do with it."

Then out of nowhere Bales stated, "I think I may have all the complaints on file."

"You have them on file? Where are these files?"

"I my file cabinet."

"Where is this cabinet located?"

"Ahh, at the school."

"So do you have any of these files with you today?"

"No."

Holly looked at Mr. Curtis Feinstein who was seated to Damon's right. "Mr. Feinstein, have you any of these files?"

"No."

"Have you seen any of these files?"

"No."

"I am requesting for the record that you get me a copy of these files that have the list of complaints and the names of the people who have filed the complaints. No matter what type of paper it may be written on."

He nodded his head up and down.

Something she would never get, even with a written request to the judge asking for all files, letters, and notes, any scrap of paper that might have anything dealing with J.P.'s name on it.

J.P. never asked Holly, after the deposition, if she could feel the evil presence in the room as he was afraid that she would think that he had lost all the "marbles" out of his bag. He could tell just by the way she handled herself that she was a hard core attorney and he could tell, come trial time, Damon Bales would not be able to withstand her hard questions, that she would trap him in his own lies and she would break him. He did not like females that were professionals and it surfaced in his tone of voice and body language. He was just glad Holly Donatello was his attorney and not Bales' and Finkel 's.

He went home and fixed himself several stiff double scotches and tried hard to block out all that he had heard. Even with a half a fifth gone by bed time, he got little sleep and his warrior instinct surfaced in its full capacity, leaving him mentally drained and totally exhausted by morning.

# Detecting Evil

J.P.'s TRIP TO DR. CELIA Flora came at the appropriate time. In the course of their talk he told his psychologist about the deposition and what he saw and felt. Then J.P. asked her if she felt if that was possible. He never really knew if she was telling him the truth, or just patronizing him, but she agreed that there were some people that could detect evil when in their presence and that he could have a special gift for just that. She did warn him that in having such a gift, it could be a curse, and that he had to be very careful about how he used it. Dr. Celia Flora sat in her chair in silence for several minutes.

"J.P.," she stated slowly, "Evil is out there, and IF you can detect it in other people you cannot let them know. You will be in danger, as well as your family. Evil is not something to take lightly. It can come in all kinds of forms, and portrays itself as being pure and very deceiving to the majority of the people. You tell me that you pray to the Blessed Mother."

J.P. paused, as if she was about to be critical of his beliefs. "Yes, I do. I also ask My Master for help as well as Saint Michael."

"Why Saint Michael?" she asked.

After a short pause, he responded, "Well, now, let us just say for the sake of this conversation, that all that I believe in actually exists. Now I do not know for sure that any of it does. But for the sake of conversation, we will say that it does, okay. Now to the Michael, Archangel aspect. Because he is a warrior, or so I have been told when I was a child by my mother and by the church. He knows what it is like to be in battle. I personally need someone who can protect me and counsel me when I am in battle. That is what I believe, at the moment at any rate."

"Do you believe that these spirits help you?"

With not a moment's hesitation he responded, "Yes! It goes beyond belief, I know for a stone cold fact they do. Look, I really do not know if there is a spirit called the Blessed Mother, or for that matter if there is a spirit called Saint Michael. I mean hell, "Doc" I am an educated person. I know that 95 % of what the Catholic Church has put out over the millenniums is crap. But for me I believe in Spirits, I believe in a spiritual world, I believe in other dimensions, I believe in multi-universes. So as far as these names we have attached to spirits are whatever one wants to label them with. For me it is whoever they might be, they and again, the "they" is something I cannot explain, aid and assist me and have for many years now."

"Then I would recommend that you request to the "Blessed Mother," and to, as you say, your Master, as well as to "Saint Michael" that they help you daily and J.P., if you so choose to change the name, that too is okay." A period of silence engulfed the room.

"Okay "Doc." Do you believe in the "Blessed Mother" and or, what is perceived to us and has been programmed into our childhood minds as the "Blessed Mother?"

"Yes J.P. I do. I too was raised with the "Blessed Mother" in my house, and yes, I do say my rosary, as I am sure you have from time to time. You know you can be very educated, and you can still question how the spirit world works, it is not a sin. Don't ever feel bad, or get on a guilt trip, if you don't have all the answers. There are special people in this world and they are here for a reason. The answers do not always come so quickly, and to question, as so many in this area, I have found at any rate, think is not right, or a sin. Never, ever feel bad about that! You keep searching for the answers and keep asking "Them" your questions. You are okay, J.P., you are not crazy. You are a bit out of balance at the moment and that is not your fault, you have had some hard years and I am sure you have had more help than you will ever imagine in this life time from your spirits but we will work on your balance as we go on, okay."

"Well, Doctor, first I do not believe in sin. It is a word that the Catholic Church created and skewed to strike fear into the masses. That way the Church could control them. Oh, and that goes for all the another "Christian" sects that followed Catholicism."

J.P.'s face broke out in a rare smile, as for the moment he felt good. He was beginning to really like his doctor and he felt that she had integrity and seemed to feel better when he left her office. His natural ebb medicine Celia Flora had him on seemed to make him feel better. He felt it could all be mental but he really did not care. He just wanted to get his life back in balance.

# Blood Line

Brian O'Francis arrived at Chicago's O'Hara's airport a day ahead of his scheduled meeting with Vincentzo Spadolini. His chauffeur was waiting for him at the hanger where his private plane was stored, and took his bags. Exiting the airport area, he took his boss via interstate W 90 to 31 to 14 North to Crystal Lake, where he had a home off North Shore Drive overlooking the lake.

Brian O'Francis stood six foot one inches tall, and weighed in the one hundred and ninety plus area, depended on the time of the year. Salt and pepper hair, more graying on the sides than anywhere, some receding in his hair line. He kept it very short, in what would be considered a "butch-cut" in the old days. He had a medium complexion and a solid framed body, clean shaven with a black mustache just starting to get some gray appearing in it.

Brian was all business and a very successful businessman. He started his career in the hotel business and had very lucrative ties in several hotel chains, aside from the outright ownership of several of his own. He had gotten interested in the shipping business, Great Lakes shipping, or "Lakers" as the Great Lake's people knew them in that business. Which by "fate" had led to Vincent Spadolini, and a partnership was born.

His service days were with the Navy SEALs. The SEALs ancestry dated back to WWII where they were known as Navy "Fog men," but the SEALs were born from John Kennedy's belief that unconventional warfare was needed to aid and assist the more conventional and traditional type of warfare the United States were more accustomed to and comfortable with. Power and overwhelming forces were used to subdue one's foes, but the 60's brought an era of warfare, the most powerful nation on earth at that point in history, that they were not accustomed to and the need for special operations' groups were badly needed. President Kennedy had the foresight for such groups and was the driving force behind them. Being a Navy man he wanted and he got a special group for his beloved Navy. By the year 1962, there was born a guerrilla warfare unit to be dubbed SEALs, an acronym for "Sea, Air and Land," an elite group of men specialized in a wide variety of skills for use in guerilla and counter guerrilla operations.

The SEALs were badly needed in the growing war in South East Asia. Their training would come from several Army schools which would prepare them for Special Forces techniques, evasion, and escape. These schools would also teach them the art of jungle warfare, the use of unconventional warfare equipment, clandestine operations to include UDT (Underwater Demolition Teams), reconnaissance, sabotage, and general guerrilla warfare, which included ambushes and counter ambushes as well as raiding techniques.

Basically they were to conduct clandestine operations on restricted waters, rivers, and canals. They were to covertly enter the enemies' shipping harbors and destroy their ships as well as their harbors, facilities, bridges, railway lines in any maritime area of operation and riverine environment.

In 1966 the Navy SEALs really went into action in Viet Nam, although their presence in Country had existed since 1961, the brainchild of the Kennedy administration using the Army as well as the Navy to conduct the kind of warfare that the "Cong" used.

Brian arrived in Viet Nam in January 1968, and was attached to Detachment Bravo and went to work almost instantly in the Mekong Delta region of the

Rung Sat, an area that could be considered the most difficult topography in all of Viet Nam. Its low lands were virtually impenetrable with large mangroves consisting of twisted roots and close growing tightly packs of Nipa Palms. Then as one went inland from the hundreds of tiny tributaries of the mighty Mekong itself, it turned into double canopy forests that could and did hide the activities of the notorious Viet Cong. Then you had the noted U-Minh forest on the southern tip of Viet Nam extending onto the Western side along the Gulf of Thailand and the famous water trail of the Sihanouk, the communist supply route by sea into the eastern shores of South Viet Nam. It also connected the notorious inland route of the Ho Chi Minh trail on the southeastern Cambodian and the South Viet Nam borders.

The Viet Cong were masters at water transportation with their famous junks, or more commonly known in Viet Nam as Sampans. For the most part the indigenous inhabitants of the Rung Sat area were all just simple rice farmers, fishermen, and woodcutters.

Vincent and Brian had been in the Great Lakes shipping business together for fifteen years and were doing extremely well. That evening Brian sat on the back deck of his lake side home, which he had designed himself, and made the living room face the lake with a walled glass doorway onto a thirty by twenty foot very private deck off the split level of his home. Here he sipped on one of his favorite scotches, 21 year old Glenfiddish single malt and smoked his favorite brand of cigars, the 50 X 7" Macanudo, a vintage from as far back as 1984 through the late 1990's. It was a very quiet evening with clear skies and he did enjoy the openness of the area, away from the big city lights and the noise. His success enabled him to enjoy the comforts of being able to own a home away from all the city life. He enjoyed just leaning back in his lounge chair and looking up at the starry skies. Even with his financial success and the hard-core business world he normally had to exist in, his days were spent in running two major businesses out of his main office, and his evenings and nights were in one of his own hotel suites in one of the many major cities spanning the length of the United States.

The quirky thing about Brian O'Francis and James O'Francis were they liked the same things. Brian had always been able to afford the things that J.P. liked.

It was not until J.P. moved west that he could and would indulge himself in the finer scotches and Irish whiskeys and cigars, and just sit out under the stars, enjoying the night air, and the open clear Montana sky. J.P. was not fond of any city, he had nothing against any one of them personally, just did not like crowds, the fast pace it took to survive. Brian had no problems with the city life, it was money to him. But it was nice to be alone out in the rural area, especially from spring through the early fall, before it turned cold.

Only a very select few people had the number to his home phone, (he always turned his business cell phone off when he wanted extreme privacy), and one of them was Vincent Spadolini. The phone rang and Brian slowly reached over and lifted the phone off its cradle, saw who it was, and pushed talk.

"O'Francis here, talk to me."

"Brian, its Vince. Sorry to disturb you on this fine evening old friend and I know you are out on that deck enjoying the evening."

Brian laughed. "You got that right! So what's up?"

"I wanted to know what your plans were beyond our meeting tomorrow, for the rest of the week."

"Have a meeting in Houston, ahhh, let me think, ahhh, Wednesday afternoon, ohhh, around three, I think. Hell I'll have to call Clara and double check, why?"

"Well, would it be possible for you to cancel the meeting?"

"Possible, depends on why."

"I would like for you to meet someone…ahhh, someone I think…you will want to meet. I am not real sure, maybe, considering all that I have learned." A rather long moment of silence occurred on the phone.

"Well, how important is this person? Is it business or something else? What is this person's name?"

"Well, let's say that I think it would be worth your time."

Brian laughed again. "Shit, I don't know, my time comes at a high price Vince."

Then more laughter by both men.

"Well, mine too. But check and see if you can postpone the meeting until Friday, if your schedule will allow it. I'll tell you more tomorrow after we handle this deal we'll be working on."

"Look, Vince I have to meet with the management of the hotel tomorrow afternoon at one, so let's make it about five, back at your office."

"Good enough, we'll have dinner together."

"Okay, I'll see what I can do about Houston. No promises you understand. Why the two day delay? I mean Vince, shit man, this that important?"

"I really think so."

"Okay."

Brian hung the phone up and began to ponder as to why Vince felt it was so important for him to meet this mysterious, unknown person in whom he would not tell him his name or why the meeting was so important. Anybody else he would have said no, to but knowing Vince, he felt it had to be something very special or he would not have asked.

Janice Jones had always been totally incompetent at her job, but Marshy and Theodoric made sure she was well taken care of. Her promotion to Reynolds County's Family Life program and her under the table graft made for a very lucrative position. She had been able to work other teachers like putty in her hands as she came in contact with them throughout the county with her mendacity and evil manipulative methods, especially when it came to O'Francis. She was being paid very well to do Master Marshey's work among the "flocks". She was such a good disciple of her "Dark Master", who could and often did control the thinking of so many.

She had been retired from the corrupt life she had led for so several years. It was Friday in the month of May in the year 2005, and Janice had been to visit with one of her old cronies. She had just left one of her disciple's as well as one of her old lover's house, and had pulled up to a stop sign on a back street in the subdivision in the town of Liberty. She was only a mile or so away from the four-lane highway that ran through the county. It was one-thirty when a plain white van bumped into the rear of her year old Volvo, breaking her right rear tail light. A woman dressed in overalls, with a heating and air condition label on her left upper breast area, got out. She stood five feet six inches and weighed one hundred twenty-five pounds. She had a cap with the same label on it covering her short dark hair, and her facial complexion revealed the natural dark brown skin of someone from the Mediterranean area. Janice slung open her door and quickly walked back to the rear of her car. And just as quickly she went into her normal mode of rapid talking which had not changed in thirty plus years, as she began verbally chastising the woman driver for her stupidity and poor driving, using "unacceptable social terms" at every other breath, which she still at the point in time claimed that she never used.

The lady asked Janice to step to her van and she would provide her with the insurance company, the number to call, and her name. She assured her that it would all be taken care of, at the same time being extremely apologetic, all the time humbling herself and asking forgiveness. Janice never stopped "jacking her jaws" the entire time they walked around the rear of the van to the passenger side. As soon as the van's passenger door opened, the sliding panel door opened. A man, mid-thirties with a well-defined body, "well cut", six two, two hundred pounds, grabbed Jones' blouse and light dress jacket at the left breast area, pulling her quickly toward him and with his right fist, hit her square in the mouth and nose area, jolting her head back violently, splattering blood over both sides of her face.

In the same fluid motion, he pulled and lifted her into the van. The woman driver of the van closed the passenger's door and then the sliding door. She walked to Janice's car, putting on a single black tight fitting driving glove on her right hand. Unfolding the green wrapping paper, she took a dark purple Lily out with her right hand and dropped it on the driver's seat. She went back to the van, got in, backed up enough to clear Janice's car, then drove off in a normal manner.

In this time period, the man had quickly injected Janice with ketamine. Janice, being in a dazed state from the "shot to the face," something that should have been done to her in the nineteen eighties, was quickly unconscious on the floor of the van.

There had been no other traffic in the area at the time of the accident, and the gray Volvo was left sitting at the stop sign, motor still running, and the driver's door closed. Her good friend had a dentist appointment at two o'clock. As she approached the same stop sign, seeing Janice's car, she got out to check the car, and not seeing Janice, knew that something was wrong. She went to her car, picked up her cell phone and called the police, who arrived in a matter of minutes.

John Frederick O'Donovan sat and read his Tuesday newspaper as he ate his evening meal, and on the front page the headlines read, EX-TEACHER MISSING. The story included loose ended details, how a full investigation was taking place by the local police, as well as the State police. He quickly got up and went to his phone, dialing the number to the newspaper office, requesting to speak to Anthony Krause.

"Krause. May I help you?"

"Anthony. John O'Donovan here."

"Hey, oldddd, bud, what's up with the easy life?" Then he laughed hardily.

"Just was reading about your story on the missing teacher. What do you know?"

"Hey John, this one is a good one. We cannot find a damn thing. It is just like she, poof, disappeared, no one saw a damn thing, and I mean nothing. The local police, welllll, they have nothing. But we expect that. The state is involved and they can turn up nothing. So they have contacted the

FBI, and I guess they are taking over. Other than that, well that's it. Why? Did you know this woman?"

"Well, indirectly, I knew of her, is about it."

"Say...maybe you can help me here, what do you say?"

"No problem, if I can, I'll let you know if I hear anything."

"Good, maybe we could work together on this one. You can come out of retirement." Then Anthony laughed. "No, seriously, what do you think?"

"Well, maybe. I may be able to dig up something for you to get a good headline or two. But forget the out of retirement. I just want a little article here and there for me, just to keep in shape."

"John, do you think, naaaa..."

"What?" John asked.

"Well, do you remember, I mean, I know you will remember, but anyway, a few months ago, well let me think, close to a year ago, the Finkel thing?"

"Yes, I remember. Why?"

"Well, do you think, that...that, what was his name...ohhh, you know, that teacher friend of yours you told me about, the one that had all the problems over the years. Hell, way back in the 80's and 90's. What was his name? Damn, why is it I can never remember that guy's name? Hold it I got it here someplace in all my old notes."

"O'Francis."

"That's it. O'Francis, yeah. Do..." John cut him off.

"No, I do not!"

"Well, just wanted to ask...you know a lot of talk went around back then, just wondered if there may be some sort of a connection?"

"I'll poke around, and if I dig up something I'll call you."

Hanging up the phone he knew that it had started. Did J.P. have anything to do with it, or did he really have friends in places that no one talked about? Was it possible that the person he told him about whomever he was, was "Blind Justice?" If J.P. had made his mind up as to the moral issue, the police and newspapers were in for a lot of mystery stories. Lots of questions went through his mind for the rest of the evening.

# The O'Francis Home Life

PATRICK O'FRANCIS HAD A VERY difficult time his freshmen and sophomore years in high school. Teachers that did not like his father would not cut him a break and gave him a difficult time with their attitude and "childish" remarks toward him in class. His math teacher refused to give him two points in his algebra one class and he failed the course. His cousin, who had the same teacher, received ten points to pass him in the course.

J.P. and Dawn did not make an issue out of the matter, as they knew if Patrick had worked he could have made an average grade or above in the course. The problem was not his intelligence, it was with Nicodemus. Patrick was becoming resentful of him, and instead of Patrick influencing him, "Nico" was influencing Patrick in his work habits. "Nico" worked the teachers, coned them, and was good at it. Patrick did not have the "gift" to con his way through his courses. He was not city street smart like his cousin was. J.P. stayed on both of the boys hard, and pushed for them to do better. J.P. had lots of problems with Nicodemus, in trying to get him on the "right" road to success, not through drugs on the street, or stealing from someone, or taking someone's auto to make a living, or the pimping for some young girl he owned. He had lots to learn, and was reluctant to accept any advice from his uncle. Nicodemus wanted to be the "bad-ass" street tough guy of Honsburg, and often displayed his attitude toward J.P., but with great care.

It was on one of these evenings that "Nico" decided that with great care, he would challenge his uncle to a physical confrontation.

"Uncle "O" are you going to work out tonight?"

"Yes, in about an hour, why?"

"Well", then he paused. Patrick sat across the living room just shaking his head from side to side, as to say, "No, you are making a mistake, you really don't want to do this."

"Ahhh... I think I can take you."

J.P. smiled, as his favorite show, Star Trek returned from a commercial. "I see. Well "Nico" let us talk about that after Star Trek is over." After Jean Luc finished his negotiations on the Klingon planet for Lt. Worf, in an effort to regain the honor and dignity of his family name, J.P. asked "Nico" just how he wanted to do the sparring match.

"I need a few minutes to get loose."

"Okay, tell you what "Nico," let me go through my regular routine, and when I am done, I will let you get loose and then we can do it any way you would like."

J.P. retired to his workout room. "Nico" seemed excited about the chance to do his uncle in. J.P. spent thirty minutes going through his stretches and a few katas. He returned to the living room and informed "Nico" that the room was all his. Nicodemus spent five minutes getting ready. Patrick came into the living room and informed his dad that "Nico" was ready.

"So soon?" J.P. asked his son.

"Hey, it's "Nico" dad. What can I say?"

"Okay uncle "O.", the rules are, I can do any street moves I like, and if I can kick your ass you will not hold it against me, right?"

"That is correct "Nico.""

"Now... I can hit you in the face, right?" "Nico" stated with a great deal confidence.

"Absolutely. You may do whatever street moves it takes. You have my word I will not hold anything against you. Nor will I get mad at you."

Patrick was standing at the far end of the family room, a fourteen foot by thirty foot open area, basically designed for J.P. to do his katas, and for the boys to play "house hoops" and general "horse play." Patrick had tried to warn "Nico" in the five minutes "Nico" had prepared himself for his forthcoming match that was to render his uncle a real city street ass kicking.

"Nico" you are crazy, no way, I am telling you." Patrick warned his cousin.

But "Nico" did not hear Patrick's words. He was the badass from Detroit's streets, and he could take an old man in his mid-forties.

"Okay, uncle "O" I am ready."

Then he took his street fighting stance, bouncing around, fists up, a poke here a jab there, going for his uncle's face. In each attempt J.P. would parry his blows, and step aside, giving him every opportunity to strike his mark, and make him feel like the "bad-ass" he thought he was, proving his "man-hood," getting the anger out of his system, taking it out on the authoritarian figure in his present life. Over and over he made his attempt to hurt his uncle, and on several attempts J.P. would give him a little taste of a counter-strike to his mid-section, with a medium amount of power, just enough to let him know that old uncle could hit his mark. After several minutes of vigorous sparring and several open hand slaps to the face to let "Nico" know he could be touched with a fist if he wanted to, which of course would have hurt much worse than a light slap to the jaws, "Nico" became mad, and began swinging wildly. J.P. put him on the floor with a few throws, as "Nico" was off balance in his attack.

He opened handed smacked him on his jaws enough to make his skin become flushed. On one of his more aggressive charges toward J.P. he used the heel of his right hand, as he parried "Nico's" right lead, stepping toward him striking him on the forehead, pushing him as he stepped through, sending him to the floor yet again. "Nico" was up quickly, making him even madder, never understanding what his uncle could have done to his face, if he had intended to hurt him instead of trying to teach him a lesson. However, "Nico" being "Nico" began running his mouth in a manner that was not respectful of any guardian and more especially one who had taken him in and was doing everything he could to get him on the correct side of the legal system.

However he was still just a teenager, and O'Francis kept that in mind, but enough was enough. "Nico" struck violently at J.P. He simply sidestepped to his left as well as leaned his upper body to his left, to avoid the thrush of the young teen, and with the back of his right fist, struck "Nico" rather hard in his right kidney area, sending him to the floor crying out in pain. Then J.P. moved quickly just as his nephew rolled over on his back arching and holding his right back with his hand.

J.P. went down on his right knee, and putting his right hand gently around his throat, he whispered in his ear, "Look mister bad-ass, you are all mine, think of what I could do to you in the position you are now in! Remember this "Nico", *never,* ever start a fight! You just do not know what the other person may know, and the next time the other person will not let you off without really hurting you. You will bleed; trust me on this one, I know! "Nico" you do not have to prove you are anything, to anybody! Just be you. Your street shit just does not work, one on one. It never has! It is and most likely will always be a group, a gang, doing some individual person in. Forget the gang shit, it will get you nowhere! Trust your dear old Uncle on this one. Please listen to me. I will not lead you in the wrong direction. Your street shit is not worth the price you will have to pay. I will not lie to you."

Then as J.P. looked him in his tear-filled eyes he saw a boy searching for a life. But the little voice in his head was telling him that his nephew would not find the good life he wanted. The moments he looked at his nephew so close he could feel his breath on his face, he feared that he would not be able to save him. He could see it deep in his eyes, but he knew he had to try, he could be wrong; it could have been just the moment. He then stood, and reached out his right hand, offering to help him up. "Nico" accepted as J.P. pulled him to his feet, put his arms around him and hugged him, patting him on the back.

"Go wash your face off and let's eat some popcorn and watch a movie, okay?"

With his tear-filled eyes and wet face, sniffling, he thanked his uncle and they enjoyed the rest of evening.

Dawn got home after eleven from her job in the video store. J.P. briefed her on what had taken place so she would have the whole story. She would be able to let her sister know, who most likely would not have approved of J.P.'s methods of educating her youngest son. But J.P. felt that she really did not know her son anymore. She had lost the once little boy, with a great deal of athletic ability and great potential, as J.P. would tell Dawn.

"She will never get him back. I do not think she understands that. I do not know if Dennis understands or not, but more so than Theresa."

Dawn sat watching television, not speaking for several minutes, appearing to J.P. to be in deep thought.

"Nico," still had the street in him and he had a bad habit of lying. "I do not want Dennis and Theresa to think I am mistreating their son."

"I don't think they will." she said quickly.

"Well I know you will be talking to Theresa this week, and I know that "Nico" will also. I want them to get the real story."

"You don't think "Nico" will tell the truth?"

"No, I do not."

"Come on J.P., he has got to know they will know if he lied."

"No, he still believes that he can con them, and, now I do not mean anything bad here, but I am willing to bet my nuts that he feels that he can con his mother any time he wants. And Dawn, I believe he can, and will. I am sorry if that sounds bad, but that is how I feel. It is what I see in him. Dennis, well, not so easy. He still has high hopes for him, but I just do not know. He has a long, long way to go. That is what dealing with the scum on the street will get you. Hell Dawn, knowing the street, and letting it control you, is two different things. "Nico" has let it control him for too long, and I really do not know if I can make him see where he is going and what is ahead of him. It depends on just how bad he wants to regain control of himself. You see, he thinks he is in control, he just does not see. They have done a number on him. "

"Well you have done it for others." Dawn quickly responded, in defense of "Nico" and her sister.

"I am aware of that. I am not saying that I am not going to try to get the street scum washed out of his mind and help mold him into a good person, using his street smarts to his advantage, and I do not mean to do illegal acts but to know who and when he is being coned by someone who just wants to use him for their good. That is not what I am telling you."

"Then just what are you saying?"

He took a deep breath. "I am telling you he is worse off than they realize. I think more than you realize. He is good at putting on faces and moods to please his mother and you. He is a good con person. He is all street boy and I do not know if I can get all of that out of him that is to be used for his good, not his bad. He really does not like me."

Dawn interrupted J.P. "Oh come on J.P., I really don't think that is true."

"No Dawn, you are wrong. He really does not. Because I know what he is and he knows I know, and he knows that he cannot con me. That is what really angers him."

She sat looking at her husband from across the room. "I still think he likes you."

"Oh, in a sense he does, and I know that, but he knows I fully understand his street instincts, and that is not all that bad. It is fine to be that way if you are on the street, but not to your parents, not to the people who care for you. He does not care. He will do whomever, makes no difference to him, and I am telling you that is the problem. I am telling you I do not know if I can make him understand that. In his mind he thinks that it is the people on the street that are his friends, and they are not! He cannot see that family is most important. He thinks his street thugs are his family."

Dawn never said another word, as the two watched television for another hour, and went to bed.

Patrick's athletic ability was starting to blossom. He was bigger than his older brother and was losing his baby fat, as he grew upward, developing a bigger chest, and broader shoulders, taking on more of his mother's side of the family than that of J.P.'s, which was tall and slender.

Both of J.P.'s sons would be by their twentieth birthdays, standing three to four inches taller than their father, something he had predicted when they were born, and something he was proud of.

Patrick's football career was starting to come together as his "sure hands" for catching the ball was evident, another tight end for the Honsburg "Cats," if Coach Hobart would be smart enough to use him. He was not as aggressive as Michael, but was still getting the job done on both sides of the ball.

Tim could not ignore his ability in baseball and once again he saw an O'Francis at second base. J.P. would, as he had done with Michael, work long hours on the field during the summer, hitting grounders to him. Nico, who had some ability, could prove to be a very good first baseman, with a lot of work, and get some playing time in under Tim Harper. He had been a goalie, playing hockey on the junior league, giving him the hands and quickness for a good first baseman. Something J.P. felt that, if he really wanted he could develop him into. Baseballs were after all much larger than a puck, and traveled somewhat slower. The glove he would wear was not all that much different, and he felt that he could make a starter out of him, even though he would not be his coach, per say.

But it would be Nico's call. He had to want it, and J.P. had his doubts, but worked him as hard as he did his own son, teaching him the proper techniques for playing at the first base position. That part he found was the easy part as Nico adapted quickly to the position. Hitting a baseball was the hard part. Teaching him how to hit, J.P. found would take a bit longer. But Nico had athletic ability in him and would, with hard work make a hitter, if, he would just believe in himself, and lose the tough guy street attitude.

J.P. had been given a key to the field, something J.P. was quite surprised at, and received permission from Tim to go to the field anytime he wanted to work with the two boys or anyone else that wished to learn the game of baseball. Tim as well as J.P. talked about Nico's throwing ability, and tested him on the mound and saw that he also could make a good relief pitcher. Although J.P. was no longer part of the official coaching staff, he put in a lot hours helping both boys improve their game. However there was something O'Francis had learned in his brief absence, the ability to see some of the trees in the forest. In the few talks he had with Harper, he was able to detect an attitude toward his nephew. Of course that in itself could have come from the incident that had occurred the year before during the spring while his mother and father were down visiting.

The Junior Varsity coach, one Mr. Robert Hastert had benched Patrick as well as Nico, for no apparent reason, other than the fact that he did not like the way they were batting. Given the fact that the two young boys were taking their batting instructions from J. Patrick O'Francis and they would not change to his style of batting, they were benched. In addition, given the fact that his comment that J.P. did not know what he was talking about when both boys tried to explain to him that was the manner in which they were told to bat from the assistant varsity coach, Nico in his best Detroit street vernacular, informed Mr. Hastert that he could suck his dick, with a few other colloquialisms thrown in for good measure. Of course he was removed from the team.

Now that in itself was not the problem. It seemed that he was also to be placed in detention for his actions. So, Dawn Christine and Joan Theresa made a trip to the principal's office and requested that the junior varsity as well as the varsity coach be summoned to the office.

In the course of an hour meeting Mr. Hastert defended his actions, however the added punishment was not acceptable to either one of the "girls" and so the principal removed the detention from the list. Throughout the entire time of the meeting Mr. Harper did not speak. Even after Theresa requested that he join in the conversation as he was the head of the entire program. The best Harper could do was spit into his tobacco bottle. Theresa was not intimidated by his often "stare down" and found it rather insulting. Not to exclude the fact, he was extremely unprofessional in his actions and his conduct. Theresa being an executive for AAA in the Detroit Metropolitan area was not used to his rudeness, given the fact that he was the head of a baseball program and was responsible for all the people working under him in whatever capacity.

What J.P. did know about Harper was that he silently held grudges, and covertly got even with those who crossed him in one form or another.

J.P. had learned that there was to be an opening at Honsburg High School, and applied for the head basketball job, as he had done twice before. This time he felt that he might have a chance, as Henry appeared on the surface at any rate, to be in favor of him getting the job. But again he had no illusions about Henry, or who "pulled his chain" but felt it was worth a "swing of the bat." *You cannot hit the ball if you do not swing the bat, he would so often tell me.* He arrived at the high school and pecked on Henry's office door.

"Hey, hi J.P., come in, come in" Henry said as he got up from his chair and walked around the old familiar desk J.P. had so often in the past sat in front of. Extending his hand out to him, they shock vigorously, surprising J.P. to some extent.

"What can I do for you today Coach?" The word coach coming out of his mouth again surprised him, as he felt it was a compliment for one to be addressed as coach, recognizing his skills as a teacher of an athletic game. J.P. smiled, as he was well aware that Henry knew why he was there.

"Well Henry, you can give me a little of your time for some serious conversation."

"No problem, what do you want to talk about? Oh, wait one minute" as he got back up from his chair and walked to the door and closed it.

"Now, what's on your mind today?"

"The basketball position Henry."

"Okay, ahhh, let me tell you this. It is open, and we are taking applications, and I am told that they will be interviewing for the job in a few weeks."

"Henry, they who?"

"Well, the central office staff."

"Okay, what about you? Where do you fit into the picture?"

"I'll be in on the interviews also, and will make the recommendations to Mr. Marshy."

"Henry, I have worked for you and with you for a long time now. I deserve the job. I have the credentials for the job and you know it. Now let's cut through the bull shit, and get right down to the chase. What is the word?"

Henry acted as if he did not know what J.P. was talking about.

"Now, Henry, let's put that front of yours down, let's talk man to man, leave off all the political bull shit, you know and I need to know."

"Okay, J.P. okay. It's your law suit."

"My law suit? What in the hell does that have to do with me getting the head-coaching job? I am not suing the school system. I am suing Damon Bales and Richard Finkel!"

"I know, but Marshy." Then he caught himself.

"Well, finish Henry, hell I do know a few things you know. I mean this is a small community, and I do have a few sources. So do not sit there and try and bull shit your way through this, okay."

"Well, it's not just Marshy. Hell Duncan Brewer has vowed that you will never get this job!"

"Why"

"Well, you know?"

"No, Henry I do not know or I would not be asking! Now what does Duncan Brewer have to do with the running of this school? And why should he give a royal rat's ass if I or anyone else gets the job?"

"Because he and Richard Finkel are big time buddies."

The conversation turned to the political machine of the county and how much power Brewer had, and all the people he influenced. The two talked about their personal relationship they had when J.P. worked at the high school, the fact that neither had any problems with each other, that Henry had been the clock keeper for J.P. during his earlier years of coaching the boys as well as the girls and was well acquainted with his coaching ability and his style. Henry told J.P. that he had no problems with him as a coach or in the classroom, stating that he had heard many people praise his teaching as well as his coaching ability, and were very thankful that there child had the opportunity to be in his class or coached by J.P.

"Okay so the bottom line here is the supervisors, along with the School Board, correct?"

"You got it. Supervisors control the School Board."

"In other words pull the "chain" for them to speak. Okay Henry, I need some advice here because I have never had to go out and politic for a coaching job, so who and how?"

He sat in his chair looking across at J.P. saying nothing, and then he slowly leaned forward in his chair and laid his arms on the top of his desk.

"First thing I want you to do is go see Cosette Cameron." He stated in a lower than normal voice as if someone was close enough to hear. Cosette was the first and only female ever to sit on an elected Board of Supervisors in the history of the county.

"I can do that. I played ball against her husband, Jake. Well I did not have to guard the big lug, that was Ira's job. God was he big in our day and time. Of course now days he is just a forward, but at any rate, I know where they live. What do I say?"

Of course, Henry did not have a clue who Ira was, or what a great athlete he was, nor did he really give a shit about J.P.'s fond memories of playing basketball with his teammate Ira and playing against Honsburg and big Jake.

"Well, let's see. Just tell her what you want and you would like her support on the matter."

Henry went through all the people he wanted J.P. to go see, which included Big Fred Houston, the supervisor at large, a towering man of six foot eight, and some two hundred and seventy plus pounds, and no fat. To be so big he spoke with a soft voice and had a pleasant personality. J.P. liked him and had the pleasure of working with his wife at the middle school as she was the music teacher. Not only was Beverly extremely good at her job, she was a very pleasant person. J.P. and Dawn always enjoyed her concerts and never missed one. Henry instructed J.P. to see three out of the six members of the board of supervisors and to see the appointed School Board member for his political district and to see them in the correct order, an important issue he insisted upon.

Toward the end of their conversation, the door opened and in walked Henry's wife, Rose. No knock, no excuse me, she just walked in and walked by J.P. as if he was not there, went behind the desk and started a conversation with Henry about where they were going for dinner. She did not speak to J.P., she did not acknowledge his presence, and she did not leave, but continued to address Henry about some trivial bullshit concerning one of the teachers. Her rudeness did not surprise J.P. as she was well known for it. By all accounts, over the years O'Francis had lived in Honsburg, no one bothered to put her in her place. Her family money and political connections kept people from doing so. Hers was one of the three main family aristocracies of Honsburg.

After several minutes, J.P. stood and interrupted her by addressing Henry and informing him he would follow his instructions to the letter, and thanked him for his time and advice. At that Rose asked what they were talking about. J.P. told Henry he would report back to him in a few days, turned and walked out of the room as Henry was desperately trying to explain away their conversation without telling her what they had discussed.

Holly called J.P. and asked him to come over to her office, which was not a scheduled appointment, as they had already gone through the deposition. J.P. had taken it and filled half a legal pad of notes concerning the massive amounts of mendacious statements both Finkel and Bales had made, supporting his notations with factual documentation he had of his own. Bales of course had more lies uttered from his evil tongue than Finkel, and had passed them along to Holly for her analysis. On his way to her office his little voice began sending him warnings that something was not right, and as he walked into her office he could tell, by the look on her face, this was not going to be a "happy day in Mudville."

Holly informed J.P. that she had health problems, and she would have to discontinue her services with J.P. but gave him an option of continuing with her father's firm and allowing her younger brother to carry on with the case, or getting someone else to represent him. J.P. had met Julius Donatello a year earlier, but knew nothing about his ability, his personality, or his approach to his one shot at getting something back that he had lost. J.P. had no real choice. He had to go with the same law firm in hopes that Julius was as good as his sister. Holly was extremely apologetic to J.P. knowing that he had placed all the surgical instruments on her tray in hopes that she could put a stop to his "bleeding."

She picked up her phone and asked the secretary to ask Julius to come to her office. In a short few very unconformable minutes, Julius walked in. He was well-dressed in a dark blue suit, a white shirt, black shoes, standing about five feet ten, cold black hair and a heavy afternoon "shadowed" beard. After a thirty minutes session with Julius and Holly, J.P. was on his way home, with a great deal of apprehension.

For two days J.P. O'Francis shook hands and politicked for the head coaching job and felt that he was received well, but knew that politicians were good at making people feel good about a meeting with them. He could only hope that they had just a little honor about them, but had no illusions. O'Francis was off to see the last person on his list of political power players Henry had given him, the oldest of them, a man by the name of Harvey Booth. Being part of the inner-circle of the teachers' association for the past three years, he had attended several School Board meetings and had observed Mr. Booth's actions and reactions to various issues that had been brought up before the School Board.

On several occasions Mr. Harvey Booth went to sleep while money issues were being discussed. J.P. noted it in his log of notes he always took while at the facade meetings. But never the less he would lobby Mr. Booth for the coaching position, as Henry had directed. In the course of an hour talking to Harvey Booth, J.P. did his best, but as he drove back home from his late afternoon meeting, he knew that Harvey did not have a clue as to what in the hell he was talking about. He actually knew nothing at all about the school system, nor did he really care. J.P. took the opportunity to test his knowledge of what was happening within his school district and to see if the man had any idea as to how the schools were being operated. He learned that he did not, was totally clueless. He basically was a joke, and as he would learn within two days of his visit to Mr. Booth, he was under the total control of Duncan Brewer.

Booth called Brewer within the hour of O'Francis' departure, and got his instructions as to what to do. Of course he never ever voiced an opinion, he just voted yes or no, or grunted once in a while as he had been told, and if he forgot what to do, he had a "coach" on the board that would let him know how to vote on whatever issue was on the table, by voting as Barnard Theodric did, always looking over to him to make sure he was doing it as he had been told.

It did not take long for Duncan to get on the phone to Henry and verbally rip him a preverbal "new ass-hole" for sending O'Francis to the various political powers, reminding him how and who got him in the position he currently held.

LaMar Marshy made his phone calls as well, not only to the power players to make sure THEY were all on the same page of music together, but called Henry into his office, giving him a good verbal tongue lashing for sending J.P. out to lobby for the coaching position.

"I told you Henry, by-god he will not coach again in this county or anywhere else if I can help it! And by-god I damn sure can help it here in this county! Do you understand Henry? DO NOT, AND I REPEAT MY SELF, which I had better never have to do again on this matter, DO NOT, EVER, do this again! O'FRANCIS IS THROUGH! DO I MAKE MYSELF VERY CLEAR?"

Henry of course sat shaking his head up and down and back and forth, never so much as opening his mouth, like one of the dogs you see in the back of some of the "goood-ole-boys" car windows throughout the south.

For the three years J.P. had been out of the High School coaching business. He was not out of the baseball business. Not just umpiring for the Appalachian Umpire's Association, but he had been asked to take a senior league team, continuing to teach the game to the younger players, in hopes that one day he would once again be back on the High School level, and then he would have already primed the players as they matured and became more skilled and stronger. He could enjoy the fruits of his hard earned labor. Tim would of course reap the benefits of J.P.'s ability to teach the game of baseball, and would never so much as receive a simple thank you, much less indicate that he had anything to do with the teaching of the game.

It did not appear that the future for O'Francis to return to the high school level for Honsburg was all that bright. Even if he did get his coaching job back, it would never be the same. J.P. had obtained too much information concerning Harper's behind the scenes activities. Which much to J.P.'s tarnished pride, he had to accept as facts, never to bring the matter to the surface in anyone's presence within the entire county.

As an observer I once brought it to J.P.'s attention by asking him if he thought maybe some of his problems on the high school level was not the fact that he was too popular among the players, but rather that Tim Harper was jealous. He stood and looked at me for the longest time, or so it appeared. I do not know where his mind was and then he looked off into the depths of the forest never to answer my question. I never asked again.

He had his problems on the senior league level also, which was unexpected. Richard Finkel's first cousin, Stuart Foster's son was playing on his team. Foster would sit on the upper bleachers in the left field area, and criticize everything that J.P. did, in practice as well as the games. J.P. played everyone, win or lose, as he knew that winning at that level in the league was not the most important thing, but learning the game itself. He also knew that the vast majority of the boys would never get another chance to play the game of baseball once they left the senior league level, so he made sure that the ones that could not really play the game, did. It made him feel good when one of the not so gifted boys got a hit, or made the simplest of catches, or scored a run. The joy he saw on their faces made his days. He was hard on them, and he demanded discipline from them, and for the most part all the parents appreciated his hard work and effort.

On several occasions while Mr. Foster was verbally chastising J.P. and his efforts, a very large man by the name of Charlie Cornett informed Foster that he had heard enough of his cussing O'Francis, that he had a son on his team also and that he was very pleased that he was being coached by a qualified coach that knew what he was doing. Foster, being the spineless bastard he was, never sat with the group of men who gathered twice a week in the evenings to watch their sons play the summer game of baseball.

But Foster was not through. In a game where Foster's son was playing, J.P. had pulled him out of the game after conferring with his assistant coach, and replaced him with another player. This of course did not sit well with Foster, and so he decided that he would challenge J.P. on the matter. J.P.'s very loyal assistant Raymond Jansen informed J.P. that Stuart Foster was waiting for him outside of the field of play. Now J.P. had been chosen as the president of the senior league and was responsible for closing down the facility, locking up the press box, turning off all the lights, which of course would make it dark when he was confronted by Foster.

As the two men walked out from the dugout an older gentlemen by the name of Eugene Bankos, who's grandson played for J.P. and had raised his entire family in Honsburg. All his boys had been supporters of the entire Honsburg baseball program as well as coaching the little league for several decades. He and his entire family had been loyal supporters of J.P. through all of his trials and tribulations. Eugene himself, a very candid, honorable person, had supported baseball and O'Francis for many years. They walked toward the gate, and at the end of the bleachers stood Foster.

"O'Francis I want to talk to you!" His voice unfriendly, J.P. stepped ahead of Raymond and Eugene.

"Okay."

"I want to know why you took my son out of the game and yelled at him!"

"Well, first I took him out of the game because he was not trying! Now as to the other, I did not yell at him!"

"You cussed him and yelled at him and."

"Hold your tongue their mister Foster! I did not cuss him! And once again, I did not yell at him! Now, is there anything else you want to talk about?"

"By-god I'll take him and go home! He'll not play for someone like you!"

J.P. paused as he looked at Foster, speaking very slowly. "Well, Mr. Foster, you do whatever you like. But you will turn in his uniform before he goes anywhere or you will pay for a new one!"

"Who in the hell do you."

J.P. took two steps toward the man who was a good four inches taller than he and thirty pounds heavier. "I will tell you who I am. I am the president of the league! I am responsible for the uniforms and the equipment! I am the coach for this team! Now is there anything else you want to know? I want the uniform, do I make myself clear! Yes, I think you should take your son off this team, because he has very poor discipline, a very poor attitude, and he refuses to follow the rules like everyone else, which is a direct reflection on his father! He does not try when he is on the field, and there ARE other's that put forth a MUCH better effort than he does! NOW, Mr. FOSTER, will there be anything else? If not, we are tired, and we would like to go home!"

Foster turned and walked away. He did have his son's uniform delivered to Raymond the very next day.

It was the second fall that Nico had graced the O'Francis home. It was squirrel season, and off the two boys went with J.P. to the hills to the north of J.P.'s home. Nico had been instructed on how to use a shotgun properly, and J.P. and Patrick had tried to teach him how to hunt, but was not having a lot of success. The same went for the river fishing. Nico just did not have the patience it took for catching small mouth bass while wading down the shallows of the river. Nor did he take the time to wait out a squirrel or try and ease up on one. Everything had to be done fast and hard. He made enough noise walking and trashing his way through the woods that nobody in the general area could hunt.

J.P. had left the two in an area where two hollows come together near the crest of a hill and he had continued following the ridgeline for some three hundred yards. He was in a forty-five degree angle from the two boys as the ridge angled southward. It had not been more than an hour when he heard one of the two stomping through the undergrowth and dried leaves almost directly below him. The slope of the hill side that led to the western most hollow in which he left the two, was very steep. J.P. knew the late afternoon hunting was over, and by the time they worked their way back to the house it would be dark, so he began working his way back the way he had come, all the time hearing Nico struggling his way back up the steep hollow.

He spotted him just as he was approaching the head of the hollow, and watched him pull his way up the hill one sapling at a time, slipping and falling, cussing the hunting adventure with every breath. Nico never saw J.P. as he moved toward Patrick, who was still sitting on an old fallen tree in the same area he had left him, his gun laying across his lap watching his cousin struggle as he climbed back up the hill he had descended. J.P. was forty feet away when Nico reached Patrick, yet unseen by either boy.

"Damn, Nico, you make so much noise you can't kill any "squacks," Patrick told him.

"Shit, ain't none in here anyway."

"Bull, if you would just sit and wait."

"Hell, I ain't doing that, ain't no fun, JUST SITTING AND WAITING!" Nico was standing to Patrick's right, and before J.P. could move, he had cocked the hammer back on the single shot 410-gage shotgun, pointed it directly at Patrick's head, and snapped the trigger. J.P. blinked his eyes. The number five-buck shot had not gone off.

"Nico," he yelled. "Put the gun down, NOW!"

The sound of his commanding voice startled Nico. J.P. moved quickly in a very few steps to where they were. He picked the gun up, broke the barrel down, and caught the shotgun shell as it ejected itself from the chamber. Laying his as well as the one Nico had been allowed to use down on the ground, he then sat down hard in a slumping manner beside his son on the log between Nico and Patrick. He looked at the end of the shell. There, dead center of the cap of the shell was the mark of the firing pen, deep enough penetration for it to discharge.

He looked up at Nico, and in a very low and calm voice asked, "Do you have any idea what you just did?"

Nico just stood looking at his uncle, not saying a word. J.P. turned the shotgun shell around so he could see the end where the firing pen had made contact with the cap.

"Do you see that?"

"Yeah."

"Nico, tell me, what do you see?"

"I don't know, a shotgun shell, WHAT?"

Holding it in his left hand, "Look here", he said as he pointed to the end with his right finger.

"This is a cap. This is the print of the firing pin on the cap, which sets off the shell. You would have killed my son! IF, the shell had not misfired."

J.P. stood, looked at Nico without feelings in his eyes. His voice turned deep in tone, cold and empty. "And I would have killed you dead as many times as I could have, with as many shells that I have here."

Then he paused, and for several minutes there was silence on the ridge. A soft breeze moved the tree limbs and leaves. Patrick remained seated on the log where his father had left him and had not spoken the entire time his father was talking to Nico. A squirrel located in the top of a hickory tree not more than twenty yards away from where he sat began to "squack."

"As of this moment, you are never too tough a weapon in my house, EVER! Do you understand?"

Nico lowered his head and spoke softly. "Yes Sir."

Patrick had not yet realized what had taken place in the moments Nico had pointed the gun at him and pulled the trigger, nor shortly afterwards until J.P. had removed the shell, and only then did he know that for whatever reason, for whatever fate, or destiny he had in his future, it was not to end on that day.

That night J.P. lay in bed looking up at a dark ceiling, thanking his Master for sparing his son's life. He thanked his beloved Blessed Mother for watching over his son. Then he thanked both his spirit guardians for his as well as his son's fate, as he knew that killing Nico for shooting his son would end in tragedy for him, especially in Reynolds County and especially for J.P. O'Francis and his Family name. He knew that there was not a thing wrong with the shell, they were new. He knew the pin had penetrated deep enough for the cap to pop, and he knew that whatever name one wanted to label the supreme powers and spirits be them male or female of the universes, that once again in his life "They" had demonstrated that they did exit.

# The Recruit

KARE' EDISON WAS A VERY attractive slender framed five foot six, one hundred and twenty pound brunette with a natural medium brown Mediterranean skin tone, a trait inherited from her grandfather who was of Greek decent. She had been raised in a small town and upon graduation went off to a rather prestigious college. Redford was not a large university but was located near a large city which supports a college atmosphere. It was not the largest university in the Southwestern part of Virginia, one that held a rather high academic standard and once held the claim of being a single gender college for females.

In Kare''s senior year she had been raped by two men as she walked from the library to her dorm. After a very long ordeal with doctors, nurses, police, campus security, and university administrators, Kare' lost. She finished her bachelors with a double major in English and moved to Texas, a state bigger than most western European Nations. She could get lost there and find herself and a new life.

Kare' entered the University of Houston and got her masters in Military Science with the idea of entering the United States Army. Kare' bought her first hand gun, found an indoor firing range, and began teaching herself how to use it. Her intent was to be good at firing a hand gun before entering the Army. Each time she went to the range to practice she would picture the two men that had defiled her body. She saw the corrupt legal system who would not believe her and the high and almighty university administration that covered the incident up and pulled all the correct strings to make it go away, and it did. Her anger burned like a glowing ember deep in her physic, releasing a rush of adrenaline that made her blood rush through her veins like hot molting lava.

Each time she had finished her practice session she repeated mentally to herself, *I will hunt these animals down and I will assassinate them.*

Jordan had been visiting a childhood friend who had moved to Missouri City, Texas a suburb on the southernmost part of Houston. It was a short drive from her home in Freeport, Texas and she enjoyed visiting a couple of times a year. She was to have spent a week with her friend Awindela, a Cherokee name meaning Morning, a girl friend she had grown up with. Awindela had gotten her master's degree from the University of Houston in computer science and now worked for a large company in Houston. She lived in Missouri City on the south side of Houston on Quail Hills Drive. Jordan used the time while Awindela was at work to shop as well as visit an indoor shooting range close by Awindela's home.

Jordan walked into the indoor gun range at 1000 hours in the morning, spoke briefly with the range officer, paid for the time to be spent using the range, and got her targets. She walked past the first four shooting stalls to the fifth stall, passing the only other person in the range at that time in the morning, a woman who was at the third stall. She placed her silver gun case on the table at the rear of the stall and opened it. It was one of four cases in which she owned and she had recently purchased a new hand gun in which she intended on doing some practicing with to get the feel of the pistol.

She looked down at the pistols securely placed in each of their slots of thick gray foam. On the upper part of the case, what would be considered the lid, two fully loaded magazines for each caliber hand gun, her Glock 28; .380, her Walther PP 7.65 MM and her new S&W M&P 40. Jordan practiced once a month somewhere, mostly around her home in Quintana Beach. She started her session with her Glock and after her first magazine she pushed the button to her right and the target started back toward her. All ten rounds were center mass, not more than a silver dollar in spacing.

She loaded her second magazine and placed a new target on the rail and sent it the twenty yards distance to the far wall. She emptied the next seven rounds in the chest and the last three in the head all grouped neatly close together.

Jordan drank her regular amount of coffee that morning and needed to use the ladies room. She placed the Glock and the magazines in their proper slots in the gun case and closed it, automatically setting the combinations. She turned and walked to the door leading out to the ladies room. As she passed the young woman at the third stall, she heard her talking to herself, "Damn, I will get better." Jordan smiled and continued on out the door.

When she returned the woman was sitting at the chair located to the rear of the shooting stall. Jordan passed without speaking and when she was about ten feet by the woman she spoke, "Excuse me madam."

Jordan stopped and turned. "Yes, are you talking to me?"

"Yes ma'am. May I ask you a question?"

"Sure." Jordan stated with a smile on her face.

Still seated the woman continued.

"Forgive me, but I looked at your target while you were gone and I truly apology for doing so, but how did you get so good?"

Jordan continued to smile but took a few seconds to answer the woman. "What is your name?"

The woman remained seated. "My name is Kare'."

"Well Kare', I spend a lot of time practicing at gun ranges just like this one."

"That's it? Just keep shooting?"

"Well yes, but to be really good you need to have a feel for shooting and you need the correct hand gun, as well as knowing the proper shooting techniques."

"Is there a school you can go to, to learn how be an expert?"

"To become an expert, haaa."

"Yes," Kare' answered.

"Why would you want to become an expert?" Jordan asked.

Kare' cleared her throat and slowly stood, placed her stub-nose .38 caliber six shot revolver in the small brown leather case. She zipped the case closed and took a deep breath and straightened her body, looked Jordan in the eyes and with an ice cold tone in her voice replied, "I have a mission."

Kare' turned and started toward the door with the case in her right hand.

Just as she opened the exit door Jordan spoke. "Kare', how serious are you about becoming an expert? I mean a real expert."

Kare' stopped with her back still to Jordan, the steel gray door still opened slightly, then she stepped back one step and let the door slowly close. She turned to face Jordan now some twenty feet away. "Dead serious."

"Then Kare' if you would be willing to allow me to finish my practice session, I will give you your first lesson free. Then if you would like we can go down the street and have lunch and talk about how serious you really are.

# Failure and Success

THE FINAL YEAR'S GRADES WERE into the O'Francis house and Nico had failed Biology. J.P. had checked with his teacher, who was Tim Harper, and had found that he failed deliberately.

A full year of some hard times had passed for both Nico as well as for the O'Francis family. Nico tested the waters more than once, and had been grounded more than once. J.P. felt that he had some good in him, and he could, at times, show it. But for the most part J.P. saw the bad side of Nico and knew he did not want to be saved from a world of crime.

J.P.'s rule was simple, if he failed anything he would go back to his parents or to an all boys' camp for uncontrollable youths. Dennis and Theresa had to make the trip to Honsburg.

It was a night at the dining room table that would catch Nico in several lies in front of his parents and he would have to come clean as to why he had done what he had in school as well as several other matters of concern for Dawn and J.P. that had taken place in the community, of which he was not aware his aunt and uncle were even remotely aware of.

He could not handle the discipline that J.P. required of him, Patrick was used to it and accepted it and adhered to it. But Nico wanted to do what Nico wanted to do, stay out late at night, come and go as he pleased, which was totally unacceptable under the O'Francis roof. Nico finally stated that he did not want to stay in the same house with his uncle. The following day, he was packed and off with his parents back to the city life. J.P. and Dawn had tried for two years to reach Nico, and had failed. Theresa did not seem too happy, J.P. did not know if she was upset with him or with her son. Maybe she thought that his rules were too stern, as she was known for giving into the demands of her son. It did not matter to J.P., his home, his rules.

Now Nicodemus would have to deal with a life that would not lead him to the riches he thought he would get out of running with the gangs on the streets of Detroit. Dennis and Theresa would suffer much heartache in the fourth coming years as well as many sleepless nights because Nicodemus did not respect nor did he care about anyone other than himself.

Another year passed and it once again was spring. O'Francis requested that his son Patrick be allowed to stay on the varsity level his sophomore year and not be sent down to the junior varsity. J.P. watched in total disgust at the manner in which the junior varsity program was being operated. Practice sessions were a joke, a mockery to the game of baseball. Patrick was not learning anything, and being told that what he had been taught by his father was incorrect and that he'd better do it the way the junior varsity coach wanted it done.

The basics were the foundation for a solid baseball player, and that is what Coach O'Francis had been teaching his son. He knew what was to be expected on the varsity level, and his son was not being treated fairly in practice as well as the games. His request was not denied, and he knew he would at least get the proper instruction by Coach Ziegler at the position he had chosen to play. He knew that he would be exposed to a better and more positive mental aspect of the game by being around the upper classmen playing varsity. He also knew or he felt that Patrick would get to play an inning or two whenever the team had a game won. He knew very well what a hard time it was to correct the bad habits developed by younger players, and he did not want Patrick to have to go through that. To J.P.'s surprise, Tim agreed and assured J.P. that he would keep him on the varsity.

Patrick played sparingly throughout the course of the season, but Coach O'Francis had expected that as a senior was playing ahead of him at second base, the position Patrick's older brother had played and the one he wanted to follow.

Patrick was a very good contact hitter for a sophomore, so Tim used him as a pinch hitter on more than one occasion for other players who were not hitting the ball, or for a particular game situation, and Patrick came through for his team with a batting average of .722 by the end of the season. He did not get to play in many games at a defensive position, so Coach O'Francis took care of that. J.P. was not allowed on the field for practice or for the games, a policy passed down by the administration. Even though he did not get to see many of Patrick's games due his full schedule of umpiring, he spent hours every weekend, weather permitting, with Patrick where they would be on the field practicing and honing his defensive skills to prepare him for a run at second base his junior year. He would hit his son two hundred balls, to his left, to his right, straight at him, soft, hard, and slow rollers where he would have to charge them. "Worm burners" as they were referred to in baseball lingo, pop flies to his left and right, and on occasion in the infield, also the ones that were commonly known as "Texas leaguers", the one's he would have to dive to make the catch, which he liked to do, especially if he made the catch.

There were weekends that his timing was off and he would become very flustered with himself, and his father would have to try and explain that he was not going to make all the plays and that he would make errors, but that he could not let that bother him. Coach O'Francis knew that all competitive high-spirited athletes were like that. He knew they expected never to make mistakes, to be one hundred per cent. He also knew that it just did not happen that way, not even on the pro level, or "The Show" as it was commonly known among baseball people. They would take breaks after every fifty balls and talk.

In order for Patrick to get his throwing in to first base, his father would take the position at first and Patrick would place baseballs at various places around second and charge them and make the throw to first. The practicing of turning the double play was another one of O'Francis' "field expedience" ideals as he would play shortstop. There was no first baseman to throw to so he took the pitching target, an angle iron frame with a black thick mining belt attached to the middle of it with five holes cut out in the shape of a square with white paint around the square. One hole in the middle at the belt level of a batter, and the other four were in the upper and lower right and left hand corners. Designed for pitcher to throw at to improve their location skills, but for J.P. it was placed across first base to be used for Patrick to throw to. If he did hit one of the holes there was a net attached to the back of the frame to catch the balls so they would not go beyond the frame itself.

After a basket of balls, working on the double play, the O'Francis "boys" (as J.P. seemed to revert back to a boy when he was on the field "playing") would walk over and collect the balls out of the catch net or just in front of the pitching frame and start again with Coach O'Francis throwing the short balls, the tosses, and the long and hard one in order for his son to work on the proper mechanics for turning the double play. That part of the practice session took longer as Patrick had to re-adjust his position after each throw. One of the most important things he taught his son was to go through the bag, getting out of the way of the player sliding, trying to take him out. He taught it for safety reasons as well as being able to complete the double play properly. He reminded both his sons of his coach, "Big Daddy's" misfortune at second base, shattering his ankle, costing him a career in professional baseball. Both of J.P.'s sons had perfected the art of turning the double play correctly.

The weekends were not just limited to defense, one day of the two was set aside for batting practice. For most of the time Coach O'Francis would use the pitching machine, his arm could not produce the speed needed for his son to get used to the speeds needed for him to become a successful hitter. On occasions he would pitch to Patrick, but his lower to mid seventy mile an hour fast balls were not much of a challenge, but it was good for BP. Often times when J.P. was on the mound, they would play a game, Coach O'Francis being the Yankees and some of the many famous Yankee pitchers, and Patrick being the White Sox, and he being whomever at the plate. J.P. was the narrator of the game, and on occasions he would K his son with a breaking ball, or a called strike, which was always a debate between the two as to the strike zone.

The imaginary runners and score was really not important to J.P., it was the learning process his son was going through. The necessary bunt to advance the runner, the do or die squeeze play to win the game, and the joy he had of being with his son on the diamond. O'Francis transformed into the boy of by gone years each time they went to the field. He could spend hours per day on a baseball field if he had not had to make a living for his family. Something most people just did not understand.

The "Cats " made the post season playoffs and won their first round, but now had to travel east to Salem to face Gerald Victor High School, who had gotten a bye the first round as they had won their conference title. They would place on the mound their much talked about and college bound ace. A ninety plus fastball pitcher, who had no loses in his high school career.

Tim had stopped by the O'Francis house, which was not at all out of the ordinary even after his departure from the team. Timing was always right for one of Dawn's super suppers, and the polite hosts the O'Francis family was, he was invited to stay. You did not have to do a lot of arm twisting, as Tim loved her cooking. Out of the blue, he asked J.P. to travel with them to Salem, as they were taking cars and vans, and none belonged to the school system. He could ride with him, that way they could not stop him from going with the team. He told J.P. he wanted him in the dugout during the game and O'Francis looked at Harper for a long few seconds his mind questioning why.

"Do you think that is a wise move Tim?"

"I think it is my move! I do not have a problem with it!"

"You may not, no. But I will bet *your* ass that "They" will have a problem with it! I know for a fact that they have eyes everywhere!"

"Look, J.P., just how many damn games have any of the ass-holes ever come to? If it was not for looks, hell they would not walk out of the school for the home games!" Several minutes of silence as they both ate, and no one else talked.

J.P. spoke slowly. "Well, it would be nice. I mean... just to be in the dug-out again during the game. Keep in mind, I am telling you that it will be reported."

Tim finished his supper, got up and went to the paper towel rack, pulled off two sheets of paper, and stuffed them into a plastic cup, then took out his Red Man and packed his left jaw with a chew. The entire time the room was silent. Patrick had finished and went to the living room to take in some television. Dawn was cleaning up the dishes and putting the leftover food in the refrigerator. It was one of her very rare days off from work. Tim of course, was very happy he had decided to stop by, because eating what J.P. would have fixed was not in the same "ball park" as Dawn's cooking and on her days off she made a point of cooking her family a full meal.

"So what do you say?"

And before J.P. could answer, Dawn spoke. "I think you should go. I mean, J.P. look, take a day off work. Hell, they damn sure won't miss you. Hell you know they don't care if you are there or not. Really they prefer you not be there. I think you should go and be with your son."

She had over the many years of marriage little by little become more and more vocal, expressing her opinion. Of course her intellect and educational background was so far ahead of ninety percent of the people in the community she had to lower her conversation to the bare nothing to communicate with them.

"Okay, I will go." Then he smiled, and a warm sensation came over him, as if someone had reached out and sprinkled him with some type of Irish magic diamond dust. He looked at Dawn, and she had that big beautiful beaming smile covering her face.

What no one knew was that when J.P. came out to his car to go home that very day he found a note on his car window. He had gotten in the car and had started it before he noticed the slip of paper tucked under the wiper blade on the driver's side. He opened the door, placed one foot on the pavement, raised up and reached out over the windshield to take the paper out. He opened it as he stood with one foot on the pavement and one in the car.

*"You have a family! Drop the suit!"*

J.P. read it several times. Typed off a computer, he knew who, but also knew he could not prove it. Hell, most people would never believe half of what he had experienced, saw, or uncovered over the years. He knew damn well they would not believe this was a note from the Bales-Finkel connection. He folded the paper and placed it in his shirt pocket. Sitting back down in his car he spoke, *"If anyone touches any member of my family I will kill them!"* He spoke to no one other than himself.

Upon arrival at the field in Salem for the regional playoffs, the team walked around the field. It was a good flat infield that was well groomed. The large outfield was somewhat bigger than their own. It was 325 feet down the lines. Dead center was 375 feet, a good pock for a high school player, but not unheard of by no means. The dugouts were set down in the ground, two steps down placing the field level at one's belt line, with a chain link wire screen in front of the face of each dugout with both ends open. A bench ran the full length of the dugout and at the home plate end, a place for the bats and helmets. The floor of the dugout was made of concrete. The wall from the floor of the dugout to the roof was concrete blocks, painted in the colors of the team, which was blue and white with a red trim.

As the team and coaches were dressing, J.P. felt emptiness inside him. He was just standing around saying nothing when he should be going through his ritual of putting on his uniform. But that was not the case, and he felt some bitterness toward the coach that had replaced him, which was unjust as it was of no fault of the coach. He was a very good person, one that appeared to have a great degree of honor and integrity. He waited to follow one of his baseball superstitions, putting a chew in his mouth before he went out on the field. As soon as he walked out of the dressing room to walk to the field he put in a piece of bubble gum in his mouth, chewing it all the way to the field and as soon as he walked into the dugout, he put the chew of tobacco in to mix with his gum.

The catcher for Harriette High School asked J.P. once why he mixed bubble gum with chewing tobacco. O'Francis was prepared to umpire a game for Harriette High School, one of his favorite schools to call at.

He told the young catcher as he watched in astonishment, "Well it makes it taste better, and it holds it together."

The catcher just stood and watched saying nothing as O'Francis finished packing his jaw with a chew.

"Are you ready to get this game under way?" J.P. asked him, smiling and putting his mask over his face. Before the catcher could answer, J.P. continued, "You know you have the best spot on the field. This game cannot be played without you. That is just how important you are."

The young catcher beamed with pride, and with a smile as broad as the Mississippi river, he stated, "Then let's get it going."

The Honsburg players went to the right field area and got into their traditional circle. They went through their stretching routine, then broke out into a long line matching up with whomever they liked to warm up their arms with. The catcher and pitchers were at one end of the line of players, something J.P. had incorporated and was still intact. The coaches were out among the players and J.P. was standing in the dugout watching. The three managers had gotten all the equipment ready and was standing alongside him. J.P. felt a million miles away, and his look reflected the hollow feeling he had. He wanted so badly to be with "his" battery, getting them ready. Ten minutes of throwing passed and Tim Harper walked toward the dugout as J.P. watched him approach.

"Coach O'Francis, go get the battery ready."

He stated it without the slightest question in his tone of voice. It was as if J.P. was still in uniform. Harper walked over to the water jug, as he had gone through his third chew since leaving home. He would go through many more before the game was over, which was his nature. J.P. had not moved, and Tim repeated himself, as he knew that J.P. was hard of hearing. Coach O'Francis walked over to Harper.

"Are you sure this is a good idea?"

Tim gave him one of his looks, no words had to be spoken.

"What about Andy?"

Then with a more stern tone in his voice, "J.P., I want you to get the battery ready!"

Tim Harper and J.P. O'Francis' eyes were locked. "Okay, consider it done."

It would be the first time in three seasons he would be doing *HIS* JOB. It would also be the first time he would be doing it without a uniform on. But it was okay with Coach O'Francis, a term of endearment the players still referred to him as, also something that he was very much aware of, that really "ate" at the administration, as well as some of the powerful political people, trivial as it was. They hated people to refer to him as Coach. His youngest son was now wearing his father's uniform. Patrick had requested that he be allowed to wear his dad's number long before the season had begun, and Tim Harper made sure that he received it. On one of the rare games he was able to attend during the regular season, when J.P. first saw it on his son, a warm feeling went through him and "goose" bumps covered his entire body as a lump emerged in his throat and tears filled his eyes.

As he began his walk toward the pitcher and catcher, O'Francis' heart began to pound hard. It was an instant good feeling that started at the top of his head and rolled down the entire length of his body like a great shock wave extending out from an atomic explosion. He had a bounce in his steps as he walked toward them. His attire was not what he would have wanted, black and tan Dockers, no socks, jeans, and a collared three button pullover black shirt. He walked down the long line of players tossing to one another and came to the end of the line, placing his left hand on Shane Mitchell's right shoulder.

Shane was born to be a catcher. J.P. had coached him in the last year of his senior league days. He had been a hard person to control because of his temper, and would get so mad at himself that one would think he was going to have a stroke as red as his face would get. He had listened and learned and now he was in his senior year of varsity baseball, and had come a long way as a catcher. O'Francis was very proud of him, as he knew that he had worked very hard to get where he was. He would, over the years J.P. had been away from the team, come to Coach O'Francis and seek advice on the techniques of catching, and would receive it. He stood five feet eleven and weighed one hundred and ninety pounds, all solid muscle. He smiled as he raised his hand, "Hi Coach." J.P. motioned for Malcolm Jennings to come with O'Francis and Mitchell. As Malcolm jogged up to the two already walking to the bullpen, J.P. told them he was going to get them ready for the game. That part of the job had not been turned over to Andy in the past three seasons. Shane spoke. "Great!"

Then Malcolm spoke. "Great Coach".

"I know I am not dressed for the occasion men, but..."

Shane interrupted. "That's okay Coach, we're just happy you are here." He was commonly referred to "Moose," which most people did not know the nickname was an Algonquian word that meant "*to strip away*".

"So, what do you think Coach?"

J.P. spit. "I think you are going to pitch a great game! I think we are going to win! I think we will hit their ace!"

One could sense the excitement in both young men, and J.P. intended on motivating them even more before the game was over. He had a rare chance to coach again, and he would do his normal encouraging pep talks to individuals as the game went on. He squatted as Shane and "Moose" got ready. He worked them slow as they had a lot of time before game time. J.P. would walk from the catcher to the pitcher talking to them building on their confidence, reminding them of the little things it took to win a big game. After returning from Malcolm back to Shane and placing himself in the batter's box to give Malcolm a body to throw to, Shane looked up at O'Francis.

"Coach are you going to call the pitches for us?"

"I do not know that Shane. That depends on what Coach Harper wants, and what I am allowed to do in the dugout."

Malcolm began his finial warm-up by firing four fastballs down the middle.

"Move him to the outside Shane." Coach O'Francis said as he still stood in the batter's box to give Malcolm a better idea of where to pitch the ball, a better look at where the ball was traveling, to see how much movement was on his fast ball. O'Francis would take a normal batting stance.

"Fast ball?" Shane asked.

"Yes." And three pitches were on the corner thigh high.

"Now inside Coach?"

J.P. looked down and smiled. "Yes, then I will switch to the left side." They worked the right and left side of the plate with his fastballs and then went through his breaking pitches in the same manner.

"You're ready." Coach O'Francis told "Moose."

Shane and O'Francis walked to the bullpen mound.

"Coach," Malcolm looked at O'Francis with a concerned look on his face, "Are you going to call the pitches for us?"

J.P. spit again, and looked down at the mound, raking some dirt off the pitching rubber. "I do not know."

They both started to speak, and then Shane continued as "Moose" stopped, "I'll talk to Coach Harper if you want me to."

"Yes I will too, Coach. We want you to call the pitches for us. It makes it a lot easier for us."

"We will see. How do you feel "Moose?"

"I feel great." He stated with excitement.

"Just remember, believe in yourself! Now you know we will not get all the pitches, and Shane you know that the umpire will miss some, so do not get down! That happens. And never, I mean never, say anything to the ump. If I get to call the pitches, and if the ump misses on the corner, nod yes. If it was a strike, you can tell."

"Okay Coach."

"Moose", you block out everything, do not listen to the noise! You must have complete concentration today, no matter what the call is. And if they get a hit, or even a home run, do not worry about it. That too will happen. Hell guys that happens to the pros. Just keep telling yourself that you are the best that ever walked to the mound and that you are going to throw strikes. Keep telling yourself that you are the best that ever squatted behind the plate! I really do not care how much news coverage this other pitcher has gotten, you are as good as he is, and do not forget it! Concentrate on where to throw the ball, think of nothing else. Shane, hold the mitt steady...do not forget to frame each pitch. Do not move your arm, only your wrist. Got it?"

"I will Coach, I will!" came a response from the battery.

While O'Francis was getting the battery ready Andy Ziegler was getting the infield and outfield ready. J.P. had informed Tim that Malcolm was ready, and was looking really good. Coach Ziegler had come into the dugout, and gathered with Harper and Teddy to look over the lineup. J.P. had walked to the other end of the dugout, when Tim looked around.

"O'Francis, what are you doing? Get over here!"

J.P. walked back to the where the three coaches were. "Well, I..."

Tim cut him off quickly, "Bull, you're still a part of this team as far as I am concerned! So what do you think?" As he showed him the lineup card.

O'Francis looked over it slowly. "No DH?"

"No, Patrick would normally be the DH, but I am thinking we may need him to pinch hit, and that would remove him if we DH'ed him."

O'Francis looked across at Andy, who was facing him. "What do you think "Zek?"

"I like the idea myself. I mean I have no problem with the idea of using Patrick as a pinch hitter. I mean he has done it all year for us, and you just don't know which one of this bunch is going to be off today at the plate."

It was set, Tim liked it, and he liked how all three would have disagreed if they did not like the lineup. If Andy had not, he was sure that Teddy and J.P. would have told him. He would have preferred to have all three on his staff, but the Honsburg administration and LaMar just would not allow it to be. It would have made the perfect baseball staff, and Marshy was smart enough to know that. He was not going to let that happen, not for Tim Harper, and not for Honsburg High School, and especially not for J. Patrick O'Francis.

The fans that would normally follow the "Cats" were in the stands by that point as the Gerald Victor Blue Devils were finishing up their infield warm ups. Several people in the stands who were not a fan of O'Francis, and who had covertly assisted Damon and Finkel in getting him removed from his coaching position, several being part of the Christian faction of the community, spotted J.P. and made several snide remarks about him not being a coach and being in the dugout. One of the more candid and very open supporters of O'Francis, overheard the comments, and made a point of getting up and walking two rows down to the three women and two men.

"Look, everybody knows what you have done, and how you feel. I am here to tell you the majority likes for O'Francis to be where he is. By-god, if you don't like it why don't you get off your asses and walk down there and tell Coach Harper you don't want him in the dugout! Matter a fact, why don't you tell Coach O'Francis to his face!"

The man stood facing J.P.'s adversaries. The people were in shock, as they had been caught character assassinating O'Francis. No one moved, no one said a word.

"Yeah, just as I thought! You'll stab him behind his back, but you haven't got the guts to tell him to his face! Damn hypocrites! Hell, we lost one of the best baseball coaches this school has ever had because of people just like you!"

His anger showed, and his words were harsh. His voice had raised and others had turned their attention to the confrontation. As he walked back to his seat several parents clapped and several patted him on the shoulder and back as he passed them and re-took his seat. The group of "assassins" slowly got up and moved to another part of the stands.

Dawn could not be at the game, as she had to work at the video store. She would have, if Damon Bales had not unjustly rejected her as a substitute teacher. Dawn was very bitter not being able to see her youngest son play in a regional play off game. This of course would have made Bales and Marshy happy if they could have known. The people she had to deal with that thought that people like Marshy and Bales were the greatest thing since peanut butter, always came in the store and seemed to always ask leading, probing questions, which Dawn was able to detect with great ease. She had without any question far superior intelligentsia than the people she had to deal with on a day in and day out basis. She would brush the probes off with a sharp response that left them dumb founded, as they did not get her whit, sharp Italian cutting sarcasm. Her responses went so far over their heads a 747 flying at maximum altitude could have not equaled it. The one thing that saved her day was that it was on the radio, and she could listen to the play by play.

Tim read the lineup and the players got ready to face the fireball ace that had taken the mound. He looked good as J.P. watched him get in his final warmup pitches before the umpire called "Play Ball." In O'Francis' mind he was not as good as some of the pitchers the "Cats" had faced in past years. He felt that the media had made more out of him than he really was. He appeared to have a fast ball ranging in the upper eighties, and his breaking ball seemed to be only fair, as it would go in the dirt three out of the five times he threw it. *Making his catcher's day a difficult one*, J.P. thought. He had been watching him in the bullpen earlier, and O'Francis had already developed an attitude about him. He was too cocky, too arrogant. He lacked discipline, he could tell, just something about his body language that gave it away. And O'Francis was good at reading people. He had become somewhat of an unofficial expert at reading people, and rarely was he ever wrong.

It was game time and the "Cats" lead off was a small-framed right hander with quick feet. He was not known for his intellect but was a very good outfielder. Anson threw him four straight balls, and Paul Steward was on first. O'Francis had taken note of the catcher's arm and speed of release and calculated that with Steward's speed coupled with Arson's high leg kick, he could take second. But Tim did not send him. When O'Francis was in his first base coaching box they had been able to signal each other, forming a communication. They had their mental connection that had allowed for the confidence in each other as to strategy.

When Harper would question himself, it had been J.P. that gave him that extra confidence to gamble. And in some cases J.P would send a player without Harper's sign, which got him into somewhat trouble with the head coach. However, in all the years he had sent a player "unauthorized" to second, he had never had one thrown out. J.P. knew his players, and could read catchers like an elementary level book. But that was not the case anymore. Zek did not have that connection with Tim, nor was he a gambler. He was not a leader, and would not question Harper.

Harper had expressed over the years they had been apart how he missed him on the field. J.P. felt that he was very sincere in his words, on the rare occasions whenever they had crossed paths. Deep in the recesses of his subconscious he hoped he was not wrong about Harper. Their relationship had been tainted and he did not know if Tim even knew it. If he did he did not show it. But J.P. also knew he was very good at hiding his feelings. And once he came out of the forest and was able to see the trees, he had a much different perspective of the person he had so loyally befriend.

Bart Milstone, the shortstop, flied out to the right fielder, and Robert Milstone, the second baseman Bart's brother, went down swinging. Mark Houston the third baseman hit a line drive to the second baseman, stranding Steward at first. In the top half of the first inning, J.P. was not impressed at all with the media's hype of Arson, but it was only the top half of the first inning and he was only a seventeen year old that was as tight as a drum.

Tim looked at J.P. when he walked into the dugout. There was no real need for words, *he needed him!* O'Francis was standing alone at the far end of the dugout and Tim walked the full length of the dugout and stood beside him for a mere moment. "Call them!" He turned and went to the water jug at the other end.

J.P. had already worked out his signals for Shane to use. J.P. stepped outside to the corner of the dugout, yelling at Shane, getting his attention and nodding his head, *yes,* and he could see a broad smile come across his face through his mask. Two pitches later, he threw down to second, a strong throw and dead on the money, a signal to the opposing team, *"just try me!"* He walked to the mound and told "Moose" that Coach O'Francis was calling the pitches, and "Moose" looked over at O'Francis, nodded his head up and down, and smiled. Shane jogged back to the plate, pulled his mask over his face, then squatted and turned his head toward J.P. Now it was Coach O'Francis who had to produce.

He called for a curve ball. Most pitchers in high school start off with a fastball in hopes of getting a strike, as it was very important to get ahead of the batter. The first batter he faced was the center fielder. He had not expected a breaking ball and swung late for a strike. Another curve ball in the dirt and a fastball off the corner, for a two and one count. He called for another breaking pitch and another ball. J.P. had to set the tone right away, and he knew his plan would work.

Tim never questioned him. He called for a fastball on the outside to the right handed batter, and he flied out to the right fielder for the first out. The next batter got a single. "Not to worry," he said, calling out to "Moose." The catcher batted third, and grounded out to the second baseman. They had avoided the double as a hit and run was on, but they had two out. Now the big ace, the pitcher, the young man who could do it all for them was at the plate. J.P. figured him for a fastball hitter, and started him with a changeup. He swung so hard he momentarily lost his balance. "Moose" delivered him a sharp breaking curve that went down and away on a right-handed batter and it worked, as he popped up to the pitcher, to end the first inning.

Anson collected three K's at the top of the second. "Moose" collected his three outs with assistance from his team mates, two fly balls to the outfield and a grounder just in front of the plate. Shane was out on it quicker than a cat pouncing on a field mouse. He scooped it up, came under control and fired a "bullet" to his first baseman, a perfect execution of how a catcher performs with a ball chopped to the infield in front of home plate. Coach O'Francis just smiled with pride at what he saw.

The third saw no score and Malcolm began to feel that he could equal the highly publicized ace. O'Francis talked to them in between each inning, motivating them, instilling in them that they were the best "battery" on the field.

In the fourth he got Hudson the catcher on a called third strike. Malcolm had run the count to a two and two. J.P. had not used the change-up but once to that point, and felt that it was time. He had called out to Malcolm to focus. "Believe in yourself," and nodded at him. Hudson took the pitch; he had been fooled. The bat barrel dropped to the ground, and he stood in the box looking back at the umpire in disbelief.

O'Francis had always feared catchers, as he felt that they were over all your best hitter. They could see the ball so much better as they saw it coming at them all the time and in many different ways. Plus he was the leadoff man, and it was extremely important to get the leadoff batter in any inning, on any level of the game. It gave the defense the better percentage. Unlike football or basketball, baseball was all about percentages. But it was baseball, and anything could happen in the game of baseball. Since it can happen it usually did.

Anson was up and got a double, followed by their DH with a single. They were on the board, a one to zip game. J.P. watched "Moose" closely. He appeared to be unrattled. Robins, the DH stole second, the throw was on line and it was there in time, the tag was down but the call was safe.

That bothered Shane. J.P. motioned for him to calm down and assured him it would work out.

Teddy screamed out from the dugout, "A little home cooking don't you think there Mr. Umpire?"

Malcolm lost one in the dirt to Shane's right, which ricocheted off his forearm, a WP and Robins was on third. Haddon, the first baseman hit a slow roller to the second baseman, leaving Milstone no choice but to go to first, allowing Robin to score. Now it was a two-zip game. Malcolm got Walls, the second baseman to "K" on two fastballs and a slow curve to end the inning.

The "Cats" left two stranded on base in their half of the inning. The fifth saw G.V. stranding two at the corners, and the "Cats" leaving two at first and second again. J.P. began to worry a little. That was four potential scorers left on base, with two innings left. "Moose" was not tired and had been doing well. He had only thrown fifty-two pitches and had been matching Mr. "Ace" who was becoming a little angered as the "Cats" were making contact with his pitches. It was unfortunate that they were hit to someone, but that was all part of the game. Sometimes they have "eyes" and hit the holes, or the gaps, sometimes they don't. In the top half of the sixth the "Blue Devils" went down in order, and it was time for the "Cats" to strike, and they did. Anson walked the first batter, got a call third strike out on the second, which Teddy went off on the call to the umpire as it was well out of the strike zone.

"Good God, Ump, he needed a ladder to reach that one! Christ, what kind of call was that?"

J.P. just smiled, he knew that Ted was correct. He either missed accidentally, which can happen, or he was playing, "help the "Ace" a little. It was to have been a blow out, the Honsburg "Cats" were not supposed to be in the game by this point. J.P. had seen it happen to them more than once in his career, so nothing surprised him. He would say nothing overt to any of the umpires. He just encouraged each batter to focus and believe in themselves.

Anson walked the next two batters, and was visibly shaken. The "Cats" had the bases loaded with one out, and their coach walked to the mound to try and calm Anson down. Instead of listening to his coach, he bitched to him the entire time about the calls he was getting. J.P. had been right, he told himself as he observed the action at the mound. The boy was out of control, he had no discipline, and the coach did not have control of his "Ace". As O'Francis stood at the opposite end of the dugout from the rest of the Honsburg staff, a conference began at the other end. Then Harper walked to J.P.

"O'Francis, what do you think about pinch hitting Patrick for Stockton?" J.P. looked at his ex-coaching partner, and then looked around him at the other two coaches at the other end of the dugout.

"Tim, what has Paul done today?"

He spit and replied, "A walk and two K's. But he had not been doing real well lately, and he is not good in a tight situation."

J.P. looked at Paul walking to the plate, The umpire was working his way to the mound, and Tim watched J.P.'s eyes.

"Do you think Patrick can come through for us?"

O'Francis did not hesitate, "Yes! He is an O'Francis. He will do it under pressure! Trust me Tim on that one!"

Tim Harper turned. "Humper" pinch-hit O'Francis. Patrick, you're batting."

"Hump" who kept the books, walked about halfway to home plate and called out to Stockton to come to him. He informed him that he was being replaced and then walked to the plate umpire and made the changes. Stockton walked into the dugout with an attitude, threw his helmet down, which was a "no-no" and got a cold hard look from both Harper and O'Francis instantly. His overinflated ego, and usually overrunning mouth, was about to get the wrath of one H. Timothy Harper.

J.P. walked over to his son, who seemed to be calm, putting his helmet on.

"Patrick. Concentrate, and believe in yourself. I have faith in you."

J.P. patted him on the butt, and he was out of the dugout and walking to the plate.

His mother was hanging on every word the play-by-play radio announcer was speaking. Her heart began to beat much faster when she heard her baby boy's name announced.

J.P. walked to the outside edge of the dugout, and stood with his hands crossed resting behind his "butt".

"My Lady, allow his God given abilities to surface. Give him the confidence he needs to perform."

Then he called out to his son once more before he stepped into the batter's box. "Patrick, believe in yourself!"

J.P. felt good, he knew that his youngest son, like his older son had done many times, would come through. It was in their genes, their blood, they were O'Francis'.

Anson took his signal and delivered a strike on the outside corner to the sophomore right handed batter. His next pitch was a strike low. Patrick had read it to be a ball. J.P. felt from his angle it was. Tim took a few steps at third and spit. J.P. never moved from his position, his mind working.

"Watch the ball, read the pitch, follow it all the way through to the catcher's mitt. Pull the trigger if it is close." O'Francis yelled to his son.

Patrick took the next one low for a ball, the same place the last pitch was. Anson delivered his famed fastball, and Patrick fouled it back into the stands. J.P. smiled to himself. *"He was on that one, and he has him! He'll not get my son on this day!"* Anson ran the count to full, and the place was going wild. The "Blue Devils" coach walked to the outside of the dugout, took three steps toward the mound and stopped, then turned and walked back to the edge of the dugout. Patrick stepped back out of the batter's box. The catcher looked up at him, and then called time and jogged to the mound.

"He's young. Hell man, you can blow this one by him! Now come on, let's do it!"

He turned and jogged back to the plate. Patrick stepped back into the batter's box, took a couple of swings, and big Anson delivered another eighty-eight mile an hour fast ball. Patrick took him hard to right field between the second baseman and first baseman with a line drive, allowing two runs to score and tying the game up.

The G.V. coach called time and went to the mound. He patted Anson on the butt, and called for the relief pitcher. As Anson went into the dugout he threw his glove against the wall then kicked the helmet rack scattering helmets over the floor of the dugout, sending his teammates running to the opposite end as he was throwing his childish uncontrollable temper tantrum. He began beating his fist against the cinder block wall of the back of the dugout cussing the young sophomore now standing on first base.

J.P. clapped his hands and pointed at his son with a wide smile. Patrick clapped and pointed back at his father, with a beaming smile on his face. Tim Harper looked across at O'Francis standing at the corner of the dugout, spit and a rare slight smile broke his face.

Dawn bounced around the video store and out into the parking lot screaming and yelling doing her Native American "around a camp fire" dance with joy and happiness.

An error on the left fielder from a sharp line drive gave the "Cats" the lead. The inning ended with a K from the second basemen.

It was the seventh inning, do or die for the power scoring "Blue Devils". They were at the top of their order. J.P. called for a change for his first pitch. The batter expected a fastball, and tried to check his swing, and dribbled one to the third baseman for the first out. They were now two outs away from a victory over one of the most over powering teams in the region, according to the press. The third baseman connected with a single to right field putting the tying run on first. Then Malcolm slipped and a running fastball tight inside hit the batter.

The next batter fouled the first pitch off, a curve ball, and then the strike zone shrank, and he could not get a strike. A walk and the game winning runner was on second. J.P. also had been here before. He knew that saying anything to the umpire would do no good. "Humper" was outraged, and let the ump know it. He was right, and J.P. knew it, but he had to concentrate and call the pitches. Malcolm was working like a finely oiled machine. Shane was working the plate like a pro, but the plate umpire, like many Coach O'Francis had seen before had no ethics.

J.P. called for a fastball. A check swing was called a strike when there was a request by Shane to the first base umpire. J.P. remembered that earlier in the game he had a problem with the slow breaking curve and called it. He blooped it to right field, an in "betweener" a "Texas-leaguer." Phillip the right fielder broke for the ball. His speed was unmatched on the team. The second baseman, Raymond Milstone the brother of Bart the shortstop, broke for the ball and the two dove for the ball at the same time colliding in midair twisting each other like a pretzel. The ball went off the heel of Stockton's glove onto the ground. The two boys lay on the ground in pain. The ball was still in play. The first baseman ran to the ball picking it up and throwing it home but not before two runs crossed the plate. The umpire called time, and the batter-runner held on second. Raymond had injured his knee. Tim replaced him with another sophomore, Jason Justin. Stockton would have a few sore spots but remained in the game.

To add insult to injury, the very next pitch the plate umpire called a balk on "Moose", which was not a balk, but again J.P. would not get into a debate over it, because he knew he could not win. It would only add more problems to his already unjust tattered and stained name. Harper remained on the surface composed. "Hump" went off again and never let up for the remainder of the game. "Zek" for the first time became vocal and joined "Humper" in their verbal barrage on the plate umpire. With one out and the bases loaded, J.P. called for a high fast ball, hoping for a pop up. Malcolm delivered, but the batter flied out to the center fielder, just deep enough for another run to score. Now the lead had switched and the "Blue Devils" held a five to three lead.

The center fielder, Nead walked to the plate with a cocky strut as J.P. called pitches and Malcolm's smoothness screwed him into the ground on three straight curve balls to bring an end to a stressful inning.

The "Cats" scored another run and left three runners stranded to end the game. Another trip to the regional playoffs, and once again Tim Harper's "Cats" had to come home without a victory.

Joy reined in the private homes of some of the anti-baseball power players of Honsburg and J.P. knew that Barnard Theodoric, LaMar Marshy and Damon Bales could not have had a better ending to another school year than with the loss to Harper's team.

It was the weekend and J.P. was not in the best of moods. It took several days for him to get over any loss, but when they came in the manner in which this one had, yet another one in his storied unofficial career, it seemed to hit harder and take longer to recover from.

The phone rang, and he heard on the other end of the line, "Will you accept a collect call from a David Higgenbottom?"

"Yes."

On the other end came, "Coach, what up?"

"Ahhh, not a lot, what's happening with you? How is our uncle treating you?"

"Country" laughed. "He's not treating me the way he should. Remember when I called a while back?"

"Yes, you were due a promotion, and due to head from Campbell to Korea. Yes I remember."

Hell, I am getting old, but still have a half ass memory. More than I can say for some of the ass-holes I have had to deal with. But hell that is another story, at another time over a few beers. So, what is the word?"

"I do not know if I told you or not, but I got my Air Assault wings. The 101st Air Borne is now the 101st Air Assault."

"So what is the difference?"

"Well we do not jump from planes; we retrograde out of Black Hawks now."

There was a pause in the conversation on the phone.

"You know, climb down from ropes out the sides of the chopper."

"You got me for a second, I did not know."

"I have put in for a TDY to Bragg to get my jump wings, but don't look like I will get a chance to get them."

"Why?"

"Ahh, ass holes are jerking me around on my stripe."

"Well, are you not due one? I mean I thought you,"

"Country" interrupted. "Hell, I have more than enough points and time in grade, but they want me to re-up before they give it to me."

"What are you going to do?"

"Not sure yet. I still have a few months, I will see."

"Well, it is your call, what did you tell them?"

"The stripe or no re-enlist!"

"Are you going to stick to what you told them?"

"Yes!"

"So, what are you going to do in the time you have left?"

"Ahhh, they got me going all over the place picking up people who have fucked-up, and taking them to Leavenworth."

"As in prison?"

"Yup, the one."

"Then someone must have really screwed up?"

"Oh, yeah, they see hard time."

"Well, that has to be a real joy."

"Ahh, it's just a thing. I finished another course in Law Enforcement."

"Gooood. So how many does that make you?"

"Ahh, I...ahhh, think about eighteen credit hours? I am not for sure, have to look."

"Hell you're close to having your associates in Law Enforcement then."

"How many hours does that take?"

"I'm not sure, but it will look good on a resume, when you get out."

"Hey, Coach I'll get back with you as to what I am going to do, may just see my ass coming Home."

"Well, do good and remember, believe in yourself, and be careful."

"Always. Later" And then the dial tone came on the line.

J.P. was very proud of Dave and his military record as well as his higher education, something most of his teachers would not have expected of him. But teachers at Honsburg were not known for encouraging the lower social economic level students to achieve a higher education in life. After discussing what the army had done, J.P. knew that he was indeed a man of his word, and he was very proud of him for that. He told Dawn that he felt that Dave would be coming home. She did not understand why they would want to lose a good soldier by playing stupid games with his life. J.P. of course did not either, as much as the military needed good people, and good career people. It was stupid to lose one because some dumb-ass wanted to play tough guy with someone's life.

"They will lose." He told Dawn as they sat at the dining room table discussing the conversation J.P. had with "Country".

"Why do you say that?"

"Because if Dave told the recruiting Officer that he wanted his stripe before he re-upped, and not to come to him the very last minute, trying to deal with him, he will stick to his word. Trust me on that."

# To Gaze upon the Beauty of Death

❧ ❧ ❧ ❧

DUNKIN BREWER RETIRED FROM THE school system in 1999. He continued his covert work in his semi-drug/gun dealing for his additional income. Not that he really needed it to make it, as he had been well cared for by the Marshy era and being the corrupt politician he had been for many years. He had scammed the county for a sizeable amount of change. 2005 made little change in how things worked in the Reynolds County area. The investigation on Dunkin left some questions for the "hit parade". Small time as he was he was a source of income for people in a business, that according to the government and its laws, was illegal. But after some evaluation, meetings, and a few phone calls to get clearance on the matter, it was decided that he could be replaced with ease, and with a better and younger operator for the area. Dunkin's activities on a daily basis had been monitored, photographed and passed to the proper people. It would be an easy job.

His lust for younger and very attractive women made him unfaithful to his wife for many years, and still at his age he thought of himself as a play-boy, playing the games that males and females have played which had not changed since the time male and female had been sexual attracted to each other, be it your bible toting people that insisted the "Word" was literally a fact, and covertly conducted their sexual games, while praising their Lord and digging deep into your household income, giving it to the church. God will surely reward you with your generous contribution.

He still had an insatiable habit of drinking, although he had cut back on it to some degree over the past few years. His habits put him in places where a job for a professional would be made "like a walk in the park".

It was late autumn and the mountain air was crisp in the evenings, a time for fireplaces and romance. Dunkin left his home with a kiss to his wife and informed her he had to be out of town for some business. She never questioned his "business" for all the years they had been married, although she knew inside he had been unfaithful for as long as she could remember back. Well maybe he was faithful to her for their first few years, but for the past thirty some odd years, he had not. A few earlier rounds of verbal confrontations resulted in some brief bitterness and she resolved herself to what he was and lived with it. She had her home and a nice one at that, something more than what a simple teacher's salary could have afforded, or for that matter what a principal's salary could have in the earlier years. LaMar had provided her husband with a very nice income through his reign and they lived very comfortably on it and the retirement it brought. It was no match to the income he received from whatever business he was in outside of the school system. She really did not care anymore. There was no real romance left in their lives, just a day in and day out routine that she was sure many other people just like her went through. What he did during his time with the school system and now after his retirement, she did not want to know.

Several years before J.P. had retired and moved from the area, he discussed the top ten people that had been slightly part of having or had been directly involved in his hardships. The list was then passed along to Joseph who had discussed it with his father-in-law in detail and had profiled what the total fifteen people had done to O'Francis and his family. Lots of questions were asked as to the "*whys*" of these people's actions, and no cause could be found to justify what they had done. It was Joseph's project all the way, as it did not involve the business directly nor did it involve any one of the people in the business. Brian O'Francis had been informed of the "*project*". Paul knew of all the people, their comings and their goings, and he knew all the connections to the *"project"*. It had been decided by Vincent and Brian that Joseph could precede with his "project" but with prudence and each part of the "project" would have to go through one of the two or both of the men.

The next part of the overall "project" was to be handled by Bruce, and he would select who he wanted to help with the operation. It had been easy to put a tracking device on Dunkin's car, and they had been following him and his activities for a period of a month. They had informed the people in the upper echelon that they would be losing one of their long time operators. Business was business, and they were prepared to have a replacement for him in a matter of days of his removal as a contact/dealer/operator/mule.

The people contracted for the job picked him up a few miles from his house and followed him for over an hour to a nice hotel, where he was to meet one of the contacts he had known for many years. Dunkin was told that because of his loyal service for the many years he had been working for them he was about to move right on up and receive a lucrative salary increase with a more executive like position, one of the operations, which would cover the entire five state area, something he could not resist. His ego had been pumped to the max and the extremely seductive female that had accompanied the two businessmen in their meeting in early fall made it more enticing, as she had played him like a fine Stradivarius.

It was wine and dine time, as he walked into the elegant dining area. "Good evening sir, may I help you"? The maitre d' spoke with a pleasant voice with a slight Italian accent to it.

"I am to meet Mr. Gabbana."

"Yes sir, if you will just follow me." He held his hand out as he began to walk to a table in a somewhat secluded area.

As Dunkin approached the table Nick Zileri raised up from his table. "Welcome Dunkin, let me introduce our business partners." He held his hand out. "Mr. Nic Gabbana, Mr. Mario Lorenzo, and Ms. Jordan Black, whom I assume you remember."

He smiled and acknowledged that he remembered her as he was being seated. The waiters approached and asked Dunkin if he would like something to drink, which he did.

During the course of the meal the business deal was discussed, and the details of what Dunkin would be doing was presented. He accepted the offer by the end of the dinner. It was now time for Jordan to play her hand, as she leaned over to Dunkin and in a whisper asked him to join her for a few after dinner drinks in the lounge. As they got up from the dining table the men all shook hands and Jordan extended her arm for Dunkin to escort her to the lounge for their drinks.

The music was leisure and the mood was being set as Dunkin began to feel his liquor. A small dance floor for some slow dancing made the night more of a seductive atmosphere for Dunkin. His thoughts had already turned to what he would be doing in a matter of a few hours. As they danced and their bodies rubbed against one another, Jordan used her skills of body movement to get a semi-erection from her would be seducer for the night. She began to nibble on his right ear and lick it with her tongue.

"I am quite tired. It has been a rather long day for me. Why don't you join me in my room?" It was an invitation that Dunkin had been waiting for, and he accepted eagerly.

A bottle of very good champagne had been chilling in a bucket of ice since Jordan had left her room for dinner. She pointed to the bottle and asked Dunkin to open it and pour them a couple of glasses to celebrate his new position in the company while she got into something more comfortable. She then turned the lights in the room down to dim. Dunkin's heart pounded as his anticipation grew for a night of lustful sex. Jordan was one of the most lustful and attractive women he had ever met.

*Could this be real* he thought, *a woman like this in a room for the evening. Was this the kind of women that he would be associating with at his new level?* She was something he had only seen in a Playboy magazine.

Her exit from the bathroom into the bedroom almost caused Dunkin to drop the bottle of champagne he was holding.

"My god", he exclaimed. He could not believe his own eyes, even with his dark rimmed glasses on. There she stood in her black, short, see through thigh length nightgown. She stood momentarily at the bathroom door letting the light of the bathroom to her back shine through the nightgown exposing all of her beauty for Dunkin to gaze upon. In her most seductive sexiest voice she requested a glass of champagne. Dunkin's hands were trembling as he poured the champagne in the two glasses. He turned and walked toward her. He handed her a glass and they tossed his new job. Jordan put her arms around his waist and pulled him to her kissing him and inserting her tongue deep into his mouth. She slowly removed his suit coat, and undid his tie, took off his glasses, then began kissing him on the neck and mouth as she undid the buttons of his shirt, pulling it out of his pants.

Jordan moved him slowly toward the edge of the bed and Dunkin lay back onto it. Jordan then removed his shoes and socks and placed them on the floor at the end of the bed. Dunkin was lying on his back looking down at the end of the bed facing her as she stood, the dim light casting a soft glow off her smooth dark skin. Jordan removed the top of her sheer nightgown letting it drop on the floor at her feet exposing her full naked body, her firm melon shaped breasts. Dunkin took a deep breath, "Oh my", was all he could mutter, and then closed his eyes and awaited her voluptuous body to accompany him on the bed.

Jordan tuned and walked to the dresser and opened her purse, withdrawing a nine-millimeter pistol, and then withdrew a silencer and attached it to the end. The entire time she was softly talking to Dunkin with words that sent him into a state of wonderfulness. She slowly approached the end of the bed raised her right hand and quickly squeezed off three rounds. One to the chest, one to the throat and one to the forehead. His body jerked only once, as his eyes rolled open, only to gaze upon the beauty of death.

Jordan turned, walked to her purse, pulled out a cell phone and dialed a number. It rang twice and on the other end of the line "yes" was the response. "It is done" she replied with a calm and cold voice.

"Get dressed, we are on the way."

By the time the knock came to her door she was clothed in a dark blue pin striped pants suit, a beige blouse and dark blue high heel shoes. She opened the door to greet Nic Gabbana and Nick Zileri.

"Any problems?" Nic asked.

"None." As she picked up her purse and small tote bag and started out the door.

"Mario is waiting in the car in the back lot. We will see you at the plane."

The two men closed the door, put on their rubber gloves and began cleaning the room. They removed the body from the bed and placed it in a body bag. Stripped the linen off the bed and replaced it with fresh new ones including the bed cover. They placed all items in a plastic bag and began to wipe down everything in the bed room, leaving nothing that could not have been touched and then cleaned the bathroom, leaving it perfectly sanitized, with no traces of anyone ever being in the bathroom or the bedroom. Dunkin had never registered in the hotel and no one dealing with the hotel or the restaurant or the lounge was ever introduced to him, just another face, with no name for the employees. He of course had not told a single person where he was going or the name of any person he was meeting.

His body was removed by way of the service elevator in a large laundry cart and loaded into a van at the rear of the hotel. It was business as usually for anyone who might see them, just a large bundle of dirty laundry being tossed into the back of the van.

Two days later his body was discovered five miles east of the city of Kinstown. It had been removed from the body bag and tossed in a field off the side of a country road. The investigation into his death posed more questions than could be answered. It once again brought out the phone tree from people that felt that he was the victim of some type of ongoing conspiracy to get rid of all of them. The more they pointed the finger at J.P. O'Francis the more questions the investigating officers would ask them. Why this man, they would ask. Why was this O'Francis behind two murders and one missing person to date? Why would O'Francis have reason for such acts?

Of course none would answer that, and the officers would then ask, "Then why are you naming this O'Francis person as the one doing or behind these acts?" Again the people making the accusations of the wrong doings would not give the officers any answers to warrant putting an APB out on J.P. O'Francis. When asked where this person was, none could give them a concrete answer. As the investigating officers probed for answers from members of the Honsburg community, they found O'Francis was living in the Atlanta area, maybe the Dallas area. They got answers from people that he moved to Dover, one stated that he had to be in one of the New England states. They were not sure which one, just that he had talked about moving there.

Several stated that they thought he had moved to South Bend to be close to Notre Dame. There were several reports that he had moved to Ireland. The police officers dismissed the notion that the O'Francis person had anything at all to do with any of the events, or for that matter if J.P. O'Francis was even alive. One report reached the desks of the investigating officers that he had died of a heart attack several years earlier, but did not know where he was at the time, just that the rumor mill was in Honsburg, where he had once lived, that he had died.

It had been three weeks since the body of Dunkin Brewer had been found naked with three holes in him and a purple lily on his chest.

Roger Bushman sat at his desk reading the morning paper and sipping his coffee. His phone rang three times before he reached over with his left hand and picked it up not taking his eyes off the article he was reading.

"Captain Bushman, May I help you?"

A momentary pause on the other end of the line and a man's voice then slowly spoke, "There is a connection to the deaths of Richard Finkel, Brewer, and the disappearance of Janice Jones."

This caught Bushman's attention. "What?"

"You heard me." Came the response on the other end of the line.

Bushman quickly picked up a pen and asked for the names again and received them. "With whom am I speaking to?" Then the phone clicked and it was dead.

"Hello, hello." Roger put the receiver down, rose from his chair and went to the door, opened it, walked out a few steps into the squad room and looked around.

"Burt," referring, to Burt Bass. "I need to see you in my office." Once inside he asked the detective who was working the Brewer case, and learned that it was Jason Branch. He then called Jason into his office.

"What have you got so far on the Brewer case?"

"Not much Captain."

"Well, what is not much?"

He hated to hear "not much" that never told him a thing.

"Well, he was from Reynolds County, Virginia. He was married with two children, who are grown with families of their own. He drank a lot, screwed around on his wife. Ahhh, let's see, ahhh. Was a retired principal, ahhhh, that's about it."

"Have you checked his wife out?"

"Yes sir I have, and she is clean. According to the coroner's time of death she had some friends, women, over to her house, some kind of bridge group. They met each week, and played cards. Goes to church regularly, seems to be an upright person."

"Did you check with all these women she associated with?"

"Yes sir. They all confirmed where she was. Even checked with some of the people in the area, about their card game, and they confirmed that they met every week, the same time."

"Any of the women absent from the card game that night?"

"No sir."

"Who is, ahhh" Roger looked down at the notes that he scribbled on his note pad. "Who is Richard Finkel?" Both detectives looked at each other, and both stated at the same time that they did not know. The name would not have keyed a thought as the Finkel 's assassination had taken place ten months earlier, and some fifty miles away from the city of Kinstown.

"Okay, who is Janice Jones?" Again they had no clue as to what their Captain was talking about, as Jones had disappeared in Reynolds County, a good ninety miles away.

"I just had a phone call, from someone who would not leave a name. Tells me that there was a connection between these people. He stated that the Finkel man was dead, and that the Jones woman was missing. Now I want you to get on this today. I want to know what the connection is."

The two detectives turned and began to exit the office when Branch stopped at the door.

"Oh, ahhh, Captain, there was one other thing about the Brewer man." He stood at the door. Roger waited for him to continue. When he didn't, "Okay, sooo, what?" he barked his question as he had been in a semi-ill mood from several other cases that were not being solved.

"Well, he had a dark purple Lily laying on him." Roger paused in thought. "Captain."

"Yeah, yeah. Look, Jason I get the feeling that there is more to this. Don't know, but... I mean, did you not think a purple Lily lying on the man's body was odd?"

"Yes sir. I mean we followed up on everything we could. We just did not turn up anything. We asked the people around where he lived. And Captain, damn, he lived, way," as he drew out the word, "back in the mountains. I mean there were lots of people living around there, but it's a hell-of a long way back in the mountains. Anyway, sorry sir, we could not find anything connected to a Purple Lily."

"You checked with the local Sheriff's department?"

"Yes sir. Hell, we would have never found the place if we had not. They knew him and told us that he was big in politics at one time, not much else. Well other than some of the same stuff we already had."

"You checked with the local political people? Of course that in itself should tell us something."

"Yes. We worked with the Sheriff's department, and they helped us get what information we have."

"Which is?"

"Well, other than he was tied into all the County politics and served as a County Supervisor for a number of years, there really was nothing to indicate that there was some type of shady dealings going on."

"Well, he was a politician, so that would mean that there was some type of shady deal somewhere. I want to find out what."

"Okay, we are on it."

"I don't know… I feel like there is something here. Re-check, find out about this person."

"Okay, we will go back over there and talk to some people. May turn up something."

"No may, I want a reason for this man's death. Oh, and I want to know what the damn lily means! Also, I want you to find out about these other two people. I want to know if they were connected and how! You get their names? Find out where this, this," he looked at his notes again, "Finkel person was and where and how he died." Then before they could take two steps, "and call the FBI and see if they have any report on a missing person in the area. If there is some sort of connection, it may be from the same county."

"Yes sir. Got it."

"Captain, I think a Purple Lily means death." Jason stated standing at the open door.

"Yeah, and just how did you come by that information?"

"I really can't remember, but I think I read it somewhere, or maybe heard on one of the Discovery channels. But I believe I am right."

"Nevertheless, what does it mean to this person. If that is what it means, then it has to be a message to someone, who? Get on this and stay on it."

# The Last Inning

IT WAS TO BE J.P.'S last year with the senior league All-Stars, and he had prepared his players well. Raymond would have to take over after he left the program. Raymond would do very well in the years to come as he had learned a great deal from J.P. He had been like a sponge absorbing everything J.P. had taught the young players as well as the strategy for playing the game. Raymond's son Jason and J.P.'s son Patrick was also playing their last All-Star games because of their age. They would now advance to the varsity level of high school. Jason aka, simple J.J., was behind the plate for most of the games. On occasions J.P. would use him on the mound as he was a God gifted athlete and had pitching skills two years ahead of his age.

Patrick was at second, following in his big brother's footsteps. When Jason went to the mound J.P. would often put Patrick behind the plate, depending on the opponents, as he was the only person with the skills to catch Jason. He would use a less skilled catcher in a less important game, to give him experience at catching a good pitcher, in hopes that the experience and instruction'swould develop the player into a good catcher, or at least give him a chance to go on to the next level with a good sound foundation, with the hope that someone would take over at that point in the player's career and advance him to a higher skill level. J.P. had Dee Bankos at firstbase, one of the best first basemen he had ever seen at that age. His stretching ability and his glove was many years ahead of his age. As his short stop he would have Bart Milstone who was as good as they came anywhere in the country, quick, great glove, and a strong arm. At third, the super quiet Samuel Langley, a teacher's son, who liked fishing just about as good as playing baseball. J.P. saw in him the ability to become a great third base-man, something the Honsburg High varsity had not had in many years. It had been for years the weak spot in the infield for the Honsburg Cats, but J.P. was about to put a stop to that, working him hard at his position.

The only open critic of O'Francis from the Honsburg section was Chris Talbert the father of Ken Talbert who liked to play third but threw side armed, which J.P. tried to get him out of, as it was a bad habit, His throws were not accurate from the third base position. Usually the ball sailed on him on its way to first base, making it impossible for Bankos to make the play. He was slow of foot, and did not have the glove that Sam had. He had an attitude that he should start because of his father's volunteering his time in helping to build the high school field and his close connection to Tim Harper. For J.P. as well as his loyal assistant Raymond, they saw Sam as the only choice and Sam had earned the position.

They were to face Liberty's best, and the animosity the two teams had toward each other was very evident even before the game started. Liberty was unbeatable, so the fans often would state, as they had swept by their opponents in their bracket with great ease. Honsburg All-Stars on the other hand had struggled to make it to the semi-finals, with good bunting, squeeze plays and a couple of special defensive plays that caught their opponents off guard. It was show down time and J.P. had prepared his team as well as anyone could have and for that matter much better than the greater majority of anyone could have done so in the community.

I had gone to several practices and observed J.P. and Raymond prepare the fifteen and sixteen year old boys for a game that for J.P. meant more than just a simple senior league game. He schooled his players on a level equal to most high school teams, with special plays of what *IFs,* programming them to react to situations *If* they should occur, so they would not have to think, and they had responded well to his teaching. The fans of all the teams that had faced the Honsburg All-Stars during the 4 of July week knew of J.P.'s dismissal from the high school level of play. Some, as I sat among the many fans, anonymous to them as to who I was, or for that matter the reason I was there, spoke often of J.P.'s ability to teach the game and the enormous response he got from his players. A few were very critical of him for what they perceived as too hard core, and a lot of *"I heard"* comments. Be it as it may, I found over the years of research and observing on my own, the teams that he coached won the greater percentage of the games they played. And in our many conversations over the years, J.P. had taught me that in baseball it was all about percentage.

I never told J.P. that I had been attending many of his games both in his league play as well as the tournament play and several of his practices over a three-year period. I really did not see the need in doing so. I wanted to find out for myself what the man was like, not from someone else's point of view, be it positive or negative. I got a lot from people sitting around me in the stands, not all conversations were about baseball, nor was it about J.P. Some of the information I gathered proved to be correct, upon further investigation. Some proved to be just what it was, gossip. I did tell J.P. that I had seen a few of his tournament games, and we often would discuss different parts of the game. I would have several questions for him, which allowed for lengthy conversations about the game he so loved.

There was a larger than normal crowd at the Honsburg vs. Liberty game, maybe it was because of the reported show down between J.P.'s team and Liberty, as the coaches for Liberty were good friends and social elites of LaMar Marshy, and most everyone knew what he had done to O'Francis. The event reminded me of the historical first large Civil War engagement at First Manassas, where the people from Washington and the near-by towns and communities poured out to watch the day's event, bringing with them their picnic lunches, the social elites in their fancy carriages, the gentlemen with their fancy suits and top hats, with their lady's at their sides in their "high-dollar" dresses and big southern antebellum hats.

I watched as the people poured into the ball park and the social elites gathered in their groups always away from the "common" folk, as if they would contract some contagious disease if they were to rub shoulders with them. I learned that a lot of the "general common folk" had grown up with J.P. and came to watch "him" perform his "Irish magic" as a baseball coach. Many were from the Fortwood and St. Pete area and had known him and his mother Catherine and were very well liked. They had come for the same reasons, in hopes that his baseball "Irish magic" as I overheard one such person phrase it, "beat the shit out of Liberty's best!"

I stood at the concession stand waiting in line to get a ball park hot dog and a coke, of which I was in no hurry, listening to a group of men talk about O'Francis and his team, of which I learned they were from the town J.P. had grown up.

A man with a rugged weathered face by the name of Tommy Davis spoke, "Now boys, you know him as well as I do. He'll have them ready. I've watched him too many years now. He should be the head coach for Liberty, if the truth be known."

Then one of the men with Tommy spoke, "Shit Davis, you know that just ain't going to happen. Marshy hates O'Francis."

"Yeah, wellll, only because he is a damn good coach, and LaMar just thinks he is."

Then the third man in the company of the group spoke as they had gotten their hot dogs and cokes, and were walking away, "O'Francis probably knows more baseball in his little finger than Marshy does in that big fat body of his. I'll agree with Davis, he'll have them ready, and I'll bet Liberty doesn't blow him out. If he does lose, I say it will be damn close. Ain't going to be like all the rest of the teams Liberty has played. I'm telling you guys that."

Tommy spoke in his usually southern Appalachian draw and dialect, "Now boys, you watch how he warms his team up and you watch how Liberty warms up. That will tell you everything. I'll put my money on J.P.

If his pitcher is right, he'll beat Liberty. If it's close, he'll out coach them, you watch."

"Yeah, and if he does, 'ole big mouth Marshy will sit in the stands and cuss him, til a fly won't land on him."

"Yeah, yo rite, but I'll bet you a dollar to a donut that he won't to his face."

"Shitttt, ain't nobody going to take that bet, you dumb-ass."

Then they laughed as they walked out of earshot toward the right field side of the ball park along the first base line.

LaMar arrived in his county supplied, high dollar car and waiting for his arrival was his slug crawling friends in the parking lot. When upon arriving they quickly gathered around him as if they were some type of secret service agents for some special government official.

I personally got a laugh out of LaMar Marshy's self-deemed importance. I could only assume that he felt very secure around his awaiting entourage, which in reality was a joke. I would learn that none of them had any real "back-bone" to them, a lot of mouth, but no more than that.

They settled at the far corner of the stands, mid-way from the top, on the third base side. I had positioned myself in an earshot area just above them. Marshy spotted J.P. in his pre-game warm up of his infield, and Raymond was preparing the outfield, going through their routine, which they did with great perfection. It was an important part of his game plan, intimidation factor, J.P. often would tell me. And in many cases it worked, if the other team had not been equally prepared both physically as well as mentally, more mental than anything else.

Marshy wasted no time in his demeaning criticism about O'Francis, and somewhere during the course of the game making the statement, "He had better enjoy what he is doing because he will never get the chance to do it on the high school level, ever again." A statement I would hear over and over again over several years.

The one thing that I did learn about J.P. O'Francis and his coaching was that he ran a class program win or lose. He and the players he coached were all class on the field, in the dugout, and as they were leaving the field.

Liberty started off with the lead and appeared to all in the stands that it was going to be another walk in the park for the All Stars from Liberty. But by the fifth inning O'Francis' all stars had regained the lead five to three. It was something that most players at that age would not have done. He had runners on first and third, with one out. The batter hit the ball to the third baseman, the runner broke for home, and the throw went to the catcher, but the runner stopped as soon as the third baseman threw the ball home and hurried back to third, preventing the double play or the out at home and no time for the play at first, loading the bases. Another one of O'Francis' IFs and it was done without thought or any game yelling or instructions from the dugout. The Liberty coaches went "nuts" yelling and screaming at their third baseman, who was embarrassed and belittled in front of a large crowd. Then Liberty's coach called time out to talk to the pitcher and catcher. I had watched O'Francis enough to know that the move by the runner on third was a designed play, and it had been performed with perfection.

Sam was due at the plate. He appeared to be as calm as an experienced senior in a high school game with a state championship at stake. J.P. never went to him for any special words. He just gave him his signals from third, and let it go, as he had all the confidence in the world in his player at the plate. His signals appeared to be a complicated jumble of hands signals from all parts of his body, and after he had completed his sign giving to Sam as well as the base runners, he really had signaled nothing, simply "hit away." Sam did, by driving a hard line drive to left center scoring two runs.

The game ended with Liberty not getting another player in scoring position in the sixth or seventh inning. J.P.'s boys did threaten with runners on base in both innings but failed to bring them home. His infield went errorless for all seven innings, with Milstone, O'Francis and Bankos turning two double plays in both the sixth and seventh to stop any late game rallies.

The loss was taken hard by the Liberty coaches as well as the players and fans. The coaches refused to shake J.P.'s hand, and shunned him as he approached them. I learned that the people that coached the senior league teams at Liberty, their conduct on that day was typical of their sportsmanship, if they lost.

The win was sweet for both players and coaches from Honsburg. The fans that were in support of J.P. went home that day as "happy campers", and Tommy repeated himself to his two friends.

"I told you guys, he would just flat outcoach them."

Marshy left cussing J.P. with a great deal of hate in his words and tone in his voice.

Dawn, J.P. and Patrick, who had a three for four day at the plate, enjoyed their late ten o'clock "Big Mac" supper, rehashing the entire game.

Knowing the game of baseball, as I do now, which I am by far no expert, I knew that Liberty had all the "guns" to win the game with ease, and if put on paper, stats wise, would have, but like the honey bee who does not know it is not supposed to be able to fly, J.P.'s boys did not know they were supposed to lose. Calling every pitch, playing the odds on every pitched ball, confident in every one of his players, J.P. worked his "Irish magic" and sent the message to all his foes both in the community of Honsburg as well as the rest of the county that had counted him out, that he was still a winner. His supporters were reminding all *"I told you so,"* rubbing it in and enjoying every minute of it.

His team fell short in their final game by a score of four to three, denying J.P. the chance to advance and coach his boys on the state level. As we talked on a later date in the early fall, while watching a Yankees' game on television, he was disappointed that they did not get to advance but he was pleased that he had prepared them for their next step up in the game of baseball.

# The Violin Plays on

J.P. HAD BEEN ATTENDING ONE of his teacher association meetings that had run longer than normal, and had adjourned shortly after eight o'clock p.m. His now, what seemed to be "friend" Emmanuel opted for a last cup of coffee at the local "Big Mac", to go over a few items of concern that had been introduced in the meeting, but tabled until the next meeting.

It was close to nine p.m. when they departed for their respective homes each heading in the opposite direction, but J.P. did not travel far, a matter of a few hundred yards before he turned into a small sub-division, and made a few lefts and rights on a few streets, and then into a small apartment building parking lot, located in the rear of the building. There were only three visitors' spaces, and one of them was occupied. J.P. pulled into the one open space on the far end of the lot, which was good for what he needed. He sat in his car for a good ten minutes in silence. He had read the second note placed on the windshield of his car several times, warning of impending danger to his family if he did not drop the suit.

He put on a pair of black driving gloves, reached into the back seat and retrieved a black Army sweater and pulled it over his head and adjusted it to his body to fit comfortable. His blue jeans and "cowboy" boots of gray with black tips made for the perfect shading for the kind of night he had to operate. He reached under the driver's seat and obtained a black full-face sky mask, and pulled it over his head. Lying at the heel of his feet was a cold black Army .45, 1911 caliber pistol, which he placed in his belt in the center of his lower back. Reaching to the overhead dome light he switched it to the off position so when he open the door it would not come on.

As he did so he picked up a 24 inch very hard oak piece of wood, about two inches in dimension, sanded smooth and treated with a coat of polyurethane, what most law enforcement people refer to as a "night stick". This was a weapon used in one of his many kata's and could bring instant death to a person, or render them immobile and in a great deal of pain, if one knew how to use it properly, which he worked at it on a weekly basis, in hopes he would prefect the skill and art of the Hon Jo kata. He placed it in his left hand and along his left inside arm cradling it in the palm of his hand.

Moving quickly to a row of pine trees, separating the parking lot from the property just to the east of the long line of pines, he wrapped himself into the lower branches of the trees and waited, concealed from the untrained eye. He waited for several minutes while the dark clouds moved to cover the full bright late autumn moon. Like the stealthiest of a cat on the prowl at night he moved across the open area of the yard to the corner of a brick house where he crouched down against a large evergreen shrub, as the brightness of the moon reappeared to illuminate the area like some giant spot light. As he waited the light from a window not more than three feet away and just overhead high came on, and voices from within indicated bedtime for the couple. Another large cluster of dark clouds once again turned off nature's spot light and only the yellow glow from the bedroom window pierced the darkness.

J.P. moved to within inches of the window, rising up just enough to peer into the room, seeing the man reaching over to turn off the night stand lamp, and darkness. *"Bang, your dead!"* he thought. He squatted by the outer wall of the house, patting it with his right hand. *"C-4, and a remote, your history!"* He then waited for ten minutes as the moon came in and out. He then reached into his sweater pocket and pulled out a blue post-it pad where he had with great care printed the words *"There is no Time Limit"* with his left hand. He was ambidextrous, of which no one actually knew outside of his family. He pulled it off the back of the pad where he had placed one and written on it to leave no trace on the next sheet. He reached up and gently placed it in the middle of the window, knowing that eventually it would be discovered. Then like the stealth he used to get to the house he retraced his steps back to the tree line, then to his car and exited the parking lot, laughing aloud, and feeling good. *"Damon Bales you are mine! You evil bastard! I can have you anytime I want!"*

What made him feel even better than the actual act itself was the fact that he knew he was within a few feet of Damon and he did not have a clue. *"How easy it could be, these stupid ass-holes just do not know. They think they are totally untouchable here in their little sanctuary, and how wrong they are!"* His oldies radio station was playing, *"we got to get out of this place, if it's the last thing we ever do."* After singing along with the song, which was a habit of J.P.'s, although he more often than not did not know all the words, spoke to himself again, *"God,..is that ever true,"* and then mentally wondered how long his Master intended for him to remain in what had become a repulsive and distasteful place to live.

# On Patroll The Fuhrer

AS THE TWO COUNTY DEPUTIES roamed the back roads of the eastern section of Reynolds County, they talked of hunting in general but most about where each was going deer hunting. They spun stories about past hunting experiences that one would have to question as to the validity of the hunting expedition, but it was entertaining for each. The gravel and dirt road meandered its way through the back farm country with large open fields on each side, up and down the hills that lay below a large bluff off a long ridge towering high above the river valley that cut its way through the mountains eons ago.

As they topped a rather high knoll they stopped and turned off the patrol car's engine. The bright moonlit night allowed them to see the road twisting and turning for a good half mile below them. A large hay field stretched, what appeared to be endless in the glowing night, toward the river more than two miles away. They opened their windows letting in the coolness of the mountain's night air, cooling the interior of the car off quickly. Their hopes was to spot some deer grazing in the field as they had done before on other nights during the earlier part of the summer months. It was now early fall and only a few of the trees had begun their metamorphosis for the upcoming season.

With only a month and a half to go before rifle season the fever was already increasing their blood to a fast flow through their veins. The two had never been hunting together, always with other parties, but this year they would join each other with two other friends for a hunting trek several counties east of Reynolds County, deep in the mountains of what was known as Big Walker, a mountain region which was part of the much larger and rather lengthy Great Appalachian Mountain Range.

Far below them, a set of car lights pierced the night and came to a stop off the side of the road in what was only a few real wide places along the rarely traveled back road. A perfect place for young teen lovers to park, something both men had done during their youth.

"Hey, what do we have here...looks like...is it...could it be...YES, it is, Parkers! Ohhhh boy, lovers, the heat of passion is on!" The deputy on the passenger side exclaimed with great excitement. They watched the car's lights go off and then the deputy behind the wheel slapped his partner on his left front shoulder and pointed toward the field. There some 100 yards away were four deer, all does. They walked around and grazed on the thick late summer grass. The moon illuminated the night so well they could see them twitching and turning their ears as they looked up and around from moment to moment surveying the area listening and smelling for predators. They sat and watched the deer as they worked their way toward the center of the field and then three more appeared only 30 yards away from them as both men got even more exited and whispered, exclaiming about the size of several of the does. Their radio was turned down to its lowest possible level, and fortunately it was a very quiet night with little or no traffic on it.

"JESUS, LOOK THERE!" The deputy on the passenger side pointed out the window, desperately trying to control himself.

The driver of the patrol car's mouth dropped open and then he slowly exclaimed, "OHHHH, MY GODDDDDD!" Strutting slowly and causelessly out of the wooded area to the east of the field was a twelve-point buck. It was an awesome sight to watch the magnificent white tail buck work his way in among his does.

It had been a good twenty minutes since the car had parked below them and the two deputies started their car. The deer broke for the woods white tails flagging as they bounced and leaped out of sight in a matter of seconds. They did not turn on their lights and slowly eased down the hill pulling up within twenty feet of the parked car. Both deputies got out and took their proper position on both sides of the car, tapping lightly on the sides of the front windows with their long black heavy flash lights. The windows were fogged up and simultaneously the side windows slowly rolled down to the halfway point.

The passenger quickly started, "Evening officer."

The deputy looking into the car with his light said, "Good evening gentlemen. What's going on here?"

"Ahhh, I spilled beer on my pants and, and I was just holding them up in front of the heater, ahhh, so they would dry."

"Ahhhha, I see, well if I may suggest, they would probably dry much quicker if the car heater was turned on."

The two deputies then looked across the top of the car at each other and then asked for the two men's identifications. As each gave the officers their ids and they looked them over. One was Dan Logger and the other was Tim Popper. The officers thanked the two and gave the identifications back to them. The deputy on the driver's side suggested that they move on and then they walked back to the patrol car. Turning the lights on the parked car and getting the tag number they called the dispatcher and asked for a check on the car's owner. It came back as belonging to Dan Logger, who was the Director of instructions for Reynolds County School System. The deputies reported the event to the night shift officer and filed their report.

It had been a while since I had talked with J.P. and I had been trying to keep up with his progress in his job as well as his court case. I became somewhat worried about him, as he did not usually go for such a long time without at least a phone call. I called him and invited him to come to my home for a Saturday afternoon football game. Not just any game, as he rarely watched any other game but Notre Dame. Since the local television station refused to show HIS, Irish when playing at home, which they were supposed to or so an NBC contract so stated, but like most things in our society some type of loophole allowed them to show the SEC games, which upset J.P. to no end. He had written letters to NBC, made phone calls to NBC, as well as to the television station to honor the contract, but like a voice in the wilderness no one heard.

I, on the other hand, had a satellite and was able to pick the home games up out of Atlanta, so I invited him to spend the afternoon with me, enjoying HIS, Irish watching him and his reactions to the good as well as the bad plays, as well as his comments on the officiating. Then I could also get answers for some unanswered questions about a few stories about his school system I had picked up and knew he would have the answers. He would never allow me to buy the beer. It was a tradition for him to bring his own and drink at least three to four of the six-pack and eat a rather large bag of pretzels during the course of a Notre Dame game. One thing I had noticed of J.P., he never criticized the coaching staff. I asked him why. With his response I learned more about this man I had come to admire and I respected his honesty. He took a few minutes to answer. I had learned over the years to wait until he answered, as he collected his thoughts.

"You know, most people do not understand coaches. Most people who watch football have never been on the field as a coach. They just do not realize that you have to make decisions, based on pre-game films and strategies, you have a matter of a few seconds to call a play, both offense and defense. Sometimes they work, sometimes you get a break, and sometimes they do not. When they work, hell, you are the greatest coach in the history of the school, but when they do not, you are the worst. You are stupid! *"Hell I could do better than that!"* is what most people will say. I have been there and it is not easy. Then when you get on the level that the Irish play, with every damn school in the country wanting to beat your ass. The greater majority of them are ranked in the top twenty, and of course because of the long tradition, it does not make any difference if they are having a good year or not, they want a piece of the Irish! And I do not give a rat's ass if, if whoever, is playing Notre Dame, they will have one of the best damn games they have ever played. Hell, they could be, haaa, shit, say, o and ten, with one game left on the season, and you know what, they play some kind of super perfect game. It has been that way, for me at any rate, ever since I can remember listening to them on the radio when I was a little boy."

Then he paused for a moment, took a drink of beer, and continued, "Okay, back to your question. You can multiply the difficultly factor by a thousand with every call."

The game went well for the Notre Dame Fighting Irish that day and J.P. was happy, which was very good for me. If it had not gone well he became very inward, closed mouth, and withdrawn. But he never did lay criticism on the coaches, and after asking his sons and wife about his love for Notre Dame and posing the question if they had ever heard him lay out the coaches, they too could not ever recall J.P. putting the blame on any coach for an Irish loss. He told me once that he had some coaches he liked better than others, and that there was one he did not like, one in particular. But even with his dislike for the coach, he just stated that he just was out of his league. He should have stayed on the high school level.

Notre Dame, he would say, "Is not just any college. It is a place that 99 % of the coaches in the country cannot handle, no matter how good they are, where they are at. I really do not care what their record is. Everything changes when a new coach takes on the helm of Notre Dame Football. It is the most unique place in the world, and has the tradition that backs it up. You either love her or hate her, there is no in between!"

There was one thing I learned, anyone who knew J.P. knew where he stood on the Irish. I found a lot of his former students in all walks of life, from professional to laborer that would tell me, "When the Irish play on national T.V., I think of O'Francis."

I had picked up on some talk concerning Dan Logger, and asked him if he could enlighten me on the "gossip". He confirmed everything I had learned and added a few facts about his activities outside the school system. Dan Logger had been caught on two other occasions by two different sets of police officers. Both incidents took place in school parking lots in the early hours of the morning, and on both occasions, the men were in a compromising position.

Then I asked him if he himself had any problems with gays, as over the years of gathering information surrounding him there were some people who were either bi-sexual or outright gays. After a rather long pause in thought he started very slowly to answer my question.

"You know, personally I really do not have any problem with anyone's choice of sexual preference. But the one thing that really bothers me is the Christian hypocrisy in, around, and among these people. Well these people in my community that is. I am sure even though it is not accepted nation-wide there are areas that accept people for who they are and not what our religious social norms proclaim is right."

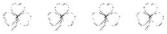

LaMar had been in power for four years and had been sued twice. His latest was a teacher at the Technical Center, Ms. Susan Arnold who had been the drafting and architecture teacher. The rumor reached her that her job was going to be terminated the forthcoming year. She was a very attractive lady and LaMar had not been able to seduce her over the years, although he had tried on several occasions. He called her to come to his office and informed her that he would have to fight the School Board to keep the course at the center, which meant he would have to fight for her job. Susan bought into his story "hook, line and sinker." Once again he made his pitch to her only this time she felt as if he would really save her position, but she would have to come through for him.

She met him in Jefferson City on several occasions over the course of the year giving herself freely, doing all the kinky sexual favors he desired. But she had been smart, and in the back of her mind felt that she needed some insurance, so she obtained the copies of the register LaMar had signed at the hotel they stayed in. To up the insurance she had a friend that followed them on more than one occasion, take pictures of them entering the hotel together. She also made tape recordings of conversations with LaMar in the hotel and on several occasions at dinner.

When it came to crunch time, LaMar cut her course and left Susan standing "naked" and used. LaMar had underestimated her intelligence, and she brought a suit against him for sexual harassment. As the case progressed and the evidence mounted against LaMar, the public became more aware of the events in the case. LaMar was good, smooth, and slick and knew how to work the court system. He agreed to settle out of court. Susan Arnold did not have to work any place for the rest of her natural born life, as the settlement left her financially stable. The School Board in all their "wisdom" supported LaMar, and the school's insurance covered the tab, as he knew it would.

He used the school system as if it were his own personal company, of which he had extracted a large sum of money from it, not to include his regular salary, which was approaching more than any superintendent in any of the eight counties surrounding Reynolds County. He ruled and covered it so well that the vast majority of the people could not see how he was working it. A master of illusion, the sleight of hand, a magician, all the things true evil is made of. As O'Francis stated once, "Evil has a way of disguising itself and making friends with the good although rather stupid people of the world and dragging them into the abyss of darkness." The appointed School Board was so dumb that they could not see, they never questioned anything he did, or said. It was, "Yes Mr. Marshy, whatever you think. You know best." They did all but bow to him each time they spoke or entered the room where he was present. J.P. once told me he thought that mentally they did, and would have physically in public, if he had requested it.

The Dan Logger affair was beginning to get hot as more and more people were becoming aware of his homosexual activities with the band director at Honsburg High School. LaMar boldly walked into Dan's office and closed the door. In the course of five minutes they were at odds with each other and angry words were being thrown back and forth. LaMar aggressively threatened Dan's job. Dan in his anger walked to his desk, opened the middle drawer, and taped under it was several sexually reveling photos of LaMar. Retrieving them and laying them out on his desk, point and tapping on the pictures and in a hate filled voice, he stated, "And YOU are going to FIRE me! Fuck you! YOU ARE NOT GOING TO FIRE ME FOR ANYTHING!" LaMar's face was crimson red. He turned and violently left Dan's office.

❀ ❀ ❀ ❀

Christmas break had arrived and the school system ground to a halt for a period of ten days. Marshy had been laying plans to correct a few mistakes he had made in his climb to the zenith of his powerhouse. He established two sets of books for his financial budget presented to the School Board and the public. He had been a quick learner. It had been pre-arranged by LaMar that on the 26th of December the School Board building would be torched. He had provided a key for the professional arsonist to enter the lower level of the building. For Marshy the cost had been pocket change compared to what he would receive. He wasted no money in getting the very best, as he knew that the local "yahoos" would never figure it was torched. He looked upon the people with utter contempt, as he placed himself high above them all.

By the time the fire department arrived all they could do was contain the blaze and keep it from spreading to other buildings. Everything had gone as planned, and all records of any importance were destroyed leaving no paper trails. Dan Logger had grossly miscalculated LaMar, and the other copies he had, had been stored in what he felt was a secure place in the basement of the building among all the thousands of files and old documents dating back to the very beginnings of the school system itself. His blood turned cold, as he knew that Marshy would be coming after him in all his fury, as no one crossed the great LaMar Marshy.

The school system relocated its central office staff into a vacant building up the street from the ruins of the School Board office. After a short time in the temporary site, LaMar walked into Dan's office and once again closed the door. Walking over to his desk, Dan stood.

"I told you not to fuck with me, you are through." LaMar's smile reflected his evilness, as he pointed his finger at Logger. He chuckled a cold, bone chilling deep hollowed laugh as he turned and walked out of the room. Before the year was over Dan would be forced to resign as Marshy gave him no choice. Resign or face public humiliation.

LaMar had become somewhat of an expert at embezzling money from the Reynolds County School System and by the middle of the 1990's he had secured away well over one and a half million dollars in a Nassau bank. Money that could have been used for the betterment of the students, or to help the employees keep pace with the rising cost of living. But Marshy was not done. Besides his lavish salary and benefits, he continued to skillfully manipulate the budget and skim off larger chunks here and there adding to his growing account. It was easy. His personal secretary/ book keeper/ budget manager was also his longtime mistress. She of course was not aware of all of his other extracurricular activities, although she suspected that he was having other encounters. She was being taken care of and for the small price she had to pay, it was well worth the cost as he took great care of her, and she had no financial worries. Whatever he requested from the School Board for her salary and benefits he got. A forty thousand dollar a year salary plus fringe benefits and trips with and without LaMar was paid for by the school system. Attire bought while on trips with LaMar was put on his expense account.

The architecture for the grand central office was orchestrated by the master himself and every detail would have to meet his approval before it was completed. When it was completed the "important" people of the county praised him and glorified LaMar in the highest. He had reached a point of supreme power. No one challenged him, as he was in complete and full control of every aspect of the school system and had an extremely strong connection to the law and judicial forces in the area. Moreover, to seal all his connections, he was a loyal and righteous member of the largest organized church in the Liberty area, a major force to contend with in any situation.

In the grand opening of the newly constructed Reynolds School System headquarters, with all the news reporters from the area present and many speeches delivered, none was more pronounced than that of the great Marshy's speech, where he referred to the Reynolds County School Board Office as Mecca, a reference to the Islamic religion and the bowing toward the holy site of Mohammed by the Muslims of the Middle Eastern world. As disrespectful as it was and a mockery of one of the world's most powerful religions, most people in the predominantly southern Baptist area did not understand his callous comment about Mecca.


For J.P. it was the ultimate insult and demonstrated his lack of respect for the Islamic faith, another clear-cut example of the evilness that LaMar was a devoted disciple of the Dark world of Satan, a word that was so misused in the Christian world. Satan, or Lucifer, a Latin word that means *The Bringer of Light,* he was able to control the very thoughts of the weak, which was most of the people. The employees feared him and came very close to bowing to him, as he would pass them when he would visit any one of the schools under his controlling power. Marshy's principals or as J.P. referred to them as his lieutenants, feared him as well, but not for the same reasons.

For them it was money. He bought them off, by getting them large raises. He did not fail to remind them, on a regular basis, as to what he had done for them. The teachers had gone four straight years without a raise, and the administrators received a whopping twenty-three per cent increase in their salaries. His Central Office Staff were rewarded even more, as did all the rest. They too were reminded of what he had done for them as well as what he could do and would do. They obeyed his every directive, even if they knew it was wrong. They never questioned LaMar. He could get rid of them in a snap of his finger, and they all knew it. The very few that did not submit to his will, he attacked with a vengeance and tried to destroy them, and in some cases he was successful in one form or another.

# Attorney's

FOR J.P. IT APPEARED THAT his attorney was a bit "wet" behind the ears. He did not have the savvy of his sister, nor was he as organized. He had a bad habit of procrastinating on matters that J.P. strongly felt was important to his case. It had been alleged in the Bales/ Finkel deposition, that J.P. had made statement to his classes that Finkel had been intimately involved with a senior, gotten her pregnant, and she had his son. J.P. had time and time again denied that he had not made such statements in front of any of his classes. He never did deny that he had not talked about what he had heard from others outside the classroom. He asked his attorney to investigate the matter and find out why Finkel had been dismissed from his previous job. Julius did not seem to want to find out, or did not appear to think that it was an important matter concerning the case.

J.P. on the other hand, did and being the reconnaissance person he was, did do the "leg" work and found that the reasons he had been dismissed was due to a multitude of reasons. The affair was with a young lady, of seventeen years of age. He obtained the information from a nurse and a friend of the family who was very willing to talk about the entire event. Nurse Davies did not like Richard and thought of him as abusive and coercing young girls into sex with him. She was not the first who had to pay the embarrassing price for her young stupidity. She informed J.P., whom she did not know, as he had identified himself as an investigator for a law firm in a court case, that the girl's parents hated Finkel so much that the father stated to several people in the tiny community of Park Lawn that if he ever saw him in the area he would kill him.

The information concerning Richard Finkel's gambling operation J.P. had gotten from the principal of the school where Richard Finkel had worked at that point in time of his career. The principal had been promoted to the central office, and although he preferred not to testify, he did reveal the facts that Finkel was running a numbers game through the school.

Finkel's physical abuse to a player also came from the ex-principal, as Finkel had physically slapped one of his football players several times during a practice session because he was not performing up to his expectations. He had knocked his helmet off and then slapped him across the side of his head literally knocking him to the ground, yelling at him even while he was laying on the ground with tears in his eyes, telling him what a *"piece of shit"* of a ball player he was.

Finkel had been named as the athletic director, which Mr. Charles freely admitted that he had made a mistake, but in the same breath defended his appointment by stating that he had only his recommendation to go by at the time and had no clue what type of person he really was. This of course led to the misappropriation of athletic funds, of which James Charles explained he used as cash flow for his own personal expenses.

J.P. never did tell Julius that he had done the leg work, but kept insisting that he get the information, as it would make it legal, and could be entered into the course of the case, if need be, showing what type of character Richard Finkel was. He felt that the defense would attack his character in court, and that Julius then could attack them with their own dark side. Julius kept insisting that it had nothing to do with the case. J.P. agreed, but that he felt they would try and attack him from that point as that was all they really had. He could catch Finkel in a lie, and establish that he could not be believed. A point J.P. felt the jury would need to hear.

It was the second time Julius met with the defendant's attorney in front of the Judge for a motion to get the case dismissed completely. Holly had met once earlier for a motion of dismissal, and once again the judge refused to dismiss the case for lack of a "case". During the hearing the defense's lawyer tried to get specific evidence removed and failed. Laying the groundwork for the case was for J.P. puzzling, as he did not understand the legal "loopholes." He dealt in logic, truth, and facts. Either you did write the letter and send it to every "dick" in the entire area or you did not! Either it was damaging to his reputation and character or it was not! All else to J.P. was totally irrelevant. But nothing in the legal system was that simple.

Julius was for the most part not forceful enough and allowed the case to drag on and on. O'Francis felt that the longer the case went without getting it into court the less chance he had of winning.

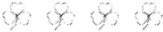

Julius had J.P. come over to his office after school, which was a good 45-minute drive. He usually was the last person he would meet with on any given day, and most of the time there was no one else in the office when they met. J.P. would have several cups of coffee while they talked over the case. The meeting would never last more than an hour at the very most. Often times O'Francis would leave wondering why he just did not call him and talk about what he needed to know over the phone, for the information he needed and J.P. would provide would have taken a lot less time. He was having a difficult time figuring Julius out and it appeared to J.P. at any rate, that he wasted a lot of his time traveling back and forth on matters that a simple phone call would have resolved. Too much logic. There had been several meetings scheduled for him to meet Julius and there would be no one there. He would wait for a period of time, ten to twenty minutes, and then go back home in disgust.

One such meeting J.P. arrived five minutes early for his 1900 hours appointment, O'Francis' use of international time, which he preferred to use and
most people referred to as military time, confused ninety-ninety percent of
the people. When he did find anyone who could relate to international time
he was pleased.

It had already turned dark as it was in the late fall of the year and the
time of course had changed, something J.P. did not like. Time was time,
if the sun was at high noon, it was 1200 hours, not some other manmade
time. But like all the rest of the people of the country he had to go along
with it, as if he had a choice, like so many other mindless edicts the legislative talking heads would pass down to party minded people who elected
them.

The evening air was cool as he parked his car across the street in a parking lot directly across from the law office of Donatello and Donatello. He
closed and locked the door to his small compact car and walked the seventy-
five feet or so, crossing the empty street to the door of the office. Turning
the doorknob he found it to be locked. Lights in the downstairs offices as
well as the upstairs indicated that there was someone inside. Usually in a
matter of a minute Julius or his father Lucius would unlock and open the
door. J.P. assumed that it was SOP for attorneys to work way pass the normal working hours of the general population.

Yet again another night meeting when no one opened the door. He then
knocked on the door with the large brass doorknocker in the middle of
the door. He stood waiting for someone to open the door. It would not be
the first time he would have to wait for Julius to arrive late for a scheduled
appointment, so he walked back to his car and sat in the dimly lit parking
lot. He reached for his half smoked cigar and lit it, then rolled the driver's
window down half way. The white smoke quickly gushed out into the night
air like some giant fan had sucked it out.

He sat looking at the large white wood framed house, probably built
in the earlier part of the century, and thought to himself that it was a great
idea to turn a house as glorious as it was into a law office. Smart move on
most likely Lucius' part. Probably bought it for a "song and dance" and

remodeled it. Great location too, another smart move, three blocks from the courthouse, walking distance. As he puffed on his cigar, he could see out but most likely no one could see him sitting in his car, except for the glow off the end of his cigar when he drew on it.

He sat in disgust for twenty minutes. He felt it was rude and inconsiderate of his attorney to treat him in such a manner. *Probably not enough money involved, his share that is,* he thought. Once he could have accepted. When he was about to give it up once more, a car pulled up and parked at the curb. Lucius Donatello emerged from the car and walked to the door, placed his key into the door, opened it and entered. J.P. waited until he was inside and got out, tossing his cigar off onto the parking lot pavement, as no one smoked in the office building as Lucius and Julius were avid walkers and bike riders, health nuts as they would be commonly called.

As he walked once again across the corner of the parking lot and across the street he could hear his cowboy boots strike the pavement with their leather heels. He knocked on the door with the doorknocker and he could hear Lucius walking toward the door. He opened it and with a surprised look, welcomed J.P. in. "Come in Mr. O'Francis," and he entered the large room made into a lobby and waiting room. It was extremely well decorated, a woman's touch he could tell, with the decor. The floors were hardwood, probably original. They had built a counter across the back section of the room separating the work area of their secretary. "What can I do for you this evening?"

J.P. stood a few feet from Lucius in the middle of the room. "I had an appointment with Julius tonight at 1900, but no one was here when I arrived."

Lucius looked at the clock on the wall over what was now an inoperative fireplace. The clock showed 1940 hours. "Well, let me call him at home." He walked behind the counter and dialed a number. As it rang J.P. walked to the edge of the counter and leaned his forearms on it cupping his hands together, waiting. It rang several times and the answering machine came on.

Lucius spoke, "Julius, this is Lucius. Mr. O'Francis is here for your seven o'clock appointment. Give me a call when you return."

He placed the phone down, looked at J.P. as their eyes met and locked. He liked that about Lucius, from the first time he had met him. He was not afraid to look you in the eyes when he talked to you. His eyes did not jump from one object to another in a room or to the walls or ceiling, they stayed locked. He was not a big man, small framed, slender, black hair, not much gray, a strong face, the kind of man you really did not want to fuck with verbally or physically, J.P. figured. A man you could not intimidate, with your looks, with vocabulary, or with physical gestures. He really did not know him well but figured he would like him, his kind of person.

"Are you sure you had an appointment today?"

J.P. opened is portfolio and checked his notes as well as his calendar. "Yes sir, it is right here." He turned it around enabling Lucius to see, there marked in red, Donatello 1900 hours, and again half way down the legal pad, he had noted Julius Donatello 1900 hours, also marked in red.

"Well, it is not like Julius to miss an appointment. Would you like a cup of coffee while we wait?"

J.P. did not tell him that he had missed several appointments. "Yes, do you have some made?"

"No, but I was going to make a new pot, as I had some work to do and would have to do so any way."

They walked to the copy room as J.P. had dubbed it. It had a small table sitting in the middle of the room, usually with legal papers on it in neat stacks. Two copiers, one not really a copier. A modern day printer sat on a long table on the back wall in front of a window and to the left of J.P. as he faced the window, a small stove, and beside it a sink. Above the sink and stove stretching from one side of the room to the other a set of cabinets, L shaping to the door they had entered. On the counter was a coffee pot, a label of a Bunn. Lucius opened the cabinet above the coffee maker and got a filter, placed it in the coffee holder, opened the top to the coffee, and placed a measuring cup of coffee in the filter.

"How do you like your coffee?" Before J.P. could answer, he continued, "Strong or weak?"

J.P. smiled. "Strong, but it is your coffee. I will drink whatever you make."

Mr. Donatello laughed. "Ahhh, an old military man like yourself, I would guess strong."

J.P. stood watching the head of the small law firm fix the coffee. He was in no mood for small talk, but wanted to be polite. J.P.'s thoughts were that he should have been the one to take the case from Holly, and not his wet behind the ears son. O'Francis had already put together that the young Donatello was to get his feet wet on J.P.'s case, his first real case other than the usual court appointed cases he was normally used to handling. He figured that Julius did not realize that each time he made a trip to his office it cost him money, money he did not have, money that had to come out of his family's operating fund.

Julius was young, just getting started, and would most likely take over the firm when his father retired. He did have a few good points, he was in the military reserves. It was not regular Army, but it was the Army, and he was serving his country, and that alone was a few points for Julius. The one thing he did not understand was that being in the reserves, he should have been more responsible. There was a long moment of silence in the room as Lucius waited for the coffee to fill the pot, which did not take long as it was a Bunn, and as soon as someone poured water in it, it started draining into the pot with hot fresh coffee.

The smell permeated the room, as Lucius broke the silence. "So, how do you think things are going?"

J.P. thought before he answered. "I do not really know."

"Well," as Lucius took out two cups from the drainer next to the sink, "How are things going at school? Have you had any more problems?"

Again J.P. thought before he answered, knowing that Lucius really could give a royal rat's ass less about how his work days were going, just idol talk to kill time. "Ah, about like one would expect working for Reynolds County!"

"That bad, huh." Then he chuckled aloud.

" That bad!" J.P. responded quickly in a cold an unemotional tone with a stone cold blank expression on his face.

Then Lucius glanced at his watch on his wrist. "Thought Julius would have called by now." he stated with a bit of concern in his voice, as well as making conversation trying to cover for his son's lack of professionalism, as well as indicating a tent of dissatisfaction that he had not kept an appointment. Again he struck J.P. as a no nonsense type of person, stern, candid, a man that had things in order, the typical military type. The type you really did not want to question you on the witness stand. He wore an old light weight flannel long sleeve shirt, plaid, beige and green in color, a tan pair of pants and a worn pair of walking tennis shoes. J.P. guessed his age to be in his early sixties and appeared to be in great physical shape. He poured two cups of coffee. "Black I suppose?" he asked as he handed O'Francis his cup.

"Yes sir, the only way."

"Have a seat and I'll go give Julius another call."

As J.P. pulled out one of the four chairs around the table Lucius walked out of the room to an office directly across a short hallway that led to a back door, which led out to a small yard in the back of the office. J.P. could hear him ask someone, most likely Julius' wife, where he was, and stated that he had a client waiting on him.

Some type of response on the other end of the line, then Lucius stated, "Well, have him call me when he returns." His voice was stern and direct. He returned and pulled out a chair directly across from J.P. and set his coffee cup down on the table.

"So", and then he took a deep breath. "Just who is this Janice Jones? What does she have to do with your case?"

Two questions in one breath. "May I?" as J.P. stood and pointed toward the coffee pot.

"Sure help yourself." he responded with a warm voice.

J.P. walked slowly over and filled his half-cup of coffee to its top and returned to his seat before answering Lucius's questions. "In response to your two questions I really do not know Mr. Donatello."

"Well, Julius says that Bales' attorney, Bales that is correct, right?"

"Yes, that is correct."

"That his attorney has stated that she will be their key witness, so I was just wondering where she fits into the picture? Have you two discussed having her deposed?"

"No sir, we have not. Point of fact sir, I am just now learning that Janice Jones is their key witness."

"Oh, I see."

As the surprised look was written all over his face, J.P. continued with the course of the conversation. "I will say this, if as you have stated, she is their key witness, I do want her to be deposed! Of course, with that, she will only character assassinate me! I mean she cannot testify to anything that had taken place between Richard Finkel and I. She cannot testify that she was a part of the letter that was sent all over hell and half of Georgia! So I really do not know what she can contribute to the case in their behalf? Wellll, other than, as I have already stated, another oratory on assassinating my character, which is nothing new for her!" J.P.'s voice trailed off in total disgust of the name itself. "Hell, Mr. Donatello, she has been doing that for the past, hell, let me think, well, shit, since I arrived at Honsburg High School!"

"She had nothing to do with ahh, what was the place called?"

J.P. interjected, "Cassey's corner. And noooo, she was not involved at all! I will add at this point, if I may, a damn liar! And she will do whatever Damon Bales tells her to do! She will do what LaMar Marshy tells her to do or say for that matter! She will lie for them! And that Sir is a stone cold fact!"

His voice became hard and Lucius could tell he was angered with the whole conversation.

"As to being a key witness, hell I do not have a clue. That is your field of play, I am not in the legal profession and I do not know what can and cannot be done. I deal in logic, and of course that damn sure does not apply to the legal profession!" Lucius did not respond to J.P.'s statement. He did take note of his dissatisfaction with the judicial process and started to change the subject.

O'Francis stated, "Look, Mr. Donatello, I really appreciate your time, the coffee and the conversation, but I am quite sure you have a lot of work to do or you would not have returned to the office tonight. Again I thank you for your politeness and your valuable time. Tell Julius to contact me. I feel there is much work to be done!"

By J.P.'s time it was 2015 hours when he got back into his car. As he drove the forty-five minutes back home he spoke aloud to himself, *"A waste of my time! My time is just as valuable as his! He probably gets two hundred per hour!"* J.P. had gone through every line of the Bales and Finkel deposition and found several blatant lies, and had highlighted each of them. He had recorded them on a legal pad, the page as well as the line. He had noted any and all discrepancies by page and line and had filled several long yellow legal pages with them. He had asked Julius on several occasions if he had read over the deposition, which had been some ten months earlier, and each time he stated he had not had time yet but would get to it. Then he asked if he could have J.P.'s notes on it in which he had made copies for Julius. Major points, if he were the attorney, J.P. felt, he would hit hard come trial time. As he drove a light rain began to fall, enough for the use of his windshield wipers.

Again he talked to himself aloud, *"Damn, just who in the hell is doing the legal work here? Damn it, he is going to lose this case! I mean Shit! One motion after another to suppress this or that, or to get the whole damn thing thrown out of court, hell, and to name Janice Jones as a key witness, I mean, f..u...c...k...! What a damn joke! Some damn delay tactic is all!"* As his voice raised, *"Fuck,..."* drawing the word out slowly, *"All she is going to do is lambast me with her lies and attack my character, A G A I N ! Which has ab..so..lutely nothing to do with the suit itself!"*

But he knew he had no choice but to stay the course with what now appeared to be an inept young attorney. He began having bad vibes about the case. It was dragging on for too long, too many delays, too many excuses. The defense had been ordered to submit all material that they were going to use in the case, and had not done so. Holly had done all the legal paperwork concerning the matter of evidence to be used, and Julius was to follow up, but they had not complied to the judge's orders, and Julius had not pressed the matter. Another point J.P. was not happy with.

J.P. asked Julius to contact the FBI, as he told J.P. that he knew the agents that worked in the field office. He was to get all the material that allegedly had been presented to them concerning J.P. According to Bales' and Finkel's key witness, Janice Jones, J.P. had been investigated by the FBI, because of terrorist activities conducted by him on her and her husband.

In an afternoon meeting some several months earlier, J.P. had been informed of the alleged charges by Jones in the presence of Julius and Lucius Donatello. J.P. laughed aloud. Julius did not, and his father had given O'Francis a cold hard look.

"Look, gentlemen, you have no idea to what lengths these people will go to discredit me! I will tell you this, you contact the FBI and get their report. I will review it with you and I will clarify any and all they have. Shittttt, FBI investigates me! Damn men, that was not too damn hard for them to do. Hell, they knew all about me! I mean I almost went to work for them. But that is another story, and it damn sure does not belong in this case! Sooo, you get the report, and we will go from there!"

They both looked at J.P. as if they were astonished at what he had said.

Julius spoke slowly, "You almost went to work for them? What do you mean?"

J.P. smiled. "Like I said, you get your report from these agents you say you are acquainted with. I will not go into it. As I have stated, that, gentlemen, is another story. But I will add at this point, the fact that I was once in line to become an employee of the FBI, that can be confirmed. Oh and for your record, it was my choice not to go to work for them. I was cleared to go to D.C."

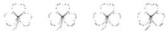

Time passed and as the case went on one month after another, J.P. never did see any report from the FBI. He questioned Julius about it on several occasions, and got no real answer. A run around about not having the time, or he could not get in contact with them. O'Francis mentally questioned his alleged acquaintance with the agents.

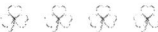

J.P. did not like what he felt. He spent long hours in the woods surrounding his home, pondering the events that seemed to be controlling his life. He began to question Holly's honesty, as she had been sick. Too sick to practice, but not too sick to run for, what he thought would be a very stressful political job. O'Francis never said a word to any of them as he remained polite, and friendly, each time he was in their presence. He was learning and quickly. He had been doing a lot of the paperwork for Julius, getting documentations in order, refining the words, listing events in chronological order and typing up effects of the events on him and his family, both emotionally as well as financially. He became deeper and deeper resentful each time he had to pay money out of his family's income toward the case as he knew that the Reynolds County School System was footing the entire legal expenses for both Bales and Finkel.

# Vitiate

EMMANUEL HAD CHALLENGED ONE OF **Marshy's** loyal lieutenants and filed a grievance. J.P. had been asked to sit on a hearing panel, which he accepted. The Superintendent's choice was another loyal principal, Levien Berghoff. He was a tall, big boned man who liked to use his bulk to intimidate teachers, especially females. He had never been married and was known for his violent temper. He ran his school like a true SS officer, with an iron hand and accepted no questioning of his policies. He let it be known on more than one occasion that he hated the teachers' association and did all he could to disrupt any meetings that anyone might want to hold at his school. When the teachers' association scheduled their monthly meetings he would schedule his monthly faculty meetings. He made a point of telling the teacher "rep" at his school that he expected him or her to attend the faculty meeting. If they chose not to, he would consider it a direct act of insubordination and would place a written reprimand in their personnel file.

Norberta Millicent had struck a personal blow to Emmanuel's character by starting a rumor that he was having an affair with a person outside of the school system. It had worked, and he and his wife began having trouble. She would plant love notes on his car, and on several occasions broke into his car and placed blond hairs on his seat, then call his wife anonymously, and inform her of his conduct. She called him into her office and officially reprimanded him for receiving personal phone calls from his "girlfriend" and then officially wrote him up. No phone calls had been received by Emmanuel, but it was his word against hers. What made matters worse was that Emmanuel was very active in the association and would attend a lot of the meetings in as well as outside of the county. This made her story even more believable that he was having an affair.

*Sylvia Wariner*

❀ ❀ ❀ ❀

Serbian Wagner was in her second year of a two-year term as the association president. A presidency she had gotten by manipulating the vote count. She was of course a loyal follower and a disciple of Marshy. It was very important for Marshy that she place herself in that position. Although the teachers' association did not have the power to bring him down, they could be a major aggravation to him, which he did not like.

He would tell Serbian, "The more I know about what is going on and who is at the core of any moves I don't like, the better I can take care of them!"

J.P. had on more than one occasion told Emmanuel and Dan that he did not trust her and that too much information about what was discussed in the association's meetings was reaching the ears of LaMar Marshy. He believed that they were close friends and that she was the source of a major leak. J.P. decided to find out and started surveillance on her out of school activities. His reconnaissance of her revealed that she and Marshy partied together and frequently visited one another's home. Her husband had been a principal and had worked under Marshy before his retirement. He and Justin Falcon another retired principal had gone into the lawn care business and Marshy had made sure that they had a yearly contract to do all the school's mowing and lawn care, a very lucrative contract.

Serbian made the mistake of appointing Emmanuel as the chairperson of the salary committee. He in turn asked J.P. to sit on his committee along with two other teachers. It was J.P. and Emmanuel who would do most of the work to prepare a salary proposal to the School Board. They would request a copy of the budget from the school's central office staff that prepared it for the School Board.

This was unexpected by Marshy and Wagner, but after several months of stonewalling and the threat of legal action if they did not meet the privilege of information act, they received a three inch thick budget. It was not a line item budget, so they had to try and figure out what all the numbers meant by each dollar figure. That proved to be an impossible task, but what J.P. and Emmanuel did find after several days of four and five hours a day was that the numbers did not match the dollars. Because they were not CPAs they were unable to match the dollars, but were able to find triple figure dollars unaccounted for. Emmanuel was very good with numbers, and after pouring over what they had found again and again, they knew they were correct. "$300,000. Holy shit."

J.P. stated to Emmanuel, "If we can find this, what can an accountant find?"

He was quick in his response. "A Lot!"

As J.P. got the last of the second pot of coffee, it was three in the morning. "So, what do we do?"

A long pause as Manual took a long deep draw off his cigarette. "I really don't know. I mean whom can we turn to? We damn sure can't tell the School Board. The association does not have the power to just walk in and go through the books."

J.P. interrupted. "Hell, it would not make any difference. They will have more than one set of books. Hell that is a no brainier! Shit Emmanuel, he is slick, and there is only a very few of us that can see it!" Another few minutes of silence in the room as they sat and looked at the walls.

"I really do not mean any...any...well I really do not know quite how to put this. But, I really do not think that Dan is willing to take LaMar on. I mean he would have to go through the VEA, and I just do not think he will do that. Do not get me wrong, I trust Dan, well to a point, I have to, and if it were not for him I would not have a teaching job. But there are times that I think that,"

Emmanuel interrupted J.P. "I know what you are saying, and I, well, I really just do not know what to do with this."

# The Unbroken Seal

BRIAN RETURNED TO THE CHICAGO area waiting for a meeting with someone he knew nothing about, nor was he told his name. He had been able to change his business meeting, but he had all but forgotten about this unknown person that seemed to be so important. Vincent had informed him he wanted him to meet with a person, but would not reveal his name, which was very unlike his friend to do. He only knew that it was *very important*, and that he thought he would be pleasantly surprised. Vincent had uncovered too many plus factors over the past several months, which the time had been good in many ways, allowing him to do some research into J.P. and Brian's past with a lot of help from Paul. For Vincent he was sure they were connected, just too much evidence for it not to be.

The entire Spadolini family was excited about the meeting, if, and there was still an IF, they were related by blood. If it did turn out that they were not blood related, then they could at least meet each other. Vincent liked J.P. and had thoughts of maybe offering him a position with his company or that Brian might have a place for him. Joseph had been encouraging his father-in- law to follow up on the matter and possibly incorporate J.P. into the business at some capacity with Brian, assuming that J.P. even wanted to come aboard.

His portfolio indicated that he was good in the management field at one time and was an extremely good organizer and a stickler for details. He needed a person at that point in time to take over some of the areas Brian and he was involved in. He needed someone he could trust, someone that displayed loyalty. There was still a lot to consider. He had no idea if J.P. would be interested in going back to work, and of course there was Brian, who would be directly involved as it would deal with his hotels. Both knew that the person had to fit the mold, to take some of the load off of them, but that *someone* would have to be *very* special.

It was late spring in the north and the morning and evening temperatures were still a little nippy, but warm enough for talking outdoors during the early afternoon. Brian, like many other Viet Nam vets, had never gotten over the war, and there were times that he drifted back and recalled his youth, both the good and the bad parts of it. His dreams like all veterans of any war never ever went away. A smell, a song, a noise would key a flashback.

The contact with Paul had been made and J.P. had been contacted. Vincent had no problem with the way J.P. was informed of his invitation. In fact he rather liked the manner in which he operated.

It had been eight months since his last trip to Chicago, and this trip seemed to bring an uneasy anticipation for him. He could not quite put his finger on it. He knew it was not Joseph, or his father-in-law, something else seemed be causing his "gut" to feel odd. It was not fear. He pondered his feelings as he made his way through his maze of airport moves and switches, again arranged by Paul. J.P. never used his name over the phone, nor had Paul used J.P.'s name over the phone. Letter or envelopes mailed to J.P. simply had his address and the word occupant on it. They always seemed to arrive without any problems.

Brian sat on his back deck reading a book, Gai-Jin. One he had been meaning to read for many years, and had been sitting on his book shelf, but he never seemed to have the time to just sit and relax and read. He had spent his R and R in Japan and had for some strange reason, one he really could never explain, not that he had to, had always liked the Japanese culture and liked reading about it. On occasion he would pause and take in the fowl and animal activities taking place on the small lake in front of him. He would drift and find himself recalling his tours in Viet Nam, something he was very proud of and of being a Navy SEAL.

The reputation of the SEALs had become so famous that the average V.C. would not face them, given the choice to fight or run. The fear of meeting the men with the green striped faces and the fact that the fear of where these illusive men of the night would strike sent bone chilling terror through the ranks of the Viet Cong in the Delta region. The SEALs seemed to be everywhere, even snatching village chiefs and high V.C. officials right out of their beds in the middle of a dark night without a sound, in the most secure and remote of places. They were like ghosts in the night appearing and disappearing without a trace, a tribute to the skills of guerilla warfare and the elite Navy SEALs.

The Delta had an estimated five million people in it. The Navy had maybe two hundred SEALs in the entire area of operation. SEALs often times when on a surveillance mission, (*which was their primary job, securing information to be passed along to the intelligence department of the military for the large scale operations*) the SEAL teams were not to engage the enemy if at all possible. Often times this was not possible and to avoid being compromised, the use of silencers on their weapons were used or personal knifes to take out the V.C. so as not be compromised. The SEALs would of course not always follow the orders of the "*great minds*" behind all the operations. They seemed to just do things on their own, which was really the correct way if anyone outside the specially trained men who played the real game in Viet Nam wanted to really win the war. Which seemed to be a question in the minds of SEALs and Special Forces/ Ranger personnel.

Maybe it was the fact that the "*brass*" and the "*great minds*" of Washington, all the politicians, really did not want the war to end so quickly, money being the major factor. Somebody was making lots of money off the grunts in Nam. But not off the elite, the very specially trained men who really knew what the war was all about and was doing it right. Now that upset the "proverbial apple cart" and upset all the real *"head dicks"* from D.C. to Nam. The elite trained just would not play by THEIR rules. On more than one occasion, from the southernmost part of the Delta to the DMZ someone that belonged to a Special Operations Unit, be it Army or Navy, got their "Balls" in a vice, because they had not "followed THEIR orders." Operating on their own just did not go over well with the "Powers in control." But true to the very nature of Guerrilla Warfare, they played the game, and played it very well. Probably the only men in the entire country that knew that the idiots calling the "shots" had no clue as to what Unconventional Warfare was all about.

Michael and Joseph once again met J.P. at the airport, and in a short time arrived at the home of Vincent Spadolini, where J.P. would be a guest. Again he was very surprised, as he had figured he would be staying at Joseph's home. Vincent had called Brian and informed him he would be arriving at his place on the lake around five o'clock, still leaving Brian in the dark as to who the mystery person was.

Salvatore was the driver for Vincent, as they rode in a four door black BMW, with J.P. and Vincent in the back. They conducted small talk about politics, a little talk about Vincent's business as they traveled toward Brian's home. J.P. was not real comfortable on the way to this unknown destination, and Vincent did most of the talking. With ten minutes left in the trip Vincent asked J.P. if he had ever considered coming out of retirement.

J.P. assumed he was talking about teaching, and quickly responded. "I got out of the teaching business for good. I am sure there are good school systems around the country, but I do not want any part of any of them. One, there is no system that will employee a person my age. Two, I do not have my Ph.D., and that eliminates the college or university aspect of employment."

Vincent smiled. "Well, J.P. I was not talking about the educational profession."

This again set J.P. back and he did not know what to say. As the car made its way into the lake area Vincent ended the conversation with, "Well I will talk to you about it at another time. We have more important things to take care of now."

The car entered a section that was sectioned off by a ten-foot chain-linked fence, which covered some ten acres of land right down to the lake water's edge. The gate entrance was made of two steel gates that rose two feet above the ten-foot stone pillars they were attached to. They were open and Salvatore drove through the entrance and down the road without any hesitation, as if he was used to coming to the place. There was only one house on the property that bordered the north side of the lake, the home of Brian Keefe O'Francis. There were other homes, on both ends and on the other side of the lake, all in the three-figure range and well above. J.P. knew he was dealing with people way out of his range financially, even with his windfall and investments, most likely in other ways also. The home on the lake was not your run of the mill lake side house. More like a small countryside summer getaway, in the two million and up range.

A maid, of Hispanic background, very attractive, small framed body, and stood no more than five feet tall, greeted them at the door, and with the welcome, J.P. knew that she knew Vincent well.

"Come in Mr. Spadolini, come in. I will tell Mr. O'Francis you are here."

J.P. was stunned at hearing his family name. He looked directly at Don Spadolini. He turned his head slightly to the right and saw the shock and puzzled look on J.P.'s face.

"No, I know where he is, we will join him on the deck. J.P. if you will join me."

He began walking through the house with J.P. two steps to his right rear. Salvatore and Mirabella turned and went in another direction.

As the two men stepped out onto the very large back deck that overlooked the lake, Brian rose from his chair. "Vincent, welcome, pull up a chair and have a seat. Been waiting for you," he said as he laid his book down on the table.

"Ahhh, had a short delay, little matter I need to take care of before we left." Vincent stated.

Before Brian could call Mirabella, she appeared at the door.

"Ahhh, could you bring us some," then he paused. "Is ice tea okay Vince? And ahhh."

For the first time he looked at J.P. and their eyes locked on each other. Vincent stood to the left of the two men with a smile on his face. Neither one was speaking. Their eyes went from one another's head to their feet. Their body frame was the same, their height was the same, and their facial features were so much alike it was scary. Brian had a salt and pepper mustache, J.P. had a salt and auburn one. J.P.'s hair was a grayish/white. Brian's hair was dark gray with very little black left in it.

Vincent broke the moments of silence. "Brian, I would like for you to meet J.P. O'Francis."

The look on Mirabella's face also told the story, and one could read the questions on her face as she stood staring at the two men. Brian extended his hand, and J.P. took it as the two shook hands, both with a firm grip, once again locking eyes with each other.

"It is good to meet you Brian O'Francis." J.P. responded with a question in his voice.

"What would you like to drink?" Brian asked.

J.P. smiled. "Tea will be fine."

Brian extended his hand outward toward the chair indicating for him to have a seat. "Sit gentlemen."

The three men took a seat around the very large round glass top table.

"Have you two had dinner yet?" Brian asked, trying not to stare at J.P.

Vincent answered, "No we have not as we came right over after J.P. arrived."

Mirabella was bringing out a tray with a pitcher of ice tea and three goblet shaped glasses. As she set them on the table, Brian asked, "What would you like for dinner? Now Mirabella is an excellent cook and she can fix anything you would like. Vince... J.P., you have a preference?"

J.P. was sitting back in his chair, his hands cupped together resting at his waist. Vince was pouring the tea for all three.

"No sir, I have no particular cravings."

Vincent smiled. "Ahhh, Mirabella, fix us some steaks, and baked potatod, and a salad, or something like that."

"J.P.," Vincent said, "she is an excellent cook, and that may be a gross understatement."

Mirabella smiled from ear to ear. "Well thank you Mr. Spadolini and that was very kind Mr. O'Francis." Then she paused and looked at Brian and then at J.P., "I mean, ahhh, Mr. Brian, ahh." She was embarrassed, and Brian knew it.

"It's okay, Mirabella. It is not often that we have another O'Francis in the house." And then he laughed. "Well hell, we have never had one, have we?" He laughed again, as he looked up at Mirabella, relieving some of the light tension that seemed to be in the air.

"I was wondering when you would like to eat." she said.

"When you get it ready just give us a yell, okay."

Then Vincent chimed in, "Take your time, we aren't in any hurry."

Mirabella was off to the kitchen to fix the men their meal.

Brian allowed her to fix anything she liked for herself. If she wanted to eat what he had or anyone of his guests she could. He rarely had anyone over to his lakeside home, but Mirabella kept a fully stocked food supply. She had worked for Brian for ten years, and had been given access to his home if he was there or if he was away on business. He preferred her to stay, but she never would, except on rare occasions, like bad weather, or late night dinner parties. She had her own room, if she needed to stay over. Her husband had left her many years earlier. She had raised her only son Rafael Angel by herself, and Brian had made sure they had money. He had employed Mirabella when Rafael was ten years old, and in a short period of time he too was working for Mr. Brian O'Francis, maintaining the grounds around the lakeside home during the summer. He too had a separate room if he needed to spend the night or several days, which often he did when he was in his late teens. In the winter he had him working for him in one of his hotels, or clearing the snow from his rather long drive-way/road that led to his home. He made sure he went to a private school, and now he was in college, at the University of Chicago.

Brian rose from his chair. "Excuse me for a moment." And in a minute he had returned with a humidor and placed it on the table and opened it.

"Have a cigar. Oh, I mean if you smoke that is J.P.? What does J.P. stand for, may I ask? I don't mean to be pushy, it is just that Vincent and I usually sit out here on occasions and smoke a cigar."

"Thank you. I believe I will. I also partake in a good cigar on occasions." Then he smiled and reached for one of Brian's Cohibas. He put it under his nose and ran it from one end to the other. He then reached for the cigar cutter, and clipped the end of it off. Reaching his left hand into his pocket and retrieving his black Zippo lighter, he toasted the end and then let the flame draw up to the end of the seven inch cigar as he puffed and got a nice glow. J.P. then laid his lighter down on the table.

"The "J" is for James. The "P" is for Patrick." Vincent and Brian were going through the same procedure in lighting their cigars.

As J.P. laid his lighter down on the table Brian looked at it and saw the 75th Ranger crest attached to the side of it. He continued to draw the fire from his lighter to his cigar. His eyes shifted toward where J.P. was seated, his head never moved. He then tilted his head back and blew the smoke upward into the late afternoon breeze that carried it in the opposite direction of where J.P. was sitting.

"A military crest I presume?"

It took J.P. a few seconds, but he caught what he was referring to.

"Yes, it was my unit's crest, the 1st of the 75th Rangers. Well, in a way. There is a story behind that also. A time factor, but we who were Ranger qualified in Vietnam at the time adopted it as our unit. They, our good people in DC, had not established a full unit of Rangers when I was in there." He reached over to the table and picked the now worn looking lighter up and reached it to Brian.

"I don't believe I know what this one is. Of course, now I was in the Navy, and if it ain't Navy I would not know."

J.P. smiled. "Well Brian, it sure ain't Navy. Nothing personal you understand."

"Oh, none taken," he said as he passed the lighter back to J.P., then took a drink of his tea.

"Army?" Brian asked, knowing it was.

"That would be a very safe bet."

He continued with the light conversation. "Rangers you say. Well now, that is impressive. Would it also be a safe bet that you are a Viet Nam Veteran?"

J.P. smiled, and took his time answering, by taking a drink of tea and slowly setting his glass down on the table. "Yes, that too would be a very safe bet. Seems you are winning this game of poker so far."

Brian patted his ashes off into a large cigar ashtray sitting in the middle of the table for all to reach.

"Well J.P., so far they were no brainers. I like the insignia. Here comes another "no brainer". The Sun represents day, the Star, night, and the lightning bolt, striking with quickness." Vincent laughed, and then both O'Francis men laughed.

"Yes you won another pot."

And just as quick as the laughter began, with a smile on his face he asked, "So where are you from J.P?"

Again he paused before he answered, but not enough to make Brian or Vincent think he did not want to answer or that he may be hiding something. "Currently living in Georgia."

"Ah yes, a southerner." Brian put on his best deep southern drawl. "Atlanta right?"

J.P. puffed on his cigar and reached over the ashtray and patted his ashes off. "Not quite, Northern Georgia, southern part of the Appalachians. You lost that one." J.P. smiled. All three laughed. The atmosphere was becoming more relaxed as the three men began to loosen up a bit.

J.P. noticed out of the corner of his eye, undetected by Vincent, that he had been watching him, his body language, and his tone of voice as he answered the seemingly meaningless questions. There was still a lot he did not know about J.P., which left a rather large void in his knowledge concerning him. A mystery, and Vincent knew that knowledge was power, and he liked to have all the answers when it came to people he dealt with or came into contact with. He liked J.P. and at the point they were at, trusted him, and simply based on Joseph's and Paul's reports on him.

J.P. did not really know just how Paul and Vincent knew each other, or how well. But he was very aware that there was some type of connection, which did not bother him, as he trusted Paul, and that was enough for J.P.

Vincent had planned a light first meeting, with casual conversations on a variety of subjects. He was in hopes that the two could get together the next day and get down to a more personal level, which is how it went. A nice dinner, some wine, a few drinks afterwards and another cigar. They departed at ten o'clock with the knowledge that J.P. would be returned tomorrow to spend the afternoon and evening with Brian, maybe even stay the night.

At precisely 1000 hours, Vincent's car pulled into Brian's driveway with only J.P. and Salvatore. J.P. picked up his two pieces of luggage out of the trunk and thanked Salvatore. He was not at all sure about this part of his trip, but he was adhering to the request of Don Spadolini, and he was at the mercy of people he really did not know, so he figured he would play the hand he had been dealt, figuring that Paul would not have advised him to stay for the entire course and that he would talk to him after he returned to Atlanta.

Brian met J.P. at the door and waved to Salvatore as he drive off down the driveway and headed back to Chicago.

"Follow me J.P. and I will show you to your room," Brian stated.

They walked up the arched stairway and down a hallway to one of three guest rooms. It was a plush room, large, thirty by twenty foot with a queen size bed done in a Western style décor, a large picture window looked out over the lake.

"Very nice Brian." J.P. stated as he laid his garment bag on the bed. Brian walked to the walk-in closet and opened a set of double-mirrored doors.

"You may hang your clothes in here if you wish. I understand how it is when you travel, things get wrinkled even with the best of packing. The dressers are empty. You may put your other clothes in them also if you wish."

Brian was trying to be the perfect host, and J.P. could tell Brian was a little tense with the arrangements that Vincent had made.

"When you are done, come downstairs and we will have coffee in the dining room. Ohhh, that is if you drink coffee, I mean, unless you prefer something else,"

J.P. cut him off. "Coffee will be fine. I like coffee, drink a lot of it, probably too much."

Brian smiled. "Yes, me too. Have you had breakfast?"

"Yes."

"I'll have Mirabella fix us a small snack. Would you like anything in particular?"

"No, just whatever you would normally have is fine." The two men stood at opposite ends of the room.

"Oh shit, forgive me. Let me show you the bathroom."

He then walked to a solid wooden door that appeared to be made of light oak and opened it. "I think you will find everything you may need, and if you do need something let me know."

"Thanks, but I think I have all I will need."

"The towels and wash cloths are here," he said as he opened a full length mirrored door opposite the wall to the shower. Then he left J.P. to put his clothes up and freshen up. After hanging his two suits, four ties, and four dress shirts up, placing his socks, three casual slacks, two pairs of jeans and casual shirts as well as his sweat shirts in the dresser drawers, and putting his two additional pairs of dress shoes at the foot of the bed, he went to the bathroom. It was large, fifteen feet by fifteen feet he figured, a shower that one could have fit three people in, two sinks, two full length mirrors. *Had to be specially made*, J.P. thought, as they opened swinging to the left and right, revealing large and small bath towels and wash cloths, enough for several people for a week, using a new one each day.

J.P. noted that he had a shelf with several new toothbrushes in sealed wrappers, three different kinds of toothpaste, two new razors and refills, and one electric razor, several bars of soap in their boxes, three different kinds of shampoo, all very neatly arranged. He noted that the house, what he had seen of it, was spotlessly clean, and appeared to have everything in a particular place. Brian O'Francis was, it appeared, a very meticulous and clean person and was quite sure that Brian's maid kept his home in that manner.

As J.P. descended the wooden staircase Mirabella, who appeared from a room to the left of the stairs, met him.

"Mr. O'Francis, Mr. O'Francis is waiting for you in the breakfast nook."

J.P. followed her across the living room to a separate room that was all windows in an arch shape from the ceiling to the floor that took up the entire corner of the west end of the house. A single swinging door led directly into the kitchen to the rear of the room, where she disappeared as soon as J.P. entered the room.

Brian rose, "Have a seat." A pot of coffee and two cups were on the thick octagon glass table. "Thanks."

"Do you take anything in your coffee?"

"No, black."

Brian smiled. "Me too." Then poured two cups.

"Mirabella will have us some Danish out in a few minutes. I asked her to fix us shrimp salad and garlic bread for lunch. I hope that will do?"

J.P. was taking a drink of coffee, and setting it down he stated, "Oh, that is more than enough. Hell, a simple bologna sandwich would have been fine with me."

Brian laughed. "Wellll, me too, but I leave the food part to Mirabella when I have a guest. Me, here by myself, sandwiches and "junk" food is about all I eat during the day. I usually have a light breakfast, and then a good dinner. Hell, I really do not have a lot of time to eat at all."

Which left an opening for J.P. "What do you do Brian? If you do not mind me asking."

"No, No, don't mind at all. I own and operate hotels. I am also in the Lake Shipping business with Vincent."

J.P.'s eyebrows went up, as he was impressed.

"So J.P., what do you do for an occupation?"

"I am a retired high school teacher. Actually for several years now. Not quite as impressive as the business world you two are in, but I was able to survive through it all."

"I take that to mean that you had difficulties?"

J.P. had a half laugh, as he took another drink of his coffee, and reached for the pot. "May I?"

"Sure, help yourself. And if we run out we'll make some more. Or I should say, Mirabella will. I am not allowed in the kitchen when she is here." And then Brian laughed.

"Are you married J.P.?"

"Yes. And no. I am a widow. I was married and still am, to the most wonderful woman. She died several years ago. Her name is Dawn Christine, and I have a son named, Michael, thirty-eight, and Patrick, who would have been thirty-three this coming year. How about yourself?"

"No, never been married. And let me inject here, I am sorry for the losses in your family. As to me I really do not think I will get married, a little late at my age, and I have no desire for a permanent companion. It is not for everyone you know."

Mirabella came through the door and placed their Danish on the table along with some raisin bread, butter and butter knife.

"Will you need anything else Mr. O'Francis?"

"I don't think so."

As the two ate their morning snack, J.P. asked Brian about Mirabella, and he enlightened him on her history. They talked about Brian's business with Vincent, and his own business of hotels, as well as where some of them were. J.P. noticed that Brian appeared to be very comfortable talking to him, as well he should have he figured, since Vincent was the one who arranged the encounter. If he could not have been trusted, he would not have been in Brian's house to start with, must less in Vincentzo Spadolini's home.

After a tour of Brian's home the two went for a walk around his land. As they walked Brian told J.P. how and why he bought the land where he had, how he had designed and overlooked the building of his home. He went into great detail about the specifics of his home displaying great pride in it.

J.P. was the one to break the ice and ask Brian specifically where he was originally from. He never said anything at the point of discovering that he was born in the same state that he was. He learned that he had family in Houston and Tulsa Oklahoma, Texas, and California. J.P. was processing the information as fast as his brain could operate without short-circuiting. He talked about where he had gone to high school, college, and that he had served in the military, the Navy, and had been a SEAL.

J.P. really did not know a lot about SEALs other than they were specially trained in Unconventional Warfare and was part of the military's elite. He'd briefly read a few articles about them, and one TV documentary, which really limited his knowledge on the elite group. He knew that for decades they had carried the repetition for lavishing great damage upon whomever they were hunting. He knew that no other nation on earth could match their skills. He was well aware of the rivalry between SEALs, Special Forces, and Rangers as to who was the *"Badest man in the whole damn town, or the meanest man alive, the king of the jungle jive."* Which simply meant for the elite special operations groups, rock/roll and count. A few motion pictures had been made about the SEALs, but that was Hollywood and J.P. was well aware that did not tell the true story of what a real SEAL was.

He had not mentioned his father's name, nor did he elaborate on the SEALs. J.P. never asked nor did he interrupt him as he was talking. He could handle just so much information at a time, and figured he had more than enough time to get down to the specifics of any part of Brian Keefe

O'Francis. They ended up at the lake where Brian had a short dock extending out into the lake, brick steps leading up to a brick patio measuring twenty by twenty feet square, several feet up from the dock. Black mesh iron rocking chairs and a mesh black iron table sat in the middle of the patio. They talked briefly about the weather and the lakeside view, small talk it appeared, avoiding what was nagging both men in the back of their minds.

Brian got around to asking J.P. where he was born, not where he was raised, but born. When J.P. responded he was looking at Brian, and saw the more than shocked look on his face. Each treaded lightly with their probing questions. J.P. had given a brief synopsis of where he was raised and why, never naming his father or mother just that he was raised with his grandparents. It did give Brian somewhat of a false impression, but it was not a total lie. Twice they had acknowledged that they looked a lot alike. But neither time did either probe any deeper.

Brian raised forward in his chair and placed his arms on the table, cupping his hands together, looking over at J.P.

"Look, I want to ask you a point blank question."

J.P. stopped rocking.

"What was the name of your father?"

J.P. never responded. He cleared his throat, slowly came forward, pulling his chair to the edge of the table and placed his arms on the table, also cupping his hands, and then looked Brian in the eyes. "George E. O'Francis. And yours?"

His eyes told him before he answered. "George E. O'Francis. What does the E. stand for? You know there could be a lot of George E. O'Francis' out there."

"Yes, you are very much correct about that, and I know. The E. stands for Eugene."

Brian plumed backward in his chair.

"Ohhh shitttt! H o l y f u c k! Are we? Could we be? I mean, what, I don't think I?"

J.P. interrupted. "Ahhh, Brian, I do not know? I...."

Brian got up. "Look, please excuse me, I am going to the house, I need a drink! I drink scotch. I will bring the cigars down also. Can I get you anything in particular?"

J.P. stood, and walked to the edge of the red brick patio, a few feet from Brian. "I drink scotch! I smoke cigars! You might better bring a full bottle, and the whole box!" Then he smiled.

"I think I will." Brian paused as he looked at J.P. for a moment and then turned and walked to the house.

As he was gathering up a new bottle of Glen Livet, he picked up the humidor and started out of his den only to be met by Mirabella.

"Brian what is wrong? You look pale."

Brian just stood at the double doors for a moment. "Mirabella, ahh," Then clearing his throat. "Ahhh, would you fix a really nice dinner for J.P. and me tonight? Something really special."

She looked puzzled, as she would have without being asked. She could tell he was visibly shaken. Something she had never seen in him before in all the years she had known him. He had always been a rock, not much emotion, all business. Hard. But the man that now stood facing her, was not the Brian O'Francis she knew.

"Is there something special you would like? Are you going to still have lunch?"

Again, he had a hard time thinking about such minor things like food at the time.

"Yes, lunch, and I really don't know about dinner, you decide, and, Mirabella...make it special." She smiled, because she had already figured the connection, a mother's instinct, although she was two years younger than Brian, she could tell before J.P. had left with Vincent the day before.

"Si, Mr. O'Francis, I will make it a very special dinner."

Brian took several steps by her, and stopped and turned. "Mirabella, Brian will do fine while J.P. his here, it's okay. And Mirabella, I think J.P. will do fine also."

He sounded totally lost at that point. Mirabella's smile covered her whole face. She beamed as if some glorious happening had just occurred to her boss. He appeared as giddy as a school boy, smiling all over his body. A light seemed to bream from his face. The business man she was so accustomed to was not present.

J.P. had walked to the edge of the pier, and was staring at the water as it moved back and forth with the light wind. His mind was numb at that point, thinking about nothing, because he could not figure all the angles, and was getting a headache trying. He heard Brian coming and rejoined him at the table. That afternoon with the spring temperature at a warm sixty-five degrees, the two men continued to talk and learn more about each other. By the time Mirabella informed the two half-brothers that dinner was ready, it was six-thirty and the temperature had become cool.

The two had not noticed the time or the temperature. J.P. had told him his story about what he knew of his mother and father, and Brian told him of his mother and father. J.P. learned that his father had died in 1990, and that Brian's mother had died in 1995. Brian could not help but to feel a void in J.P., growing up not knowing the same father he knew. They learned that one had lived poor, and grew up on a river and in the streets of a small town, the other rich, living in a city and attending a private school. J.P. learned that Brian had been told that their father had been married before and had one child, but he never told him anything other than that. He had to admit to J.P. that he had all but forgotten about it, as he was thirteen when he had been told. He apologized to J.P. at least five times, and had been told five times that he need not.

By midnight, the two had finished off a liter and a half of scotch, and had smoked several cigars. Mirabella informed them that she was retiring for the evening at ten. Their conversations had become more and more personal. J.P. learned that Brian, as a Navy SEAL, had served in Nam, doing basically the same jobs as he had done, just at opposite ends of the country. It had been Brian that had broken the ice about Viet Nam.

"There were large mangroves that produced a very large variety of insects. Mosquitoes of course, by the billions. I think I hate that one insect more than anything. Snakes of what would seem to be a fuck'en zoo, with all the different kinds *and* most very venomous! Now I damn sure don't want to forget the fuck'en blood-sucking leeches! Nor the damn spiders, where one could find, *I am sure*, the world's largest as well as variety! The entire area was a fuck'en nightmare! It had to be the most treacherous place in all of Viet Nam! Forgive me J.P. I mean no disrespect to what you all did and where you were. Hell I have heard of the horror stories about the northern sector. I am sure where you were was not a picnic. But the Delta, well the VC, well this is where they made their home. You know, looking back on it, and I have often looked back on it, I wish they had let the little bastards keep it! We could have found another way for stopping the flow of supplies! But on the other hand, I know that there was no other way! Shit!"

He got up and walked to the fireplace tossing another cigar stub into it. The scotch had begun to work on Brian, and J.P. understood completely. Brian turned to face his "new blood brother." J.P. knew he wanted to talk, and he could tell that he felt at ease talking to him, for so often the combat veteran had no one to talk to that understood. Only another combat veteran could understand what another combat veteran had gone through. The classic comment from people who had not been there and really knew nothing about it, which included all the educated medical profession, physiologist included, was "I understand." And the usual bobbing of the head up and down as one would talk, seeking counseling, trying to make the veteran think that they understood.

"Often we would go on surveillance missions. We were not to engage the enemy. That was not possible all the time. We were often compromised, and we carried with us silencers. When we were too close we used knifes to take them out."

Then he looked at J.P. who had refilled both scotch glasses, and placed a couple of ice cubes in each. Odd he thought as Brian talked to him, how both of them liked scotch on the rocks. He handed the glass to Brian.

"You know J.P., it probably sounds like I hated being a SEAL. But that is not true!" As he began to slur some of his words, and pointed his glass at J.P. "I love being a SEAL! I don't regret doing my time in Nam! But...goddamn it..." he sat down hard in his chair and leaned his head back and looked up at the ceiling. "J.P., tell me, have you ever gotten over it?"

"No. Not really Brian. I do not think in our lifetime we will ever get over it."

"Did you like what you did?"

"Meaning?" J.P. responded.

"I mean, did you get to the point that you liked the stalking, and the hunt, the kill?"

A long pause, Brian's rather lavish den seemed to succumb with the sense of danger. The moments before the hunt began. The seconds before the encounter, the heart pounds so hard the hunter can hear it in his ears. His mouth goes dry, even to the seasoned veteran. The adrenaline begins to flow, that addictive substance that makes one feel they can do anything.

"Amphetamine high," J.P. finally spoke. "That is what Rusty and I would call it. We got to the point that we really liked killing. It consumed us. We competed for the most scores."

"How did you know who got the kill?"

"Ears!"

Brian rose forward in his large soft pillow overstuffed chair. "Ears?"

J.P. turned his glass up to his mouth and finished off another glass of scotch, and walked to the small table that had the ice bucket, opened it, plucked three small ice cubes out and dropped them into his glass. Picked up the bottle of scotch, that was half full, poured a two finger amount into his glass. He stood with his back to Brian, swirled the scotch around a moment and then turned.

"Ears, Brian. I collected ears for each personal kill. I cannot tell you how many people I have actually killed. I do not think any combat vet can do that. However, I can confirm the ones I have ears. I should say, had. I mean... I did not bring them home. Brian, I have a lot of problems with the rules of combat! WE, like you, fought in a war where our idiot government officials wanted rules of the game to play by. Of course they were sitting in Washington, but I won't get into that. WE fought an enemy that had no rules. So WE were trained to fight like they did. My point here is, besides being drunk, and going to places I do not like to go, and talking too much. My point, ahhhh, hell, I think I have forgotten the point. Shit! Ahhh, hell, Brian. Yes I really liked what I did, and it took me a long, long, I mean a long time to get over it.

"What about food?"

J.P. asked, "Food?"

Brian repeated. "Yes, the food you ate while in Nam. I mean we ate things like fish and rice all the time. Well, we did have access to some of the local places where we got fairly good food. On occasions we ate American. Wellll, most all of us did at any rate. So, what type of food did you eat?" Brian asked J.P.

"Well, my situation was a little different. Some did eat dehydrated rations or C-rations, or LRRP food we called it. I or rather we lived with the Montagnard. We ate their food. Well, most of the time. Well, ninety-nine per cent of the time. Oh, we would on a very rare occasion eat some dehydrated shit or even C-rats while we were out for a long time. I mean away from the village, or the base camp. But as far as the basic diet, we ate lots of rice, monkey, chicken, and on special occasions, buffalo, and ate dog a few times."

Brian smiled as J.P. talked.

"They had a salad they fixed a lot. Do not ask what it was made up of, hell I really do not remember, but it was good. Wellll…good at the time. We drank lots of rice wine, lots. Especially during their ceremonies, we dressed in their traditional attire during these things."

Then he trailed off into silence, staring into the void of the fireplace. A few moments passed and J.P. spoke very softly, as if he did and did not want Brian to hear what he was saying but wanted to say what was on his mind, "I still to this very day have the desire for that addictive substance."

Until the short oratory of J.P.'s, Brian had been doing most of the talking but the scotch had gotten to J.P. and he felt comfortable enough to speak his mind to Brian. It did not take a lot for the bitter feelings of J.P.'s experience with the Reynolds School System to surface, even after the many years of his retirement. The bitterness triggered his Viet Nam experiences, which made him a danger to himself.

"Odd you would say that."

J.P. never got to respond to his statement.

"I too have the desire for that high as you put it. It was an addiction. I really did not think about it in that manner, but you are right. You just did not think about the fact that it was another human you were stalking. It was the hunt, a game of sorts. Like these old movies or documentaries about African big game hunters. You know, we were special people, weren't we?"

Silence again permeated the room as the two looked at each other from across the room. J.P. sat in his chair, his arms relaxed on the arms of his chair, his drink in his left hand, his cigar smoking in his ashtray to his right.

"Yes, we were very special people."

"We people never really did get credit for the job we did for the military, or for our country, I don't think. Of course you have your famous press, the good ole on the spot reporter who shoved a black tennis ball size "mike" in your face and his loyal dumb-ass camera man recording every detail for the good folks back home to up their nightly news ratings. Now they were not to be found in our area. I am sure they were not where you were either! J.P., don't get me wrong on this one. Hell, I would have hated the bastards if they had been anywhere around! I don't know that I would not have shot one of them. But even now I have little for the media and how they report a war."

Then he paused in his conversation. "Well, I guess some books and some articles have surfaced praising the accomplishments, the SEAL team's achievements. Oh, and I am sure the Special Forces and Rangers have a few books written about them also. But hell, it was the men who served, the ones who were really there that have written them. But it has been a long, and I mean long time after we have come home. Ahhhh, I have seen a few film documentaries on Viet Nam over the years. Shit! By-god I damn sure did not see them in the Delta!"

His scotch was getting to him, and he was rambling.

"Of course I am sure you are aware that if it were not for JFK there would not have ever been a COIN (counter insurgency)! No Special Forces, NO, Rangers, LRRP's that is. It was us, J.P.! I mean it was us that really knew what the war was all about!"

Holding his Cohiba toward J.P. he stated, "We were the ones that slowed down the flow of supplies, not the damn bombs!"

The two men never went to bed, instead they stopped drinking and went to the kitchen and made coffee, and continued to talk about each other's lives, their parents, and their ancestral background.

Mirabella entered "Her" kitchen at seven A.M. The two O'Francis men had stepped out on the back deck, to continue their talk and drink their coffee. They were almost sober by that point. The fact that they had not slept in twenty-four hours had not hit either one yet.

Mirabella walked out onto the deck. "Good morning Mr. O'Francis." And then she smiled a warm bright smile. "Would you two men like for me to fix you something special for breakfast?"

As both looked up at her from where they were seated, and then back at each other, J.P. spoke. "I really would like to have a good western omelet, with some toast, if you do not mind?"

"And you Brian?" Mirabella asked.

"That will be good, with a lot of beacon, please."

Mirabella turned and went to "Her" kitchen to make the two men what they requested. The morning air was a little crisp, and Brian had provided J.P. with a light coat. Brian went in to get both a new cigar, and to tell Mirabella that they were going for a walk, and to take her time fixing breakfast. It was during their walk that J.P. learned about Brian's connection to Vincent, and his connections to other people. He learned about Brian's own men who took care of his business for him. J.P. found that he was very powerful, both financially as well as influentially. Brian found out that J.P. was a lot like him, without the "money" and connections.

"You know Brian it was altogether different for me. I grew up in a small town." He then stopped and began to laugh. Brian was smiling, but did not understand what had struck J.P. to be so funny.

As he continued to laugh, Brian looked at him. "What?"

"Have you ever heard of or listened to a singer by the name of John Mellencamp?"

"Yes, why?"

"He wrote a song a long time ago, called *Small Town*. It struck a chord in me the first time I heard it, and just suddenly the song came to mind."

He paused and slowly his laughter faded and the smile on his face slowly went away. "God… it really is weird what a song will do to your mind."

A few minutes of silence as the two continued to walk, and then Brian looked over at J.P. "Hey…only in America."

"No,No.No, It's, *Ain't that America..*"

"Ohhh, Yaaa, it was." The two men laughed together. Brian had not been so relaxed since his college days, when life was just fun to live.

"J.P., tell me, I understand we have a mutual friend down south."

They continued to walk. J.P. had not responded to his question.

"Look, J.P., I am not trying to probe, nor am I testing you. Paul has known Vincent and I for some years now. I have only recently learned of you and the acquaintance you have with Paul. J.P., I really did not know nor did I have a clue we were brothers. Vincent simply told me he had someone he wanted me to meet and that you knew Paul."

"Well, yes I do know Paul. But I am not connected with him as far as his business goes. Hell, I really do not know exactly what business he is in. Well, that is not exactly true. I mean I do know he has a PI business, but I mean I really do not know what his background is. He has helped me some, by his ability of obtaining information. For us, that is "recon" and surveillance of some… let me put it this way, some undesirables."

They had reached the crest of the gentle sloping hill that overlooked Brian's property.

"J.P., please don't take this the wrong way. I really don't mean to get personal here, although we have been for the past, ahhh, every how many hours it has been. I do not intend to pry into your private life. But, how are you financially?"

J.P. took a long drag off his once seven inch cigar, which was about at the half way point. He blew the smoke upward into the crisp early morning air. Extending his right arm outward and holding the "stodgy" as if he were examining it.

"This is a very expansive cigar. Or to me it is!" Brian never answered.

He stood beside his newly found brother, paused only for a moment and continued, "You have never wanted for much have you? I mean, you have always been financially well off, correct?"

Brian started to speak and then paused and removed his cigar from his mouth. "Yes, J.P. that is correct. And I am very…"

J.P. cut him off in mid-sentence. " No! You owe me no apology. Nor do you owe me any type of explanation. That is just how the cards were dealt! I had to play my hand and you had to play yours. Now, to your question: I am not rich by any means! But at this point in my life I am above water! It has not always been that way, as you know now."

They spent the entire day together sharing everything they could with each other, and learning just how much they were alike. With different mothers, Brian's being of Italian background and J.P.'s being German/Irish background, their father's genes were dominate in both of the O'Francis men. J.P. learned a lot about the father he had never seen, and yet he had always felt that he and his father were very much alike. As he would learn, he had been correct, they were. As his mother had often stated, "You're just like your damn father!"

Brian had taken on more of the Italian skin pigmentations and hair color. J.P. had gotten his skin tone and hair from his grandmother O'Francis. But the structure of their faces left no questions. Brian was kind enough to share the pictures he had of his father with J.P., and there had been no question as to the father and son connection. J.P. kept looking at the pictures of his father, as if he were burning the images into his mind, so as not to forget. But he had not needed to worry. He left with several pictures, compliments of his brother.

His stop off in Atlanta was pleasant. J.P. did not learn how Paul knew Brian and Vincent. But he did not care. They had a good conversation. His biggest concern was the fact that sooner or later they would learn that he did not live in Georgia. Paul informed him that he would take care of that end of the connection in due time, that it would not be a major problem.

"Paul, did you know that I had a brother? Well, I guess he would be considered a half-brother. I mean according to socially correct terms that is."

"Not at first, to be completely honest with you J.P."

He drank his coffee, and the waitress arrived and filled his cup, and looked over at J.P. "More sir?"

J.P. just nodded, yes. J.P. was looking down at his cup as she filled it to the brim.

"J.P., what are your thoughts?"

"Do you know how long," he paused, and Paul finished his sentence.

"You looked for your father."

"Yes."

"Well, no I really do not. But, I made the connection between you two, in 1997. I really came about it by accident. I had not really given it a lot of thought, until I was sitting in Don Spadolini's den and Brian came in. The more I looked at him the more I made the connection. Or thought I did. I mean, damn, J.P., you two, well I mean it would take a blind person not to see the similarities. I never said anything to anyone. I did not know all the connections. So when I got back home I started doing some checking, and called in a few low cost favors, and bang, there was the connection."

"All these years you have known that I had a brother, and you did not tell me."

"It was not my place to tell you. And besides I did not know at the time you had or was trying to locate your father."

There were several minutes of silence, with only the sounds of the other people in the lounge, utensils touching the plates, and some music being played in the background.

"You know Brian is a very powerful person, don't you?"

J.P. did not respond. Paul sat looking at him. J.P. slowly looked up from staring into his coffee cup.

"I did not. Well I should say I really do not know. I mean I figured. Hell I am not a complete idiot. I know he has and is in a very powerful financial world with very powerful and wealthy people."

"I know you're no idiot. I think you could have fit into..." another pause as Paul seemed to be choosing his words very carefully.

"I think you would have worked out very well in the business."

"The business?"

"Yes."

J.P. looked down at his watch. He had forty-five minutes before his flight left. His thoughts were that Paul seemed to be different. He seemed to look at him in a different perspective, than he had. Maybe he did not. Maybe it was just his paranoia surfacing. He knew that he was in a world with people that could control the destiny of people with the flip of a coin.

Paul did not interrupt J.P.'s thoughts. He knew he was doing just that, figuring, calculating, and putting together pieces of a puzzle. He had a total military mind. Even at his age he had not lost the sharpness. Not that sixty-five was old, maybe at one time, but not now. He was one that planned, and calculated even move, figuring the odds. That was why he knew that he would fit into the business. He knew that Vincent and Brian would see it also, if, they got anywhere close to J.P. That is, if, he would let them. Paul could not blame him if he did not, but he also knew that he was not totally wealthy, and that he could be, with a little help from people like Vincent and Brian. Brian was, why not J.P. He deserved it.

J.P. got up without speaking and tossed five dollars on the table.

"Let's take a walk toward the gate." He was halfway to the gate before he spoke again.

"So when are you going to come to see me, Paul?"

The statement took Paul by surprise, and it was several moments before he could answer. "I don't know. I guess whenever you want."

"Well the weather is turning early this year. Spring should be getting an early start. Fishing is really good in the early spring. Why not give me a call?"

"Okay." Was all Paul said and then he gave him a new password, and they parted. J.P. headed to the northwest by way of the southwest and Paul to the northeast by way of a car and both with a lot to think about.

# The Cage

IT WAS 7:00 A.M. WHEN the phone started to ring in O'Neill's office. After the fifth ring the answering machine picked up. *You have reached Blue Ridge Investigation. Leave your name and number and a short message. I will return your call.*

"This is Henry David Thoreau. Call me."

It was 10:00 a.m. when Paul walked into his office.

"Good morning Judy, you're looking bright and spiffy for a Monday morning."

Mary Judy Pendergrass smiled. "Thank you Mr. O'Neill. Your mail is on your desk, and you have had three phone calls this morning. I left the messages on your desk. Coffee?"

"Yes please." Paul O'Neill went into his office. The answering machine was on the right corner of his desk, the light flashing. Paul sat down in his old battered chair and began opening his mail, most of which was junk. Three were checks for services rendered. Judy came in with coffee in his favorite mug, a faded tan mug with an Irish and American flag unfurled, crossed in the center and wrapped around the sides to the handle of the mug.

"Thanks Mary. Would you put these checks in the bank for me this morning?" He signed the backs of each and handed them to her.

"Do you want me to go now or do you need me for anything right away?"

"I'll be here for a while, you can go this morning. Oh, Mary would you be so kind as to pick us up some breakfast while you are out? Would you please?"

"The usual?" Mary asked.

Paul smiled. "Yes, I guess. No, no, on second thought, surprise me this time." Then Paul smiled and winked at his loyal secretary of ten years.

Mary J. turned and walked out of his office closing the door behind her as she left.

Paul took a drink of coffee while he reached over to the corner of the desk and pushed play on the answering machine. "Damn, she makes good coffee," Paul spoke out loud to himself. He swung his old chair around and placed his feet on the low windowsill and leaned back, the chair squeaking as it went back. He enjoyed just looking out of the two corner windows down on the street below. Paul enjoyed watching the people and traffic going about their daily routines. The first message was a female needing his services, the second an attorney who frequently required his services, the third a voice he had not heard in some time.

"Hmmmm. Now that is a pleasant surprise," he said as he once again spoke aloud. He leaned to his right and picked up the phone. He was aware that only a few people had J.P.'s number, or knew where he was for that matter. It had to be important for him to place a call to him. Paul had his number stored in his memory banks and punched in the number on the phone.

It was 7:25 a.m. in Montana. J.P. was at the kitchen table eating his breakfast. He had fixed oatmeal and toast. The early spring weather on O'Brian Creek was still cool, upper 40's during the day and then drop-ping to the mid-twenties on often time lower at night. Snow still covered the ground, and the sun was extremely bright as it brightly illuminated the O'Francis kitchen.

The phone rang for the third time by the time he reached it on the wall on the far side of the kitchen. He looked at the caller ID. It read Blue Ridge Investigation.

"This is Thoreau, talk to me."

"This is Longfellow."

"How goes business in the hustling bustling big city?" J.P. started the conversation.

"Oh, I'm staying as busy as I want. Same old stuff, someone wants to find out who is cheating on someone. How are things in your neck of the woods?" Paul asked.

"Well, we still have a good blanket of snow on the ground but it is getting warmer by the day though," J.P. said.

Paul laughed. "Yeah, I bet it's up to zero by now." Then he continued to chuckle.

"Oh we're up to the upper 40's during the days. It does seem warmer when the sun is out. The reflection will just about blind you though. Ahhh, give Mother Nature a few weeks and she will have her green carpet covering everything," J.P. said as if to defend the weather at the foothills of the Bitterroot Mountains.

Paul was well aware that J.P. did not call for a friendly chat. "So, my good friend, what can I do for you?" Paul's voice became serious.

"Can you meet me in Minneapolis?" J.P. said.

A short pause in the conversation as Paul took his feet off the windowsill, leaned forward in his chair, with the chair squeaking as he came forward and scooting it toward the edge of the windows, looking down on the people coming and going on the sidewalks, entering and exiting the stores in the renovated new downtown, as the 60-degree spring morning seemed to motivate people to get out and about.

"Yes. Sure. Why Minneapolis?" Paul asked.

"No real reason just figured to be about halfway for the both of us. Would you not say?" J.P. answered.

"Yeah, not a problem. So where and when do we meet?" Asked Paul.

"Don't know yet. I'll make the arrangements and call you back this afternoon," J.P. said.

"Okay. I'll be in the office all day." Paul told J.P. Then without any good bye or so longs J.P. hung up. Paul knew him well, and although it may have bothered most people and most would have thought it rude, Paul accepted the way Jim operated.

It was early Friday morning when J.P. checked into the Hilton and Towers on 1001 Marquette Avenue in downtown Minneapolis 18 days later. Paul was due to arrive Saturday morning. J.P. had reserved a room next his. After getting settled into his room J.P. strolled out on the sidewalk of Marquette Avenue and hailed a cab, telling the driver to take him to First and Marquette. He paid the fare and got out and walked the short distance to Riverside Park on the shores of the mighty Mississippi River. He found a park bench and took a seat. The air was a cool 50 degrees at eleven o'clock and a mild breeze blew from the north down the river making it feel like it was 30 degrees. J.P. had dressed for the weather, jeans, western light tan snakeskin boots, blue denim shirt and his favorite cowhide sheep lined coat. He sat with his hands in his coat pockets staring out at the almond shaped island splitting the Mississippi. He watched the busy traffic on the river as well as the bridge leading across the river to the island. But his mind did not comprehend any of it. He was pondering what he was about to set in motion.

It was Saturday morning 9:00 a.m. when Paul entered the hotel restaurant. There were just a few people in the room, maybe ten or twelve. He paused and scanned the room for J.P. as he had received a message at the desk to meet him in the restaurant when he was settled in. The hostess approached Paul and before she could ask him where he would like to be seated, he informed her that he was meeting a gentleman and had located him. J.P. was in the far corner of the restaurant, and had seen Paul enter. He stood and raised his arm so he could locate him. Paul thanked the hostess and made his way across the room to J.P.'s table.

"Good morning, Paul." J.P. said. "Good flight?"

"Ahh, no problems, enjoyed it. Good to do a little long distance traveling again. I think I miss it." Paul said with a smile on his face.

They had no more than sat down when the waitress arrived. "Good morning gentlemen. May I get you something to drink?"

"Coffee and plenty of it please." Paul told her.

"I'll be right back." And she was off.

"So, J.P. you look like you have been keeping in shape."

"Don't look to0 shabby yourself ole boy." J.P. replied.

The waitress returned with a container of coffee and turned each cup over on the saucers and filled them. "May I take your order now? Or would you like some time to look at a menu?"

Paul looked at her nametag. "Well, Carol, I think I'll have your house special."

J.P. stated that he would have the same.

"Would you like to know what it is?" Carol asked.

"No, I am sure it is good." Paul stated.

"Okay gentlemen, it'll be a few minutes." Carol turned and was off again.

"Well my good friend, why are we here in the great Viking city of Minneapolis?" Paul opened the business conversation up. J.P. took a long drink of coffee, set his cup gently down in his saucer and looked across the table at Paul.

"I want to build a cage." J.P. said with calm, an almost coldness in his voice.

Paul put his cup down. "A cage?" Paul asked.

"Yes a cage, a Viet Cong cage," J.P. answered.

"I don't think I understand," Paul stated with a very puzzled expression on his face.

"Do you know anyone in the Bayous of Louisiana?" J.P. continued.

Paul took another drink of coffee. He thought for a few minutes, his hands wrapped around his cup. J.P. sat in silence as Paul pondered. Some small conversation took place between the two, politics, weather, travel and what J.P. had been doing with himself on a ranch he was still learning how to operate. The waitress arrived with their breakfast.

"Well that didn't take long," J.P. stated.

"Well, it is easy when you order the house special." Carol answered with a friendly smile. Then continued to place each plate down, telling them what they were having. "Two eggs, scrambled, three pieces of bacon, three pieces of toast and a bowel of fruit, gentlemen. Will there be anything else?"

"No. It looks good. Just keep us filled with coffee," J.P. told Carol.

She picked up the container and was off with a response of, "Yes sir. I'll be right back."

As the two men ate their breakfast they continued their talk about the politics of the Nation, the weather, and J.P.'s Buffalo ranch. Carol returned with a full container of coffee.

As soon as the men were finished, Carol was at their table taking their plates away. "Fresh coffee gentlemen?" She asked pleasantly.

"Yes, if you don't mind." Paul told her.

"No problem. I'll be right back," Carol stated and took the plates and container with her.

"I think I can locate a source in the swamp land. Why do we need someone in the deep swamps of the Louisiana?" Paul picked up on the business end of the conversation again.

"The first thing I want is someplace deep in the swamps, an island. I want to build a cage 6 X 6X 5 feet, top, bottom, and sides, with three inches between each pole. I want the poles to be three inches in diameter. I want the cage to be three feet off the ground. I want one bamboo mat placed on the floor of the cage. I want one door in the center of the top of the cage. I want it built so no one can escape! Can that be done?" J.P. stated with hardness in his voice.

Paul looked at him for a long few seconds before he spoke. "J.P. what is going down my friend?"

J.P. did not answer right away. "Can you get what I am asking for?" J.P. stated, without answering Paul's question.

"Well I'll have to make some phone calls. But, yes, I can get what you want. Now, my question is why?" Paul picked up his cup to take another drink.

"I am going to have someone placed in it, for a long time. They will not return from the swamp. They will not be found. I want someone we can trust that will provide two meals per day to this individual. I want them to be fed one fish and one cup of white rice at each meal." J.P. continued with his request. "Then after one month I want the person to forget where the cage is."

"Damn J.P. you turning V.C. on me? That is cold," Paul stated.

"No, but I learned. I remembered. I know what it will do to even the very well trained, experienced hardened person. Yes, but not cold enough," J.P. said.

Paul looked across at O'Francis and saw in his eyes that there was absolutely no feeling at all.

"What about the cost?" Paul asked knowing that J.P. was not wealthy. However, knew he was not hurting for money and knew that he had a brother with the finances that could handle any cost for whatever J.P. wanted.

"The cost will be covered!" The reply came from J.P.

"Who's the mark J.P.?" Before he could answer Paul asked, "Have you made arrangements for this person to be abducted? Have you got your ass covered on this mission?"

J.P. finished off yet another cup of coffee and poured another cup. "To answer all your questions, affirmative and the mark is a female and a deadly enemy." J.P. said without feelings.

Carol brought the check and J.P. placed fifty dollars in with the bill then handed it to her. "Keep the change." He and Paul rose and exited the restaurant, with a quick stop by the restroom. "Let's go for a walk Paul," as they walked out on Marquette Avenue.

"Which way and I know you have already reconned the area," Paul said with a bit of a laugh.

"Ahhh, come on Paul, why would you think that?"

J.P. nodded his head toward the river. "It's not far by country boys' standards. We'll walk to the great and mighty Mississippi. There is a real nice park at the end of Marquette and First Street," O'Francis stated.

At the end of the block, a matter of a few hundred feet from the hotel, Paul looked at the cross street. "Damn, this is Tenth Street. And we are going to First. You have got to be kidding, right?" Paul stood as the light changed and people began crossing the street.

"Let's go city boy." J.P. stepped off the curb and crossed the street toward Riverside Park.

# The Nail

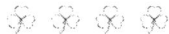

J.P. HAD BEEN A "BURNED out" teacher for several years, one absurd conflict after another, never seeming to let up. His thoughts turned to how Ho Chi Minh had defeated not only the French but also the United States, with staying power, constant pressure on your foe until they broke. It seemed to O'Francis the son of bitches in the political arena in Reynolds County had adopted his philosophy. Instead of the lead from the end of an AK-47, something he could counter, they were attacking his character, his name, his family. There seemed to be no defense against this tactic.

O'Francis' will of self-discipline was once again at the very breaking point. How often would it reach that point without snapping? Like a rubber band, stretched back and forth time and time again until it finely weakens to the point that stretching it to it maximum point, it breaks. Stress was a constant companion again, creating anxiety and chest pains on a frequent basis.

Andrew Duponte' and Linnet Thomas, supervisors from the central office, had requested J.P. to report to his principal's office. Over the years, he had been investigated so many times by the same two supervisors that he began to like them. Not for what they were doing so much, but because he knew they were doing what they were told by their Fuhrer. Good soldiers, just doing the job they were hired to do. The pattern had become routine. He could never figure whether the two liked harassing him or if they were really just doing their job. If it was just a job, he could handle that. However, if it was the enjoyment of harassment, he had a major problem with both of them. That question was something he would deal with in time.

He entered Mr. Wolffe's office. Ms. Thomas was behind Wolffe's desk, and Duponte' was in a chair to the left of the door. J.P. smiled and placed his tape recorder down on Wolffe's desk.

"You folks are really going to have to stop meeting me like this. You know people are beginning to talk about us."

Duponte' forced a half laugh, and Thomas just smiled. J.P. took a mental note of the fact that she had a warm genuine smile. He never figured her for the Gestapo type, but felt that she most likely could be rather harsh if she needed to be. Yet, over the course of several meetings and investigations, there was something about her in which he had dictated just did not fit the Marshy storm trooper mentality.

"I want to inform you two that this conference will be recorded. Present here on this date 28 May in the year 1998 is the good Dr. Thomas and Mr. Duponte'. Both are supervisors from the Center Office staff. Now since I only see you two whenever someone files an observed, mendacious complaint, and I might add brought on by some nefarious person, what have we got today?" O'Francis did not let the supervisors speak. He was irritated and lashed out with a sarcastic remark.

"Let me see. Grades! No, too much homework! No, could not be that because I give very little of that and we have covered all that several times. Ahhh yes, I broke up a fight the wrong way. Maybe I corrected someone of my precious little students in a manner that they did not like. Or is it another child whose daddy or mommy is politically connected and they just do not like the manner in which I am teaching? AHHH that is it!" J.P. exclaimed in excitement.

"Teaching. Now that is a real joke. That's it. I am trying to teach. Nowwww, we all know at this point that is really not allowed in my classroom! Trying to pass along knowledge, oh, my, out of the question!"

Both supervisors sat in silence as if O'Francis' oratory and seemingly insane statements stunned them. By all appearances James Patrick O'Francis had finally broken. Duponte' in his usual deep voice, which by his appearance he would not have such, spoke, "No actually, Mr. O'Francis we are here today to make you an offer. There have not been any complaints," Andrew replied.

"You are kidding. No complaints. Geez, I am really in a state of total shock! Now that is a real news item. Point of fact is, it should make headlines. Hell maybe CNN! Ahhh wait. You stated you were here to make me an offer. Now that would not be an offer I cannot refuse, would it?"

J.P. did not smile with his own statement. He looked directly at Duponte'. His eyes were filled with the emptiness of a black hole. Duponte''s statement of "an offer he could not refuse" implied more to J.P. than either one of the two could have possibly imagined.

"No, we are not kidding." Andrew laughed a true laugh and J.P. thought he would never see Duponte' really have a true joyous laugh in his presence.

"J.P., we are here to offer you a job." Then Andrew paused for a moment waiting for a response from James P. There was none. O'Francis sat in silence looking at Duponte'.

"Okay, ahhh," Andrew continued, "We have an opening for a secondary homebound teacher. We would like for you to take it."

Again he paused and waited for J.P. to say something. He did not. He broke his eye contact with Duponte' and went to Thomas.

Several more seconds of unconformable silence passed before O'Francis spoke, "What are the requirements for doing this job?" O'Francis asked with a degree of less anxiety in his voice.

"Now J.P. you are really going to like it." Andrew spoke with excitement and moved up to the edge of his chair. "You will meet with the students that are homebound and make sure they get the work from their regular teachers and get it back to the students' teachers."

"Do I have to grade their work?"

Duponte' looked at Thomas, and for the first time in the meeting, she spoke, "No. You will not have to grade any papers." She stated firmly in a pleasant voice.

"And that is it?" J.P. responded.

"Well," Andrew continued, "That is about it."

J.P. sat in silence looking at first one then the other.

"What about a car?" O'Francis inquired.

"Well, ahhh." Duponte′ was caught off guard by the simple question.

"Look Andrew" J.P. continued, "I sure am not going to drive my car all over the county, to whatever God forsaken place, up some God forsaken hollow. So you will just have to come up with one of your old best Junkers for me. Now of course," then O'Francis paused and a smile slowly creeped across his face. "If ole LaMar," he spoke slowly, "wants to give me one of those big fancy county cars that you all drive all over hell and half of Georgia. Oh, I am so very sorry." J.P. drew out his words as if he had just spoken a bible belt go to hell statement. "I mean Tennessee. Georgia and Alabama are not where you would find Marshy, would you?"

Andrew did not respond to J.P.'s sense of humor. He was so wrapped up in his blind devotion to LaMar that any satirical humor directed toward Marshy was considered blasphemy.

"Naaa, I did not think neither you nor good ole' LaMar would go for that. But do I get a county car?" J.P. concluded with a more serious tone. He noticed out of the corner of his eye that in his moment of humor that Thomas had broken yet another smile.

"Yes we think we can arrange that," Andrew answered.

"No, not quite yet they're Mr. Duponte′. You stated, I think. I would like a confirmed yes or no on my request."

Again Andrew looked over at Thomas. And for the second time she spoke, "Yes J.P., we can provide you with transportation."

"Thank you, now what about an office?"

"An office, well, ahhh?" Andrew responded with a large question in his voice.

"Yes, an office. I do not expect I will be in a car the entire year. I mean I can do some quick calculating. I will have paperwork of some type. Where will I do this work?"

No one was talking. J.P. looked over at Linnet Thomas. "Well Dr. Thomas, do I get my own office to do my work or not?"

"Yes I think we can provide you with an office. And J.P. before you say anything about "*I think*" I have to check on a place and run it by Mr. Marshy. But I really do believe we will find you a place."

O'Francis smiled. "One more question Dr. Thomas. Who will be my direct supervisor?"

"That would be Ms. French."

With a surprised tone in his voice J.P. responded quickly, "Rebecca Ellen French?"

"Yes. Why, is that a problem?" Andrew questioned.

"Well, Mr. Duponte', given the fact that according to my sources, she does not like me at all. Well, let me re-phrase that a little bit. She despises me! Yes, I would safely say that is a problem."

"Now Mr. O'Francis. Ms. French has never said she did not like you," Andrew stated, hoping to smooth out what he himself knew to be true.

"Right! And I believe in the Easter bunny Andrew! Look, I really do not care. If she can work with me, I can work with her. Adjust and overcome. I tell you what Andrew." Then J.P. paused, his mind working rapidly to get his thoughts gathered before he spoke.

"You ask her to come by my room Friday and we will go over what she expects of me and how she wants the job done. Maybe we can reach some sort of compromise. Hell Andrew, who knows, we may even get to know each other to the point of understanding and actually liking one another. Now would that not be a real ass kicker for everyone in the central office? French and O'Francis working together and getting along and actually getting to like each other."

Andrew only responded to O'Francis' request for a Friday meeting. "Okay. I don't see that is a problem. Do you Dr. Thomas?"

"No. I really do believe that you and Ms. French will work well together." Thomas stated.

"Okay, I accept the job." J.P. rose, picked up his tape recorder then thanked the two lieutenants from LaMar Marshy's headquarters, and walked happily out of the office and down the long hallway to his room.

He would begin a new job, one of being the secondary homebound teacher. J.P. accepted the job with joy much to the surprise of Duponte'. He knew it was yet another demotion, and most likely forced into if he had not accepted. But what they did not know was that he had been looking for anything to get away from the insanity of the junior high school class room and the whining—obnoxious parents, the maliciously conspiring principal and his sidekick, and School Board representative, Barnard Theodoric for a long time. As long as he had a job so he could provide for his family.

Teaching really was dead. It really did not matter to the people any more. They did not care if their children learned or not, just as long as they were given their A's. Work for a grade? Not anymore. Not in the Reynolds County Public School System. Not just the county, but the state as a whole. SOL's, which J.P. opposed and wrote several letters in protest to the promoters of such a statewide plan, which all ended up on Marshy's desk along with their own letter to J.P.'s Superintendent. This was an opportunity for him to get out of the classroom just before the state regulations handcuffed the real teaching teachers.

After reviewing the offer with Dawn that evening they came to the conclusion that Dr. Thomas may have had something to do with the offer to J.P. Dawn and J.P. liked Dr. Thomas and did not figure her to be the type to lower herself to the level of the rest of the people she had to work with. Especially LaMar, but she needed a job, as well as her husband, who was a principal at the middle school, so they did what they had to do and left it at that. J.P. told Dawn that he thought that Dr. Thomas' intellect was so far above that of the rest of the people that she probably had a difficult time communicating with them.

He met with his new supervisor before the school year was over for the summer vacation, ironing out the details of his job. Much to J.P.'s utmost surprise Ms. Rebecca Ellen French was quite receptive to his ideas about how the program could be improved and protect the teacher at the same time. Rebecca told J.P. she would incorporate them into the program. Rebecca had not been an advocate of J.P. She had been part of the SS team that had destroyed his coaching career, had supported Damon Bales, and had helped bring J.P. to the point he was at. He made up his mind if the position went as it had been laid out for him, he would change Rebecca's mind about all she had heard about him. Of course he was fully aware that the entire position that "they" were so in need of someone to fill was a complete setup to put the final nail in his coffin. But he would not let that happen. He would play the game, just as he had played the game in the jungles, and he would win. He would adapt and he would overcome. He would not let them bring him to his knees. He would succeed much to the aversion of the people who had given him the job.

# Surprise Visit

I HAD NOT SEEN J.P. in several months, so I decided to pay him a surprise visit at his school. It was during the time teachers were finishing up for the year and there were no students, so I figured I would not be disrupting anything, and that we might have some time to talk. I wanted to see his junior high classroom and just touch base with him, just to see how the end of the year had gone for him.

After following the proper protocol and getting directions from the assistant principal I made my way down the very long hallway to his room. His door was open and I pecked on the side of the door. J.P. looked up from what he was doing at his desk, a smile came across his momentarily stern face. "Oh my, come in John. What in the world brings you to this neck of the wood?"

"Ah, just thought I would stop by to see if you were still breathing. Have not heard from you in some time. And I actually wanted to see where you worked."

As I walked across the room, and he had risen from his chair and was approaching me, he waved his arms open and looked around the room as to indicate this is it, stating, "You have it, my little world of education."

As I surveyed the layout of his room, it was not what I expected. Instead of the usual classroom desks, he had tables with chairs at the tables. It looked more like a lunch room setting than a classroom. But I knew that J.P. was different and did not fit the round holes that most if not all schools, teachers, and classrooms were made up of.

"So J.P., what is with the tables?"

"Ah, yes. The tables. Well, I got this idea of making the setting more of a social atmosphere than the usual stressful, same ole same ole boring classroom the students have to walk into on a daily basis. So, I was able to gather up enough unused tables and chairs to cover the 25 or so students I usually have. Hey, they liked it, and my productivity improved, in addition to the music I play for them. Well with the few exceptions of music choices that I will not allow."

I stood and looked at all the posters, some commercially bought, some I could tell was hand drawn by J.P., all with educational messages, scattered about the room. In the upper right hand corner of the chalk board was a section blocked off with the words: Welcome to O'Francis' Think Tank. Rules:

Words you can use in the classroom: YES; NO; PLEASE; THANK YOU; MAY I. Words you cannot use in the classroom: YEAH, NAA, NOPE. Always remember, The most powerful weapon on earth is? The worst think you can waste is?

"Interesting. One question."

"Okay, shoot."

"How long has the message been up in the corner?" I indicated with my head.

"All year, every year."

"I am sure they know the answer to the two questions, correct?"

"Yes. Gave them the answer at the first of the year, once. It is on every test I give. I make my own tests. No commercially made tests in my class. Never have, never will."

"The answers are?"

At that J.P. broke out into a full face smile. "Oh my John. One time only. Knowledge. The mind."

"Ah, okay. One more question, if I may."

"Sure."

"How do you keep the students from, shall I use the word, cheating? Or looking off someone else's paper while taking a test?"

J.P. smiled and started walking toward his desk, which was to the far right corner of the room, just in front of the row of windows that stretched the length of the room. I followed him. He pulled out one of the chairs and placed it beside his desk as he sat in his chair.

"Have a seat John. Now to my students cheating. Well, let me state for your record, as I know you are mentally recording all of this. I have had few students cheat in any of my classes here at the junior high level and at the high school level, where they are more brave and daring and more likely to attempt to cheat. Now before you ask why. Well they learn quickly that they do not have to cheat to pass my classes. Together we will find a way for them to learn and pass my course, if, they have a desire to obtain knowledge and move forward in their education. We establish the honor system. For the most part, that has worked for me through the years. I am sure I have missed on some occasions, but I will say, 95% of the time my students adhere to "O's" honor system."

This was the first time I had heard him refer to himself in such a manner. I had heard his students and ballplayers do so, but not J.P. "I got it, understood. Just did not think anything like that existed in a public school setting."

"Can I offer some coffee? I have my own coffee maker." As he pointed over to a sink and a counter with a coffee maker and three cups upside down on the counter, along with a roll a paper towels.

"You are set here, you are in the same room."

"One does not have to move. Little different here than at the high school. Well, for me at any rate." He got up and made his way to the far side of the room. "Black I still presume?"

"Yes." As he poured, he stated that it was fresh, maybe an hour old, and that was fresh for J.P.

"So, my friend, tell me about your year as we have not seen each other in eight months."

J.P. smiled. "Well, it has been interesting to say the least." I was not for sure how to take that, given the pattern of his past years. I automatically presumed given his nature and ideology about his students that he had spent more time in the office than any of his students had. And given the facts that 98% of the faculty was female, I knew he had more than any one of them.

"Well, John, let me start by saying this is my last year at this school. I have been given an "offer I cannot refuse." He proceeded to tell the events that had transpired over the course of the last few weeks. By that time I had retrieved my tape recorder and had placed it on the corner of his desk. He just smiled and never missed a beat in telling me what had gone down.

"I have no idea as to what to expect in this new position I am about to enter into. I do know one thing, I will miss the interaction with the students in the classroom. Well, for the most part."

"Bet you have had some good ones, and interesting ones, ha."

"Well, yes point of fact I have."

As he looked across the empty room toward the door, we sat in silence for a good three minutes. He took a sip of his coffee, turned his head toward me. "You see John, when you have students like, ah, let me think for a second. Ah, Jose Pickens, whose mind is about three years ahead of everyone in his class, and to some extent above some of his other teachers, not too sure he was not above mine, you can really enjoy teaching. And let me add his sister Heather was not far behind him. Jose was like a giant sponge, soaking up every bit of knowledge he could about the subject matter in which I was presenting to him. I will tell you this, I will predict that the high school teachers who encounter him will be challenged to keep him from being bored out of his gourd. He thinks way ahead of most everyone. But hell, he was not the only one. Shit, let me think. You have had several that just popped out at you and you know they are special. Some in their own way, some a little on the odd side, but that does not diminish the quality of their young minds. Minds that are ahead of their ages."

He was up and across the room for a refill, then he walked to the door and closed it. As he walked back across the room, in his jeans, polo shirt, and sandals, he continued, "Jesus wegons," as he always referred to them, "Echo, John. Sound travels out into the hall, ears are atoned to anything I say, do, or company I may have. Anybody else, no one gives a flying fuck!"

"I understand J.P."

"I have a couple more days to put in and pack my shit and clear out, to the joy, I am sure, of some several teachers. Well, there is one, across the hall, a really good teacher, caring, professional, has been a great asset to me over the past several years I have been here."

"What about the current principal?"

J.P. had a little chuckle, before he answered. "Well, he is all part of the establishment. Part of the plan I have learned, and I might add John, my sources are solid."

"Oh, I have no doubt."

"But here again you see just how a negative can creep into a conversation about the joy of teaching good students, and the joy I get from watching them as they absorb knowledge."

"Yes J.P. I know, and I know what you have endured over the years. I, well to be honest with you, and as a Brother, cannot for the life of me figure out how or for that matter why you and Dawn stayed in this community, or this county. I know, your sons. But damn, man." He did not say anything for a few minutes, then with a smile, as if he just thought of something pleasant, he said, "Take Nobel Bryan, big for his age, gentle giant, never said spit, quiet, kind of shy, but damn, was he smart. Shit, eat you up with knowledge. Sucked it in like a vacuum cleaner. Aced 99% of all my tests. He will be another one that will challenge his high school teachers. Or of course, be bored to death with their same ole same ole shit out of an outdated text and method of delivering knowledge to the students. Now John, do not get me wrong here with all my negativity of the high school teachers. There are a few over there that are damn good, challenge their students, stay on top of new educational ideals. However, I do not use the word few lightly."

"How do you remember these, well, for a lack of another word at the moment, so called stand outs, or extra smart ones?"

"Because that is what they are, standouts, shit there are a lot really. This area is full of really smart students, students that will go on to do and be great in whatever chosen fields they settle on. I mean you have Blake Vanpelt, who I am sure will make it in a field that will carry him far into the future. Now, he is all boy at the present, but he is smart. Oh, cannot forget Jonathan Bentley Hogg, now you talking about an odd duck in class. You can just tell, he will add gray to his mother's and dad's hair before it's all said and done. But, John, all that does not take away from the mind. You have students like him who at his age think out of the box. Students like him I can relate to, you can give them so many tools to carry forward in their minds that will challenge others including teachers, who in all likelihood will be offended by their intellect, and will not want or allow them to think out of the preverbal box, especially in such a conservative cultural area like this one. I mean, John, you still have people out in the public who think that in order to have any type of real discipline in the school you have to take a goddamn piece of wood and beat the hell out of them, and then you have control. Does that tell you anything?"

I sat and looked at J.P., as to say, you are kidding, right. But I could see the expression on his face that he was not kidding at all. "So you have had a good few years?"

"For the most part. A few encounters, a few investigations."

I got up and got myself a fresh cup of coffee, which really was not bad at all, sure had had a lot worse. "May I ask why you were investigated?"

"Sure. Because I used excessive force in breaking up a fight, right there." As he pointed to the center of the room.

"Care to elaborate?"

"Not at all. I had stepped outside momentarily to speak with Mrs. Mazo, the teacher I told you about across the hallway, and in a matter of three minutes this rather large boy, slightly bigger than I, had decided that he would take it upon himself to beat the shit out of a much smaller boy. I heard the "fight," and rushed back into the room. As I reached both boys, jerking the larger one away from the smaller one, who had him in a headlock pounding his face, my feet slipped with the leather sole shoes I had on at the time, and we all went to the floor together. I was up quickly and got both of them by the arm, told them both that there will be no fighting in my classroom, and went toward the door. Now as I got to the hall, I took note of the fact that the principal had arrived at Mrs. Mazo's room door and was talking to her. I marched both boys right by him, and he not so much as inquired as to what I was doing, if I needed his assistance, not jack shit was said. Which of course left my class of students unattended as I heading down the very long hallway to his office. Not so much as a word. Now you would think that the two boys would have gotten in trouble, right? I mean, I took them to Mr. Cosworth's office, gave him my assessment of the situation, left them with him, and returned to the classroom. It was at the end of the last period of the day and school was about to be let out."

"By that J.P. I am safe to assume that the end of this story is you got the short end of the shit stick?"

"You got it. Central office sent in their two best investigators, and a full scale investigation took place, and I had to get my representative in on it to defend me. To top it all off, I had to apologize to the class, the two students, and to the parents with the principal and central office Gestapo, all present right over there." He pointed to the front of the room.

"J.P., I do not quite understand. What did you do wrong? I mean what were you supposed to do?"

"I was too rough with them."

"That is it. You are kidding me right? I mean is that what you were told, I mean really?"

"Yes John, that is exactly what I was told. That is exactly what went down, just like I have described to you."

"Well, why didn't the principal take over from the beginning when you passed him across the hallway?"

"Shit!" Is all he said, and he moved on to several other not so pleasant events that had occurred, with the same group investigating O'Francis for what appeared to me as bullshit. I wondered what these people would do in a large city school, where I went. My god they would not survive more than a week, where they had real problems to contend with. Everything about J.P. and his trials and tribulations ceased to amaze me. He had a target, not just on his back, his entire body was a target, and one would have to be totally blind, as well having their head stuck in a pile of sand not to have seen it.

He related to me a story about a student that was not allowed to go to the restroom and she urinated on herself at her desk. Totally embarrassing to anyone, especially a girl in the seventh grade. The sad part of the story was even though the parent filed a complaint on the teacher, not one thing was done. No central office staff, no apology. Nothing. One point I must make about the teacher, it was a she.

I spent several hours with him that day, recounting the good and the not so good of his years on the Middle School level of teaching. I could only wonder how somebody was setting him up with his new position, and how he would handle it, if he could. Knowing him as I did, and knowing PTSD veterans, there was a point where everything fell apart. Usually, when that occurred, somebody got hurt.

# Homebound

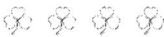

O'FRANCIS HAD BEEN WORKING HIS new job as a homebound instructor for two years and had not had one complaint. No parents, no principals, no visits from Marshy's Schutzstaffel troops. J.P. had gone the extra mile for the students he had to teach as well as going that mile with the supervisors he had to mingle with in and around the central office from time to time. He was not completely at ease in and around several of them, but for the most part he was not under any stress and was for the first time in many years enjoying his job. He was not really teaching but he knew they did not want good creative minded teachers, especially the one that made learning fun. He enjoyed the freedom of being out of the confines of a classroom, as well as being away from so many that had no desire to learn. He enjoyed being away from the ignorant bitching parents on some form of welfare, complaining about how hard he was and how much work he put on their "kid". A word in which I learned that he actually hated. A kid, he told me once, when I used the word referring to students/children, is a goat. A student is a child or children. I never made the mistake again.

He and Rebecca became very good working partners for the most part. J.P. did the job he had been assigned and she let him perform in his own way. It was possible that in the two years that she just might have seen that he was not what she thought or what she had heard. However, he had no illusions about her or anyone else she worked directly with or for. After all, he knew he was in the center of the viper pit. So he stepped very carefully. Trust was measured, zero. Nothing for anyone.

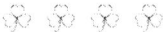

Reynolds County School System set up a program that would remove the misfits, devious, disruptive and violent students out of the regular classroom and place them in what was known as Alternative Education. A place J.P. was told was being funded by the state government. He also had been informed that for the most part the teachers that had been assigned to teach at the AE couldn't really care less about most of the students as they were going to end up in some jail cell within a few years because the students in which they had to deal with were alleged drug users as well as dealers or associated with the likes of people on the streets.

On several occasions J.P. had been assigned AE students that could not make the adjustments even in the environment of Alternative Education. As homebound students O'Francis fared well with them. He even made some progress with a few and successfully had them complete the required courses needed to graduate. These were the exceptions, but there were always exceptions to most everything in life. J.P. was street wise enough to know the ones that he could reach and the ones that had no hope. The reality was in our society there was a percentage of students that would end up on the wrong side of the law and ultimately find themselves in a prison or dead in some alley or street.

Now homebound students ran the gamut of intellect, attitudes, living environments, and parents. But there was one J.P. told me about that probably stands out as being unusual. This case, as I will refer to it as his miracle case, is unusual because it happened a year after LaMar Marshy left his position as superintendent of Reynolds County Schools, and the first female took his place. A female that J.P. had a year before Marshy's departure in a private conversation, had in fact encouraged her to "throw" her "hat" into the ring for the job of superintendent. As J.P. learned through his sources and some very reliable inside information of the "beltway" of the school system, information that stated Marshy was on his way out.

Lora informed J.P. there were three things she did not have for her to obtain such a powerful position. One she was a female. Two she was from Danway. She paused and added, "J.P., you know how people feel about that small town." And third, she told him, "I have no political connections. I owe no allegiance to anyone."

Of course being J.P. and being a strong supporter of the female movement, he insisted Lora "Swing the bat. You cannot hit the ball if you do not step up to the plate and swing the bat." Now this was the same female that had investigated J.P. on a number of cases for being a teacher "out of control." She stepped to the plate and got a hit. She became the first female superintendent of Reynolds County.

"LT" as J.P. called her in private, gave her the respect of Dr. Tanner when in the presence of others because he knew she had earned it, not bought it.

He returned to his office late in the afternoon, as he had been overloaded with homebound students, and being the person he was, he gave each equal time on a daily basis, which extended his hours of work from eight to ten hours per day. He checked his voice messages on his office phone. "J.P., this is Dr. Tanner, come by my office when you get in." J.P. looked at his watch, it was 1720 hours. Pausing, he figured it was not a good thing if the superintendent was working that late and wanted him in her office, as she was aware of his work habits. So off he went to "LT's" office. After getting access to the main building, via the custodian, he made his way to the superintendent's office. Her door was open. J.P. stepped to the door and spoke. She waved him in as she was on the phone.

After the phone conversation was finished, a matter of about five minutes, she got up and went to a small round table to the right of her large office desk indicating to J.P. to join her. Being polite she offered him something to drink and he took a bottle of water. "LT" was not one for wasting words, she got to the point. She had a special case for him, a very special education girl that was on homebound. She was aware that he was primarily high school, and was not educated in teaching special education students, but for "LT" this was a special case and the current homebound teacher just was not cutting it, as "LT" had had a multitude of complaints concerning Ms. Swift and her incompetence. She asked J.P., as a favor for her. J.P. did not hesitate in his answer. She gave him the file on Karen Friday, a young eighth grader who had suffered through a horrific auto accident and was scarred physically and mentally and on a walker. Even with the walker her movement was with great difficultly.

His first visit was longer than normal, as he wanted to get a feel of the single parent, her daughter, and what progress they had made in her education over the first half of the year. What he learned from the mother was not a surprise to him, but was disappointing. "LT" had instructed him to give her a weekly report on Karen's progress after the first two weeks on the case, as well as a report on what had been done to that point. The first thing he had to do was verify some of the information Mrs. Friday had given him concerning Karen's teacher. So off he went to Liberty High to meet with Karen's teacher, informing her that he would be taking over for the previous homebound instructor.

After meeting with Ms. Imogene Onager, Karen's primary teacher, he realized that she couldn't care less about Karen and her education. Her demeanor on their first meeting told J.P. she did not like him, even though he had never had any association with her and knew nothing about her.

Ms. Onager had already written Karen off. J.P. did as "LT" had asked, and turned in a preliminary report to her at the end of the first couple of weeks, which included the educational material he had received from Ms. Onager and the first little bit of progress he had made, along with his professional recommendation.

Dr. Tanner made a phone call to the principal of Liberty High, Mr. Andrew Duponte' who had accepted a new position from center office staff to principal. When J.P. went to pick up Karen's lessons for the week, he was intercepted by Mr. Duponte, who informed J.P. he needed to meet with him. After a short meeting J.P. learned that he would be doing all the teaching, planning, and testing of all the subjects for Karen Friday. Now J.P.'s job profile was not to teach any subject, but to instruct and assist in what the students regular teachers provided for them while they were homebound. Monitor all tests, and return all materials back to the appropriate teacher. When O'Francis gave Mr. Duponte' a questioning look, he said, "Dr. Tanners' request."

J.P. would over the course of the next four years, not only teach Karen, he would get her off her walker, slowly, but he achieved his goal and had her walking on her own by the end of her senior year. However, following his "LT's" instructions were not without controversy. Imogene Onager took exception to J.P.'s teaching Karen, exceeding all expectations. Her close ties to Ms. Robbys, a teacher who loathed J.P., led to two confrontations and allegations by Onager concerning O'Francis' teachings and comments to Onager.

The one good part of this segment of J.P. O'Francis' saga, he had done his due diligence, and had followed his boss' instructions to the letter. His second unprovoked encounter with Ms. Onager was the last one he had to worry about. Dr. Tanners' one trip to Liberty High and a meeting in the principal's office with Ms. Onager, ended all communications with J.P. when he had to be in the building.

However that being a happy ending to a remarkable story about O'Francis and what he achieved with a little girl named Karen Friday, all his encounters with homebound students were not so happy. Several years earlier, before Lora Tanner came to power, J.P. O'Francis' life was turned to total disarray.

It was now August and it had been six months since the events at the Alternative Education building had taken place. At 3:00 a.m. he was still awake listening to the sounds of rain. He had retired for the night at 11:30

p.m. and had quickly gone to sleep only to be awakened at 1:00 a.m. by rolling thunder echoing through the mountains. He lay in his bed beside his soulmate looking at the ceiling listening to Dawn breathe. For an hour he tried to sleep, hoping that the sounds of rain would drive away the violent thoughts that permeated his mind. Their cat "LaLa" had joined J.P. as she so often did, on his side of the bed, and had curled up and was purring to her little heart's content. Somewhere in the mist of the rain, the purring, and his prayers he drifted off to sleep.

It was seven in the morning and J.P. had been up long before the alarm had gone off. He had showered, shaved, dressed and was drinking coffee while watching CNN news, even though he really did not like the manner in which they reported what was happening throughout the world, but it sure was better than Fox News, which he considered a joke, especially when the word "news" was attached to Fox. But CNN was the only way in which he could keep up with world events.

By eight in the morning he was meeting with John S. Marshall, his attorney in an office inside the court house. After reviewing a few courtroom procedures and how John Marshall expected J.P. to act or not react to what he was about to have to go through, they went directly to the courtroom and took a seat. By 10:00 a.m. he had been witness to several cases that he thought were rather trivial to have been taking up the time of Juvenile Judge James M. Madison. Judge Madison was forty-two years old and a native of Reynolds County. He had short cropped hair of salt and pepper color with a neatly trimmed mustache which had not begun the change to salt. He wore round wire rimmed glasses and a Masonic ring on his right hand and a wedding band on his left. His wife, J.P. had learned, was also a teacher in the same county.

A brief conversation ensued between Judge Madison and John Jay the Assistant Commonwealth Attorney who had been assigned to the case by the Commonwealth Attorney Mark Bosch, whom J.P. knew because of the political machine. He had to be elected to the position and J.P. had not only voted for him but had campaigned for him, because he knew him as a Mason as well as him being an honorable person.

Judge Madison looked around the courtroom for a few moments then spoke with a stern and clear voice, "This next case will require a closed hearing. Anyone not connected to the Commonwealth verses James Patrick O'Francis will need to leave the court room."

April in the mountains was fresh with blooms on the trees and the early flowers of tulips. Daffodils brightened the landscape. It was a good warm spring morning and O'Francis had been invited to have lunch with the Alternative Education personnel. He would be finished with his morning student and would have a brief break before he met with his afternoon student. His spirits were high and he looked forward to a brief socialization with the teachers and the director he had to work with from time to time.

*Tracy Short* was a thirty-five year old with dark Native American skin, dark hair and dark eyes. She was very well proportioned, extremely good looking, and stood five foot four and weighed one hundred and twenty-five pounds.

*Alicia Hyden* was a young lady in her late twenties and a former student from Honsburg High, black hair, very attractive, still not married and a health enthusiast. She worked out at the local gym to keep her one hundred and ten pound body in near perfect shape.

*Linda Hawkins* the assistant director of the Alternate program, fifty-five years old, a little overweight but acceptable for her age. She had a good personality, talked all the time, was very knowledgeable about a wide array of topics and was a very staunch Democrat. She had a happy laugh and on the surface she appeared to like J.P and often times over the past two years they would discuss the pluses and minuses of the school system as well as politics, and would for the most part agree with each other. However there was just a little bit of a whisper from J.P.'s little voice that kept him on alert when he was around her or dealing with any type of school/student issue with her.

*Steward Brittin* was the director of the program. He was a rather large man, a bit overweight, as was shown in his gut. However his six foot five height did allow him to carry his excess weight a little better. Stewart spoke with a very deep voice, the kind one would have expected from a hard-core drill sergeant. His sixty year old body and facial features had not suffered a decline in appearance. His hair was not fully white, but maintained a good portion of its brown tone. He was a very intricate part of the political machine of Reynolds County. J.P.'s connection to Steward went back many years and he was well aware of his political power in the county. There were times that J.P did not know whether to believe him or not as he was very much the politician, but he would play the game he was entrenched in and hoped he did not make any fatal mistakes.

J.P. was sitting at the very end of a ten foot long dark wooden, much worn pew in the front row as one entered the court room. The benches extended some fifteen rows deep with an aisle way separating the same number of benches to his left. He figured this was done in order to separate the warring parties at any one time having to be in the courtroom. Directly in the center of the aisle at the very front of the courtroom, three steps higher than the level of the main floor, was where the Judge sat behind his seven foot wide and three foot deep dark wooden podium. There was a witness chair directly in front of the Judge's podium one step up from the courtroom floor and a rail separating the bench pews from the witness chair. To the left and right about ten feet from the Judge was a rail separating the attorneys and the Judge's podium. Each attorney had a large wooden table six feet by two feet with two office chairs covered in brown cloth.

As O'Francis looked around the courtroom, he saw four other people remaining in the room, including Bruce McCloud, the alleged victim. John Marshall instructed J.P. to join him at his table. As he looked directly across the room to the Prosecuting side of the courtroom, a young John Jay was seated arranging his papers in some order, preparing himself for his case. He was a good looking young man six foot tall, one hundred and eight pounds, wearing wire round rimmed glasses. J.P. wondered to himself if the round wire rimmed glasses was an attorney thing. He had brown short cut hair parted in the middle, with a dark blue suit with a white shirt and dark blue tie. He wore a wedding band on his left hand and a Mason ring on his right.

Then his eyes traveled beyond the Assistant Prosecuting Attorney to the one pew that sat behind John Jay. There seated on the bench were two social workers, a man he did not know and the female that sat beside him. J.P.'s eyes narrowed with hardness as he looked at the female. *Just two more members of the Marshy Schutzstaffel, he thought to himself.*

J.P. went to his office after taking the next two days off from his encounter at the A.E. school with Bruce. He spent the weekend reliving the events and putting them down on paper for documentation for his supervisor. On Monday, he returned to work and hand delivered the report to Rebecca and went about his job going from one student's house to another. He had worked very hard trying to put the events into some sort of perspective as well as working on putting it behind him. The only real good thing about the day as he entered his office was that it was Wednesday, "hump" day as the working world referred to it. He was tired and in a very ill mood because of the lack of sleep since he had been attacked. He had been fighting a series of not welcomed flashbacks that always seemed to leave him totally drained.

The light was flashing on his answering machine so he reached over and pushed the button as he set his coffee mug down on his desk.

"Mr. O'Francis this is Rebecca. I need to see you as soon as you get into the office. Do not go to your regularly scheduled student before you talk to me."

J.P. stood for a moment letting the message ramble through his mind, then he spoke aloud to no one as if someone were in the room listening to him, "Welll shit, this can't be good! I am in no mood for any Buffalo Chips being thrown at me today."

His eyes indicated his lack of sleep as they were blood shot with dark shadows under them. He sat down at his desk for a moment and looked out of the window at the lush greening mountains far to the north and wished he were in them instead of where he was.

He then tried to become more positive in his thoughts and self-verbal conversation. "Ahhh, maybe she has yet another student and most likely one more that is pregnant and needs to give me some inside information on the parents."

He got up and went out his door and headed to Rebecca French's office. But the little voice in his head began sending him warnings that this was not going to be a good meeting.

J.P. pecked on Rebecca's door and entered with a warm and friendly, "Good morning Rebecca."

"Good morning J.P. How are you today?"

"Ahhh, I am doing well under the circumstances, I guess. Hey crap happens in our business, just got to adjust and move on. So, what's up?" His mind instantly flashed to his son's term of what's up, as "SAUP", and a smile crossed his face.

She had been sitting at the table behind her desk doing some paperwork, then pulled her seat back around to her office desk. She stated, "J.P. I have some bad news for you. Social Services have charged you with child abuse."

J.P. continued to smile as he stood directly in front of her desk and then responded sarcastically, "Child abuse, right."

Rebecca was not smiling nor did she give any hint of a practical joke on her face that J.P. could detect.

"J.P. I am very serious. Someone called them and filed a complaint"

J.P. kind-of half laughed. "Look Rebecca this had better be a joke."

"I assure you J.P. that it is not a joke at all. It is very serious. I have nothing for Social Service and anytime they get involved in the school business there are big problems."

The warm smile that J.P. had adorned for only a few moments had now left and a stone expressionless look graced his tired looking face.

"Rebecca, I can assure you I have not abused anyone. Just whom does Social Services claim that I have abused? I mean they must have me confused with someone else. Right?"

"Bruce McCloud."

"Who?" He responded as the name did not register as it was not on his list of the nine students he had on homebound.

"Bruce McCloud. J.P., the boy you had the altercation with a few days ago at the Alternative Education Building.

"Rebecca there is no way. I mean you read my report. Rebecca, I did not lie, I told you the truth, all facts and no fabrications."

"J.P. I believe you, I really do. But what we have here is a bunch of Social Service idiots who are running amuck and doing what they want to any teacher they can get their fangs into to suck the blood out of. They're ass holes! Believe me I know because I have had to deal with them on several occasions in the past."

"Rebecca I do not even know this...this piece of shit! No, shit can be used for some good use...this whatever he is...I cannot even come up with a word. He had no real purpose. I mean this is a stack of buffalo chips."

J.P. then sat down very heavily in the chair to the left of Rebecca's desk. "Look Rebecca I really do not know who the hell these people are but they have the wrong information. Child abuse! Great God Almighty, I have not gotten my glasses back yet, which by the way cost me two hundred dollars to get repaired. Now who is going to pay for my loss? And I have been charged with child abuse. Damn, what kind of FUBAR do we have here?" He thought Rebecca did not know what the anagram stood for.

"You are correct J.P. this is a FUBAR...and yes I do know what it means."

"Who called Social Services anyway?" O'Francis inquired.

"I really don't know J.P."

"Okay, well think about it. I mean there were just a few who could have. These few are in the Alternative Program and there is," He paused momentarily. "Who was it, Linda Hawkins?" J.P. stated with a harsh tone and a degree of disgust in his voice. "I mean, she thinks these little bastards are to be treated like all other students in our system. Hell if that were the case they would not be in alternative education now would they. I mean, that is why they are where they are, for Christ's sake!"

J.P. stopped venting and just looked at his supervisor. "Sorry I went off like that Rebecca. It is not your fault. I have not been sleeping well lately and I am just a little on edge."

"J.P. there is no need for an apology. I understand completely. It is a FUBAR and the fact of the matter is these people can do whatever they want and we are at their mercy. J.P., believe me when I tell you they really like going after teachers. Now, you have to give your testimony in front of a Social Service case worker in two days and she is a real bitch. I will set it up in the small conference room. I want you to call Dan Jakes and tell him to get John Marshall as your attorney. He is the best attorney in these matters."

J.P. knew at that moment that it was a very bad situation for Rebecca to tell him to place a call to Dan Jakes because he was the one person she had battled for years over school related issues and she had no love for him at all.

J.P. rose from his chair. "I will do as you have instructed. Child abuse. Christ, Rebecca."

He then went out the door, stopped and returned quickly. "I want to know who made the call to the Social Services. This is a school matter. Also did Mr. Brittin do anything to the boy?"

"I am not sure."

"You are not sure? Have you talked to Mr. Brittin about what took place? I gave him the same detailed account of what took place."

"Yes, he and I talked briefly."

"And...?"

"He did not indicate that he was going to do anything to the boy."

"Well now that tells you volumes."

Rebecca French did not respond to J.P.'s comment, they just looked at each other for several seconds. "J.P. I want you to go and make the call to Dan Jakes before you do anything else today. Trust me on this one, these people are totally ruthless."

O'Francis turned and went back to his office. As he sat for several minutes thinking before he called Dan, he reflected on Rebecca's last words.

*Totally ruthless. What in the hell does she think LaMar and his SS troops have been over the past decade?* Knowing that Rebecca had been part of that SS group herself. *Hell I wonder if she thinks that people have such a short memory that they do not remember what she herself has done to people and that includes me. I wonder if she made the call and is trying to implicate the people at Alternative.* Then J.P. prayed softly aloud, "My Master, it appears that I am in yet another quagmire and will most likely need your guidance and help."

He was taken aback by Rebecca's support of him. Something he did not expect and would have bet against. He was not sure if it was support or not. Just covering her ass was more like it. He kept looking for the bullet coming toward his head. O'Francis put in the call to Dan Jakes and by that afternoon he was in John Scott Marshall's law office telling him what had gone down as well as providing him with a copy of the documentation he had given to Rebecca French.

The central office phone rang and the secretary Grace Cater answered, "Reynolds's County Schools. May I help you?"

"I need to speak to LaMar." The tone on the other end of the line was curt and direct.

"Who is calling please?"

"This is Mr. Bales."

"Just a moment please." She pushed the hold button and rang Marshy's office. "Mr. Marshy there is a Mr. Bales on line one for you. Do you want to take the call?"

"Yeah put him through."

In his usually vociferous and façade voice he answered, "Damon, what can I do for you on this fine day?"

"LaMar it has been brought to my attention that O'Francis is in a world of trouble."

"Well, I don't know, what are you talking about?" LaMar was trying hard to sound as if he did not know anything about the charges.

"Ahhh, LaMar you know damn well what trouble he has and the charges that have been brought against him."

"Yes I have heard something about some trouble with a student and Social Services." He was grinning from ear to ear as he leaned back in his heavily padded office chair swiveling to place his feet on his desk.

"I think we have his ass this time." Damon stated with a venomous tone to his voice.

"Welll, Damon I don't know about that. We may have."

"Have you made the call to Social Services?"

"I have spoken to the case worker concerning the matter, yes."

"Have you talked to Randy Dowell?" Knowing that LaMar knew Dowell was the director and knew that he was politically connected to him covertly, LaMar informed Damon that he had spoken to him. Damon reminded LaMar that he had a chance to get rid of O'Francis and allow the legal system to do his work for him. Damon reminded him that he had better call Judge MacMuller and get him to put the pressure on Judge Madison. LaMar quickly became agitated at Damon and cut him off in one of his mid-sentences informing him he would do everything he could and said his goodbyes and hung up the phone.

Janet Sheffield picked up the phone and dialed the Alternative Education Center.

"Mrs. Hawkins, please."

"Speaking."

"Mrs. Hawkins this is Janet Sheffield at Social Services. I need the home number for Bruce McCloud." There was a short pause on the phone.

"Just a moment please, I will get it for you."

Linda went to her file cabinet and pulled Bruce McCloud's file. "Okay, it is 883-4856. Is there anything else I can do for you?"

"Yes you might. I think Mrs. McCloud should press criminal charges against Mr. O'Francis. I know you have helped greatly already but maybe you can assist us in persuading her to press assault charges against O'Francis."

Linda Hawkins never responded for several seconds. "Well Mrs. Sheffield I am not at all sure I can do that. I really do not want to get involved in anything like that."

Janet Sheffield continued, "Mrs. Hawkins I don't think you have to worry about that. He will never know that you have talked to Mrs. McCloud. We could use your assistance on this matter. I mean his father has just been killed and to have a person like O'Francis do what he did, well... it's inexcusable don't you think?"

"Mrs. Sheffield, I really don't think I should be the one to get involved in any legal matter concerning your case against Mr. O'Francis."

"Well think about it and I will get back to you."

Linda Hawkins went straight to Steward Brittin's office and informed him of the conversation she had with Janet Sheffield. Steward leaned back in his worn tattered office chair and looked out the window for a long time. Linda kept talking and when she had finished, Steward spoke in his usual groggy voice, "Linda, I think you need to stay out of the legal matter on this. J.P. will fight this and you know it. Hell I don't know that he is guilty of anything. I mean..." then he stopped short of what he was about to say. "Anyway, let's keep out of this mess as much as we can."

The door to the court room was closed and the room was silent. Judge Madison then spoke. "Is the Commonwealth ready?"

"Yes your Honor." John Jay replied.

J.P.'s mid-section became as tight as a drum.

"Is the defense ready?"

"Yes your Honor." John Marshall replied.

Judge Madison looked at J.P. and stated, "James Patrick O'Francis you have been charged by the Commonwealth with assault and battery. How do you plead?"

Marshall leaned over to J.P. and whispered in his right ear, "Not guilty."

"I plead not guilty your Honor."

Looking back to his right he addressed John Jay, "You may call your first wittiness."

John Jay called his first witness, a girl by the name of Kelli Bartals. J.P. sat and listened to her version of what had taken place that day and it did not sift out exactly the way it actually went down. John Marshall took his time getting up for his cross exam of Kelli Bartals.

"Tell Me Miss Bartals. Did you see Mr. O'Francis hit Bruce McCloud?"

"No," was her response.

"Did you see Bruce hit Mr. O"Francis?"

"Yes."

"Miss Bartals you stated that you saw Mr. O'Francis put his hands around Bruce's neck. Is that correct?"

"Yes."

"Was Mr. McCloud turning blue?"

"I don't understand what you mean."

"Well, Miss Bartals, if you saw Mr. O'Francis choking Bruce, he would be cutting off his supply of air. He would not be breathing. Now, was he gasping for air?"

"Well no, not really."

"Okay Miss Bartals was Bruce talking or saying anything while Mr. O'Francis had him by the throat as you have so stated?"

"Ahhh, I think so. I am not for sure. But he was choking him. He just walked over and grabbed him by the throat and that is what started the fight."

"Was he using any foul language while all this was taking place?"

"Well... yeah."

"Miss Bartals after the altercation occurred, what happened then?"

"Well Mrs. Hawkins came in and took Mr. O'Francis out of the room."

"How did she do this?"

"Well she got in front of him and pushed him backward out of the room."

"Did Mr. O'Francis resist?"

"Well no, I don't think so."

"Where did all the students go after all this took place?"

"Well, all the teachers went into one of the offices and they put all of us in a class room."

"So you are stating that every one of the students was in a class room by yourselves just after the altercation between Bruce McCloud and Mr. O'Francis had occurred."

"Yes."

"Were there any teachers in the room with you and the rest of the students?"

"No."

"Were there any teachers' aids present?"

"No."

"Was Bruce McCloud in the same room with the rest of the students?"

"Well, yeah, I mean he is a student too."

John Marshall went back to the table and picked up a written statement Bartals had given to the Social worker. He turned back toward the witness with the paper in his hand. "Miss Bartals, you have stated that you heard Bruce McCloud tell Mr. O'Francis that his father had been killed in an automobile accident and that you heard Mr. O'Francis say, 'So.' Now I ask you, where were you sitting when this conversation took place?"

"Well I was across the room at my table."

"Was Mr. O'Francis facing you when he was having this conversation with Bruce?"

"No, he was looking at Bruce."

"So is it possible that you could have misunderstood what he said. Yes or no?"

"I don't think so. I heard him say, 'So.' That is when Bruce got all mad and started cussing Mr. O'Francis and he just went after Bruce."

"Miss Bartals, just answer the question yes or no. Could you have misunderstood Mr. O'Francis?"

"No."

"Miss Bartals, could Mr. O'Francis have said 'Oh,' instead of 'So'?"

Kelli Bartals paused before she answered and looked at John Marshall. "I am sure. I thought he said, 'So'."

"Did Mr. O'Francis cuss Mr. McCloud?"

"No."

"How far away would you say you were sitting when this conversation took place?"

"Across the room."

"I understand that Miss Bartals, but give me a guess. How many feet would you say you were from Mr. O'Francis?"

She began looking around the room… "Ahhh, oh maybe from here to the wall over there." As Kelli pointed toward the left side wall from the witness stand.

"So you would guess that you were oh, let's say about thirty feet, would that sound about right?"

"Yeah, I guess. Ever how far that is."

John Marshall turned to the Judge. "That is all I have at this time your Honor."

The other two witnesses testified and all had the same exact story, including Bruce McCloud, who played the humble poor little heartbroken boy over the loss of his father. But what did not come out in the case was that he and his father did not get along, and from time to time they had come to physical blows. It also did not come out that Bruce had even become physically violent with his mother, that Bruce as well as Rhymes were not only drug users but had begun the process of being dealers in the small town in which they hung out in. J.P. knew all this but knew that bringing it to the surface would only make his defense look as if he was attacking the character of the heartbroken boy who had lost his beloved father.

After going through all the witnesses J.P. was called to the stand and gave his testimony as to the events that had occurred on that late morning in April. After being cross examined with a good deal of intensity by John Jay, he informed the Judge that the prosecution rested its case.

J.P. was pleased with the manner in which his attorney had defended him. He now sat straight in his chair and watched the Judge as he pondered the evidence of the case before him.

After a good five minutes of silence in the room Judge Madison briefly went over the case and all the testimony presented. J.P.'s gut tightened as he listened to what the Judge was saying. He tried to keep a positive attitude about the case, but it appeared that the Judge was leaning in favor of the prosecution. He knew that the witnesses as well as McCloud had lied as to what had taken place. He knew that all the students had made up what they were going to say and had stuck together with their story.

J.P. had little faith in the judicial system and feared that the Judge would believe the acting role of the good little students and the very bad teacher who had just walked into their little world and attacked one of their own without cause. J.P. knew that this was the one area that would put the nail in his coffin with the superintendent and the School Board. If he lost this case it would mean that his career as a teacher was over and he feared what the sentence would be. His greatest fear was the damage to his character and what it would mean to his name. He had no expression on his face as Judge Madison came to a close of the facts presented to him.

"I have considered all part of this case and I believe that even though Mr. O'Francis should have never used such language in the presence of a student, he was not the one who provoked the attack and that he is innocent as to the charges of assault and battery. Court is adjourned."

He reached over, picked up his gavel, and hammered it onto the hard oak surface sending an echo throughout the court room. J.P. remained motionless as Judge Madison rose and went out the door to the rear of where he was sitting. J.P. looked across at the Assistant Commonwealth Attorney and he was looking at J.P. John Jay then broke a slight smile, picked up his papers, put them in his briefcase, and closed the lid.

J.P. rose and faced John Marshall. "Thank you so very much. Believe me when I tell you this. I was for the first time in a long time afraid that I was about to lose not just my job with the loss of this case, but my character as a person."

John Marshall smiled from ear to ear. "You doubted me? Why J.P. I am shocked. J.P. this case had no merit. Judge Madison knew that they were lying as well did John Jay, but they had to go through the process. You had some very powerful people on your side today, but I think you know that. Now, we still have to get ready for Social Services."

"I do not understand. I thought this was it?"

John laughed as he placed his files into his briefcase. "Oh no J.P., not by a long shot. Social Service will come after you with a vengeance. They have their own set of laws in which our court system has nothing to do with. And that woman over across the room is not a very happy person in case you have not noticed."

"But John, the law is the law and I have been acquitted of all the charges, correct?"

"Yes you have been acquitted of all charges brought against you in a court of law. But like I have stated, Social Services has their own laws and they are not governed by our legal system. But do not worry, we will get through all that in due time."

# Spoiled

DAMON BALES WALKED INTO THE central office of the Reynolds County School System in an angry and disturbed state of mind.

A dark silver van pulled into the far end of the Food City parking lot one hundred and fifty yards away as the crow flies, from the office of the superintendent's side of the building. The driver parked the van and turned off the engine, then got out and closed and locked the door. He walked around to the right side of the van and opened the sliding door and got in and closed it behind him and then locked it. The cargo section of the van had no windows, and he reached to his right to a custom made wall behind the driver's and passenger's seats of the van and flipped a switch that lit a dim light on the ceiling of the cargo section.

The floor of the cargo section was covered with indoor and outdoor light gray carpet. The section had two comfortable office chairs that were bolted to the floor, one on each side of the van. The right side chair was toward the front, the left side chair was toward the back. The walls were filled with a wide selection of high tech, state of the art electronic equipment, monitors and taping equipment with a table two feet wide extending from the front of the cargo section to the back doors, gracing both sides of the cargo section. The back doors had been welded together. Note tablets hung from hooks on the front edges of the tables. Pens and pencils were placed in cups in circular holes that were cut out of several places on the tops of the table.

He sat in the chair on the right side of the van and began to flip switches to ease-dropping electronics. On top of the van a dish shaped sphere elevated upward. At its pinnacle of two feet it stopped and another bright silver sphere began to unfold. When it stopped, a pencil shaped rod began to extend outward for eighteen inches and stopped.

Inside a reel to reel tape began to turn as the man placed a set of ear phones over his ears.

"Good morning, my name is Damon Bales and I want to see Mr. Marshy." He addressed the receptionist.

"Mr. Bales, do you have an appointment?"

"No."

"I will see if Mr. Marshy will see you."

"He will." His tone of voice was curt and demanding.

She picked up the phone and pushed a button.

"Mr. Marshy, a Mr. Bales is here and wants to talk to you."

"Do I have an appointment with him?" LaMar asked. As Grace looked over at Damon who had taken several steps away from the receptionist desk, she answered, "No sir. I do not have one on the appointment sheet. Mr. Marshy, you do have a Mr. Gardner coming in at ten o'clock today."

"Okay, send him in." She placed the phone down and looked up at Bales. "You may go back. Just..."

Bales rudely cut her off. "I know where it is!"

Damon Bales walked out of the lobby to the circular hallway, turned left and with a fast pace walked to Marshy's office that was on the back side of the building facing the Food City's parking lot. He entered the secretary's office and went by Sally without speaking and entered Marshy's very large thirty feet by forty foot office and closed the door behind him.

"Well Damon, come in." LaMar did not get out of his chair. His desk set in the middle of the quarter moon shaped room. Two tan leather chairs were placed to the front on each side of his desk. "Have a seat Damon."

"What in the hell is going on!"

"What do you mean?"

"I mean with that god damn O'Francis!"

"Hell, Damon I don't know. What are you talking about? You come storming in here mad as a wet hen and demand the answer to a question of which I don't know what the hell you are talking about."

"Damn it, LaMar I am talking about the trial! You mean you don't know that he got off on the assault and battery charges!"

"Yes. I am very much aware of the fact. So?"

"So! So! Hell, how did he do that?"

"He had a good attorney?"

Damon sat red faced at Marshy's smart ass remark. "Well Damon you were the one who told me that you could get Judge MacMullur to get Judge Madison to convict him. What more can I say?"

"Well you were going to get some political pressure put on Madison. What the hell happened to that?"

"I did my best. I can't go to Madison and tell him how to rule on a case. I do have limits you know. You were the one who seemed so convinced that he would rule to convict. If he had, then we could recommend to the Board to dismiss O'Francis as a teacher. Damon, it didn't work. So don't get your shorts in a squeeze."

"God-damn it! That sonavabitch! How does he keep getting off?" Marshy grinned.

"So what is so damn funny LaMar?"

"I thought you didn't like the word son of a bitch?"

"Ahh, fuck you LaMar!"

"Well, you were the one who wanted him fired for calling you a son of a bitch, not me."

"So now what?"

"Well he still has to face charges of child abuse. The Social Service board will have a hearing on that sometime soon. We will see what happens there."

"You have connections there?"

"Yes."

"And?"

"I have made in-roads. We will see."

The phone rang. Marshy reached over and picked it up. "Yes."

Grace, the receptionist spoke, "Mr. Marshy, your ten o'clock appointment is here."

"Okay, give me a few minutes." Then Marshy laid the phone down on the receiver. "Look Damon I have someone I have to talk to. Calm down, things will work out."

Damon got up still agitated, turned, and walked out of Marshy's office.

The man in the van spoke softly, "Very good."

# O'Donavan

I WANT TO TAKE YOU back a few years in my story about O'Francis. This was not the first time J.P. had to be in court, a legal system in which he did not have any faith in because of its corruption. He talked to me shortly after the trial and in the course of our conversation we rehashed the events that led him to distrust the legal system. He was completely surprised at the outcome of the child abuse trial even though he told me that he felt he would have a better chance of having the truth surface and for the Judge to believe his testimony as to the event that had occurred at the Alternative School Building simply because of the brotherhood in which he belonged.

I myself felt that real justice would be served because I also belonged to the same brotherhood and being a brother felt that if, they were true brothers, then the fraternal order would be true to the oaths in which we have taken. Although I did not attend my home lodge as it is in another state I kept my membership paid up and being a part of this great brotherhood is another reason why I learned to believe in what J.P. told me when we got together and talked. I did not reveal to him that I was part of the same organization as he was as I felt that it would complicate the matter.

Although O'Francis' will was like steel and it appeared that he could endure anything, I had my doubts as to how long the steel well in him would last under the stress and pressure in which he seemed to have to endure on a monthly and yearly basis. I have seen strong willed people like him before break like glass just when you least expected them to. People, I have learned over my life time of covering one story after another, can only take so much and then when you least expect it they come apart, usually at their own demise leaving a destroyed family with questions that can never be answered.

But J.P. was different, and as I have stated before in my story to you, he is one that I do not believe I will ever come across again in my lifetime. What I uncovered on my own as well with the help of J.P. of which I still do not know how he was able to obtain such covert information, although I do believe there is someone else in his life in which he has never made any reference to, that provided him with such secret information. Someone that has the training and the means of obtaining information that is not supposed to be obtained by any means. Which leads me to believe that this other person has some type of governmental connection, which really does not surprise me, considering the type of people J.P. was once connected too? As a good journalist should, on several occasions I inquired as to where the information he was passing along to me was obtained and its validity in other to tell my story, but as I expected I got no answers. But this is not taking you back to the mid-nineties when he lost his faith in our legal system. I can fully understand why he ended up the way he did.

# The Clerk

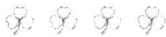

Jarvis picked up the phone and dialed the number of Damon Bales. After three rings the connection was made.

"Hello," Damon said.

"Damon, this is Jarvis. I need to speak with you. Can you come by my house tonight, ohh, say about seven?"

"Why?"

"Well, I don't want to talk on the phone. It is important."

"I guess." Then there was a long pause.

"It's about your case," Jarvis stated.

"Say at seven?" Damon said.

"Yeah."

"Okay, I'll be there."

Damon arrived at Jarvis's house on time. They went to Jarvis's den and sat in two large well-padded high backed chairs with a glass-topped table between them. Jarvis had provided ice tea to drink as they talked.

"So what is new?" Damon started the conversation.

"I have this juror that we can reach. Well, kind of. Let me explain what I have in mind. I think you will like it."

"How do you know this person? How do you know if he can be trusted?"

"Let me explain. First I know him. Let it go at that. Second, what I have in mind is we pay him some money to say that O'Francis has talked to him about the case. That will look bad on O'Francis with the Judge."

Damon interrupted. "We have the Judge."

"I know. This will help the Judge out and will impact the rest of the jurors in the case."

Jarvis continued, "I know he is on jury duty, and I know he does not want to be there. This will get him out of jury duty and give him a little cash on the side. Also it will make O'Francis look real bad. I can announce to the Judge that he has been approached by O'Francis as we are going through the process of selecting a jury. Your attorney will request that he be removed. Like I said, it will look real bad on O'Francis."

Damon smiled. His blood rushed through his veins at such a speed it warmed his whole body.

"Do you have someone in mind that can get him the money? And how much are we talking about?"

"Oh yes. I know he will do what I ask of him. Let's say two hundred."

Damon took a drink of tea. He slowly put the glass down and looked at Jarvis. "Let's make it three hundred. Just to be sure because I want to ruin O'Francis." His voice was filled with hate. "The three hundred, in one hundred dollar bills is more impressive. That's more of an impact when he gets it."

"Okay, three hundred it is."

"Now, is this 100 % sure?" Damon asked.

"Yes. I am dead sure!"

"Okay, I will have three one hundred dollar bills here tomorrow for you."

"Put them in a regular legal envelope," Jarvis told Damon.

"You will take care of all the details, right?"

"Yes. It will be handled. No one will ever know. Trust me. I know he will do it and I know it will work," Jarvis stated with a great degree of confidence.

# Grift

RICHARD FINKEL PULLED INTO THE paved blacktopped driveway of Damon Bales' home as requested at 12:30 p.m. The noon sun was warm for a mid-October Sunday. None of his neighbors were out in their yards, as most were still in church or about to leave church.

Richard pulled his car in front of the closed garage doors, got out, and walked along the thirty-foot brick sidewalk passing a large picture window with pulled drapes. He stepped to the door and rang the doorbell. The doorknob turned as soon as Richard removed his finger from the button. Damon stood looking at Richard from behind a full glass storm door with a smile on his face that would have put the Cheshire cat to shame.

"Come in, come in," Damon spoke with an excitement in his voice, closing the door after Richard entered the living room.

"Thank you. You sure are in a good mood today Damon," Richard stated with a question in his voice as if it was rare to see him happy.

Damon walked across the room continuing to talk, "Follow me Richard, " his voice displaying a touch of excitement. He entered the kitchen, and opened the door leading to the basement. As they reached the basement floor, Damon walked across the concrete floor to the glass sliding door and opened it. "We'll talk out here. It is a warm day. I have some ice tea for us and a few snacks." Richard continued to follow Damon saying nothing.

They walked out onto the deep red brick 16 by 20 foot patio. A black mesh iron patio table and chairs set in the middle of the patio. On the table was a large pitcher of ice tea beading with condensation. Two glasses also adorned the middle of the table. A serving tray filled with half cut tuna sandwiches and a large bowl of plan potato chips set off to the right side of the rectangular table.

"Have a seat Richard. Would you care for some tea?" Damon asked as he indicated the tea with his open right hand, simultaneously pulling his chair out with his left hand and sat down.

As Richard sat down he replied, "I do believe I will."

Damon filled both of their glasses with the sweetened ice tea. "Would you like something to eat? I made these sandwiches myself."

"Thank you, I think I will," Richard said.

As Richard began eating, Damon explained why he called Richard to his home, which was extremely rare for him to have anyone in the school system at his house. Only his elite social political buddies were ever invited to his house.

"Richard, the reason I asked you here today was because we need to come up with sixty thousand dollars. Thirty apiece."

Finkel took a drink of tea before he spoke. "So, why do we need that kind of money? I mean, I thought the School Board was paying for the attorney and all that stuff? You know, legal fees and so forth." Richard's tone of voice was filled with sarcasm.

Damon was very quick to answer his question, "Ohhh, they are."

"Okay so why the money?" Richard said.

"Insurance," Damon stated with confidence in his voice.

"Insurance?" Richard asked as he finished his first half of his sandwich.

"Yes. Insurance Richard. It will take us about sixty thousand, I think, maybe less, I don't think more, to ensure us a win," Damon said.

There was a long pause in their conversation. Richard reached to his right and got another sandwich. His ice tea was half gone. Without asking, Damon refilled his glass.

Damon continued, "A far less amount than if we should lose the case! I mean, as I have told you, the School Board agreed to pay for the lawsuit, not the appeal if we were to lose this case. Do you have a problem coming up with half?"

"No, no, not at all. Hell Damon, you should know that," Richard said scoffing.

Damon smiled, and then continued to divulge the grand plan. "I have Jarvis Griffith, you know, the clerk, working with us. Now that will cost five thousand and Judge MacMuller will cost five. Also Judge Munis will be five."

Richard interrupted, "Ten thousand to two judges? You are kidding, right?"

"Noooo, that is the price for insurance," Damon said.

"Why Judge Munis? And who is Judge Munis?" Richard said.

"Welll because he will be the one sitting on the bench. And since he and Judge MacMuller are good friends, I have asked Jarvis to make arrangements for him to see to it that we do not lose." Damon stated in a stronger tone.

"So, why doesn't Judge MacMuller hear the case?" Richard said.

"I thought you knew," Damon said as he refilled his glass and reached for a sandwich for the first time.

"No. Know what?" Richard said, knowing at that point that he had been cut out of the loop.

"Oh, well, I guess I had better fill you in on a few things." Damon said in his best innocent voice.

"Yes, Damon I think you should since you have asked me to fork out fifteen thousand dollars." Richard 's voice had become a little harsh.

"Okay, okay. I just assumed that you had been informed. At any rate, here is what has happened. O'Francis and his split tailed bitch lawyer have requested that Judge MacMuller remove himself from the case as he was indirectly involved."

Richard cut him off. "How?"

"Well, O'Francis had applied for some sort of police license, and Daniel refused to issue it to him."

Richard sat looking at Damon with a question written all over his face. Damon saw he was not aware of the letter sent to Daniel MacMuller.

"Okay, so what does that have to do with this case?" Richard said.

"Well, the letter we sent to the School Board was also sent to MacMuller," Damon firmly stated with a bit of pride in his voice.

"Oh, I was not aware that anyone outside the School Board had received the letter." Richard said.

"Oh, yeah," Damon replied quickly.

"Okay, who else got the letter?" Richard said.

"Well, let me think. Well of course the School Board, MacMuller, then there was all the local police. Ahhh, the county police, ahhh, the state police, and ahhh, the F.B.I., ahhh, I think that is all." Damon sat back in his chair, an evil smile slowly crept across his face, one that would have rivaled that of the Grinch himself.

Richard sat in his chair in shock. "You are shitting me!" he said.

"No!" Damon stated.

"Jesus Damon! Why did you do that? I mean hell, the School Board would have been good enough!" Then there was a slight pause, and Richard continued, "Damn man, you know what will happen if these people start looking into all this. I mean, hell man...I mean I make my real money from a business that is not exactly legal you know! Or have you forgotten! Damn!"

"Oh hell Richard, don't worry about that. No one will be looking at us. They are going to be looking at O'Francis. I really fucked him this time! I mean really good! He will not get out of this one!"

Again Damon spoke with a great deal of pride in his voice.

"Oh, really! Yeah, you did that! But when you bring in the fuck'en F.B.I., you can bet they will look at all of us! Not just O'Francis!" Richard's voice and expression on his face was one of total disapproval of what Damon had done. But Richard was a much more streetwise person than Damon would ever hope to be. Richard had never had the support of a corrupt political machine to protect him.

For a moment, a concerned look crossed Damon's face. Then Richard continued as he moved forward in his chair, leaning onto the table, his head tilted to his right looking somewhat sideways at Damon, "Damon! What were you thinking? Hell, the local boys, well I mean that was okay. Even the state, since we do have someone on the inside there also. But the fuck'en F.B.I.! You know anybody there?" Sarcasm filled Finkel's voice as he looked at Damon.

"Well, no," Damon spoke, his voice indicating some concern at that point of the conversation.

Damon quickly defended his action. "Look, Griffith is a personal friend of mine. MacMuller is a personal friend of mine. And he and Munis are really close. They will handle everything. There is nothing to worry about. We have everything worked out. They will help us in anyway. Trust me."

Richard Finkel slid back in his chair, reached for his glass of tea, and was sipping on it as he continued to look at Damon Balcs.

Damon had totally dismissed the concern for the Fed's being remotely involved as he continued with the grand plan. "Okay. Now Richard what I need is for you to get one of your people to make the deliveries."

"What deliveries?" Richard asked. His mind was on the Fed's, and his connection with the drug lords in the area, as well as the gambling connections he had.

"Well, the money. I think it should be done with someone no one knows. Also, we will need to get Janice Jones paid."

"Janice Jones? What does she have to do with this? And why do we have to pay her?" Finkel responded with some agitation in his voice.

"Well, Richard she is our key witness you know," Damon said.

"Noooo. I didn't know. Besides, how can Janice be a key witness? Hell, she wasn't anywhere around that morning."

Richard was becoming more irritated as he was figuring out that he had been cut out of the loop on more than just the judges on the case. Since it appeared to him that he did have a major say in how the case was to be handled, he was becoming a bit testy.

"Well, I brought Janice in on the case because she will be willing to testify to the terrorist acts that O'Francis has done to her and Gil and their family." Damon said with a more, *I am in control of this case*, tone in his voice. "She has agreed to do it for five thousand."

Finkel didn't respond. Damon continued.

"Then I think we can get that woman in the store to testify, for, let's say, fifteen hundred."

"Who? Bankos?" Richard said.

"Yes." Damon said as if money would buy anybody.

"Nooo. Damon you won't get Bankos! I am telling you that now!"

"Why? I hear she could use the money." Damon said.

"Yeah, well, she may. I don't know. But she is loyal to O'Francis. Hell that whole fuck'en family is! I know!" Then he stopped. "Well, maybe not all of them." Then a slight smile crossed his face. "But, Mary Jo and her husband and her sons are, that I do know!"

"Okay. Who else works at the store?" Damon said.

"What about Garry? I mean, didn't you talk to him?" Richard said.

"Yes." Damon said.

"Well? How much for him to testify for us?" Finkel stated.

"He won't." Damon said.

"He won't. Why? I mean he was there. He saw what went on. I talked to him just after it happened. Hell, I told you that. I mean, what is his problem?" Richard said with contempt in his voice toward Garry Bare.

"He just told me that he would not get involved in the case," Damon said.

"He is involved. What does he mean, not get involved?"

"All I know is that he stated to me in the office that he and O'Francis had something in common. That he would not breach that common bond. Now what that is I don't have a clue. Hell, I didn't even know he liked him. I thought all along that he was with us. Did Gerry ever indicate to you that he and O'Francis had anything going?" Damon said.

"No, not at all. What does that mean, a common bond?" Finkel asked.

"I don't know," Damon replied.

"Well don't you think we need to find out? How do you know he will not testify for O'Francis? I mean we need to know where Gerry stands on this. He knows too much. Hell, he has heard too much," Richard said.

"Yeah. I know, but he said he was not going to get involved one way or the other. To me, that tells me he will not testify on O'Francis' behalf," Damon stated.

They both ate another half of a sandwich and drank another half glass of tea. Richard pushed his chair back and stood. "I need to use the bathroom."

"Sure, sure, there is one in the basement, just through the doors and to the right, just beyond the stairs," Damon said.

When he returned Richard began the conversation, "I think I can get Joan Dobson. I have had some dealings with her in the past. I think we can count on her to testify for us."

"She really was not there. Correct? I mean in the store at the time all this took place, right?" Damon asked.

"Right. But she will testify that she was. Ahh, we can get her to say she was in the back at the time the conversation took place in the front of the store," Finkel stated with an assured tone in his voice. "I believe fifteen hundred will take care of that."

Damon again smiled and nodded his yes in the affirmative. Then he softly spoke, "Yes!" He picked up his glass and took a long slow drink of tea.

"Let's make this happen." Damon looked over at Richard and spoke with confidence in his voice.

Richard Finkel shook his head yes, stating, "Yes. No problem."

The sun was shining bright in the mid-October Sunday with the temperature reaching in the mid 70's. There was silence between the two men as they sat looking at empty space, but not at each other. Richard leaned forward in his chair placing his half empty glass back on the table. Then he leaned back in his chair, placed his hands behind his head, interlocking his fingers, looking slightly upward, but not at Damon. "Okay, let's talk a little about Janice Jones."

"Okay. What about her?" Damon said.

" Well you say she will testify for five grand. Now is that a firm price?" Richard asked with a degree of doubt.

"Well, yes. I mean that is what she said to me," Damon answered. "I mean, why do you question her?"

"Because." Then there was a moment of silence. "Because I know her and her type. She will blackmail you in a beat of your heart. She would sell her own mother out. She will sell her soul for a price. Damon, you should know her by now. You have seen her operate. There is nothing she will not do for the right price! I question if she feels that what she is going to do is the right price. Now don't read me wrong here. I think five grand is more than enough. But I damn sure ain't fool enough to think she thinks that is enough giving her time to think about it and then come back and tell you that she has had a change of mind. It will not be beyond her to ask for more."

Richard then took his hands from behind his head and raised forward placing his arms on the table, looking at Damon.

"Well, Richard, she has always been very loyal to me. You know that. I mean she has done a lot for me and well for you too." Damon defended their key witness.

"Yeah, well, you have done her lots of favors along the way, Damon. You know it! Hey, don't get me wrong here. I mean I'm all for it. The question I am asking is how much?"

"Well, it may cost a little more. I am not for sure. I mean she will have to give a deposition and then she will have to testify in court," Damon stated with a degree of confidence.

"I still can't see them letting her be a key witness. I just have a hard time figuring how we are going to get that by the judge. You know that O'Francis' attorney will object to that. He will question how she can be witness to something she knows nothing about."

Richard shook his head. Damon turned his glass slowly on the table, looking at it, thinking.

"I mean we pay all this money out, and she screws it up," Richard continued.

Damon continued turning his glass, still not looking at Richard. "We lose and we lose more than just a case against O'Francis. We lose our ass. Now Damon, you know how she is. She has a mouth that won't quit. She starts running it, and she does all the time. She damn sure could say the wrong thing, and then we are dicked! I mean more than this damn court case! I will be very surprised if she does just what she is told to do, or say. I worry about her story, and if it will hold under pressure."

Damon shook his head slowly indicating the gravity of the now reality of the situation using Janice Jones in a case he so desperately wanted to win. He then looked up at Richard Finkel. "Not to worry. She will have her story rehearsed. She will have it down smooth. I will make sure she knows not to say more than she should. We have an attorney that will get her ready. She will be convincing. Besides, remember, we have the Judge on our side."

"Yeah, well, that is all fine and good. What about O'Francis appealing the case when he loses? I mean your money damn sure don't reach up to the appeals court. We make any slips, the case can get overturned. Damon, there can be no room for error here. Do you understand?" Finkel 's voice indicated the seriousness of the case as well as the game they were playing.

"Can you get someone to deliver the money rather soon?" Damon asked.

"Yes I have told you I could take care of that," Richard said.

"Who? And how much will that cost?" Damon asked.

"The who, I can't tell you, and the how much, I don't know." Richard replied.

Damon looked down at his glass of tea, frowned at the tone and the arrogant demeanor that Richard was displaying. But he said nothing, which was out of character for him.

"Okay." Damon rose from his chair. "We are set right?"

Richard scooted his chair back, and rose. "I would say we are."

"Okay, let me know when you are ready for the delivery. We need to get this done in the next two weeks. That way we have everyone in place," Damon stated displaying his superior authority over Richard.

Richard Finkel smiled. "I will let you know."

# The Trial

Michael had taken off work and traveled six hours to be with his family for the trial. All three of the men in the O'Francis family wore double breasted blue pin striped suits with light blue button down collared shirts and highly shined black shoes. They met Julius Donatello at the courthouse. It was thirty minutes before the trial was to begin. Julius had a box of files he was carrying.

They entered the courtroom and took their seats on the left side of the Judge's chair. Dawn, Michael, and Patrick took a seat on the first row behind the rail on the same side as J.P. and Julius.

Across from J.P. and Julius were Richard, Damon, and their attorney, Curtis Feinstein. J.P. did not hesitate in looking at all three with utter contempt. Their posture depicted smugness and confidence. Julius was placing his files on the table in front of O'Francis. J.P. noted that he had not brought the poster that listed the incidences that had taken place over the years that would show Damon's pattern of harassment as well as his character assassination of J.P. He also noted that he did not have the pictures of the area where the incident between Richard and J.P. had taken place. J.P. had been requested by Julius to take the pictures and make the poster listing a pattern that reflected the letter that brought them to court. He had enlarged the pictures to a ten by twelve, labeled each, and had given all the items that Julius had requested of him, two weeks earlier.

Manuel and Nina Reuben entered the courtroom and sat at the back of the room. Also sitting in the back of the room was John O'Donovan, and a late arrival was Paul O'Neill. J.P. observed that John wore casual attire and that Paul had a suit on. The two did not know each other and sat in separate pews.

He also took note of the fact that a reporter from the newspaper was present, dressed in casual attire that appeared as if he had slept in them all night. He knew him from the many times he had been at the School Board meetings. His accounts of the School Board meetings always seemed to portray LaMar and company in glorious light and the teachers' association seemed to be the villain's. On several occasions the teachers' association's president questioned the reporter as to the manner and accuracy in which he had reported what had taken place at the School Board meeting. As usual he responded with a sarcastic answer. J.P. figured that he was at the trial upon the request of Marshy, to portray him in the worst manner possible and portray Bales and Finkel as the poor victims.

J.P. also had expected the director over all the teachers in the first district, Dan Jakes, to be present in support of him, if only for a short time, but he did not show. For J.P. it was a disappointment. Dan's old school idea of doing business behind the scenes philosophy, was for J.P., just that, old school. It was now the mid-nineties, and as far as he was concerned the old school mentality went out of style long ago. He logged it away as yet another lesson in loyalty and importance in the game he was now playing, as well as maybe he did not know Dan as well as he may have thought. *Maybe he was the old school one in the game, and he was the one who needed to change*, he thought. *It is time, let me get my shit together here, damn.*

Two county police officers, Charles Kuntz and James Fleming, entered the courtroom. J.P. knew both men well. Moments later the Judge entered the room and Charles Kuntz announced his presence. "All rise." He spoke loud and clear, "The honorable Dan Munis presiding."

"Be seated," Charles stated as Judge Munis took his seat.

The clerk of the court read to the court the case number as well as what the case was about and who was bringing suit and by whom.

"Is the defense ready?" Judge Munis asked.

"Yes your honor," came the response from Curtis Feinstein

"Is the plaintiff ready?" he asked.

"Yes your honor," Julius stated.

"Will the clerk call in the jurors?" Judge Munis stated.

With those instructions the clerk of the court Jarvis Griffith went to the back of the court room and went out the large double door and returned with fifteen people, of which five would be picked for the trial.

As the men and women were taking their seats, Jarvis Griffith announced to Judge Munis that he had been informed that Mr. O'Francis had been in contact with one of the jurors.

Judge Munis asked which one.

"Your honor Mr. Brian Weber," Jarvis announced.

"How?" Judge Munis asked.

"Your honor, according to Mr. Weber, Mr. O'Francis went to his place of employment, Food City, and spoke with him concerning this case."

The Judge look down and over at J.P. and Julius.

"Do you know this person?" Julius asked.

"No."

"Did you talk to him at any time?"

"No." J.P. stated with a harsh tone in his voice.

"Are you sure?" Julius asked again.

J.P. looked over at his attorney. His eyes were cold and without feeling. "I said no! That statement is a lie! And Julius, I expect there will be more as the day goes on, just like there was when your sister questioned them in the deposition. I have tried to tell you!"

"Mr. Weber you are excused. You may leave," Judge Munis stated.

Damon smiled and leaned back in his seat crossing his arms over his chest.

At that point J.P. knew that he had been set up. A cold chill raced over his body leaving "goose" bumps all over his back and arms.

The clerk would call the names of each juror and asked each if they knew either one of the people involved in the case. Julius and Curtis would strike the one they did not want. J.P. had only known one of the fifteen men and women sitting in the juror's box, Mr. Jerry Jensen who was from Honsburg and had known J.P. for several years. He was a very large man, six foot six, and a solid two hundred and fifty pounds. J.P. had never spoken to him concerning the case. But he knew that he was a straight up, point of fact talking man. He would tell the truth. But he also knew that was not what the Judge nor Curtis Feinstein were after.

One juror stated that he knew Damon and that he did not like him. He went one step further and stated that he was a crook. Curtis excused him from jury duty. No one else spoke and the two attorneys went through the process of striking the jurors until they got the required number needed for the case.

The entire process took thirty minutes to seat five jurors. Jerry was not one of the ones that made the list, which did not surprise J.P. as he would learn later that the leg work had been done on each juror and they were well aware that Jensen liked O'Francis and would most likely support him.

Just to the left of Dawn, Michael, and Patrick was Mr. Lucius Donatello. J.P. had requested that Holly be part of the team at his table. He wanted her to question Damon. He knew that she could bring the very worst out in him, as he hated any female that held a professional position and could not be controlled and had power over him. She was not present. This was a major disappointment. He began to feel very uneasy, and a bit angry. On the other side of the room was the current wife of Damon and several members of the Honsburg community that did not have what would have to be considered the best of reputations. However with J.P.'s knowledge of the people in the community over the years, it did not surprise him at all.

Julius Donatello then stood and delivered his opening statement to the jury.

"Ladies and gentlemen of the jury, this trial is about character assassination. It is about slander, it is about libel, and it is about defaming the character of one Mr. J.P. O'Francis. This case is about Mr. Bales and Mr. Finkel conspiring to destroy the reputation of my client. This case is about a letter in which Mr. Bales wrote and sent to the Reynolds County School

Board in hopes that they would fire Mr. O'Francis from a job he has held in this county for over twenty years. In fact Mr. Bales did indeed get him fired from his coaching job, a job that provided ten percent of his family's income, placing them in a financial burden.

"Mr. Bales has not provided any solid proof as to why Mr. O'Francis was dismissed from his coaching position, one that he has held for thirteen years. Mr. O'Francis was a very well respected coach among not only his own coaching colleagues, but among his opponents, as well as among the officials that oversee the games he was involved in. Mr. Bales has not provided any evidence of any sort that has proven otherwise. Mr. Bales went one step further. He sent a copy of this defaming letter to all law enforcement agencies throughout the entire area including the FBI to cast a dark cloud over Mr. O'Francis, labeling him as a terrorist.

"Now let me define a few words for you so you will fully understand the extent of the damage this letter Mr. Bales wrote, with the help of Mr. Finkel.

"First, let's take the word slander: a false report maliciously uttered and tending to injure the reputation of a person." Julius then walked back toward the table where J.P. sat. Half way he turned in a sharp military manner.

"Second, Libel: spoken or written," he put a lot of emphasis on the word written, "Statement, which gives an unjustly, unfavorable impression of a person. That letter that Mr. Bales wrote did both. Now..." as he walked in front of the jurors, he placed his hands on the railing in front of them, putting the weight of his upper body entirely on his arms.

"Let's take the word defamation, to injure, to destroy the reputation by means of either libel or slander. That ladies and gentlemen of the jury is just what Mr. Damon Bales with the aid of Mr. Richard Finkel did to Mr. O'Francis. His good name, his good character, was assassinated. This letter was only one in a long series of letters that has emanated from Mr. Damon Bales' office. My client has been attacked by Damon Bales repeatedly for five years." He held his hand up, spreading his fingers out wide swinging his arm from the far right juror to the far left, making eye contact with each one.

"Ladies and gentlemen, the fact is in print. There can be no disputing the facts. He, Damon Bales, has been the author of not only this," Julius held up the letter.

"But we have proof that he was the author of many more that has out and out character assassinated my client." Then he paused and started walking back toward the table. Half way Julius stopped. His back to the jury, he slowly turned to face them. "Do you know what assassinate means? To kill! To end a person's character, their good name, their repartition, in as well as throughout, not only the community, but the entire area in which the person lives." He turned slowly, then slowly walked to the table and took a seat.

Curtis Feinstein sprang up like a jack-in-a-box, just as Julius' ass hit the seat.

"I intend to show you," he pointed to each of them, "That it has been my client that has been injured here. Not Mr. O'Francis!"

This opening pitch was a curve ball. J.P. could not figure how in the hell he was going to prove that he had damaged Bales or Finkel.

"Ladies and gentlemen, let me tell you what Mr. O'Francis has done to my clients, Mr. Bales and Mr. Finkel. They have been living in total fear for the past five years. Living in fear I tell you! Do you know what it is like to live in fear every single day of your lives?"

His voice raised, he placed emphasis on each of the words, "*living in fear every single day of your lives.*" He paused for a good ten seconds, a long time for a lot of people. Then he continued. "This man," he turned sideways from the jury, and pointed at O'Francis.

"This man is not what he appears. He is not just a simple teacher. Ohhh, no! He is a terrorist! He has struck fear into the daily lives of my clients! He has defied his boss, the principal of the school in which he worked, on everything he asked him to do. He has received numerous written reprimands by his boss, Mr. Bales. This we can prove. He has been called into the superintendent's office on a number of occasions for disobeying Mr. Bales' orders. He has been a total disruption to the running of Mr. Bales' school. He has verbally threatened Mr. Finkel, as well as several other teachers in the school. This man, who has claimed that MY clients have injured HIM, is not what he appears! Oh he sits there and he appears to be a simple teacher. But he is much more than an ordinary teacher. I ask you. Do not let his innocent looking teacher appearance fool you."

Then he walked halfway to his table, stopped and turned as if he had forgotten something.

"He claims he was fired unjustly from his coaching job. Ladies and gentlemen of the jury, he was fired from his coaching job because of all the complaints that my client, Mr. Bales, had received from a large number of parents and his fellow coaches, other principals, and officials. His firing was justified. He was not fit to be a coach. He was an embarrassment to the school. That is why Mr. Bales had to fire Mr. O'Francis."

At that point J.P. had reached his breaking point. His mind was about to short fuse. He had sat stone still through yet another character assassination. For J.P. his family name was now being publicly tarnished in a court of law. The very reason he brought the suit. His jaws hurt from gritting his teeth. J.P. felt that he was being bated. Curtis Feinstein was in hopes that his opening to the jury slandering O'Francis would be enough to break O'Francis and cause him to verbally comment in an angry manner toward him, winning his case before it even got started. J.P. had come too far and went through too much to lose control at this late inning of the game. He quickly regained control of his mind and took a deep breath tying to relax.

As Curtis Feinstein walked slowly back to his chair, he concluded, "Ladies and gentlemen, please do not fault Mr. Bales for doing his job in the manner of a true professional. A man who has devoted his entire life to the teaching profession. A man who has given over forty years to education. A man who did not want the school he worked at to be tarnished by one bad apple." He had reached his seat as he uttered the last word. He smiled at the jury. "I think after you hear all the evidence presented here today you will make the correct decision. I think you will know the difference between right and wrong. You will know at the end of this trial that my clients have done no wrong." Then he pulled his chair out and sat.

J.P. thought, *he has done well. He would have received a "B" in acting class. Of course he would have gotten an "A" in Lying 101. He gives attorneys a bad name. Of course then again attorneys have a job to do. If it means lying to get the job done, then so be it. Hell it is just money for anyone of them. He couldn't care less about the truth. But his opening curve ball went in the dirt.* He felt a great deal of anger and his military instincts bubbled up inside. O'Francis was not intimated by Curtis Feinstein and looked directly across the room at him and locked his eyes on him. In O'Francis' mind he could only see the enemy, someone you take out with one shot.

But he quickly regained his thoughts and brought himself back to the reality of a courtroom setting. He was not in a combat setting. He had to focus on what was at the moment. That was not looking down the sights of an M-16 lying in the bush.

Julius began to call his first witness, Mr. George Rake.

"Your honor," Mr. Feinstein rose and spoke. "I do not have this witness on my list."

J.P. looked over at Julius. Julius quickly rose.

"Your honor, I have provided the clerk with a list of all my witnesses, which included Mr. Rake. Mr. Feinstein should have received this list."

"Approach. You too Mr. Griffith." Judge Munis stated. Feinstein, Donatello, and Griffith went to the Judge.

"Mr. Feinstein, would you care to explain?"

"Yes sir. I do not have Mr. Rake on my list."

"Your honor," Julius stated. "I have provided the clerk as well as Mr. Feinstein with a current list of all the people I intend to call as witnesses."

"Do you have a list of people you intend to call?"

"Yes sir." Julius quickly returned to the table and picked up his list of witnesses and returned, handing the Judge the list.

"And you Mr. Feinstein." Judge Munis asked.

"Yes." Already having the list in his hand, he handed him his list. Judge Munis looked at both lists.

"Gentlemen we seem to have some problem with communications here. Mr. Donatello, your list does not match the one Mr. Feinstein has.

Mr. Griffith, do you have a list of people both parties are going to call in this case?"

"Yes your honor." Having the list with him he handed the Judge the list. Munis looked at the list. "Mr. Donatello, Mr. Griffith's list does not match yours. I see here that there are ahhh, four people on your list that does not appear on either Mr. Griffith's or Mr. Feinstein's list."

"Your honor, I really do not understand. I am quite sure I provided each with the list of witnesses I intended to call."

"Well, I can't allow these people to be called as witnesses." He placed check marks beside the names and handed the list back to Julius.

"If you would like to reschedule this case for a later date we can. Or would you like to continue with the people you have?" Judge Munis was cold and unfeeling in his tone of voice.

"I will confer with my client your Honor."

"You may step back," Judge Munis stated.

Julius walked back to the table where J.P. was seated.

"We have a slight problem." J.P. did not respond. He just looked at Julius with no surprise on his face. He expected glitches in the case, as there had been over the past five years of just getting the case to trial.

"It seems that our witness list is incomplete. They do not have all our witnesses listed. The Judge will not allow us to use these four as witnesses."

J.P. looked down at the list of key people in his case: *Greg Roscommon,* Athletic Director and teaching colleague who was very much aware of some of Damon's underhanded tactics toward J.P. and would have been very open and trustful in answering any questions. *Stewart Brittin,* well-known powerful member in the Democratic political machine in the county, now a supervisor in the school system, who was willing to testify (J.P. and Julius thought)to Damon's character and the fact that Damon Bales was well known throughout the county for his character assassination and dislike for O'Francis. He was also willing to testify to several conversations that took place when he was present where Damon openly and blatantly slandered J.P.

*Dave Hobart,* head football coach at Honsburg High School would testify, although not so willingly, but would tell the truth if asked about conversations he had with Richard Finkel that were demeaning to J.P. as well as his son Michael.

*Belinda Bookmann,* secretary at Honsburg High and had been there since J.P. arrived and knew of and had seen as well as heard Bales and Finkel discrediting J.P.

O'Francis looked up at the Judge, who sat looking toward J.P. and Julius. The courtroom was deadly silent. J.P. then slowly turned his head toward the Clerk, who was leaning against the far wall directly across from him and directly behind Damon's table. Jarvis Griffin had a smirk expression on his face. Damon leaned back in his chair, with a smile on his face. Feinstein was looking across at Julius waiting to see what he was going to do.

"Do you want to continue with what we have? Or do you want to get the trial put off until a later date?"

J.P. knew at that moment the case was doomed. He knew at that moment that it was no use in postponing the trial. It would be a waste of his time and his money. The cards were stacked. It was crunch time. The bases were loaded. There were two outs, and it was the bottom of the ninth inning. He had to swing away and hope for a hit to win the game. His mind was racing. It appeared that everything was going in slow motion. The room was deadly silent. J.P. looked first at his attorney, and then across the room to his enemies. He slowly turned his head and looked diagonally to the far back of the court room at John and Paul. He paused for several minutes while looking at them. They returned the look and J.P. knew that they knew that something was not right. He then looked over at his wife and sons, pausing again for several seconds.

" Delay, reschedule. How long, when?"

"I do not know that J.P."

"No." Then he paused for a good five seconds. "I want to proceed. Julius, you did send in all the proper paperwork or whatever you attorneys have to do to get ready for a trial, did you not?"

"Yes." Came the response without hesitation.

"I see. Well this is Reynolds County, and we are fighting the great political machine here! Which includes the Clerk, and most likely the Judge. Fuck-it! The odds are against us! Let's do what we can! Swing away! Hope for a hit," J.P. responded in total disgust. Julius looked at him for just a moment, and then understood his analogy and rose from his seat.

"Your Honor, we will proceed with what we have." Julius informed the Judge.

"Very well, then is the defense ready? Judge Munis asked.

"We are your honor."

J.P. mentally began to talk to himself. *It was after all Reynolds County. Anyone that was living here knew that it was the most political and most corrupt county in the entire region. What sounded good and was the truth was not always the way the legal system worked in Reynolds County. What more could I have expected. Take total control of your emotions. Do not break. Do not show any emotions. I have rolled the dice. I knew it was a big gamble from the very beginning. I knew the odds were against me. What the fuck was I thinking, that some fairy tale story will come out of all this. That is okay. I will give it my best shot. If I lose this fucking case, I will have justice.*

It appeared at that point, to all that had their eyes on J.P. that a calming came over him. He appeared as if he had been relieved of an overloaded burden. He even broke a slight smile as he lowered his head as if he was looking at something on the table in front of him. He looked up, took a deep breath, looked at his family, let the air out of his lungs, sat up straight in his chair, and thought to himself, *Let's get this thing over with.*

Judge Munis looked over at Donatello. "Are your witnesses ready Mr. Donatello?"

"They are your Honor."

J.P. thought, *Yeah all two of them you mother fucker! You corrupt bastard!*

"Then call your first witness."

"Your honor, we call Mr. Tim Harper to the stand."

J.P. had a great deal of doubt whether Tim Harper would make a good testifying witness, as did Julius. His performance during practice was not all that great. In baseball terms he struck out every time he was asked a question. He would not follow up on the leads that Julius would give him. He wanted Julius to ask him direct questions. Julius explained to Tim that he could not get what he wanted by doing so. That he would be able to ask him some direct questions, but that he would have to take the lead and elaborate on the questions he asked.

As J.P. told me several months later, the problem with Harper was that if he elaborated on anything it made him look as if he was volunteering information. However, if Julius asked him direct questions, he could state that he was under oath and had to answer the questions.

After going through the name, occupation, where he worked, and how long he had worked for the school system, Julius got down to some of the more leading questions for Tim.

"Mr. Harper, how would you describe Mr. O'Francis and Mr. Damon's relationship?"

Tim paused in thought, longer than he should have for a key supportive witness. The one thing he could not do was spit into one of his soda bottles or cans.

He spoke slowly as he began, "I would describe his relationship as being very poor." Then he stopped, which was not what Julius wanted. He did not want to have to drag the answers out of Harper.

J.P. had a cold chill run over his body once again, even with the court room temperature a very hot 80 degrees. He knew with his first answer that Tim was not going to do him any favors. He knew what the problem was. He was on the "hot seat." He was in front of everybody. He could not use anyone to cover for him. His answers were being recorded. He had to take the lead, placing himself in direct line of fire, so to speak, something

Tim Harper did not do. There was no one else to talk for him. He had to answer the questions presented to him. Julius needed for him to go into a lot of detail about events in which he was very acquainted with.

Julius walked from one side of the witness stand to another as he waited for Tim to go on with more detail. When he didn't, he continued with his questions. He had no choice.

In an instant J.P. reflected back to the events of the baseball field and his standing in his classroom window. He knew at that moment Harper was a user and a coward, just like Decal and the rest of the staff he had worked with over the many years. He could not believe he had not seen it before. His abdomen became extremely tight as he slowly began to mentally assault himself for not seeing the big picture before that moment. He became mentally angry at himself for being used, then he spoke mentally to himself, *"Well you idiot, that is what you get for being a loyal friend, no one to blame but yourself!"*

"Mr. Harper, how would you characterize Mr. Bales' attitude toward Mr. O'Francis."

Now J.P. knew that Tim could really elaborate on this question with all the times he had seen Bales go off on J.P. singling him out, not only in conferences with Tim as a witness, but in front of the entire faculty. At least he could get an objection from the plaintiff's attorney, if he went into details.

"Well, I would say he did not like him." Then he just stopped.

J.P.'s jaws tightened as his teeth pressed together.

"Mr. Harper have you ever heard Mr. O'Francis threaten either Mr. Finkel or Mr. Bales?"

"No."

"Have you ever been in a position where Mr. Bales and Mr. O'Francis had a heated confrontation?"

"Yes sir I have." Another leading question, but nothing followed. Harper was not going to elaborate on anything. The question J.P. had to ask himself at that point was why?

"Well Mr. Harper did Mr. O'Francis ever threaten Mr. Bales in any of these confrontations?"

"No sir."

"How about Mr. Finkel? Did Mr. O'Francis ever to your knowledge threaten him?"

"No sir."

"Ever hear them get into a verbal exchange?"

"No, I don't think so."

*Christ*, J.P. thought. *What the fuck is he trying to do? Shit, he is not helping me at all!*

The same line of questioning went on for thirty more minutes, and Julius got frustrated with the manner in which Tim was not answering the questions with follow up information that could greatly help J.P.'s case. He sat down and it was Curtis Feinstein's time to cross examine, which did not take long, as he did not have to counter but just a very few questions.

"Mr. Harper, do you like Damon Bales?"

"No."

"Have you ever had any problems with Mr. Bales?"

"Yes. Matter of fact..." he was cut off with, "Just answer the question yes or no Mr. Harper."

This thought flashed through J.P.'s mind like lightning, *Jesus Christ, you want to elaborate now? What the fuck. Oh lets everybody look at poor old Tim and what Bales has done to Tim. God-damn-it. That son-of-a-bitch has totally sold me out!*

"Have you ever been in the presence of Mr. O'Francis and Mr. Bales when Mr. O'Francis was rude and insubordinate to Mr. Bales?"

Tim took another long pause before he answered.

"I really don't recall."

"Mr. Harper were you not present when Mr. O'Francis called Mr. Bales a son-of-a-bitch?"

"Well, yes. But," Curtis Feinstein did not give Tim a chance to elaborate.

"Then it is your testimony here today that you did in fact hear Mr. O'Francis insult Mr. Bales by using a word that would characterize his mother as a bitch? Answer yes or no."

Again he paused. He was caught in a typical attorney's ploy. The pause was too long for Feinstein.

His voice raised a notch, "Mr. Harper, answer the question, yes or no."

"Yes."

"This is all I have your honor." Tim Harper was dismissed. He had basically done nothing to help J.P.'s case. He could have, all he needed to do was expound on some of the lead questions Julius had asked which would have allowed Julius to extend his questions to areas of damaging testimony against Bales and Finkel. But he did not. Mr. Tim Harper, the one person who could have set the tone for the case against Finkel and Bales, had failed miserably. J.P. could tell that Julius was not a happy person. Hell, he was not a happy person. His "friend" for the past fifteen years had just shown his ability to defend the person HE claimed was his friend.

It was now 1130 A.M. and Judge Munis called for a lunch break.

Outside the courthouse, Julius, Dawn, and J.P. stood beside Julius' car talking, and Harper walked up. As J.P. looked around as Tim approached, he saw walking across the street at the end of the block, Judge Munis, Curtis Feinstein, Damon Bales, Richard Finkel, and Jarvis Griffith, by appearances laughing and having a grand time as they entered the restaurant just on the other side of the street from the courthouse.

In J.P.'s mind there was something very wrong with the picture. He became very agitated.

Tim Harper began running his mouth about himself and the case and Julius cut him to the bone. "Look, this case is not about you, Mr. Harper! It is about J.P." Then the good looking well-dressed Italian stood a foot away from Tim staring at him with a very cold expressionless face. Tim turned and walked away. J.P. looked at Dawn and then at Julius, then just a little smile broke at the corner of his mouth.

"Julius, I am going to have lunch at the Teachers' Association office. Would you like to join Dawn and I?"

"No, but thank you. I am going to have lunch with my dad. We have a few things I need to go over before this afternoon."

"Julius," then J.P. paused and stood looking into his eyes, in the 75 degree warm weather on the fourth of October. "You did what you could do with Tim. Hell, it was not your fault. He had his chance to nail their asses to the wall. Hell, I do not understand either. By all appearances today in public, it is all about Tim Harper. What can I say?"

"You can say nothing. A person would have to blind and deaf not to have seen what took place this morning with him." He then took a step away from O'Francis and then stopped and paused as if in careful thought. Then he spoke with what appeared to be with great care, "James Patrick O'Francis, I truly do hope that all your so called friends are not like that." Then he took a few more steps toward his car, stopped some ten feet from J.P. turned and stated in an emphatic manner, "You will say all you want when I call you to the stand. You are ready. I have no doubts about your testimony."

"Well we have one left. Maybe he will do better?"

"Yeah, maybe?" Julius turned to get in his car.

"Go have a good lunch, see you at 1300 hrs."

J.P. and Dawn walked the two blocks to the Teachers' Association office where Nina and Emmanuel met them for lunch. They had gone to Wendy's and picked up hamburgers and fries for all. For J.P. and Dawn, them being there was very important. For J.P. it showed that they truly were good friends. Nina had taken off work, using one of her personal leave days that even though it appeared to be a minor item, for J.P. it was major. Even though he did consider them as real friends, in the future he would become even closer to both of them and the real friendship would blossom like the flowers of the spring cherry tree, big and beautiful.

Dan Jakes had left for the day, which at that point did not surprise J.P., as his none appearance in the courtroom had set the tone as to where he fit on the scale of importance.

As he ate, his thoughts were on Dan, *That is okay, a lesson to be learned. I will make it with his support or without. He talks a good game, but he does not do much walking. But I knew that he likes the old style of politics, back room, and smoke filled, old school philosophy, which I really do not think works any more. Well, maybe it does. Hell I do not know. I know that I do not work that way. So fuck him too!*

His silence brought a question from Emmanuel. "J.P. you alright?"

"What?'

"I asked if you were alright. You have been very quiet for a good ten minutes."

"Ahhhh, just thinking. I am all right. Not to worry. But thanks for asking."

The rest of the lunch hour and a half was spent talking about the morning session and what had gone wrong with Tim's testimony, what they thought Teddy would say, and if he would help or hurt. Then of course how J.P. was going to be on the stand was hashed over.

They all arrived back at the courthouse thirty minutes before the afternoon session began, and Julius and J.P. talked over the line of questions he was going to give Teddy Hauler.

Julius stood and called his next witness, Mr. Teddy Hauler. After all the facade of swearing to God was over, Julius began his line of questions.

"Mr. Hauler, how long have you known Mr. O'Francis?"

"Twenty some odd years, I met him when he first moved to Honsburg."

"Could you tell the court how that came about?"

"Sure. I met him when he was coaching basketball, boys at the time and then got to know him even better when he took over the girls' program. That is where my sister played for him. Good coach by the way."

"Okay, have you worked with him in any other capacity?"

"Yes. I worked with him in football and in baseball. I worked with him in the training room. He was the official/unofficial athletic trainer for the football team. I use the term unofficial because the school officially does not have an athletic trainer. Well you know, they do not pay for a person to do that. He was really a good one, and I learned a lot from him. Really cared for the safety of our players, well, plus he coached the defensive backs and the offensive receivers."

Well J.P. thought, give "Humper" a lead and he will run with it.

"You stated that you also worked with him in baseball, is that correct?"

"Yes. He was the assistant to Coach Harper for ten years. Actually it was kind of like having two head coaches. Which was really good, and that is why they won so many of their games. It was very hard to outsmart both of them."

"You stated he was like a head coach, correct?"

"Yes, and he was. I mean, he really is as good a head coach as Tim, it is just that Tim has the title as the head and J.P. as his assistant. But really again I say, he was also the head coach just really hard to outsmart two head coaches." Then there was just a slight hesitation. "Ah, sure would like to see them play against each other with equal quality players. Boys, what a game that would be." Then Teddy smiled from ear to ear.

Just as Julius started to ask another question, Teddy continued. "Actually I really do not know which one is the better. Coach O'Francis is more aggressive than Coach Harper, but if they had to go head to head it really would be a real game, if they both had the same talent, that is."

"Ever hear of anyone complaining about Mr. O'Francis?"

"Meaning like players or things like that?"

"Yes," Julius stated.

"Lord no. Nor did I ever hear of any parents complaining. My God, oops sorry about that."

"That is okay, continue if you will please," Julius instructed Teddy. He did not want him to stop, he was on a roll.

"Okay, ahhh, I mean not only did the players have a great deal of respect for him, so did their parents. You know a lot of parents would come to practices, not just pick up their kid, well son, but to watch how he worked the players. Hey, a lot of these players played football also and they had been in J.P.'s training room. He cared for them. They knew it, and he was good at what he did. I will tell you this, I learned a lot from him. I have stated this more than once, and I will tell all here, I wished he had been around when I was in school."

"Mr. Hauler, have you ever heard of any official or unofficial complaints filed against Mr. O'Francis from any umpire, referee in any of the sports in which he coached?"

"No. Matter of fact in a football game at Gardner he was the only coach who did not get a flag thrown on him, and that is saying a lot considering the circumstances of the game. Now as far as baseball goes, an umpire has never even warned him. I was also with him the entire time he coached both boys' and girls' basketball and he never had a technical foul called on him. He was an emotional coach, but he knew his limits."

"You said that you have been around him in the classroom, is that correct?"

"Yes, both as a substitute as well as just sitting in on his class."

"Have you ever heard him use any language that would not be considered appropriate?"

"Not any more than I have heard from other teachers and I have been around a lot of them."

"Okay Mr. Hauler, are you aware of any parents filing any complaints about his teaching?"

"Well yes I have, but if I may, I would like to explain."

"You may, continue."

"Okay, Mr. O'Francis was not your normal type of teacher. He did not follow the usual method of teaching. He made his classes fun to be in. Matter of fact there has always been a problem of too many students wanting to be in his class and there was not enough room, well I mean seats. He was always fair with all students. It did not matter who you were or where you came from. He was a strong disciplinarian, but if you worked for him and you tried, he would grade you on your ability. Gaining Knowledge was his key concern, not finishing a textbook."

"Mr. Hauler you stated you were in the training room with Mr. O'Francis. Did you ever see or hear of him mistreating any athlete?"

"Absolutely not. He was one of the most caring coaches and trainers on the staff. He went out of his way caring for not just the boys but also the girls. He saved many knees with his treatment of the athletes. Matter of fact even after they removed him from his coaching duties, parents would call on him for advice when one of their children would get hurt either in school or outside of school. The door to his home was always open and many students graced his home for advice as well as assistance in their schoolwork."

"Did you ever hear or were you ever aware of Mr. O'Francis making or conducting any type of terrorist acts on anyone at Honsburg High School?"

"No."

J.P. had looked across the room at the three stooges. They were not smiling anymore, and they had no smirk grin on their faces. They sat with faces of gloom and doom. "Humper" was doing a number on them, with little or no prompting by Julius.

He continued with J.P. in the classroom, as he had substituted on a number of occasions for him. His praises for his ability to reach the students in and out of the classroom rolled off his tongue with great ease. The question J.P. began running through his mind was how he would handle the cross examination.

After Julius finished, Curtis Feinstein was not as quick to get up. He sat for a good thirty seconds before slowly rising and asking his questions. After the cross examination of Teddy Hauler and not tripping him up once and not getting anything negative from anything he had stated, he ended and Teddy was excused. He had been on the witness stand for a little over an hour and had not "struck out" a single time. Yet he had gotten a hit each and every time a question had been asked as he would freely elaborate on each question.

J.P. broke a small smile, as he knew that it struck a blow to the scum sitting across the room. He thought, *Your efforts to "K" Teddy failed. At the end of an inning! We scored runs. Even with Harper "K'ing" each time.*

J.P. knew he was behind in the game, and feared that he would not have enough witnesses to counter the lies that were going to be told. And in the end, it was who won the game, not just an inning.

"I would like to call Mary Jo Bankos, as my next witness."

Again they went through all the buffalo dung and Julius got down to business.

"Mrs. Bankos, on the morning of the 31 of October 1990, were you working at the corner service station and convenience store?"

"Yes I was."

"Did Mr. O'Francis come in and get gas that morning?"

"Yes he did."

"Would you tell us what took place that morning?"

'Well, I will tell you what took place inside the store. I do not know exactly what took place outside, other than I could see Mr. O'Francis and Mr. Finkel talking."

"Okay, then tell the court what took place inside the store."

"Well, Coach O'Francis got gas, and came in to pay for it. Gerry Bare was standing at the counter drinking a cup of coffee. Coach bid him a good morning and then asked him if he could not find someone better to ride with than the ass-hole he was with. I told him to be nice, and he told me he was sorry."

"Okay, what did Mr. Bare say, or did he say anything?"

'"Well, I probably will not get the words exact, but he stated that he had to get a ride with whom ever. And then, let me think, I think Coach O'Francis and Gerry just kind of talked to each other for maybe a couple of minutes and he left."

"Who left?"

"Mr. O'Francis left."

"Well was the conversation pleasant with Mr. Bare?"

"Oh, yes. They smiled and shook hands and wished each other a good day."

"Can you remember any of the conversation?"

"Well, let me think, ahhh, I am not real sure, but I remember Coach O'Francis asking him how his season was going. Ahhh, not really a lot, but they were only talking just a very few minutes."

"Mrs. Bankos, what took place then?"

"Well, I really do not know what was said, but I saw Mr. Finkel approach Coach O'Francis and they were talking for maybe five minutes, then Coach O'Francis went to his car and drove off. Oh wait a minute, Coach O'Francis took his sunglasses off and dropped them to the ground."

"Okay, and then what happened?"

"Well, nothing. I mean it appeared that words were being exchanged. Other than that, Coach picked up his glasses and went to his car."

"Where did Mr. Finkel go?"

"He came into the store to pay for the gas."

"Did he say anything?"

"Well not really, he just paid for the gas and he and Mr. Bare then left."

"Well, how did he appear to you?"

"Ahhh, well, he appeared to be a little nervous."

"How could you tell he was, as you say, a little nervous?"

"Well, his hand was shaking when he paid for his gas. He did not look real happy. He looked a little pale."

"Did he say anything to you?"

"No, just paid for the gas and left."

"Did he say anything to Mr. Bare?"

"Not while he was in the store."

"Okay, Mrs. Bankos, how long have you know Mr. O'Francis?"

"Oh, Lord, I guess for ahhh, maybe twenty years. Well, way back when he was coaching the girls' basketball. Then of course he had my sons in school and coached them and they were in his classroom also."

"Ever had any complaints about his teaching or coaching?"

"Coach O'Francis? Lord no. I have a few complaints about the principal, but not Coach O'Francis. I heard about how he was giving Coach O'Francis a hard time."

At that Feinstein spoke, "Objection your honor, hearsay."

"Sustained. The witness will not repeat what others have stated."

Okay, Mrs. Bankos, have you ever heard either Mr. Bales or Mr. Finkel make any negative comments about Mr. O'Francis?"

"Well, Mr. Bales would never talk to me anyway, but I have heard Mr. Finkel talk badly about Coach O'Francis."

"Can you remember where and what was said."

"Well, I can remember where but as to exactly what, I may miss a few words, but I can get close. That is if I am allowed?"

"Sure, go ahead, do your best, please."

Curtis Feinstein quickly objected, "Hearsay your honor."

To J.P.'s utmost surprise the Judge informed the witness that she could answer.

"Well, when my son was playing senior league and playing on Coach O'Francis' team, Mr. Finkel was there with his cousin and they were telling everyone how he was able to get Coach O'Francis removed from the high school and out of coaching and that he thought that Mr. O'Francis was a very poor teacher and a bad coach. He was not fit to be a coach at the high school. I can't remember his exact words but that was generally what he was saying."

"Mrs. Bankos, this was in public, correct?"

"Yes it was. Also he made some statements to my husband concerning Mr. O'Francis when he was coaching the high school team."

"When you say statements, what do you mean?"

Again, Feinstein objected. "Hearsay your honor."

Julius quickly informed the Judge that he would withdraw the question.

"Have you ever heard anyone complain about his teaching or coaching?"

"No. Well, I might say I have heard that he was a hard coach, a very strict discipline coach. That he demanded a lot from his players as well as his students. Well, also if I may."

"Sure, go right ahead," Julius stated as he gestured with his right hand.

"He was always fair. I mean he treated everyone equal, fair, you know what I mean."

Mr. Donatello asked, "Is that correct?"

"Yes, that is correct. Can I state what I heard Mr. MacNolin say about Coach O'Francis?"

"Were you present at the time of the conversation Mrs. Bankos?"

"Yes I was."

"Okay, continue."

Again to J.P.'s surprise Feinstein did not object.

"Well, when my husband and I were at a girls' softball game, we were standing next to MacNolin and Richard and Stan..."

Julius interrupted her. "Who is Stan?"

"Oh I am sorry, that is Mr. MacNolin."

"Okay, continue."

"Anyway, Stan was talking to Richard and Richard told him that he and Mr. Bales had plans that would mark the doom for Coach O'Francis as a coach and a teacher at Honsburg. That they had everything in order and that they may need his help if need be."

"How did Mr. MacNolin respond to his statement?"

"He stated that he did not like Coach O'Francis and that he had tried to get him to do what they had planned, but that he would not admit that he had said anything bad about Richard when they were at the barn."

"Do you know what he was referring to?" Julius asked.

"Not really but he did say that he had his tape recorder going and that he would have bet that O'Francis would have admitted to what he had heard."

"Mrs. Bankos when you stated, what he had heard, who was the he?"

"That would be Stan. Stan was telling Coach O'Francis what he had heard."

"When was that?"

"I don't know. But I heard that..."

"Objection your honor she cannot testify to something that she heard or learned through hearsay from someone else."

"Mrs. Bankos, you can only testify to what you yourself have heard." The Judge told her.

"Mrs. Bankos did you ever hear Mr. Bare make any negative statements about Mr. O'Francis?"

"No. I do know that he liked him and he always stated that he really knew his baseball. That he had heard that he was a really good basketball coach. That he was a winner and that the school was lucky that they had him as a coach. He did tell Dallas, my husband, that he was an extremely good teacher and that the students really liked him."

"Thank you, I have no further questions at this time." Julius turned and went to his seat.

Curtis Feinstein slowly got up from his table and slowly walked in front of Mary Jo Bankos.

"Mrs. Bankos, in all these years you have never heard anyone say anything about Mr. O'Francis in a negative way?"

"No."

"Are you sure?"

"Yes. Well other than he was a hard teacher and coach. But not that he was bad or anything like that."

"Has anyone ever complained about his classroom teaching methods?"

"To me personally?"

"Yes."

"No. But I have heard that others have, but the judge told me I could not tell what I heard from others. Right your honor?" She asked as she looked directly at Judge Minus.

"Okay, Mrs. Bankos let's focus on the day of the incident at the service station. Was there anyone else in the store at the time Mr. O'Francis came in the store to pay for his gas?"

"Mr. Bare."

"Okay. Was there anyone else in the store?"

"Yes."

"Who?"

"Mrs. Joan Dobson. But she was in the back of the store putting up stock, and-

Feinstein cut her off. "Mrs. Bankos, Mrs. Dobson ever come into the part of the store where you, Mr. O'Francis, and Mr. Bare were?"

"No."

"How can you be sure she did not hear the entire conversation?"

"Well, because you just can't when you are in the supply room."

"But you are not sure that Mrs. Dobson did not come into the store part where she could hear, are you?"

"Well, yes, I am pretty sure."

"But not positive, right?"

"Well, I think."

"Yes or no, Mrs. Bankos."

"Yes."

"Okay Mrs. Bankos, you have stated that you have known Mr. O'Francis for a long time. Has he ever stated to you or your husband that he didn't like Mr. Finkel or Mr. Bales?"

"No. Not to my knowledge. Now as to Dallas, you would have to ask him. I do know that there are a lot of people unhappy about him being removed from the high school and from coaching. I am not happy about it either."

"I have no more questions your Honor."

"Your Honor." Julius rose quickly. "I have one more question for Mrs. Bankos."

"Mrs. Bankos, you stated yes, that you were not sure if Mrs. Dobson came into the store from the supply room. Is that correct?"

Mary Jo paused as she processed the question. "I tried to say, that I think I would have noticed her if she had come into the store from the supply room because you can see from the counter to the door of the supply room."

"Did you see her come into the store from the supply room while any of the conversation between Mr. O'Francis, Mr. Bare, Mr. Finkel and you were taking place?"

"No sir, I did not."

"So, it is safe to say that Mrs. Dobson did not know that any of the men involved in this conversation was ever in the store?"

"She didn't. They were gone before she was done putting up the supplies and came out to the counter."

"Thank you, Mrs. Bankos. I have no further questions."

The Judge looked over to Feinstein.

"Do you have any further questions?"

"I have nothing further your honor."

"You may step down," the Judge stated.

Julius walked to the table were J.P. sat. "Are you ready?"

"Well, since I am all that is left, I guess I had better be. Let's do our thing."

"Remember, J.P., relax, you know they will come after you."

J.P. spent the greater part of the afternoon on the witness stand going through a multitude of questions and elaborating on each of them in hopes that the jury understood why he was suing them for tainting his name. Julius worked him to perfection and J.P. took each lead as it was handed to him.

As Julius ended J.P. injected in a timely fashion, "My father gave me this name without spot or blemish. I have passed my name to my sons without any blemish, and now because of many false allegations, it now has been stained. What's in a name is not just a bunch of words slung together. It is very important to me as it was to my father and to his father and to his father who arrived in this country in 1872 without any blemishes on the O'Francis name."

The cross examination by Feinstein was harsh and he did everything he could to trip J.P. He came at him soft and then hard, redirecting several questions in hopes that J.P. would falter, but he did not. He remained very calm and even as physically hot as it was, he did not so much as break a bead of sweet on his brow which, unlike Feinstein, who on several occasions had to wipe his forehead. As the five o'clock hour approached Feinstein finished his cross examining of J.P. and the Judge adjourned court for the day leaving Feinstein to call his first witness at 9:00 A.M. on the second day of the trial.

The next morning found J.P. in an ill mood as he had gotten little sleep over the night. He did not have a good feeling and his little voice kept telling him to prepare himself for the worst.

Julius seemed to be in a pleasant mood and his father was present at the same place he was the day before. But there was no Hope present, something J.P. was extremely disappointed in, as he did not think that Julius would have the same impact on Damon as Hope would have in his cross examination. After all the buffalo chips was over, the Judge asked if the defense was ready to call their first witness and he informed the judge that he was.

"The defense calls Mrs. Janice Jones."

J.P.'s eyes narrowed as Janice bounced into the courtroom and took her seat on the stand.

*Ah, yes, their key witness, he thought. The one person who was supposed to have so much information concerning me that she is their major contributor to this case. Now if that is not just a major pile of camel dung! Key witness my ass! Hell, she is part of the whole damn conspiracy. She has been from the day I started in this damn corrupt frigging county! Now you, bitch, I could pop a cap on you here and now and sleep much better tonight!*

After she swore to tell the truth and nothing but the truth, Curtis Feinstein started his questions. J.P.'s thoughts raced like a modern high tech computer. *Now if that just ain't a joke. Hell it's done in every courtroom in the entire country. Do you swear and all in the name of God. Hell that is no different than the real terrorist of the world, killing hundreds in the name of Allah. Shit, lies are told in volumes on the witness stand. Just her sitting there is a lie! Damn, I hate the hypocrisy in our system! The people just buy into all this shit! And all this legal crap is based on the good ole holy bible. What a pile of dung!*

They went through all the information about her name, where she lived, for how long, and all the useless information that is spouted in court cases. Did she know the plaintiff...how long, da,da,da,...

"In your own words, tell the court a little about your relationship with Mr. O'Francis."

"Objection your honor. Relevance."

"I will allow it."

"Well, I can tell you that he caused a lot of trouble from the time he arrived at Honsburg High School. He did not get along with any of the teachers. He was not well liked among the staff as well as the administration. He was always in trouble with the administration."

"Mrs. Jones, what do you mean, he was in trouble with the administration?"

"Well, he did not follow the rules the administration set for the teachers in the school. He would be called to the office a lot for breaking the rules. He would have trouble with parents of the students."

"Objection your honor. She cannot possible know if he violated any rules or had trouble with any parent or parents unless she was directly involved as an administrator."

"Overruled, you may answer the question."

"The principals would have to have parents come to the school because he would not teach the same way as the rest of us. Oh and he would use foul language all the time."

"Objection, your honor. She cannot possible know if Mr. O'Francis allegedly used foul language in class."

"Overruled."

"Where would he use this foul language?"

"In his classroom, oh and on the basketball court."

"Object your honor. She was not present in all these places."

"Overruled."

"Did you hear Mr. O'Francis use any of this foul language?"

"Yes."

"Where did you hear him use this foul language?"

"While he was coaching basketball."

"Mrs. Jones, did you have any personal conflicts with Mr. O'Francis?"

"Yes."

"Tell the court about some of these conflicts."

"Objection your honor. This has nothing to do with this case."

Fienstein turned to the judge and quickly spoke, "Your honor it speaks to the character of the plaintiff."

"Overruled." Judge Minus quickly replied. "You may answer the question."

After a very long oratory of all the terrorist acts done to her family and others, and with a multitude of objections, she was allowed to continue with the character assassination of J.P.

Again Julius objected. "Your honor, Mr. O'Francis is not on trial here for these alleged terrorist acts. This is about a letter that the defendant has written."

Nevertheless, the judge overruled the objection once again.

"Mrs. Jones, did you report all these incidents to the police?"

"Yes, we reported all this to the police. As did others." She looked over to Julius and stated, "And, yes I happen to know that for a fact."

Julius objected, but nothing was done.

"They never did arrest him for any of it. We even called the FBI and reported it. They, I guess, investigated Mr. O'Francis."

"Mrs. Jones do you know where Mr. O'Francis is from?"

Donatello stood and in a more than normal tone and volume in his voice stated, "Objection your honor!" In a more than demanding voice he continued, "I really do not see the relevance in where Mr. O'Francis is from."

Judge Munis paused before he ruled. "Sustained." J.P. knew where Feinstein was heading with his question. O'Francis was from the Detroit metropolitan area, and he wanted the jury to get the idea that O'Francis was connected to the Mob in some manner as the people in the area thought that all mob connections were in Detroit, New York, or Chicago, and really knew nothing about them other than what they may have seen on television, which would have given the jury the idea that Jones' testimony had some credibility.

Feinstein took his time, and the questions went on for close to two hours, with Janice character assassinating J.P. with every word she spoke. The question in J.P.'s mind was, is the jury buying into all the garbage she was dumping out? None of it had anything to do with why the case was in court. But, if they were buying her tales of woe, then the case was doomed from the get-go. If they found that all she stated could not have been true or even a part of it, then he had a fighting chance. He tried to read the faces of each juror.

The cross examination was rather short, shorter than J.P. would have liked.

"Mrs. Jones, was Mr. O'Francis ever arrested for these alleged acts you have stated to the court?"

"No. But that..."

"Did the FBI ever contact you concerning these alleged acts?"

"No. But let me…"

"So you don't know for sure if it was Mr. O'Francis that committed any of these acts of, as you have stated here today under oath and to the this court, terrorism?"

"Well," Julius interrupted her. "Yes or no, Mrs. Jones."

"Well, ah, no, but…"

"Mrs. Jones." Julius continued before she could finish whatever she was going to say. "Were you present at any time during any of the alleged threats made by Mr. O'Francis to Mr. Finkel at the service station?"

"No."

"Have you seen the letter that Mr. Bales wrote and sent to all the law enforcement agencies throughout the area?"

"No."

"Mrs. Jones, have you ever been present at any time when Mr. O'Francis verbally threatened either Mr. Bales or Mr. Finkel?"

"I have heard a lot of people-"

"Mrs. Jones, have you been present, at any time, when Mr. O'Francis allegedly threatened either Mr. Bales or Mr. Finkel ? Answer yes or no." Julius voice was stern and commanding as if he was totally agitated.

"Ahh, no."

"Mrs. Jones, have you ever seen Mr. O'Francis at any time anywhere around your home, your farm, or any vehicle that you or your husband owns?"

"Well, no but…"

Julius sharply cut her off. "So you cannot testify here on this day in this court of law that any of these alleged acts of terrorism that you claim took place was done by my client, Mr. James Patrick O'Francis?" Julius' voice was up another notch and even more stern, as he pointed to J.P.

"Mr. ahhh," Janice did not know his last name.

Julius, again with a sharp tone, asked her to answer the question with a simple yes or no.

"NO." Janice was pissed. The tone of her answer gave her away. Her body language was very evident as she had begun to move her shoulders in the normal manner in which she usually did when she was verbalizing anger.

"Were you aware of any of the activities that took place in Mr. Bales' office, or were you aware that Mr. Bales ever wrote or sent any letter concerning Mr. O'Francis to the School Board, law enforcement agencies, or judges surrounding this case?"

"Ahhh, NO." Again, her tone of voice was filled with anger. She was not allowed to verbally continue, which was her normal mode of operation.

"Mrs. Jones, has Mr. O'Francis ever personally threatened you?"

"Well, let me tell you…"

Again, Julius cut her off. "Answer the question Mrs. Jones with a simple yes or no."

"I would like to tell you…"

Julius interrupted her quickly. "Mrs. Jones I asked you a question. Give me a yes or no answer."

Janice puffed up like a toad, and sat silent.

"Your Honor, would you please instruct the witness to answer the question."

"Mrs. Jones, you have to answer the question." His voice was not one of a stern judge, but of a more polite, "Would you please?" tone to it. One that J.P. took note of instantly. It appeared to J.P. that the Judge was reluctant to instruct Janice to answer the question. However, J.P. had already resigned himself to the fact that the Judge was impartial in the case. Something he would learn later.

"I would like to but he won't let me."

J.P. was not at all surprised at her comment to the Judge.

At that point, Julius stated, "Your Honor."

Judge Minus, in what appeared to be a nice tone, instructed Janice to answer the questions as presented.

Feinstein rose at that point and stated that Julius was harassing his witness. To J.P.'s surprise Judge Minus dismissed the objection.

"Now, Mrs. Jones let me ask you again. Did Mr. O'Francis, at any time, during the time you and he worked in the same school, ever threaten you?"

"NO!"

Julius turned to the Judge. "You honor I have no further questions for this witness. I do reserve the right to recall her."

"You may step down Mrs. Jones," Judge Munis stated.

Feinstein quickly rose from his seat. "Your Honor, the defense calls Mr. Stan MacNolin to the stand."

After all the I swear to God crap, who he was, as well as who he worked for and where he lived was through, Feinstein started his questions.

"Mr. MacNolin, have you ever had any private conversations with Mr. O'Francis?"

"Yes."

"If you would, tell the court where and what was discussed."

"Well, Mr. O'Francis came to my horse barn one evening and we were talking about my horses as I knew that he liked horses. We started talking about the school system and he just started talking about Mr. Finkel and the affair he had been having with Ms. Alcott and how he thought that it was wrong for teachers to have affairs while working in the same school."

"What did you say when he told you about this alleged affair?"

"I told him that I did not believe that Richard and Maura were having any affair."

"What was Mr. O'Francis' reply to your disagreeing with his allegation?"

"He told me that he had proof of the affair and that it was a fact."

"Mr. MacNolin, do you have any children who have played under Mr. O'Francis' direction?"

"Yes."

"How many?"

"One."

"Would you tell the court what kind of coach he was?"

MacNolin went through all the dislikes of J.P.'s coaching and his teaching, more of the same type of character assassination Jones had uttered from her mendacious mouth.

Again Julius objected to MacNolin knowing what went on in O'Francis' classroom, as it was from his son's perspective.

"Sustained."

"Okay, are you aware of any problems with Mr. O'Francis in the classroom?"

"Object, your Honor, that would be hearsay."

"Sustained."

Curtis Feinstein started to his table and turned. "I have one more question. Mr. MacNolin, have you and Mr. Harper ever had any discussions concerning Mr. O'Francis' coaching?"

"Yes."

"Would you tell the court about what was discussed?"

"Well, Mr. Harper told me that he was disappointed in his conduct and that he was becoming an embarrassment to him and the school. That he had to talk to him on several occasions about how he acted."

"Did Mr. Harper ever tell you that he had to report this conduct to the principal or the athletic director?"

"Yes."

"No further questions at this time your Honor."

Julius turned to J.P. and asked, "Are you aware of any of this?"

"Some."

Judge Dan Munis looked at Julius. "Do you wish to cross examine Mr. MacNolin?"

"Yes your Honor. One moment please."

"Some, what does that mean?" Julius asked O'Francis.

"It simply means that the only thing in the entire testimony that had any truth in it, to my knowledge, was that I did go to the horse barn, just as I have stated in my testimony to Feinstein. As to anything else I have no knowledge what so ever. And I repeat myself here Julius, I did not have any conversation concerning Maura Alcott with Stan at the barn or anywhere else. Julius, that just did not, happen. Fact!"

Julius rose slowly but stayed at the table beside J.P.

"Mr. MacNolin, do you like Mr. O'Francis?"

"Well, I don't know."

"Well, either you do or you don't, which is it?"

"Well, I guess I would say I don't."

"How often did you talk to Mr. O'Francis?"

"Very little."

"So, you could say you really do not know him very well, do you?"

"Ahhh, well, no I don't guess so."

"Did you attend all your son's home games?"

"Yes and several that were away."

"Have you ever seen Coach O'Francis thrown out of a game?"

"I don't think so."

"Have you ever seen him in an angry confrontation with an umpire?"

"Ahh, I don't believe I have."

"You don't think so? Either you have Mr. McNolin or you have not. Which is it?"

"Well I would have to say no."

"Have you ever seen or have you ever been present when Coach Harper had to confront Coach O'Francis about anything he may or may not have done during the course of a game or at any practices?"

There was a rather long pause as if Stan was thinking.

Julius did not let it linger. "Your answer please, Mr. McNolin."

"Ahhh, no I don't believe I have."

"Mr. MacNolin, have you seen the letter Mr. Bales and Mr. Finkel wrote concerning Mr. O'Francis?"

"No."

"Did your son ever tell you that he did not like Coach O'Francis?"

"Ahhh, no."

"Did he ever complain about him as a teacher?"

"No."

"What kind of grades did he make under Mr. O'Francis?"

"Good ones."

"What does that mean, good ones? Give me a letter grade so the jury can understand what you mean by good ones."

"He made A's and B's in his class."

"So you can testify here today that you had no complaints concerning Mr. O'Francis teaching your son?"

"Well, not really. But I heard..."

"Thank you. I have no more questions for the witness at this time."

Judge Munis excused MacNolin from the stand.

After going through both Bales' mentally deranged skewed testimony as well as Finkel's, which took up the rest of the day, the trial was done and all that remained was the closing by both attorneys. Julius' cross examination of both was done fairly well, but not as well as Hope Donatello's would have been. Julius did not have the skills to bring the very worst out of Damon or for that that matter, Finkel. She was a very skilled attorney and could set one up with her questions and have you telling the lies that they themselves thought to be the truth, revealing the person, who they really were. However, there was nothing J.P. could do about her absence. He just had to go with what cards he had in his hand and hope that Julius could win the game with his closing statement.

# Judges and Jurors

THE JUDGES HAD DONE THEIR jobs. They had communicated with each other, as they had done in other cases, and the Clerk of the Reynolds County Court provided them with a reward of a small bit of graft. The amount was nothing compared to larger and more important cases, which he had done for both judges depending on who was sitting on the Circuit Court bench at the time, and of course depending on the person or persons involved in the case before either judge. Never the less, a little cash in the pocket never seemed to bother either of the Judges or Jarvis, who got a moderate fee for his part in making sure that certain cases went the way of the cash flow.

Of course for Judge MacMuller, his situation was just a little different. He was in debt up to his eyeballs from his divorce from his lovely wife, of which was questionable as to the lovely part, that was not of a mutual agreement. The ugly surfaced in both of them, and their pompous snobbiness seemed to dissipate if for only a short while. The divorce left him rather short of money, something he was not accustomed to, not even as he grew up from childhood as he had come from a very prominent political family who had obtained their wealth from the hard work of their father, who made it big in the coal field. Judge Daniel MacMuller had been deep in the pockets of the heavy hammers of the political party of Reynolds County and had been well taken care of by a few of the larger and more powerful companies located within the county. The counties surrounding Reynolds also had a few large companies that paid a rather nice fee for services to the

Judge when cases came before him. So, taking graft for making the law work for whoever could afford the cost for blind justice had slowly become a source of substantial income.

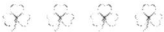

Judge Dan Munis had his own closet of secrets. His drug and prostitute habit grew with each passing year and his lucrative salary for sitting on the bench was being strained to the max. The extra payments for favorites passed on in the name of blind justice, be it large or small, was all welcomed.

The jury had been given their instructions from the Judge, of which J.P. was savvy enough to have caught the intent of his instructions and knew that his case was in the "shitter," depending on whether or not there were any honest people on the jury, and that was very unlikely, J.P. calculated. As Judge Munis finished his "little according to the law" instructions, he looked over at J.P., who had locked his eyes on the Judge. For just a mere moment Dan Munis paused in speech and movement as O'Francis' cold hard look caught his attention. At that moment J.P. knew that he knew. But J.P. also knew that he had the power, and that was all that mattered, no matter how small and insignificant his case may be. Judge Munis' pompous attitude quickly returned as he instructed the jurors to retire to the jury room.

The five jurors rose and strolled out to a conference room beside the Judge's office. O'Francis took a deep breath and looked over at his family. He scanned the room and saw that Holly had arrived after it was all was over. No consolation for J.P., who at that point was in no mood for her conversation and for that matter, outside of his family he really did not care to talk to anyone. For all his earlier beliefs in Holly and her family of attorneys, he felt betrayed by the lack of interest in his simplyecivil suit and the fact that they used him to get the newest member of the firm some experience other than court appointed cases.

He wandered off to himself for a short period of time to gather his thoughts and to mentally prepare himself for the outcome that his little voice was telling him would be. *It is human nature for people to be corruptible,* he thought. His little voice continued to talk to him telling him that everything about the trial had been corrupted. It would not have made any difference if he had had F. Lee Bailey as his attorney, the die had been cast. This was Reynolds County and it had earned its reputation long before his little case had made its way to the courtroom. Clerks, attorneys and judges, they all were tainted, and J.P. O'Francis' belief in honor and integrity in the judicial system was as dissipating as a fart in the wind.

Inside the jury room a problem seemed to have arisen. All the jurors did not seem to adhere to what the Judge had instructed them to consider. For two of the jurors, the fact that the letter was written and that it was sent was enough to cast their vote for J.P. The other three insisted that the Judge instructed them to consider the fact that O'Francis still had his teaching job and that he had not really lost any significant money from his family income.

For Jarvis, who was now in the Judge's office, stated that he felt that it had gone well and that the verdict would come quickly. Then he and Judge Munis laughed.

Inside the jury room the conversation continued.

"Look, the principal, what's his name?" Harold asked.

"Damon Bales." Tamura replied.

"What he did was out and out wrong. Hell, I sure would not like for someone to write a letter to all the police forces and tell them I was a terrorist. Look people, in this day and time police take that kind of stuff real serious."

"I think he brought it on himself," Tamura stated.

"How?"

"Well according to the testimony of that Jones woman..."

She was cut off by Pauline. "You know people, you may believe her if you want. But for me, I think she lied through her teeth! Just something about her. I just don't believe a word she said. My vote stays the same. Also, how in the world did she get involved in this case anyway? I mean, wasn't the case about the letter? All she did was lambast Mr. O'Francis, right?"

"I have to agree with Pauline," Harold said. "I think several people lied for Bales. And another thing, isn't lying under oath some kind of a crime? I mean you take an oath to tell the truth on the witness stand, right? I think I heard that somewhere."

Several moments passed and no one commented on the lying aspect of the question.

"I just don't think Mr. O'Francis was damaged all that much from just a single letter. I mean he still has his job. Right?" Randall stated.

J.P. paced back and forth from outside the building to the long corridor that led past the offices and the courtroom. The entire Donatello legal counsel was now present in the corridor. J.P. talked a few minutes, then walked and got some fresh air. He was still running the whole ordeal over in his mind. Every word the witnesses said, he was good at remembering what people said. The way Julius handled the case. The fact that Holly just could not be present on the day they put Damon on the stand. The entire thing began to smell of a dead fish.

He rested his hands on the gray painted rail that connected the build-ing and led some ten feet out toward the parking lot. Stepping back several steps, leaving his hands on the rail, J.P. stretched his back. Several upper disks popped as he arched his body down between his arms. His little voice was telling him that the day was not going to end good for him. He should be mentally prepared for the worse. *Fuck! I just do not like the way Julius handled the entire frigging thing! What the fuck! His first real case or was it the fact that I just would not settle with what the son-of-bitches were offering me to settle out of court?*

Then he began to speak aloud very softly to himself. "I really do not give a royal rat's ass what they think. I know that Julius damn sure did not do all that he could have done. I wonder just why all my witnesses were left off the fucking list! I mean come on here. Would not a good attorney have all that shit checked and double-checked? I tell you something is just not right! And why did he not present the poster, the pictures..."

It was a good thing no one was present, or they would have thought J.P. had lost his mind because he was talking to someone that was damn sure not present, or at least not anyone else that would have seen him and heard the conversation. He walked his feet forward, standing erect. He looked out over the back side of the town and the business and government building with people coming and going all with their own problems. He turned sharply to his right. He went back in the building to put on his best political face, telling himself all the time to choose his words with care. He tried staying close to his wife and sons. That way he was less likely to speak ill of his counsel or any member of the counsel's family.

Jarvis had left for a good 45 minutes, and returned to the Judge's office.

"What the hell. I know it don't take that long to find in favor of Defense. Hell-O, Dan, did they not get what you were telling them? This was to be a done deal. Who did we miss?"

"The We part is, I don't know. The question is who did you miss? There are no we in that." As Judge Munis curtly corrected the clerk of the court.

"Well you know what I mean."

"I will admit this is taking a little longer than I expected," Munis confessed.

"Hell, people! This is a simple civil case, not a murder case, what's the problem? Look, I want to go home. It's late, we have gone over this too many times already," Kermit stated in a strong voice.

"I really don't care. I think the letter is damaging!" Pauline insisted.

"Look Pauline," Randall stated, trying to plead with her to vote in favor of the defense so they could get out and go home. "O'Francis is really not out of anything. He has not lost his job, I mean, as I have stated several times now, as has Kermit. He still has his teaching job. Now if he lost his job, and all that, then I would be all for you. But, there is no real damage done. Right?"

Harold left most of the talking to everyone else in the room. Pauline was doing his talking, and he felt she was right, so he felt no need in repeating the same thing she was stating.

"So Harold, you have not said anything in a long while. What do you say? You are voting with the rest of us, right?" Tamura asked.

"I keep thinking about what he said when he was on the stand."

"He who?" Tamura stated in an agitated voice.

"O'Francis."

"Okay, so what?" Kermit said.

"He stated that a name is special, that our name is special. That to tarnish that name is damaging. I know it's not his exact words, but something like that. Oh yeah, and what was that about his father passed it to him and he wanted to pass it to his sons. Oh yeah and with a clean slate."

"So, what's your point?" Tamura stated, her voice displaying her dislike for the long debate.

The room was very quiet for several minutes.

"Okay, Tamura, I don't think you will ever understand his point. But you know, I do. But for the sake of dragging this out any longer…"

It had been three hours since the jury had been deliberating. J.P. had just returned from another walk outside and had sat by his sons and wife when

Officer Kuntz came out into the hallway and announced that the jury was returning. Last scene of a five-year play, one that J.P. had not liked, and would not likely ever be in the presence of again.

J.P. was standing at parade rest alongside Julius. Judge Dan Munis asked, "Has the jury reached a verdict?"

"We have your Honor."

"You may read the verdict."

"We the juries find in favor of the defense."

J.P. never moved. The gang of Jackals celebrated with their friends and witnesses. His little voice had tried to prepare him, and yet he was crushed inside. His outer demeanor was professional, never expressing any emotion.

The clerk rushed to the Judge and handed him a piece of paper and spoke with him for a moment. Judge Munis looked over toward Julius and J.P., and then requested that Julius approach.

J.P. was still standing at parade rest, motionless. He slowly turned his head toward his family and their faces told how they felt. His eyes shifted to the back of the courtroom. "The Man" and O'Donovan were standing separated on the long benches in the courtroom, one at the far end next to the wall and the other at the entrance to the courtroom, both looking toward J.P., neither one showing as if either knew him.

Julius returned to the table. "We need to talk in a room in the back." Julius requested that his father join them, as they made their way to a conference room. After they sat Julius asked, "J.P. did you discuss Richard Finkel's alleged affair openly in your classroom?"

"No. Why?"

"Because the clerk presented this letter to the judge."

He handed the letter to J.P. to read. He quickly read it. A student, one that had never been in any of his classes signed it. Jenny Bosworth claimed that J.P. had talked to his History class about Finkel and Maura Alcott.

J.P. exploded. He held the letter up toward Julius and Lucius and stated loudly, "This is a god-damn lie!"

"All that may be true, but you are going to be investigated for perjury by the Commonwealth attorney."

"I, am going to be investigated for PERJURY? Is this some kind of sick damn joke?"

"Not so loud J.P., someone will hear you. The Judge is in the next room."

"Well, Julius, at this point I really do not give a damn! Go tell the "good" judge to come in here and I will state the same to his corrupt face!"

Julius and Lucius just looked at one another.

J.P. tossed the letter toward Julius. It slid to him on the shiny, highly polished table.

"Another thing Julius!" In an instant his voice had turned to a very calm and deadly cold tone. "Jenny Bosworth was never in my class. So how did she hear me discuss anything she claimed in her letter to Mr. Finkel?"

"Well, I don't know that J.P. All I know is that the clerk informed the Judge that you had committed perjury during your testimony."

"The clerk told the Judge? Now I am not in a really good, frame of mind now. But how in the hell would the CLERK know if I had or had not committed perjury? I mean can you tell me that!"

"No, J.P. I cannot."

"Well Mr. Lucius Donatello, you are the experienced one here, can you tell me?"

"No Mr. O'Francis, I cannot."

"Well, I am telling YOU, AND YOU," O'Francis indicated with a nod of his head to both the Donatello attorneys. "That I did not commit perjury! FACT! Now IF there is anyone in this GREAT judicial system that really wants to find the REAL truth, and find who really did commit perjury, then they only need to look as far as Bales, Finkel and their witnesses! BUT, we all know that, that just ain't going to happen! Hey, let me tell you two something, let them investigate me. Hell it will not be the first time I have been investigated. I have been cleared each time. You know why? Because I tell the truth and that gentleman is the real problem in this great judicial system we have!"

Then there was a rather long pause. "Let me end this little meeting by stating I will never make this mistake again! Never!" Then he stood.

Just as he began to turn, the elder of the Donatello legal minds spoke. "Mr. O'Francis, may I ask what you mean?"

"What I mean what?"

"With the statement, you will never make this mistake again."

J.P. took several steps around the corner of the table toward the two attorneys, and in a very low unemotional voice stated, "It is quite simple Mr. Donatello. I will be the legal system. I will receive a rightful justice. Your system is corrupted. I may not be some great legal mind, but even this simple teacher can see through this."

In a quick defense of the great legal system the United States has in place, Julius spoke. "It is better than any place else in the world, Mr. O'Francis."

"That Mr. Julius Donatello is very debatable! Sir!"

J.P. left the two attorneys that day, in the hopes that he would only have to meet one more time to discuss if he wanted to appeal the verdict in his case, which he could not afford, and if he could, the outcome would be the same, because in J.P.'s mind it would still be the same corrupt judicial system.

# The Insanity of War

O'FRANCIS MIND COULD NOT LET the events of the day go and his night was filled with the events of anger and violence. His psychologist had told him that anger, fear and guilt were the results of his nightmares. J.P. did not always agree with what his mental doctor had to say, although she was a renowned expert in her field. His reaction to the death of Rusty still, after so many years, haunted his nights and out of all the horrors of Vietnam he had experienced, the one that seemed to reoccur more often, the death of his closest friend. Although his nightmares had not been occurring as often over the past several years, his own personal analysis was because he had not been under any work related stress.

He still had no clue as to what triggered his nightmares. It did not make sense to O'Francis. If nightmares were triggered because of anger, fear or guilt, how could one explain away the fact that there were times when he would have a good day, filled with happiness, lots of smiles and laughter, joy and love, always coming home to a wife that he adored and knew she loved and supported him, but yet, in the middle of what had started out as a peaceful night's sleep, he would experience the sights, sounds, and smells of Viet Nam, finding himself on the floor beside his bed in the prone position in a cold sweat, breathing heavily, looking across a dark room for something that was not there?

Another simple mission, recon an area that really did not need to be reconned or so O'Francis thought. Hell everyone knew who and what was there. But someone, some big ass brass bastard needed the information, the "Spooks" the good ole military intelligences. SOG, CIA ran the operation. They needed this very important information. Pure bullshit O'Francis thought as he readied himself for a four-day trek through the fuck'en jungle, which often times more than not turned out to be more than four days. He had been in an ill mood for over a month. He had no one to talk to, so he bottled everything up inside. He spoke to no one, did his job with reckless disregard for his life.

The orders were to "nab" a VC, or even better a North Vietnamese Regular, preferably an officer. Captain Thompson's last words to O'Francis was not to take any unnecessary chances. He himself was not all that sure that it was all that important. Just get what you can and get the hell out of the valley. It was not a good place to be, as the activity was heavy and everyone knew it. Two Americans, one Special Force staff sergeant named Michael Grooms from Georgia and one Ranger, along with four well trained "Yard's" left the compound on a mission of doom for O'Francis.

It was near nightfall when they lifted off from camp, a very short flight, and by darkness they were in position for their first night under a star filled sky, if one could see the little twinkles in the sky from the depth of a heavy jungle canopy. He had gotten to the point that everything bothered him. The bugs, which had not really bothered him before, or so he had thought, seemed to just irritate him more than ever. Sounds, any sound bothered him. He would snap at the "Yards" when they asked him questions for guidance. Then he would apologize moments later, realizing what he had done. He knew they had lost much more than he had, but yet he just could not let it go. As he lay silent on the floor of the jungle, the anger built inside. He got little sleep when he was in camp, and on patrol he could not rest at all. Not that one could rest on patrol, but one learned that you got what you could when and where you could.

Day light and they were up and moving like some camouflaged jungle cat searching out their prey. One enemy patrol passed after another, unknowing that they were being watched, all wearing black, hauling their supplies from one point to another. Deeper and deeper they went into the mouth of the valley of doom. It was truly insane what they were doing, but *"It was very important now,"* to get a live North Vietnamese Regular. O'Francis thought as yet another patrol passed within a few feet of him, *like the son of bitch is really going to tell "whomever" anything.*

Grooms was not at all happy about the mission himself. He was a veteran Special Forces sergeant on his third tour. He knew how O'Francis felt about it, but they were good soldiers, and did what they were told. The odds were that IF they could nab one, and they would, because they were good at playing the game of guerrilla warfare, as good if not better than the very people who they played against, "they" wouldn't get "jack" out of him.

Day two and day three were repeats of day one. No Regulars. If none decided to stroll by, they would have to settle for a simple V.C. Something they knew they could get in places a hell of a lot safer. Not that they ever went anywhere safe, but there were worse places to be caught in a firefight then others, and a hell of a lot easier to nab a simple V.C. Now getting a Regular, and an officer to boot, well then one must go where the "big dogs" ran. The next big problem was picking a very small patrol. Which was not all that easy, and from where they were, getting out after a firefight, even a small one, did not have the best of odds, something Jim was sure the odd makers would not place their money down on.

It was very late in the afternoon. O'Francis had just looked at his watch, 1715 hours, when movement was spotted. Again they prepared for the snatch, and as "luck" would have it, if one would like to consider having a ten man patrol with three North Vietnamese Officers in the very middle of the patrol, "luck," then the "Sheep Dog" patrol were the luckiest bunch of guerrilla fighters that ever rolled the dice.

O'Francis' eyes got big, and his heart began to pound heavily when he saw the three tan uniforms trimmed in red stroll by. The "Cong" wore sandals, the Regular's wore boots. Everyone down to the last man knew just what to do. The trap, so to speak, was sprung. A very short firefight and all three Regulars were now officially POW's. One was wounded in his right upper thigh and lower left abdomen. The other two were unharmed. Two V.C. were also captured, but they were not needed, and O'Francis was in no mood for any of their mouth. Nor was he about to drag five POW's through an enemy infested jungle just so some starched fatigued high ranking numb nutted, pencil dicked officer could interrogate them, and get squat. Without warning he drew his .45 from his shoulder holster and walked up to the two V.C. and popped a cap on each, "dead" center of the forehead, and replaced his pistol in his black shoulder holster. He reached his right hand to his upper left shoulder and removed his knife from the black leather sheath. Placing the blade against the side of the dead V.C.'s right head he sliced the right ear off like a surgeon with a scalpel. He repeated the same to the second one and replaced the knife in the sheath, then he turned and walked ten feet to the wounded North Vietnamese Regular officer.

Grooms quickly moved to his side and in a low voice asked, "O'Francis, what the hell are you doing? For Christ sakes man."

O'Francis' eyes told him everything. There was nothing there. An abyss of darkness.

He turned to face Timothy M. Grooms and in a very low voice that had no feeling in it at all he answered, "This is personal! It's for Rusty. We will have two to haul back, for who the fuck ever!"

As the two stood a few feet away from the NVA officer, he spoke, "Ban lâ nguoi lay-tai" (*You are the ear taker.*) The officer spoke in Vietnamese in a painful voice.

Jim slowly turned his head to look down at the Officer. As he turned his head he slowly removed his pistol from the holster and slowly cocked the hammer back. He dropped his arm to his side. He looked directly into the eyes of the man. "Phen. Ai em nguoi lay-tai." (*Yes. I am the ear taker.*) He had learned enough Vietnamese to understand some of their language and speak some.

Grooms did not respond. He had been where Jim was. Their eyes locked once again. Timothy Grooms saw nothing but a deep black void. He turned and moved back down the trail some fifty or so feet to help bind the two other Regulars' hands behind their backs. The "Yards" and Grooms started off on their escape route. O'Francis looked into the officer's eyes. From 36 inches away he raised his arm extending it straight down toward the officer's head and popped the cap, leaving the man limp with just his leg muscles twitching. O'Francis felt nothing as he slowly replaced his pistol in the holster. He then removed his knife and took the North Vietnamese Captain's right and left ear placing them in his left fatigue pocket with the other two. He stood for a moment, silence filled the air, not so much as a sound, not even a breeze. He stood looking at the three soldiers. It was as if he was not where he was, as if he was removed from all the insanity that had engulfed him for the past few months. "Damn this place!" He then turned and in moments had rejoined his patrol, hoping to make the PZ without meeting any of their Guerrilla counterparts.

He awoke sweating, and then he shook his entire upper body as if the temperature was in the teens. His heart was beating overtime. Looking around the dark room, orienting himself, he quietly got out of the bed where Dawn was soundly sleeping and went to the living room where he spent the next two hours pondering and talking with his Master.

Several months passed and the short walks in the forest were not doing a lot of good for J.P. He liked walking in the forest in the winter, especially when there was snow on the ground. The cold winds turned his face red and the stinging tingling followed. He loved the pure silence of it all. Just the wind was all one could hear.

The early spring arrived. As the trees were putting on their new green clothes, he would take longer walks, observing the small animals and on a rare occasion a deer. However, that was not helping his mental state. He would have to return home to face yet another day of work. He knew he had to get away for a long while. He had to go somewhere he could think, somewhere he felt safe, somewhere he could breathe, somewhere he could feel the earth under him at night, where he could smell the forest floor of decayed leaves and deep dark soil on his clothes, hands, face and arms. Some place he did not have to return home and wash off the forest smell. He desperately needed time away, night and day spent alone with just the forest. His soul mate knew her soul mate was in deep pain, and there was not a thing she could do. Dawn knew that he would not talk about it, and she never ever inquired. She just did her best to try and understand her husband's mood swings.

# Retreat

IT WAS LATE JULY AND he had gone to the mountains once again to recover. He could not shake the loss of the trial that had all the signs of political corruption. He was very bitter over the manner in which his attorney had handled the entire case. Poorly and incompetent would be a light verbal tongue lashing. Hate was eating him alive. It had been the death of Rusty that hate had made him imprudent to the perils of his job at the time. He knew these feelings very well, but he was not in Vietnam. He was in the good ole U.S. of A. He could not do what he did then.

For days he had moved from one campsite to another, finding a spot he liked and felt secure to camp for a night. When the sun rose, he was up and broke camp, walking through the mountain forest with stealth, observing the wild life enjoying the peacefulness of Mother Nature. Often a deer would stop suddenly and look at the strange figure twenty-five yards away. They would smell the air, turn one ear then another, using all their senses to try and detect what it was that was not normal to the area they traveled, a stare down between homo- sapient and deer. J.P. would never move when these events would occur, often remaining motionless for as long as five to eight minutes. The deer would then flicker their tails a few times and stroll off and disappear into the thickness of the forest. Most of the wildlife was small, and paid little attention to O'Francis as they went about their daily routine of survival. Something J.P. was trying extremely hard to do. His mental game had to be put back on track and he had to overcome his present adversities and move on with his life.

J.P. had been walking the strip job for miles, the ever continuous or what would seem, one to two hundred yard wide path, cut off the near tops of mountains to extract the rich mineral called coal. A snake like lush green carpet of grazing area, restored by the mine owners, ordered by the federal government, which had in essence turned into a positive environmental project. He never made camp on the "stripped" land. He would calculate his daylight and make sure he found a break in the "high wall" so as to go to the top of a ridge or part of a mountain top. He never went down off the "strip job" to find a campsite.

Usually in the very early morning hours he was able to catch the wild-life as they too stirred from a night of rest. His "field glasses" as he often referred to them, most people just called them binoculars, were used often during his trip, not just to observe the wildlife, but to make sure he did not come upon any humans.

He had paused for a rest and some map and compass readings as he decided to follow the ridgeline for the morning instead of the easier travel-ing on the ribbon of tall grasses with the few saplings that dotted the old "strip job" below him. He had never seen a bear in all the times he had been in the forest surrounding the area. As he sat on the top of a peaked point and major out-cropping before the topography dropped sharply downward to a natural break in the ridge, with a breeze blowing through the trees, below him he heard an abnormal amount of noise being created. His "topo" map indicated there was a brook leading down the south side of the moun-tain. With field glasses in hand he scanned the thick underbrush carefully, seeking any small open areas between the trees where he could see what the noise was.

Then he saw movement, a black bear with two cubs working their way up the hill directly toward him. He waited and watched as the cubs played and the mother looked for food. She took her cubs around the north side of the ridge some fifty yards from where J.P. sat. For the moments he had watched these magnificent creatures his mind had been free, at peace. He was relaxed and felt at ease. Calm had come over him.

He was on his fourth day and according to his map there was a road about five miles in the westerly direction he was traveling. It appeared to lead off the mountain, most likely an old logging road, or maybe a "strip mining" road. He took his time going up and down the hump-backed ridge, as he did not really want to return to "civilization." He was very much at ease by himself in the arms of Mother Nature. His mind often went to Dawn, and what she was doing, or what she would do if something were to happen to him. His adoration for her was immeasurable. He knew he needed to get his "shit" together and get back home and do what needed to be done that made her home a home.

It took J.P. the better part of the morning to trek the five miles he had set for himself, arriving at the top of a bluff overlooking the road leading out onto the flat grasses of the "stripped" land. He was soaked from sweat, a light breeze swept across the top of the ridge. He removed his backpack and then he stripped to his waist draping his gray tee shirt on one bush, his "jungle" fatigue top on another to dry. He preferred the old fatigues he had used in his youth to the modern day type of fatigues. He searched for several years before he found the Vietnam era fatigues, and wore them each time he escaped into his forest world. His leather shoulder holster was just as wet, which he hung on yet another branch of a bush. He removed his boots and his socks, and then removed a gun cleaning kit from his pack, wiping down his .357 but not removing the "snake" shot in the cylinder.

His line of sight to the field below was fairly good. Placing his field glasses to his eyes, he scanned the area of view, spotted two does at the edge of the field grazing. As he observed the deer with his natural sight, he ate another pack of dehydrated food and two-granola bars. His water was now running low, but knew he would be home by nightfall. He could not stand to be without water, he had gone through that once in his life and knew the value of the precious liquid. His planned path to descend the mountain would lead him to his friend Emmanuel's farm. There he would call Dawn to come get him, yet knowing that Emmanuel would insist on taking him home.

He had been resting for two hours, writing in his journal, laying back on the ground watching the clouds passing overhead, absorbing the sounds of nature, dozing off to a light nap. The crows in the area began to sound a "news signal" moments later. J.P.'s ears caught the sound of something not natural to nature, the sound of a human machine, a motorized vehicle approaching in the distance. It seemed odd to J.P. with his hearing as bad as it was, but when he was alone in the forest it appeared to him, he could pick up sounds one hundred per cent better, more prominent, at a father distance.

He rose quickly, gathered his not yet dry clothes, strapped on his holster, shoved his gun in its place, put his socks and boots on in a hurry, slung his back pack on and worked his way some fifty yards down the bluff to a point he could observe the approaching vehicle. As he settled into the thick undergrowth, his thoughts went to the sounds of the crows...*Nature at its best, crows, "the news reporters" of nature.* In a matter of minutes a sports utility vehicle came to a stop at a rusty-chained gate. A man on the passenger side got out with a set of heavy duty bolt cutters and cut the chain, swinging the gate open, allowing the Chevrolet Blazer to enter the flat. They drove directly toward J.P., coming to a stop a quarter of a mile from the gate in a concave area of the high wall, out of view of the gate area.

J.P. sat high above the two men looking almost straight at them. From his concealed vantage point, using his field glasses, he could see directly into the Blazer. Ten minutes passed, then the two got out and looking around the area, both men relieved themselves of a full bladder, one looking directly up at J.P.'s observation point. In O'Francis' camouflaged position he looked directly into the whites of the man's eyes. For O'Francis, he was in his element, cloaked and observing his "enemy." So many times he had been in the very position he was now in. His veins felt hot with the unexpected rush of adrenaline.

Like a bolt of lightning he was in the jungles of Eastern Laos, looking down on a patrol of Viet Cong working their way through the twisting, winding foot trails leading to a base camp they had been sent to gather intelligence on. Sergeant O'Francis, Sergeant Skelton and four Montagnard had been searching for three days for the camp. Now all they had to do was follow the patrol to their jungle sanctuary, plot it on a map, work their way to their PZ, be extracted and let the "Fly Boys" do their thing. But that would be too easy. Patrols did not always go the way they had been planned. This one was to be no different. One day from the discovery of a major supply camp, the small patrol ran into an unexpected equally small patrol of Viet Cong at the bottom of a long ridge they had descended. The advantage went to O'Francis and company, as the Viet Cong were not expecting intruders into their covert world of thick jungle foliage. It was over in a matter of minutes, with seven Asian "enemy" dead, and one slightly wounded Montagnard.

The men remained out of their vehicle as J.P.'s ears picked up the sound of another approaching vehicle. He turned his field glasses ever so slightly toward the open gate. Another SUV rose up over the steep road leveling off just at it entered through the gate. It paused for a moment and began its approach toward the awaiting party. They moved very slowly. When it came into sight of the tan Blazer, it stopped.

J.P. knew that this was not just some of the good 'ole boys meeting on top of the mountain to discuss coon hunting while drinking a few beers. The smell of something major was about to go down.

The Explorer began its slow approach and came to a stop some fifty feet from the awaiting men. Three men emerged. J.P. could hear their voices but could not determine what they were saying. The two men in the blazer retrieved a briefcase from the back seat and walked toward their "guests." One of the three men was standing at the rear of the Explorer. He opened up the hatch and carried a medium size tote bag to the hood. Both parties placed their articles on the hood, each examined the others goods. J.P.

could not see what the items were because of the men's positions, but had no problem surmising what it was.

A brief conversation took place, and the tote bag was zipped close, the briefcase was closed. The two men took the tote bag, turned and began to walk away. The man handling the briefcase turned and walked toward the passenger's side of the Explorer. One of the men had gotten into the back seat of the Explorer. The third man reached the driver's door, which had been left open. The man in the back seat closed his door. At that point the two men from the Blazer wheeled around. The one with the tote bag dropped it to the ground, pulling from under their light wind-breaker jackets their weapons and fired rapidly. The driver and passenger went down instantly. The man in the back seat quickly opened the door and began firing his 9mm short barreled Uzi, striking both his attackers, sending them tumbling to the ground. He stepped from behind the door and had taken no more than three steps toward the front of the Explorer when one of the two men rose to his knees, popped off three rounds hitting his intended target twice in the chest and once in the abdomen, sending him wheeling back against the door, forcing it closed, as he staggered for two more steps and then flattened face down on the ground. In a New York minute, five men lay motionless on the flat grassy "strip job."

O'Francis lay totally motionless as he watched the deal go south. Twenty minutes passed as he went from one to the other examining each body through his field glasses. Looking in both directions from the scene, he saw no one approaching, nor did he hear any approaching vehicles.

It took him another thirty minutes to work his way down onto the flat, from the natural break in the ridge and the high wall. He moved slow and cautious, crouching in the tall grass. The breeze moved the grass back and forth like the waves of an ocean, birds began chirping once again, the usual crows flying about seemed to be announcing the events that had occurred, like some on the spot reporter broadcasting live on CNN.

J.P. stayed close to the high wall taking another ten minutes as he approached the two vehicles. He went to a low crouching position, almost a crawl, approaching the Explorer first. When he was within ten yards of the vehicle he pulled his weapon, and paused. Squatting in the thirty-inch high grass, he thought about switching his ammo, "snake" shot to his .357 hollow point Teflon tipped ones, but did not. He eased to the back of the Explorer and looked at the man who went down last. He laid face down fifteen feet away. The grass concealed him from any further distance. He moved to the man, kneeling on his right knee. He checked the pulse on his neck with his left index and middle finger. Nothing. Moving methodically he went to each of the other men who had arrived in the Explorer, checking for signs of life. He found none.

J.P. paused for a few moments at the front edge of the Explorer, as he had become aware the crows had stopped their "on the spot broadcasting." The breeze had picked up slightly, and he sat down, waited and listened. Ten minutes passed and the crows began their "broadcasting" once again. He became weary and rolled his left leg under him, crossed his right foot over, placing it flat on the ground, and rose with ease. Remaining crouched, he moved to the remaining men, both on their backs. They had been hit several times in the chest area, one had been hit in the right forehead. He felt no pulse from either man. Looking around he located the tote bag. The black canvas bag lay a few feet from the feet of the man he had checked first. He reached into his left pocket of his fatigues and pulled out a pair of tan soft leather cowhide gloves. Replacing his weapon in his shoulder holster, he then put his skintight gloves on. Moving to the bag, he zipped it open. He saw rectangle brown paper packages, each securely taped. Reaching to his right hip he retrieved his knife and inserted it into the center of one of the packages and touched the tip to his tongue.

"Ahhha, yes, pure White Snow." He counted the packages. Ten. "Damn!" He spoke softly to himself. "This has to be at least, oh man, hell maybe two maybe three million on the street. Hell maybe more. Somebody is going to be really pissed!"

The body of the man who had picked up the briefcase was six feet to the right of the passenger's door. As the bullets had entered his upper back, he had wheeled and stumbled for a few steps and fell. J.P. turned and looked over at the man face up. He had not turned loose of the brown leather briefcase. He squatted beside the man, removed the case from his hand, walked to the Explorer's passenger's door, opened it and placed it on the seat. Popping it open, J.P. looked down at a lot of neatly wrapped money. He looked up and through the opposite side of the SUV, and then looked around at the bodies on the ground. He picked up one stack, flipped the bills with his thumb, which appeared to be all hundreds.

"Holy Shit!" he said softly to himself.

At that point he knew he could not go down the road he had planned to descend the mountain, so out came the topography map. Getting his bearings, he thought briefly, *I need to walk on the edge of the strip job, no trail going through the grass.* He walked directly to the very edge of the "strip job" where it dropped off at a ninety-degree decline, then headed in the opposite direction with the briefcase in hand. He had not gone more than twenty-five yards when he stopped. He backtracked to where he had left the canvas bag and zipped it up, picked it up, and headed east. He walked more briskly along the flat-stripped grassy terrain making sure he did not make any trail through the tall grasses. For an hour and a half he traveled before he took his first break. Sitting on a large boulder he reviewed his map. Looking up and back down he figured that two maybe three more miles and there should be a hollow leading to the bottom of the mountain.

Talking to himself, and tapping his finger on a point on the map he said, "This should put me about here. Oh well, a few more days in the mountains, I'll need it to think."

Looking back to his map, he figured two more days of moderate trekking would put him home.

He made camp at the top edge of the long hollow leading to the foothills of Copper Ridge. Making no fire, he sat and counted the money stack by stack, before darkness fell. After the last stack was counted, he sat looking at the money.

"Christ! Seven hundred and fifty thousand dollars! Damn! Lottery time! There will be more than one somebody pissed!"

Then he looked over at the tote canvas bag, stating in disgust, "Now what in the hell do I do with that shit?" He stated as if he were talking to someone. An hour before dark, he got up and walked around the area where he was to camp for the night. On the northeast side of the concaved head of the hollow, he carefully removed the topsoil from the side of the hill placing it to the side. With his entrenching tool he dug an eighteen-inch hole, placed the canvas bag in one of the plastic trash bags he had and dropped the tote bag in, covered it up, smoothing the earth and carefully replacing the topsoil leaving an area that did not look disturbed. Then he carefully notated the trees around the area, measured the distance from four different trees, crossing the imaginary line over the buried "Coke." He returned to his camp, removed his gloves, ate his dry food, then carefully marked the area on his "topo" map with a grease pencil. Then he enjoyed the sounds of the night residences and the clear star filled sky, until sleep over took him.

Dawn came at 0530 hours and he was up with the alarm of birds and of course his favorite, the ever clever and observant crows. He placed the money in his backpack, and then went three hundred yards down the hollow, where he stopped to dig another hole and placed the empty briefcase in it, taking the same care he had with the hole he had dug for the "coke".

His return home was the usual, how bad he smelled and looked, but after a long clean up, he was what Dawn was used to. He was happy to be home. Her ever present smile, and usual "wise-cracking" comments about something, just made him smile. He often looked at her and realized how fortunate he was to have her as a soulmate. Her quick wit and sometime sarcasm did not always set well with J.P., however that was his mate for life, forever.

J.P. shared his adventure with Dawn, as he knew she could be trusted not to reveal to anyone what had happened. They had to do some very careful planning. However what J.P. did not know, and could not foresee, was that his beloved Dawn would be leaving him for a dimension not of this earth.

# Vultures

JOHN MARSHAL MET J.P. AT the courthouse at high noon. It was a rather warm day for October. J.P. wore a light blue long sleeve shirt, light gray tie, with a fountain pen print on the lower tip of the tie, khaki docker slacks, dark blue knee high socks, and brown loafers. John Marshal wore a dark blue three-piece suit, white shirt, red tie and black lace up shoes.

John had arranged to use a conference room off the lobby of the court-room. It was a small room, one window facing Main Street. A small well-worn desk and two wooden chairs were in the room.

John took out several files and a law book. He handed J.P. a file and asked him to read it, that he needed to go to the restroom and would return in a few minutes.

As J.P. read, his blood pressure began to rise. His skin became flushed, his heart began to increase in beats. Ms. Sheffield had presented John with the copies of the interviews she had with people in her investigation of J.P. Her report was not good. J.P. was a very bad person according to her sources, both in school as well as out.

J.P. had finished the report by the time John returned.

"So, J.P. what do you think?"

"I think..." then he paused, trying to gain his composure. "I think whomever she got her information from, does not like Mr. O'Francis very much. I think that this report is spurious." Then he paused for several moments. John did not say anything. He sat and waited.

"I think the report really pisses me off! I hate people to lie about me! I hate people who are afraid to give their names when they are making statements about me. Well for that matter anybody! Point of fact is John, I am really upset over this! Who are these people? Why can I not have them face me and make these very outlandish, absurd statements?"

"Well, I was afraid you would be upset. I did not give this to you to make you upset. But, you needed to know what you were about to face with the Department of Social Services.

"In answer to your questions. First, they, the Social Services, do not have to reveal the names of the people that gave them the information. Second, you do not have the right to face your accusers in the world of Social Services. They have their own laws."

"I do not think so John! Excuse me sir, but, they cannot be above the law! I mean I am not an attorney, not by a very long shot. However, I do know about the government, and the constitution, both state and federal. I have studied it, taught it."

John smiled. "J.P...yes and no."

"Yes and no? You cannot have it both ways," J.P. protested.

Again, John Marshal smiled at J.P., and warmly stated, "J.P. they have their own set of rules they are allowed to go by. The state legislators are the very people who gave them all this power. Therefore, yes they can be above the law, because the law so states. J.P., no they cannot, or are not supposed to be able to convict anyone when the laws of the State of Virginia are in direct conflict with their policies. However, they do, have, and will continue to do so."

"Well, that is just, excuse me please, fucking great! So, why in the hell are we wasting my time as well as yours?"

"Because we are going to win this case, if not here in Reynolds County, then in the appeals hearing in Richmond. That is why."

He sat and looked directly at J.P., eye to eye, something J.P. liked about him from the first day he met him. He was not afraid to hold eye contact with him.

"Here is how the hearing is going to go. Dear sweet Janet will present all this damaging material in her best, feel sorry for the poor little boy fashion, to the director, Mr. Randy Dowell. Therefore, I do not want you to lose your cool. I want you to sit and take what she will be stating to the director as fact, because she will state that she has done an in depth and honest investigation into the matter as well as into your background and character. I want you to respond in a calm and controlled manner when it is your turn to tell your side of the story. You may respond to any of the past-alleged events that you want to. That will be your call. I really do not know any of the details about any of…" he paused and pointed to the large document lying on the table given to him by Janet Sheffield, "these very vague statements about your alleged abuse to students. She will go into detail when she presents her case to Randy Dowell. Now can you do that?"

"Oh yes, I can do this. Point of fact is John, there has never ever been any abuse to any child! I mean ever! I resent the implications here! If she does go into this, and spouts out details, I want to be able to ask where she got her information! Also I want to respond to any and all child abuse statements that I have been involved in!"

"Well, like I told you J.P., you may respond to any of the statements she makes. But she will not give you the names of the people she got the information from."

"So just how does one know if the information is true or not?"

"Well, they are supposed to conduct a fair and impartial investigation, without any biases."

"Right! And I am supposed to sit here and believe all that."

"No, I didn't say you had to believe it. It is just what the Department of Social Services will tell you. Moreover, they will stick to what they say. They will not change."

"Well hell John, with what is in that report, along without the details, it is already a damn lie! The report is tainted from the very get-go!"

"I know. I believe you. I am on your side. If I did not believe you, I would have never taken your case. I do not take every case that crosses my desk J.P. That is not the point here. I want you to handle this like a professional. She will expect you to go off. That is what she is hoping for J.P. Sweet Janet is mad as a wet hen because you were acquitted of the assault charges. We have blown holes in the stories these students have portrayed as facts. Now again, bear in mind, this did not set well with sweet Janet."

"Well I have one thing to say about sweet Janet. Get a real life! Let me get just one more thing out of my system before we gladiators adjourn to the arena. Janet and her cohorts do not have an F'en clue as to what it is like to be a teacher in a public school system and to deal with these insubordinate, rude, impolite thuds! And also, these types of students are in the rural areas, not just in the city school that you hear about on TV. Sweet Janet lives in a world that does not exist! She is a total idiot!" J.P. took a deep breath and smiled. "Damn I feel much better having said that."

J.P. stood. "Okay. I will handle this thing. You do not have to worry. Hell, I will not blow the case. I work better under pressure anyway. Trust me John on this one." Then he smiled again, looked at his watch. And said, "I am ready. Let's go to battle."

The two men got in John Marshal's dark blue SUV and traveled the quarter of a mile to the headquarters of the Reynolds County's infamous S.S. Office. The scheduled appointment was set for 1300 hours. They walked through the door at 1258 hours. John approached a large glass window where a woman sat.

She pulled opened a sliding section of the glass. "May I help you sir?"

"John Marshal and James Patrick O'Francis to see Mr. Randy Dowell. We have a 1:00 o'clock appointment."

The woman closed the glass back, picked the phone up, and spoke. Several seconds passed and she slid opened the glass window.

"Just have a seat Mr. Marshal and he will be right with you."

J.P. and John walked across the room and sat in a not so comfortable chair. A woman with a little girl was sitting across the room. The girl was a typical, what appeared to be, five year old. Poorly disciplined, her mother was constantly correcting her, with little or no effect. J.P. looked upon the child as just another generation of rude, impolite, problem children, that would most likely cause some future generation teacher problems and most likely have them brought up on some bogus charge that Social Services would get involved with and once again try to destroy the character of a teacher.

Ten minutes passed and J.P. took note of the fact that they had a scheduled appointment, just another tactic to demonstrate that "They" were the real power.

The woman behind the glass slid it open and called to John. "Mr. Marshal, you may go through that door." The woman pointed to her right. Just as they approached the steel door the lady pushed a button and the buzzer sounded. The door unlocked, allowing them to enter. After entering a long corridor that ran to their left, another woman, who looked to be in her fifties, directed them to the last door on the right at the end of the hall. As they entered a room twenty by forty feet, to their right along the wall sat Sweet Janet Sheffield. The chair, in which she was sitting, was not big enough for her obese frame. Her mo-mo attire did nothing for her appearance. Her hair was a dirty blond color and shabby looking, as if it needed to be washed and some type of style done to it. The man seated to her right was the same man from the courtroom who had accompanied Janet on the day of the trial. Mr. Randy Dowell pulled a chair from behind a desk, which was at the far end of the room and placed it in the middle of the room between four chairs on the social worker's side and the four on the opposite side.

"Good afternoon gentlemen."

"Good afternoon Mr. Dowell. I would like to introduce J. Patrick O'Francis."

"Mr. Dowell," J.P. responded. He did not shake his hand.

Mr. Dowell then introduced Janet and Edward Houston. He was a well-built man, five ten or eleven, one hundred and eighty pounds, dressed casual, tan slacks white shirt, blue tie and brown slip on shoes. Again, J.P. only nodded toward them. Dowell instructed them to have a seat. All introductions were done as a professional courtesy for

O'Francis, as John knew all of them and they knew him from previous cases. He had to defend teachers from the ever-ravaging vultures of Social Services.

After a few moments of preliminaries, Randy Dowell instructed Janet that she could begin her report. Janet's story rolled out like a Steven King horror novel. In her portrayal of O'Francis, it made Hannibal Lector look like Pope Paul II. She stated as fact that her true and unbiased investigation into Mr. O'Francis had revealed that he had in his past molested young high school girl students, girl and boy athletes, injected football players with morphine so that they could play in games even though they were injured. O'Francis, according to Janet, had struck male students physically, and had in the course of breaking up fights between students, used unreasonable and unnecessary force to do so. She also stated that he had been accused of mentally abusing students in his class and that his conduct outside of school was just as abusive. She went into detail about each incident. She then went into the events of 5 April weaving a story even better than the students had in court. Of course, she had a lot more practice at storytelling.

J.P. tried to humor himself with his thoughts. *She should write a fuck'en book! This is as good as a Steven King novel. She would make a Fuck'en fortune. At least she would be leaving teachers alone.*

At the end of the forty five minute report she stated that Mr. O'Francis had terrorized several teachers as well as several of his supervisors and that several principals had stated that they feared for their very lives. She reported that he had even sued one of his principals. She stated that she had gone to the courthouse to obtain the records of the case but they were missing. She implied that Mr. O'Francis had in fact been able to get rid of the files from the court records. Ms. Sheffield concluded that several of the people in which she spoke with had warned her that she was putting her life in grave danger by investigating O'Francis.

Then she twisted and turned in her seat, as best she could, arched her shoulders back as if she had just presented the world with the facts that would win her the Pulitzer Prize in Literature.

J.P. sat very erect in his most uncomfortable chair, feet flat on the floor, and his hands cupped together in his lap through it all without making a sound. He had not moved his body in any manner. He sat as if he was a stone statue. He had not made any expressions on his face, and he had looked directly at her the entire time she presented her report. He was aware that Mr. Houston, her associate he presumed, seated directly across from him, was watching his every move which was part of the grand scheme of the SS department.

Mr. Dowell took a few seconds before he addressed Mr. Marshal. "Mr. Marshal, would you like to respond to any of the report presented here today by Mrs. Sheffield?"

"Well, Janet certainly portrayed my client as a villainous person. I truly am surprised that he is still working for Reynolds County School System. In all fairness Mr. Dowell, I would like to let Mr. O'Francis respond to any or all of the alleged statements in which Ms. Sheffield has obtained from her unbiased investigation. He would have more insight to all these improprieties and illegal acts than I would." John then turned his head to his left. "J.P., you may respond to any of the statements or you may just tell your side of the story that took place the day of the incident in which we are here for."

O'Francis took his time, looked at each of the Social Service people present. "Well, I would first like to respond to some of the allegations Ms. Sheffield has presented to you today, Mr. Dowell."

"You may make any statements you wish, Mr. O'Francis." Mr. Dowell stated.

"Thank you sir." J.P. then crossed his right leg over his left and placed his hands on his lap.

"First and foremost Mr. Dowell, Ms. Sheffield has gotten false information from someone, or she has misquoted whomever she got this information from. Now if I may, Mr. Dowell, I would like to ask a question."

"You may." He nodded as he spoke.

"Ms. Sheffield, where did you obtain this information in which you have presented here today?"

She squirmed in her seat, moved her shoulders back and forth. "I am not at liberty to give you that information."

"Well, that tells me a lot. I have heard that same statement from the person in whom you obtained the information many times before, which was typical of his response when he was telling one of many of his lies."

"Mr. O'Francis..."

J.P. cut Janet off. "Ma'am, you had your turn to make all the statements you wanted. It is my turn to respond to them without being interrupted."

Sheffield frowned at J.P. and moved her upper body back and forth in an agitating manner.

"I have never ever mistreated a student! I have never mistreated an athlete! I have never struck a student or an athlete. I have never injured a student when breaking up any fight, which is more than I can say for Damon Bales, who for the record broke a student's shoulder, who also slapped a student at a football game when he spoke to him in a disrespectful manner! He also addressed the student and the two other students accompanying him with several sentences of very colorful metaphors. I have no doubts that most if not all of your information came from Bales, and or any one of his loyal cronies." At that point he deliberately paused for a good three minutes as if he were getting his thoughts in order.

Then with a calmness to his demeanor and sternness in his voice he continued, "Now if you had asked the right people who were with me during my coaching years, you would have found out that the information you have presented here today depicting my character was not who I am. If you were to have asked some of my fellow colleagues in which I worked with and knew me and the manner in which I have taught in the classroom over the past 25 years, again you would have gotten the truth. Instead, I am of the belief that you sought your answers from people who in fact have over the years slandered as well as libeled my good name! By all appearances here today with your report, they still are! If that is what you were looking for, and I am of the belief at this point in this unbiased report you have rendered, that is exactly what you were looking for! Then you found it. The people with whom you have sought out to give you the information you wanted, do not like me and will do anything that they can to discredit my name!"

Another short pause in his rebuttal. "I do not agree with your policy that I cannot face my accusers. They would not have made these statements in the presence of my attorney, where they could have been cross-examined. They are and have always been mendacious cowards! I do not agree that I cannot get the names of the people you have obtained this slanderous information and in my opinion, another biased cowardly act!"

Janet's face was becoming red, she twisted more in her seat. Her face became more distorted. Edward remained calm, showing no emotion to anything J.P. said.

"Now to a few specifics. I have broken up a few fights in my day. Never have I been charged with any wrongdoing in any of them. There is one exception. I broke up a fight when I was teaching on the junior high level and the parents of the boy who had started the fight and was in fact beating up a boy much smaller than he was, filed a complaint with the principal. That principal was Mr. Wolffe. I would like to know what he had to say about the complaint. I would also like to know what Mrs. Linnet Thomas and Mr. Anthony Duponte' would have to say concerning the incident, as they had to do an investigation into the matter at the request of the superintendent and a School Board member, Mr. Theodoric, who was a friend of the guilty boy. I did nothing wrong concerning that particular incident either! I did the job as I was required to do as a teacher in this county and by the school's policy manual. Your information is tainted!"

Janet started to speak. J.P. just held up his arm, four figures folded, index finger extending upward, as to indicate that he was not finished.

"I did in fact sue a principal. Now that, you did get correct Ms. Sheffield. I sued Damon Clay Bales and Richard Finkel for libel and slander."

"Excuse me Mr. O'Francis for interrupting," Mr. Dowell stated. "But what does any of this have to do with what went on with you and this boy at the, ahhh whatever it is?"

"Alternative school, and it has absolutely nothing to do with it sir."

"Then let's just get to the incident that you are here being charged for."

"No problem sir, I was just responding to these observed allegations that Ms. Sheffield has presented to you depicting my character and my past as well as, as she has stated, and using her very words, showing a pattern of behavior. And before I go to the incident of 5 April, I would like to state that I can and would, if you so desired, present witnesses to any and all of these alleged events and they would I am quite sure tell a much different story, in spite of what Ms. Sheffield has presented here today as facts, which I might add, you allowed her to present."

"Mr. O'Francis, that will not be necessary."

"Very well. Now to the events of 5 April..." J.P. went through the entire events that had taken place just as he had in court and just as he had written up in his documentation. After he had finished, Edward requested to ask J.P. a question.

"Mr. O'Francis. If you were to have to do it all over, would you have handled the matter in a different way?"

"Knowing what I know now? Yes!"

"Do you think this has changed you as a teacher?"

"Yes!"

"In what way?" Mr. Edwards inquired.

At that, J.P. paused for a long two minutes. He felt he was being set up with the question. Then he slowly answered Edwards' question. "I think, as of now, I will not ever get involved with any type of confrontation with a student. I will not be the caring person I have been in the past. Caring as far as concern for the welfare of the students."

At that, John Marshal interjected before any more questions were asked. He presented to the local Social Service board the legal side of the issue. He presented each of the parties a copy of the written law concerning the matter between Bruce McCloud and J.P. O'Francis. After hearing his statement, pointing out what the laws of the State of Virginia had on its books as well as the policies of the county school system, Janet Sheffield made a statement that totally stunned J.P.

"Mr. Marshal, these laws or school policies do not apply to Social Services' policies."

John Marshal broke a smile. "Ms. Sheffield, these laws apply to all people in the State of Virginia. No other law or policy can supersede the laws of the state. And the state laws cannot supersede the laws of the United States."

"Well, Mr. Marshal, that may be true, but they do not apply to our policies. We have our own policies that we go by."

"Mr. Dowell, I have given you legal room to find my client innocent of these charges if you so desire. We thank you for your time today. We'll be in touch."

John Marshal looked at J.P. His eyes told O'Francis that it was time to leave. He rose from his chair, John was already standing, and they walked out of the room.

They rode in silence to where J.P. had his truck parked before O'Francis said anything.

"John, is Sheffield as stupid as she presented herself today?"

"Yes."

"John, I have taught political science for many years, and I do not think that any law or policy can supersede the laws of a state and so on up the line."

"You are correct. They cannot."

"Look, I hope I did alright in there today...hell I really did not know what to say about all the bullshit she presented. I mean bullshit is an understatement. There is no way, John...believe me...no way that any of that shit is true! Crap like that is exactly why I sued Damon Bales! Hell he is a sick and very dangerous bastard anyway. That is where she got all that stuff. I mean she went back to a period of time before Bales was even a principal at Honsburg. Now the only person she could have gotten that from was Bobby Simms. Well, no let me retract that. She could have gotten it from Carl Decal. He did not like me either. He did everything in his power, which at the time he was at Honsburg, he did a lot to discredit me.

However, that is another story altogether. He and Bales were big buddies. In the first meeting of her investigating me at the School Board office she requested me to give her a list of names in which she might talk to concerning me as a teacher and a coach. I have a record of what was talked about that day. So, why ask me for names if she was not going to talk to them in the first place? People I worked directly with, people who knew me for what I am?"

"Because she could not get the answers she was after if she did that. Not to worry. You did well. You have the right to defend yourself from all the allegations, as did you with Bruce attacking you. Remember he hit you. You did not hit him. The law gives you due deference. O'Francis that is the law despite what sweet Janet would like to think."

"I do not know John. I have a bad feeling here."

"Look, even if they do find you guilty, we have the right to appeal to Richmond. They do have some knowledge of the law there. You will be alright. I think we will win in the long haul. Okay. Now don't worry yourself about this. We'll be alright. Trust me O'Francis. Trust me."

J.P. shook his head. "Okay, I will. You know I have little faith in our judicial system."

"Ahh, but wait my find Irish friend. The system did right by you in the assault charges. Right? I mean you told the truth, and the judge saw it was the truth. Right?"

"Yeah, you're right on that one. I will give credit where it is due. But this. Hell they act like the law does not even apply to them. I mean, just how ignorant can they be?"

"Ah yes. How ignorant you asked? Well you saw for yourself today. This is not the first time I have had to dance with these people. The very same ones with a case much harder than yours, and in the end they lost and we won."

"You had to appeal to the state?"

"Yes. O'Francis they do look at the facts on both sides without bias and more objectively in Richmond than they do here in Reynolds County. Believe me."

The two parted with John Marshal telling J.P. that he would be in contact with him and that if he had any questions or anything was bothering him that he could call him at his office or at his home anytime he wanted or needed to.

# *Deliverance*

J.P. ARRIVED AT HIS OFFICE at his usual time of 8:20. His official time started at 8:30 a.m. but for him that was a pile of buffalo dung, as his hours did not reflect that of a normal teacher.

Sometimes he arrived at 9:00, sometimes at 10:00 a.m. but on the other hand, when the normal teacher was at home in the afternoon, J.P. was still working. Sometimes at 7:00 p.m., he was leaving a student's house headed for the office to swap out his very used county car he had nicknamed "*The Blue Goose*" for his black Nissan truck.

J.P. had two students on this day, one on the far western end of the county, a thirty-five minute drive from the central office and one on the eastern end of the county with a 45-minute drive from his office. By the time he left his morning student, stopped by the high school, then drive to the high school on the eastern end of the county, got her work from the teachers, then drove to where his afternoon student lived, it would take two hours and fifteen minutes.

The school year had only three weeks left in it. A year J.P. would like to forget. It had been a little over a month since the incident at the alternative school and O'Francis faced yet another major battle to keep his name intact. However, he tried to keep an upbeat attitude, as he was well aware that the students he had to go see had no clue as to his problems. For most of them, the problems they had were of major proportion. Little did they know what life was going to throw at them. Then they would look back at their teens and think, and I thought...was a problem.

He arrived back at the office from his morning student at 1:00 p.m. He took all the needed material from the light blue county car and put it on the floor and seat of the passenger's side of his black truck. When he was finished with his afternoon student, he would go straight to his home. There would be no need for him taking the *"Blue Goose"*, as it would be asinine to travel the forty minutes or so back to the office then thirty minutes back home, a waste of time and money. Some would have, instead of taking their own vehicle, being stubborn, showing the school system that "they" would not use their own vehicle for work. However this student lived in an area that the "Blue Goose" as good as it was, would not make the trip. It took a four wheel drive vehicle to get up on top of the mountain. So J.P. used his own truck for the trek.

J.P. told me that the previous homebound teacher would not even go to the homes J.P. visited. Not clean enough. But in checking out his story I found that most people thought Frank Hanover had been and still was an obnoxious individual, bordering on being insane, even after his retirement, as the southern saying goes, once an ass-hole always an ass-hole. J.P. of course referred to him in an odd sort of way, just a pile of buffalo dung that needed to be spread over a field for fertilizer.

Melissa Casey was yet another one of the girls that was pregnant and which was allowed to go on homebound for medical reasons. Something J.P. really did not approve of but he would say nothing, he just did his job as assigned, like the good soldier he was. "It is not for us to asked why, but to do and die." A Marine saying J.P. would say, "Even though I was not a "jar-head", as he referred to them.

I always heard them called "Leather-necks," I said to J.P.

"One in the same," J.P. replied.

He had been going to Melissa's home for the past six weeks and had learned a lot about her home life. Her mother did a lot of talking to J.P. who was a very good listener.

His first trip to the house was a trip in itself. Six miles east of Honsburg, turn right on route 614, go one mile, turn right on the first dirt road you come to. Follow that road up the mountain until you come onto the "strip job". Travel out the "strip job" for about a mile, then turn right up the hill off the strip job for another mile or so, then turn left and just follow that road until you come to the old home place. Turn left just as you enter the gate and go a quarter of a mile to the trailer.

Now the trailer was setting on top of a ridge overlooking an array of magnificent mountains. J.P. stood and admired the view and thought it would make a place for a nice home, but that was not the case. The old home place was, by all appearances, at least seventy-five years old.

To quote J.P. on this part of his story, "Now people in general think that the movie Deliverance was just a movie, but a point of fact is there are many places in the Appalachian mountains that are like the people in the movie. Mountain people. Nothing wrong with mountain people you understand. Again, point of fact is, I like them. Well for the most part."

J.P. had learned much about the broken family he was now visiting on a weekly basis. The mother, Lara, had left her husband, Bob, or rather it would be best to phrase it, that Bob went back to the home place to stay with his mother.

Bob was an abusive husband and drank more often than he should. He would be working on his "toys," motorcycles, Harley-Davidsons, in an old shed, what appeared to be a garage, each time J.P. went by the home place on his way to the trailer. Bob would be playing music from the sixties, which was not all bad as far as J.P. was concerned. He looked to be in his late thirties and by all appearances someone that was caught in a time-warp from the late sixties or early seventies.

J.P. arrived at the trailer at 2:30 in the afternoon. Melissa had two tests to take, which would take up the afternoon session. By three-thirty, she had finished the first test. Lara had expressed concern several times about Bob coming down to the trailer as he had been drinking all day. J.P. paid little attention to the comments that Lara had made.

After Melissa finished her first test, Lara stepped out on the porch to smoke a cigarette. Melissa got up and got her a glass of water, looked out the kitchen window. J.P. sensed that both women were on edge a few minutes after his arrival. Melissa returned to the dining room table and the look of fear had taken over her face.

"Mr. O'Francis, when daddy is drunk he is very violent. I do not think it is safe for you to be here today. I am so very sorry."

"Melissa." J.P. stated in a calm and firm voice. "Not to worry about things you have no control over. You have enough to worry about with the baby you are carrying. You are a week maybe two the doctor said, correct?" She nodded her head, to confirm. "Well, you worry about the next test we have to take and do not worry about Mr. O'Francis. Okay?"

J.P. reviewed for the test before Melissa began to take the rather long test. One that he was sure was not given to the students that were in the regular classroom, but he had no control over that, and he did not worry himself over the fact that teachers had no concern about the students he had on homebound. J.P. just made sure that they knew the material well enough that it really did not matter what type or how long of a test the teachers chose to give, they would pass it.

Thirty minutes passed and Lara came into the kitchen.

"Mr. O'Francis, Bob is coming and he is drunk. I think you should leave. I don't mean to offend you, but he is really not a very nice person when he is drunk."

"Mrs. Casey, I will do so just as soon as Melissa finishes her test. It will only take a short while. Her education is very important. I will be fine. Do not worry yourself about me."

A few minutes passed and Bob came into the living room of the rather old trailer, with an addition added to the living room and bedrooms. Lara kept it very clean inside and had her home in order and items neat and in what appeared to be their proper place. It had a clean smell to it, which J.P. was glad as there were some that the odors would gag a maggot.

Lara began pleading to Bob to leave, that Melissa's teacher was present and that she had to take a test. She tried to get him to understand that her education was important. Bob was the very typical backwoods "redneck" mountain man who was in all reality just mean when he was drunk. He was the type that would cut you with a knife without a second thought. The type you saw in a bar that after a few drinks wanted to take on anyone and everyone. The type of person that could spoil a person's beer when all one wanted was to be left alone to have a cold one and leave. The type of person that most people called a "mean ass-hole drunk!"

Bob started into the kitchen, Lara tried to step in front of him, but with no success. Melissa had stopped taking her test. Tears swelled up in her eyes. J.P. very slowly moved his legs from under the table and positioned himself to where he could rise up without having the table to contend with in front of him. The kitchen was rather small. The table, old, chrome legs, looked to be the type you saw in homes in the late fifties and early sixties. Four matching chairs with chrome legs and plaid seats and backs, a brown colored refrigerator, a sink with a small amount of counter space. There was one window over the sink and one beside the table where J.P. and Melissa were sitting.

Bob walked into the kitchen. J.P. knew at that moment that he had but one choice, take him out before he could strike his first blow. He had seen Bob's type so many times before in his earlier days, when he made his rounds to the local bars in the towns and cities he had traveled to.

As Bob approached, O'Francis saw in his eyes that he intended to show him just how mean he was and to set a tone for future visits if at all. J.P. came out of his chair like a bolt of lightning driving his left extended fingers into his throat. Both of Bob's hands instantly went to his throat as he gasped for air. His knees were slightly bent and J.P. drove his open right hand like the back edge of a knife upward into his groin. His left hand now firmly grasped Bob's shirt at his upper chest, lifted him upward and back with force against the wall beside the refrigerator.

J.P. moved close to Bob's right ear and whispered, "Do not, ever, threaten me! I personally couldn't give a good god-damn what you do up on this fuck'in mountain, or for that matter anywhere else. But, do not ever, never, ever, threaten me!"

As he was whispering, he had rolled his hand over to grasp Bob's testicles and was squeezing them. Bob was still struggling to get his breath.

"I am not your little chicken shit Reynolds County teacher! When I leave this fuck'en mountain today, this event had better stay up on this fucking mountain! You understand me Bob! I have nothing personal against you. Let me and you just leave it at that!"

J.P. let go of Bob's shirt and testicles. Bob dropped to the floor on his knees still gasping for air. J.P. turned to Melissa. "You finish the test later, or tomorrow, just whenever you feel like it."

With tears streaming down her cheeks, she spoke with a "crackling" voice, "But aren't you supposed to be here when I take the test?" she stated.

"Yes. I was here. As far as completing your test, well, you let me worry about that. Just use the honor system is all I asked." He gathered up his file case he had made that contained his students' records and began walking out of the house.

As he passed Lara who was standing at the entrance of the kitchen with eyes the size of golf balls, J.P. paused. "Sorry Mrs. Casey, but I had no choice. Hope you understand. If you do not want me to return for next week's session, just call the office and let me know. You all have a nice day."

All Lara did was nod her head, and then smiled.

O'Francis walked through the living room and spoke as he exited the trailer, "Melissa, I will see you next week, okay? You work hard for me."

"Okay, Mr. O'Francis I will. Thanks." Still with a slight crackle to her young teen voice.

As J.P. walked out onto the porch, he spoke loud enough so Bob could hear him, "I really like your Harleys. You play good music also Bob."

He walked the forty feet to his truck, put his file case on the floorboard of the passengers side of the truck, then walked to the driver's side of his truck and got in. He then unzipped a section of his soft brown leather case that was sitting on the passenger's seat, pulled out his .380 automatic and set it beside him. He started the truck, pushed in a tape by Bob Seger, took the time to load his pipe and then lit it, took a few puffs to get it going good, then backed out of the dirt driveway to a wide spot, turned the truck around and slowly drove down the mountain. He smiled as he thought of what had taken place.

Then he talked to himself, "Just ain't going to happen again. Never! Adult, teen, male, female. Just ain't going to ever happen again!" Then he started singing along with Bob Seger, *"STOOD THERE BOLDLY SWEATING IN THE SUN, FELT LIKE A MILLION, FELT LIKE NUMBER ONE..."*

# The Yellow House

RANARD WOLFFE WAS ENJOYING AN evening of drinking and sex with another of his women who, legally by social standards, belonged to another man. They had spent the greater part of the night engaged in consuming alcohol, watching X rated movies, and partaking in their own form of sex.

At 2:00 a.m. Ranard's phone rang. On the fifth ring, he managed to roll over and reach to his nightstand to drag it from the receiver.

"Hello," Ranard answered with a very groggy voice, his eyes still closed, his head on the pillow.

"Ranard, this is Marshy."

"Who?" Ranard replied not awake, his body in the long process of recovering from all the alcohol he had consumed and the sex he had with a woman fifteen years his younger.

"God-damn-it, I said this is LaMar Marshy! Now wake your ass up and talk to me!"

The voice registered in his mind and his eyes opened wide and quickly. He sat up in bed as if someone had suddenly fired a gun into the air.

"LaMar," as Ranard looked at the clock on his nightstand. "What are you calling me at, ahhh, damn, 2:05 in the morning?"

"I need your assistance."

"Okay, what?" Ranard answered in an obedient manner.

"I am in the Princeton jail. I need you to come bail me out. Now!"

A long pause on the phone, leaving Marshy to think no one was on the other end of the line. "Ranard, you there?"

"Yes sir. I am here. Just, ahhh, what."

He did not get to finish his question. "Look, don't ask, just get your ass up here as soon as you can and get me the hell out of here!"

"Yes sir. I will be there in, ahhh, about an hour." Then he hung the phone up. The young twenty-five year old teacher, whose husband had gone on a fishing trip for an entire week, rolled over and inquired as to what was going on. Ranard informed her he had to leave for a few hours to take care of some emergency business.

Aileen rolled back over on her right side. "Okay."

Ranard got dressed and was on his way in a matter of five minutes.

Linda Diamond had bought the large Victorian home in 1981 and had totally refurbished it in grand style. Linda was a self-made millionaire and had moved to the small city to open a business she had longed to operate all her adult life. She painted her house yellow and nicknamed it the "Yellow House." She ran her house of prostitution with classy women she had imported from the northern city of New Jersey. Her prices were high, and catered to the upper middle class and wealthy clientele of the surrounding area. They arrived at the "Yellow House" by appointment only.

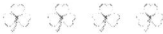

The reverend Paul Lina and his Bible belt Southern Baptist congregation had been politically putting pressure on the Mayor and the city council for ten years to close the "Yellow House" down. However, he had little success, as Ms. Diamond had been a major financial contributor to the Mayor and several of the council members that had been elected to power. Ms. Diamond played the political game well, and knew what it took to keep her business open. Her clients were well shielded from the public and any scandals.

Nevertheless, the pressure had been mounting, and the Mayor and the police department had to make some type of showing to get the Christian faction off their backs.

Even though ninety-ninety percent were as hypocritical as the day is long, this was quite normal for the sounding area. Ms. Diamond had been pre-warned as to when the raid would take place. Linda Diamond made sure that none of the local affluent clientele would be present on the night of the "surprise" raid on her business. The ten women she had working for her were also informed as to what would be taking place and were prepared for the police when they arrived. The clients on the other hand were not enlightened as to any of the mock raid, and were arrested along with all the workingwomen.

Linda Diamond had her attorney on call, and by the time LaMar had been allowed to make his one call, Linda Diamond had her women out on bail and back at the "Yellow House."

Ranard Wolffe arrived one hour and twenty minutes after LaMar's call to him. He posted bail and they were on their way by five o'clock. After picking up LaMar's car, they stopped at a local coffee house in the city of Blue Ridge.

The server came up to them in a matter of minutes after arriving. "May I get you gentlemen something?"

"Coffee please." LaMar informed her.

"So, LaMar what the hell happened?" Ranard inquired.

"Hell, I don't know. One minute I was having a good time and the next thing I knew all hell broke loose. Son of a bitch Ranard, I thought you said this place was safe?"

"Well it is. I mean I have been going there, off and on for several years and nothing ever happened. I mean, the women who ran the place assured me that I would be safe, no one would ever know. Hell, it is, was a real professionally run place."

Several minutes passed without either one speaking. The server brought their coffee and left. The two men sat and sipped their hot coffee in total silence.

Then LaMar broke the silence. "Damn! Five hundred for the whore, two hundred for bail. What the hell will the fine be? We have to keep this quiet! Understand! I may need your help on this."

"Not a problem, I'll help you. Hell ain't anyone going to find out, too far from home. Where is Sandy?"

"Ahh, she is gone to some kind of conference in Richmond."

After thirty minutes of conversation and planning, they parted to their homes, a one hour drive.

# Labor Day

I HAD DRIVEN BY THE O'Francis home several times just to see where he lived and how. I had never stopped by for a visit nor requested to come by for a visit. Being the old journalist I am, I just more or less wanted to see things for myself and make a judgment call on observation.

It had been a while since I had talked to J.P., and I had made myself aware of some of the problems he was encountering with the school system and social services. Being the veteran journalist, I was able to establish several contacts in Reynolds County and after some extensive research, it amazed me how someone so dedicated to the betterment of his students got in so much trouble. What further amazed me was that the leadership of the school system did not see his good work. They sure were quick in seeing and reacting to anything controversial that surrounded O'Francis. Yet he stood his ground against whomever or whatever.

I made up my mind to go for a visit. Just drop in without notice. I entered the section of town he lived in, and as I approached where Hickman turned into Maple, I stopped. Up the street, I saw O'Francis laboring away. I backed my Jeep up to a wide spot on the street and decided to observe for a few minutes. He was carrying the remains of a tree, which appeared to have been recently cut. From where I sat, I could see the remains of a stump next to his privacy fence. The line of fifty-foot pine trees that lined the boundary of his land that ran along Maple Street extended from the fence for a good 200 hundred feet to the front section of his property.

I sat and watched him haul an entire tree to some point to the back of his house. I could only see him enter his privacy gate, which he had secured open, and walk toward the hill to the back of his home. Back and forth he went, first the trunk, which had been cut into what appeared to be about four foot lengths. He would heave them up on his shoulder and one by one he would haul them to some point on the hill, then all the limbs and small branches. All this took a bit of time. After he had what appeared to me at any rate, finished, he came to the street with a shop broom and swept the street clean of all small scrap pieces from the tree.

I shook my head. Who in the hell would take the time to clean the street after they had spent close to an hour carrying an entire tree off the side of the street? I told myself I would ask him that very question. It was now shortly after 10:00 a.m. and I felt it was time for a short visit.

As I entered his driveway, his wife Dawn was hanging clothes on the line to the north side of their house. I had never met her, and I heard her call for J.P., informing him that, "someone was here." She did not seem overly joyous. I was aware of their exclusion, even with neighbors. His corner lot with large pine trees covering all of Maple Street and half way up Pine Street helped a great deal, he often times would tell me. He did not mind having "Country" across the street from him. Also facing his property across the street was Alicia, who bought that property off her mother Betty, who he told me had only lived there for about five years. He and Dawn thought a lot of them. Hard workers he would tell me, in addition she kept her place up. She only had one daughter Alicia, and between the two of them, they kept their place in top shape. Just really good people, he would tell me.

J.P. came from the back of their home. His Notre Dame tee shirt was soaked with sweat, and his black headband which had been cut out of a black tee shirt, a strip of cloth about thirty-six inches long was tied at the back of his head with tails of some six to eight inches long, hanging down onto his upper back, was also soaked in sweat. He had a cigar in the left side of his mouth and a bottle of water in his right hand. He was wearing gray shorts, white socks and brown ankle high work boots. As soon as I saw him I began getting out of the jeep. A smile crossed his face as soon as he saw me.

"Hey, John Frederick," he exclaimed with a joyful, warm voice. "Come in, my good friend."

"I assume it will be safe for me to park here."

"Yeah, sure. Hell we ain't going anywhere."

"I mean your sign."

O'Francis turned and looked at the four by four posts that held the cross four by four that held the ends of four clothes lines.

The sign read, *If you are not Irish, your vehicle will be towed away.*

"Oh yes, you are safe." Then he turned as Dawn walked to his side. I had walked to within six feet of them.

"Dawn, this is John Frederick O'Donovan."

"Oh, are we, a wee bit of Irish also?" She spoke in her best Irish brogue, which was quite good.

"Oh yes. Just a wee-bit," I replied with a smile.

We retired to the back of the house where he had built a rather large deck that extended some fifty feet along the house. As I walked to the far end of the deck and turned to look up on the hill he had been hauling the tree to, I saw another very large deck setting some hundred feet toward the top of the incline, that he called his hill. Pine trees surrounded his property. Out from his deck on the hill was a large pine grove.

"Nice place you have here J.P."

"Well thank you. We like it. It has taken us some thirty years to get it the way we want it. But I have enjoyed working on it."

"May we walk up there?" As I pointed to the deck on the hill.

"Sure."

After getting to the twenty-five foot squared deck, I could see what he had been doing with the tree. In between the pine trees, he had over the years built a barrier fence with limbs of trees as well as trees that had been cut into sections of four to six foot lengths. The barrier was three feet high and extended completely around the exterior of his property.

"J.P. I have to ask you a question."

"Okay."

"Why were you sweeping the street?"

"Oh that. Well you see "County" and his nephew, Lloyd help me cut down a very large pine tree that had died. Hell I asked for the power company to come out and cut it, as I was afraid it would fall onto the electrical lines. However, as usual, big companies have little time for the common consumer. Hell, I called them in April. Well, anyway," then he paused and lit his cigar. "As I was telling you, "Country", oh that is a nickname, David is his name. Anyway, David, Lloyd and I cut it down in sections. David hooked a long rope to his truck, then attached it to the upper sections. As Lloyd would notch each one David would ease his truck up the street, and the sections would just miss the power lines as it fell. We finished the cutting late yesterday evening. Well, all that had to be cleaned up. I did not get to it until this morning. The street had many little tiny bits and pieces scattered all over the place. Looked bad, and besides, I made the mess, I needed to clean it up. You know what I mean?"

"Yes I do." Then I smiled at J.P.

"Have you had lunch?" he asked me.

"Well. No, but." He cut me off.

"There will be no buts. I will see if Dawn can fix us a little bit to eat."

By eleven-thirty we were eating. The lunch lasted for two hours. Dawn was the perfect host. J.P., Dawn and I sat in the tranquility of his back deck and talked about the joys of life. Of course, I had to answer a load of questions from Dawn, concerning myself, which I actually found rather enjoyable. I learned another important trait about J.P. He did not talk much when Dawn took the stage. She dominated the discussions. She would have made one hell-of a reporter. I found her intellect to be challenging, her humor extremely joyful, and her wit sharp. I invited her to accompany J.P. sometime on one of his retreats to my home in the mountains. She accepted.

# "Mary Jane"

IT WAS AN OVERCAST DAY with a light rain falling. J.P. was lining the ditch line that went along two sides of his corner property with number five gable stones. "Country" had gotten in from working the post office, his second job, and had come over to see how J.P. was doing.

"What are you doing?"

"Playing in the ditch." J.P. answered. He always liked it when people asked him a rhetorical question.

"Looking good J.P., looking real good."

"I think it will work better. I think the water will flow better and not wash out the ditch as much on these hard ass rains." Then he rose up straight, spit a mouth full of tobacco juice.

"What are you doing in about an hour?" 'Country' asked.

"Working here most likely. Do not see me finishing this soon, slow process, placing rocks in the ditch properly, you know."

"Want to do some recon work?" Dave asked.

"On what?"

"I have a report on some Marijuana plants down where we got the last bunch we found. Thought we might go and see if we can locate the patch, take some pictures."

"Yeah, sure, why not."

"Let me change clothes, take a shit and go get the camera and I will be right back." 'Country' informed J.P.

"I should be about done with this section by then," J.P. stated.

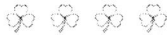

The two traveled the county gravel road down along the tributary creek to the Clinch River for several miles and then turned up through a culvert where a large brook flowed through. The tributary brook flowed directly into the main creek. After exiting the culvert, they traveled along the side of the brook and up the hollow for about a half mile. The going was rough and they had to go slow. The tracker 'Country' had chosen to take, rolled back and forth, as they went up the old rutted out road crossing over the brook twice before coming to a stop.

According to the Chief of Police, Dave Higgenbottom's source, the plants were in a field along the tree line to the upper side of an old house. In addition, according to his source, the people who had the plants had placed steel traps around the area protecting the plants. An old house set some fifty yards up an adjoining hollow from the large brook. A smaller brook to the left of the house, as one faced it, came out of a steep hollow extending further up behind the old unused house. The area was heavily laden with large groves of thick green biars, tall weeds, and grasses of various types and small saplings.

David had his nine M.M. on his hip. J.P. had his .357 in his shoulder holster. Both had walking sticks to test the ground as they walked, to trip the traps, if any were around. They crossed over the brook and worked their way up toward the house. David took the lead with J.P. some ten feet behind walking slowly and probing the ground with every step as they moved through the thick waist high weeds that covered the area of land between the house and the brook. They moved toward the upper side of the house crossing a boggy area that covered some fifty yards square, sinking up to the tops of their boots, as the rain continued to fall. The area would go from marsh to solid ground.

J.P. had his bonnie hat on, jeans, a dark blue lightweight weather jacket and Viet Nam style jungle boots, and a large chew of tobacco in his left cheek. Dave had on a baseball hat with a Norfolk and Southern emblem on it, jeans and camouflage jacket, with black police style boots on.

They crossed several hundred yards of bottom area, when J.P. heard the first trap go off. They froze.

"Damn!" J.P. spoke softly.

"We're close." 'Country' stated. Then he took his camera out and took a picture.

"Felony." David stated and pointed toward the steel trap and looking back at J.P.

Another few feet and another trap went off.

Another picture was taken. J.P. began looking around. "I am about to get a real bad feeling about this 'Country'." The light drizzle continued to fall. J.P.'s mind began to drift. He told himself to get a grip, this was not the time to have a flashback, although he could recall when a similar time took place many years in the past. Instead of steel traps, trip wires. When they went off someone died. He told himself to be alert. The little voice started talking to him. "*You are in danger, be sharp.*"

J.P. unbuttoned his jacket with his left hand. He put the staff in his left hand, reached into his jacket and felt his gun as if to check to see if it was there. He had no idea why he made the move, he just felt as if he needed to. He knew it was there because of the weight of the gun itself.

A large briar patch ten feet high crossed three quarters of the bottom land. The two moved to the upper side of the patch through the weeds. The steep hillside began at the corner of the briar patch. An old rusted fence line partly torn down, some twenty feet up on the side of the hill just where the tree line began, was a path that 'Country' elected to travel. Three more traps were sprung before they came upon a large patch of plants. They were just starting to grow. They were not very tall, maybe two feet tall at the most. They stood side by side looking at the marijuana plants.

"Son of a bitch." Then J.P. started counting.

"I count one hundred and fifty. You count?" he asked Dave.

"Yeah. I got one fifty five." Dave stated in a very low voice.

"Did your source tell you who owned this?"

"Nope. Just where."

"Got any ideas?"

"Yeap." David said. Then he took several pictures of the plants.

"Let's set the traps as we go out. Be careful where we are stepping, probably more all around here."

As the two backtracked out of the marijuana patch, they set the traps and covered them up again.

"'Country,'" J.P. stated as they made their way back across the bottom land. "I do not think we should tell the county about this. I think we should let someone with the state know."

"Yeah, I know. Hell, they'll help them move the damn stuff to a safer place. Ass holes!"

Just as they reached the front of the house, a shot rang out striking the front wall of the house, maybe a foot from J.P.'s right chest area. Both men flattened themselves to the ground.

"Where did the shot come from?" David asked.

"Other side of the hill," J.P. stated. Another rifle shot rang out hitting two feet to the right of the two men, digging up the ground.

"'Country,'" J.P. said, "You break to the left side of the house and I'll go to the right. We'll get behind the house."

"Ready?" David asked.

"Now!" J.P. said. They jumped up and broke in two different directions. Another shot toward J.P.'s side of the house caught the corner of the house, ripping off the wood on the corner six feet high on the house. They both made it to the back of the house at the same time.

"Son-of-a -bitch!" Higgenbottom stated with excitement in his voice.

J.P. looked at his military watch he had put on before he left the house. It read 1600 hours.

"Dave, can you make it to that brook coming out of the hollow?"

"Yeah. Why?"

"You work your way down the brook, should have good cover with all the briers, and little saplings. I will make for the barn then along the briar patch to the main brook. We'll get the sons of a bitches."

Dave looked at J.P. with a question on his face.

O'Francis spoke in a very harsh voice with anger in his words. "Fuck a bunch of legal shit 'Country'! We are at war here. We'll make it legal by god!"

"We going at the same time?" 'Country' asked?

"Yeah. When we move they'll fire, look and see where they are firing from, then we will get close and open up."

"Damn, J.P., I don't know. I mean..."

O'Francis cut him off, and in a commanding voice asked, "You got an extra magazine?"

"Yeah."

J.P. responded, "I got an extra six rounds, including what's in the cylinder now. That's enough to either kill the bastards or run them off."

David checked his magazines. "I have two full mags."

"Okay, you see them, you fire, don't wait on me. Same goes for me. You ready?"

"Ahh, hell I guess. J.P.? Ain't never been in a firefight."

"Hell, 'Country', nothing to it. Believe in yourself. You win!" He took a deep breath.

"Okay, I'm ready," David stated.

"Go!" They broke at the same time. "Country" darted over the bank to the smaller brook, J.P. to the barn to the left of the house. The brook coming out of the hollow was about twenty-five yards away. The barn was about twenty-five yards. Another shot rang out, echoing through the hills. J.P. looked. He did not know which one they were shooting at, but he saw where the shot was coming from. He made it to the barn, in hopes that "Country" made it to the creek. The shooter was about thirty yards up on the side of the opposite hill one hundred and fifty yards on a straight line from the house.

J.P. quickly moved along the edge of the briar patch hugging the ten-foot high wall of briars. The large green vines ripped at his jacket and face as he quickly worked his way to the large brook. A line of trees ran along the brook edge giving him cover from the shooter. He slid to the edge of the brook taking cover behind a medium size tree. He scanned the hillside for any sign of movement. Several minutes passed and then movement. J.P. knew they could not sit still for long. No training. Two men to his right front, a little higher than he had estimated. He pulled his Smith and Wesson blue steel .357 out of his holster and took careful aim with both hands. Slowly he squeezed.

The gun jumped in his hand. The bullet was true but not deadly. It caught one of the two men in the left shoulder spinning him to the ground. The second man quickly turned his rifle toward J.P.'s position. Just as he was about to fire, three quick shots rang out from "Country's" position. Two out of the three missed the man aiming at J.P.'s position, but the one hit the left hip sending him to the ground. J.P. could see both men on the ground, but did not know what their condition was.

O'Francis moved into the brook, and then quickly ran to the side of the hill opposite the brook landing on his belly, aiming his pistol toward the position of the two men now lying on the hillside. To his right "Country" darted across the rutted out road leading up the main hollow, and took a position against the hill. J.P. rose up enough to look toward "Country." He whistled and "Country" raised up enough to look toward J.P.

O'Francis pointed toward the position of the two men, indicating to move up the steep hill. Crawling from tree to tree on their bellies and hands and knees, they slowly moved up the side of the hill. When J.P. got to within twenty feet of the two snipers he could see them lying on the ground. He could hear them moaning in pain. He quickly moved to the next tree aiming his pistol toward the wounded men. "Country" mirrored his every move. They both got even with them on the side of the hill then simultaneously they moved out the side of the hill pointing their pistols at both men.

"Do not move," 'Country' stated. "You are under arrest."

"I'm dying." The one moaned that 'Country' had hit.

The one J.P. had hit in the shoulder had rolled several feet from the other shooter, and was holding his shoulder.

"You son of a bitch! You shot me."

"You think. You fuck!" J.P. snapped, grabbing his rifle by the barrel and tossing it down the side of the hill.

"Hey! Mother-fucker! That is an eight-hundred dollar gun you just threw on the ground!"

O'Francis did not respond to the sniper's lame-brained statement.

"You got that one, Dave?"

"Yeah. Fucked his hip up." 'Country' had picked up the rifle, which had a sling and had slung it over his shoulder. He then put his pistol in his hostler on his side. J.P. had holstered his pistol also.

"Get up," J.P. stated. The man struggled to get his footing.

"I'll kill you, you sonavabitch!" he stated.

"Yeah, yeah, I know. Just shut the fuck up or I'll shoot you in the knee." J.P. told the man.

"Start walking down the hill. If you start to run I'll shoot you in the back of the head!"

J.P. picked up the rifle as they started side stepping down the hill, the only way down without falling.

"I can't walk." the other man stated. "I am bleeding to death."

"Country" looked at the man with a cold careless expression on his face.

"Then I guess you will just have to slide, or crawl down the hill. I ain't going to help you. One way or the other you're going."

"Damn, man you shot me in the hip. I can't."

David cut him off. "Oh yeah you can and you're going too! Now start crawling!" The man rolled over on his belly and began to drag himself down the side of the hill.

When they got to the tracker, "Country" got some rope out of the back and tied the men's hands behind their backs.

"'Country'," J.P. stated. "Run the rope down to his ankles. Put him on his belly." David did.

"Now pull his legs back up toward his back and tie him off."

"Damn man you hurting me." Dave did not respond, he just pulled his legs up toward the back of his head and tied the rope off.

"God-damn it! I said, you are hurting me. I'm shot, you ass hole!"

"Ahh, shut the fuck up!" David cut the rope and gave it to J.P. who repeated the method of securing the men. The man J.P. had shot complained about his shoulder as he pulled his arms behind him. After he had him securely tied up, he leaned down and whispered in his ear.

"You're lucky, you fuck! You are still breathing. If you were dead, I would have your fucking ears!"

David took out his radio off his hip, turned it on, and as all police radios do, it started crackling with activity and squealing. He called the Honsburg P.D., told the dispatcher to get the state police and the rescue squad and gave them directions as to where they were.

"David," J.P. said. "Call the dispatcher back and ask them if Vaga is on duty. If he is not, tell them to call this number." Then he gave it to him. "Tell them to call Vaga first. If Vaga is on duty, he will come. If he is not, tell him I am requesting his assistance. If you cannot reach him with this number, call him at this one." Then he gave that number to David. "He will be at this one for sure."

"Got it." David did as he was requested.

"'Country'," J.P. stated. "It will be dark soon."

"I know."

"While you are doing that, let me get those rags out of the back, and I'll try and stop some of the bleeding on these two yahoo bad asses."

A light rain continued to fall. The two had all but forgotten about the rain and how wet and muddy they now were. J.P. did some medical work on the two, hoping to stop some of the bleeding. The man shot in the hip had passed out.

Forty-five minutes later a cavalry of law enforcement officers had arrived along with the rescue squad. Vaga was on duty and took charge of the crime scene when he arrived. For J.P. it was a relief, as he was the only one he would trust.

The marijuana that was confiscated, when it was harvested at full growth, would have produced a street profit of two hundred thousand dollars or more.

After all had paraded back out of the hollow, leaving only Dave and J.P., the rain was still falling, dark, flashlights giving off the only light. They looked at each other. A smile crossed their faces at the same time. "I think it is time for a bud," David said. "Roger that! Let's get the hell out of here!"

# Religious Sects of the World

As J.P. BEGAN HIS WORLD Geography class to his junior high students, he realized that the material he was about to place on the chalkboard was the same material in which he had been forbidden to ever teach again, according to Damon C. "Himmler" Bales, the head of the LM Gestapo at Housburg High. As J.P. sat at his desk looking at the board a good 30 minutes before his first junior high student would walk through the door, he thought back on that day, which had been one of many infamous days in Bale's office. However, this was not Bale's school. Now would the parents of the junior high students file a complaint with Wolffe and would he have to go through yet another round of why he should not be teaching the major religions of the world to the student. Was it worth the stress of fighting the administration and some of the more narrow-minded people of the community? Blinded by the religious propaganda in which they had been programed to believe. He talked to himself, *"religion is the opium to the mindless masses of the world."*

Was passing along knowledge that important at this point in his teaching career?

It was the start of just another week for O'Francis as he prepared himself for whatever Bale and his disciples would throw at him. Just as the first period began and students entered into his World Geography class, the PA system came on and Belinda was on the other end.

"Mr. O'Francis."

"Yes."

"Mr. O'Francis, Mr. Bale wants to see you in his office during your planning period."

"Okay, thank you Ms. Bookmann."

Jim's planning period was the second period and he knew his trip to the office was not one of congratulation. He could not figure what he was to have done, according to "someone" but it really did not make any difference, it could simply be that he had farted incorrectly. Then he smiled to himself and began his second week of lecturing to his students about the major religions of the world, which included maps, diagrams, and charts of the history of each. He usually like to make it a one-week section, but because of all the interruptions that had taken place the previous week he did not get to finish. So he had two more days of notes to give, one day for review and two tests, one note test and one map and chart test to give, which covered his week in world geography.

Jim had notice that the interest in the subject had perked up with several lackadaisical students, which excited him as more and more questions were being asked concerning all the different religions. He was aware of the religious propaganda that permeated the entire region and stifled the young minds from becoming independently thinking. But he would present them with some facts and maybe it would spark enough interest that a few would become thinkers and not blindly following what "someone" who claimed that God, or Jesus had deemed them the messenger of the word.

He quit his lecture three minutes before the bell rang; bells were something Jim hated, he told me on several occasions as if I had forgotten or that he had over looked telling me;

"The only two institutions in the United States with bell are prisons and school. Now that should tell you something."

Jim went to his brief case and withdrew his tape recorder, checked the batteries and checked the tape, turned sharply to his left, walked out of his

room and headed down the long hallway to the office. As he approached
the office outer door, he clicked on his tape recorder, opened the door and
walked to Belinda's desk.

"Ms. Bookmann, Mr. O'Francis to see Mr. Bale."

She just smiled at Jim, got up and went to Damon's office door;

"Mr. Bale, Mr. O'Francis is here to see you."

All Jim could hear was a grunt, and Belinda came back to the center of
the office area and informed O'Francis to go in.

Jim walked into Bale's office and stood an arm's length from the corner
of his desk.

"Have a set Mr. O'Francis."

Jim did not respond he just took the first chair to his right, which left
one empty chair an arm's length to his right and more in the corner. Both
chairs were the same, deep dark brown with wooden frames, which also
formed the arms of the chair with medium brown leather seating and backing. Jim crossed his left leg over his right and placed his hands in his lap,
cradling his tape recorder in his left hand. Bale had not looked up at Jim,
as he continued to write on a legal pad on his desk. A full minute went by
before he looked up at O'Francis.

"Now Mr. O'Francis, I have here your lesson plans for last week as well
as this week." Then he saw the tape recorder in Jim's hands. He pointed
toward the recorder; "You can turn that off."

"Well, in all due respect to your present position Mr. Bale, I do not
think so."

"Yes, I told you to turn THAT, off. I don't mind you taking notes, but
you will not use a tape recorder in any of our conversations."

"Well, Mr. Bale, if you prefer taking notes I do not mind at all, but as
for my choice of recording any of our conversations it will be done via taping. Moreover, sir, I do believe we have had this conversation once before.
Now if you have nothing you would like to discuss with me that is notewor-
thy of recording, I have papers I need to grade, so if you will excuse me."

Jim stood, but before he could make his now infamous military turn, which
he knew irritated his principal, Bale commanded him to set down.

"Find! As I was about to say, your lesson plans are unacceptable."

Expecting a response from Jim, Bale paused. Jim said nothing, he just sat in his chair, leg crossed, hands in his lap, looking directly at Damon.

"Okay, if that is the way you are going to be." He held the two sheets of paper up and directed them at Jim.

"I just want to know why you are teaching about religion in your class. More especially these other religions: Just how is it that you think you are some sort of expert on these things. Mr. O'Francis, I am getting real tired of having parents call me and complaining about your classroom lectures on matter that these students do not need to know anything about. I really do not understand you. I do not have these problems out of my other teachers. Why can't you just go along with everyone else and follow the curriculum?"

Jim cleared his throat, "Wellll, Mr. Bale, let me just start by stating that I am following the curriculum." Bale started to speak; Jim held his right hand up in the air with only his index finger extended upward. "Sir, if I may be allowed to continue without interruption." Bale's face began to turn rose colored.

"Now according to the text and according to the county curriculum, world geography encompasses all the major religions of the world. In order for the student to get a better understanding of all these religions I have provided them with factual information, maps and charts as to their time of origin up to the present day, as well as all the branches of the origin or the roots of each of the religions. As to the expert part, I have done extensive research on the subject matter and have had 15 hours of college courses in the subject. An I might add, from an extremely reputable University. Now as to parents calling you, well I do not understand why they would call you. I am the person teaching the course and I am the one who could answer any of their questions concerning the material in which I am teaching. I will say that my students are enjoying the subject matter and are quite interested in gaining knowledge. I have not had one to complain to me about any of the notes or material in general in which I have provided for them. Point of fact is they are asking a lot of really good questions and the subject matter has sparked a great deal of interest."

By that time, Bale's face had slowly changed color from a very light rose to a dark blood red. His hands had cured up into a fist as they rested on the top of his desk. Jim's voice remained a calm steady level the entire time he was talking. He had finished his comments concerning his lesson plans. He calmly sat very erect in his chair, and for thirty seconds there was silence in the office. Jim never took his eyes off Bale. It was as if an eruption was building deep inside the very bowels of a human volcano and the magma was rapidly making its way up through the vents with a major eruption about to occur, blowing the very top off the "mountain".

"Let me tell you something. I do not intend on you continuing on the same path you are going. I will not allow you to teach any religion in your classroom, other than that which is the true religion in this area, which is the only real religion of the entire world. Do I make myself clear on that matter?"

"I understand what you have said Sir. However, the fact remains that there are other religions of the world, the course itself calls for the introduction of these other religions, and they are incorporated into the text. All I am doing is providing a more clear understanding of these religions. I am not teaching the theology of these religions, but the historical facts about them. The text does not do so, and as a teacher, it is my duty to provide the students with as much knowledge about the subject in which we are encountering as possible."

"I personally do not care about the other religions of the world, and the parents in this area do not either. Now you will stop teaching about any of these religions at once."

"Does that include this religion you are referring too?"

"You just do not get it do you. You are in the Bible belt Mr. O'Francis. This is not some school up north. If you want to tell the students about the true religion, I do not have a problem with that. But you are not to talk about any of the other religions."

"Well, okay Mr. Bale. But you have really not told me just what religion I am to enlighten the student on?"

"What?"

"Well, you stated the true religion of the area, correct? Well sir, just what religion is that?"

"Are you just totally incompetent?"

"Sir, I am neither incompetent on the subject matter nor am I violating any school policy or state policy in relations to the subject matter."

"Mr. O'Francis", as he drew out his last name, "have you ever really read the good book?"

"Mr. Bale, if you are referring to the "Book," in which you all have dubbed the "Bible," yes I have. I have found it to be fractured with a great deal of anomalies, a not so greatly written history book, I might add."

"Did you say history book?"

"Yes, I did. It is very subjective to say the very least."

"What?"

"Knowledge, Mr. Bale is the most powerful weapon on earth. Something you and your kind fear more than death itself."

"You are really a heretic"

"Ahhh, yes, Mr. Bale, Simply and correctly put, choice. It is mind to make."

"Do you not go to church?" He lashed out, not recognizing what O'Francis had just stated.

Jim set saying not a word knowing that Damon did not caught the meaning of heretic. "Well, do you Mr. O'Francis?" Jim still did not respond.

"The protestant religion is, the only religion, the true religion of the world. It is the only real Christian religion of the world. It is the only way to real salvation. It is the word of God. I am a deacon in my church and I am telling you that is the way it is going to be as long as I am the principal of this school. You will obey me and you will not make any reference to any of these other so called religions in your classroom."

Jim began a slow smile, which eventually crossed his entire face.

"Do you find this to be humorous Mr. O'Francis?"

"Well sir, point of fact is, I do."

At that Bale stood, shoving his chair backward: "What are you anyway? Are you some kind of devil worshiper?"

"No Mr. Bale I am not. Point of fact is I was baptized Catholic in a cathedral in Tulsa Oklahoma. However, I do question your devotion to this religion you are referring too."

"What?"

"I think you heard me correctly sir. I need not repeat myself."

"That explains a lot."

"Which means what Mr. Bale?"

Bale paused for a moment looking at O'Francis as if he had made a statement that troubled him, then seat back down in his chair in a heavy manner. He pulled himself back up to his desk, his facial expression, strained. Picking up his pen, he began to write on his legal pad. Jim remained seated in his chair in silence. He put his pen down and leaned forward slightly over onto his desk.

"Mr. O'Francis, I personally do not conceder Catholic's Christians. You can believe what you like of course, but you will not teach anything other than the facts about the protestant religion in your class. It is what has saved this Nation, it is what this Nation believes in and I will not have you corrupt these children's minds with false information, is that clear."

Before Jim could respond Damon continued; "I think you have covered enough about religion in your class as it is. Move on to the next section. Whatever that is?" Then he looked down at his paper as if he was reading what he had written, and then picking up his pen began to write again.

"Mr. Bale, before I go, I would like to tell you that in order for me to teach about the origins of your protestant religion I had to incorporate the religion of Judaism and Catholicism and their origins. I did not mean to influence any one's personal way of thinking; I simply wanted to present the students with some basic facts about the different religions. I simply want them to learn to think, to question, to seek knowledge."

Again he put his pen down and with his body gesture of discuss slowly leaned back in his chair, took a deep breath.

"I do not know where you get all this insane information about the protestant religion, you are wrong! Catholic and Judaism, teaching them to think, gaining knowledge, you apparently do not know what you are talking about! Now, you are not to teach any other religion in your class!"

Then he leaned forward onto the top of his desk, his teeth were locked together as he spoke through them.

"Do I make myself clear, Mr. O'Francis! Your teachings are insane!"

"Sir, insane?"

Damon's voice lowered, a first for J.P., his eyes looked dark, and his facial expression turned hard. "That is correct, insane! You really do not know whom you are dealing with here. I know all about the bible and I am well aware of what the true religion is. You apparently are confused. You really do not want to cross me."

His intimating performance did not frighten Jim and he began laughing, "You have got to be kidding me. Mr. Bale, in all due respect, you are sadly misinformed. Moreover, as far as the roots of the Christian religion goes, your religion or the one in which you sat in that chair at this present time and calm is your religion, as well as the one I was born into comes from Judaism. That is a fact. Facts are all I have ever dealt in. Since I do not have the time to educate you about Judaism as well as Catholicism, maybe you should join my class and learn about the roots to this religion you clam you believe in. And since I have never been bias when it comes to any religion, you also could get educated on the basic beliefs of the other religions of the world. Furthermore, if you want to talk about who and what you worship, we could schedule an afternoon and you and I can get down to the real issues. Evil."

Bale became so angered his hands began to tremble, his face became distorted and he looked as if his blood pressure was off the scale.

"I have heard enough of this blasphemous. You will not teach anything related to any religion in your class I don't care if it is in the text or not. Skip it! I do not want to hear of you teaching anything related to religion! If I do, I am recommending your immediate dismissal. Now get out of here."

As he waved his right arm, foreword and flipping his hand as if to back slap some insect away, then looked down at his note pad picked up his pen and began to write quickly. Jim stood, turned and as he walked to the door, stopped turned back around took two steps back toward Bale's desk. "Mr. Bale, to answer your question, I know exactly who you are. It is the people that are exposed to you that do not know. You have a blessed day now, you hear."

Jim turned sharply and exited the office. He was but a few steps from Bale's office door, when he heard him state; "Pagan!" O'Francis smiled when he heard what he had said, as he walked by Belinda's desk and wished her a good day and thanked her, he walked out of the office, mid-way down the hall he clicked off his tape recorder. Talking aloud to himself, *"well, that went rather nicely. Damn, he really would have blown a fuse if I had told him I included the teaching of Paganism in my lectures."* Then he laughed aloud.

# The Abduction

DAMON BALE HAD BEEN A frequent visitor to the Cellar lounge for many years. The lounge was located in the lower part of a very plush hotel in the middle of Abetton, a historical town with lots of 1700 and 1800 buildings.

The timing was critical and there had been many hours put in on surveillance to make sure the mission was completed without any hitches.

Damon and his wife arrived at 8:30 P.M.. they went into the more plush room off to the right of the dance floor where live music was being played for the younger crowds that came to be entertained for a Friday night. The Plush room had a more casual relaxed atmosphere with four plush large soft, badge colored, heavily padded chairs and two large soft padded couches. There were four modern hard wood square tables with four chairs and two with two chairs located about the room. A television was located to rear of the room usually carrying the news channel. A long bar was located to the left of the door as one enters the room with ten hard oak wood, soft padded seated bar stools with concaved backs and a television in the center of the back and above the bar usually carrying the sports channel.

As you entered into the more popular forty by forty foot, entertainment room there was a stage where the live bands would play. Just to the front of the stage was a dance area that could accommodate thirty to forty people. Just to the rear of the dance floor there were ten tables with four chairs per table and to the far left side of the entertainment room there as a separate room with a large opening with an old antique decor with eight tables with four chairs and four with two chairs scattered about the room. One could set and enjoy the sounds and sights of the band as well as the people dancing and not be on top of them. A fire place was located at the very back of the room which was usually lit with gas logs and gave off a warm glow in the dimly lit room during the late fall and throughout the winter months. To the right of the fire place was an exit door with two steps leading out into the back of the hotel parking lot. As one entered the rustic room to the right was a short hallway that lead to the restrooms, the women's room was the first on the left as one went down the hallway and the men's was at the far end of the corridor.

Brian O'Francis' Hawker Siddeley HS 125 arrived at Missoula, Montana at 0600 hours and taxied to the hanger and stopped.

J.P. O'Francis waited until the plane came to a stop before he got out of his truck. He stood by the open truck door dressed in Wrangler blue jeans, long sleeved blue denim shirt, brown western boots, and tanned leather coat with a sheep lining. The early morning fall Montana air was quite cool and J.P. had his winter gear on as the warm air exhaled from his lungs, his breath gave the temperature away.

As the hatch of the plane was opened and the steppes were lowered Bruce Beck exited from the plane, looked toward the few parking slots at the far end of the hanger. He walked down the steps and toward O'Francis.

"Good morning J.P. how are you this great morning?"

"I am doing well Bruce. Good to see you."

"Are you ready?"

"Yes. Let me get my bag." J.P. reached across the seat and picked up his small leather dark blue travel bag. Closed the door to the truck, clicked his electronic door lock twice and walked with Bruce toward the plane.

The pilot revved the jet engines up and they moved to the runway.

"I will get us some coffee as soon as we are air borne."

"Nice plane Bruce." As J.P. examined the light tan leather seats.

"Yes it is. Brian has several. Not all like this one, but they all are fast and comfortable."

In a matter of minutes they were in the air and cruising at twenty thousand feet.

Nick Zileri, was forty-five years old, black hair with a touch of gray on the sides. He was six foot two and weighted an even two-hundred pounds with dark tanned skin. Tony Mauriello, was thirty-five years old with short dark brown hair, cut in a military style, olive skin tone, stood six foot two and weighted two hundred and twenty pound. Joseph Scirrotta was the youngest of the three, 33 years old smooth Mediterranean complexion, black hair, six foot four and two hundred and thirty solid muscular pounds.

They had arrived at the Cellar at 7:45 P.M. and had taken the last table next to the rest room hallway. Every ten minutes Joseph would make the trip from the rustic section to the less noisy plush section and scan the room. By 8:45 P.M. they knew that Damon Bale was present in the lounge. Damon usually only stayed at the Cellar for about two hours each time he came, which was twice a month.

At 9:30 P.M. Damon passed in front of the table where the three men sat and went down the hallway to the restroom. Nick rose from his seat first, and then Joseph and Tony, Nick took a position at the door and Joseph and Tony went into the restroom. Two other patrons were departing the restroom as Joseph and Tony went in. They quickly check the room for anyone else and found that other than Damon they were alone. Tony stepped back out the door and told Nick.

Two minutes later two other young men came down the hallway as they approached the restroom door Nick flashed a badge and informed them that there was a little problem inside and could they give him a few minutes. The two young men stated that they had no problem with that and returned down the hallway.

Damon finished urinating and stepped to the sink to wash his hands; Joseph walked quickly over to him from his rear and with the force of a vice placed a chloroform cloth over his nose and mouth. Within moments Damon's body was as limp as a wet dish rag. Tony and Joseph lifted him up placing his arms over their shoulders and came out the door. Nick led the way down the hall and to the right to the exit door. The few patrons in the room at the time looked but said nothing. Most were dancing in the entertainment room to the loud music being played by a local band.

They quickly carried him to the SUV that had been parked as close as possible to the exit door. Nick opened the right back door and Joseph and Tony shoved Damon into the back seat. Tony got into the passenger's seat and Nick had gotten into the driver's seat and had started the SUV. Three minutes later, they were out on the main street headed to the signal light at the end of the street. They made a left and two minutes later they were entering onto the interstate headed south.

Within thirty minutes they drive up to the private hanger where the private jet was already prepared to taxi out onto the runway for takeoff. Paul walked over to the SUV as the three men unloaded Damon and carried him onto the plane.

Nick smiled at Paul as he approached.

"It went like clockwork."

"I'll take care of the rental." Paul stated. "You all have a safe trip, oh, and tell J.P. I said hello and that I would be in touch."

"Will do; later Paul, and thanks for the help."

"Hey, not a problem, glade to be of service."

Within minutes the plane was air borne heading west.

Ten minutes had passed, Damon had not returned, and his wife got up and approached the manager Ted Mason, who was standing at the door entrance to the lounge. They knew Mason, as they had been regulars for several years.

"Mason would you check on Damon as he went to the restroom ten minutes ago and has not returned."

Mason informed her he would and walked to the men's room. There were four other men in the room and he looked around, checked the stales and found that Damon was not there. He came out of the restroom and back into the rustic room scanned it for Damon, then he stepped to the large opening that lead to the dance floor room and scanned it and no Damon. He returned to the Plush Room and informed Mrs. Bale that Damon was nowhere to be found and asked if he could have stepped out with someone to the patio which was to the rear of the lounge by way of the exit door. She informed him that she did not know, but did not think so? Mason told her he would check for her, and did so. Returned to inform her he was not there. A since of panic come over Evelyn Bale and Mason could see it in her face. Mason called security and they began a search for Damon. When he was not found they began asking the patrons in the lounge if they had seen an older man anywhere and gave them the description and what he was wearing. After forty-five minutes of inquiring two couples setting next to the fire place informed the two security men that three men had helped an old man out the exit door about an hour earlier and that it appeared that he was passed out and that they were just helping him. When asked to describe the three men, none could, as they had not given much thought to the matter. At that point, Ted Mason called the police and in a matter of minutes, they had arrived at the Cellar. Evelyn went into a hysteric mode clamming that something bad had happened to him and then began going on about a J.P. O'Francis. The police questioned her in Mason's office and inquired as to who O'Francis was and she inform them that he was Damon's sworn enemy and that he was very dangerous. Continuing the investigation throughout the rest of the night and into the morning hours they had learned nothing. No one had seen anything nor heard anything. All they had was three men helping an old man out of the exit door.

Bruce and J.P. arrived at Hunt Airport in Portland, Texas at 9:00 A.M. and get into a rental SUV. They drove south on 181 to 358 south to 22 south to State Park road 53, turned north to Port Aransas then turned north on 361 to Avenue G, made a left onto Port Street and went to the end of the street where they pulled up to an abandoned warehouse at 11:00 A.M.

Nick and company had arrived at the same airport at 2:00 A.M. with a confused and scared Damon Bale. They loaded him in a Jeep Grand Cherokee, then taken the same route as Bruce, and was awaiting the arrival of Bruce and J.P.

Damon sat at the end of a ten foot long, five foot wide old dusty work table and had been told to keep his mouth shut. The large building was dark with the exception of a Coleman lantern that burned at the far end of the table opposite of where Damon sat. There were no sounds to be heard other than the burning of the lantern. Damon was exhausted, his eyes were heavy from lack of sleep, and he would drift off from time to time and jerk himself awake only after a few minutes.

The faint light of the morning sun filtered through the breaks in the old broken windows high above from where Damon sat alone. The streams of sun light reviled the dust in the air as he looked around trying to locate someone and then he spoke.

"Who are you and where am I?"

From a distant to Damon's rear, a deep voice relied.

"I would suggest that you sit in your chair and say nothing."

Damon did not respond for a few seconds, and then he spoke again.

"I need to stand up."

Joseph appeared from the rear of where Damon was seated.

"You may stand."

Damon slowly rose his legs were numb and stiff, his buttock was sore from the hard wooden chair he had been sitting on. He turned slowly to face Joseph. In a slow old man's sounding voice he asked.

"Who are you and where am I?"

Joseph stood ten feet away from Damon and did not respond to his question.

"Can I walk around?" Damon asked.

"Yes." As Joseph stood erect his arms to his side his feet shoulder width apart. "You may walk around the table and that is all."

Damon's insides quivered, his skin became covered with bumps as he began slowly walking around the table. The floor of the warehouse was covered in two inches of very fine dirt which had been collecting for many years. Pigeons began their morning activity of flying in and out of the many openings in the upper parts of the building. As Damon circled the table he looked around the large empty space and saw nothing other than the man standing at the far end of the table. He could not see to the far end of the warehouse some fifty yards away because of the dark shadows. The sound of a door being opened was heard in the far distance to the rear of where Damon was at.

Joseph spoke in a calm deep voice; "you may take a seat now."

Damon stopped at the only chair at the table and stared at Joseph. Joseph never said a word, he just stared at Damon and the look along was all it took for Damon to obey his request. Fear reflected on his face and in his eyes as he finally took a seat.

Damon heard a vehicle enter the confines of the warehouse, the engine being turned off and then several doors being closed. His heart begin to beat faster, his skin became hot and beads of sweet appeared on his forehead. He placed his hands on the dusty table, and then he lifted them and looked down at the dust on his hands. Slowly and softly wiping them he placed them in his lap. To his back he could hear men's voices. Several minutes passed and then there was silence. He sat looking around from side to side but he did not turn and look to his rear. It was if an eidolon had manifested at the end of the long gray-white dust covered table. The lowly flickering lamp gave off a shadowy figure of a man, his head was tilted downward; he had a large flat-brimmed dark brown western style hat on. His thick full extended white mustache trailing down to the very top of the upper part of his each side of his chin. The man stood motionless for several minutes.

Silence permeated the large warehouse. Damon sat starring toward the person opposite of him. Slowly the man reached his left hand up, removed his hat, and placed it on the end of the dusty table. His head was still tilted downward. Damon could see he had gray-white closely trimmed hair and a mustache that matched in color, but because of the lack of illumination, he could not see the man's face.

Slowly the man looked up and directly at Damon. At that moment, he saw his face and took a deep gasping breath as if he was looking directly at an apparition. Then he stated.

"YOU!"

The response was; "Time has come today."

The man raised his right hand, holding a black cylinder magnum Smith & Wesson .357, and he squeezed the trigger once. The bullet struck Bale in the center of his forehead sending his body backward over the chair and onto the dusty warehouse floor, spraying a smattering of dust upward. The echoing sound reverberated throughout the building sending the pigeons and other birds fluttering and flying about the large empty area.

Moments passed and the man with the pistol stood motionless, his arms to his side. He slowly reached down and picked up his hat placed it on his head and calmly walked to the far end of the table where Bale lay. The chair lying on its back, Damon's arms lay outward from his lifeless body. Pieces of his skill and brains lay a few feet from his head. Blood being soaked up by the thick dust on the floor turning it an even darker color red.

The man looked down at Damon, without a word, he walked to the awaiting vehicle, handed the pistol to Bruce and got into the back seat of the passenger side.

Ten minutes later, the warehouse was once again silent and empty of any human life.

John O'Donovan got up at his regular time of 7:00 A.M. showered, got dressed, went to the kitchen and put on a pot of coffee. He then went down to the garage clicked open the garage door and drive down the mountain to his paper box, retrieved his Monday morning paper and returned to his home at the top of the mountain. The morning mountain air was a bit cool, mid 40's and with the slight breeze it felt as if it was in the mid 30's. John went back into the kitchen got his oversized coffee cup, filled it and went into his great room to his favorite chair, placed his cup on the rustic pine table to the left of the chair and sat down. The chair faced the east side of the great room, which had solid glass window from the ceiling to the floor. There was no deck on the outside which allowed him to view the forest and its creatures without obstruction. The great room was on the second floor allowing him to look down and over the cleared land some twenty yards to the edge of the tree line. He enjoyed just setting and looking out at the forest and on occasion deer that would graze on the soft grass between the tree line and his home.

Just as he got comfortable and ready to read his paper his cat "Boaz" jumped into his lap for his morning petting session. "Boaz" had showed up at John's home some five years earlier and had taken up residence with John. He enjoyed his company and had taken him to the vet and got him the proper shots and had him fixed. "Boaz" was a rather large black and white cat with three white paws. John had no idea what kind he was but had become very attached to him. He administered his morning petting as "Boaz" purred in his lap as they sat and looked out the window while John took a sip of coffee from time to time. Then suddenly "Boaz" jumped down and strolled over to his hand build bed/chair/perch at the base of the full window to observe what was happen below him, if anything. John reached over and picked up his paper and began to scan the front page.

"Well, now let's see what has been taking place over the week-end "Boaz" as if his cat understood him. "Boaz" looked over at him and gave a soft mow in response to John's statement and then looked back out the window and laid down folded his front paws inward, settling on his perch for the morning. John looked over the front page quickly reading a few articles scanning as he usual did as most of the time nothing really interested him. However on this day one article did catch his attention. There on the right side was the heading; Damon Bale missing. He read the article and quickly got up went to the kitchen for more coffee and went to his den for his file on Bale. As he re-entered the great room the phone rang. He picked the phone up and walked to his seat.

"Hello, John O'Donovan here."

"Morning John, its Anthony Krause. How are you this fine Monday morning?"

"I am doing well; how about you?"

"I am fine. Say, I have some questions for you. Have you read the morning paper yet?"

"Well, yes, but just started. Why?"

"Well, have you read the article on Damon Bale yet?"

"Yes just finished it."

Anthony proceeded to tell him that he just so happened to be present at the Cellar Friday night when he had disappeared in front of everyone and that no one knew who had abducted him. He was following the investigation and was in hopes that he could tell him a little about the man and his wife's accusation that O'Francis had something to do with his disappearance.

"Well Anthony to tell you the truth I have not seen O'Francis in several years and I really do not know where he went. However, I serious doubt that he had anything to do with Damon's disappearance. By the way where were you when all this took place?"

"I was in the Plush Room where Damon and his wife were. Several of us guys had a night out together and just out of nowhere, there were police all over the place asking everyone in the place all kinds of questions. His wife went off the chart. The par-medic's had to be called in and had to take her to the hospital as she was having heart palpitations and they thought she was going to stroke out on them."

"Well Anthony sounds as if you had an exciting evening."

"John, did he and O'Francis have some problems back in the earlier nineties?"

"Yes, but my God, he had problems with a lot of people. Just because his wife stated that J.P. would have had anything to do with his disappearance is a stretch I would think?"

"I don't know John, she seems to think that Bale was in constant fear that he would do something to him. And it is the only name that seems to be coming up."

"Well what have you turned up? What have the police found out?"

"Nothing, absolutely nothing. I think the local police have turned it over to the F.B. I. and they are treating it like a missing person's case. No one even knows O'Francis. They have been over to Honsburg to see if anyone knew where he had moved to and found nothing. They went by the county school system and I guess all the people there were relativity new and had heard of him, but did not know where he was located. Didn't he retire from the school system?"

"Yes, he did."

"Well, I followed up on the school lead, but no one knew anything. Hell, retiree have to get a check don't they?"

"I would assume so."

"Isn't that part of the VRS."

"I really don't know Anthony."

"It is as if he just disappeared himself from the face of the earth. That is what makes this even more intriguing. So, can you help me out here?"

"Tell me Anthony, have you been to Honsburg yet?"

"Oh yes, but the people there do not seem to know where he went to."

"Have you talked to the town police yet?"

"Yelp, did that too. However, he told me after his son and his wife's death that O'Francis left about five years ago to parts unknown. I even tracked down and talked to the retired police chief. By the way, wasn't O'Francis and the re-tired Chief over there good friends?"

"Yes, to the best of my knowledge they were."

"Well, do you think he was telling me the truth about where O'Francis could have gone?"

"Yes, I would say he was. I think O'Francis just up and left without telling anyone where he was going. Actually he was more of a recluse than anyone realized. So, I actually do not think he told anyone. "

"Well, tell me this John, did he not give you any idea as to where he would have gone? I mean you and him were tight, weren't you?"

"Well I would say we were well acquainted, but tight, well I would not say that. He just walked off one evening and I never heard from him again. Tried locating him, even went by where he lived and he had sold his home to someone, cannot remember their names, a young couple. I asked them but they did not know, said they had gone through a local realtor. And before you ask Anthony, yes I went by the realtor's office and spoke to the person who sold the home for him and they knew nothing."

John sat in his chair and smiled as Anthony continued to probe in hopes that he might get a lead on O'Francis' where bout's for a big new story. After a fifteen minute conversation of which Anthony had gotten no new information he asked John one question before bidding John a good-bye and requested that he contact him if he could think of or that if he happened to come across anything of importance or news worthy, from one semi-retired reporter to one working a case.

"John, do you have any idea as to what a black lily means?"

John paused in conversation. "No, I don't think I do. Why?"

"Well the police found one lying on the sink of the restroom at the Cellar. I just thought it might have some type of significance?"

"Well, I really cannot help you there Anthony."

# Investigation

CAPTAIN BUSHMAN STEPPED TO HIS office door and called detectives Branch and Bass into his office.

"Yes Sir."

"I have been looking over your note on this Brewer case. I think there is more to the case than meets the eye. I want you to go to Honsburg and do some investigating. I want to know what the connection is between the other cases. I have been on the phone with the Chief in Liberty and Jefferson City and Abetton, they are going to provide us with all the information they have on their cases. I want you to find out all you can on this, ahhh," He turned over the two pages of note on his desk, "Ahh, O'Francis. I want to know if there is any connection. His name has cropped up several times according to these other police departments. Find him."

"Okay. But…we have been over it with several people, including the Reynolds County Sheriff's Department and really they had very little to help us. Captain, apparently no one really knows where this guy is."

"Do it again. They may remember something. Talk to the local's; find something we can go on. There is just something about this that is nagging at me, I think they maybe something to that phone call."

The two detectives left the office and headed for Reynolds County.

They arrived in Honsburg at 11:00 o'clock in the morning, and as they approached the town's post office, they pulled in the parking lot thinking that the post master knew everyone in a small town and would be able to at least give them a lead on O'Francis.

Burt had on a blue sports coat, white shirt, red tie, tan slacks, and brown loafers. Jason had on a tan jacket, light blue shirt, dark blue tie, tan slacks, and brown loafers. They approached the counter inside the post office and requested to see the Post Master. In a few seconds, Mr. Jon Waldon came to the counter.

"May I help you?"

"Yes you may." Burt said.

"I am detective Bass and this is detective Branch. We are from Kinstown, is there some place we can talk to you privately?"

"Yes, in my office. It is that door over there, as he pointed to the far side of the room. I will open it for you." Jon left and in a few seconds he opened the door and the two detectives stepped into Waldon's office.

"Gentlemen, how may I help you? Have a seat," as Jon pointed to two chairs sitting in from of his desk. Jon's office was rather plain with a few pictures of postal history on the wall, nothing else. His desk was clear of any paper work. He had a stapler, tap dispenser, and one penholder on his desk with three pens in it.

"We are investigating the death of one of your county residences, a Dunkin Brewer. Did you know him?"

"I knew of him."

"You did know he was found dead down in our area a while back, didn't you?"

"Yes, read about it in the paper."

"How about a Richard Finkel?"

"Yes, hear about that one also, but did not know him."

Bass paused for a few seconds thinking the Post Master would continue with the conversation but Jon sat in his chair waiting on the next question.

"Okay. Mr." Bass paused as he forgot the Post Masters name, Jon answered.

"Waldon."

"Yes. Sorry Mr. Waldon."

"It's okay."

"Okay, what about a women by the name of Janice Jones. Do you know her?"

"Yes. I knew her, have not seen her in many years. Think she moved away. Ahh, maybe up in northern Virginia not real sure about that part but that was what the gossip in the town was at one time."

"Well, actually Mr. Waldon, she is on a missing persons list. She disappeared about six months ago from the town of Liberty. The FBI are looking into that.

"Oh, I was not aware of that." Jon said.

"Well that is okay. We are looking into the possible connections between these people since they all seem to be from this area."

"Branch spoke for the first time in the conversation." He opened his note pad and looked at it.

"Do you know a man by the name of Damon Bale?"

"Yes, I knew of him. He was a principal here at the high school for a time back in the, ahhh, let me think…I think maybe in the 1980's. Not real sure about that, I was not around here back then."

"Well, were you aware that he is also listed as a missing person?"

"No, I was not aware of that either. I am assuming that the F.B.I. is looking into that one also?"

"Yes they are, as well as us."

"Well, how about a man by the name of O'Francis? Did you know him?"

"Yes."

"Know where we can find him?"

"No."

"Know anyone who might?"

"Well, O'Francis use to live around here but he moved several years ago. I really don't know where. He never left any forwarding address for us, he just up and left after he lost his wife."

The two detectives continued to ask the post master questions about the people that were missing or dead, figuring that being a small town he would know. They ask him about the police chief, and was informed that he probably would not know much. Told them of the retired chief and told them where he live. Stating he might be able to help them?

Finding out that Jon wife, Rachel also knew O'Francis they got directions to her work place, which the local elementary school where she was a secretary.

After going through a multitude of questions with Rachel and checking with the town police chief who gave them nothing as he had not known any of the people. However learning that the Mayor, Mr. Charles Headley Winslow might know as he had been around a long time. Stopping by the local mayors place of business, they gathered information on all the people on their list. However none of it seem to get them any closer to finding the whereabouts of J.P. O'Francis. So they headed to the retired police chiefs house, who lived several mile away.

Running the back roads and getting lost twice, they found former Chief Higgenbottom. After thirty minutes of probing they ended up with no more than they had when they left Honsburg. Which after returning to report to their Captain, did not go over well at all.

# Legs

LA MAR MARSHY'S CORRUPT ACTIONS of hiding money and shifting it around so many times that no one really knew where or what the school budget money really was. There had been questions by the newly elected school board, but no one seemed to be able to get any real straight answers. He had for years been funneling large sums of money into an unknown account, using various means and personal primarily his loyal book keeper and lover. But the time had come when to many questions were being asked and legal charges were being discussed by the new board, a board in which he had only two members he could control and would support him, leaving four that would probe deeper and expose him for what he really was, a thief. The cost for such a legal undertaking would be long and costly, and the Board elected to buy Marshy's contract out, still leaving him with over two hundred and fifty thousand dollars in walk away money in his pocket. Something J.P. and the teachers association was not in favor of, but had no control over.

La Mar moved on to newer and better ground, east, to the far end of Virginia where he would begin a new career as a superintendent of a school system that did not know what they were getting. When he left he hung everyone remotely connected to him out to dry, including his lover and book keeper who lose her job but without jail time for her part in the alleged embezzlement that no one wanted to pursue in a court of law.

Bruce was once again clicking roll after roll of film of Marshy, when he left his home to his arrival at his new school's central office to his social events to his extra martial affairs which he continued with his new found lady's at his new school district.

Bruce had logged his travel times to and from various places and had plotted a drafted plan of action for Marshy's abduction. O'Francis was not to be involved in the actual abduction however would to be involved on the finial end of the mission. Bruce and Paul had meet with Brian in St. Louis at one of Brian's hotels. They had discussed the mission in every detail, and were putting the final touches of it. Once again, Jordan was to be involved as Marshy's weakness was attractive women.

Marshy had trimmed down his weight from two hundred seventy pounds to a more present appealing two hundred pounds. Jordan and Bruce arrived in Richmond via Brian's private jet and Paul arrived via car and picked them up and checked into the Holiday Inn-Airport on Williamsburg Road. Having dinner and reviewing the finial plans for the pick-up of Marshy and then they retired for the evening. By 0600 on Friday morning, they were on the road headed west weaving their way through the city of Richmond on route 60 and into the countryside to the small town of Buckingham.

Jordan Black had made an appointment with Marshy two weeks in advance; she was representing a private computer software company that wanted to test their new math and science software on real students before releasing it to the public. It was at no cost to the school district and the school district would be allowed to keep the new software. Marshy agreed to talk to her and gave Ms. Felice Eugena an appointment for 1030 A.M.

Jordan walked into the central office at 1015 A.M.

"Ms. Felice Eugena to see Mr. Marshy. I have an appointment at 1030."

At 1030 on the dot Marshy walked out into the lobby of the central office. Jordan was setting with her left leg crossed over her right and Marshy almost gave himself away by taking in a gasping breath when his eyes gazed upon the stunning beauty of Jordan, her smooth dark Native American legs was exposed up to the middle of her thigh and his eyes flashed instantly to them and Jordan watch his eyes as he approached and knew she had him. She was dressed in a black sleeveless body fitting top of the knee dress that outlined the shape of her hour glass body, with black high heel opened toe shoes, she stood as he approached and Marshy's eyes gave himself away once again as they traveled the entire length of her body.

She stuck her hand out, "Mr. Marshy, I am Felice Eugena, thank you for seeing me."

Marshy smile went from ear to ear. "No, thank you for coming." Then he held his hand out indicating for her to go through the door to the far right of the receptionist. As she went by him, her very expensive perfume penetrated LaMar's nostrils sending "goose" bumps down the middle of his back.

They retired to his office where she gave him her pitch and presented him with the factitious portfolio. Shifting her legs several times from left to right and from right to left as she went over each page of what the software company was offering. Jordan watched his eyes and each time she shifted her legs LaMar looked up from the portfolio and looked at her. After a forty-five minute conversation of all the company was willing to do for his school district, Jordan made her move.

"Mr. Marshy...," he interrupted her, "you can call me LaMar." Okay, LaMar, as I was saying, it has been a rather long trip from Texas and I was wondering if there is a place one can stay overnight as my flight back does not leave until late Saturday evening."

Marshy of course informed her where she might stay and instantly lost his train of thought as he mind went to a half of a night in bed with her.

"Mr. Marshy, is there anywhere one can go to lunch in your town?"

"Oh yes, there is a very nice restaurant five minutes from here?"

"Would you like to join me for a bit of lunch? It will be on the company and we can continue our conversation over lunch, as I am a little hungry. I came straight here from the airport and have not had anything to eat."

Marshy gladly accepted the invitation and they walked out of his office, as he went past his secretary, he informed her he was going out to lunch and would be back by one o'clock. As they went through the lobby and by the receptionist he also informed her that he was going out to lunch and would be back by one.

As they exited the central office building Felice, informed him that they could take her car and promised that she would not kidnap such a hunk of a man. Marshy laughed loudly; "Felice, being kidnapped by you might prove to be interesting."

"Yes LaMar, I think it would." As she smiled and made eye contact with him.

He agreed to take Felice's car as they walked toward a black Chrysler 300. The sides and back of the windows of the car were darkened and Marshy could not see the two men setting inside the front seat as they approached the car from the rear. Paul and Bruce watched them through the side mirrors as they walked the twenty-five yards from the front door of the central office across the parking lot. Being the gentleman he was, he walked Jordan to the driver's side as she clicked the key chain to unlock the doors. As he opened the driver's side door, Jordan was standing beside the left rear door, talking and smiling keeping LaMar's total attention.

"LaMar, you are such a southern gentleman." Which prompted him to turn his head to the right and look at her for just an instant and in that moment of time Bruce wheeled out from under the steering wheel and sent a breath exhausting blow to LaMar's mid-section bending him over. Marshy only saw an instant of a blur of a figure emerging from the car. Bruce grabbed his suit coat at the right upper shoulder and presented a pistol in his face and in a low deep voice, ordered him to get into the back seat as Jordan had opened the left rear door just as Bruce struck him. LaMar was still gasping for air to refill his lungs and could not respond as Bruce forcefully moved him into the back seat, and got in beside him closing the door behind him. Jordan got in the driver's seat and closed the door. Paul had reached over and started the engine just as Bruce had struck Marshy, Jordan backed out of the parking spot, shifted to drive and pulled out heading for the parking lot exit. The entire sequence of events had taken place in a matter of less than a minute. There had not been anyone leaving or coming during this minute. As they exited the school board office parking lot a FedEx truck and a car were entering, but not being able to see into the side windows of the car they had no idea as to who was in the car. Marshy was still trying to get his breathing back to normal as he laid his head back and sucked in air, his mid-section ached with pain; "What are you doing?" he finely gasped out.

"Kidnapping you." As Bruce leaned over and softly spoke into his left ear. Marshy's eyes were fully dilated as he slowly looked over and gazed into the dark brown almost black, cold hard eyes of Bruce Beck.

# Impending Danger

His contact with the DEA was done covertly. He used an alias and mailed the information to the only honest State Trooper he knew, Lenny Vaga.

J.P. had tried for several years to work with the Reynolds County drug agency, but had gotten little or no success. It had taken several years before learning that several county deputies plus the sheriff himself either turned their heads or held out their hands when it came to certain people who were directly or indirectly involved in trafficking drugs within the county which resulted in being well rewarded for not doing their jobs.

J.P. had gone down town to obtain material from the hardware store. Where he tried to do as much business as he could. As he believed in supporting the local businesses. While there getting what he needed for yet another small project, he took the opportunity to talk to the Mayor, C.H. Winslow about a bit of a traffic problem in his neighborhood, which J.P. knew was drug related.

O'Francis came out of the Winslow's hardware store, walked the few steps to his pick-up truck and opened the door, he looked down the street to the corner, standing at the corner were two former students and a man he did not know. Bobby Joe looked toward J.P., O'Francis closed his truck door and walked the half block to the corner.

Bobby Joe had been a favorite of his when in school. He encouraged him to get off the pills and marijuana each time he saw him. O'Francis did not walk away or shun him when they passed on the street, or when he crossed paths in one of the stores in the town.

Bobby had always liked O'Francis, because he was one of the very few teachers in Honsburg High that had helped him as well as pushed him so he could graduate. Bobby knew that if it were not for J.P.'s guidance he would have never graduated. Bob knew that O'Francis did not like what he did, but he knew he always spoke and ask how he was doing. He knew that he always had something positive to say to him before they parted.

J.P. approached the group and spoke to Bobby first.

"What's up Bobby?"

Ahhhh, nothing much, Coach." J.P. looked at Darrell and Spoke.

"How you doing Darrell."

"Okay Coach. How you?" J.P. smiled at the two former students, as he spoke to them.

"Ahhh, I am doing well I guess, same ole same ole, you know how this school system is run."

As both nodded their heads yes they spoke in unison. "Oh, yes we know."

J.P. then addressed Bobby Joe.

"So, what are you doing now days Bobby?"

"Ahh, working as a flag man on that construction job over next to Liberty."

"Well good. Do you like it?"

"Well, yeah, I guess. It's a job Coach."

"Well, you never know, you stick with it you may get a chance to move up to something better, working for a company like that." Then J.P. looked at Darrell.

"So, Darrell what are you doing with yourself?"

"Nothing. Just hanging out."

"No job?"

"Nope."

"Well did you check with the construction company that Bobby is working for? They may need something done. Or at least they will have your application on file."

O'Francis' peripheral vision caught the frond expression on the face of the man of what J.P. figured to be a thirty year old. J.P. did not know the man and did not bother to introduce himself nor ask his name. About the time J.P. started to ask Darrell another question, the man with a full black beard, black hair down to his shoulders, faded out jeans, and jean jacket tattered at the ends of the sleeves, spoke in a rather deep voice. "Sure do ask a lot of questions mister." J.P. did not look at him nor did he comment on his statement.

"Darrell, you need help getting a job some place, a reference maybe?"

When Darrell answered O'Francis, his tone of voice had changed slightly to a harsher one.

"No man, I don't need nothing." J.P. smiled as he spoke. "Well, if you ever do, just let me know. If I can, I will help. Okay." Darrell never answered O'Francis.

O'Francis patted Bobby on his left shoulder; "Bobby you need anything you know where I live."

Bobby smiled at O'Francis. "Okay Coach, I will. Thanks Coach."

"Hey, no problem, be glad to help. See you two guys. Do good now, you hear." Bobby was the only one who replied. "Okay Coach."

J.P. turned and walked back to his truck, get in and drove by the corner waving at the two young mid twenty year olds as he passed.

At 10:30 that night, the phone rang at the O'Francis house. Patrick answered, J.P. heard him coming down the hall to the den.

"Dad, it is for you."

"Who is it?"

"Don't know? It's a man, calling from a pay phone."

"Okay, thanks." He pivoted in his swivel chair and reached for the phone.

"Hello."

"Coach. It's Bobby."

"Well...Bobby my man. What can I do for you?"

"Coach I really need to talk to you."

"Okay. I am all ears."

"No coach, not on the phone." J.P. paused, knowing that it was not for advice from his former teacher.

"Okay. When would you like to talk?"

"Coach, I know it's late, but could you meet me tonight?" O'Francis thoughts were that it was very series by the tone of his voice.

"Okay. Ahhh, where are you at now Bobby?" J.P. could hear people talking in the background as well as the sounds of automobiles. Bobby cleared his throat.

"I am at the Exxon now. I know it's late Coach, but ahhh, can you meet me down on Lewis creek?"

"Okay, Bobby. I can handle that, where at?"

"Howbout where the road turns up from the river, you know where that white church is?"

"Yes. Give me twenty minutes."

"Coach it's really important."

"Bobby, I'll be there. I promise. Have I ever made a promise I did not keep."

"Nope, not to me."

"Right. Then I will be there in twenty minutes."

"I'll be there Coach. See you in twenty." Then he hung the phone up. J.P. waited for several seconds listening before he placed the receiver down.

As J.P. was putting on his western boots, Dawn came down the hallway and into the bedroom.

"Who was that?"

"An ex-student."

"Who?"

"Bobby Lebert."

"What did he want?"

"He needs to talk to me about something." J.P. went to the nightstand on his side of the bed. Went down on his right knee, lifted the nightstand with his left hand, reached under it with his right hand, and pulled out a .357 wrapped in a black cloth and laid it on the bed. Then he opened the drawer of the nightstand, took out his shoulder holster, and put it over his Notre Dame tee shirt. Took the cloth off the revolver, opened the cylinder, checked the shells, position the cylinder where the first shell would be the quarter shot shall to fire. Every other shell was a .357 hollow point.

"J.P. what is going on?"

"Don't know? He just wants to meet me and talk about something important."

Dawn's voice expressed concern. "Don't worry. I'll be careful." He gave Dawn a kiss and went out the back door grabbing his Levi jacket off the coat rack as he went out.

He traveled the dirt road following the creek until it emptied into the river, then followed the dirt road that ran alongside the river, passing one house after another, some with lights on some with no lights. He arrived at the church within twenty minutes. He pulled up beside the driver's side of the dark blue 1987-chevy cavalier with gray primer paint on the left front fender and the right quarter panel. Turned the lights off, then the engine. Rolled down the window. It was very dark, no streetlights. His eyes adjusted quickly to the dark.

"Hello Bobby, fancy meeting you here."

"Hi Coach. Sorry for the late night call."

"Ahhh, it's okay. I assume this is really important for such a covert meeting?" The look on Bobby's face told J.P. that he did not know what the word covert meant. J.P. told him.

J.P. opened his door and stepped out. Bobby opened his door and got out. J.P. noted that his dome light did not come on in his car.

"Okay Bobby, let's talk over on the steps." The two walked the one hundred feet to the church steps. They sat on the second of the five steps that lead to the church doors.

It was a cool night, fifty degree. Bobby took out a pack of cigarettes and lit one. J.P. pulled a cigar out of his inside pocket of his jacket. Reached into his right outside pocket and took out a cigar cutter, clipped the end off, licked the cigar from one end to another. Put the cutter back into the pocket, took out his lighter, and lit his cigar.

"Coach, I know you know I smoke pot and I know you don't tell nobody. I know you don't like drugs." J.P. said nothing; he just let Bobby talk as he puffed on his cigar.

"You know that guy that was with me and Darrel today." J.P. looked at Bobby in the dark of the night.

"Didn't know him."

"Well. He was a dealer. He wants me to work for him. He wants me to push the hard stuff for him. Said he would pay me well."

"Ah-huh."

"But that is not what I want to talk to you about." O'Francis did not say anything. There were a few moments of silence as Bobby gathered his thoughts.

"Look coach, he knows you are trying to stop the drugs in Honsburg."

"Hammmm. I see." J.P. responded.

"Coach, you know that there are cops working for the county that are working for the drug pushers in the county?"

"I see." Was all the response that J.P. gave?

"They know about you Coach."

"Okay. So, they know. I do not make any secret about my efforts to stop the drug traffic in Honsburg as well as the county."

"I know. But…" Then Bobby stopped talking." A long moment of silence and all that could be heard was the flowing of the river some fifty yards over the bank. Then J.P. spoke.

"But what Bobby… hell man, don't stop now. You wanted to talk to me. Shit man, just come out with it."

"Okay… I was told that they are going to put a stop to you. That you are costing them too much."

"How?"

"I don't know. I guess by telling somebody about the drug deals in Honsburg. You know that several people have gone to jail."

"Yes, but not the ones that should be in jail. It is the users, not the dealers! People like you Bobby. I do not want you all. I want the dealers. I want the money man or men whichever the case may be! I want the people at the top. And for the record Bobby, I do know a few people that are deeply involved and they are at the top, your good upstanding church going citizens that is who I want the legal system to nail."

"Well, that is what I mean. The cops are involved. They are on the take. And they are the ones that are telling on you."

"Well, Bobby how do the cops know that I am the one telling about the drug dealers?"

"I don't know. I just know that they have been talking about you."

"Well, tell me Bobby who are they." Bobby had put out his cigarette and lit another. J.P. sat quietly with his arms resting on his knees, taking a puff off his cigar once every minute or so.

"Coach this is really serious. I mean these people are really bad. I mean you can't tell nobody we are talking."

"Bobby. You do not have to worry about that. I give you my word that no one, I mean no one will know we talked."

"I mean..." Then he stopped. Took a deep drag off his cigarette, flipped the ashes off the end. He took the same position as O'Francis looking out into the dark of the night. He finished his second cigarette, dropped it at his feet, lifted his left foot, and crushed it out. J.P. held his cigar in between his left index finger and his middle finger. He touched the half inch of ashes at the end of his cigar to his left knee and they dropped at his feet. Put the cigar to his mouth and puffed on it a few times.

"I mean what Bobby?"

"Well, there are some talk that...well that they are, ahhh, they are going to ahhh take you out." J.P. never moved. He did not talk. He just looked out toward the river. The night carried the sound of the water rolling across the rocky shallows of the river as it turned and followed the mountain ridge as it had done for thousands of years. An owl pierced the silence of the night.

"I really don't know the main man. I just know that the two county cops that are working with the people I know."

"Who's the guy on the street with you today?"

"That would be Jake Salvador. Or that is what I know him as."

"Soo, where he from?"

"Don't know."

"Who's the cops?"

"Sam Crouse, Greg Felton, Danny Vachel and John Lakeland."

"Anybody else."

"Not sure. Don't think so, could be. Hell Coach, I think the Sheriff is in on the deals too."

"So how they supposed to do me in?"

"Don't know? Just that some of the guys been talking about it. You know some of the guys don't like you Coach."

"Yeah, well...I don't like some of them either." Then there was silence for two minutes or so.

"Know who is supposed to do me?"

"Nope."

"So who told you that somebody was going to do me in?"

"Got it from James and Ted. They don't like you. Said they hoped somebody did."

"Where they get the info?"

"They didn't say. Just said they had heard."

"James and Ted have any dealings with the cops."

"Yeah."

"How you know that?"

"They told me."

"Why?"

"Why what?"

"Why they tell you?"

"I don't know. Just was talking one night. Said they wouldn't bust them if they worked with them. Lakeland and Vachel met with the dealers."

"How you know that?"

"Hey Coach, we see things. We know who doing the deals and who getting the money. Ahh, once in a while they get us some fee stuff. You know how it is." J.P. never answered.

"Which ones does the most contact with the dealers?"

"Lakeland and Vachel for sure. Not sure about the others." J.P.'s cigar was three quarters of the way smoked. He reached the cigar down between his feet and touched the long ashes to the concrete steps. They broke off smooth. He straightened his back, arching his shoulders back, several spinal desks popped.

"Well Bobby, this is real interesting."

"Got anything else for me?"

"Nope. Just that."

"You think they, whoever they might me, are serious?"

"Yeah Coach. I mean Jake, is one of them I think."

"One of the ones going to get rid of me?"

"I think so."

"Soo, Bobby, why you telling me?"

"Cause, I like you. I know you don't like what I do, but I am trying to stop. You know, cut back. I don't like all this talk about getting rid of you. You help me when I was in school, and all. I just think you should know. I mean you might be able to, you know, stop them or something."

"Ah-huh. I see. Well, maybe." J.P. stood, then Bobby.

"Tell you what Bobby, let's call it a night. You let me know if you get anything new on getting rid of me okay."

"Okay Coach, I will." J.P. shook his hand and thanked him for the warning. They got in their vehicles and departed.

# Turning Point

PATRICK WAS NOT AS FORTUNATE as his older brother when it came to his high school days. Patrick's class was generally made up of losers, people who were drug users and would in time become dealers and movers of the cancer that beleaguered the community in which Patrick lived and grew up in, a place where J.P. had moved to escape the blights of the big cities of America. However the cancer that griped all cities, large and small in its death grip, had spread to the small towns and rural communities.

Dawn and J.P. worked hard to stay on top of Patrick and his attitude toward his academic's, which had started back in his junior high school days with his science teacher who should have been removed from the system. But like most if not all public school systems throughout the United States, either because of unions or just the fact that the administrators were incompetent to do the jobs they were supposed to do, making sure the students got a good education, and weed out the dead wood, non-caring and incompetent teachers. Teachers like Fred had done more damage to more students and their overall attitudes toward learning than any the O'Francis' had ever seen. Patrick was one of his victims, and it was up to his parents to try and correct the damage. His athletic career did not fair a lot better. The administration at the school was extremely poor, with little or no leadership, not that it had been all that good over the years the O'Francis family had lived in the community. All the negatives of the school atmosphere as well as the community were carrying a heavy toll on Patrick and his parents. They had tried to keep a positive attitude about his

596

career, pushing him to excel, trying to overcome the negative that he was exposed to on a daily basis.

Patrick's high school day's ended with a bitter taste in his mouth, both athletically and academically. He went off to college, but he did not have the desire to excel on a higher educational level. His intelligence level was there, his will was not. Two years and he dropped out to go to work in the oil and gas drilling profession. The students who had skimmed by in high school had graduated to the street, where they made more money selling and dealing in the drug world than Patrick did in his profession as a driller and with a lot less physical labor. Patrick had reached the age of 21 and had yet to escape the clutches of marijuana, which could be obtained with ease most anywhere. J.P. had mixed feeling about "MJ", he knew it was no worse of a substance abusing product than that of alcohol. In some cases, less of a problem for society as a whole. It was just that it was currently illegal, which put his son in jeopardy.

It was another normal teenage and post teen party and Patrick was in attendances, like many others of his high school days. Beer and marijuana were the main course for the night. Pills of assorted degrees of highs and the ever present coke provided by the more affluent filtered through the ones who could pay for it. The ages ran from seventeen to twenty-six, with a social economic class ranging from the poor side of town to the very rich side of town had gathered for a night of alcohol, drugs and sex. When it came to ADS, class distention, wealth, race, gender or intelligence did not play a factor in the end game.

As it was BYO, Patrick chose his favorite, Crown Royal. It was one thirty in the morning, when the drug task force rolled in on the house, grabbing one after another slinging them to the floor striking them with their batons. Anyone with long hair, boy or girl clothed or necked were grabbed and pulled or slung against a wall or onto the floor. One would have thought by the manner in which the local police officers were conducting themselves that it was 1968, and the protest riots, instead of 1998, and a drug bust on a group of youths. The Reynolds County Police had slept through the class on police abuse. The Reynolds County drug task force had to put on a good show for the members of the State drug enforcement agency.

Patrick had never been a violent person, a little on the passive side unless pushed, and then his Irish surfaced. He was clean-shaven with a military haircut. He was no angel of course nor was all the others gathered that evening, as one after the other were arrested and drug out of the house.

Patrick raised his arms high in the air to the approaching county deputy, "Hay man, I am going, no problem." He stated clearly to the county deputy. But that was not enough, he could not grab his hair, so he took his baton and struck him behind his knees sending his six foot two, two hundred pound Patrick to the floor. Using his black Gestapo style boots, the deputies' foot caved in his left rib cage, then a blow to the right side of his head with his baton, bringing forth a gush of blood. A State Trooper had walked into the room just as the County Deputy had struck Patrick across the head with his baton.

"What the hell are you doing?" He yelled in a deep voice.

"Teaching this piece of shit a lesson!" Replied the deputy in his toughest, tough cop tone.

The Trooper stepped between the deputy and Patrick. Reaching down and assisted Patrick to his feet, even with the blood covering his head and the side of his face he recognized who it was.

"Holy shit!" The Trooper exclaimed. Then he helped Patrick to a county police car, told him to stand by the door and not move. The County deputy watched as the Trooper walked away. Then he walked toward Patrick, stopped and looked at him, Patrick's head was lowered, his right hand over the gash on the side of his head, blood dripping between his fingers to the ground.

"Yeah; I know who you are too! I never liked your piece of shit old man anyway! Fuck him too!" He stated with bitterness in his voice. Then with a quick violent motion, his right elbow caught Patrick's left jaw sending him to the ground putting Patrick's mind in a semi mental state. He then took his right foot drove it into his face; breaking his nose and gashing open his lips. Trooper Vaga had been talking to two of the States drug agents and had looked toward the squad car where he had placed Patrick just as Couch's foot made contact with Patrick's face. He instantly broke into a run toward Couch from some thirty feet away, with his large hands grabbed the deputy by his coat and slinging him away from Patrick to the far side of the squad car. Vaga's structure was much larger than that of Couch and had no problem man handling him to the far side of the car.

"You know; you are one stupid son of a bitch! You know who that boy is?" He yelled at the county deputy. His face inches from deputy Couch's face the brim of his hat touching Couch's forehead like the old days of the military D.I.'s . With a smirk on his face and a sarcastic tone to his voice, Couch replied.

"Yeah, I know who the little son of a bitch is! So, what makes him so god damn special!" Deputy Couch snapped back.

Trooper Lenny Franklin Vaga, L.F. for the people who knew him, had known J.P. for over forty years, and J.P. had provided Vaga with information that had led to several rather large drug busts throughout the county. To Trooper Vaga, J.P. was one of the "good guys" as well as a very good friend. Vaga knew J.P.'s background, knew he had worked under William Peng and had been trained by him. Anybody in law enforcement in the entire state knew if you worked for and had been trained by William Peng you had to be a clean Law Enforcement Officer. Vaga also knew of J.P.'s elite military background. Vaga himself was a veteran of the Viet Nam Conflict and like Peng had served the Marine Corp with pride and honor.

As he was having his "man to man" with Deputy Couch, Lt. Samuel Drake, the Reynolds County Officer in charge of running the drug task force, seeing the conflict between the two men approached the scene.

"L.F.; What the hell is going on?" He asked.

"One of your finest here has most likely cost us one of our best supporters and a valued link to information we normally cannot get!" Lieutenant Drake had a look of puzzlement on his face. Vaga saw it.

"Follow me!" He stated harshly, his voice strong and filled with anger with both hands still holding onto Deputy Couch's coat. Vaga shoved him hard against the squad car, stating. "Stupid! Just plain damn stupid!" Vaga walked Lieutenant Drake around the car where Patrick lay on the ground dazed. Vaga squatted and helped Patrick set up, telling him who he was as he leaned him against the cars back door. Samuel squatted and shined his light to his now cut and blooded face.

"God damn-it!" Drake yelled out. "Well Fuck! I don't believe this shit!" He continued his colorful metaphors. He stood, took two steps away, turned and looking back at Patrick, "God-damnit!" Taking his hat off and slamming it to the ground, yelling at the top of his voice, "Couch!"

Couch had gone to mingle with the other corrupt deputies that riddled the County police Department. He did not hear Drake yell for him as he was bitching about how Patrick O'Francis was being treated different from the others they had arrested. As he spouted off at the mouth about the special treatment of Patrick O'Francis.

"I don't know why Drake likes O'Francis so god-damn much. Hell I think he is a piece of shit!" Deputy Brent Whit spoke; "Well, I'll tell you why." As his face became crimson and his voice denoted his anger. "The same reason I like him! He was our teacher and coach. He was a damn good one. The only one who really gave a rat's ass about others and me in high school. Now Couch I really don't know why you don't like Coach O'Francis, but some of us do. I have heard enough. So, just keep your fuck'en comments to your fuck'en self."

"I can't stand the son of a bitch! Hell Brent, you know god damn well where he is when it come to our, and by god that includes you, side job! Soo, why should you give a fuck about O'Francis!" Then he paused. None of the other four deputies was saying anything. Then Couch continued. "Hell man, he would hang your ass just as quick as any of the others we deal with and you know it."

At that point big Jamie "Red" Flennor came walking over to the group. He was one of only a few that had not caved in to the temptation of the extra money from the dealer. Big "Red" as he was known and for good reason. Jamie Flennor stood six foot six, and weight three hundred plus pounds. His strength appeared to be beyond human. He was a close acquaintance and considered the O'Francis family friends. J.P. had taught his daughter and son in school, and had work with "Big Red" during the time when there was no corruption in the County Police Department under William Peng.

"What is this I hear about Patrick O'Francis being hurt?" He asked the group. Couch knew that Flennor also liked O'Francis. He did not like Flennor, and spoke.

"Yeah. He's over there." As he point toward Trooper Vaga and Drake. Drake called out Couch's name the second time. "COUCH!"

Flennor looked at Deputy Couch.

"Drake wants you." As both walked over to where Drake and Vaga were.

Flennor walked to the side of Vaga.

"What's this about J.P.'s son Patrick? I didn't see him when we went in."

"Come with me." Vaga stated. Drake and Couch walked off in the opposite direction.

Patrick had lain down on the ground against the back wheel of the squad car. Vaga and Flennor walked to where he was. Jamie squatted down placed his mage light on the ground, and like a giant grizzle bear gently raised Patrick up and leaned him against the back wheel. Vaga shined his light onto Patrick's face.

"Oh my God." We need to get him to the hospital L.F., like now! Shit. Who did this?" As the gentle giant rose to tour over his longtime friend, Lenny Vaga who was a very large man himself..

"One of Drakes boys!" Lenny stated.

"Who?" Jamie asked.

"Couch. I saw him hit him twice. Don't know how many more time. Bastard. You know "Big Red" what this means." As both men looked at each other and shook their heads.

"I know we had better get Patrick to the hospital. I damn sure know that. Damn, Lenny, he is hurt bad."

"Help me get him in my car. I'll go ahead and take him. You tell Drake." Trooper Vaga stated as he squatted down to assist Patrick up. Patrick was still dazed and was not feeling the full pain of his bruised ribs and busted up face. His legs were like rubber, as Flennor and Vaga carried him to Vaga State Police Car.

It was 2:30 a.m. when the phone startled J.P. awake, a parent's greatest fear, a phone call in the middle of the night.

"J.P., Coach" The unrecognized voice on the other end of the line said.

"Yes speaking." O'Francis said, his heart beginning to pound harder each second.

"Samuel Drake here. Sorry to bother you at this hour of the morning, but you need to come over to the jail." J.P. set up in the bed becoming instantly awake. Dawn being awakened by the phone felt his sudden movement and raised up. "What's wrong?" She said with the fear of a mother's voice. J.P. remained calm, "Brother Drake," as both belonged to the same Masonic Lodge, "What is it?"

"Well it's Patrick." Samuel stated.

"What?" J.P. replied.

"J.P., he was at the wrong place at the wrong time tonight. He is okay, just a small problem. Look, I will handle it. Just get dressed and come over to my office. I'll be up stairs, okay." Samuel stated firmly.

The twenty-minute drive seemed to take longer than twenty minutes. Maybe it was because both he and Dawn rode in silence the entire way.

As they climbed the wooden stairs to Samuel Drakes office, their footsteps seem to echo loader than normal in the old narrow wooden stairwell. He opened Samuel's office door at the top of the stairs, and was met by Samuel with a cup of coffee in his hand. He handed it to J.P.

"How about you Mrs. O'Francis?" He asked. Trooper Vaga was seated to the left of the door entrance and rose, all six foot four and two hundred thirty pounds, sticking his hand out greeting J.P., In his deep voice, "Morning J.P., sorry about this. Mrs. O'Francis." As he nodded at Dawn.

"Okay gentlemen, where is Patrick?" J.P. asked. Samuel answered.

"J.P. he is at the hospital." Samuel looked quickly at Dawn. "Now look Mrs. O'Francis," as the look on her face told them everything, "He'll be alright."

J.P. looked around the room before he spoke. Lenny Vaga was still standing, Samuel was to Dawns left, Officer Wilson, plains cloths officer and sometimes undercover officer for a regional drug task force, was setting to the far right hand corner as you entered the room.

"Well this must be really bad, both of you are out tonight." Then he turned and looked at Wilson, "And you. You part of this. So let's have it." J.P. stated in a military tone of voice.

J.P. was not expecting what he heard. Both he and Dawn had taken a seat, as Samuel and Lenny explained what had gone down. After all had been said, a moment of silence. Lenny looked over at J.P.

"We are not going to charge Patrick with anything. Our undercover man told us he was only drinking, stated that he had brought his own bottle of Crown to the party. Continuing, he had stated that he had not seen him doing any of the drugs. He was a little high, but not drunk."

More silence as J.P. took all that was being said in and running it through his mind. He looked at Wilson. "You there?" Asked J.P.

"No." Came the first response he had made since the O'Francis' had entered the room.

"We had someone their age working. He has being working undercover for some time now. He is a good man." Brad Wilson stated.

"J.P." L.F. continued, "He was just at the wrong party at the wrong time." Samuel spoke.

"Coach, look, I will take care of the over reaction by my officer. I truly want to apologize for all this. It is wrong and I will take care of it. Please let me handle it okay?"

J.P. never said a word, just set looking at Samuel, L.F., and Brad. The phone rang; Brad picked it up, and by the conversation, J.P. and Dawn knew that their son was down at the jail. He hung the phone up, turned in his chair.

"J.P. you can pick up Patrick and take him home now." Lenny Vaga stood and as J.P. and Dawn stood, Vaga placed his large hand on his friend shoulder.

"He'll be all right. I'll talk to you in a few days. J.P., let us handle this, I promise you it will be handled properly. I promise."

As Dawn went out the door J.P. followed, stopped at the top of the stairs looked at Samuel. Samuel Drake stepped close to J.P. placed his hand on J.P.'s back, whispered in his ear,

"Brother to Brother; I will take care of this. Take Patrick home, and care for him."

J.P. thanked Lenny and Samuel, then giving Samuel a Masonic hand-shake, stepped back to the doorway and shook Vaga's hand. He and Dawn went down to their son and departed.

It had been three month since the incident had occurred with Patrick, when O'Francis was exiting David's grocery, deputy Couch was entering. He had been suspended for one month without pay and had been removed from the drug task force and was bitterer than ever at O'Francis.

The County Sheriff was retiring at the end of the year and Sam Drake would run for the High Sheriff and get elected. He would in time change the image of the department and would with time get rid of the corrupt officers within the department. Trooper Vaga would leave the State Drug Task Force and retire because of politics and corruption within the State Police.

J.P. waited on Couch outside the store, and as he exited he spoke. "Deputy Couch." He turned to face J.P., "Just wanted you to know that there is no time limit." J.P. stated with a smile on his face.

"Just what does that mean?" Couch puffed up in a manly posture, as if he was about to exert his police powers on James Patrick O'Francis.

"Just what I said." O'Francis stated. Waved and smiled, then J.P. turned and went to his car. As he drove off, he vowed to himself, no more police help.

# A Pleasant Encounter

O'FRANCIS HAD BEEN WORKING IN his new job for several years, and had become attached to it, as he found that he could achieve a great deal with students one on one. The students that were on the higher intellectual level, he did not have to help a lot, but enjoyed talking to them as they became more comfortable with each other and were able to expand into areas and topics that were taboo in the classroom. The students that did need a lot of help with whatever subject, he enjoyed, because he was able to get them through the courses and raise their GPA, as well as he was able to see the joy on their faces when they got their tests back with high grades and the grades for any given six weeks. It also made very happy parents. He also was able to learn about teachers in the other three high schools in the county. Some were very good, a low per cent were very bad, but yet were able to maintain their jobs, doing great damage to certain students that were not able to overcome their none caring, biases and callousness. A concern for J.P. when it came to students on home bound, which lead to more than one confrontation with certain teachers. However with the aid of very good record keeping and the support of principals and a newly appointed super-intendent, J.P. never loss a single "battle" and the students he had on HB, won. Which was all that mattered to O'Francis.

As the years past, so very quickly, he found that two of his former student had entered into the field of IT. They had gotten a job working for Reynolds County as the county was attempting to more forward into the world of high tech. Not that anyone in control really wanted to, as none really understood the world of computers, and it would mean that the county would have to put forth more money to educate the student body. Not to exclude that they would have to hire people who actually knew what they were doing in the world of high tech. It was a matter of necessity, that anyone on the school board approved any budget remotely connected to the field of IT. Reynolds County and the "know it all's" entered into the IT world as slow as the state and federal subsidizing would allow. Never leading in anything, but rather being forced to obtain materials and personnel to maintain the needed equipment to operate in a world of computers.

J.P. was a forward think individual, always thinking out of the preverbal box, and enjoyed conversing and associating with people who did also. Upon his arrival to his office at 0900 hours, and having no students scheduled for that morning, due to two cancelations, he wondered into the IT department. Much to his surprise there were two former students, Nobel Bryan and Blake Vanpelt, working away at repairing computers and operating some individual school computer system that was ran through their department. Upon seeing their former teacher, all work stopped for a cup of fresh coffee, and a long break. The conversation went from how they got there, and had it been that long, to a general "bitch" session of the lack of intelligence of the higher echelon that ran the school system.

J.P. would over time, learn that both were extremely gifted in what they did, and were way above the level of intelligence of the people that did the hiring for the system as a whole. Every chance he could, which was not often, due to his schedule, but would pop in on them and spend a little time talking to both Noble and Blake. It seemed to lift his sometime unpleasant day, to a higher level when he could spend a few minutes with both, as they were positive, progressive thinking young men. It also did his "soul" good to see his former students achieving success. And of course a few good laughs when they would remind him of something that had happened in their class, or something that he had told them and that they had never forgotten. J.P. marveled at the "things" he did not remember taking place, that they did. He did appreciate the fact that they did not forget "O'Francis Think Tank," the nick name of his room, and the answer to the questions, "What is the most powerful weapon on earth? And what is the worst thing a person can waste?"

The one thing I learned about J.P. and his relationship with any one of his students, that it would last far into the future, and that they would carry with them more than he would have ever though they had learned.

# The Hit

AT THREE A.M., A SUV pulled into the parking lot of the Honsburg fire department. Since the mountain town's fire department was made up of volunteers, there was no one on duty at the fire station. The driver of the SUV turned off the engine and sat in the semi-dark of the parking lot observing the houses leading into the Holliman section of the town. He remained in his vehicle for ten minutes. No automobiles came into or exited during this period. The driver opened the door, no dome light came on, he stepped out, opened the back driver's side door and retrieved a 12 gage modified; cut down to 18 inches Winchester model 700 pump shot gun. He closed the back door and then the driver's door quietly. Standing motionless for several minutes, he then jacked one shall into the chamber. He wore black ankle high soft sole shoes; black leather paints; black turtle neck sweater; full length black leather coat; black leather gloves; and a black leather flat brimmed western hat. He opened the left side of his coat and slid the barrel of the shotgun down into the special pocket sown into the coat. He walked across the parking lot and onto Hickman Street where he continued walking toward his assignment. In a few minutes, he came to the first intersection, Hickman and Maple, where he veered onto Maple. He continued on Maple until he came to Pine and Maple, where he turned onto Pine Street. The streetlights were far enough apart that he became a shadowy figure as he made his way to his point of destination, which was the corner house. The night was cold, 28 degrees in the late month of February. The weather report had called for a light snow flurries. The night sky was dark with clouds, and a very light mist had begun to fall. There was no natural illumination and the night seemed darker than normal. There were no dogs barking, no sound at all. A deathly silence seemed to cover the northwestern section of the town. He stopped at 1700 Pine Street; entered the drive way, and then to the far corner of the yard, where an eight foot private fence separated the two houses. Directly across Pine Street at 1701 was the home of David "Country" Higgenbottom.

He stood in the dark of the corner of the yard, observing the ranch style home. The yard was sixty feet from house to street, with a row of pine trees along the Maple Street side of the yard and then hafts way up the Pine Street side. A three layered split rail fence lined the outside of the pines and ended at the driveway. An open driveway and then a short section of split rails continued to the corner to the privacy fence. The privacy fence continued across the north side of the yard separating the house at 1702. The ranch style home was an unusually lone house for the area, some eighty feet. The front door of the house was just off to the right of the driveway, then a bay window then two-bed room windows; a deck four feet off the ground started some six feet from the second bedroom window. A large glass door allowed entrance from the front deck to the master bedroom.

It was now 3:30 a.m. and he walked to the back of the house by way of the private fence. The backdoor of the house opened onto a one hundred year old handmade brick patio. The outer door was a full glass wooden framed storm door. He tried opening it; it was not locked. The inter door was a solid wood door, he turned the knob slowly, it too was unlocked. Slowly he opened it looking carefully into the room, the man slowly stepped down into a laundry room. The room was an eight by ten with shelves lining the walls, a washer and dryer at opposite ends of the room. Another door, located in the middle of the wall directly opposite of the outside door, it too was closed but as he slowly turned the knob he found it not locked. He gently turned the knob and opened it slowly, as he opened the door, it squeaked. He stood motionless for several minutes as he peered into a large room, which was the O'Francis entertainment room. Then he reached into his right inside coat pocket and removed a set of night vision goggles. Removed his hat with his right hand, placed the goggles over his head, and adjusted them to his face. Replaced his hat then he scanned the room he was about to enter. At the far end of the room was a bar, behind the bar the wall to the front side of the house were two small windows head high off the floor. A bumper pool table was in the middle of the twenty by twelve foot room.

The master bedroom was located at the far end of the house. The bedroom was rather large, thirty by twenty. Off the bedroom were a den, a walk-in closet, and the master bedrooms private bath. A set of double solid cherry wood door separated the closet from the bedroom. A small eight by eight room separated the bath from the closet. That room led to a den fourteen foot long and seven foot wide. The queen size bed was at the south end of the room with a large window over the bed. In front of the glass wall, facing the front deck was a vanity table with a flower arrangement on it. At the end of the bed a short couch the same width of the bed. To the right of the entrance to the master bedroom was a full wall entertainment center. Several of O'Francis drawings lined the walls of the bedroom.

The bedroom door was open; J.P. abruptly opened his eyes. He had been sleeping on his back; he heard the squeak of the laundry room door. His youngest son Patrick had left at 11:30 with his girlfriend, and had informed his parents that he would be spending the night with her. Michael was in his final year of service for the military and stationed in Maryland working at the NSA headquarters. Normally if one of the sons came into the house late at night, the first thing they did was whistle. A special whistle the family had come up with to identify each other when entering the house, or to locate each other when separated in a large store.

J.P.'s hearing intensified greatly at night, something he could never understand, but welcomed the sense as a gift. He became cold, even though his house was kept warm at a steady 70 degrees by the heat pump. He and Dawn slept in the nude under a sheet, a light cover and a bedspread if needed. Dawn was soundly sleeping as usual with the security of her soulmate to protect her. She was on her right side, her back to J.P. He touched her on the shoulder gently; she was startled awake with a "Ha, what?" J.P. leaned over to her left ear and whispered, "I do not want you to say a word. Just listen." She turned her head and looked at her Husband in the darkness of the room trying to adjust her eyes. He put his left index finger over her mouth.

"I want you to slide out of the bed on my side, quietly, get on the floor, get as much of your body under the bed as you can." She did and J.P. put several pillows over her, "say nothing!" He whispered as she became scared, her body began to tremble, tears gathered in her eyes. She did what her husband told her. To the right of J.P.'s side of the bed was a nightstand that fit flush against the thick tan carpet covering floor. Normally he kept two pistols under the night stand. One on the left side was a .357 Smith and Wesson revolver; blue steel with a four-inch barrel. In the cylinder were alternating 1/4 oz. shot shells and hollow point .357's. On the right side was a military .45 caliber with a full clip with one in the chamber. Both would have been wrapped in a soft black cotton cloth. But, he had removed them and place one each in each of the night stands draws. He pulled the top draw out and removed the .357.

Stepping into the large room, he located the door leading from the game room to the kitchen, he stepped into the kitchen then he scanned the room, he then turned right and passed through the door that lead into the living room. He stopped, looked about the room. He faced the bay window side of the house. To his right was a love seat; his left a long couch; in the middle of the room a hand carved wooden oriental coffee table. Across the room in front of the window, a lazy-boy chair. The wall to his left was a full wall entertainment center and then a long hallway leading to the back of the house. He looked down at the floor, hard wood. He walked around the center of the room passing by the coffee table and stopped at the entrance of the hallway.

J.P. had slid out of the bed onto the floor. He reached down to his side of the bed to the floor and pulled two of the larger pillows up and placed one on each side of the bed pulling the covers over them. After quickly arranging the pillows to appear as if someone was under the covers, he dropped to his knees, and stretched out to the end of the left side of the couch facing the bedroom door. The heat pump kick on, just as it did he cocked the hammer back on the pistol. Several years earlier while working with Chris Whitley he had the trigger adjusted to a hair touch. The room was pitch-black; he could not see anything, not even the white dots on the front and rear sights. The roman shades had been let down as usual, preventing any light from the outside from penetrating the room at night. J.P. lay in the prone position pointing his pistol at the master bedroom door entrance.

The intruder looked down the hallway, he could see to the far end of the hall, and the door that entered into the master bedroom. As he took his first step into the hall, the floor squeaked. He stopped.

J.P. had laid the hard wood floor himself, and had made the wood to give and squeak if someone stepped on it, another security measure for him. At the end of the hallway three steps before one entered to his bedroom he had done the same with the floor.

Slowly he put his foot down on the floor, no sound. He moved slowly, one step at a time pausing with each step. He paused at the first room, the central bathroom. Looked to his left and scanned the room, then a few steps and scanned Patrick's bedroom to the left. Then the O'Francis library. The next room was the guest bedroom. The night vision goggles made everything appear pale green. Ten feet of hallway was left before he reached the master bedroom door. Step, then he pause, step, pause, step pause, and then a squeak as he placed his right foot down on the floor. He stopped. Peering through the bedroom door he could only see a fourth of the room.

⚜ ⚜ ⚜ ⚜

J.P.'s heart began to pound in his ears. Dawn had pulled one of the pillows over her head exposing only the right half of her body. O'Francis held the pistol in his right hand; his left cupped under his right. His left thumb crossed the back of his right thumb. He was trying hard to see through the door, his eyes had adjusted to the dark but could not see anything. J.P.'s aim was chest high to what he perceived to be the center of the door.

⚜ ⚜ ⚜ ⚜

He pulled the shotgun to his right shoulder, then stepped, no sound, he stepped again. He was one-step away from entering the bedroom. He could see the bed and two large mounds on the bed in a ghostly pale like shape at the far end of the twenty-foot long room. He heard nothing. He stepped into the room onto the thick tan carpet and fired once at the left side of the bed.

The red flame exiting from the end of the barrel of the shotgun told J.P. what he needed. He raised the pistol barrel up slightly, and fired two quick shots; just as the assassin jacked, another shall into the chamber. J.P.'s first shot was the 1/4 oz. shot shall that hit the man in the face. The second was the hollow point .357, hitting the man in his upper chest cutting across the right lung through his left back. The second shot sent the man backward into the hallway and onto the floor. As he fell backward he dropped the shotgun. J.P. heard it hit the floor in the hallway. He was up and moved quickly to the handmade entertainment center to the right side of the door. He paused; he had to get his eye's adjusted again as the flash from the shots fired had left white spots in his vision. He heard no movement, no sound.

He stood with his back against the entertainment center, his arms folded up at the elbows and against his chest, the pistol pointing upward. He took a deep breath, in one smooth quick motion he pivoted on his left foot, crossed the right over and moved across in front of the bedroom door, pointing the pistol down at the floor and fired two more shots. Shot shall first and another .357 hollow point, continuing across to the double doors leading into Dawn's large walk-in closet. He pressed his back against the double doors and waited. His arms were in the same position as he had before; his cross over in front of the bedroom door had placed him only two feet from the entrance of bedroom door. He heard no sound.

Dawn had buried her face into her hands. She was crying without any sound, her body trembled uncontrollably.

J.P. took his left hand off the pistol and reached to his left to the doorknob of the closets right door. He turned the knob and swung the door open without a sound. He slid to his left and into the closet. Then he stepped back to the wall, taking the standing ready position, his gun pointing forward. He reached to the wall and flipped on the closet light. Still silence. Quickly swinging outward pointing his gun toward the bedroom door, the light pierced the bedroom and illuminated down the hallway. He slid to the two feet space between the closet door and the bedroom door, paused. Pistol pointing forward, he edged to the door facing; quickly he looked to his right, down the hallway taking a mental picture of the hallway and then back. He had seen a body lying in the floor a foot from the bedroom. Again, he repeated the move, the same scene. He then looked around the door opening without withdrawing. Stepped out into the hall standing at the feet of the body lying in his hallway, pointing his pistol at the man, the hammer cocked, he stepped to the left of the man, as he occupied the right side of the hallway. The shotgun lay at his right knee on the floor. His left arm stretched out over his head, his right arm to his side. His head lay to his right, the night-vision goggles still over his eyes. J.P. eased by the still body, and around to the top of his head. Holding his pistol in his right hand, pointing it at the man's head he reached down with his left hand, placed his index and middle finger on the side of his neck. There was no pulse. J.P. then moved back to the side of the dead man, reached down, picked up the shotgun by the stock, and laid it on the bedroom floor as he went to his wife.

"Dawn, it J.P., it's okay, come out." She slowly rose out from under her cover. Grabbed her husband and hugged him tightly, breaking down and sobbing aloud.

"What the hell is going on?" She stated as she cried.

"Get dressed. I'll call the police." J.P. went to the phone on the nightstand, called "Country" first and told him he needed him to come over. David knew that he did not call him over just anything, that this had to be an emergency. J.P. then put on his jeans and Notre Dame Sweatshirt which were lying on the couch at the end of the bed. "Country" was entering the front door by the time J.P. was getting off the phone with the county police. He knew that the state police as well as the county would be at his home in a matter of ten minutes. Dawn was in the kitchen trying to get control of herself and putting on a pot of coffee. As "Country" entered the O'Francis house, he called out.

"J.P. What's up?"

"Dawn is in the kitchen." O'Francis yelled from his bedroom. "I'll be there in a second."

Maw, as David had always referred to Dawn, walked into the kitchen to see his surrogate mother totally in emotional shambles, which did not set well with him at all. J.P. went to the kitchen; Dawn was trying to tell David what had happened, her voice still trembling, tears still filled her eyes and running down her face. Clearly shaken from the events that had just occurred. J.P. walked in and looked at David.

"Come with me." They walked to the hallway and he flipped on the light. "Country" squatted down and removed the goggles from the man's face. Small pellet shots dotted the right side of the man's his face.

"You know him?" J.P. asks.

"No."

"Do you?"

"No. Someone put a hit on me and my family "Country!""

"What the hell is going on J.P.?" David rose to face his longtime friend, teacher and coach.

"I really do not know. But I intend on finding out."

Dave squatted down again, examining the dead man's chest. "Hit him twice."

"No, four times." Dave turned his head and looked up at J.P.

"Pellets from the shot shells got him in the face twice. Hollow points got him in the upper chest and through the heart."

"Country" being the chief of police for many years in the town of Honsburg, rolled the body over to see his back. Two large holes in his back indicating the exit of the hollow point shells, one had cut his upper spine the other came out just below the shoulder bone. "Country" rolled him back. Looked up at the wall in the hall, then raised up and reached over and rubbed his fingers over a hole in the painted beige paneling. "First shot went through the middle of his back probable severing his spine?"

J.P. looked at "Country",

"You'll find the next shot in the floor under him." Then he proceeded to explain how it went down.

The County and State arrived, and David Higgenbottom let them into O'Francis' home, proceed to explain what had taken place. J.P. stayed in the kitchen with Dawn drinking coffee. Of the four county deputies and the two state police that had arrive on the scene, three were Masonic Brothers and former students.

The rest of the night was long with lots of talking. No one seemed to know who the man was. No one seemed to know why he was trying to kill J.P. and his wife. O'Francis knew, but said nothing. He knew he would be getting a visit from the 29th District Drug Task Force in the next few days. J.P. had questioned some of the people connected the task force, but had no hard evidence to link anyone to any of the top drug pushers in the area.

Two days after the attempt on him and his family, he called O'Neill. It was arranged for J.P. to meet him at his office. The following morning he was in Paul's office drinking coffee and giving Paul all the details of the events that had taken place. Paul sat in his old squeaky wooden office chair listening to every word. When J.P. was finished, he got up and went to the coffee pot poured another cup, held the pot up and toward Paul.

"Yes please." J.P. walked to the desk refilled Paul's cup returned it to the Bunn holder put the pot back, returned to his semi comfortable office chair and sat.

"J.P., this is big. You have struck a major nerve. This is not a small town move."

"Yes I am well aware of that. The question is who? I mean." Then he stopped, took a drink of coffee.

"I do not think I really did all that much to curtail the flow of drugs into the area. I mean hell Paul, a street dealer here and there, a few users, nothing to the real money people. What the hell?"

"The what the hell, is that you have gotten someone's attention. That someone is afraid that your little one-man crusade against the flow of drugs will expose whomever, because that street person you have identified will talk too much and that their name will surface. J.P., it may seem like minor money, but it is not. The money is big. We are not talking a few thousand dollars here. We are talking hundreds of thousands of dollars. The kind of money that leads to someone in Miami, New York, places like that."

"Damn Paul, I really do not." Paul cut him off.

"J.P. no offense here, I mean you are yourself street smart. When the money trail goes up it get big. You are costing these people some big dollars. And again, more important than the money, which they can absorb, is names."

They sat and looked at each other for several minutes without speaking. Paul continued.

"Someone in your little neck of the woods, so to speak, someone most likely very paramount in your community, a church goer, a business person, a civic leader, someone who has got some connections has requested a little assistance from the heavy hitter. People, who have pros on their pay roll, people who take care of business when needed. You were a minor problem. Not a major job, simple. They, whoever they might be, simply under estimated you. Someone did not do there reconnaissance well at all."

J.P. sat in his chair, both hands on his cup looking down into his half-drunk coffee. Paul never said anything, rocked back again in his chair. Only the squeak was heard in the room.

"Okay," J.P. finally stated. "It is time for me to leave. I will tell you this Paul. I will, be back, in due time. I will be back to take care of business. Point of fact is, several pieces of business. That is a promise. It will take a while to get things in order, but Paul, I am out of here."

"Will you need help getting where you want to go?"

"No, I do not think so. I will talk to you before we leave. Will be a while getting things in order."

"J.P., if you need anything, I mean anything..."

"Yes, I know. I really do appreciate the offer. As well as all the help you have given me over the years."

"J.P. I have some connections that can help in these matters."

"Paul, I am aware you do. However, well, we will see. Let me do some thinking, some planning, I have a lot to sift through. I just need time."

Paul interrupted. "J.P., I"

J.P. cut him off. "Paul, look, I like the "Company," really, I do. I support them. I really do not give a royal's fat rats whether what they do is legal or illegal. However, it is the government. I hope you understand, nothing personal, okay. I know you use to work for them."

"Nothing personal taken. J.P. there is several things you are not aware of but in due time my friend. Just remember there is no time limit."

J.P. looked at Paul for a long minute, "oh, you are talking about...then he stopped."

Then for the first time since he got into Paul's office he broke a slight smile.

"Now, do you need any help moving?"

"No Paul. I think I can handle all that myself. Besides, I really think that it would be best that you did not know exactly where I will be relocating. No offense meant."

"Oh, believe me, I do understand."

"Well I thought you might. Tell you what; let us just say for the hell of it, that I am somewhere in the northern part of Georgia. Just in case, some-one might ask. Okay."

"Hey, good enough for me." Then Paul smiled, got up from his squeaky chair walked around his well warn desk, stuck his hand out. J.P. rose as he approached and they gripped and held it looking into each other's eyes.

"Thanks Paul. Thank you for everything. I owe you a lot."

"No, you don't owe me a damn thing. I will do some leg work for you and when you are ready, the report will be ready."

James Patrick O'Francis would find a way to get even. He and Dawn had already decided after all that had taken place in the past year that it was time for them to move from the area.

But J.P. O'Francis would suffer through two more heart breaking events in his life before he was able to move from the area. He would never recover from the loss of his youngest son and his beloved wife. He would never return to the area.

However, there was no time limit for the Irishman to seek restitution for the hardships that had been bestowed onto him and his family.

# So Let Be Said; So Let It Be Written

BRUCE HAD RETURNED FROM HIS last trip to the south and had placed a call to Brian to let him know that all the Intel and recon had been done that could be done on the next mission.

Over the course of two years, the missing or dead's was up to five and the list had shrunk to the last three people that had been a major player in the character assassination, as well as the attempted assassination on the O'Francis family as well as the questionable death of his son and the sudden and unexpected death of his beloved soul mate. J.P. had requested of Brian, specific ways in which each mission was to be carried out and he and Vince had honored his requests.

J.P. and Brian had become rather close and he had in one of their earlier business meetings along with Vince Spadolini reviled to them his true place of residence. J.P. had misjudged both of them. He was pleasantly surprised to find out that they admired him for the manner in which he had handled the entire sequence of events.

James Patrick had learned that Paul was an intricate part of the O'Francis /Spadolini business operations, which made it much easier for him to be accepted by both men into their business world.

Dawn had died a few years before his move to the Big Sky Country, and J.P.'s bitterness ran deeper than ever toward the people who had driven him from their home in Virginia, a place they had spent thirty plus years getting it the way they liked it. Dawn love the little village and the place they together had created at the foot of the mountains in Virginia, because she had been such an intricate part in the design of the interior as well as the landscape surrounding their home.

His coldness and calculations for planning, his attention to the minuteness of details surprised Vince, but not Brian, Bruce nor Paul.

J.P. had begun to enjoy the hotel business that Brian had talked him into taking a part in. He enjoyed the involvement and association with the people he was getting to know in both Brian's and Vince's world. Which was a surprise to even himself. His entire life had flipped to the other side of the pancake. An entire world far different from that of just a simple teacher, which was all he wanted to be.

Decal was going to be a special treat for J.P. The orchestration of his ultimate demise was to be, once again by his request, at his own hands.

# The Narrator

I HAD RECEIVED MANY PHONE calls from the reporters at the local newspaper, but I had nothing for them. I really did not know where J.P. was. I do not think that any of the reporters believed me, and I do not believe if I did, that I had it in me to tell them. The investigation into the mysterious disappearance and deaths of so many people in such a small area eventually made its way to the national headlines and special interest stories. However, with all the sources the law enforcement as well as the news media and newspapers had, no one could pin point any one person behind what seemed to be a string of mystery occurrences. J.P.'s name soon faded into the mysteries of the missing or dead.

I often sat on my deck on my mountain in my little isolated world with Boaz close by or on my lap and when the late afternoon sun drifts slowly down into the west, I think about the not so simple teacher I had gotten to know. As a journalist over the years, you develop a certain instinct, and I knew that he was not dead. Missing, perhaps, from though who he wanted to be missing from. My thoughts turn of how he was doing and if he had a forest that he could go walking. J.P. had gotten me into the habit of walking and thinking and had taught me to listen to the forest and to all the animals seen as well as unseen and I continue to go for my early evening strolls along the same paths that he and I once walked. I never did create any new ones in the additional acres I had obtained. I could only hope that he had found the peace he had been searching for.

He was a man of his word. I have given a lot of thought to this man and his philosophy and concluded that those whose words are void of honor and integrity and are filled with mendacity, their actions shrouded in deceit, should never test such men. For such men, there is no time limit, and the ultimate consequences can only result in their loss. I wonder how long it would go on. How many would he feel was enough before justice was reached?

CHRISTINE JANE COUNTS O'CONNOR

"You ask how much I need you, must I explain?
I need you, oh my darling, like roses need rain.
You ask how long I'll love you; I'll tell you true:
Until the twelfth of never, I'll still be loving you."
Song by: *Johnny Mathis Lyrics by: Jerry Livington and Paul Francis Webber*

CPSIA information can be obtained at www.ICGtesting.com
Printed in the USA
LVOW11s0513260816

501862LV00001B/36/P